Baen Books by
A. Bertram Chandler

To the Galactic Rim (omnibus)
First Command (omnibus)
Galactic Courier (omnibus)
Ride the Star Winds (omnibus)
Upon A Sea of Stars (omnibus)

UPON A SEA OF STARS

A. Bertram Chandler

UPON A SEA OF STARS

A Baen Books Original

Baen Publishing Enterprises
P.O. Box 1403
Riverdale, NY 10471
www.baen.com

ISBN: 978-1-4767-3636-5

Cover art by Alan Pollack

First Baen paperback printing, April 2014

Distributed by Simon & Schuster
1230 Avenue of the Americas
New York, NY 10020

Library of Congress Cataloging-in-Publication Data

Chandler, A. Bertram (Arthur Bertram), 1912-1984.
 [Short stories. Selections]
 Upon a sea of stars / A. Bertram Chandler.
   pages cm
 ISBN 978-1-4767-3636-5 (omni trade pb)
 I. Title.
 PR6053.H325A6 2014
 823'.914--dc23
                                    2013049451

Printed in the United States of America

10 9 8 7 6 5 4 3 2 1

CONTENTS

INTO THE ALTERNATE UNIVERSE

DEDICATION
For my nose-to-grindstone keeper

⤳ Chapter 1 ⤳

THE INEVITABLE FREEZING WIND whistled thinly across the Port Forlorn landing field, bringing with it eddies of gritty dust and flurries of dirty snow. From his office, on the top floor of the Port Administration Building, Commodore Grimes stared out at what, over the long years, he had come to regard as his private kingdom. On a day such as this there was not much to see. Save for *Faraway Quest*, the Rim Worlds Government survey ship, the spaceport was deserted, a state of affairs that occurred but rarely. Soon it would resume its usual activity, with units of the Rim Runners' fleet dropping down through the overcast, from Faraway, Ultimo and Thule, from the planets of the Eastern Circuit, from the anti-matter systems to the Galactic West. But now there was only the old *Quest* in port, although a scurry of activity around her battered hull did a little to detract from the desolation of the scene.

Grimes stepped back from the window to the pedestal on which the big binoculars swiveled on their universal mount. He swung the instrument until *Faraway Quest* was centered in the field of view. He noted with satisfaction that the bitter weather had done little to slow down the work of refitting. The flare of welding torches around the sharp stem told him that the new Mass Proximity Indicator was being installed. The ship's original instrument had been loaned to Captain Calver for use in his *Outsider*, and the *Outsider*, her Mannschenn Drive unit having been rebuilt rather than merely modified, was now falling across the incredibly wide and deep gulf of light years between the island universes.

And I, thought Grimes sullenly, *am stuck here. How long ago was my last expedition, when I took out the old* Quest *and surveyed the inhabited planets of what is now the Eastern Circuit, and the anti-matter worlds to the Galactic West? But they say that I'm too valuable in an administrative capacity for any further gallivanting, and so younger men, like Calver and Listowel, have all the fun, while I just keep the seat of my office chair warm. . . .*

"Commodore Grimes!"

Grimes started as the sharp female voice broke into his thoughts, then stepped back from the instrument, turning to face his secretary. "Yes, Miss Willoughby?"

"Port Control called through to say that they've just given landing clearance to *Star Roamer.*"

"*Star Roamer?*" repeated the Commodore slowly. "Oh, yes. Survey Service."

"Interstellar Federation Survey Service," she corrected him.

He smiled briefly, the flash of white teeth momentarily taking all the harshness from his seamed, pitted face. "That's the only Survey Service that piles on any gees." He sighed. "Oh, well, I suppose I'd better wash behind the ears and put on a clean shirt. . . ."

"But your shirts are *always* clean, Commodore Grimes," the girl told him.

He thought, *I wish you wouldn't take things so literally*, and said, "Merely a figure of speech, my dear."

"ETA fifteen minutes from now," she went on. "And that's the Survey Service for you," he said. "Come in at damn nearly escape velocity, and fire the braking jets with one-and-a-half seconds to spare. But it's the Federation's tax payers that foot the fuel bills, so why should we worry?"

"You were in the Survey Service yourself, weren't you?" she asked.

"Many, many years ago. But I regard myself as a Rimworlder, even though I wasn't born out here." He smiled again as he said, "After all, home is where the heart is . . ." And silently he asked himself, *But where is the heart?*

He wished that it was night and that the sky was clear so that he could see the stars, even if they were only the faint, far luminosities of the Galactic Rim.

Star Roamer came in with the usual Survey Service *éclat*, her exhaust flare a dazzling star in the gray sky long before the bellowing thunder of her descent reverberated among the spaceport buildings, among cranes and gantries and conveyer belts. Then the long tongue of incandescence licked the sparse drifts and frozen puddles into an explosion of dirty steam that billowed up to conceal her shining hull, that was swept from the needle of bright metal by the impatient wind, fogging the wide window of Grimes' office with a fine drizzle of condensation.

She sat there on the scarred concrete—only a little ship, and yet with a certain air of arrogance. Already the beetle-like vehicles of the port officials were scurrying out to her. Grimes thought sourly, *I wish that they'd give our own ships the same prompt attention.* Remembering his own Survey Service days he felt a certain nostalgia. *Damn it all,* he thought, *I piled on more gees as a snotty-nosed Ensign than as Astronautical Superintendent of a shipping line and Commodore of the Rim Worlds Naval Reserve. . . .*

He stood by the window, from which the mist had now cleared, and watched the activity around *Star Roamer*. The ground vehicles were withdrawing from her sleek hull, and at the very point of her needle-sharp prow, the red light, almost painfully bright against the all-surrounding grayness, was blinking. He heard Miss Willoughby say, "She's blasting off again." He muttered in reply, "So I see." Then, in a louder voice, "That was a brief call. It must have been on some matter of Survey Service business. In that case, I should have been included in the boarding party. As soon as she's up and away, my dear, send word to the Port Captain that I wish to see him. *At once.*"

There was a flicker of blue incandescence under *Star Roamer's* stern and then, as though fired from some invisible cannon, she was gone, and the sudden vacuum of her own creation was filled with peal after crashing peal of deafening thunder. Grimes was aware that the speaker of the intercom was squawking, but could not make out the words. His secretary did. Shouting to be heard over the dying reverberations she cried, "Commander Verrill to see you, sir!"

"I should have washed behind the ears," replied Grimes. "But it's too late now."

Chapter 2

SHE HASN'T CHANGED MUCH, thought Grimes, as she strode into his office. She was wearing civilian clothes—a swirling, high-collared cloak in dark blue, tapered black slacks, a white jersey of a material so lustrous that it seemed almost luminous. *And that outfit,* went on the Commodore to himself, *would make a nasty hole in a year's salary. Rob Roy tweed and Altairian crystal silk . . . The Survey Service looks after its own.* Even so, he looked at her with appreciation. She was a beautiful woman, and on her an old flour sack would have looked almost as glamorous as the luxurious materials that adorned her fine body. In her pale blonde hair the slowly melting snow crystals sparkled like diamonds.

"Welcome aboard, Commander," said Grimes.

"Glad to be aboard, Commodore," she replied softly.

She allowed him to take the cloak from her, accepted the chair that Miss Willoughby ushered her towards. She sat down gracefully, watching Grimes as he carefully hung up her outer garment.

"Coffee, Commander Verrill? Or something stronger?"

"Something stronger." A smile flickered over her full lips. "As long as it's not your local rot-gut, that is."

"It's not. I have my sources of supply. Nova Caledon Scotch-on-the-rocks?"

"That will do nicely. But please omit the rocks." She shivered a little theatrically, "What a vile climate you have here, Commodore."

7

"It's the only one we have. Say when."

"Right up, please. I need some central heating."

And so you do, thought Grimes, studying her face. *So you do. And it's more than our weather that's to blame. You did what had to be done insofar as that mess involving you and Jane and Derek Calver was concerned, but to every action there's an equal and opposite reaction—especially once the glow of conscious nobility has worn off.*

She said, "Down the hatch."

"Down the hatch," he replied. "A refill?"

"Thank you."

He took his time about pouring the drinks, asking as he busied himself with glasses and ice cubes and bottle, "You must be here on important business, Commander. A courier ship all to yourself."

"Very important," she replied, looking rather pointedly towards Miss Willoughby, who was busying herself with the papers on her desk in a somewhat ostentatious manner.

"H'm. Yes. Oh, Miss Willoughby. I'd like you to run along to the Stores Superintendent, if you wouldn't mind, to straighten up the mess about *Rim Falcon*'s requisition sheets."

"But I still have to run through *Rim Kestrel*'s repair list, sir."

"*Rim Kestrel*'s not due in for a week yet, Miss Willoughby."

"Very well, sir."

The girl straightened the litter on her desk, got up and walked slowly and with dignity from the office.

Sonya Verrill chuckled. "Such sticky-beaking would never be tolerated in the Service, Commodore."

"But you don't have to put up with civilian secretarial staff. Commander. Come to that, I well recall that when I was in the Service myself an occasional gift of some out-world luxury to a certain Lieutenant Masson—she was old Admiral Hall's secretary-could result in the premature release of all sorts of interesting information regarding promotions, transfers and the like."

"Things are different now, Commodore."

"Like hell they are. Anyhow, Sonya, you can talk freely now. This office is regularly debugged."

"Debugged, John?"

"Yes. Every now and again high-ups in the various Ministries decide that they aren't told enough of Rim Runners' affairs—of course, the *Aeriel* business made me very unpopular, and if Ralph Listowel hadn't got results, serendipitous ones at that, I'd have been out on my arse. And then *your* people manage to plant an occasional bug themselves."

"Come off it, John."

"Still playing the little wooly lamb, Sonya?"

She grinned. "It's part of my job. Perhaps the most important part."

"And what's the job this time?"

"There won't be any job unless our Ambassador to the Rim Confederation manages to talk your President into supplying help. But I think that he will. Relations have been fairly friendly since your autonomy was recognized."

"If you want a ship," said Grimes, "the charter rates will be favorable to ourselves. But surely the Federation has tonnage to spare. There are all the Commission's vessels as well as your own Survey Service wagons."

"Yes, we've plenty of ships," she admitted. "And plenty of personnel. But it's know-how that we're after. You hardly need to be told that your people have converted this sector of Space into your own backyard, and put up a big sign, *No Trespassing*. Even so, we hear things. Such as Rim Ghosts, and the winds of it that blew your pet *Aeriel* through about half a dozen alternative time tracks. And there was that business of the wet paint on Kinsolving's Planet years ago—but that, of course, was before you became autonomous, so *we* had the job of handling it. . . ."

"And the Outsider's ship . . ." supplied Grimes.

"No. Not in the same class, John. She'd drifted in, or been placed there, by visitors from another Galaxy. And, in any case, we're already in on that." She held out her glass for a refill.

"You're welcome, Sonya, but . . ."

"Don't worry, John. Olga Popovsky, the Beautiful Spy with hollow legs—that's me."

"You know your own capacity."

"Of course. Thank you. Now, as I was saying, our top brass is interested in all the odd things that seem to happen only in this sector of Space, and the Rhine Institute boys are interested too. It was decided that there was only one Intelligence Officer in the Service with anything approaching an intimate knowledge of the Rim. I needn't tell you who that is. It was decided, too, that I'd work better if allowed to beg, borrow or steal Rim Worlds' personnel. Oh, the Service can afford to pay Award rates, and above. Frankly, when I was offered the job I almost turned it down. I know the Rim—but my memories of this sector of Space aren't all too happy . . ." She leaned forward in her chair, put her slim hand on Grimes' knee. "But . . ."

"But what, Sonya?"

"All this business of Rim Ghosts, all these theories about the curtains between the alternative universes wearing thin here, on the very edge of the expanding Galaxy . . . You know something of my history, John. You know that there have only been two men, real men, in my life. Bill Maudsley, who found the Outsiders' quarantine station, and who paid for the discovery with his life. And Derek Calver, whose first loyalties were, after all, to Jane . . . Damn it all, John, I'm no chicken. I'm rather tired of playing the part of a lone wolf—or a lone bitch, if you like. I want me a man—but the right man—and I want to settle down. I shall be due a very handsome gratuity from the Service when I retire, and there are still sparsely settled systems in this Galaxy where a little, one-ship company could provide its owners and operators with a very comfortable living. . . ."

"So?"

"So it's bloody obvious. I've been put in charge of this wild goose chase—and with any luck at all I shall catch me my own wild gander. Surely there must be some alternative Universe in which I shall find either Bill or Derek, with no strings attached."

"And what if you find them both at once?" asked Grimes.

"As long as it's in a culture that approves of polyandry," she grinned. Then she was serious again. "You can see, John, that this—this research may well fantastically advance the frontiers of human knowledge."

"And it may well," he told her, "bring you to the haven where you would be." He raised his glass to her. "And for that reason, Sonya, I shall do everything within my power to help you."

✑ Chapter 3 ✑

AFTER SONYA HAD LEFT he pottered around his office for a while, doing jobs that could have been done faster and better by Miss Willoughby. When his secretary returned from her visit to the Stores Superintendent and, with a display of efficiency, tried to take the work from his hands, he dismissed her for the day. Finally, realizing that he was accomplishing nothing of any value, he put the papers back in their files and, having drawn himself a cup of coffee from the automatic dispenser, sat down to smoke his battered pipe.

He felt sorry for Sonya Verrill. He knew much of her past history—more, in fact, than she had told him. He was sorry for her, and yet he envied her. She had been given fresh hope, a new goal towards which to strive. Whether or not she met with success was not of real importance. If she failed, there would be other goals, and still others. As an officer of the Survey Service Intelligence Branch she was given opportunities for travel denied even to the majority of professional spacemen and women. Grimes smiled at the corniness of the thought and muttered, "Someday her prince will come . . ."

Yes, he envied her. She, even within the framework of regulations that governed her Service, had far more freedom of movement than he had. He strongly suspected that she was in a position to be able to select her own assignments. *And I,* he thought, *am marooned for the rest of my natural—or, if I so desire, unnatural—life on this dead-end world at the bitter end of sweet damn' all . . .*

Come off it, Grimes, he told himself. *Come off it, Grimes, Commodore Grimes, Rim Worlds Naval Reserve. Don't be so bloody sorry for yourself. You've climbed to the top of your own private tree.*

Even so . . .

He finished his coffee, poured himself another cup. He thought, *I should have offered to put her up during her stay on Lorn.* And then he was glad that he had not made the offer. She was used to luxury—luxury on a government expense account, but luxury nonetheless—and surely would have been appalled by his messy widower's establishment. His children were grown up, and had their own homes and, in any case, incurable planetlubbers that they were, would have little in common with one who, after all, was a professional adventuress.

So . . .

So I can enjoy adventures—although not in the same sense—vicariously, he thought. *I'll do what I can for Sonya, and hope to receive in return a firsthand account of all that happens to her. She said that she would want a ship—well, she shall have* Faraway Quest. *It's time that the poor old girl was taken for another gallop. And she'll be wanting a crew. I'll put out the call for volunteers before I get definite word that the expedition has been approved—just quietly, there's no need to get the politicians' backs up. Rimworlders, she specified. Rimworlders born and bred. I can see why. People raised on the Rim are far more likely to have counterparts in the alternative Universes than those of us who have, like myself, drifted out here, driven out here by the winds of chance. I shouldn't have much trouble in raising a team of officers, but a Master will be the problem. Practically all our Captains are refugees from the big, Earth-based companies, or from the Survey Service.*

But there was no urgency, he told himself.

He drew yet another cup of coffee and, carrying it, walked to the wide window. Night had fallen and the sky had cleared and, work having ceased for the day, there was no dazzle of lights from the spaceport to rob the vision of keenness.

Overhead in the blackness was one bright star, the Faraway sun, and beyond it lay the faint, far nebulosities. Low in the east the Lens was rising, the upper limb only visible, a parabola of misty light. Grimes looked away from it to the zenith, to the dark immensities through which Calver in his *Outsider* was falling, perhaps never to return. And soon Sonya Verrill would be falling—but would she? could she?—through and across even stranger, even more fantastic gulfs, of Time as well as of Space.

Grimes shivered. Suddenly he felt old and alone, although he loathed himself for his self pity.

He left his office, fell down the dropshaft (what irony!) to the ground floor, got out his monocar from the executives' garage and drove home.

Home was a large house on the outskirts of Port Forlorn. Home was a villa, and well kept—the maintenance service to which Grimes subscribed was highly efficient—but sadly lacking in the touches of individuality, or imagination, that only a woman can supply.

The commodore drove his car into his garage and, after having shut off the engine, entered the house proper directly from the outbuilding. He did not, as he usually did, linger for a few minutes in the conservatory that housed his collection of exotic plants from a century of worlds. He went straight to his lounge, where he helped himself to a strong whisky from the bar. Then he sat down before his telephone console and, with his free hand, punched the number for library service.

The screen lit up, and in it appeared the head and shoulders of a girl who contrived to look both efficient and beautiful. Grimes smiled, as he always did, at the old-fashioned horn-rimmed spectacles that, some genius had decided, made the humanoid robot look like a real human librarian. A melodious contralto asked, "May I be of service, sir?"

"You may, my dear," answered Grimes. (A little subtle—or not so subtle—flattery worked wonders with often temperamental robots.) "I'd like whatever available data you have on Rim Ghosts."

"Visual sir, or *viva voce?*"

"*Viva voce*, please." (Even this tin blonde, with her phony femininity, was better than no woman at all in the house.)

"Condensed or detailed, sir?"

"Condensed, please. I can always ask you to elaborate as and if necessary."

"Very good, sir. The phenomenon of the Rim Ghosts occurs, as the name implies, only on the Rim. Sightings are not confined to single individuals, so therefore cannot be assumed to be subjective in nature. A pattern has been established regarding these sightings. One member of a party of people will see himself, and be seen by his companions, in surroundings and company differing, sometimes only subtly, from those of actuality. Cases have been known in which an entire group of people has seen its Rim Ghost counterpart.

"For a while it was thought that the apparitions were prophetic in character, and the orthodox explanation was that of precognition. With the collection of a substantial body of data, however, it became obvious that prophetic visions comprised only about 30% of the total. Another 30% seemed to be recapitulations of past events, 20% had a definite here-and-now flavor, while the remaining 20% depicted situations that, in our society, can never arise.

"It was in the year 313 A.G. that Dr. Foulsham, of the Terran Rhine Institute, advanced his Alternative Universe Theory. This, of course, was no more than the reformulation of the idea played around with for centuries by speculative thinkers and writers, that of an infinitude of almost parallel Time Tracks, the so-called Worlds of If. According to Dr. Foulsham, on Earth and on the worlds that have been colonized for many generations, the barriers between the individual tracks are . . ." The robot paused.

"Go on, my dear," encouraged Grimes. "This is only a condensation. You needn't bother trying to break down fancy scientific terminology."

"Thank you, sir. The barriers, as I was trying to say in suitable language, are both high and thick, so that a break-through is almost impossible. But on the very rim of the expanding Galaxy these barriers are . . . tenuous, so that very often a fortuitous breakthrough does occur.

"An example of such a breakthrough, but visual only, was that achieved by Captain Derek Calver and his shipmates when he was serving as Chief Officer of the freighter *Lorn Lady*. The ship was proceeding through deep space, under Mannschenn Drive, when another vessel was sighted close alongside. In the control room of the other spacecraft Calver saw himself—but he was wearing Master's uniform—and most of the others who were with him in *Lorn Lady*'s control compartment. He was able, too, to make out the name of the strange ship. It was the *Outsider*. Some months later, having become the recipient of a handsome salvage award, Calver and his shipmates were able to buy a secondhand ship and to operate as a small tramp shipping company. They christened her the *Outsider*. This, then, was obviously one of the precognitive apparitions, and can be explained by the assumption that the Alternative Universe in which Calver's career runs almost parallel to his career in *this* Universe possesses a slightly different time scale.

"Physical breakthrough was inadvertently achieved by Captain Ralph Listowel in his experimental light jammer *Aeriel*. Various members of his crew unwisely attempted to 'break the light barrier' and, when the ship was proceeding at a velocity only fractionally less than that of light, discharged a jury-rigged rocket hoping thereby to outrun the photon gale. They did not, of course, and *Aeriel*'s crew became Rim Ghosts themselves, experiencing life in a succession of utterly strange cultures before, more by luck than judgment, returning to their own. The unexpected result of this ill-advised experiment was the developing of a method whereby atomic signs may be reversed, thereby making possible intercourse between our planets and the anti-matter worlds.

"There is no doubt that the Rim Ghost phenomenon is one deserving of thorough investigation, but with the breakaway of the Rim Worlds from the Federation it has not been possible to maintain full contact with either the Survey Service or the Rhine Institute, which bodies, working in conjunction, would be eminently capable of carrying out the necessary research . . ."

"You're out of date, duckie," chuckled Grimes.

"I beg your pardon, sir?"

"You're out of date. But don't let it worry you; it's not your fault. It's we poor, inefficient humans who're to blame, for failing to feed new data into your memory tanks."

"And may I ask, sir, the nature of the new data?"

"Just stick around," said Grimes, "and some day, soon, I may be able to pass it on to you."

If Sonya comes back to tell me, he thought, and his odd mood of elevation evaporated.

⇜ Chapter 4 ⇝

A WEEK PASSED, and for Commodore Grimes it was an exceptionally busy one. *Rim Mammoth—ex-Beta Geminorum—*had berthed, and that ship, as usual, was justifying her reputation as the white elephant of Rim Runners' fleet. A large consignment of fish had spoiled on the passage from Mellise to Lorn. The Chief Reaction Drive Engineer had been beaten up in the course of a drunken brawl with the Purser. The Second, Third and Fourth Officers had stormed into the Astronautical Superintendent's presence to aver that they would sooner shovel sludge in the State Sewage Farm than lift as much as another centimeter from a planetary surface under the command of the *Mammoth*'s Master and Chief Officer. Even so, Grimes found time to initiate his preliminary inquiries. To begin with, he had his secretary draw up a questionnaire, this asking for all relevant data on the sighting of Rim Ghosts. It seemed to him that Sonya Verrill would require for her crew personnel who were in the habit of sighting such apparitions. Then, having come to the reluctant conclusion that a lightjammer would be the most suitable research ship, he studied the schedules of such vessels as were in operation, trying to work out which one could be withdrawn from service with the minimal dislocation of the newly developed trade with the anti-matter systems.

Rather to his annoyance, Miss Willoughby issued copies of the questionnaire to the crew of the only ship at the time in port—*Rim*

Mammoth. The officers of that vessel were all in his black books, and it had been his intention to split them up, to transfer them to smaller and less well-appointed units of the fleet. Nonetheless, he studied the forms with interest when they were returned. He was not surprised by what he discovered. The Master and the Chief Officer, both of whom had come out to the Rim from the Interplanetary Transport Commission's ships, had no sightings to report—Captain Jenkins, in fact, had scrawled across the paper, *Superstitious Rubbish!* The Second, Third and Fourth Officers, together with the Psionic Radio Officer, were all third generation Rim Worlders, and all of them had been witnesses, on more than one occasion, to the odd phenomena.

Grimes ceased to be annoyed with Miss Willoughby. It looked as though the manning problem was already solved, insofar as executive officers were concerned. The Second, Third and Fourth Mates of *Rim Mammoth* were all due for promotion, and Captain Jenkins' adverse report on their conduct and capabilities could well result in the transfer of their names to the bottom of the list. So there was scope for a little gentle blackmail. Volunteers wanted for a Rim Ghost hunt! You, and you, and you!

But there was a snag. None of them had any sail training. How soon would Sonya Verrill want her ship? Would there be time to put the officers concerned through a hasty course in the handling of lightjammers? No doubt he would be able to find a team of suitably qualified men in the existing lightjammer fleet, but all of them were too useful where they were.

It was while he was mulling this problem over in his mind that Commander Verrill was announced. She came into his office carrying a long envelope. She held it out to him, grinning. "Sealed orders, Commodore."

Grimes accepted the package, studying it cautiously. It bore the crest of the Rim Confederation.

"Aren't you going to open it?"

"What's the rush?" he grunted.

But he picked up the paper knife from his desk—it had been the deadly horn of a Mellisan sea unicorn—and slit the envelope, pulling out the contents.

He skipped the needlessly complicated legal language while, at the same time, getting the gist of it. As a result of talks between the President of the Rim Worlds Confederation and the Ambassador of the Interstellar Federation, it had been decided that the Confederation was to afford to the Federation's Survey Service all possible assistance—at a price. One Commodore Grimes was empowered to negotiate directly with one Commander Verrill regarding the time charter of a suitable vessel and the employment of all necessary personnel. . . .

Grimes read on—and then he came to the paragraph that caused him to raise his eyebrows in surprise.

Commodore Grimes was granted indefinite leave of absence from his post of Astronautical Superintendent of Rim Runners, and was to arrange to hand over to Captain Farley as soon as possible. Commodore Grimes was to sail as Master of the vessel chartered by the Survey Service, and at all times was to further and protect the interests of the Rim Confederation. . . .

Grimes grunted, looked up at the woman from under his heavy eyebrows. "Is this your doing, Sonya?"

"Partly. But in large measure it's due to the reluctance of your government to entrust one of its precious ships to an outsider."

"But why me?"

She grinned again. "I said that if I were obliged to ship a Rim Confederation sailing master, I insisted on exercising some little control over the appointment. Then we all agreed that there was only one Master of sufficiently proven reliability to meet the requirements of all concerned . . ." She looked a little worried. "Aren't you glad, John?"

"It's rather short notice," he replied tersely and then, as he watched her expression, he smiled. "Frankly, Sonya, before you blew in aboard *Star Roamer* I'd decided that I was sick and tired of being a desk-borne Commodore. This crazy expedition of yours will be better than a holiday."

She snapped, "It's not crazy."

His eyebrows went up. "No? An interstellar ghost hunt?"

"Come off it, John. You know as well as I that the Rim Ghosts are objective phenomena. It's a case of paranormal physics rather than paranormal psychology. It's high time that somebody ran an investigation—and if you people are too tired to dedigitate, then somebody else will."

Grimes chuckled. "All right, all right, I've never seen a Rim Ghost myself, but the evidence is too—massive?—to laugh away. So, while Miss Willoughby starts getting my papers into something like order for Captain Farley—he's on leave at present, so we won't have long to wait for him—we'll talk over the terms of the charter party.

"To begin with, I assume that you'll be wanting one of the lightjammers. *Cutty Sark* will be available very shortly."

She told him, "No. I don't want a lightjammer."

"I would have thought that one would have been ideal for this . . . research."

"Yes. I know all about Captain Ralph Listowel and what happened to him and his crew on the maiden voyage of *Aeriel*. But there's one big snag. When *Aeriel*'s people switched Time Tracks, they also, to a large extent, switched personalities. When I visit the Universe next door I want to do it as me, not as a smudged carbon copy."

"Then what sort of ship do you want?"

She looked out of the window. "I was hoping that your *Faraway Quest* would be available."

"As a matter of fact, she is."

"And she has more gear than most of your merchant shipping. A Mass Proximity Indicator, for example . . ."

"Yes."

"Carlotti Communication and Direction Finding Equipment?"

"Yes."

Then, "I know this is asking rather much—but could a sizeable hunk of that anti-matter iron be installed?"

He grinned at her. "Your intelligence service isn't quite as good as you'd have us believe, Sonya. The *Quest* has no anti-matter incorporated in her structure yet—as you know, it's not allowed within a hundred miles of any populated area. But there's a suitably sized sphere of the stuff hanging in orbit, and there it stays until

Faraway Quest goes upstairs to collect it. You know the drill, of course—the antimatter, then an insulation of neutronium, than a steel shell with powerful permanent magnets built into it to keep the anti-matter from making contact with normal matter. A neutrino bombardment and, presto!—anti-gravity. As a matter of fact the reason for the *Quest's* refitting was so that she could be used for research into the problems arising from incorporating anti-gravity into a ship with normal interstellar drive."

"Good. Your technicians had better see to the installing of the anti-matter, and then ours—there's a bunch of them due in from Elsinore in *Rim Bison*—will be making a few modifications to the Carlotti gear. Meanwhile, have you considered manning?"

"I have. But, before we go any further, just what modifications do you have in mind? I may as well make it clear now that the Carlotti gear will have to be restored to an as-was condition before the ship comes off hire."

"Don't worry, it will be. Or brand new equipment will be installed." She paused and glanced meaningfully at the coffee dispenser. Grimes drew her a cup, then one for himself. "Well, John, I suppose you're all agog to learn what's going to happen to your beloved *Faraway Quest*, to say nothing of you and me and the mugs who sail with us. Get this straight, I'm no boffin. I can handle a ship and navigate well enough to justify my Executive Branch commission, but that's all.

"Anyhow, this is the way of it, errors and omissions expected. As soon as the necessary modifications have been made to the ship, we blast off, and then cruise along the lanes on which Rim Ghost sightings have been most frequent. It will help, of course, if all members of the crew are people who've made a habit of seeing Rim Ghosts . . ."

"That's been attended to," said Grimes.

"Good. So we cruise along quietly and peacefully—but keeping our eyes peeled. And as soon as Ghost is sighted—Action Stations!"

"You aren't going to open fire on it?" demanded Grimes.

"Of course not. But there will be things to be done, and done in a ruddy blush. The officer of the watch will push a button that will convert the ship into an enormously powerful electro-magnet, and the same switch will actuate the alarm bells. Automatically the projector of the modified Carlotti beacon will swing to bring the Ghost into its field. The boffins tell me that what *should* happen is that a bridge, a temporary bridge, will be thrown across the gulf between the Parallel Universes."

"I see. And as *Faraway Quest* is an enormously powerful magnet, the other ship, the Ghost, will be drawn into our Universe."

"No," she said impatiently. "Have you forgotten the anti-matter, the anti-gravity? The *Quest* will have one helluva magnetic field, but no mass to speak of. She'll be the one that gets pulled across the gap, or through the curtain, or however else you care to put it."

"And how do we get back?" asked Grimes.

"I'm not very clear on that point myself," she admitted.

The Commodore laughed. "So when I man the *Quest* it will have to be with people with no ties." He said softly, "I have none."

"And neither have I, John," she told him. "Not any longer."

~ Chapter 5 ~

CAPTAIN FARLEY was somewhat disgruntled at being called back from leave, but was mollified slightly when Grimes told him that he would be amply compensated. As soon as was decently possible the Commodore left Farley to cope with whatever problems relative to the efficient running of Rim Runners arose—after all, it was Miss Willoughby who really ran the show—and threw himself into the organizing of Sonya Verrill's expedition. What irked him was the amount of time wasted on legal matters. There was the charter, of course, and then there was the reluctance of Lloyd's surveyors to pass as space-worthy a ship in which Mannschenn Drive and antimatter were combined, not to say one in which the Carlotti gear had been modified almost out of recognition. Finally Sonya Verrill was obliged to play hell with a Survey Service big stick, and the gentlemen from Lloyd's withdrew, grumbling.

Manning, too, was a problem. The Second, Third and Fourth Mates of *Rim Mastodon* agreed, quite willingly, to sign on *Faraway Quest's* articles as Chief, Second and Third. The Psionic Radio Officer was happy to come along with them. After a little prodding at the ministerial level the Catering and Engineering Superintendents supplied personnel for their departments. And then the Institute of Spacial Engineers stepped in, demanding for its members the payment of Danger Money, this to be 150% of the salaries laid down by the Award. Grimes was tempted to let them have it—after all, it was the Federation's taxpayers who would be footing the bill—and then, on second thoughts, laid his ears back and refused to play. He got over the hurdle rather neatly, persuading the Minister of Shipping and the Minister for the Navy to have *Faraway Quest* commissioned as an auxiliary cruiser and all her officers—who were, of course, reservists, called up for special duties. Like Lloyd's, the Institute retired grumbling.

As a matter of fact, Grimes was rather grateful to them for having forced his hand. Had the *Quest* blasted off as a specialized merchant vessel only, with her crew on Articles, his own status would have been merely that of a shipmaster, and Sonya Verrill, representing the Survey Service, would have piled on far too many gees. Now he was a Commodore on active service, and, as such, well and truly outranked any mere Commander, no matter what pretty badge she wore on her cap. It was, he knew well, no more than a matter of male pride, but the way that things finally were he felt much happier.

So, after the many frustrating delays, *Faraway Quest* finally lifted from her berth at the Lorn spaceport. Grimes was rusty, and knew it, and allowed young Swinton—lately Second Officer of *Rim Mammoth*, now Lieutenant Commander Swinton, First Lieutenant of R.W.S. *Faraway Quest*—to take the ship upstairs. Grimes watched critically from one of the spare acceleration chairs, Sonya Verrill watched critically from the other. Swinton—slight, fair-haired, looking like a schoolboy in a grown-up's cut-down uniform—managed well in spite of his audience. The old *Quest* climbed slowly at first, then with rapidly increasing acceleration, whistling through the overcast into the clear air beyond, the fast thinning air, into the vacuum of Space.

Blast-off time had been calculated with considerable exactitude—"If it had been more exact," commented Grimes, "we'd have rammed our hunk of anti-matter and promptly become the wrong sort of ghosts . . ."—and so there was the minimum jockeying required to match orbits with the innocent-looking sphere of shining steel. The *Quest* had brought a crew of fitters up with her men with experience of handling similar spheres. Working with an economy of motion that was beautiful to watch they gentled the thing in through the special hatch that had been made for it, bolted it into its seating. Then it was the turn of the physicists, who set up their apparatus and bathed the anti-iron in a flood of neutrinos. While this operation was in progress, two tanker rockets stood by, pumping tons of water into the extra tanks that had been built into the *Quest's* structure. This, Grimes explained to his officers, was to prevent her from attaining negative mass and flying out of her orbit, repelled rather than attracted by Lorn and the Lorn sun, blown out of station before the landing of the assorted technicians and the loading of final essential items of stores and equipment.

At last all the preliminaries were completed. *Faraway Quest* was fully manned, fully equipped, and all the dockyard employees had made their transfer to the ferry rocket. This time Grimes assumed the pilot's chair. Through the viewports he could see the globe that was Lorn, the globe whose clouds, even from this altitude, looked dirty. Looking away from it, he told himself that he did not care if he never saw it again. Ahead, but to starboard, a lonely, unblinking beacon in the blackness, was the yellow spark that was the Mellise sun. The commodore's stubby fingers played lightly over his control panel. From the bowels of the ship came the humming of gyroscopes, and as the ship turned on her short axis the centrifugal force gave a brief illusion of off-center gravity.

The Lorn sun was ahead now.

"Sound an alarm, Commander Swinton," snapped Grimes.

The First Lieutenant pressed a stud, and throughout the ship there was the coded shrilling of bells, a succession of Morse R's short-long-short, short-long-short. *R is for rocket,* thought Grimes. *Better than all this civilian yapping into microphones.*

Abruptly the shrilling ceased.

With deliberate theatricality Grimes brought his fist down on the firing button. The giant hand of acceleration pushed the officers down into the padding of their chairs. The Commodore watched the sweep-second hand of the clock set in the center of the panel. He lifted his hand again—but this time it was with an appreciable effort—again brought it down. Simultaneously, from his own control position, Swinton gave the order, "Start Mannschenn Drive."

The roar of the rockets cut off abruptly, but before there was silence the keening song of the Drive pervaded the ship, the high-pitched complaint of the ever-spinning, ever-precessing gyroscopes. To the starboard hand, the great, misty lens of the Galaxy warped and twisted, was deformed into a vari-colored convolution at which it was not good to look. Ahead, the Mellise sun had taken the likelihood of a dimly luminous spiral.

Grimes felt rather pleased with himself. He had a crew of reservists, was a reservist himself, and yet the operation had been carried out with naval snap and efficiency. He turned to look at Sonya Verrill, curious as to what he would read in her expression.

She smiled slightly and said, "May I suggest, sir, that we splice the mainbrace?" She added, with more than a hint of cattiness, "After all, it's the Federation's taxpayers who're footing the bill."

~ Chapter 6 ~

THE SHIP having been steadied on to her trajectory, Grimes gave the order that Sonya Verrill had suggested. All hands, with the exception of the watch-keeping officers, gathered in *Faraway Quest's* commodious wardroom, strapping themselves into their chairs, accepting drinking bulbs from the tray that Karen Schmidt, the Catering Officer, handed around.

When everybody had been supplied with a drink the Commodore surveyed his assembled officers. He wanted to propose a toast, but had never possessed a happy knack with words. The only phrases that came to his mind were too stodgy, too platitudinous. At last he cleared his throat and said gruffly, "Well, gentlemen—and ladies, of course—you may consider that the expedition is under way, and the mainbrace is in the process of being spliced. Perhaps one of you would care to say something."

Young Swinton sat erect in his chair—in Free Fall, of course, toasts were drunk sitting—and raised his liquor bulb. He declaimed, trying to keep the amusement from his voice, "To the wild ghost chase!"

There was a ripple of laughter through the big compartment—a subdued merriment in which, Grimes noted, Sonya Verrill did not join. He felt a strong sympathy for her. As far as she was concerned this was no matter for jest, this pushing out into the unknown, perhaps the unknowable. It was, for her, the fruition of months of scheming, persuading, wire-pulling. And yet, Grimes was obliged to admit, the play on words was a neat one. "Very well," he responded, "to the wild ghost chase it is."

He sipped from his bulb, watched the others doing likewise. He reflected that insofar as Rim Worlds personnel was concerned it would have been hard to have manned the ship with a better crew— for this particular enterprise. All of them, during their service in the Rim Runners' fleet, had acquired reputations—not bad, exactly, but not good. Each of them had exhibited, from time to time, a certain ... scattiness? Yes, scattiness. Each of them had never been really at home in a service that, in the final analysis, existed only to make the maximum profit with the minimum expense. But now—the Federation's taxpayers had deep pockets—expense was no object. There would be no tedious inquiries into the alleged squandering of reaction mass and consumable stores in general.

Insofar as the Survey Service personnel—the Carlotti Communications System specialists—were concerned, Grimes was not so happy. They were an unknown quantity. But he relied on Sonya Verrill to be able to handle them—after all, they were her direct subordinates.

He signaled to Karen Schmidt to serve out another round of drinks, then unstrapped himself and got carefully to his feet, held to the deck by the magnetized soles of his shoes. He said, "There's no need to hurry yourselves, but I wish to see all departmental heads in my day room in fifteen minutes."

He walked to the axial shaft, let himself into the tubular alleyway and, ignoring the spiral staircase, pulled himself rapidly forward along the guideline. A vibration of the taut wire told him that he was being followed. He turned to see who it was, and was not surprised to see that it was Sonya Verrill.

She sat facing him across his big desk.

She said, "This is no laughing matter, John. This isn't just one big joke."

"The wild ghost chase, you mean? I thought that it was rather clever. Oh, I know that you've your own axe to grind, Sonya—but you have to admit that most of us, and that includes me, are along just for the hell of it. Your people, I suppose, are here because they have to be."

"No. They're volunteers."

"Then don't take things so bloody seriously, woman. We shall all of us do our best—my crew as well as yours. But I don't think that anybody, apart from myself, has any clue as to your private motives."

She smiled unhappily. "You're right, of course, John. But . . ."

There was a sharp rap at the door. "Come in!" called Grimes.

They came in—Swinton, and the burly, redhaired Calhoun, Chief Mannschenn Drive Engineer, and scrawny, balding McHenry, Chief Reaction Drive Engineer. They were followed by the gangling, dreamy Mayhew, Psionic Radio Officer, by little, fat Petersham, the Purser, and by the yellow-haired, stocky Karen Schmidt. Then came Todhunter, the dapper little Surgeon, accompanied by Renfrew, the Survey Service Lieutenant in charge of the modified Carlotti gear.

They disposed themselves on chairs and settees, adjusted their seat straps with practiced hands.

"You may smoke," said Grimes, filling and lighting his own battered pipe. He waited until the others' pipes and cigars and cigarettes were under way, then said quietly, "None of you need to be told that this is not a commercial voyage." He grinned. "It is almost like a return to the bad old days of piracy. We're like the legendary Black Bart, Scourge of the Spaceways, just cruising along waiting for some fat prize to wander within range of our guns. Not that Black Bart ever went ghost hunting. . . ."

"He would have done, sir," put in Swinton, "if there'd been money in it."

"There's money in anything if you can figure the angle," contributed McHenry.

This was too much for Sonya Verrill. "I'd have you gentlemen know," she said coldly, "that the question of money doesn't enter into it. This expedition is classed as pure scientific research."

"Is it, Commander Verrill?" Grimes' heavy eyebrows lifted sardonically. "I don't think that we should have had the backing either of your Government or of ours unless some farsighted politicians had glimpsed the possibility of future profits. After all, trade between the Alternative Universes could well be advantageous to all concerned."

"If there *are* Alternative Universes," put in Calhoun.

"What do you mean, Commander? I specified that the personnel of this ship was to be made up of those who have actually sighted Rim Ghosts."

"That is so, sir. But we should bear in mind the possibility—or the probability—that the Rim Ghosts *are* ghosts—ghosts, that is, in the old-fashioned sense of the word."

"We shall bear it in mind, Commander," snapped Grimes. "And if it is so, then we shall, at least have made a small contribution to the sum total of human knowledge." He drew deeply from his pipe, exhaled a cloud of blue smoke that drifted lazily towards the nearest exhaust vent. "Meanwhile, gentlemen, we shall proceed, as I have already said, as though we were a pirate ship out of the bad old days. All of you will impress upon your juniors the necessity for absolute alertness at all times. For example, Commander Swinton, the practice of passing a boring watch by playing three-dimensional noughts and crosses in the plotting tank will cease forthwith." Swinton blushed. This had been the habit of his that had aroused the ire of the Master and the Chief Officer of *Rim Mastodon*. "And, Commander Calhoun, we shall both of us be most unhappy if the log desk in the Mannschenn Drive Room is found to be well stocked with light reading matter and girlie magazines." It was Calhoun's turn to look embarrassed. "Oh, Commander McHenry, the Reaction Drive was in first class condition when we blasted off from Port Forlorn. A few hours' work should suffice to restore it to that condition. I shall not expect to find the Reaction Drive Engine Room littered with bits and pieces that will eventually be reassembled five seconds before planetfall." The Surgeon, the Purser and the Catering Officer looked at each other apprehensively, but the Commodore pounced next on the Psionic Radio Officer. "Mr. Mayhew, I know that it is the standard practice for you people to gossip with your opposite number all over the Galaxy, but on this voyage, unless I order otherwise, a strict listening watch only is to be kept. Is that understood?"

"You're the boss," replied Mayhew dreamily and then, realizing what he had said, "Yes, sir. Of course, sir. Very good, sir."

Grimes let his glance wander over Todhunter, Petershamm and Schmidt, sighed regretfully. He said, "I think that is all. Have you anything to add, Commander Verrill?"

"You seem to have cleared up all the salient points insofar as your own officers are concerned," said the girl. "And I am sure that Mr. Renfrew is capable of carrying out the orders that he has already been given."

"Which are, Commander?"

"As you already know, sir, to maintain his equipment in a state of constant, manned readiness, and to endeavour to lock on to a Rim Ghost as soon as one is sighted."

"Good. In that case we all seem to know what's expected. We stand on, and stand on, until . . ."

"I still think, sir," said Calhoun, "that we should be carrying a Chaplain—one qualified to carry out exorcism."

"To exorcise the Rim Ghosts," Sonya Verrill told him, "is the very last thing that we want to do."

～ Chapter 7 ～

THEY STOOD ON . . .

And on.

Second by second, minute by minute, hour by hour the time was ticked away by the ship's master chronometer; watch succeeded watch, day succeeded day. There was normal Deep Space routine to keep the hands occupied, there were the frequent drills—at first carried out at set times and then, as every officer learned what was expected of him, at random intervals—to break the monotony. But nothing was sighted, nothing was seen outside the viewports but the distorted lens of the Galaxy, the faint, far, convoluted nebulosities that were the sparse Rim stars.

Grimes discussed matters with Sonya Verrill.

He said, "I've been through all the records, and I still can't discover a pattern."

"But there is a pattern," she told him. "On every occasion at least one member of the group to sight a Rim Ghost has seen his own alternative self."

"Yes, yes. I know that. But what physical conditions must be established before a sighting? What initial velocity, for example? What temporal precession rate? As far as I can gather, such things have had no bearing on the sightings whatsoever."

"Then they haven't."

"But there must be some specific combination of circumstances, Sonya."

33

"Yes. But it could well be something outside the ship from which the ghost is sighted, some conditions peculiar to the region of Space that she is traversing."

"Yes, yes. But what?"

"That, John, is one of the things we're supposed to find out."

Grimes said, "You know, Sonya, I think that perhaps we are on the wrong track, We're trying to do the job with technicians and machinery . . ."

"So?"

"How shall I put it? This way, perhaps. It could be that the best machine to employ would be the human mind. Or brain."

"What do you mean?"

"That Calhoun may have something after all. It will not surprise you to learn that I have, on microfilm, a complete dossier on every Rim Worlds' officer in this ship. I've been through these dossiers, hoping to establish some sort of pattern. As you know, every Rim Worlder in this ship has at least one Rim Ghost sighting to his name. Now, our Mr. Calhoun, or Commander Calhoun if you like—you recall his remarks at our first conference, just after we'd lined up for the Mellise sun?"

"I do. He was saying that the Rim Ghosts might be *real*—or should one say *unreal?*—ghosts."

"Yes. Anyhow, Calhoun was born on the Rim. On Ultimo, to be exact. But his parents were migrants. From Dunglass."

"Yes. . . ."

"You know Dunglass?"

"I was there once. An odd world. Ruled by a theocracy . . . Or is 'theocracy' the right word? But the United Reformed Spiritualist Church runs the show, after a fashion."

"Probably as well as any other government on any other world. Anyhow, the U.R.S.C., as no doubt you know, has its share of heretics. Calhoun's parents were such. Apparently the house in which they lived was haunted, and they employed a bootleg exorcist to lay the ghost. This was frowned upon by the authorities, so much so that the Calhouns decided to emigrate. Now, one can be a heretic without being either an atheist or an agnostic. The Calhouns still *believe*, although reserving the right to believe in their own way. Their only son was brought up in their religion."

"And so what?"

"So—ignoring telepathy, telekinesis, teleportation and the like— what proportion of psychic phenomena is due to the activities of the dear departed, and what proportion is due to a . . . leakage—from one Universe through to another?"

"H'm. I must confess that this was a line of approach that never occurred to me. I don't pretend to be an expert on so-called psychic matters, but if we did hold a seance, shouldn't we require a medium?"

"We have one—Mr. Mayhew."

"Yes. But as you know, all these Rhine Institute graduates insist that there's nothing supernatural about their psionic talents. Furthermore, one can be telepathic without being clairvoyant."

"Can one, Sonya? I'm not so sure. There are quite a few recorded cases of clairvoyance, and many of them can be explained by telepathy. Even the premonitory ones can be accounted for by assuming the reception of a telepathic broadcast from a Universe with a slightly different Time Scale. There is no need to assume that the Rim Ghosts are a supernatural phenomenon. If we do pay lip service to one of the supernatural religions it will only be to create the right conditions for our own experiments."

She said, "You rank me, John, and you're in command of this ship and this expedition. But I still don't like it."

"You think that we're selling out, as it were, to the supernaturalists?"

"Frankly, yes."

"I don't see it that way. What is natural, and what is supernatural? Can you draw a dividing line? *I* can't."

"All right." She unstrapped herself and got to her feet, the slight effort pushing her up and clear from the chair. She hung there, motionless, until the feeble gravitational field of her shoe soles pulled her back to the deck. Then, contact having been made with solidity, she flung her hands out in an appealing gesture. "Do what you can, John, any way you like. But do it. You've guessed how hard it was for me to persuade our top brass to pour time and money into what your Commander Swinton called a wild ghost chase. Unless we get results, there'll never be another one. And you know that I want results. And you know the sort of results I want." Her hands fell to her sides. "Only—only I've stood on my own flat feet for so long that it rather hurts to have to call in outside assistance."

"It won't be outside assistance, Sonya. We shall be working with and through our own people, aboard our own ship. All that we shall be trying to do will be the creation of conditions favorable to a leakage from one Universe to another."

"As you say. As you say." She laughed briefly. "After all, men and women have been in the habit of selling their souls to the Devil from the very beginnings of human history. Or mythology." She paused. "No, history is the better word."

He said, exasperated, "But we won't be selling our souls to the Devil. If it makes Calhoun any happier to think that he's gained a few converts to the odd faith of his parents, what does it matter?" He reached out for his telephone, pressed a numbered stud. "Mr. Mayhew? Commodore here. Can you spare me a moment?" He pressed another stud. "Commander Calhoun? Commodore here. Would you mind stepping up to my quarters?"

Sonya Verrill pulled herself back into her chair, buckled herself in and she and Grimes sat back to wait.

Mayhew was first to arrive in Grimes' day cabin. He was untidy as always, his uniform shirt sloppily buttoned, one shoulderboard hanging adrift, his wispy gray hair rumpled, his eyes vague and unfocused. He stifled a yawn. "Yes, sir?"

"Take a seat, please, Mr. Mayhew." There was a sharp rap at the door. "Come in!"

Calhoun entered, somewhat ostentatiously wiping his hands on a piece of waste. He, too, was told to be seated.

"Commander Calhoun," said Grimes, "I believe that you were brought up in the beliefs of the United Reformed Spiritualist Church?"

"No, sir." The engineer's reply was a stressed negative. "No, sir. I was brought up in the beliefs of the United Primitive Spiritualist Church." He seemed to realize that his answer had caused a certain confusion in Grimes' mind, so went on, "You will know something of Dunglass, sir. You will know that there were people, my parents among them, who advocated a return to the old beliefs, the old, the only true faith. The right to exorcise, for example . . ."

"Yes, Commander. I understand. But you believe in the existence of the Rim Ghosts?"

"Of course, sir—although it has yet to be determined if they are good or evil manifestations. If they are evil, then exorcism should be practiced."

"Yes, of course. As you are well aware, most of us in this ship do not hold the same views as yourself regarding the phenomena of the Rim Ghosts. But you will agree that it is desirable that contact be made with one or more of the apparitions—after all, this is the purpose of this expedition. And if such contact is made . . ." Grimes paused. "If such contact is made, it might well be to the advantage of your church."

"That is so, sir."

"Perhaps you might help us to make such a contact."

"How, sir? I do not think that tampering with the Drive controls will achieve any useful result."

"That was not in my mind. But it had occurred to me, Commander, that there are certain rites practiced by your Church . . ."

"A seance, you mean, Commodore? But I have no mediumistic talents. If such had been the case I should not be here now; I should have entered our priesthood."

"But you know the drill?"

"Yes, sir. I am conversant with the rites and ceremonies. But without a medium they are valueless."

"Here is our medium," said Grimes, nodding towards the almost asleep Mayhew.

The Psionic Radio Officer jerked awake. "Come off it!" he ejaculated. "I'm a technician, not a cheap fortune teller!" Then, "I beg your pardon, sir. What I meant to say is that the Rhine Institute has always been opposed to superstition."

"Religion is not superstition, you half-witted teacup reader!" shouted Calhoun.

"Gentlemen, gentlemen . . ." soothed Grimes. "Need I remind you that we are under Naval discipline, and that I could order you, Commander Calhoun, to organize a seance, and you Mr. Mayhew, to officiate as medium?"

"Even in the Navy, *sir*," said Calhoun, his freckles standing out sharply against the suddenly white skin of his face, "there are lawful and unlawful commands."

"And," Grimes told him coldly, "bearing in mind the peculiar purpose of this expedition, such a command made by myself would be construed as lawful by the Board of Admiralty. But many centuries ago, back in the days when navies were made up of wooden ships sailing Earth's seas, there used to be a saying: 'One volunteer is worth ten pressed men.' Surely, Commander, you will not hesitate to volunteer to play your part in an experiment that, when made public, could well result in a flood of converts to your faith?"

"If you put it that way, sir, But . . ."

"And surely, Mr. Mayhew, you will not hesitate to play your part? After all, it could well lead to a Fellowship of your Institute. . . ."

"But, sir, the superstition . . ."

"If you dare to use that word again, Mayhew . . ." threatened Calhoun.

"Commander! Please remember where you are. And Mr. Mayhew, I am asking you to respect Commander Calhoun's beliefs. If that is ineffective I shall order you to do so—with the usual penalties if the order is willfully disobeyed."

The pair of them lapsed into a sulky silence.

Grimes went on, "I shall leave matters in your hands, Commander. You are the only person in the ship qualified to carry out the necessary organization. And you, Mr. Mayhew, will co-operate fully with Commander Calhoun." He smiled briefly. "And now, gentlemen, perhaps a little refreshment before you engage yourself upon what are, after all, somewhat unusual duties. . . ."

When they were gone, mellowed by the alcohol, almost friendly towards each other, Sonya Verrill said, "The big stick and the carrot . . . I hope the combination gets results."

"I hope it gets the results we want," replied Grimes. "We don't want to raise any ghosts of the wrong sort."

"No," whispered Sonya, her face suddenly pale and strained. *"No."*

❧ Chapter 8 ❧

THE PREPARATIONS for the seance took much longer than Grimes had anticipated. But it was obvious that Calhoun, religiously as well as professionally, was a perfectionist. The most time-consuming operation was the construction of a harmonium, during which the wardroom piano was cannibalized for its keyboard, this being cut down from seven and a half octaves to five. The engineer's workshop was able to turn out the necessary bellows and treadles, and the brass vibrators or "reeds." The ivory from the surplus keys was utilized in the manufacture of the various stops. Grimes, watching with interest the fabrication of the archaic instrument, listening wincingly to the caterwauling notes of its initial tests—"We must *get* the *wheezing* quality . . ." insisted Calhoun—was inclined to deplore the sacrifice of what had been a well-cared-for and versatile music maker, the life and soul of many a good party during previous expeditions in *Faraway Quest*. But the seance had been his idea initially, so he felt that he had no right to criticize.

Then the wardroom was stripped of its fittings. The comfortable, well padded chairs were removed and replaced by hard metal benches. The paneling was covered by dingy gray drapes—bedsheets that had been passed through a dye concocted from peculiar ingredients by Dr. Todhunter and Karen Schmidt. Dimmers were fitted to the light switches, and some of the fluorescent tubes were removed and replaced by bulbs giving a peculiarly dingy red illumination. And there were other accessories to be made: A tin speaking trumpet, and a tambourine, both of which were decorated with lines and blobs of luminous paint.

At last everything was ready.

Grimes sent for his First Lieutenant. "Commander Swinton," he said, "we shall hold our seance at 2100 hours this evening, ship's time. Please see to it that all departments are notified."

"Ay, ay, sir."

"And wipe that silly grin off your face!"

"Sorry, sir. But you must admit that after that toast, when we spliced the mainbrace, this is turning out to be a wilder ghost chase than any of us anticipated."

"From Commander Calhoun's viewpoint it's somewhat less wild than it was, Swinton. As far as he's concerned we're dropping all the scientific flummery and returning to the primitive methods, the tried and trusted methods, of his religion. And all the evidence indicates that these methods do work after a fashion. They create the right atmosphere. They raise—*something*. From inside, a release of the wild talents possessed by those present at the seance? From Outside? From the next Time Track but three? I don't know, Swinton. I don't know—yet."

"It will be an interesting experiment."

"Yes. And I'm pleased that Mr. Mayhew has been persuaded to look at it in that light."

"I suppose that he *has* got mediumistic talents, sir?"

"He must have, Swinton. What is a medium but a telepath?"

"Could be, sir. Could be. But . . ."

"Don't say that Commander Calhoun has converted *you?*"

"He's tried hard enough, sir. Oh, I'm willing to believe that his Church, in either the Primitive or the Reformed versions, has produced some interesting phenomena, but I've yet to be convinced that they're supernatural, any more than the Rim Ghosts are. I can't understand why the Rhine Institute hasn't done more to investigate Spiritualism."

"Because, my boy, it hasn't been allowed to. It's *scientific*. Every time that one of its investigators sniffs around a Spiritualist Church he's given either the cold shoulder or the bum's rush. You know the line of talk—'There are some things that we aren't *meant* to know. Faith is all-important; knowledge is a device of the Devil.' And so on. And so on."

"Then I'm surprised that Calhoun was among the volunteers for this expedition."

"You shouldn't be. Commander Calhoun has an axe to grind. He hopes that something will be discovered that will be useful to his Reformed Church. Exorcism by remote control, for example . . ."

"But that would be dragging in Science."

"As a servant, not as a competitor."

"I think I see . . ." The young man still looked dubious, however. "Will that be all, sir?"

"Yes, thank you, Commander Swinton. Oh, just one more thing. As soon as this . . . experiment is over, please get the wardroom looking like a wardroom, and not like a down-at-the-heels meeting house."

"That, sir, will be a pleasure."

Grimes dined in his own quarters that night—the wardroom, as it was at this time, was far too comfortless. Sonya Verrill kept him company. They enjoyed their meal together. Although it was simple it was well cooked and nicely served, and the wines from the Commodore's private stock were an excellent accompaniment to the food. While they were eating they chatted about minor matters and listened to the background music softly tinkling from Grimes' playmaster.

And then, after Grimes had produced two bulbs of vintage port and a box of fine cigars imported from Caribbea, they talked more seriously.

She said, "I hate to admit it, John, but I'm rather frightened."

"You, of all people? Why, Sonya?"

"As long as this expedition was being run on scientific lines it was . . . How shall I put it? It was, in spite of my own private reasons for being here, *fun*. Something in it, as you said, of the old days of piracy—but only playing at pirates. A Carlotti beacon instead of a real gun or laser projector, and a sort of atmosphere about it all of,

"Bang! You're dead!" But now . . . As I told you, I've been on Dunglass. It's a dreary world, with cities that are no more than straggling towns, streets and streets of mean little houses and Meeting Halls that are just sheds designed, one would think, with a deliberate avoidance of pleasing proportion. And the feeling all the time that one is being watched, disapprovingly, by the ghosts of all the countless millions who have gone before.

"I went to one or two of their services. Partly out of curiosity, and partly because it was my job, as an Intelligence Officer. Cold, cold halls—with a chill that didn't seem to be natural—and dreary hymn singing by drab people, and dim lights, and a voice that seemed to come from nowhere giving advice about the most trivial matters—and some that weren't so trivial. . . .

"Yes, I remember it well. There was this voice—a man's voice, deep, although the medium was a skinny little woman. The man sitting next to me whispered that it was Red Eagle, a Spirit Guide. He went on to say that this Red Eagle was, or had been, a Red Indian, an American Indian. I wondered what Red Eagle was doing so many light years away from home, but it occurred to me that Time and Space, as we know them, probably mean nothing to spirits, so kept quiet. The voice said, 'There is a stranger here tonight, a woman from beyond the sky.' Well, most of those present must have known who I was. The voice went on, 'I have a message for the stranger. I see a ship. I see a ship falling through the emptiness, far and far away . . .' Once again, so what? I was a spacewoman and it was no secret. 'Far away, far away, where the stars are few and dim, far and few . . . And I see the name of the ship, in gold letters on her prow . . . I can read the name . . . *Outsider*. . .' And that meant nothing to me—*then*. 'I see the Captain, brave in his black and gold. You know him. You will know him again . . .' And then there was a description of the Captain's appearance, and I knew that it was Derek Calver. As you are aware, I first met Derek when he was Second Mate of the old *Lorn Lady*. There is another man. He is one of the officers, although he, too, has been a Captain. He is afraid, and he is disgraced, and he is locked in his cabin . . .' And once again there was the description—even to the laser burn on the left buttock and the funny little mole just above the navel. It was Bill all right. Bill Maudsley. 'He is sick, and he is afraid, and you are not with him, and he knows that he has lost you forever. There is a bottle, and he drinks from it, and the spilled fluid drifts around the air of the cabin in a mist, in a spray. He looks at the empty bottle and curses, then smashes it on the wall. The broken, splintered neck is still in his hand, and he brings the sharp, jagged end of it across his throat . . .'

"I just sat there, in a sick, numb silence. I wanted to ask questions, but I couldn't in front of all those strangers. But there was nothing more. Nothing at all. Red Eagle had said his piece as far as I was concerned, and passed on all sorts of trivial messages to other members of the congregation. Bill Brown's grandmother was concerned because he wasn't wearing his long underwear, and Jimmy Smith's Aunt Susan wanted to tell him that trade would pick up next year, and so on, and so on.

"After the . . . meeting? Service? After the service I stayed on to have a talk with the minister. He was very sympathetic, and arranged for me to have a private sitting with the medium. It wasn't very satisfactory. Red Eagle seemed to be somewhat peeved at being called away from whatever it was that he was doing, and just told me that I should search long and far, and that I should and should not find that for which I was searching. "And what can be made of that? Shall I succeed in my search by becoming a ghost myself, before my time? I hope not. I'm too fond of life, John—life on this gross physical plane. I like good food and wine and tobacco and books and music and clothes and . . . and all the other things that make life, in spite of everything, so well worth living. There's far too much vagueness about what comes after. Oh, there are the stock protestations—'It is very beautiful here, and everybody is happy . . .'—but . . . It could be faulty transmission and reception, but I always get the impression that the After Life is lacking in character, and color and, but of course, the good, lusty pleasures of the flesh . . .

"Even so, I was shaken. Badly shaken."

"It could be explained by telepathy, Sonya."

"No, John, it couldn't be. I was not thinking about Bill Maudsley at the time—not until that message came through, and even then I was thinking only about Derek Calver. I didn't know that Bill had shipped as his Mate. And as for . . . And as for the shocking manner of his death, that I did *not* know about. I did not know about it officially for a matter of months, which was the time it took for the news to drift in from the Rim. But I checked up. I ran all available data through one of our Master Computers, and got one of our Specialist Navigators to run his own check, and there were no two ways about the answer. Bill must have taken his own life at the very time that I was sitting in that dreary Meeting Hall in Dovlesville, on Dunglass. . . ."

"It might be as well if you didn't attend the seance, Sonya," Grimes told her.

"And leave the show to you lousy secessionists?" she flared, with a flash of her old spirit. "No sir!"

⁓ Chapter 9 ⁓

WHEN GRIMES and Sonya Verrill went down to the wardroom they found that all was in readiness for the seance. The uncomfortable benches—it was fortunate, thought the Commodore, that the ship was falling free so that the only contact between buttocks and an unyielding surface was that produced by the gentle restriction of the seatbelts—had been arranged in rows, facing a platform on which were a table, three chairs and the harmonium. Calhoun, contriving to look like a nonconformist minister in spite of his uniform, occupied one of the chairs at the table. Mayhew, his usual dreaminess replaced by an air of acute embarrassment, sat in the other. Karen Schmidt was seated at the musical instrument.

As soon as the Commodore and Sonya had taken a bench in the front row the engineer, unbuckling his seat belt, got carefully to his feet. His voice, as he made the initial announcement, was more of a street corner bray than a pulpit bleat. "Brethren," he said, "we are here as humble seekers, gathered in all humility, to beg that our loved ones on the Other Side will shed light on our darkness. We pray to Them for help—but we must, also, be prepared to help Them. We must cast out doubt, and replace it by childlike faith. We must *believe*." He went on in a more normal voice, "This, I assure you, is essential. We must put ourselves in a receptive mood, throwing our minds and our hearts open to the benevolent powers on the other side of the veil . . ." Then, the engineer briefly ascendant over the lay preacher, "We must strive to create the right conditions insofar as we are able . . ."

Meanwhile, one of his juniors was making his way along the tiers of benches distributing mimeographed sheets. Grimes looked at his curiously. It was, he saw, a hymnal.

"Brethren!" cried Calhoun, "we will join in singing the first hymn."

Karen Schmidt was having trouble with the harmonium—the operation of treadles in the absence of a gravitational field requires a certain degree of concentration. At last, however, she got the thing going and suddenly and shockingly the introductory chords blared out.

Then they were all singing to the wheezing, gasping accompaniment:

"*Lead, Kindly Light, amid the encircling gloom,*
"*Lead Thou me on . . .*"

The hymn over, Calhoun prayed. Although himself an agnostic, Grimes was impressed by the sincerity of the man. He began to wish that he could believe in something.

There was another hymn, and then the lights were dimmed until only the dull-glowing red globes remained. The lines and blobs of luminous paint picking out the simple apparatus—the speaking trumpet and the tambourine—on the table gleamed eerily. Suddenly it was very quiet in the wardroom; the muted noises of machinery, the sobbing of pumps and whizzing of fans, the thin, high keening of the Mannschenn Drive, accentuated the silence rather than diminished it. It was very quiet—and very cold.

Physical or psychological? Grimes asked himself as he shivered.

His eyes were becoming accustomed to the almost-darkness. He could see the dark forms of Calhoun and Mayhew, sitting motionless at the table, and Karen Schmidt hunched over the harmonium. He turned his head to look at Sonya. Her face was so pale as to seem almost luminous. He put out his hand to grasp hers, gave it a reassuring squeeze. She returned the pressure, and seemed reluctant to relinquish the physical contact.

Mayhew cleared his throat. He said matter-of-factly, "There's something coming through. . . ."

"Yes?" whispered Calhoun. *"Yes?"*

Mayhew chuckled. "It's only a routine message, I'm afraid. *Flora Macdonald* . . ."

"But you must have heard of her," insisted Calhoun in a low voice. "She lived in the eighteenth century, on Earth. She was a Jacobite heroine. . . ."

Mayhew chuckled again. "Not this *Flora Macdonald*. She's a Waverley Royal Mail cargo liner, and she's off Nova Caledon . . . All the same, this is remarkable range I'm getting, with no amplifier. It must be that the brains of all you people, in these somewhat peculiar circumstances, are supplying the necessary boost. . . ."

"Mr. Mayhew, you are ruining the atmosphere!"

"Commander Calhoun, I consented to take part in this experiment on the understanding that it was to be treated as an experiment."

Something tinkled sharply.

At the table, forgetting this disagreement, Calhoun and Mayhew were staring at the tambourine. Grimes stared too, saw that something had broken its magnetic contact with the steel surface, that it had lifted and was drifting, swaying gently, carried by the air currents of the ventilation system.

But the exhaust ducts were in the bulkhead behind the platform, and the thing, bobbing and jingling, was making its slow, unsteady way towards the intake ports, on the other side of the wardroom.

Grimes was annoyed. This was no time for practical jokes. Telekinesis was an uncommon talent, for some reason not usually found among spacemen, but not so uncommon as all that. There was, the Commodore knew, one telekineticist in *Faraway Quest*'s crew— and he would be on the carpet very shortly.

But . . .

But he was the Third Mate, and he was on watch and, in any case, all the tests that he had undergone had proven his incapability of any but the most trivial telekinetic feats.

So this, after all, was no more than some freak of air circulation.

The harmonium wheezed discordantly.

Calhoun was on his feet, furious. "Can't you people take things seriously? This is a religious service! Miss Schmidt, stop that vile noise at once! Stop it, I say! Lights, somebody! Lights!"

The incandescent tubes flared into harsh brilliance. The tambourine steadied and hung motionless, and then behaved in the normal manner of a small object floating loose in Free Fall, drifting very slowly with the air current towards the exhaust ducts. But at the harmonium Karen Schmidt still twitched and shuddered, her feet erratically pumping, her hands falling at random on the keyboard. Her eyes were glazed and her face vacant; her mouth was open and little globules of saliva, expelled by her sterntorous breathing, hung about her jerking head in a glistening cloud.

Grimes unsnapped his seat belt and got to his feet. "Dr. Todhunter! See to Miss Schmidt, will you?"

But all Calhoun's anger had evaporated.

"No!" he shouted. "No! Be seated, everybody!"

"Like that woman," Sonya Verrill was whispering tensely.

"Let me pass!" It was Todhunter, trying to make his way through the packed rows of benches. "Let me pass."

And then Karen Schmidt spoke.

But it was not with her own voice. It was with the voice of a man—deep, resonant. At first the words seemed to be an unknown language—a strange but hauntingly familiar tongue. And then, with a subtle shift of stress and tempo, they were understandable.

"Falling . . . falling . . .

"Through the night and through the nothingness you seek and you fall . . .

"But I am the onlooker; I care not if you seek and find, if you seek and fail.

"I am the onlooker."

Calhoun was taking charge. "Who are you?"

"I am the onlooker."

"Have you a message?"

"I have no message." There was laughter that seemed to come from nowhere and everywhere. "Why should I have a message?"

"But tell us. Shall we succeed?"

"Why should I tell you? Why should you succeed? What is success, and what is failure?"

"But there must be a message!" The initial awe in Calhoun's voice was being replaced by exasperation. Grimes was reminded of those primitive peoples, sincere believers, who maltreat the images of their gods should those deities fail to deliver the goods.

Again the uncanny laughter. "Little man, what message do you want? Would you know the day and hour and manner of your death? Would you live the rest of your life in fear and trembling, striving to evade the unavoidable?" The hands of the medium swept over the keyboard, and the instrument responded—not discordantly, not wheezingly, but with the tones of a great organ. And the music was the opening bars of the "Dead March" in *Saul*. "Is this the message you crave?"

Sonya Verrill, standing stiff and straight, cried, "Is this all you have for us? Is that the limit of your powers—to tell us all what we know already, that some day we must die?"

For the last time there was the sound of laughter, and the voice said quietly, "Here is your message." And then came the shrilling of the alarm bells, the repetition of the Morse symbol A, short long, short long, short long . . . Action Stations.

≈ Chapter 10 ≈

SHE HUNG THERE on *Faraway Quest's* port beam, matching velocity and temporal precession rate, a big ship, conventional enough in design, nothing at all strange about her, except that both radar and mass proximity indicator screens remained obstinately blank. Already the oddly twisted directional antenna of the *Quest's* Carlotti apparatus was trained upon her, like the barrel of some fantastic gun, already the whine of the emergency generators, feeding power into the huge solenoid that was the ship, was audible over and above the still ringing alarm bells, the sounds of orderly confusion.

"Nothing showing on the screens, sir," the Third Officer was reporting. "And the transceiver is dead."

Swinton was already at the huge mounted binoculars. He muttered, "I think I can read her name ... *Rim Ranger* ..."

"And that," said Grimes, "is what I had in mind for the next addition to our fleet.... Interesting ..."

"Call her on the lamp, sir?"

"No. If all goes well we shall soon be able to communicate through the usual channels. Ready, Mr. Renfrew?"

"Ready and standing by, sir," answered the Survey Service lieutenant.

"Good." And then Grimes found that he was groping for words in which to frame his order. He had almost said, "Fire!" but that was hardly applicable.

"Make contact!" snapped Sonya Verrill.

Renfrew, strapped into his seat at the controls of his apparatus, did look like a gunner, carefully laying and training his weapon, bringing the target into the spiderweb sights. One of his juniors was snapping meter readings: "Red twenty five, red fifty, red seventy five, eighty five . . . Red ninety, ninety-five . . . six . . . seven . . . eight . . . nine . . ."

There was a long pause and the men around the modified Carlotti gear were muttering among themselves. Swinton, who was still watching the other ship, announced, "She's flashing. Morse, it looks like . . ."

"Stand by!" shouted Renfrew. "Now!"

The Carlotti gear whined intolerably, whined and crackled, and the men serving it sneezed as arc-engendered ozone stung their nostrils. There was tension, almost unbearable strain, a psychological rending—and Grimes realized that he was seeing double, that every person, every piece of apparatus in the control room was visually duplicated. But it was more than a mere visual duplication—that was the frightening part. One image of Swinton was still hunched over the eyepieces of the binoculars, the other had turned to stare at Renfrew and his crew. One image of Renfrew still had both hands at the console of his apparatus, the other had one hand raised to stifle a sneeze. And there was a growing confusion of sound as well as of sight. It was—the old, old saying flashed unbidden into Grimes' mind—an Irish parliament, with everybody talking and nobody listening.

And it was like being stretched on a rack, stretched impossibly and painfully—until something snapped.

The other ship, *Rim Ranger*, was there still, looming large in the viewports, close, too close. A voice—it could have been Swinton's— was yelping from the transceiver, "What ship?" Then, "What the hell are you playing at, you fools?"

Grimes realized that he was in the Captain's chair, although he had no recollection of having seated himself. His own control console was before him. There was only one way to avoid collision, and that was by the use of rocket power. (And he had given strict orders that the Reaction Drive was to be kept in a state of readiness at all times.) There was a microsecond of hesitation as his hand swept down to the firing key—the jettison of mass while the Mannschenn Drive was in operation could have unpredictable consequences. But it was the only way to avoid collision. Even with the solenoid cut off there was enough residual magnetism to intensify the normal interaction due to the gravitational fields of the two vessels.

But he was gentle, careful.

From aft there was only the gentlest cough, and acceleration was no more than a nudge, although heavy enough to knock unsecured personnel off balance and tumble them to the deck.

And outside the viewports there was nothing—no strange ship, no convoluted, distorted Galactic lens, no dim and distant luminosities.

This was the Ultimate Night.

~ Chapter 11 ~

SOME HOURS LATER they came to the unavoidable conclusion that they were alone in absolute nothingness. Their signaling equipment—both physical and parapsychological—was useless, as were their navigational instruments. There was nobody to talk to, nothing to take a fix on. Presumably they were still falling free (through *what?*)—still, thanks to the temporal precession fields of the Drive, proceeding at an effective velocity in excess of that of light. But here—whatever *here* was—there was no light. There was no departure point, no destination.

After conferring with his senior officers Grimes ordered the Mannschenn Drive shut down. They had nowhere to go, and there was no point in wasting power or in subjecting the complexity of ever-precessing gyroscopes to unnecessary wear and tear. And then he passed word for a general meeting in the wardroom.

That compartment was, of course, still wearing its drab camouflage as a meeting house. The tin speaking trumpet adhered to the surface of the table still; the tambourine clung to the bulkhead hard by one of the exhaust ducts. But this time it was Grimes who took the main platform seat, with Sonya Verrill at his side. Pale and shaken, still dazed after her involuntary mediumism, Karen Schmidt seated herself again at the harmonium. Grimes looked at her curiously, then shrugged. She might as well sit there as anywhere else.

He called the meeting to order. He said, "Gentlemen, you may carry on smoking, but I wish to point out that it may be some little time before we are able to lay in fresh supplies." He was grimly amused as he noticed Todhunter, who was in the act of selecting a fresh cigarette from his platinum case, snap it hastily shut and return it to his pocket. He went on, "Gentlemen, I accept the responsibility for what has happened. I know that the reduction of the ship's mass while the Mannschenn Drive is in operation may, and almost certainly will, have unpredictable consequences. I was obliged to throw away reaction mass. And now we don't know where—or *when*—we are."

Sonya Verrill interrupted him sharply. "Don't be silly, John. If you hadn't used the rockets there'd be no doubt as to our condition, or the condition of the people in the other ship. A collision, and none of us wearing suits . . ."

"She's right," somebody murmured, and somebody else muttered something about proposing a vote of confidence.

But this, thought Grimes, was no time to allow democracy to raise its head. He had nothing against democracy—as long as it stayed on a planetary surface. But in Deep Space there must be a dictatorship—a dictatorship hedged around with qualifications and safeguards, but a dictatorship nonetheless. Too, he was not sure that he liked Sonya Verrill's use of his given name in public. He said coldly, "I appreciate your trust in me, but I do not think that any useful purpose would be served by putting the matter to the vote. As commanding officer I am fully responsible for this expedition." He allowed himself a brief smile. "But I am not omniscient. I assure you that I shall welcome any and all explanations of our present predicament, and any proposals as to ways and means of extricating ourselves from this . . ." he finished lamely, "mess."

Swinton, seated in the front row with the other departmental heads, started to laugh. It was not hysterical laughter. Grimes glared at the young officer from under his heavy brows, said icily, "Please share the joke, Commander Swinton."

"I'm sorry, sir, but it *is* rather funny. When we had the seance Miss Schmidt, at the console of that most peculiar poor man's organ, played on the white keys, and on the black keys. But *you*, at *your* console, played in the cracks."

"What do you mean, Commander Swinton?"

"That we're in one of the cracks. We jumped tracks, but when we tried to jump back we didn't make it. We fell into the crack."

"Very neat, Swinton," admitted Grimes. "A very neat analogy. We've fallen into the gulf between Universes. But how are we to climb out?"

"Perhaps Commander Calhoun could help. . . ." suggested Renfrew. "When we held the seance we got in touch with . . . something."

Karen Schmidt cried, "No! No! You've not had something utterly alien taking charge of your mind and your body. I have, and I'll not go through it again!"

Surprisingly Calhoun also showed a lack of enthusiasm. He said carefully, "That . . . entity was not at all helpful. If we had succeeded in making contact with one of the regular Guides, all would have been well. But we didn't. And I fear that should we succeed in getting in touch with that same entity we shall merely expose ourselves in further derision."

"Well?" asked Grimes, breaking the silence that followed Calhoun's little speech.

Once again the Survey Service lieutenant spoke up. "I see it this way, sir. The Mannschenn Drive got us into this mess, perhaps it can get us out of it. Although the fact that my own apparatus was functioning at the time has some bearing on it. But, putting it crudely, it boils down to the fact that the mass of the ship was suddenly reduced while two Time-twisting machines—the Mannschenn Drive and the Carlotti Beacon—were in operation. As you know, experiments have been made with both of them from the Time Travel angle; no doubt you have heard of Fergus and the crazy apparatus he set up on Wenceslaus, the moon of Carinthia. . . . Well, I shall want the services of the Mannschenn Drive engineers and of everybody in the ship with any mathematical training. I think I know what we can do to get out of this hole, but it would be as well to work out the theory, as far as is possible, first."

"And what do you have in mind, Mr. Renfrew?" asked Grimes.

"Just this, sir. A duplication as far as possible of the conditions obtaining when, as your Commander Swinton puts it, we fell into the crack, *but with those conditions reversed in one respect.*"

"Which is?"

"The running of the Mannschenn Drive in reverse."

"It can't be done," stated Calhoun flatly.

"It can be done, Commander, although considerable modification will be necessary."

"We can give it a go," said Swinton.

"Yes," agreed Grimes. "We can give it a go. But it is essential that nothing be done in practice until the theory has been thoroughly explored. I have no need to tell you that a reversal of temporal precession might well age us all many years in a few seconds. Or there is another possibility. We may be flung into the far future—a future that could be extremely un-hospitable. A future in which the last of the suns of this Galaxy are dying, in which the worlds are dead. Or a future in which one of the non-humanoid races has gained supremacy—the Shaara, for example, or the Darshans. Oh, we maintain diplomatic relations with them, but they don't like us any more than we like them."

"Mr. Renfrew," said Sonya Verrill, "holds a Master's degree in Multi-Dimensional Physics."

"And I, Commander Verrill, hold a Master Astronaut's certificate. I've seen some of the things that happen when a Mannschenn Drive unit gets out of control, and I've had firsthand accounts of similar accidents, and I've a healthy respect for the brute."

"But it is essential that no time be wasted," said Renfrew.

"Why, Lieutenant? What Time is there in this . . . Limbo? Oh, there's biological time, but as far as air, water and food are concerned the ship is a closed economy. I regret that the bio-chemists failed to plant a cigarette tree in our 'farm,' but we still have the facilities for brewing and distilling."

"Then, Commodore, at least I have your permission to make a start on the math?"

"Of course."

Renfrew spoke half to himself. "To begin with, all three executive officers are qualified navigators. There is no reason why, with two of them working in their watches below, the third one should not do his share of the calculations."

"There is a very good reason why not," remarked Swinton.

"Indeed, Commander? I was forgetting that in spite of your status as a Reserve Officer you are really a civilian. Would that be breaking your Award, or something equally absurd?"

Swinton flushed, but replied quietly. "As long as we are serving in what, legally speaking, is a Rim Worlds warship, governed by the Articles of War, we are not civilians. My point is this—that it is essential that a good lookout be kept at all times, by all means. The officer of the watch must be fully alert, not tangled up in miles of taped calculations spewing from the control room computer."

"But we're in absolute nothingness," growled Renfrew.

"Yes, but . . ."

"But we're in a crack," finished Grimes for him, feeling a childish happiness at having beaten his First Lieutenant to the draw. "And all sorts of odd things have the habit of falling into cracks!"

⇜ Chapter 12 ⇝

FARAWAY QUEST fell through the nothingness, drifting from nowhere to nowhere, a tiny bubble of light and heat and life lost in an infinite negation. Her electronic radio apparatus was useless. And Mayhew, the Psionic Radio Operator, crouched long hours in his cabin, staring into vacancy and listening, listening. He resorted to drugs to step up the sensitivity of both himself and the dog's brain that was his organic amplifier, but never the faintest whisper from Outside disturbed the telepath's mind. And the work went on, the laborious calculations that, even with the ship's computers fully employed, took days, longer in the programming than in the actual reckoning. There were so many variables, too many variables. There were so many unknown quantities. There were too many occasions when the words *Data Insufficient* were typed on the long tapes issuing from the slots of the instruments.

And Grimes, albeit with reluctance, held himself aloof from the activity. He said to Sonya, "Why keep a dog and bark yourself?" But he knew that he, at least, should be free to make decisions, to take action at a second's notice if needs be. He was grateful that the woman was able to keep him company. She, like himself, could not afford to be tied down. She was in command of the Survey Service personnel and directly subordinate to the Commodore insofar as the overall command of the expedition was concerned. And there were administrative worries too. Tempers were beginning to fray. The

59

latent hostility between members of different services, and between members of different departments, was beginning to manifest itself. And as Grimes knew full well, unless something happened soon there would be other worries.

They were castaways, just as surely as though they had been the crew and passengers of a ship wrecked on some hitherto undiscovered planet. There were thirty of them: eight Survey Service officers, twenty-two Rim Worlds Naval Reservists. Of the thirty, eight were women. As long as this had been no more than a voyage—not a routine voyage, to be sure, but a voyage nonetheless—sex had not been a problem. As long as all hands were fully occupied with mathematical work and, eventually, the modifications of the Mannschenn Drive, sex would not be a problem. But if every attempt to escape from the crack in Time failed, and if the ship were to drift eternally, a tiny, fertile oasis in a vast desert of nothingness, then something would have to be done about it. Spacemen are not monks, neither are spacewomen nuns.

"We may have to face the problem, Sonya," said Grimes worriedly as the two of them, cautiously sipping bulbs of Dr. Todhunter's first experimental batch of beer, talked things over.

She said, "I've already been facing it, John. The disproportion of the sexes makes things awkward. Oh, I know that in one or two cases it doesn't matter—my own Sub-Lieutenant Patsy Kent, for example. But even if she doesn't draw the line at polyandry, there's no guarantee that her boyfriends will take kindly to it."

He said, "We may be crossing our bridges before we come to them, if we ever do come to them. But that's one of the things that a commanding officer is paid for. It looks as though we may have to devise some workable system of polyandry. . . ."

"Include me out," she said sharply. "By some people's standards I've led a far from moral life, but I have my own standards, and they're the most important as far as I'm concerned. If the microcosmic civilization aboard this ship degenerates to a Nature red in tooth and claw sort of set-up, then I'm looking after Number One. The best bet will be to become the private, personal popsy of the Old Man of the tribe."

He looked at her carefully as she sat there in the armchair, contriving to loll even in conditions of Free Fall. She was wearing uniform shorts and her smooth, tanned legs were very long, and her carelessly buttoned shirt revealed the division between her firm breasts. He looked at her and thought, *The Old Man of the tribe . . . But it's a figure of speech only. I'm not all that old.* He said drily, "I suppose that rank should have its privileges. And if I'm the Old Man of *my* tribe, then you're the Old Woman of yours."

She said, "You flatter me, sir."

He said, "In any case, all this talk is rather jumping the gun. Your Mr. Renfrew and my own bright boys may come up with the answer."

She said, "They may not—and a girl has to look after herself."

He murmured, more to himself than to her, "I wish that there were some other reason for your . . . proposition."

She laughed, but tremulously, "And do you really think that there's not, John?"

"But these are exceptional circumstances," he said. "I know your reasons for embarking on this expedition. There were two men in your life, in our own Continuum, and you lost both of them. You're hoping to find what you lost."

"And perhaps I have found it. We've been cooped up in this tin coffin together long enough now. I've watched you, John, and I've seen how you've reacted to emergencies, how you've kept a tight rein on your people without playing the petty tyrant. They all respect you, John, and so does my own staff. And so do I."

He said, a little bitterly, "Respect isn't enough."

"But it helps, especially when respect is accompanied by other feelings. It would help, too, if you were to regard me, once in a while, as a woman, and not as Commander Verrill, Federation Survey Service."

He managed a grin. "This is so sudden."

She grinned back. "Isn't it?" And then she was serious again. "All right. I don't mind admitting that the jam we're in has brought things to a head. We may never get back again—either to our own Continuum or to any of the more or less parallel ones. We may all die if one of our bright young men does something exceptionally brilliant. But let's ignore the morbid—or the more morbid—possibility. Just suppose that we do drift for a fair hunk of eternity on our little, self-sustaining desert island. As you know, some of the old gaussjammers have been picked up that have been adrift for centuries, with the descendants of their original crews still living aboard them. . . .

"Well, we drift. You're the boss of your tribe, I'm the boss of my smaller tribe. Our getting together would be no more than a political alliance."

He said, "How romantic."

"We're rather too old for romance, John."

"Like hell we are."

He reached out for her, and she did not try to avoid him.

He reached out for her, and as he kissed her he wondered how long it was since he had felt a woman's lips—warm, responsive—on his. *Too long,* he thought. And how long was it since he had felt the rising tide of passion and let the softly thunderous breakers (her heart and his, and the combined thudding loud in his ears) bear him where they would? How long since he had felt the skin—firm, resilient, silken-soft—of a woman, and how long since the heat of his embrace was answered with a greater heat?

Too long . . .

"Too long . . ." she was murmuring. "Too long . . ." Then was silent again as his mouth covered hers.

And outside the cabin was the ship, and outside the ship was the black nothingness. . . .

But there was warmth in the cabin, and glowing light, a light that flared to almost unendurable brilliance and then faded, but slowly, slowly, to a comforting glow that would never go out, that would flare again, and again. There was warmth in the cabin and a drowsy comfort, and a sense of security that was all wrong in these circumstances—and yet was unanswerably right.

Grimes recalled the words of the medium—or the words of the entity that had assumed control of her mind and body. *"Through the night and through the nothingness you seek and you fall . . ."*

And he and Sonya had sought, and they had found.

They had sought, and they had found—not that for which they were seeking—or had they? She had been seeking a lover, and he? Adventure? Knowledge?

But all that was worth knowing, ever, was in his arms. (He knew that this mood would evaporate—and knew that it would return.)

She whispered something.

"What was that, darling?"

She murmured, "Now you'll have to make an honest woman of me."

"Of course," he replied. "Provided that the Federation taxpayers kick in with a really expensive wedding present."

She cast doubts on his legitimacy and bit his ear, quite painfully, and they were engaged in a wrestling match that could only have one possible ending when the alarm bells started to ring.

This time their curses were in earnest, and Grimes, pulling on his shorts, hurried out of the cabin to the control room, leaving Sonya to follow as soon as she was dressed.

But it made no sense, he thought, no sense at all—Action Stations in this all pervading nothingness.

∾ Chapter 13 ∾

GRIMES, whose quarters were immediately abaft the control room, was in that compartment in a matter of seconds. He found there young Larsen, the Third Mate, and with him was Sub-Lieutenant Patsy Kent, of the Survey Service. Larsen flushed as he saw the Commodore and explained hastily, "Miss Kent was using the computer, sir . . ."

"Never mind that. What is the emergency?"

The officer gestured towards the globe of darkness that was the screen of the Mass Proximity Indicator. "I . . . I don't know, sir. But there's something. Something on our line of advance."

Grimes stared into the screen.

Yes, there was something there. There was the merest spark just inside the surface of the globe, and its range . . . The Commodore flipped the switch of the range indicator, turned the knob that expanded a sphere of a faint light from the center of the screen, read the figure from the dial. He muttered, "Twelve and a half thousand miles . . ." and marveled at the sensitivity of this new, improved model. But the target could be a planetoid, or a planet, or even a dead sun. Somehow he had assumed that it was another ship, but it need not be. Twelve and a half thousand miles, and *Faraway Quest's* initial velocity before proceeding under Interstellar Drive had been seven miles a second . . . (But was it still? Where was a yardstick?) Contact in thirty minutes, give or take a couple or three . . . But there should be ample time to compute the velocity of approach . . .

The others were now in the control room: Swinton, and Jones, the Second Mate, and Renfrew. And Sonya. He could smell the faint, disturbing perfume of her and he asked himself, *What am I doing here?* He stared at the spark of light, brighter now, and closer, with a certain resentment. *Come off it, Grimes,* he thought in self-admonishment, *it's years since you were rosy-cheeked, snotty, sulking hard because a call to duty interfered with your very first date. . . .*

"Your orders, sir?" Swinton was asking politely, yet with a touch of urgency.

"Action Stations was sounded, and Action Stations it is. I take it that the laser projectors and the missile launchers are closed up?"

"They are, sir."

"Good. Mr. Jones, please work out velocity of approach and estimated time of contact. Mr. Renfrew, please use the Carlotti gear for the purpose for which it was originally invented and try to initiate radio communication. Mr. Larsen, get on the blower to Mr. Mayhew and shake him up. Tell him that there's something ahead—a ship? a planet?—and that I want to know if it has a crew, or a population." Then, to Swinton, "I shall be going below for a few seconds, Commander. If anything happens you will know where to find me."

He dropped down the axial shaft to his day cabin, went through to his lavatory cubicle and hastily tidied himself up. He dressed rapidly, but with care. If this were to be a first contact with some alien race he would, at least, try to look the part that he was playing, that of leader of an expedition of Earthmen into the Unknown. He snared an undergarment of filmy crystal silk that was drifting in the air currents, stowed it hastily in a convenient drawer. It was just possible that he would be entertaining guests shortly.

Then, back in the control room, he received the reports of his officers. *Faraway Quest*, they told him, was closing the target at twelve miles a second. (So *it*, whatever *it* was, was not hanging motionless in Space. Or was it?) It had now been picked up by the radar, and the indications were that it was a metallic structure, not overly large. Neither electronic nor psionic radio had been able to establish contact.

So . . .

So it was a dead ship, a vessel that years—or centuries—ago had fallen out of its own continuum, a ship whose crew had died, or whose descendants were no longer able to operate any of the machinery except what was essential for the maintenance of life? Or was it a ship in fighting trim manned by possibly hostile beings with itchy trigger fingers, maintaining a cautious silence until the *Quest* was within range of the homing missiles, the flickering laser beams?

The Commodore went to the telephone, pressed the selector stud. "Mr. Mayhew. We are closing the target. Do you hear anything?"

"No, sir."

"The target appears to be a ship. Suppose that her Captain has ordered radio silence, what then?"

"Any unshielded mind must radiate, sir. Only trained telepaths can establish and maintain an effective shield, but even then there is leakage, a gabble of scraps of nonsense verse, meaningless mathematical formulae and the like."

"So you think that there's nothing living there, Mayhew?"

"I'd bet on it, sir."

"I hope you're right." He snapped orders to the First Lieutenant. "Commander Swinton, take the controls, please. Match velocities with the target and maintain a range of one mile."

"Ay, ay, sir." And then Swinton, seating himself in the Master Pilot's chair, was snapping his own orders, his manner assured and competent, in startling contrast to his usual callow youthfulness.

Grimes, strapped into a convenient acceleration chair, watched the young man appreciatively. He heard the whine of the stabilizing gyroscopes and felt the vibration as the ship was turned end for end— and it was odd for this maneuver to be carried out without, as a visual accompaniment, the drift of stars (even the few, faint stars of the Rim) across the viewports. And then, relatively speaking, the target was astern—astern, but still closing rapidly. *Faraway Quest's* rocket drive coughed briefly, and coughed again. The target was still closing—but slowly, slowly.

For the last time there was the subdued rumble of the rockets, the gentle pressure of deceleration, and Swinton announced, not without pride, "Target abeam, sir. Velocities matched. Range one-point-oh-five of a mile."

Grimes swiveled his chair so that he could look out of the viewports. And outside there was nothing but blackness.

In a matter of seconds the probing beam of the searchlight found the target.

It was a ship, but no ship such as any of those in the control room had ever seen. There was a long hull that looked as though the conventional torpedo shape had been sliced in two longitudinally. At one end of it there was what looked like an assemblage of control surfaces. Grimes, out of his chair and monopolizing the huge mounted binoculars, studied it carefully. There was a rudder, and there were two screw propellers. It could be, he thought, a lightjammer, similar to the ones that he himself had designed, capable of being handled in a planetary atmosphere like an airship. But the rudder was too small, and those propellers were too heavy and had too coarse a pitch to be airscrews.

But there were the lofty masts, one forward and one aft, protruding from the flat deck . . . But that would be an unusual, and not very practicable arrangement of spars to carry a lightjammer's suite of sails. . . . And between the masts there was a structure, white-painted, that looked more like a block of apartments, complete with balconies, than part of a ship. Roughly in the middle of this there was another mast. . . . No, decided Grimes, it wasn't a mast, it was too thick, too short. It, too, was white-painted, but with a black top, and carried a design in blue. Grimes studied it carefully, decided that it was supposed to be some sort of grapnel or anchor.

He relinquished the binoculars to Sonya Verrill. When she had had time to study the weird derelict he asked, "Well, Commander, what do *you* make of it?"

She replied doubtfully, "It *could* be a lightjammer, sir. But all those ports . . . It'd be hard enough to make a thing like that watertight, let alone airtight. . . ."

"H'm. But those ports seem to be on one half of the hull only, the half with all the odd superstructures . . . Like half a ship, and half—something else . . ."

"After all, sir," put in Swinton, who had been studying the thing with a smaller pair of binoculars, "there's no reason why a spaceship should be symmetrical. As long as it never has to proceed through an atmosphere it can be any shape at all that's convenient."

"True, Swinton. True. But if that thing's designed for Deep Space only, why those screw propellers? Aerodynamically speaking it's a hopeless mess, and yet it's equipped for atmospheric flight. . . ."

"But is it?" queried Sonya Verrill. "Those absurdly heavy screws with their fantastically coarse pitch . . ."

"But where's the planet?" asked Swinton.

"Come to that," countered Grimes, "where's *our* planet?" He added, "Who knows what odd combinations of circumstances threw us here, dropped us into this crack in Time? Who knows what similar combinations have occurred in the past?" And then, in a whisper, "But we're such a long way from Earth . . ."

"Are we?" asked Renfrew. "Are we? What does the word 'dimension' mean in this dimensionless Limbo?"

"So I could be right," said Grimes.

"What are you driving at, John?" demanded Sonya Verrill.

"I'd rather not say, yet. It's too fantastic." He turned to his First Lieutenant. "I'll leave you to hold the fort, Swinton. I shall take away the boarding party."

Chapter 14

THEY ASSEMBLED in the after airlock of *Faraway Quest*: Grimes, and Sonya Verrill, and Jones, and Dr. Todhunter. They waited until they were joined by Calhoun and McHenry. When the two senior engineers put in an appearance they were hung around with an assortment of tools that would have been impossible to carry in any appreciable gravitational field: hammers, and wrenches and pinch bars and burning equipment. All members of the party, of course, carried reaction pistols and, on Sonya Verrill's insistence, all were armed—Grimes with the heavy projectile pistol that he favored, the others with hand laser projectors. In addition, the Surgeon carried a small battery of cameras.

They had put on their helmets and then Grimes, plugging the lead from his suit radio microphone into the telephone socket, ordered Swinton, in the control room, to evacuate the airlock. They watched the needle of the gauge drop slowly, finally coming to rest on Zero. And then the valve opened.

The strange ship hung out there in the absolute blackness, every detail picked out by the harsh glare of the searchlight. Her colors were bright, garish—the red that was almost purple, the broad band of pink paint, and then black, and then the white of the superstructure and the yellow of that odd assemblage of spars, of masts and booms.

She looked, thought Grimes, out of context.

But to any dweller in this nothingness—if there were any such dwellers—*Faraway Quest* would look out of context too.

With an odd reluctance Grimes shuffled to the sill of the airlock door, made the little jump that broke contact between his magnetic boot soles and the steel deck. His reaction pistol was ready, and with economical blasts he jetted across the mile of emptiness. And then that odd expanse of red-purple plating was before him—and with a sudden shift of orientation he had the sensation of falling toward it head first. He used his pistol to turn himself and then to brake his speed. His landing was gentle, his boot soles making contact with the metal with no more than the slightest of jars. They made contact and they held. *So*, he thought, *this ship is made of iron, or steel. But if I am right, when she was built nobody had thought of using aluminum as a structural material, and plastics had not been dreamed of . . .*

He felt the shock as Sonya Verrill landed beside him, and then Jones came in, and Todhunter, and the two engineers. Grimes waited until Calhoun and McHenry had sorted themselves out—hampered as they were by their equipment, they had fallen clumsily—and then led the way along the surface of painted metal.

It was not easy going.

A spaceman's shuffle is a quite effective means of locomotion over a perfectly flat and smooth surface—but when the surface is made up of overlapping, riveted plates the feet must, frequently, be lifted, and there is the fear that, with magnetic contact broken, a long fall through emptiness will ensue.

But they made progress, trudging towards a near horizon that was a purple painted angle-bar, glowing dully against the blackness.

Todhunter called a halt, contorting himself so that his magnetic knee-pads touched the plating. He said, "This is odd. It looks like clumps of some sort of living organism growing on the plates. It's dead now, of course."

"What I expected," Grimes told him.

"What you expected, sir?"

"If and when we get back to Port Forlorn, Doctor, you must read a few of the books in my rather specialized library. . . . I remember that a bright young journalist from the *Lorn Argus* once did a feature article on it. She cooked up rather a neat title, *From Dug-Out Canoe to Interstellar Liner.*"

"I don't understand, sir."

"Neither do I, Doctor. But those barnacles will keep. They've been keeping for one hell of a long time."

They negotiated the angle-bar—like a ridge, it was, like the ridge of a roof with a pitch of 45 degrees—and beyond it was more of the purple-painted plating, and beyond that a stretch of pink paint, and beyond that was the dull-gleaming black. Grimes stopped at the border between the two colors, looked down at an odd, white-painted design—a circle, bisected by a line that had at one end the letter L, at the other the letter R. And from the right-hand end of this line was another line at right angles to it, and this was subdivided and lettered: IT, T, S, W, WNA. . . .

"So this is—or was—one of *our* ships. . . ." Sonya Verill's voice was faint yet clear in his helmet phones. "Of course, those letters could be odd characters from some utterly alien alphabet, but they don't look like it to me."

"They're not," Grimes told her. "The L and the R stand for Lloyds' Register. TF is Tropical Fresh, T is Tropical, S is Summer, W is Winter, and WNA is Winter North Atlantic."

"But what does it mean? And how do you know?"

"I know because the history of shipping—all shipping—has always fascinated me. I should have recognized this ship at first glance, but I did not, because she has no right here. (But have we?) But here she is, and here we are—and we're luckier than her people because we shall be able to survive even if we can't find our way back . . ."

And then, still in the lead, he was shuffling over the black-painted plating until he came to a section of white-painted rails. He threw his body forward, grasped the rails with his gloved hands. He remained in this position until he had once again oriented himself, until his "up" and "down" were the "up" and "down" of the long-dead people of the dead ship. He was looking into a promenade deck. There was the scrubbed planking, and ahead of him was white-painted plating, broken by teakwood doors and brass rimmed ports—and with dense, black shadows where the glare of the *Quest's* searchlights did not penetrate. With a nudge of his chin he switched on his helmet lantern; he would be needing it soon.

The wooden deck would effectively insulate his boot soles from the steel plating beneath it, so he made a scrambling leap from the rail to one of the open doorways, pulled himself into the alleyway beyond it. There were more doors—some open, some ajar and secured by stay hooks, some shut. Grimes waited until the others had joined him, then pulled himself along a sort of grab rail to the first of the partially open doors. His gloved fingers fumbled with the stay hook, finally lifted it. The door swung easily enough on its hinges, which were of polished brass.

He let himself drift into the cabin, the glare of his helmet light gleaming back at him from burnished metal, from polished wood. There was a chest of drawers, and there were two light chairs that seemed to be secured to the deck, and there were two bunks, one above the other. The upper bunk was empty.

The Commodore stared sadly at the pair of figures in the lower bunk, the man and the woman held in place by the tangle of still-white sheets. He had seen Death before, but never in so inoffensive a guise. The bodies, little more than mummies, had been drained of all moisture by their centuries-long exposure to a vacuum harder even than that of normal interstellar Space, or even that of intergalactic Space, and yet lacked the macabre qualities of the true skeleton.

Todhunter's voice was hushed. "Do you think, sir, a photograph?"

"Go ahead, Doctor. *They* won't mind."

It's a long time, he thought, *it's a long, long time since you minded anything. . . . But how did it come to you? Was it sudden? Did the cold get you first, or did you die when the air rushed out of your lungs in one explosive burst?* He turned to look at Sonya, saw that her face was pale behind the visor of her helmet. He thought, *We should be thankful. We were lucky.* He said, "We shan't learn much by looking in the other cabins."

"Then where can we learn something?" asked Calhoun in a subdued voice.

"In the control room—although they didn't call it that."

He led the way along alleyways—in some of which drifted dessicated bodies—and up companionways, careful all the time to maintain the sense of orientation adapted to the derelict. Through public rooms they passed, the glare of their helmet lanterns, broken up into all the colors of the spectrum, flung back at them from the ornate crystal chandeliers. And then, at last, they came out into the open again, on to a great expansive of planking on either side of which the useless lifeboats were ranged beneath their davits. All around them was the emptiness, and there was *Faraway Quest*, her searchlights blazing, no more than a bright and lonely star in the black sky.

From handhold to handhold they made their way, following the Commodore, until they came to more ladders, leading to a bridge that spanned the fore part of the superstructure. In the center of this bridge was a house of varnished timber with big glass windows, and in the forward compartment of this house there was the body of a man. He was standing there, held in position by the grip of his hands on a big, spoked wheel, an ornate affair of polished wood and burnished brass. He was wearing an odd, flat blue cap, and a blue, wide-collared jumper, and blue trousers that were tucked into short black boots. The skeletal face still—after how many centuries?—wore an expression of concentration as the eyes, no more than depressions in the taut skin, stared sightlessly at the compass, at the lubber's line that had not shifted a microsecond of arc from the quarter point in half a millenium. Eerily the card swung as Grimes looked at it, pulled away from its heading by the magnetic field generated by his suit transceiver.

Abaft the wheelhouse there was another compartment. In it were two men, both attired in uniforms that still, to a shipman, made sense. Grimes murmured, "Sorry, Captain," and gently lifted the body of the tall, thin man, the almost-skeleton with the neat gray beard and the four gold bands on the sleeves, away from the chart table. He looked down at the chart, at the penciled courseline, at the circled intersections of cross bearings. "Yes," he whispered. "As I thought. The South African coast . . ."

"And where is that, sir?" asked Calhoun.

"On Earth. And the time? Towards the beginning of the Twentieth Century . . ."

By his side Sonya Verrill was looking at the open pages of the Log Book. She said, "The watchkeeper recorded thunder and exceptionally vivid lightning, and also makes mention of an unusual display of phosphoresence."

"But who were they?" Todhunter was demanding. "How did they get here?"

"I can answer the first question," Grimes replied gravely. His gloved forefinger indicated the heading of the Log Book path. "'*Waratah,* from Durban towards Liverpool.' But she never got there."

∾ Chapter 15 ∾

THERE WERE SEVERAL BIG, glazed frames on the after bulkhead of the chartroom, and in one of them was a detailed plan of the ship. Grimes and his officers studied it with interest. McHenry said suddenly, "I'd like to see what their engines are like."

"I can tell you now, Commander," Grimes told him. "Steam. Reciprocating. Coal burning. As I remember the story, she put into Durban for bunkers on her way home from Australia."

"But I'd like to see them, sir." The engineer's forefinger was tracing out a route on the plan. "As long as we keep amidships and carry on down we're bound to come to the stokehold, and from there to the engine room."

"Then carry on," said Grimes. "But I don't want you to go by yourself."

"I shall be with him," said Calhoun, and Jones said that he wanted to make a further exploration of the derelict, and Todhunter wanted to take more photographs.

Grimes and Sonya went out to the wing of the bridge, keeping a firm grasp on the teakwood rail, and watched the two engineers, the Second Mate and the Surgeon making their way along the boat deck, saw them open a door in the fiddley casing below and just forward of the funnel and vanish, one by one, into the black opening.

He heard the girl ask, "But how do you explain all this, John?"

"I can't, Sonya—although this could be the explanation of a number of mysteries. As you know, I'm something of an authority on the history of shipping. You'd think that even as far back as the Twentieth Century it would be impossible to lose, completely, anything so large as a ship. After all, in those days there was quite efficient diving gear, and sonic sounding apparatus—and, even though it was in its earliest infancy, there was radio.

"But ships did vanish—and vanish without trace.

"Take this *Waratah*, for example. She was a new ship, owned by the Blue Anchor Line, built for the cargo-passenger trade between England and Australia. On her maiden voyage she carried freight and passengers outwards, and then loaded more freight—frozen meat and general cargo—in Australia for England, also embarking passengers. She was scheduled to call at Durban on the homeward passage to replenish her coal bunkers, also to disembark and to embark passengers. One odd feature of the voyage was the number of intending travelers who experienced premonitory dreams of a warning character and, as a result of these, canceled their passages.

"Anyhow, she arrived in Durban, and bunkered, and sailed. She exchanged visual signals with another ship shortly afterwards. And that was all.

"Oh, plenty of surface ships did founder, some of them with all hands, and the loss of *Waratah* was explained away by the theory that she was extremely unstable, and rolled so badly in a heavy swell that she capsized and went down suddenly. But this was not in the loneliness of mid-ocean. This was in soundings, in relatively shallow water, and on a well-frequented shipping route. But no bodies were ever found, and not a single fragment of identifiable wreckage. . . ." He pointed to a lifebuoy in its rack, the white and scarlet paint still bright, gleaming in the beams from *Faraway Quest's* searchlights, the black lettering, *Waratah, Liverpool*, clearly legible. "Even if she had gone down suddenly *something* would have broken free and floated, something with the ship's name on it. . . .

"She was a passenger liner, and so she became better known than a smaller ship would have done, and her name joined that of *Marie Celeste* on the long list of unsolved ocean mysteries that, even to this day, are occasionally rehashed by journalists as fillers for Sunday supplements. As a matter of fact that wench from the *Lorn Argus* who was writing up my library said that she was going to do a series called *Maritime Mysteries of Old Earth* and spent quite a few evenings browsing among my books. . . .

"But there was *Waratah*, and there was *Anglo-Australian*, and there was *Cyclops*. . . . And there were the ships like *Mary Celeste*, found drifting in perfect order without a soul on board. . . .

"Well, I suppose we've found out *what* happened. But how? *How?*"

Sonya said, "That analogy of playing on the black keys, and playing on the white keys, and playing in the cracks, was a good one. But as an Intelligence Officer I've had to do quite a deal of research into this sort of thing. Oceangoing ships have vanished, but so have aircraft, and so have spacecraft. And there have been many, many cases of the inexplicable disappearances of people—the crew of your *Mary Celeste*, for example, and the famous man who walked round the horses, and Ambrose Bierce, and . . . and . . ."

"And?"

"I suppose you're wondering why I haven't cited any modern cases. The trouble, of course, is that Space Travel has given the explainers-away far too easy a time. A ship goes missing on a voyage, say, from Port Forlorn to Nova Caledon, as the Commission's *Delta Eridani* did a couple of years back. But Space is so vast, and when you throw in the extra dimensions added by the use of any sort of Interstellar Drive, it's vaster still. When a ship is overdue, you know as well as I do that any search would be quite useless. And men and women still go missing—but if they go missing on any of the frontier planets there are so many possible causes—usually some hitherto undiscovered life form that's gobbled them up, bones, boots and all."

"Even so, records are kept."

"Of course. It takes a small city to house all the Intelligence Department's files on the subject."

They went back into the chartroom. Grimes looked at the desiccated bodies of the Captain and his watch officer, wished that the two men were able to speak to tell him just what had happened. Perhaps, he thought, they would be able to do so. Results, of a sort, had been achieved by that first seance aboard *Faraway Quest*. He wondered, too, if Todhunter would be able to revive any of *Waratah's* people, but he doubted it. In the early days of intersteller expansion a deep freeze technique had been used, but all of those making a long, long voyage in a state of suspended animation had undergone months of preparation before what had been, in effect, their temporary deaths—and in many cases, in far too many cases, the deaths had been all too permanent. It was easy enough to say the words, "Snap-freezing and dehydration," but the actual technique had never been easy.

Carefully Grimes examined the Log Book. The pages were brittle, all moisture leeched from them by their centuries of exposure to hard vacuum. He deciphered the crabbed handwriting in the *Remarks* column. "Mod. beam sea, v. heavy beam swell. Vsl. rolling heavily. O'cast, with occ'l heavy rain and violent thunderstorms. Abnormally bright phosphorescence observed."

Thunder and lightning and abnormally bright phosphorescence . . .

So what?

He muttered, "The electrical storm may have had something to do with it. . . . And possibly there was some sort of disturbance of the Earth's magnetic field in that locality, and something just right—or just wrong—about the period of the roll of a steel hull . . ."

"Or possibly," she said, "there was somebody aboard the ship who was a sort of catalyst. Remember all the dreams, all the premonitory, warning visions, that were experienced just before her disappearance? Perhaps there are people—in fact, our researches hint that there are, and always have been such people—who can slip from one Time Track to another, in many cases quite inadvertently. As well as the records of inexplicable disappearances there are also the records of equally inexplicable appearances—men and women who have turned up from, literally, nowhere, and who have been strangers, lost and bewildered, in a strange world. . . .

"In our own case, how much was due to Mr. Renfrew's fancy apparatus and your own tinkering with anti-matter and anti-gravity, and how much was due to the mediumistic powers of your Miss Karen Schmidt?"

"Could be . . ." he admitted. "Could be . . . It's a farfetched theory, but . . ."

"Farfetched?" she scoffed. "Here we are, marooned in this absolute nothingness, and you have the nerve to accuse me of drawing a long bow!"

"Not quite nothingness," he corrected her. "The indications are that we may be in a sort of graveyard of lost ships. . . ."

"And lost people. The unfortunates who, somehow, have missed their footing from stepping to one track to the next . . . As *Waratah's* people did."

"And as we did."

"But we're lucky enough to have a self-sustaining economy."

Grimes broke off the conversation to keep Swinton, back in the control room of *Faraway Quest*, up to date with what was happening and what had been discovered, including in his report the tentative theories that had been, so far, advanced. The First Lieutenant acknowledged, then said, "I don't want to hurry you, sir. But Mr. Mayhew informs me that he's receiving very faint signals from somewhere. It could either be something or somebody extremely distant, or something quite close but transmitting feebly."

"So we aren't alone in the junkyard," said Grimes. Then, switching frequencies, he succeeded in raising the Second Mate, the doctor and the two engineers, who were still prowling in the bowels of the ship and who were most reluctant to break off their explorations. He ordered them to report to the bridge at once.

At last they appeared, babbling of pistons and furnaces and boilers and refrigerating machinery, carrying lumps of coal that they had taken from the bunkers. *Odd souvenirs,* thought Grimes—and decided that if he were able he would acquire something more useful, the books from the library, for example, or the grand piano from the First Class lounge. . . . And with the thought he looked at the long dead Captain and whispered, "It's not theft. I know you wouldn't object to making a gift to a fellow shipmaster."

"What was that, sir?" asked Jones.

"Nothing," snapped Grimes. "Now let's get back to our own wagon and find out what fresh surprises they've cooked up for us."

⤠ Chapter 16 ⤟

ONCE BACK ABOARD HIS OWN SHIP, Grimes went straight from the airlock to the control room, pausing only to take off his helmet. Swinton greeted him with the words, "Mayhew is still picking it up, sir."

"Good. Can he get any kind of directional fix on it?"

"He says not. But you know what Mayhew is like, impossibly vague unless you can nail him down."

Grimes went to inspect the screens first of the radar, then of the Mass Proximity Indicator. Both instruments had been reset for extreme long range. Both showed nothing.

He went to the nearest telephone, put out his hand to take the handset from the rack, then changed his mind. He said, "I shall be with Mr. Mayhew if you want me, Commander Swinton." He made a beckoning nod to Sonya Verrill, who followed him from the control room.

He knew that it would be a waste of time tapping on the door to the Psionic Radio Officer's cabin, but did so nonetheless. He waited for a decent interval and then slid the panel to one side, letting himself and Sonya into the room. Mayhew had his back to them; he was strapped in his seat, his body hunched as though it were being dragged from an upright position by a heavy gravitational field. He was staring at the transparent cylinder, nested in its wires and pipes, in which, submerged in the bath of nutrient fluid, hung the small, gray-white mass, obscenely naked, that was the living brain of one of the most telepathic of all animals, a dog, that was the amplifier with the aid of which a skilled telepath could span the Galaxy.

They may have made a slight noise as they entered; in any case Mayhew turned slightly in his chair and looked at them with vague, unfocused eyes, muttering, "Oh. It's you." And then, in a more alert voice, "What can I do for you, sir?"

"Just carry on with what you *are* doing, Mr. Mayhew. But you can talk, I think, while keeping a listening watch."

"Of course, sir."

"This signal you've picked up, can it be vocalised?"

The telepath pondered, then said, "No, sir. It's emotion rather than words. . . . It's a matter of impressions rather than a definite message. . . ."

"Such as?"

"It's hard to put into words, sir. It's dreamlike. A dim dream within a dream . . ."

"'And doubtful dreams of dreams . . .'" quoted Grimes.

"Yes, sir. That's it."

"And who, or what, is making the transmission? Is it human? Or humanoid? Or a representative of one of the other intelligent races?"

"There's more than one, sir. Many more. But they're human."

Sonya Verrill said, "There's a chance, John, that there may be some flicker of life, the faintest spark, still surviving in the brains of those people aboard *Waratah*. What are their dreams, Mr. Mayhew? Are they of cold, and darkness, and loneliness?"

"No, Miss Verrill. Nothing like that. They're happy dreams, in a dim sort of way. They're dreams of warmth, and light, and comfort, and . . ." he blushed " . . . love . . ."

"But it could still be *Waratah's* people."

"No. I probed her very thoroughly, very thoroughly. They're all as dead as the frozen mutton in her holds."

"How did you know that?" demanded Grimes sharply.

"It was necessary, sir, to maintain telepathic contact with the boarding party. I 'overheard' what you were telling the others about *Waratah's* last voyage."

"Sorry, Mr. Mayhew."

"And the only telepathic broadcast from the derelict was made by you and your party, sir. With these other signals I get the impression of distance—and a slow approach."

"But who the hell is approaching whom?" exploded Grimes. Then, "I was talking to myself. But we still don't know at what speed we're traveling, if we are traveling. When we matched velocities with *Waratah* did we reverse our original motion, or did we merely come to rest, or are we still proceeding the same way as we were when we fell into this bloody crack?"

"I'm not a navigator, sir," said Mayhew stiffly.

"None of us is, until there's something to navigate with. But we're interrupting you."

"Not really, sir. This is no more than one of those pleasant dreams you have sometimes between sleeping and waking. . . ." He stiffened. "There's one coming through a little stronger than the others. . . . I'll try to isolate it. . . . Yes. . . .

"There are blue skies, and white, fleecy clouds, and a river with green, grassy banks . . . Yes, and trees . . . And I am sitting by the river, and I can feel the warmth of the sun, and the breeze is bringing a scent that I know is that of new-mown hay . . ." He paused, looked at the others with a wry grin. "And I've never seen hay, let alone smelled it. But this is not *my* dream, of course. Yes. There's the smell of new-mown hay, and there's the song of birds in the trees, and my pipe is drawing well, and my rod is perfectly balanced in my hands, and I am watching the—the bait, the fly that I tied myself, drifting on the smooth surface of the stream, and I know that sooner or later a trout will rise to take it, but there is no hurry. I'm perfectly happy where I am, doing what I am, and there's no hurry . . .

"But there is. Behind it all, underneath it all, there *is* a sense of urgency. There's the guilty feeling, the guilty knowledge that I'm late, that I've overslept, and that something dreadful will happen if I don't wake up. . . ."

"Odd," commented Grimes. "Do you know Earth, Mayhew?"

"No, sir."

"Do you know anything about dry flies?"

"What are they, sir?"

"You were talking about tying one just now. They're a form of bait used by fishermen who do it for sport, not commercially. The really keen anglers tie their own flies—in other words they fabricate from feathers, wire, and the odd Gods of the Galaxy alone know what else, extremely odd—but as long as the trout also think that they look edible, why worry?"

"So," said Sonya, "we have a nostalgic dry fly fisherman from Earth, who's dreaming about his favorite sport, marooned, like ourselves, in this crack in Time-Space. Or Space-Time. But, for all we know, we may be picking up this dream from Earth itself. Dimensions are meaningless here. After all, there's *Waratah* . . ."

"She's had a long time to drift," said Grimes. "But go on, Mr. Mayhew."

"He's drifted back into the happy dream," murmured Mayhew. "He's not catching anything, but that doesn't worry him."

"And can you isolate any of the others?" asked the Commodore.

"I'll try, sir. But most of them are about long, timeless days in the air and the warm sunshine . . . There is a man who is swimming, and he turns to look at the girl beside him, and her body is impossibly beautiful, pearl-like in the clear, green water. . . . And there is a woman, sitting on velvet-smooth grass while her sun-browned children play around her . . .

"But they're getting closer, whoever they are. They're getting closer. The dreams are more distinct, more vivid. . . .

"The air is thin and cold, and the hard-packed snow is crunching under my heavy, spiked boots. It seems that I could reach out now to touch the peak with my ice-axe. . . . It's close, close, sharp and brilliantly white against hard blue sky. . . . There's a white plume steaming from it, like a flag of surrender. . . . It's only snow, of course, wind-driven snow, but it is a white flag. It's never been conquered—but in only a few hours I shall plant my flag, driving the spiked ferrule deep into the ice and rock . . . They said that it couldn't be done without oxygen and crampon-guns and all the rest of it, but I shall do it. . . ."

"It would be quite a relief," remarked Sonya, half seriously, "if somebody would dream about a nice, quiet game of chess in a stuffy room with the air thick with tobacco smoke and liquor fumes."

Grimes laughed briefly. He said, "I have a hunch that these are all hand-picked dreamers, hearty open air types." The telephone buzzed sharply. He reached out, took the instrument from its rest. "Commodore here . . . Yes . . . Yes . . . Secure all for acceleration and prepare to proceed on an interception orbit."

☙ Chapter 17 ☙

OUTSIDE THE VIEWPORTS there was nothing but blackness, and the old steamship was no more than a spark of light, a dimming ember in the screens of radar and Mass Proximity Indicator. A gleaming bead threaded on to the glowing filament that was the extrapolation of *Faraway Quest's* orbit was the new target, the ship that had drifted in from somewhere (nowhere?) on a track that would have carried her all of a thousand miles clear of the *Quest* had she not been picked up by the survey ship's instruments.

Grimes and his officers sat in their chairs, acceleration pressing their bodies into the resilient padding. Swinton, as before, had the con, and handled the ship with an ease that many a more experienced pilot would have envied. At a heavy four gravities *Faraway Quest* roared in on her interception orbit and then, with split second timing, the rockets were cut and the gyroscopes brought into play, spinning the vessel about her short axis. One last brief burst of power and she, relative momentum killed, was herself drifting, hanging in the emptiness a scant mile clear of the stranger.

The searchlights came on.

Faraway Quest's people stared through the ports at the weird construction, only Grimes evincing no surprise. Her appearance confirmed his hunch. She was an affair of metal spheres and girders— a small one, its surface broken by ports and antennae, a large one, with what looked like conventional enough rocket lifecraft cradled about its equator, then another small one, with a nest of venturis protruding from the pole like a battery of guns. There were no fins, no atmospheric control surfaces.

Swinton broke the silence. "What the hell is that?"

"I suggest, Commander, that you take a course in the history of astronautics. That is a relic of the days of the First Expansion, when Man was pushing out toward the stars, without any sort of reliable interstellar drive to cut down the traveling time from centuries to weeks." He assumed a lecture room manner. "You will observe that the ship was not designed for blasting off from or landing on a planetary surface; she is, in fact, a true spaceship. She was constructed in orbit, and stores and personnel were ferried up to her by small tender rockets—quite possibly those same tenders that are secured about the central sphere.

"The small, leading sphere is, of course, the control room. The central sphere contains the accommodation—if you can call it such. The after sphere is the engine room."

Swinton said thoughtfully, "And I suppose that she's manned— no, 'inhabited' would be a better word—by the descendants of her original crew and passengers. And they don't know how to use the radio. Judging by all those antennae she's not hard up for electronic gadgetry! And so they haven't heard our signals, or if they have heard them they've not been able to answer. They probably don't even know that we're around."

Grimes laughed gently. "You haven't quite got it right, Commander. She was on a long, long voyage—far longer than her designers anticipated!—but there was no breeding *en route*."

"But there's life aboard her, sir. All those queer psionic signals that Mayhew's been picking up . . ."

"Yes. There is life aboard her. Of a sort."

"I'm sorry, sir. I don't quite get you."

Grimes relented. "As I said, she's a relic of the First Expansion. In those days, thanks to the failure of anybody, in spite of ample forewarning, to do anything about it, the Population Explosion had come to pass, and both Earth and the habitable planets and satellites of the Solar System were overcrowded. But it was known that practically every sun had its family of planets capable of supporting our kind of life. So there was a siphoning off of surplus population—mainly of those who could not and would not adapt to life in the densely populated cities. Techniques for the suspension of animation were already in existence and so each of the big ships was able to carry an enormous number of passengers, stacked like the frozen mutton in the holds. The crew too spent most of the voyage frozen, the idea being that the spacemen would keep watches—relatively short intervals of duty sandwiched between decades of deep freeze—so that they, on arrival at their destination, would have aged only a year or so. The passengers, of course, would not have aged at all.

"Finally, with the ship in orbit about the planet of her destination, everybody would be revived and ferried down to the surface of their new home."

"I'm not sure that I'd care for that, sir."

"Neither should I. But they had no Interstellar Drive. And they didn't know, Commander, as we now know, how many of those ships were to go missing. Some of them must have fallen into suns or crashed on planetary surfaces. Others are still wandering. . . ."

"The Survey Service," put in Sonya Verrill, "has satisfactorily accounted for all but thirteen of them."

"And this one brings the number down to twelve," remarked the Commodore.

"But how did she wander *here?*" demanded Sonya.

"We can find out," Swinton told her.

"We can try to find out," she corrected him.

Grimes stared through the big binoculars at the archaic interstellar ship, carefully studied the forward sphere, the control compartment. He could make out what looked like a manually operated airlock door on its after surface. It should be easy enough, he thought, to effect an entrance.

"Surely the duty watch will have seen the glare of our lights," Swinton was saying.

"I fear that the watch will have been too long for them," said the Commodore quietly.

As before, the boarding party was composed of Grimes, Sonya Verrill, Jones, Calhoun, McHenry and Dr. Todhunter. This time, thought Grimes, there would be something for the engineers and the Surgeon to do. The big ship could be restored to running order, her thousands of people rescued from a condition that was akin to death. *And then?* wondered Grimes. *And then?* But that bridge could be crossed when it was reached, not before.

He led the way across the emptiness between the two vessels—the sleek, slim *Faraway Quest* and the clumsy assemblage of spheres and girders. He turned in his flight to watch the others—silver fireflies they were in the beam of the *Quest's* lights, the exhausts of their reaction pistols feeble sparks in the all-pervading blackness. He turned again, with seconds to spare, and came in to a clumsy landing on the still-burnished surface of the control sphere, magnetized knee and elbow pads clicking into contact with the metal. He got carefully to his feet and watched the others coming in and then, when they had all joined him, moved slowly to one of the big ports and shone the beam of his helmet lantern through the transparency.

He saw what looked like a typical enough control room of that period: acceleration chairs, radar and closed circuit TV screens, instrument consoles. But it was all dead, dead. There were no glowing pilot lights—white and red, green and amber—to present at least the illusion of life and warmth. There was a thick hoar frost that sparkled in the rays from the helmet lanterns; there was ice that gleamed in gelid reflection. The very atmosphere of the compartment had frozen.

He made his way from port to port. It was obvious that the control room was deserted—but the control room occupied only a relatively small volume of the forward globe. The rest of it would be storerooms, and hydroponic tanks, and the living quarters for the duty watch.

He said to Sonya, "We may find somebody in the accommodation. Somebody whom we can revive. And if we don't—there are the thousands of dreamers in the main body of the ship. . . ."

He led the way around the curvature of the metal sphere, found the door that he had observed from *Faraway Quest*. He stood back while McHenry and Calhoun went to work on it. They did not have to use any of their tools; after a few turns of the recessed wheel it opened easily enough, but the inner door of the airlock was stubborn. It was only after the little party had so disposed itself in the cramped compartment that maximum leverage could be exerted that it yielded, and then barely enough for the Commodore and his companions to squeeze through one by one. It was a thick drift of snow, of congealed atmosphere, that had obstructed the inward swinging valve. The snow and the frost were everywhere, and the ice was a cloudy glaze over all projections.

They proceeded cautiously through the short alleyway, and then through a hydroponics chamber in which the ultraviolet and infra-red tubes had been cold for centuries, in which fronds and fruit and foliage still glowed with the colors of life but shattered at the merest touch. Grimes watched the explosion of glittering fragments about his inquisitive, gloved finger, and imagined that he could hear, very faintly, a crystalline tinkling. But there was no sound. The interior of the ship was frighteningly silent. There was not even the vibration of footsteps transmitted through metal plating and suit fabric; the omnipresent snow and ice muffled every contact.

They came to a circular alleyway off which numbered doors opened.

Grimes tried the first one, the one with the numeral 4. It slid aside with only a hint of protest. Beyond it was what had been a sleeping cabin. But it was not now. It was a morgue. It held two bodies. There was a big man, and he held in his right hand a knife, and the frozen film on it still glistened redly. There was a woman who was still beautiful. Todhunter's specialized knowledge was not required to determine the cause of death. There was a clean stab wound under the woman's left breast, and the man's jugular vein had been neatly slit.

They went into the next cabin. Its occupants, lying together in the wide bunk, could have been asleep—but in the clip on the bulkhead to which it had carefully returned was a drinking bulb. It was empty—but the label, upon which was a skull and crossbones in glaring scarlet, made it obvious what the contents had been.

In the third cabin there was shared death too. There was an

ingenious arrangement of wires leading from a lighting fixture to the double bunk, and a step-up transformer. The end might have been sudden, but it had not been painless. The two frozen bodies, entangled in the lethal webbing, made a Laocoon-like group of statuary—but that legendary priest of Apollo had perished with his sons, not with a woman.

And in the fourth cabin there was only one body, a female one. She was sitting primly in the chair to which she was strapped, and she was clothed, attired in a black uniform that was still neat, that did not reveal the round bullet hole over the breast until a close inspection had been made.

"Cabin Number One . . ." said Calhoun slowly. "Could she have been the Captain?"

"No," said Grimes. "This, like the others, is a cabin for two people. And there's no sign of a weapon. . . ." Gently he brushed a coating of frost from the woman's sleeve. "Gold braid on a white velvet backing . . . She will have been the Purser."

They found the Captain in a large compartment that lay inboard from the alleyway. He, too, was formally clothed in gold-buttoned, gold-braided black. He was huddled over a desk. The automatic pistol was still in his hand, the muzzle of the weapon still in his mouth. Frost coated the exit wound at the back of his head, robbing it of its gruesomeness. Before him was a typewriter and beside the machine was a small stack of paper, held to the surface of the desk by a metal clip.

Grimes read aloud the heading of the first page:

"TO WHOM IT MAY CONCERN . . .
"IF AND WHEN . . .
"WHEN AND IF . . .
"IF EVER."

It was gallows humor, and it was not very funny.

⋙ Chapter 18 ⋘

"JUST POSSIBLY (Grimes read) somebody, somewhere, may stumble upon us. When we pushed off from Earth there was talk of an interstellar drive that would enable ships to take short cuts through sub-Space. I suppose that it's sub-Space that we're in now. But I don't know how we got here, and I don't know how we can get out. If I did know I would not have sanctioned the use of the Euthanol—and how was I to know that all but one of the containers had leaked?—and, in the case of the Gallaghers, the Nakamuras and ourselves, the rather messy substitutes. We could have finished our watch, of course, and then awakened Captain Mitchell and *his* staff so that they could have returned us to the state of suspended animation—but we talked it over and we decided against it. Our dreams, during our long sleep, our long watch below, would not have been happy ones. All the others are dreaming happily of the lives that they will lead on the new world to which we are bound, the lives of which their rationed vacations in Earth's fast dwindling Nature Reserves were brief forecasts. But our dreams, now, would be full of anxiety, of cold and loneliness, of the black emptiness into which we have fallen.

"*But how?*

"*How?*

"It's the odd flotsam that we've sighted, from time to time, that has made up our minds. What laws of motion are valid in this Limbo

91

we do not know. Perhaps there are no laws. But, appearing from nowhere, there was that corpse that orbited for some hours about the control sphere. It was that of a man. He was wearing archaic clothing: a gray top hat, a stock and cravat, a frock coat. Mary Gallagher, whose hobby is—*was*, I should say—history, said that his dress was that of the early Nineteenth Century. And then there was an aircraft, a flimsy affair of fabric and stays and struts. Centuries ago they must have fallen here—they and the other briefly glimpsed men and women, and a surface ship from the days of steam on Earth's seas, and a clumsy looking rocket (not that we can talk!) bearing on its side characters that bore no resemblance to any Earthly alphabet.

"But I feel that my time is running out. All the others are dead. Sarah asked me to dispose of her, giving as her reason her nervousness with firearms. But the others are dead. The Browns were lucky—when I dealt the cards she got the ace of spades, and with it the only intact bulb of Euthanol. The rest of us could have shared the pistol, but Nakamura preferred something more traditional (although, at the end, he didn't use the knife in a traditional way) and Gallagher was an engineer to the end. But my time is running out. When I have finished this I shall shut down the machinery and then come back here to use the pistol on myself.

"So here is the story—such as it is. If whoever finds it—and I feel that it will be some castaway like ourselves—can read it, it might be of value.

"Fully manned, provisioned and equipped, with a full load of passengers, we broke away from orbit on January 3, 2005. (Full details will be found in the Log Books.) Once we were on the trajectory for Sirius XIV, watches were set. First Captain Mitchell, as senior officer, did the first year, so that he and his staff could make any necessary minor adjustments. The rest of us, after the period of preparation, went into the Deep Freeze. First Captain Mitchell was succeeded by Second Captain von Spiedel, and he was succeeded by Third Captain Geary. So it went on. It was a routine voyage, as much as any interstellar voyage is routine.

"We relieved Captain Cleary and his people.

"There was a period of three weeks, as measured by the

chronometer, during which we were able to mingle socially with our predecessors, whilst Pamela Brown, in her capacity as Medical Officer, worked with Brian Kent, Cleary's M.O., to restore us to full wakefulness and to prepare the others for their long sleep. And then, after Cleary and his team had been tucked away, we were able to get ourselves organized. The control room watches, of course, were no more than a sinecure. Routine observations were taken and told us that we were exactly on course and that our speed of advance was as predicted. The last observation, made at 1200 hours on the day that it happened, gave our position as 1.43754 Light Years out from Earth, and our velocity as 300 m.p.s. Full details are in the Log Book.

"That night—we divided our time, of course, into twenty-four hour periods—all off-duty personnel were gathered in the wardroom. There was the usual rubber of bridge in progress, and the playmaster was providing light background music. Nakamura and Mary Gallagher were engaged in their habitual game of chess. Brown had the watch and his wife was keeping him company. It was typical, we all thought, of a quiet evening in Deep Space. Those of us who were on duty were keeping the machines running, those of us off duty were relaxing in our various ways.

"So the sudden ringing of the alarm bells was especially shocking.

"I was first in the control room, but only by a very short head. There was no need for Brown to tell us what was wrong; it was glaringly obvious. No, not *glaringly* obvious. It was the absence of glare, of light of any kind, that hit us like a blow. Outside the viewports there was only a featureless blackness.

"We thought at first that we had run into a cloud of opaque dust or gas, but we soon realized that this hypothesis was untenable. Until the very moment of black-out, Brown told us, the stars ahead had been shining with their usual brilliance, as had been the stars all around the ship. Furthermore, one cannot proceed through a cloud of dust or gas, however tenuous, at a speed of 300 m.p.s. without an appreciable rise in skin temperature. An appreciable rise? By this time the shell plating would have been incandescent and all of us incinerated.

"I'll not bore you, whoever you are (if there ever is anybody) with a full account of all that we did, of all that we tried, of all the theories that we discussed. Brown stuck to his story. At one microsecond the viewports had framed the blazing hosts of Heaven, at the next there had been nothing there but the unrelieved blackness. We thought that we might be able to learn something from the radio, but it was dead, utterly dead. We disassembled every receiver and transmitter in the control sphere, checked every component, reassembled. And still the radio was dead. There were no longer the faint signals coming in from Earth and from other interstellar ships. There were no longer the signals emanating from those vast broadcasting stations that are the stars.

"But there were no stars.

"There are no stars any more.

"And then, over the weeks, there were the—apparitions?

"No. Not apparitions. They were real enough. Solid. Brown and Nakamura took one of the tenders out, and ran right alongside an ocean-going ship out of Earth's past. Her name was *Anglo-Australian*, and on her funnel was a black swan on a yellow field. They were wearing their spacesuits, so they were able to board her. They found— but could it have been otherwise?—that all of her crew was dead. There were no entries in the Log Book to account for what had happened to her. As in our case, it must have been sudden.

"There was the flotsam—the bodies, some clothed in the fashions of bygone centuries, some not clothed at all. The sea-going ships and the aircraft—and some of them could have come from Earth. There was the huge affair that consisted of a long fuselage slung under what must have been an elongated balloon—but the balloon had burst— with a crew of insects not unlike giant bees. There was that other construction—a relatively small hull suspended amid a complexity of huge sails. We never found out who or what had manned her; as soon as we turned our searchlights on her she vanished into the distance. A sailing ship of Deep Space she must have been—and we, unwittingly, provided the photon gale that drove her out of our ken.

"And we worked.

"But there was no starting point. We had fallen somehow into sub-Space—as had all those others—but how? *How?*

"We worked, and then there were weeks of alcoholic, sexual debauch, a reaction from our days of wearisome, meaningless calculation and discussion. And when, sated, we returned to sobriety we were able to face the facts squarely. We were lost, and we did not possess the knowledge to find our way out of this desert of utter nothingness. We considered calling the other watches—and then, in the end, decided against it. They were happy in their sleep, with their dreams—but we, we knew, could never be happy. We knew too much—and too little—and our dreams would be long, long experiences of tortured anxiety. We could see no faintest gleam of hope.

"And so we have taken the only way out.

"But you, whoever you are (if there ever is anybody) will be able to help.

"The other watches are sleeping in their own compartments in the northern hemisphere of the main globe. The waking process is entirely automatic. Give First Captain Mitchell my best wishes and my apologies, and tell him that I hope he understands.

"John Carradine,
Fourth Captain."

Chapter 19

THEY LEFT THE CONTROL SPHERE then, and made their way through an airlock to the tube that connected it with the large globe that was the main body of the ship. They found themselves in a cylindrical space with a domed deck head, in the center of which was the hatch through which they had entered. In the center of the deck there was a similar hatch.

There were doors equally spaced around the inside surface of the cylinder. All of them were labeled, having stenciled upon them names as well as rank "First Captain Mitchell . . ." read Sonya Verrill. "Chief Officer Alvarez . . . Second Officer Mainbridge . . . Third Officer Hannahan . . . Bio-Technician Mitchell . . ." She paused, then said, "I suppose that a husband-wife set-up is the best way of manning a ship like this . . ."

Grimes slid the door aside.

The helmet lanterns threw their beams onto eight tanks—a tier of four, and another tier of four. They looked, thought the Commodore, like glass coffins, and the people inside them like corpses. *(But corpses don't dream.)*

Four of the tanks held men, four held women. All of them were naked. All of them seemed to be in first-class physical condition. Mitchell—his name was on a metal tag screwed to the frame of his tank—was a rugged man, not young but heavily muscled, robust. He did not need a uniform as a professional identification. Even in repose, even in the repose that was almost death, he looked like a master of men and machines, a man of action with the training and intelligence to handle efficiently both great masses of complex apparatus and the mere humans that operated it.

Grimes looked at him, ignoring the other sleepers. He wondered if Mitchell were the fisherman whose pleasant dreams were being spoiled by the sense of anxiety, of urgency. It could be so. It probably was so. Mitchell had been overdue to be called for his watch for a matter of centuries, and his was the overall responsibility for the huge ship and her cargo of human lives.

Todhunter was speaking. There was a certain disappointment in his voice. "I don't have to do anything. I've been reading the instructions, such as they are. Everything is fully automated."

"All right, Doctor. You can press the button. I only want First Captain Mitchell awakened." He added softly, "After all, this is his ship. . . ."

"I've pressed the button," grumbled Todhunter. "And nothing has happened."

McHenry laughed. "Of course not. The dead Captain in the control sphere, in the wardroom, said that he'd shut down all the machinery."

"As I recall it," said Grimes, "these things were powered by a small reactor. It will be right aft, in the machinery sphere. Carradine was able to shut down by remote control, but we won't be able to restart the same way. The batteries must be dead."

"As long as the Pile is not," contributed McHenry.

"If it is, we shall send for power packs from the *Quest*. But I hope it's not."

So they left Mitchell and his staff in their deep, frozen sleep and made their way aft, through deck after deck of the glass coffins, the tanks of the motionless dreamers. Jones paused to look at a beautiful girl who seemed to be suspended in a web of her own golden hair, and murmured something about the Sleeping Beauty. Before Grimes could issue a mild reprimand to the officer, McHenry pushed him from behind, growling "Get a move on! You're no Prince Charming!"

And Grimes, hearing the words, asked himself, *Have we the right*

to play at being Prince Charming? But the decision is not ours to make.
It must rest with Mitchell . . .

Then there was the airlocked tube leading to the machinery sphere, and there were the pumps and the generators that, said McHenry, must have come out of Noah's Ark. "But this *is* an Ark," said Jones. "That last deck was the storage for the deep-frozen, fertilized ova of all sorts of domestic animals. . . ."

There were the pumps, and the generators and then, in its own heavily shielded compartment, the Reactor Pile. McHenry consulted the counter he had brought with him. He grunted, "She'll do."

Unarmored, the people from *Faraway Quest* could not have survived in the Pile Room—or would not have survived for long after leaving it. But their spacesuits gave protection against radiation as well as against heat and cold and vacuum, and working with bad-tempered efficiency (some of the dampers resisted withdrawal and were subjected to the engineer's picturesque cursing) McHenry got the Pile functioning.

Suddenly the compartment was filled with an opaque mist, a fog that slowly cleared. With the return of heat the frozen air had thawed, had vaporized, although the carbon dioxide and water were still reluctant to abandon their solid state.

McHenry gave the orders—he was the Reaction Drive specialist, and as such was in charge, aboard his own ship, of all auxiliary machinery. McHenry gave the orders and Calhoun, assisted by the second Mate, carried them out. There were gauges and meters to watch and, finally, valves to open. Cooling fluid flashed into steam, and was bled carefully, carefully into piping that had been far too cold for far too long a time. And then hesitantly, complainingly, the first turbine was starting to turn, slowly, then faster and faster, and the throbbing whine of it was audible through their helmet diaphragms. Leaping from position to position like an armored monkey, McHenry tended his valves and then pounced on the switchboard.

Flickering at first, then shining with a steady brilliance, the lights came on.

They hurried back through the dormitory sphere to the

compartment in which First Captain Mitchell and his staff were sleeping. There Todhunter took charge. He slid shut the door through which they had entered and then pulled another door into place, a heavier one with a thick gasket and dogs all around its frame. He borrowed a hammer from McHenry to drive these into place.

Grimes watched with interest. Obviously the Surgeon knew what he was doing, had studied at some time the history of the "deep freeze" colonization ships, probably one written from a medical viewpoint. He remarked, "I can see the necessity for isolating this compartment, but what was that button you pressed when we first came in here? I thought that it was supposed to initiate the awakening process."

Todhunter laughed. "That was just the light switch, sir. But once we've got over these few preliminaries everything will be automatic. But, to begin with, I have to isolate the other bodies. Each tank, as you see, is equipped with its own refrigeration unit, although this transparent material is a highly efficient insulation. Even so, it will be as well to follow the instructions to the letter." He paused to consult the big, framed notice on the bulkhead, then went to a control console and pressed seven of a set of eight buttons. On seven of the eight coffins a green light glowed. "Now . . . heat." Another button was pressed, and the frost and ice in the wedge-shaped compartment began to boil.

When the fog had cleared, the Surgeon muttered, "So far, so good." He studied the tank in which lay the body of First Captain Mitchell, put out a tentative hand to touch lightly the complexity of wiring and fine piping that ran from its sides and base. He said, "You will have noticed, of course, that the arrangements here are far more elaborate than those in the main dormitory decks. When the passengers are awakened, they will be awakened *en masse* . . ."

"Get on with it, Doctor!" snapped Sonya Verrill.

"These things cannot be hurried, Commander. There is a thermostatic control, and until the correct temperature is reached the revivification process cannot proceed." He gestured towards a bulkhead thermometer. "But it should not be long now."

Suddenly—there was the whine of some concealed machinery

A. Bertram Chandler

starting, and the stout body of the First Captain was hidden from view as the interior of his tank filled with an opaque, swirling gas, almost a liquid, that quite suddenly dissipated. It was replaced by a clear amber fluid that completely covered the body, that slowly lost its transparency as the pneumatic padding upon which Mitchell lay expanded and contracted rhythmically, imparting a gentle agitation to the frame of the big man. The massage continued while the fluid was flushed away and renewed, this process repeated several times.

At last it was over.

The lid of the coffin lifted and the man in the tank stretched slowly and luxuriously, yawned hugely.

He murmured in a pleasant baritone, "You know, I've been having the *oddest* dreams . . . I thought that I hadn't been called, and that I'd overslept a couple or three centuries. . . ." His eyes opened, and he stared at the spacesuited figures in the compartment. *"Who are you?"*

≈ Chapter 20 ≈

GRIMES PUT UP HIS HANDS to his helmet, loosened the fastenings and gave it the necessary half turn, lifted it from the shoulders of his suit. The air of the compartment was chilly still, and damp, and a sweet yet pungent odor made him sneeze.

"Gesundheit," muttered the big man in the coffin.

"Thank you, Captain. To begin with, we must apologize for having boarded your ship uninvited. I trust that you do not object to my breathing your atmosphere, but I dislike talking through a diaphragm when I don't have to."

"Never mind all that." Mitchell, sitting bolt upright in his tank, looked dangerously hostile. "Never mind all that. Who the hell are you?"

"My name is Grimes. Commodore. Rim Worlds Naval Reserve. These others, with the exception of the lady, are my officers. The lady is Commander Verrill of the Federation Survey Service."

"Rim Worlds? Federation?" He looked wildly at the other tanks, the transparent containers in which his own staff were still sleeping. "Tell me it's a dream, somebody. A bad dream."

"I'm sorry, Captain. It's not a dream. Your ship has been drifting for centuries," Sonya Verrill told him.

Mitchell laughed. It was a sane enough laugh, but bitter. "And while she's been drifting, the eggheads have come up with a practicable FTL drive. I suppose that we've fetched up at the very rim

101

of the Galaxy." He shrugged. "Well, at least we've finally got some place. I'll wake my officers, and then we'll start revivifying the passengers." His face clouded. "But what happened to the duty watch? Was it von Spiedel? Or Geary? Or Carradine?"

"It was Carradine." Grimes paused, then went on softly, "He and all his people are dead. But he asked to be remembered to you."

"Are you mad, Commodore whatever your name is? How did you know that it was Carradine? And how can a man who's been dead for centuries ask to be remembered to anybody?"

"He could write, Captain. He wrote before he died—an account of what happened. . . ."

"What did happen, damn you? And how did he die?"

"He shot himself," Grimes said gravely.

"But what happened?"

"He didn't know. I was hoping that you might be able to help us."

"To help you? I don't get the drift of this, Commodore. First of all you tell me that you've come to rescue us, and now you're asking for help."

"I'm deeply sorry if I conveyed the impression that we were here to rescue you. At the moment we're not in a position to rescue anybody. We're castaways like yourselves."

"What a lovely, bloody mess to be woken up to!" swore Mitchell. He pushed himself out of the tank, floated to a tall locker. Flinging open the door he took out clothing, a black, gold-braided uniform, a light spacesuit. He dressed with seeming unhurriedness, but in a matter of seconds was attired save for his helmet. He snapped to McHenry, who was hung about with his usual assortment of tools, "You with all the ironmongery, get ready to undog the door, will you?" And to Grimes and Sonya Verrill, "Get your helmets back on. I'm going out. I have to see for myself . . ." And then he moved to the tank beside the one that he had vacated, looked down at the still body of the mature but lovely woman. He murmured, "I'd like you with me, my dear, but you'd better sleep on. I'll not awaken you to this nightmare."

Mitchell read the brief account left by Carradine, then went to the next level, the control room, to inspect the Log Book. He stared out through a port at *Faraway Quest*, and Grimes, using his suit radio, ordered Swinton to switch off the searchlights and turn on the floods. He stared at the sleek, graceful *Quest*, so very different from his own ungainly command, and at last turned away to look through the other ports at the unrelieved emptiness. His suit had a radio of sorts, but it was A.M. and not F.M. He tried to talk with Grimes by touching helmets, but this expedient was far from satisfactory. Finally the Commodore told McHenry to seal off the control room and to turn on the heaters. When the frozen atmosphere had thawed and evaporated it was possible for them all to remove the headpieces of their suits.

"Sir, I must apologize for my lack of courtesy," said the First Captain stiffly.

"It was understandable, Captain Mitchell," Grimes told him.

"But Captain Carradine should have called me," Mitchell went on.

"And if he had, Captain, what could you have done? In all probability you would have died as he died. As it is, you know now that you stand a chance."

"Perhaps, sir. Perhaps. But you haven't told me, Commodore, how you come to be marooned in this Limbo."

"It's a long story," said Grimes doubtfully.

"And we've all the time in the Universe to tell it, John," put in Sonya Verrill. "Or all the time out of the Universe. What does it matter?"

"All right," said Grimes. "It's a long story, but you have to hear it, and it could well be that you might be able to make some suggestion, that there is some important point that has escaped us but that you, with a mind fresh to the problem, will seize upon."

"That's hardly likely," The First Captain said. "When I look at your ship out there, and envisage all the centuries of research that have gone into her building . . . But go ahead, sir. At least I shall be privileged with a glimpse into the future—although it's not the future now."

Grimes told the story, trying to keep it as short as possible, but obliged, now and again, to go into technical details. He told the story, asking his officers to supply their own amplifications when necessary. Mitchell listened attentively, asking an occasional question.

"So," he said when at last the Commodore was finished, "we are not the only ones to have fallen into this hole in Space-Time. There was the old surface ship that you boarded; there was the surface ship that Carradine's people boarded. There were the aircraft that Captain Carradine mentioned . . . That dirigible airship, sir, with the crew of beelike beings . . . ?"

"The Shaara, Captain. They, too, have interstellar travel."

"There's some sort of a connection, Commodore. You got here, you think, by the use of your fantastic electronic gadgetry. But we didn't. And those old surface ships and aircraft didn't . . . And those people, sighted by Carradine, with no ships at all . . . These Shaara, Commodore, what are they like?"

"To all intents and purposes, Captain, they're highly evolved honey bees."

"H'm. But they have something that *we* have, otherwise they'd never have gotten here. Intelligence, of course. Technology. The airship that Carradine saw, and the spaceships that you say they have now . . . But there must be something else."

"There is," stated Calhoun flatly.

"And what is that, Commander?" asked Grimes.

"It's a matter of . . . Well, I suppose *you'd* call it Psionics, sir."

"But the Shaara are an utterly materialistic race."

"I agree, sir. But they still possess certain abilities, certain talents that were essential to their survival before they started to climb the evolutionary ladder. Such as dowsing . . ."

"*Dowsing*, Commander Calhoun?"

"Yes. According to some authorities, the ability of the honey bee on Earth, and on the other worlds to which it has been introduced, to find nectar-laden blossoms is akin to dowsing, for water or minerals, as practiced by human beings."

"H'm. This is the first time that I've heard that theory."

"It's not a new one, sir."

Mitchell smiled for the first time since he had been awakened. It was not a happy smile, but it brought a momentary easing of the stern lines of his face. "Dowsing . . ." he whispered. "Yes. There could be a connection . . ."

"Such as?" asked Sonya Verrill.

The First Captain replied in a voice that was again doubtful, "I don't know. But . . ." He went on, "As you must know, this ship is one of the specialized vessels built for large scale colonization. I've no doubt that in your day, Commander Verrill, newly discovered worlds are thoroughly surveyed before the first shipment of colonists is made. But in my time this was not so. The big ships pushed out into the unknown, heading for sectors of Space recommended by the astronomers. If their first planetfall was disappointing, then they proceeded to an alternative objective. And so on. But the crews and the passengers of the ships were themselves the survey teams.

"I need hardly tell you what such a survey team would have to look for. Water, on worlds that were apparently completely arid. Necessary ores. Mineral oil. The necessary electronic divining apparatus could have been carried, but in many ways it was better to carry, instead, a certain number of men and women who, in addition to their other qualifications, possessed dowsing ability."

"I think I see what you're driving at, Captain," objected Sonya Verrill. "But those surface ships and aircraft would not have carried dowsers as an essential part of their crews."

"Perhaps not, Commander Verrill. But—"

Calhoun broke in. "Dowsing ability is far more widespread than is generally realized. Most people have it to some degree."

"So the Shaara can dowse, and we can dowse," said Grimes. "But what *is* the connection?"

"You know where the dowsers among your passengers are berthed, Captain?" asked Calhoun. "Or should I have said 'stowed?'"

"Stowed is the better word," Mitchell admitted. "I don't know at the moment where they are, but as soon as I've consulted the passenger list and the plans . . ."

"I'm sure that they've something to do with it," Calhoun stated firmly. Then, to the Commodore, "I suggest that you tell Commander

Swinton to get Mr. Mayhew into a suit, and send him across here. As soon as possible."

"Who is Mr. Mayhew?" asked Mitchell.

"Our Psionic Radio Officer. A trained telepath."

"So that idea was developed after all. There was talk of it in my time. So you think he may be able to read the minds of my dowsers?"

"I hope so," said Grimes. Then, "I'll get Swinton to send one of our suits across for you. It will make things easier if we're able to speak with each other when we're suited up again." He put his helmet back on, called his First Lieutenant aboard the *Faraway Quest* and gave him the orders.

⤳ Chapter 21 ⤲

THEY DID NOT HAVE LONG to wait for Mayhew.

They watched him, accompanied by one of the junior engineers, jetting across the emptiness between the two ships. Jones squeezed through the sphincter airlock that sealed the hatch in the control room deck, and went down to the airlock proper in the after-hemisphere of the globe. He must have flashed his helmet lantern as a signal, as the two spacesuited figures veered abruptly in midflight and, shortly thereafter, were lost to view from the control room ports. Grimes, still wearing his helmet, heard Jones say, "Mr. Mayhew and Mr. Trent are aboard, sir."

"Good. Bring them up here, will you?" The diaphragm in the deck bulged and developed a hole in its center, through which appeared the head of the Second Officer, and then his shoulders and finally, after a deal of squirming on his part, the rest of his body. The transparency of his helmet and the fabric of his suit were immediately bedewed with condensation. He stood there to help Mayhew through the Sphincter and, when he was in the control room, the junior engineer. They had been exposed to the cold for a longer period, and the congealing atmospheric moisture clothed them in glittering frost.

The three men put up their gloved hands to remove their helmets.

"You wanted me, sir?" asked Mayhew vaguely.

"Of course," Grimes bit back a sarcastic retort.

The telepath ignored him, turned his attention to First Captain

Mitchell. "You're the fisherman. You were the one who was dreaming of sitting by a sunlit stream with rod and line—"

"Never mind that now," snapped the Commodore. "Just listen to what we want, please."

"I already know, sir."

"H'm. Yes. I suppose you do. But isn't it rather against the Institute's Code of Ethics to eavesdrop?"

"Not in these circumstances, sir. My duty was to receive and to record every impression emanating from the minds of the boarding party."

"Well, it saves time. As you know, First Captain Mitchell, as soon as he's got himself into the spare suit you brought, is going to take us into the dormitory sphere, to where the team of dowsers is stowed. There may be some connection between them and the transference of ships and people to this . . . What did you call it, Captain? To this sub-Space."

Mitchell, out of his own spacesuit but not yet into the one from *Faraway Quest*, was standing by an open filing cabinet, had pulled from it a bulky folder. "C Level," he was muttering, "Sector 8. Tanks 18 to 23 inclusive . . ." He put the folder back into the cabinet and then was helped into the suit by Sonya Verrill.

With the Captain to guide them, it did not take them long to find the tanks in which the dowsers slept. There were six of them—two very ordinary looking men and four women, one of whom looked far from ordinary. The telepath stood by the first of the transparent containers, staring at the man inside it, his face behind the helmet viewplate wearing an expression of deep concentration.

"This man," he said at last, "is dreaming of food . . . I can see a table, a table covered with a snow-white cloth, and an array of crystal goblets, and gleaming silverware. There are other people around the table, but they are blurred, indistinct. They are not important. But the waiter holding up the bottle of wine for my inspection is . . . He is an elderly, portly man, with a ruddy face and gray, muttonchop whiskers. He smiles as he pours a few drops from the bottle into my glass. I sip it. It is a white wine, very dry. I nod my approval.

"Another waiter is bringing in the first course: the oysters, the brown bread and butter, the lemon wedges . . ."

"Not much for us there," interrupted Grimes.

"Oh, all right. All right. But I was just beginning to enjoy it. It was the first time that I'd seen oysters—*me*, I mean, not the man who's having the dream—and I wanted to know what they taste like. But it's too late now. Time is accelerated in dreams, and he's polished them off . . ." He glowered moodily at the tank below the first one. "This man *works* in his dreams. He's striding up a hillside, over short, springy turf. He is holding a forked twig in his hands. I can feel the odd, soft roughness of it, the—the aliveness of it. There's a tension, a feeling of pleasurable anticipation, and it comes from the twig itself and from the ground over which I am walking, and from me . . . And I can feel the twig twitching, and I know that it's water under my feet, running water. . . . But I carry on. There's no urgency. I can *feel* all the mineral wealth beneath me, around me—the metals, the radio-actives . . ."

"No," said Grimes. "That's not it."

"I wish you'd let me finish a dream, sir, even though it's not my own."

Mayhew moved to the next tank. In this one there was a woman, a tall, angular woman with a narrow face, sharp features. There was a drabness about her—a drabness, Grimes somehow knew, that would still have been there had she been awake and clothed, a coldness that was more intense than the frigidity of her physical environment.

The telepath stared at her, her face frightened. His lips moved, but no sound came. He muttered at last, "She's dead. She's dead, but . . ."

"But what?" demanded the Commodore sharply.

"There's . . . How shall I put it? There's a—a record . . ."

"A ghost," said Calhoun.

"No. Not a ghost. There's the record of her last thoughts still in her brain. . . . But I can't play it back. There's the sense—no, not even the sense, just a hint—of some orgasmic experience, something that was too intense, something that was too much for her mind. . . ."

Todhunter said, "But there was no physical cause of her death. In her condition there couldn't have been. Perhaps we could still revivify her . . ." He turned to Mitchell. "As I understand it, Captain, it would be impossible to deal with people on these dormitory decks individually. If we revive one, we revive them all."

"Yes," agreed the First Captain. "That is so."

"Then would you have any objection if we used the empty tank in your sleeping quarters for this woman?"

"Yes," replied Mitchell. "I most certainly should." His manner softened. "But there are eight empty tanks in Carradine's compartment, and neither he nor his officers are in any state to object."

"Good."

"Check the other dowsers first, Mr. Mayhew," said Grimes.

Mayhew did so. The three remaining women were all alive—if their state of suspended animation could be referred to as life—and all peacefully dreaming. The pictures in their minds were pleasant, humdrum pictures of husbands and homes and children.

The tank was opened, and the rectangular block of solid-frozen gas in which was the woman's body lifted out quite easily. Even so, it was an awkward burden, even under conditions of free fall. Todhunter and Jones maneuvered it through the tiers of containers to the cylinder that was the axis of the globe, and then it had to be carried from level to level until the final deck was reached, the deck on which were the crew dormitories.

The doctor left Jones in charge of the body, went with Mitchell and Grimes and Sonya Verrill into what had been the Fourth Captain's compartment. All the tanks, of course, were empty. Mitchell satisfied himself that Carradine's container was ready for occupancy, and the ice-encased corpse was brought in, lowered into the rectangular box. Then, when all members of the party were in the wedge-shaped room, the double door was dogged tight and the automatic revivification process initiated.

There was the gradual rise of temperature and the thawing and evaporation of the frozen gases, and there was the thawing of the frozen gas in the coffin. There was the influx and the drainage of the colored fluids, the rhythmic massaging action of the pneumatic padding. Slowly the skin of the woman changed from silvery gray to a yellowish pallor, and then was suffused with the faintest of pink flushes. The eyelids flickered, and one leg began to twitch.

"She's not dead," murmured Grimes.

"But she is," contradicted Mayhew. "And there's just a spark . . . Just a spark, no more. *And I don't like it.*"

The lid of the casket lifted, and as it did so the woman slowly assumed a sitting posture. Her eyes opened and she stared mindlessly. Her jaw hung slackly and saliva dribbled from her mouth. She was making a coarse, disgusting grunting noise.

"The blue sky . . ." Mayhew whispered. "The clear sky, and the aching blue of it . . . And it's rending, like a piece of cloth between two giant hands. . . . It's rending, and the noise of its tearing is louder than the loudest thunder. . . . And beyond it is the blackness, the dense blackness, and it's empty. . . . But it's not empty. They are there, company after company of them, robed in shining white and with great white wings that span the heavens. . . . And they raise their golden trumpets to their lips, and the sound is high and sweet, high and impossibly sweet, long, golden notes rolling down through that rent in the sky, and the voices, the golden voices and the silver voices, and the flaming swords lifted high to smite the unrighteous, and . . . And . . .

"And that was all," he concluded. "She's gone now, finally gone. What's in the box is no more than a mindless hunk of flesh. But she's gone . . ."

"So that was what she dreamed?" asked Mitchell in an almost inaudible voice. "So that was what she—dreamed, and with such intensity as almost to drag the ship with her through that rent in the blue sky. . . . But was it her? Could it possibly have been her?"

"Have you any better explanation?" countered the telepath.

"Is it an explanation?" asked Grimes tiredly.

❧ Chapter 22 ❧

IT WASN'T MUCH OF AN EXPLANATION, but it was the only one that they had had. What *Faraway Quest's* people had achieved by a sophisticated juggling with the laws of physics (but the juggling had not been sufficiently sophisticated, or the laws not properly formulated) these others had achieved, inadvertently, by the function or malfunction of parapsychological principles. Throughout human history—and the history of other intelligent beings in the Galaxy—dowsers had sought, and they had found. And some of these diviners, in dream states, had sought for things and places beyond the bounds of Space and Time. Perhaps some of them had attained their dream countries, but the majority must have fallen into this Limbo, this gulf between the Universes, dragging, in so many cases, their hapless shipmates with them.

"Commodore," whispered Mitchell, "that's how it must have been. Our ship isn't like yours. She's just an iron drive rocket, archaic by your standards. We've no fancy dimension-twisting gadgetry."

"That's how it could have been," admitted Grimes guardedly, but already he was considering ways and means, already he was trying to work out methods whereby both ships, his own as well as First Captain Mitchell's, could be saved. He was trying to recall all that he had read of the First Expansion, the Interstellar Arks. As in the Ark of Biblical legend the passengers had boarded two by two, an even distribution of the sexes being maintained. *So . . .* he thought. *So . . .*

there's just a chance that I may be able to salvage this hunk of ancient ironmongery and, at the same time, exact a fee for the operation. . . .
He saw that Sonya was looking at him, realized that already there was a strong bond between them, more than a hint of the telepathy that springs into being between people in love. She was looking at him, and an expression that could have been maternal pride flickered briefly over her face.

"Out with it, John," she murmured.

He smiled at her and then turned to the Psionic Radio Officer. "Mr. Mayhew, can you enter minds?"

"How do you mean, sir?" countered the telepath cautiously.

"To influence them."

"It's against the rules of the Institute, sir."

"Damn the Institute. Its rules may hold good throughout the Galaxy, but we're not in the Galaxy. As far as our own ship is concerned, I am the Law, just as Captain Mitchell is the Law in this vessel. Can you enter another person's mind to influence it?"

"Sometimes, sir."

"The mind of one of the sleepers aboard this ship. One of the dreamers."

"That would be easy, sir."

"Good. Now, Captain Mitchell, this is what I have in mind. You have five diviners, five dowsers, still dreaming happily in their tanks. Mr. Mayhew is going to—to tamper with the dreams of four of them. Mr. Mayhew is a very patriotic Rim Worlder and thinks that Lorn is the next best place to Eden, and he's going to use his talents to sell Lorn in a big way to the dreaming dowsers. My idea is this. Each of them will dream that he is lost in a dark emptiness—as, in fact, we all are. Each of them will dream that he has his rod in his hand—his hazel twig, or his length of wire or whatever it is that he favors. Each of them will dream that the wand is leading him, pulling him towards a pearly globe set in the black sky. He'll know the name of it, and Mayhew will be able to supply details of the outlines of seas and continents. The sky isn't always overcast, and all of us have seen Lorn a few times from Outside with all details visible.

"I'm not saying that this will work, Captain, but it just might. If it doesn't work we shall none of us be any worse off. And if it does work—well, you'd better get your rockets warmed up before Mr. Mayhew goes to work, so you'll be able to throw yourself into a safe orbit."

"It sounds crazy, Commodore," Mitchell said. "It sounds crazy, but no crazier than all of us being here. I shall have to call my officers first so that all stations are manned."

"Of course. Dr. Todhunter will lend you a hand."

Mitchell's expression was still dubious. "Tell me, sir, why did you make it quite plain that four of the dowsers are to be set to dreaming of Lorn? Why not all five?"

"If this works out, Captain, it will be an act of salvage. And I think that *Faraway Quest* will be entitled to some reward. I know how the crew and passenger lists of these ships were made up. Male and female, in equal numbers. Husbands and wives. There's a hunch of mine that the husband of the mindless woman, the religious fanatic who got you into this mess, is one of the five remaining dowsers."

"I'll check the passenger list, Commodore."

Mitchell went to the cabinet and pulled out the files.

"So if it works," murmured Sonya, "we shall have our own dowser to do the same for us."

"Yes."

Mitchell put the papers back into their file. He said, "The mindless woman, as you have called her, is—or was—Mrs. Carolyn Jenkins. Her husband, John Jenkins, is also a member of the dowsing team. And now, if you'll excuse me, I'll see about waking my staff." His was somber. "I hope, for all our sakes, that I'm not waking them for nothing."

They were down once more in the dormitory sphere, on C Level, in Sector 8. There was Grimes, and there was Sonya Verrill, and there was first Captain Mitchell. There were Todhunter and McHenry, and there was Mitchell's Medical Officer, a woman whose hard, competent features were visible behind the transparency of her helmet and who, when awakened and apprised of the situation, had wished to discuss medical matters with her opposite number from *Faraway Quest*. And, of course, there was Mayhew.

First of all there was the tank in which slept Carolyn Jenkins' husband to disconnect from its fittings. Jenkins was the man who had been dreaming about food, and who was now dreaming about other pleasures of the flesh. Grimes felt more than a little relieved. This dreamer would not object to his being press-ganged away from his own ship and would not feel the loss of his wife too deeply. The nature of his dreams told of years of hunger, of frustration.

McHenry and Todhunter maneuvered the clumsy tank through the cramped space, vanished with it in the direction of the control sphere. It was to be taken to the *Faraway Quest*, where the engineers would be able to set up the apparatus for maintaining the sleeper in his condition of suspended animation and for awakening him if Grimes' gamble paid off.

And then Mayhew went to the second of the male dowsers, the one who, in his dream, was still engaged in the exercise of his talent. The telepath vocalized his thoughts, and his voice was an eerie whisper in the helmet phones of his companions.

"You are lost. . . .

"You are lost. The sky is dark. There is no light anywhere. There is nothing anymore anywhere . . . Nothing . . . Nothing . . . Emptiness around you, emptiness underfoot . . . You are falling, falling, through the nothingness, and the rod is dead in your hands. . . .

"You are falling, falling . . .

"But not for always. The rod twitches. You feel it twitch. Feebly, but it twitches. That is all—now. That is all. But there will be more. In precisely one hundred and twenty minutes there will be more. The rod will twitch strongly, strongly, and pull you with it. You will see that it is pointing to a spark in the darkness—a golden spark. And the spark becomes a globe, becomes a fair world hanging there. There is the blue of seas, the green of continents, the gleaming white of the polar ice caps, and on the night hemisphere the sparking lights of great cities. . . . There is the blue of seas and the green of continents, and the great land mass, hourglass-shaped, that sprawls from pole to pole, with its narrow waist on the equator. . . . And the chain of islands that forms a natural breakwater to the great eastern bay. . . . But you do not see it yet. The time must pass, and then you will see it. Then the rod will come alive in your hands and will draw you, pull you, to the fair world of Lorn, the world of your fresh start, to the sunny world of Lorn . . ."

Grimes thought, *I hope that they aren't too disappointed. But even Lorn's better than Limbo . . .*

And so it went on.

Each of the four remaining dowsers was thoroughly indoctrinated, and by the time that the indoctrination was finished only thirty minutes remained before the posthypnotic command would take effect. Grimes and the others made their way back to the control sphere.

Mitchell's officers were in full charge now, and the pilot lights glowed over instrument consoles. With the exception of Grimes, Sonya Verrill and Mayhew, all of *Faraway Quest's* people were back aboard their own ship. The Commodore turned to Mitchell. "I'll leave you to it, Captain. If things work out for all of us, I'll see you on the Rim."

Mitchell grinned. "I hope so, sir. But tell me, are the Rim Worlds as marvelous as your Mr. Mayhew makes out?"

"You have to make allowances for local patriotism, Captain."

"But you needn't stay on the Rim," Sonya Verrill broke in. "I am sure that my own Service will be happy to assume responsibility for the settlement of your people on any world of their choice."

"The Federation's taxpapers have deep pockets," remarked Grimes.

"That joke is wearing a little thin, John."

"Perhaps it is, Sonya. But it's still true."

The Commodore shook hands with Mitchell and then pulled on the gloves of his spacesuit, snapping tight the connections. His helmet on, he watched Sonya Verrill and Mayhew resume their own armor and then, with one of Mitchell's officers in attendance, the party made its way to the airlock. They jetted across the emptiness to the sleek *Faraway Quest*, were admitted into their own ship. They lost no time in making their way to the control room.

And there they waited, staring at the contraption of globes and girders floating there in the nothingness, bright metal reflecting the glare of the *Quest's* searchlights. They waited, and watched the control room clock, the creeping minute hand and, towards the end, the sweep second pointer.

Grimes consulted his own watch.

Mayhew noticed the gesture. He said quietly, "I'm still in touch. They can see the spark in the darkness now. They can feel the rods stirring strongly in their hands. . . ."

"I don't see how it can work," muttered Renfrew.

"They got here without your gadgetry, Lieutenant," Calhoun told him sharply. "They should be able to get out the same way."

And then there was nothing outside the viewports.

Perhaps, thought Grimes, *our searchlights have failed. But even then we should see a dim glimmer from her control room ports, a faint flicker from her warmed-up drivers. . . .*

"The screens are dead," announced Swinton.

"She made it . . ." whispered Mayhew. "She made it. Somewhere."

~ Chapter 23 ~

SO IT HAD WORKED for First Captain Mitchell and his Erector Set of an emigrant ship. It had worked for First Captain Mitchell, and so it should work for *Faraway Quest* and her people. The shanghaied dowser was sleeping in his tank, still dreaming orgiastic dreams, and Mayhew was working on him, entering his mind, trying to introduce the first faint elements of doubt, of discomfort, trying to steer his imaginings away from overpadded comfort to the cold and emptiness of the Limbo between the Universes.

But it was hard.

This was a man who had lived in his dreams, lived for his dreams. This was a man whose waking life was, at best, purgatorial—a man who never knew in his own home the sweet smoothness of flesh on flesh, a man who was denied even such simple pleasures as a glass of cold ale, a meal more elaborate than a spoiled roast and ruined, soggy vegetables. This was a man who lived in his dreams, and who loved his dreams, and who had fled to them as the ultimate refuge from an unspeakably drab reality.

Mayhew persisted, and his whispering voice, as he vocalized his thoughts, brought a chill of horror into the section of the auxiliary motor room in which the tank had been set up. He persisted, and he worked cunningly, introducing tiny, destructive serpents into the fleshly Eden—the tough steak and the blunt knife, the corked wine, the too-young cheese and the rolls with their leathery crusts. . . . The

118

insufficiently chilled beer and the hot dog without the mustard. . . .
The overdone roast of beef and the underdone roast of pork. . . .

Small things, trivial things perhaps, but adding up to a sadistic needling.

And then there was the blonde who, when she smiled, revealed carious teeth and whose breath was foul with decay, and the voluptuous brunette who, undressed, was living proof of the necessity of foundation garments. . . .

So it went on.

The dream, perhaps, had not been a noble one, but it had been healthily hedonistic, with no real vice in it. And now, thanks to Mayhew's probing and tinkerings, it was turning sour. And now the man Jenkins, fleeing in disgust from the lewd embraces of a harridan in a decrepit hovel, was staggering over a dark, windy waste, oppressed by a sense of guilt and of shame, fearing even the vengeance of the harsh deity worshipped by his unloving wife. He was fleeing over that dark windy waste, tripping on the tussocks of coarse grass, flailing with his arms at the flapping sheets of torn, discarded newspaper that were driven into his face by the icy gusts.

The cold and the dark . . .

The cold and the dark, and the final stumble, and the helpless fall into the pit that had somehow opened beneath his feet, and fall into Absolute Nothingness, a negation worse than the fiery hell with which his wife had, on more than one occasion, threatened him.

The cold and the dark and the absolute emptiness, and the rod of twisted silver wire to which he still clung desperately, the only proof of his identity, the only link with sanity, the only guide back to Space and Time . . .

The twisted wire, the twitching wire, and the insistent tug of it in his frozen hands, and ahead of him in the darkness the faint yellow spark, but brighter, brighter, golden now, no longer a spark but a fair world hanging there in the blackness, a world of beautiful, willing women, of lush gardens in which glowed huge, succulent fruit, a world of groaning tables and dim, dusty cellars in which matured the stacked bottles of vintage years . . .

But not Lorn . . . thought Grimes.

"But not Lorn . . ." echoed Sonya.

"Lorn is hanging there in the darkness. . . ." Mayhew was whispering. "A fair world, a beautiful world . . . And the divining rod is rigid in your hands, a compass needle, pointing pointing. . . . You can cross the gulf. . . . You can bridge the gulf from dream to reality. . . . Follow the rod. . . . Let the rod guide you, draw you, pull you. . . . Follow the rod. . . ."

"But where?" interrupted Grimes. "But *where?*"

"To Lorn, of course," whispered Mayhew. And then, "To Lorn? But his dreams are too strong . . ."

Shockingly the alarm bells sounded, a succession of Morse "A"s. Once again—Action Stations.

Chapter 24

THERE, TO PORT, was the lens of the Galaxy, and to starboard was the gleaming globe that was Lorn, the great, hourglass-shaped continent proof positive. From astern came the rumble of the gentle blasts fired by Swinton, intent on his instruments, that would put *Faraway Quest* into a stable orbit about the planet. From the speaker barked an oddly familiar voice, "What ship? What ship? Identify yourself at once." And at the controls of the transceiver Renfrew made the adjustments that would bring in vision as well as sound.

"What ship?" demanded the voice. "What ship?"

From his chair Grimes could see the screens of both radar and Mass Proximity Indicator. He could see the bright and brightening blob of light that gave range and bearing of another vessel, a vessel that was closing fast. She was not yet within visual range, but that would be a matter of minutes only.

"What ship? What ship?"

Grimes accepted the microphone on its wandering lead, said, "*Faraway Quest*. Auxiliary Cruiser, Rim Worlds Confederation Navy. *What ship?*"

The voice from the bulkhead speaker contrived to convey incredulity with an odd snorting sound. "*Faraway Quest?* Rim Worlds Confederation? Never heard of you. Are you mad—or drunk?"

"No," Sonya Verrill was whispering. "No. It can't be. . . ."

Grimes looked at her, saw that her face was white, strained.

The big screen over the transceiver was alive with swirling colors, with colors that eddied and coalesced as the picture hardened. It showed the interior of another control room, a compartment not unlike their own. It showed a uniformed man who was staring into the iconoscope. Grimes recognized him. In his, Grimes', Universe this man had been Master of *Polar Queen*, had smashed her up in a bungled landing at Fort Farewell, on Faraway. Grimes had been president of the Court of Inquiry. And this man, too, had been an officer of the Intelligence Branch of the Survey Service, his position as a tramp master being an excellent cover for his activities. And he and Sonya . . .

The Commodore swiveled in his chair. He rather prided himself on the note of gentle regret that he contrived to inject into his voice. He said to the woman, "Well, your quest is over. It's been nice knowing you."

She replied, "My quest was over some time ago. It's nice knowing *you*."

"I've got their picture," Renfrew was saying unnecessarily. "But I don't think that they have ours yet."

"*Starfarer* to unknown ship. *Starfarer* to unknown ship. Take up orbit and prepare to receive boarding party."

"You'd better go and pretty yourself up," said Grimes to Sonya. He thought, *It's a pity it had to end like this, before it got properly started even. But I mustn't be selfish.*

"You'll be meeting . . . him. Again. Your second chance."

"*Starfarer* to unknown ship. Any hostile action will meet with instant retaliation. Prepare to receive boarders."

"Commander Swinton!" There was the authentic Survey Service crackle on Sonya Verrill's voice. "Stand by Mannschenn Drive. Random precession!"

"Ay, ay, sir." The young man flushed. "Ma'am." Then he swiveled to look at the Commodore. "*Your* orders, sir?"

"John!" Sonya's voice and manner were urgent. "Get us out of here."

"No. This was the chance you were wanting, the second chance, and now you've got it."

She grinned. "A girl can change her mind. I want my own Universe, where there's only you . . ." She laughed, pointing to the screen. A woman officer had come into *Starfarer's* control room, was standing behind the Captain's chair. He outranked her, but her attitude was obviously proprietorial. "Where there's only you," repeated Sonya, "and only one of me . . ."

"Mannschenn Drive," ordered Grimes. "Random precession."

"Ay, ay, sir," acknowledged Swinton, and with the thin, high keening of the precessing gyroscopes the screen blanked, the speaker went dead and, on the port hand, the Galactic lens assumed its familiar distortion, a Klein flask blown by a drunken glass blower.

"Sir," growled Renfrew, obviously in a mutinous mood, "they could have helped us to get back. And even if they couldn't, I'm of the opinion that the Rim Worlds under Federation Rule would have been somewhat better than those same planets under your Confederacy."

"That will do, Lieutenant," snapped Sonya, making it plain that she was capable of dealing with her own subordinates. "Both the Commodore and myself agreed upon our course of action."

"This was supposed to be a scientific expedition, Commander," protested Renfrew. "But it's been far from scientific. Séances, and dowsers . . ." He almost spat in his disgust.

"You can't deny that we got results," muttered Calhoun.

"Of a sort."

Grimes, seated at the table on the platform in the still unreconverted wardroom, regarded the squabbling officers with a tired amusement. He could afford to relax now. He had driven the ship down the warped Continuum in an escape pattern that had been partly random and partly a matter of lightning calculation. He had interrogated Maudsley—the other Maudsley—after the Polar Queen disaster and had not formed a very high opinion of that gentleman's capabilities as a navigator. And even if this Maudsley were brilliantly imaginative, a ship in Deep Space is a very small needle in a very big haystack. . . .

"Gentlemen," he said, "the purpose of this meeting is to discuss ways and means of getting back to our own Space-Time. Has anybody any suggestions?"

Nobody had.

"The trouble seems to be," Grimes went on, "that although the dowser technique works, Mayhew is far too liable to look at his home world through rose-colored spectacles. Unluckily he is the only one among us capable of influencing the dreams of the hapless Mr. Jenkins. No doubt the Rim Worlds are better off, in some respects, under Federation rule than under our Confederacy. Weather control (which is far from inexpensive) for example, and a much higher standard of living. But I've also no doubt that the loss of independence has been a somewhat high price to pay for these advantages. And, even you who are not Rim Worlders, would find it hard to get by in a Universe in which somebody else, even if it is *you*, has your job, your home, your wife."

"So—what are we to do?"

"We still have Jenkins," contributed Calhoun.

"Yes. We still have Jenkins. But how can we use him?"

"And you still have *your* talent," said Sonya.

"My talent?"

"Your hunches. And what is a hunch but a form of precognition?"

"My hunches," Grimes told her, "are more a case of extrapolation, from the past at that, than of precognition." And sitting there, held in his chair by the strap, he let his mind wander into the past, was only dimly conscious of the discussion going on around him. He recalled what had happened when *Faraway Quest* had been drawn into the first of the Alternative Universes before falling into Limbo. He remembered that odd sensation, the intolerable stretching, the sudden *snap*. Perhaps . . . "Mr. Mayhew!" he said.

"Yes? Sorry. Yes, sir?"

"What sort of feeling do you have for this ship?"

"She's just a ship."

"You don't, in your mind, overglamorize her?"

"Why the hell should I? Sir."

"Good. Please come with me again to this man Jenkins, the

dowser. I want you to take charge of his dreams, the same way that you did before. I want you to lose him in nothingness again, and then to let his talent guide him out of the emptiness back to light and life and warmth."

"But you said that *my* vision of Lorn was too idealistic."

"It is. It is. I want you to envisage *Faraway Quest*."

"*Us*, sir?"

"Who else?"

"The cold . . ." Mayhew was whispering. "The cold, and the dark, and the absolute emptiness. There's nothing, nothing. There's not anything, anywhere, but that rod of twisted silver wire that you hold in your two hands. . . . You feel it twitch. You feel the gentle, insistent tug of it. . . . And there's a glimmer of light ahead of you, faint, no more than a dim glow. . . . But you can make out what it is. It's the pilot lights of instrument panels, red and green, white and amber, and the fluorescent tracings in chart tanks. . . . It's the control room of a ship, and the faint illumination shows through the big, circular ports. By it you can just read the name, in golden lettering, on her sharp stem, *Faraway Quest*."

And Mayhew went on to describe the ship in detail, in amazing detail, until Grimes realized that he was drawing upon the knowledge stored in the brains of all the technical officers. He described the ship, and he described the personnel, and he contrasted the warmth and the light and the life of her interior with the cold, empty dream-Universe in which the dowser was floating. He described the ship and her personnel—and, Grimes thought wryly, some of his descriptions were far from flattering. But she was Home. She was a little world of men in the all-pervading emptiness.

She was Home, and Grimes realized that he, too, was feeling the emotions that Mayhew was implanting in the sleeping dowser's mind. She was Home, and she was close, and closer, an almost attained goal. She was Home, and Grimes knew that he could reach out to touch her, and he reached out, and felt the comforting touch of cool metal at his fingertips, the security of solidity in the vast, empty reaches of Deep Space. . . .

She was Home, and he was home at last, where he belonged, and he was looking dazedly at the odd, transparent tank that had appeared from nowhere in the Auxiliary Machinery Room, the glass coffin with a complexity of piping and wiring extruded from its sides, the casket in which floated the nude body of a portly man.

He turned to Sonya Verrill, and he heard her say, "Your hunch paid off, John."

He remembered then. (But there were two sets of memories—separate and distinct. There were the memories of Limbo, and all that had happened there, and there were the memories of a boring, fruitless cruise after the first and only Rim Ghost sighting and the failure to establish even a fleeting contact.) He remembered then, and knew that some of the memories he must cling to, always. They were all that he would have, now. There were no longer any special circumstances. There was no longer the necessity for—how had she put it?—the political marriage of the heads of two potentially hostile tribes.

He muttered, unaware that he was vocalizing his thoughts, "Oh, well—it was nice knowing you. But now. . . ."

"But now . . ." she echoed.

"If you'll excuse me, sir, and madam," broke in Mayhew, "I'll leave you alone. Now that we're back in our own Universe I'm bound by the Institute's rules again, and I'm not supposed to eavesdrop, let alone to tell either of you what the other one is thinking." He turned to the Commodore. "But I'll tell you this, sir. I'll tell you that all the guff about political marriages *was* guff. It was just an excuse. I'll tell you that the lady has found what she was looking for—or whom she was looking for—and that his name is neither Derek Calver nor Bill Maudsley."

"In the Survey Service," remarked Sonya Verrill softly, "he could be court martialed for that."

"And so he could be," Grimes told her, "in the Rim Confederacy Navy. But I don't think that I shall press any charges."

"I should be rather annoyed if you did. He told you what I should have gotten around to telling you eventually, and he has saved us a great deal of time."

They did not kiss, and their only gesture was a brief contact of hands. But they were very close together, and both of them knew it. Together they left the compartment, making for the control room.

Grimes supposed that it would be necessary to carry on the cruise for a while longer, to continue going through the motions of what young Swinton had termed a wild ghost chase, but he was no longer very interested. A long life still lay ahead of him, and there were pleasanter worlds than these planets of the far outer reaches on which to spend it.

For him, as for Sonya Verrill, the faraway quest was over.

CONTRABAND
FROM
OTHERSPACE

DEDICATION
For who else but Susan?

❧ Chapter 1 ❧

TO A CASUAL OBSERVER his seamed, deeply tanned face would have appeared expressionless—but those who knew him well could have read a certain regret in the lines of his craggy features, in the almost imperceptible softening of the hard, slate-gray eyes.

The king had abdicated.

The Astronautical Superintendent of Rim Runners had resigned from the service of the Rim Worlds Confederacy—both as a senior executive of the government owned and operated shipping line and as Commodore of the Rim Worlds Naval Reserve. His resignations were not yet effective—but they would be, so soon as Captain Trantor, in *Rim Kestrel*, came dropping down through the overcast to be relieved of his minor command prior to assuming the greater one.

On a day such as this there was little for Grimes to see. Save for *Faraway Quest*, the Rim Worlds Government Survey Ship, and for *Rim Mamelute* the spaceport was deserted. Soon enough it would resume its normal activity, with units of the Rim Runners' fleet roaring in through the cloud blanket, from Faraway, Ultimo and Thule, from the planets of the Eastern Circuit, from the anti-matter systems to the Galactic West. (And among them would be Trantor's ship, inbound from Mellise.) But now there were only the old *Quest* and the little, battered space-tug in port, silent and deserted, the survey ship a squat, gray tower (that looked as though it should have been lichen-coated) half obscured by the snow squall, the

Mamelute huddling at its base as though seeking shelter in the lee of the larger vessel.

Grimes sighed, only half aware that he had done so. But he was not (he told himself) a sentimental man. It was just that *Faraway Quest* had been his last spacegoing command, and would be his last command, ever, out on the Rim. In her he had discovered and charted the worlds of the Eastern Circuit, opened them up to trade. In her he had made the first contact with the people of the antimatter systems. In her, only short weeks ago, with a mixed crew of Rim Worlds Naval Reserve officers and Federation Survey Service personnel, he had tried to solve the mystery of those weird, and sometimes frightening phenomena known as Rim Ghosts. And whilst on this Wild Ghost Chase (as his second in command referred to it) he had found in Sonya Verrill the cure for his loneliness—as she had found, in him, the cure for hers. But his marriage to her (as do all marriages) had brought its own problems, its own responsibilities. Already he was beginning to wonder if he would like the new life the course of which Sonya had plotted so confidently.

He started as the little black box on his desk buzzed. He heard a sharp female voice announce, "Commander Verrill to see you, Commodore Grimes."

Another voice, also female, pleasantly contralto but with an underlying snap of authority, corrected the first speaker. "*Mrs. Grimes* to see the Commodore, Miss Willoughby."

"Come in, Sonya," said Grimes, addressing the instrument.

She strode into the office, dramatic as always. Melting snow crystals sparkled like diamonds on her swirling, high-collared cloak of dull crimson Altairian crystal silk in the intricate coronet of her pale blonde hair. Her face was flushed, as much by excitement as by the warmth of the building after the bitter cold outside. She was a tall woman, and a splendid one, and many men on many worlds had called her beautiful.

She reached out, grabbed Grimes by his slightly protuberant ears, pulled his face to hers and kissed him soundly.

After she had released him, he asked mildly, "And what was that in aid of, my dear?"

She laughed happily. "John, I just had to come to tell you the news in person. It wouldn't have been the same over the telephone. I've just received two Carlottigrams from Earth—one official, one personal. To begin with, my resignation's effective, as and from today. Oh, I can still be called back in an emergency, but that shouldn't worry us. And my gratuity has been approved . . ."

"How much?" he asked, not altogether seriously.

She told him.

He whistled softly. "The Federation's more generous than the Confederacy. But, of course, your taxpayers are richer than ours, and there are so many more of them. . . ."

She ignored this. "And that's not all, my dear. Admiral Salversen of the Bureau of Supply, is an old friend of mine. He sent a personal message along with the other. It seems that there's a little one ship company for sale, just a feeder line running between Montalbon and Carribea. The gratuity barely covers the down payment—but with *your* gratuity, and our savings, and the profits we're bound to make we shall be out of the red in no time at all. Just think of it, John! You as Owner-Master, and myself as your ever-loving Mate!"

Grimes thought of it as he turned to stare again out of the wide window, his mind's eye piercing the dismal overcast to the nothingness beyond. Light, and warmth, and a sky ablaze with stars instead of this bleak desolation . . .

Light and warmth . . . And a milk run.

And Sonya.

He said slowly, "We may find it hard to settle down. Even you. You're not a Rimworlder, but your life, in the Federation's Naval Intelligence, has been adventurous, and you've worked out on the Rim so much that you almost qualify for citizenship . . ."

"I qualified for citizenship when I married you. And I want to settle down, John. But not here."

The black box on the desk crackled, then said in Miss Willoughby's voice, "Port Control is calling, Commodore Grimes. Shall I put them through?"

"Yes, please," Grimes told her.

≈ Chapter 2 ≈

"**CASSIDY HERE,**" said the box.

"Yes, Captain Cassidy?"

"Orbital Station 3 reports a ship, sir."

"Isn't that one of the things they're paid for?" asked Grimes mildly.

"Yes, sir." Cassidy's voice was sulky. "But there's nothing due for almost a week, and . . ."

"Probably one of the Federation Survey Service wagons," Grimes told him, flashing a brief smile (which she answered with a glare) at Sonya. "They think they can come and go as they damn well please. Tell Station 3 to demand—*demand*, not request—identification."

"The Station Commander has already done that, Commodore. But there's no reply."

"And Station 3 doesn't run to a Psionic Radio Officer. I always said that we were ill advised to get rid of the telepaths as soon as our ships and stations were fitted with Carlotti equipment . . ." He paused, then asked, "Landing approach?"

"No, sir. Station 3 hasn't had time to extrapolate her trajectory yet, but the way she's heading now it looks as though she'll miss Lorn by all of a thousand miles and finish up in the sun. . . ."

"They haven't had time?" Grimes' voice was cold. "What the hell sort of watch are they keeping?"

"A good one, sir. Commander Hall is one of our best men—as

you know. It seems that this ship just appeared out of nothing—those were Hall's own words. There was no warning at all on the Mass Proximity Indicator. And then, suddenly, there she was—on both M.P.I, *and* radar. . . ."

"Any of your people loafing around these parts?" Grimes asked Sonya. "No," she told him. "At least not that I know of." "And you are—or were—an intelligence officer, so you should know. H'm." He turned again to the box. "Captain Cassidy, tell Station 3 that I wish direct communication with them."

"Very good, sir."

The Commodore strode to his desk, sat down in his chair, pulled out a drawer. His stubby fingers played over the console that was revealed. Suddenly the window went opaque, and as it did so the lights in the office dimmed to a faint glow. One wall of the room came alive, a swirl of light and color that coalesced to form a picture, three dimensional, of the Watch House of Station 3. There were the wide ports, beyond the thick transparencies of which was the utter blackness of Space as seen from the Rim Worlds, a blackness made even more intense by contrast with the faintly glimmering nebulosities, sparse and dim, that were the distant, unreachable island universes. Within the compartment were the banked instruments, the flickering screens, the warped, convoluted columns, each turning slowly on its axis, that were the hunting antennae of the Carlotti Beacon. Uniformed men and women busied themselves at control panels, stood tensely around the big plotting tank. One of them—the Station Commander—turned to face the camera. He asked, "Have you the picture, Commodore Grimes, sir?"

"I have, Commander," Grimes told him. "How is the extrapolation of trajectory?"

"You may have a close-up of the tank, sir."

The scene dissolved, and then only the plotting tank was in Grimes' screen. In the center of it was the dull-glowing (but not dull-glowing in reality) globe that represented the Lorn sun. And there was the curving filament of light that represented the orbit of the strange ship, the filament that extended itself as Grimes and Sonya watched, that finally touched the ruddy incandescence of the central sphere. This was only an extrapolation; it would be months before it actually occurred. There was still time, ample time, for the crew of the intruder to pull her out of the fatal plunge. And yet, somehow, there was a sense of urgency. If a rescue operation were to be undertaken, it must be done without delay. A stern chase is a long chase.

"What do you make of it?" Grimes asked Sonya.

She said, "I don't like it. Either they can't communicate, or they won't communicate. And I think they can't. There's something wrong with that ship. . . ."

"Something very wrong. Get hold of Cassidy, will you? Tell him that I want *Rim Mamelute* ready for Space as soon as possible." He stared at the screen, upon which Commander Hall had made a reappearance. "We're sending the *Mamelute* out after her, Hall. Meanwhile, keep on trying to communicate."

"We are trying, sir."

Cassidy's voice came from the black box. "Sir, Captain Welling, the skipper of the *Mamelute*, is in the hospital. Shall I . . . ?"

"No, Cassidy. Somebody has to mind the shop—and you're elected. But there's something you can do for me. Get hold of Mr. Mayhew, the Psionic Radio Officer. Yes, yes, I know that he's taking his Long Service Leave, but get hold of him. Tell him I want him here, complete with his amplifier, as soon as possible, if not before. And get *Mamelute* cleared away."

"But who's taking her out, sir?"

"Who do you think? Get cracking, Cassidy."

"You'll need a Mate," said Sonya.

He found time to tease her, saying, "Rather a come-down from the Federation Survey Service, my dear."

"Could be. But I have a feeling that this may be a job for an Intelligence Officer."

"You'll sign on as Mate," he told her firmly.

Chapter 3

RIM MAMELUTE, as a salvage tug, was already in a state of near-readiness. She was fully fueled and provisioned; all that remained to be done was the mustering of her personnel. Her engineers, pottering around in Rim Runners' workshop on the spaceport premises, were easily located. The Port doctor was conscripted from his office, and was pleased enough to be pulled away from his boring paperwork. The Port Signal Station supplied a radio officer and—for Rim *Mamelute's* permanent Mate made it plain that he would resent being left out of the party—Sonya agreed to come along as Catering Officer.

Grimes could have got the little brute upstairs within an hour of his setting the wheels in motion, but he insisted on waiting for Mayhew. In any salvage job, communication between the salvor and the salved is essential—and to judge by the experience of Station 3, any form of electronic radio communication was *out.* He stood on the concrete, just outside the tug's airlock, looking up at the overcast sky. Sonya came out to join him.

"Damn the man!" he grumbled. "He's supposed to be on his way. He was told it was urgent."

She said, "I hear something."

He heard it too, above the thin whine of the wind, a deepening drone. Then the helicopter came into sight above the high roof of the Administration Building, the jet flames at the tip of its rotor blades a bright, blue circle against the gray sky. It dropped slowly, carefully,

137

making at last a landing remarkable for its gentleness. The cabin door opened and the tall gangling telepath, his thin face pasty against the upturned collar of his dark coat, clambered to the ground. He saw Grimes, made a slovenly salute, then turned to receive the large case that was handed him by the pilot.

"Take your time," growled Grimes.

Mayhew shuffled around to face the Commodore. He set the case carefully down on the ground, patted it gently. He said, mild reproof in his voice, "Lassie's not as used to traveling as she was. I try to avoid shaking her up."

Grimes sighed. He had almost forgotten about the peculiar relationship that existed between the spacefaring telepaths and their amplifiers—the living brains of dogs suspended in their tanks of nutrient solution. It was far more intense than that existing between normal man and normal dog. When a naturally telepathic animal is deprived of its body, its psionic powers are vastly enhanced—and it will recognize as friend and master only a telepathic man. There is symbiosis, on a psionic level.

"Lassie's not at all well," complained Mayhew.

"Think her up a nice, juicy bone," Grimes almost said, then thought better of it.

"I've tried that, of course," Mayhew told him. "But she's not. . . she's just not interested any more. She's growing old. And since the Carlotti system was introduced nobody is making psionic amplifiers anymore."

"Is she functioning?" asked the Commodore coldly.

"Yes, sir. But . . ."

"Then get aboard, Mr. Mayhew. Mrs. Grimes will show you to your quarters. Prepare and secure for blast-off without delay."

He stamped up the short ramp into the airlock, climbed the ladders to the little control room. The Mate was already in the co-pilot's chair, his ungainly posture a match for his slovenly uniform. Grimes looked at him with some distaste, but he knew that the burly young man was more than merely competent, and that although his manner and appearance militated against his employment in a big ship he was ideally suited to service in a salvage tug.

"Ready as soon as you are, Skipper," the Mate said. "You takin' her up?"

"You're more used to this vessel than I am, Mr. Williams. As soon as all's secure you may blast off."

"Good-oh, Skip."

Grimes watched the indicator lights, listened to the verbal reports, aware that Williams was doing likewise. Then he said into the transceiver microphone, "*Rim Mamelute* to Port Control. Blasting off."

Before Port Control could acknowledge, Williams hit the firing key. Not for the *Mamelute* the relatively leisurely ascent, the relatively gentle acceleration of the big ships. It was, thought Grimes dazedly, like being fired from a gun. Almost at once, it seemed, harsh sunlight burst through the control room ports. He tried to move his fingers against the crushing weight, tried to bring one of them to the button set in the arm rest of his chair that controlled the polarization of the transparencies. The glare was beating full in his face, was painful even through his closed eyelids. But Williams beat him to it. When Grimes opened his eyes he saw that the Mate was grinning at him.

"She's a tough little bitch, the old *Mamelute*," announced the objectionable young man with pride.

"Yes, Mr. Williams," enunciated Grimes with difficulty. "But there are some of us who aren't as tough as the ship. And, talking of lady dogs, I don't think that Mr. Mayhew's amplifier can stand much acceleration. . . ."

"That pickled poodle's brain, Skip? The bastard's better off than we are, floatin' in its nice warm bath o' thick soup." He grinned again. "But I was forgettin'. We haven't the regular crew this time. What say we maintain a nice, steady one and a half Gs? That do yer?"

One G would be better, thought Grimes. *After all, those people, whoever they are, are in no immediate danger of falling into the sun. But perhaps even a few minutes' delay might make all the difference between life and death to them . . . Even so, we must be capable of doing work, heavy, physical work, when we catch them.*

"Yes, Mr. Williams," he said slowly. "Maintain one and a half gravities. You've fed the elements of the trajectory into the computer, of course?"

"Of course, Skip. Soon as I have her round I'll put her on auto. She'll be right."

When the tug had settled down on her long chase, Grimes left Williams in the control room, went down into the body of the ship. He made his rounds, satisfied himself that all was well in engine room, surgery, the two communications offices and, finally, the galley. Sonya was standing up to acceleration as though she had been born and bred on a high gravity planet. He looked at her with envy as she poured him a cup of coffee, handing it to him without any obvious compensation for its increased weight. Then she snapped at him, "Sit down, John. If you're as tired as you look you'd better lie down."

He said, "I'm all right."

"You're not," she told him. "And there's no need for you to put on the big, tough space captain act in front of me."

"If you can stand it . . ."

"What if I can, my dear? I haven't led such a sheltered life as you have. I've knocked around in little ships more than I have in big ones, and I'm far more used to going places in a hurry than you."

He lowered himself to a bench and she sat beside him. He sipped his coffee, then asked her, "Do you think, then, that we should be in more of a hurry?"

"Frankly, no. Salvage work is heavy work, and if we maintain more than one and a half Gs over a quite long period we shall all of us be too tired to function properly, even that tough Mate of yours." She smiled. "I mean the Mate who's on Articles as such, not the one you're married to."

He chuckled. "But she's tough, too."

"Only when I have to be, my dear."

Grimes looked at her, and thought of the old proverb which says that there is many a true word spoken in jest.

~ Chapter 4 ~

THE STRANGE VESSEL was a slowly expanding speck of light in the globular screen of the Mass Proximity Indicator; it was a gradually brightening blip on *Mamelute's* radar display that seemed as though it were being drawn in towards the tug by the ever decreasing spiral of the range marker. Clearly it showed up on the instruments, although it was still too far distant for visual sighting, and it was obvious that the extrapolation of trajectory made by Station 3 was an accurate one. It was falling free, neither accelerating nor decelerating, its course determined only by the gravitational forces within the Lorn Star's planetary system, and left to itself must inevitably fall into the sun. But long before its shell plating began to heat it would be overhauled by the salvage ship and dragged away and clear from its suicide orbit.

And it was silent. It made no reply to the signals beamed at it from *Rim Mamelute's* powerful transmitter. Bennett, the Radio Officer, complained to Grimes, "I've tried every frequency known to civilized man, and a few that aren't. But, so far, no joy."

"Keep on trying," Grimes told him, then went to the cabin that Mayhew, the telepath, shared with his organic amplifier.

The Psionic Radio Officer was slumped in his chair, staring vacantly at the glass tank in which, immersed in its cloudy nutrient fluid, floated the obscenely naked brain. The Commodore tried to ignore the thing. It made him uneasy. Every time that he saw one of the amplifiers he could not help wondering what it would be like to be, as it were, disembodied, to be deprived of all external stimuli but the stray thoughts of other, more fortunate (or less unfortunate) beings—and those thoughts, as like as not, on an incomprehensible level. What would a man do, were he so used, his brain removed from his skull and employed by some race of superior beings for their own fantastic purpose? Go mad, probably. And did the dogs sacrificed so that Man could communicate with his fellows over the light years ever go mad?

"Mr. Mayhew," he said.

"Sir?" muttered the telepath.

"As far as electronic radio is concerned, that ship is dead."

"Dead?" repeated Mayhew in a thin whisper.

"Then you think that there's nobody alive on board her?"

"I . . . I don't know. I told you before we started that Lassie's not a well dog. She's old, Commodore. She's old, and she dreams most of the time, almost all of the time. She . . . she just ignores me. . ." His voice was louder as he defended his weird pet against the implied imputation that he had made himself. "It's just that she's old, and her mind is getting very dim. Just vague dreams and ghostly memories, and the past more real than the present, even so."

"What sort of dreams?" asked Grimes, stirred to pity for the naked canine brain in its glass cannister.

"Hunting dreams, mainly. She was a terrier, you know, before she was . . . conscripted. Hunting dreams. Chasing small animals, like rats. They're good dreams, except when they turn to nightmares. And then I have to wake her up—but she's in such a state of terror that she's no good for anything."

"I didn't think that dogs have nightmares," remarked Grimes.

"Oh, but they do, sir, they do. Poor Lassie always has the same one—about an enormous rat that's just about to kill her. It must be some old memory of her puppy days, when she ran up against such an animal, a big one, bigger than she was. . . ."

"H'm. And, meanwhile, nothing from the ship."

"Nothing at all, sir."

"Have you tried transmitting, as well as just maintaining a listening watch?"

"Of course, sir." Mayhew's voice was pained. "During Lassie's lucid moments I've been punching out a strong signal, strong enough even to be picked up by non-telepaths. You must have felt it yourself, sir. *Help is on the way.* But there's been no indication of mental acknowledgement."

"All we know about the ship, Mayhew, is that she seems to be a derelict. We don't know who built her. We don't know who mans her—or manned her."

"Anybody who builds a ship, sir, must be able to think."

Grimes, remembering some of the unhandier vessels in which he had served in his youth, said, "Not necessarily."

Mayhew, not getting the point, insisted, "But they must be able to think. And, in order to think, you must have a brain to think with. And any brain at all emits psionic radiation. Furthermore, sir, such radiation sets up secondary radiation in the inanimate surrounding of the brain. What is the average haunt but a psionic record on the walls of a house in which strong emotions have been let loose? A record that is played back given the right conditions."

"H'm. But you say that the derelict is psionically dead, that there's not even a record left by her builders, or her crew, to be played back to you."

"The range is still extreme, sir. And as for this secondary psionic radiation, sir, sometimes it fades rapidly, sometimes it lingers for years. There must be laws governing it, but nobody has yet been able to work them out."

"So there could be something . . ."

"There could be, sir. And there could not."

"Just go on trying, Mr. Mayhew."

"Of course, sir. But with poor Lassie in her present state I can't promise anything."

Grimes went along to the galley. He seated himself on the bench, accepted the cup of coffee that Sonya poured for him. He said, "It looks, my dear, as though we shall soon be needing an Intelligence Officer as well as a Catering Officer."

"Why?" she asked.

He told her of his conversation with Mayhew. He said, "I'd hoped that he'd be able to find us a few short cuts—but his crystal ball doesn't seem to be functioning very well these days . . . If you could call that poodle's brain in aspic a crystal ball."

"He's told me all about it," she said. "He's told everybody in the ship all about it. But once we get the derelict in tow, and opened up, we shall soon be able to find out what makes her tick. Or made her tick."

"I'm not so sure, Sonya. The way in which she suddenly appeared from nowhere, not even a trace on Station 3's M.P.I. beforehand, makes me think that she could be very, *very* alien."

"The Survey Service is used to dealing with aliens," she told him. "The Intelligence Branch especially so."

"I know, I know."

"And now, as I'm still only the humble galley slave, can I presume to ask my lord and master the E.T.C.?"

"Unless something untoward fouls things up, E.T.C. should be in exactly five Lorn Standard Days from now."

"And then it will be *Boarders Away!*" she said, obviously relishing the prospect.

"Boarders Away!" he agreed. "And I, for one, shall be glad to get out of this spaceborne sardine can."

"Frankly," she said, "I shall be even gladder to get out of this bloody galley so that I can do the real work for which I was trained."

∽ Chapter 5 ∾

SLOWLY THE RANGE CLOSED, until the derelict was visible as a tiny, bright star a few degrees to one side of the Lorn Sun. The range closed, and *Rim Mamelute's* powerful telescope was brought into play. It showed very little; the stranger ship appeared to be an almost featureless spindle, the surface of its hull unbroken by vanes, sponsons or antennae. And still, now that the distance could be measured in scant tens of miles, the alien construction was silent, making no reply to the signals directed at it by both the salvage tug's communications officers.

Grimes sat in the little control room, letting Williams handle the ship. The Mate crouched in his chair, intent upon his tell-tale instruments, nudging the tug closer and closer to the free-falling ship with carefully timed rocket blasts, matching velocities with the skill that comes only from long practice. He looked up briefly from his console to speak to Grimes. "She's hot, Skipper. Bloody hot."

"We've radiation armor," said Grimes. The words were question rather than statement.

"O' course. The *Mamelute's* ready for anything. Remember the *Rim Eland* disaster? Her pile went critical. We brought her in. I boarded her when we took her in tow, just in case there was anybody still living. There wasn't. It was like bein' inside a radioactive electric fryin' pan . . ."

A *charming simile* . . . thought Grimes.

He used the big, mounted binoculars to study the derelict. They showed him little more than had the telescope at longer range. So she was hot, radioactive. It seemed that the atomic blast that had initiated the radiation had come from outside, not inside. There were, after all, protuberances upon that hull, but they had been melted and then re-hardened, like guttering candle wax. There were the remains of what must have been vaned landing gear. There was the stump of what could have been, once, a mast of some kind, similar to the retractable masts of the spaceships with which Grimes was familiar, the supports for Deep Space radio antennae and radar scanners.

"Mr. Williams," he ordered, "we'll make our approach from the other side of the derelict."

"You're the boss, Skipper."

Brief accelerations crushed Grimes down into the padding of his chair, centrifugal force, as *Mamelute's* powerful gyroscopes turned her about her short axis, made him giddy. Almost he regretted having embarked upon this chase in person. He was not used to small ships, to the violence of their motions. He heard, from somewhere below, a crash of kitchenware. He hoped that Sonya had not been hurt.

She had not been—not physically, at any rate. Somehow, even though the tug was falling free once more, she contrived to stamp into the control room. She was pale with temper, and the smear of some rich, brown sauce on her right cheek accentuated her pallor. She glared at her husband and demanded, "What the hell's going on? Can't you give us some warning before indulging in a bout of astrobatics?"

Williams chuckled to himself and made some remark about the unwisdom of amateurs shipping out in space tugs. She turned on him, then, and said that she had served in tugs owned by the Federation Survey Service, and that they had been, like all Federation star ships, taut ships, and that any officer who failed to warn all departments of impending maneuvers would soon find himself busted down to Spaceman, Third Class.

Before the Mate could make an angry reply Grimes intervened. He said smoothly, "It was my fault, Sonya. But I was so interested in the derelict that I forgot to renew the alarm. After all, it was sounded as we began our approach. . . ."

"I know that. But I was prepared for an approach, not this tumbling all over the sky like a drunken bat."

"Once again, I'm sorry. But now you're here, grab yourself the spare chair and sit down. This is the situation. All the evidence indicates that there's been some sort of atomic explosion. That ship is *hot*. But I think that the other side of the hull will be relatively undamaged."

"It is," grunted Williams.

The three of them stared out of the viewports. The shell plating, seen from this angle, was dull, not bright, pitted with the tiny pores that were evidence of frequent passages through swarms of micrometeorites. At the stern, one wide vane stood out sharp and clear in the glare of *Mamelute's* searchlights. Forward, the armor screens over the control room ports were obviously capable of being retracted, were not fused to the hull. There were sponsons from which projected the muzzles of weapons—they could have been cannon or laser projectors, but what little was visible was utterly unfamiliar. There was a telescopic mast, a-top which was a huge, fragile-seeming radar scanner, motionless.

And just abaft the sharp stem there was the name.

No, thought Grimes, studying the derelict through the binoculars, *two names.*

It was the huge, sprawling letters, crude daubs of black paint, that he read first. *Freedom*, they spelled. Then there were the other symbols, gold-embossed, half obscured by the dark pigment. There was something wrong about them, a subtle disproportion, an oddness of spacing. But they made sense—after a while. They did not belong to the alphabet with which Grimes was familiar, but they must have been derived from it. There was the triangular "D", the "I" that was a fat, upright oblong, the serpentine "S" . . .

"*Distriyir. . .*" muttered Grimes. "*Destroyer?*" He passed the glasses, on their universal mount, to Sonya. "What do you make of this? What branch of the human race prints like that? What people have simplified their alphabet by getting rid of the letter 'E'?"

She adjusted the focus to suit her own vision. She said at last, "That painted-on-name is the work of human hands all right. But the other . . . I don't know. I've never seen anything like it before. There's a certain lack of logicality—human logicality, that is. Oh, that stylized 'D' is logical enough. But the substitution of 'I' for 'E'—if it *is* a substitution . . . And then, as far as *we* are concerned, a destroyer is a class of ship—not a ship's name . . ."

"I seem to recall," Grimes told her, "that there was once a warship called *Dreadnought*—and the dreadnoughts have been a class of warship ever since the first ironclads were launched on Earth's seas."

"All right, Mr. amateur naval historian—but have you ever, in the course of your very wide reading on your favorite subject, come across mention of a ship called *Destroyer*—and spelled without a single 'E'? There are non-humans mixed up in this somewhere—and highly intelligent non-humans at that."

"And humans," said Grimes.

"But we'll never find out anything just by talking about it," grumbled the Mate. "An' the sooner we take this bitch in tow, the shorter the long drag back to Port Forlorn. I'd make fast alongside— but even here, in the blast shadow, that hull is too damn' hot. It'll have to be tow wires from the outriggers—an' keep our fingers crossed that they don't get cut by our exhaust . . ."

"Take her in tow, then board," said Sonya.

"O' course. First things first. There'll be nobody alive inside that radioactive can . . ."

The intercommunication telephone was buzzing furiously. Grimes picked up the instrument. "Commodore here."

"Mayhew, sir." The telepath's voice was oddly muffled. He sounded as though he had been crying. "It's Lassie, sir. She's dead. . . ."

A happy release, thought Grimes. *But what am I supposed to do about it?*

"One of her nightmares, sir," Mayhew babbled on. "I was inside her mind, and I tried to awaken her. But I couldn't. There was this huge rat—and there were the sharp yellow teeth of it, and the stink of it. . . . It was so . . . it was so real, so vivid. And it was the fear that killed her—I could feel her fear, and it was almost too much for me. . . ."

"I'm sorry, Mr. Mayhew," said Grimes inadequately. "I'm sorry.

I will see you later. But we are just about to take the derelict in tow, and we are busy."

"I . . . I understand, sir."

And then Grimes relaxed into the padding of his chair, watching, not without envy, as Williams jockeyed the salvage tug into position ahead of the derelict, then carefully matched velocity. The outriggers were extruded, and then there was the slightest shock as the little missiles, each with a powerful magnetic grapnel as its warhead, were fired.

Contact was made, and then Williams, working with the utmost care, eased *Rim Mamelute* around in a great arc, never putting too much strain on the towing gear, always keeping the wires clear of the tug's incandescent exhaust. It was pretty to watch.

Even so, when at last it was over, when at last the Lorn Star was almost directly astern, he could not resist the temptation of asking, "But why all this expenditure of reaction mass and time to ensure a bows-first tow, Mr. Williams?"

"S.O.P., Skipper. It's more convenient if the people in the towed ship can see where they're going."

"But it doesn't look as though there are any people. Not live ones, that is."

"But we could be putting a prize crew aboard her, Skipper."

Grimes thought about saying something about the radio-activity, then decided not to bother.

"You just can't win, John," Sonya told him.

⇜ Chapter 6 ⇝

IN THEORY one can perform heavy work while clad in radiation armor. One can do so in practice—provided that one has been through a rigorous course of training. Pendeen, Second Engineer of *Rim Mamelute*, had been so trained. So, of course, had been Mr. Williams—but Grimes had insisted that the Mate stay aboard the tug while he, with Sonya and the engineer, effected an entry into the hull of the derelict. Soon, while the boarding party was making its exploratory walk over the stranger ship's shell plating, he had been obliged to order Williams to cut the drive; sufficient velocity had been built up so that both vessels were now in free fall away from the sun.

Even in free fall it was bad enough. Every joint of the heavy suit was stiff, every limb had so much mass that great physical effort was required to conquer inertia. Weary and sweating heavily, Grimes forced himself to keep up with his two companions, by a great effort of will contrived to maintain his side of the conversation in a voice that did not betray his poor physical condition—

He was greatly relieved when they discovered, towards the stern, what was obviously an airlock door. Just a hair-thin crack in the plating it was, outlining a circular port roughly seven feet in diameter. There were no signs of external controls, and the crack was too thin to allow the insertion of any tool.

"Send for the bell, sir?" asked Pendeen, his normally deep voice an odd treble in Grimes' helmet phones.

"The bell? Yes, yes. Of course. Carry on, Mr. Pendeen."

"Al to Bill," Grimes heard. "Do you read me? Over."

"Bill to Al. Loud an' clear. What can I do for you?"

"We've found the airlock. But we want the bell."

"You would. Just stick around. It'll be over."

"And send the cutting gear while you're about it."

"Will do. Stand by."

"Had any experience with the Laverton Bell, sir?" asked Pendeen, his voice not as respectful as it might have been.

"No. No actual working experience, that is."

"I have," said Sonya.

"Good. Then you'll know what to do when we get it."

Grimes, looking towards *Rim Mamelute*, could see that something bulky was coming slowly towards them along one of the tow wires, the rocket that had given the packet its initial thrust long since burned out. He followed the others towards the stem of the derelict, but stood to one side, held to the plating by the magnetic soles of his boots, as they unclipped the bundle from the line. He would have helped them to carry it back aft, but they ignored him.

Back at the airlock valve, Sonya and Pendeen worked swiftly and competently, releasing the fastenings, unfolding what looked like a tent of tough white plastic. This had formed the wrapper for other things—including a gas bottle, a laser torch and a thick tube of adhesive. Without waiting for instructions Sonya took this latter, removed the screw cap and, working on her hands and knees, used it to describe a glistening line just outside the crack that marked the door. Then all three of them, standing in the middle of the circle, lifted the fabric above their heads, unfolding it as they did so. Finally, with Grimes and Pendeen acting as tent poles, Sonya neatly fitted the edge of the shaped canopy to the ring of adhesive, now and again adding a further gob of the substance from the tube.

"Stay as you are, sir," the engineer said to Grimes, then fell to a squatting position. His gloved hands went to the gas cylinder, to the valve wheel. A white cloud jetted out like a rocket exhaust, then faded to invisibility. Around the boarding party the walls of the tent bellied outwards, slowly tautened, distended to their true shape by the expanding helium. Only towards the end was the hiss of the escaping gas very faintly audible.

Pendeen shut the valve decisively, saying, "That's that. Is she all tight, Sonya?"

"All tight, Al," she replied.

"Good." With a greasy crayon he drew a circle roughly in the center of the airlock door, one large enough to admit a spacesuited body. He picked up the laser torch, directed its beam downwards, thumbed the firing button. The flare of vaporizing metal was painfully bright, outshining the helmet lights, reflected harshly from the white inner surface of the plastic igloo. There was the illusion of suffocating heat—or was it more than only an illusion? Pendeen switched off the torch and straightened, looking down at the annulus of still-glowing metal. With an effort he lifted his right foot, breaking the contact of the magnetized sole with the plating. He brought the heel down sharply. The *clang*, transmitted through the fabric of their armor, was felt rather than heard by the others.

And then the circular plate was falling slowly, into the darkness of the airlock chamber, and the rough manhole was open so that they could enter.

Grimes was first into the alien ship, followed by Sonya and then Pendeen. It was light enough in the little compartment once they were into it, the beams of their helmet lights reflected from the white-painted walls. On the inner door there was a set of manual controls that worked—once Grimes realized that the spindle of the wheel had a left handed thread. Beyond the inner door there was an alleyway, and standing there was a man.

The Commodore whipped the pistol from his holster, his reflexes more than compensating for the stiffness of the joints of his suit. Then, slowly, he returned the weapon to his belt. This man was dead. Radiation may have killed him, but it had not killed all the bacteria of decay present in his body. Some freak of inertial and centrifugal forces, coming into play when the derelict had been taken in tow, had flung him to a standing posture, and the magnetic soles of his rough sandals—Grimes could see the gleam of metal—had held him to the deck.

So he was dead, and he was decomposing, his skin taut and darkly purple, bulging over the waistband of the loincloth—it looked like sacking—that was his only clothing. He was dead—and Grimes was suddenly grateful for the sealed suit that he was wearing, the suit that earlier he had been cursing, that kept out the stench of him.

Gently, with pity and pointless tenderness, he put his gloved hands to the waist of the corpse, lifted it free of the deck, shifted it to one side.

"We must be just above engineroom level," said Sonya, her voice deliberately casual.

"Yes," agreed Grimes. "I wonder if this ship has an axial shaft. If she has, it will be the quickest way of getting to the control room."

"That will be the best place to start investigations," she said.

They moved on through the alleyway, using the free fall shuffle that was second nature to all of them, letting the homing instinct that is part of the nature of all spacemen guide them. They found more bodies, women as well as men, sprawled in untidy attitudes, hanging like monstrous mermen and merwomen in a submarine cave. They tried to ignore them, as they tried to ignore the smaller bodies, those of children, and came at last, at the end of a short, radial alleyway, to the stout pillar of the axial shaft.

There was a door in the pillar, and it was open, and one by one they passed through it and then began pulling themselves forward along the central guide rod, ignoring the spiral ramp that lined the tunnel. Finally they came to a conventional enough hatchway, but the valve sealing the end of the shaft was jammed. Grimes and Sonya fell back to let Pendeen use the laser torch. Then they followed him into the control room.

～ Chapter 7 ～

THERE WERE MORE BODIES in the control room. There were three dead men and three dead women, all of them strapped into acceleration chairs. Like all the others scattered throughout the ship they were clad only in rough, scanty rags, were swollen with decomposition.

Grimes forced himself to ignore them. He could do nothing for them. Perhaps, he thought, he might someday avenge them (somehow he did not feel that they had been criminals, pirates)—but that would not bring them back to life. He looked past the unsightly corpses to the instruments on the consoles before their chairs. These, at first glance, seemed to be familiar enough—white dials with the black calibrations marked with Arabic numerals; red, green, white and amber pilot lights, dead now, but ready to blossom with glowing life at the restoration of a power supply. Familiar enough they were, at first glance. But there were the odd differences, the placement of various controls in positions that did not tally with the construction and the articulation of the normal human frame. And there was the lettering: MINNSCHINN DRIVI, RIMITI CINTRIL. Who, he asked himself, were the builders of this ship, this vessel that was almost a standard Federation Survey Service cruiser? What human race had jettisoned every vowel in the alphabet but this absurdly fat "I?"

"John," Sonya was saying, "give me a hand, will you?"

He turned to see what she was doing. She was trying to unbuckle a seat belt that was deeply embedded in the distended flesh at the waist of one of the dead men.

He conquered his revulsion, swallowed the nausea that was rising in his throat. He pulled the sharp sheath knife from his belt, said, "This is quicker," and slashed through the tough fabric of the strap. He was careful not to touch the gleaming, purple skin. He knew that if he did so the dead man would . . . burst.

Carefully, Sonya lifted the body from its seat, set it down on the deck so that the magnetized sandal soles were in contact with the steel plating. Then she pointed to the back of the chair. "What do you make of that?" she asked.

That was a vertical slot, just over an inch in width, that was continued into the seat itself, half bisecting it.

It was Pendeen who broke the silence. He said simply, "They had tails."

"But they haven't," objected Grimes. It was obvious that the minimal breech-clouts of the dead people could not conceal even a tiny caudal appendage.

"My dear John," Sonya told him in an annoyingly superior voice, "these hapless folk are neither the builders nor the original crew of this ship. Refugees? Could be. Escapees? A slave revolt? Once again—could be. Or must be. This is a big ship, and a fighting ship. You can't run a vessel of this class without uniforms, without marks of rank so you can see at a glance who is supposed to be doing what. Furthermore, you don't clutter up a man-o-war with children."

"She's not necessarily a man-o'-war," demurred Grimes. "She could be a defensively armed merchantman. . ."

"With officers and first class passengers dressed in foul rags? With a name like DESTROYER?"

"We don't *know* that that grouping of letters on the stern does spell DESTROYER."

"We don't *know* that this other grouping of letters"—she pointed to the control panel that Grimes had been studying—"spells MANNSCHENN DRIVE, REMOTE CONTROL. But I'm willing to bet my gratuity that if you trace the leads you'll wind up in a compartment full of dimension-twisting gyroscopes."

"All right," said Grimes. "I'll go along with you. I'll admit that we're aboard a ship built by some humanoid—but possibly non-human race that, even so, uses a peculiar distortion of English as its written language. . . ."

"A humanoid race with tails," contributed Pendeen.

"A humanoid race with tails," agreed Sonya. "But *what* race? Look at this slot in the chair back. It's designed for somebody—or something—with a thin tail, thin at the root as well as at the extremity. And the only tailed beings we know with any technology comparable to our own have thick tails—and, furthermore, have their own written languages. Just imagine one of our saurian friends trying to get out of that chair in a hurry, assuming that he'd ever been able to get into it in the first place. He'd be trapped."

"You're the Intelligence Officer," said Grimes rather nastily.

"All right. I am. Also, I hold a Doctorate in Xenology. And I tell you, John, that what we've found in this ship, so far, doesn't add up to any kind of sense at all."

"She hasn't made any sense ever since she was first picked up by Station 3," admitted Grimes.

"That she hasn't," said Pendeen. "And I don't like her. Not one little bit."

"Why not, Mr. Pendeen?" asked Grimes, realizing that it was a foolish question to ask about a radioactive hull full of corpses.

"Because . . . because she's *wrong*, sir. The proportions of all her controls and fittings—just wrong enough to be scary. And left-handed threads, and gauges calibrated from right to left."

"So they are," said Grimes. "So they are. But that's odder still. Why don't they write the same way? From Right to Left?"

"Perhaps they do," murmured Sonya. "But I don't think so. I think that the only difference between their written language and ours is that they have an all-purpose 'I', or an all-purpose symbol that's used for every vowel sound." She was prowling around the control room. Damn it all, there *must* be a Log Book. . . .

"There should be a Log Book," amended Grimes.

"All right. There should be a Log Book. Here's an obvious Log Desk, complete with stylus, but empty. I begin to see how it must have been. The ship safe in port, all her papers landed for checking, and then her seizure by these people, by these unfortunate humans, whoever they were . . . H'm. The Chart Tank might tell us something . . ." She glared at the empty globe. "It would have told us something if it hadn't been in close proximity to a nuclear blast. But there will be traces. Unfortunately we haven't the facilities here to bring them out." She resumed her purposeful shuffle. "And what have we here? SIGNIL LIG? SIGNAL LOG? A black box that might well contain quite a few answers when we hook it up to a power supply. And that, I think, will lie within the capabilities of our Radio Officer back aboard *Rim Mamelute*."

The thing was secured by simple enough clips to the side of what was obviously a transceiver. Deftly, Sonya disengaged it, tucked it under her arm.

"Back to the *Mamelute*," said Grimes. It was more an order than a suggestion.

"Back to the *Mamelute*," she agreed.

The Commodore was last from the control room, watched first Pendeen and then Sonya vanish through the hatch into the axial shaft. He half-wished that enough air remained in their suit tanks for them to make a leisurely examination of the accommodation that must be situated abaft Control—and was more than half-relieved that circumstances did not permit such a course of action. He had seen his fill of corpses. In any case, the Signal Log might tell them far more than the inspection of decomposing corpses ever could.

He felt far easier in his mind when the three of them were standing, once more, in the plastic igloo that covered the breached airlock, and almost happy when, one by one, they had squeezed through the built-in sphincter valve back to the clean emptiness of Space. The harsh working lights of Rim *Mamelute* seemed soft somehow, mellow almost, suggested the lights of Home. And the cramped interior of the tug, when they were back on board, was comforting. If one has to be jostled, it is better to be jostled by the living than by dead men and women, part-cremated in a steel coffin tumbling aimlessly between the stars.

⊸ Chapter 8 ⊸

IT WAS VERY QUIET in the radio office of *Rim Mamelute*. Grimes and Sonya stood there, watching chubby little Bennett make the last connections to the black box that they had brought from the control room of the derelict. "Yes," the Electronic Radio Officer had told them, "it *is* a Signal Log, and it's well shielded, so whatever records it may contain probably haven't been wiped by radiation. Once I get it hooked up we'll have the play-back."

And now it was hooked up. "Are you sure you won't burn it out?" asked the Commodore, suddenly anxious.

"Almost sure, sir," answered Bennett cheerfully. "The thing is practically an exact copy of the Signal Logs that were in use in some ships of the Federation Survey Service all of fifty years ago. Before my time. Anyhow, my last employment before I came out to the Rim was in the Lyran Navy, and their wagons were all Survey Service cast-offs. In many of them the original communications gear was still in place, and still in working order. No, sir, this isn't the first time that I've made one of these babies sing. Reminds me of when we picked up the wreck of the old *Minstrel Boy*; I was Chief Sparks of the *Tara's Hall* at the time, and got the gen from her Signal Log that put us on the trail of Black Bart"—he added unnecessarily—"the pirate."

"I have heard of him," said Grimes coldly.

Sonya remarked, pointing towards the box, "But it doesn't look old."

"No, Mrs. Grimes. It's not old. Straight from the maker, I'd say. But there's no maker's name, which is odd. . . ."

"Switch on, Mr. Bennett," ordered the Commodore.

Bennett switched on. The thing hummed quietly to itself, crackled briefly and thinly as the spool was rewound. It crackled again, more loudly, and the play-back began.

The voice that issued from the speaker spoke English—of a sort. But it was not human. It was a thin, high, alien squeaking—and yet, somehow, not alien enough. The consonants were ill-defined, and there was only one vowel sound.

"*Eeveengeer* tee *Deestreeyeer. Eeveengeer* tee *Deestreeyeer.* Heeve tee. Heeve tee!"

The voice that answered was not a very convincing imitation of that strange accent. "*Deestreeyer* tee *Eeveenger.* Reepeet, pleese. Reepeet. . ."

"A woman," whispered Sonya. "Human. . ."

"Heeve tee, *Deestreeyeer.* Heeve tee, eer wee eepeen feer!"

A pause, then the woman's voice again, the imitation even less convincing, a certain desperation all too evident: "*Deestreeyer* tee *Avenger. Deestreeyeer* tee *Eeveengeer* . . . Eer Dreeve ceentreels eer eet eef eerdeer!"

Playing for time, thought Grimes. *Playing for time, while clumsy hands fumble with unfamiliar armament. But they tried. They did their best. . . .*

"Dee!" screamed the inhuman voice. "Heemeen sceem, dee!"

"And that must have been it," muttered Grimes.

"It was," said Sonya flatly, and the almost inaudible whirring of what remained on the spool bore her out.

"That mistake she made," said Grimes softly, "is the clue. For *Eeveengeer,* read *Avenger.* For every 'E' sound substitute the vowel that makes sense. But insofar as the written language is concerned, that fat 'I' is really an 'E'. . . ."

"That seems to be the way of it," agreed Sonya.

"'Die,'" repeated the Commodore slowly. "'Human scum, die!'" He said, "Whoever those people are, they wouldn't be at all nice to know."

"That's what I'm afraid of," Sonya told him. "That we might get to know them. Whoever they are—and wherever, and whenever. . . ."

≈ Chapter 9 ≈

THE DERELICT HUNG IN ORBIT about Lorn, and the team of scientists and technicials continued the investigations initiated by *Rim Mamelute's* people during the long haul to the tug's home planet. Grimes, Sonya and the others had been baffled by what they had found—and now, with reluctance, the experts were admitting their own bafflement.

This ship, named *Destroyer* by her builders, and renamed *Freedom* by those who had not lived long to enjoy it, seemed to have just completed a major refit and to have been in readiness for her formal recommissioning. Although her magazines and some of her storerooms were stocked, although her hydroponics tanks and tissue culture vats had been operational at the time of her final action, her accommodation and working spaces were clean of the accumulation of odds and ends that, over the years, adds appreciably to the mass of any vessel. There were no files of official correspondence, although there was not a shortage of empty filing cabinets. There were no revealing personal possessions such as letters, photographs and solidographs, books, recordings, magazines and pin-up girl calendars. (The hapless humans who had been killed by the blast seemed to have brought aboard only the rags that they were wearing.) There were no log books in either control or engine rooms.

The cabins were furnished, however, and in all of them were the strange chairs with the slotted backs and seats, the furniture that was evidence of the existence of a race—an unknown race, insisted the xenologists—of tailed beings, approximating the human norm in stature. Every door tally was in place, and each one made it clear that the creatures who had manned the ship, before her seizure, used the English language, but a version of it peculiarly their own: KIPTIN . . . CHIIF INGINIIR . . . RIICTIIN DRIVI RIIM . . . HIDRIPINICS RIM. . . .

Even so she was, apart from the furniture and the distortion of printed English and—as the engineers pointed out—the prevalence of left-handed threads, a very ordinary ship, albeit somewhat old fashioned. There was, for example, no Carlotti navigational and communications equipment. And the signal log was a model the use of which had been discontinued by the Survey Service for all of half a standard century. And she lacked yet another device, a device of fairly recent origin, the Mass Proximity Indicator.

She was, from the engineering viewpoint, a very ordinary ship; it was the biologists who discovered the shocking abnormality.

They did not discover it at once. They concentrated, at first, upon the cadavers of the unfortunate humans. These were, it was soon announced, indubitably human. They had been born upon and had lived their lives upon an Earth-type planet, but their lives had not been pleasant ones. Their physiques exhibited all the signs of undernourishment, of privation, and they almost all bore scars that told an ugly story of habitual maltreatment. But they were men, and they were women, and had they lived and had they enjoyed for a year or so normal living conditions they would have been indistinguishable from the citizens of any man-colonized world.

And there was nothing abnormal in the hydroponics tanks. There were just the standard plants that are nurtured in ships' farms throughout the Galaxy—tomatoes and cucumbers, potatoes and carrots, the Centaurian umbrella vine, Vegan moss-fern.

It was the tissue culture vats that held the shocking secret.

The flesh that they contained, the meat that was the protein supply for the tailed beings who should have manned the ship, was human flesh.

"I was right," said Sonya to Grimes. "I was right. Those people—whoever, wherever (and whenever?) they are—are our enemies. But *where* are they? And when?"

"From . . . from Outside . . . ?" wondered the Commodore.

"Don't be a bloody fool, John. Do you think that a race could wander in from the next galaxy but three, reduce a whole planet of humans to slavery, and worse than slavery, without our knowing about it? And why should such a race, if there were one, have to borrow or steal our shipbuilding techniques, our language even? Damn it all, it doesn't make sense. It doesn't even begin to make sense."

"That's what we've all been saying ever since this blasted derelict first appeared."

"And it's true." She got up from her chair and began to pace up and down Grimes' office. "Meanwhile, my dear, we've been left holding the baby. You've been asked to stay on in your various capacities until the mystery has been solved, and my resignation from the Intelligence Branch of the Survey Service has been rescinded. I've been empowered by the Federation Government to co-opt such Confederacy personnel to assist me in my investigations as I see fit. (That means you—for a start.) Forgive me for thinking out loud. It helps sometimes. Why don't you try it?"

"All we know," said Grimes slowly, "is that we've been left holding the baby."

"All we know," she countered, "is that we're supposed to carry the can back."

"But why shouldn't we?" he demanded suddenly. "Not necessarily this can, but one of our own."

She stopped her restless motion, turned to stare at him. She said coldly, "I thought that you had made a study of archaic slang expressions. Apparently I was wrong."

"Not at all, Sonya. I know what 'to carry the can back' means. I know, too, that the word 'can' is still used to refer to more and bigger things than containers of beer or preserved foods. Such as . . ."

"Such as ships," she admitted.

"Such as ships. All right. How do we carry the can, or *a* can back? Back to where the can came from?"

"But where? Or when?"

"That's what we have to find out."

She said, "I think it will have to be *the* can. That is, if you're thinking what I think you're thinking: that this *Destroyer* or *Freedom* or whatever you care to call her drifted in from one of the alternative universes. She'll have that built-in urge, yes, urge. She'll have that built-in urge to return to her own continuum."

"So you accept the alternative universe theory?"

"It seems to fit the facts. After all, out here on the Rim, the transition from one universe to another has been made more than once."

"As we should know."

"If only we knew how the derelict did drift in. . . ."

"Did she *drift* in?" asked Grimes softly. And then, in spoken answer to his wife's unspoken query, "I think that she was blown in."

"Yes . . . yes. Could be. A nuclear explosion in close, very close proximity to the ship. The very fabric of the continuum strained and warped. . ." She smiled, but it was a grim smile. "That could be it."

"And that could be the way to carry the can back."

"I don't want to be burned, my dear. And, oddly enough, I shouldn't like to see you burned."

"There's no need for anybody to be burned. Have you ever heard of lead shielding?"

"Of course. But the weight! Even if we shielded only a small compartment, the reaction drive'd be working flat out to get us off the ground, and we'd have damn all reaction mass to spare for any maneuvers. And the rest of the ship, as we found when we boarded the derelict, would be so hot as to be uninhabitable for months."

He gestured towards the wide window to the squat tower that was *Faraway Quest.* "I seem to remember, Sonya, that you shipped with me on our Wild Ghost Chase. Even though you were aboard as an officer of the Federation's Naval Intelligence you should remember how the *Quest* was fitted. That sphere of anti-matter—now back in safe orbit—that gave us anti-gravity. . . We can incorporate it into

Freedom's structure as it was incorporated into Quest's. With it functioning, we can afford to shield the entire ship and still enjoy almost negative mass."

"So you think we should take *Freedom*, or *Destroyer*, and not *Faraway Quest*?"

"I do. Assuming that we're able to blow her back into the continuum she came from, she'll be a more convincing Trojan horse than one of our own ships."

"Cans," she said. "Trojan horses. Can you think of any more metaphors?" She smiled again, and her expression was not quite so grim. "But I see what you mean. Our friends with the squeaky voices and the long, thin tails will think that their own lost ship has somehow wandered back to them, still manned by the escaped slaves." Her face hardened. "I almost feel sorry for them."

"Almost," he agreed.

⮞ Chapter 10 ⮜

THE BOFFINS were reluctant to release *Freedom,* but Grimes was insistent, explaining that disguise of *Faraway Quest*, no matter how good, might well be not good enough. A small, inconspicuous but betraying feature of her outward appearance could lead to her immediate destruction. "Then what about the crew, Commodore?" asked one of the scientists. "Surely those tailed beings will soon realize that the ship is not manned by the original rebels."

"Not necessarily," Grimes told the man. "In fact, I think it's quite unlikely. Even among human beings all members of a different race tend to look alike. And when it comes to members of two entirely different species . . ."

"I'm reasonably expert," added Sonya, "but even I find it hard until I've had time to observe carefully the beings with whom I'm dealing."

"But there's so much that we could learn from the ship!" protested the scientist.

"Mr. Wales," Grimes said to the Rim Runners' Superintending Engineer, "how much do you think there is to be learned from the derelict?"

"Not a damn thing, Commodore. But if we disguise one of our own ships, and succeed in blowing her into whatever cosmic alternative universe she came from, there's far too much that could be learned from *us*. As far as shipbuilding is concerned, we're practically a century ahead."

"Good enough. Well, gentlemen?"

"I suggest, Commodore, that we bring your *Freedom's* armament up to scratch," said Admiral Hennessey, but the way that he said it made it more of an order than a suggestion.

Grimes turned to face the Admiral, the Flag Officer commanding the Naval Force of the Confederacy. Bleak stare clashed with bleak stare, almost audibly. As an officer of the Reserve, Grimes considered himself a better spaceman than his superior, and was inclined to resent the intrusion of the Regular Navy into what he was already regarding as his own show.

He replied firmly, "No, sir. That could well give the game away."

He was hurt when Sonya took the Admiral's side—but, after all, she was regular Navy herself, although Federation and not Confederacy. She said, "But what about the lead sheathing, John? What about the sphere of anti-matter?"

Grimes was not beaten. "Mr. Wales has already made a valid point. He thinks that it would be imprudent to make the aliens a present of a century's progress in astronautical engineering. It would be equally imprudent to make them a present of a century's progress in weaponry."

"You have a point there, Grimes," admitted the Admiral. "But I do not feel happy in allowing my personnel to ship in a vessel on a hazardous mission without the utmost protection that I can afford them."

"Apart from the Marines, sir, my personnel rather than yours. Practically every officer will be a reservist."

The Admiral glared at the Commodore. He growled, "Frankly, if it were not for the pressure brought to bear by our Big Brothers of the Federation, I should insist on commissioning a battle squadron." He smiled coldly in Sonya's direction. "But the Terran Admiralty seems to trust Commander Verrill—or Mrs. Grimes—and have given her on-the-spot powers that would be more fitting to a holder of Flag Officer's rank. And my own instructions from Government House are to afford her every assistance."

He made a ritual of selecting a long, black cigar from the case that he took from an inside pocket of his uniform, lit it, filled the already foul air of the derelict's control room with wreathing eddies of acrid blue smoke. He said in a voice that equaled in acridity the fumes that carried it, "Very well, Commodore. You're having your own way. Or your wife is having her own way; she has persuaded the Federation that you are to be in full command. (But will you be, I wonder. . .) May I, as your Admiral, presume to inquire just what are your intentions, assuming that the nuclear device that you have commandeered from my arsenal does blow you into the right continuum?"

"We shall play by ear, sir."

The Admiral seemed to be emulating the weapon that he had just mentioned, but he did not quite reach critical mass. "Play by ear!" he bellowed at last, when coherent speech was at last possible. "Play by ear! Damn it all, sir, that's the sort of fatuous remark one might expect from a Snotty making his first training cruise, but not from an allegedly responsible officer."

"Admiral Hennessey," Sonya's voice was as cold as his had been. "This is not a punitive expedition. This is not a well organized attack by naval forces. This is an Intelligence operation. We do not know what we are up against. We are trying to find out." Her voice softened slightly. "I admit that the Commodore expressed himself in a rather un-spacemanlike manner, but playing by ear is what we shall do. How shall I put it? We shall poke a stick into the ants' nest and see what comes out. . . ."

"We shall hoist the banner of the Confederacy to the masthead and see who salutes," somebody said in one of those carrying whispers. The Admiral, the Commodore and Sonya Verrill turned to glare at the man. Then Sonya laughed. "That's one way of putting it. Only it won't be the black and gold of the Confederacy—it'll be the black and silver of the Jolly Roger. A little judicious piracy—or privateering. Will Rim Worlds Letters of Marque be valid wherever we're going, Admiral?"

That officer managed a rather sour chuckle. "I think I get the drift of your intentions, Commander. I hate to have to admit it—but I wish that I were coming with you." He transferred his attention to Grimes.

"So, Commodore, I think that I shall be justified in at least repairing or renewing the weapons that were damaged or destroyed by the blast—as long as I don't fit anything beyond the technology of the builders of this ship."

"Please do that, sir."

"I shall. But what about small arms for your officers and the Marines?"

Grimes pondered the question. There had been no pistols of any kind aboard the derelict when he had boarded her. It could be argued that this was a detail that did not much matter—should the ship be boarded and seized herself there would be both the lead sheathing *and* the sphere of anti-matter that would make it obvious to the boarding party that she had been . . . elsewhere. Assuming, that is, that the last survivors of her crew did not trigger the explosive charge that would shatter the neutronium shell and destroy the magnets, thus bringing the sphere of anti-iron into contact with the normal matter surrounding it. Then there would be nobody to talk about what had been found.

But *Freedom*—as a pirate or a privateer—would be sending boarding parties to other ships. There was the possibility that she might have to run before superior forces, unexpectedly appearing, leaving such a boarding party to its fate. Grimes most sincerely hoped that he would never have to make such a decision. And if the boarding party possessed obviously alien hand weapons the tailed beings would be, putting it very mildly, suspicious.

"No hand weapons," he said at last, reluctantly. "But I hope that we shall be able to capture a few, and that we shall be able to duplicate them in the ship's workshop. Meanwhile, I'd like your Marines to be experts in unarmed combat—both suited and unsuited."

"And expert knife fighters," added Sonya.

"Boarding axes and cutlasses," contributed the Admiral, not without relish.

"Yes, sir," agreed Grimes. "Boarding axes and cutlasses."

"I suggest, Commodore," said Hennessey, "that you do a course at the Personal Combat Center at Lorn Base."

"I don't think there will be time, sir," said Grimes hopefully.

"There will be, Commodore. The lead sheathing and the anti-matter sphere cannot be installed in five minutes. And there are weapons to be repaired and renewed."

"There will be time," said Sonya.

Grimes sighed. He had been in one or two minor actions in his youth, but they had been so . . . impersonal. It was the enemy ship that you were out to get, and the fact that a large proportion of her crew was liable to die with her was something that you glossed over. You did not see the dreadful damage that your missiles and beams did to the fragile flesh and blood mechanisms that were human beings. Or if you did see it—a hard frozen corpse is not the same as one still warm, still pumping blood from severed arteries, still twitching in a ghastly semblance to life.

"There will be time, Commodore," repeated the Admiral.

"There will be time," repeated Sonya.

"And what about you, Mrs. Grimes?" asked Hennessey unkindly.

"You forget, sir, that in my branch of the Federation's service we are taught how to kill or maim with whatever is to hand any and every life form with which we may come into contact."

"Then I will arrange for the Commodore's course," Hennessey told her.

It was, for Grimes, a grueling three weeks. He was fit enough, but he was not as hard as he might have been. Even wearing protective armor he emerged from every bout with the Sergeant Instructor badly bruised and battered. And he did not like knives, although he attained fair skill with them as a throwing weapon. He disliked cutlasses even more. And the boarding axes, with their pike heads, he detested.

And then, quite suddenly, it came to him. The Instructor had given him a bad time, as usual, and had then called a break. Grimes stood there, sagging in his armor, using the shaft of his axe as a staff upon which to lean. He was aching and he was itching inside his protective clothing, and his copious perspiration was making every abrasion on his skin smart painfully.

Without warning the Instructor kicked Grimes' support away with a booted foot and then, as the Commodore sprawled on the hard ground, raised his own axe for the simulated kill. Although a red haze clouded his vision, Grimes rolled out of the path of the descending blade, heard the blunted edge thud into the dirt a fraction of an inch from his helmeted head. He was on his feet then, moving with an agility that he had never dreamed that he possessed, he was on his feet, crouching and his pike head thrusting viciously at the Instructor's crotch. The man squealed as the blow connected; even the heavy codpiece could not save him from severe pain. He squealed, but brought his own axe around in a sweeping, deadly arc. Grimes parried, blade edge to shaft, to such good effect that the lethal head of the other's weapon was broken off, clattering to the ground many feet away. He parried and followed through, his blade clanging on the Instructor's shoulder armor. Yet another blow, this time to the man's broad back, and he was down like a felled ox.

Slowly the red haze cleared from the commodore's vision as he stood there. Slowly he lowered his axe, and as he did so he realized that the Instructor had rolled over, was lying there, laughing up at him, was saying, "Easy, sir. Easy. You're not supposed to kill me, sir. Or to ruin my matrimonial prospects."

"I'm sorry, Sergeant," Grimes said stiffly. "But that was a dirty trick *you* played."

"It was meant to be dirty, sir. Never trust nobody—that's Lesson One."

"And Lesson Two, Sergeant?"

"You've learned that too, sir. You gotta *hate*. You officers are all the same—you don't really hate the poor cows at the other end of the trajectory when you press a firing button. But in this sort of fighting you *gotta* hate."

"I think I see, Sergeant," said Grimes.

But he was not sorry when he was able to return to his real business—to see *Freedom* (or *Destroyer*) readied for her expedition into the Unknown.

∾ Chapter 11 ∾

FREEDOM was commissioned as a cruiser of the Navy of the Rim Worlds Confederacy, but the winged wheel of the Rim Worlds had not replaced the embossed lettering of her original name or the crude, black-painted characters that had partially obscured it. *Freedom* was manned by spacemen and spacewomen of the Reserve and a company of Marines. But there was no display of gold braid and brass buttons—marks of rank and departmental insignia had been daubed on the bare skin of wrists and upper arms and shoulders in an indelible vegetable dye. Apart from this crude attempt at uniform, the ship's complement was attired in scanty, none too clean rags. The men were shaggily bearded, the roughly hacked hair of the women was unkempt. All of them bore unsightly cicatrices on their bodies—but these were the result of plastic surgery, not of ill-treatment.

Outwardly, *Freedom* was just as she had been when she suddenly materialized in her suicidal orbit off Lorn. Internally, however, there had been changes made. On the side that had been scarred by the blast, the weapons—the laser projectors and the missile launchers—had been repaired, although this had been done so as not to be apparent to an external observer. In a hitherto empty storeroom just forward of the enginerooms the sphere of anti-matter had been installed—the big ball of anti-iron, and the powerful magnets that held it in place inside its neutronium casing. And within the shell plating was the thick lead sheathing that would protect the ship's personnel from lethal radiation when the nuclear device was exploded, the bomb that, Grimes hoped, would blow the vessel back to where she had come from. (The physicists had assured him that the odds on this happening were seven to five, and that the odds on the ship's finding herself in a habitable universe were almost astronomical.)

There was one more change insofar as the internal fittings were concerned, and it was a very important one. The tissue culture vats now contained pork, and not human flesh. "After all," Grimes had said to a Biologist who was insisting upon absolute verisimilitude, "there's not all that much difference between pig and long pig. . . ."

The man had gone all technical on him, and the Commodore had snapped, "Pirates we may have to become, but not cannibals!"

But even pirates, thought Grimes, surveying the officers in his control room, *would be dressier than this mob.* He was glad that he had insisted upon the painted badges of rank—the beards made his male officers hard to recognize. With the female ones it was not so bad, although other features (like the men, the women wore only breech clouts) tended to distract attention from their faces.

Clothes certainly make the man, the Commodore admitted wryly to himself. *And the women—although this very undress uniform suits Sonya well enough, even though her hair-do does look as though she's been dragged through a hedge backwards.* And it felt all wrong for him to be sitting in the chair of command, the seat of the mighty, without the broad gold stripes on his epaulettes (and without the epaulettes themselves, and without a shirt to mount them on) and without the golden comets encrusting the peak of his cap. But the ragged indigo band encircling each hairy wrist would have to do, just as the coarse burlap kilt would have to substitute for the tailored, sharply creased shorts that were his normal shipboard wear.

He was concerning himself with trivialities, he knew, but it is sometimes helpful and healthy to let the mind be lured away, however briefly, from consideration of the greater issues.

Williams—lately Mr. Williams, Mate of *Rim Mamelute*, now Commander Williams, Executive Officer of *Freedom*—had the con. Under his control the ship was riding the beam from Lorn back to the position in which she had first been picked up by Orbital Station 3. It was there, the scientists had assured Grimes, that she would stand the best change of being blown back into her own continuum. The theory seemed to make sense, although the mathematics of it were far beyond the Commodore, expert navigator though he was.

The ship was falling free now, her reaction drive silent, dropping down the long, empty miles towards a rendezvous that would be no more (at first) than a flickering of needles on dials, an undulation of the glowing traces on the faces of monitor tubes. She was falling free, and through the still unshuttered ports there was nothing to be seen ahead but the dim, ruddy spark that was the Eblis sun, and nothing to port but a faint, far nebulosity that was one of the distant island universes.

To starboard was the mistily gleaming galactic lens, a great ellipse of luminosity in which there were specks of brighter light, like jewels in the hair of some dark goddess.

Grimes smiled wryly at his poetic fancies, and Sonya, who had guessed what he had been thinking, grinned at him cheerfully. She was about to speak when Williams' voice broke the silence. "Hear this! Hear this! Stand by for deceleration. Stand by for deceleration!"

Retro-rockets coughed, then shrieked briefly. For a second or so seat belts became almost intolerable bonds. The Executive Officer emitted a satisfied grunt, then said, "spot on, Skipper. Secure for the Big Bang?"

"You know the drill, Commander Williams. Carry on, please."

"Good-oh, Skipper." Williams snapped orders, and the ship shivered a little as the capsule containing the nuclear device was launched. Grimes saw the thing briefly from a port before the shutters—armor plating and thick lead sheathing—slid into place. It was just a dull-gleaming metal cylinder. It should have looked innocuous, but somehow it didn't. Grimes was suddenly acutely conscious of the craziness of this venture. The scientists had been sure that everything would work as it should, but they were not here to see their theories put to the test. *But I must be fair,* Grimes told himself. *After all, it was our idea. Mine and Sonya's. . . .*

"Fire!" he heard Williams say.

But nothing happened.

There was no noise—but, of course, in the vacuum of Deep Space there should not have been. There was no sense of shock. There was no appreciable rise of the control room temperature.

"A missfire?" somebody audibly wondered.

"Try to raise Lorn," Grimes ordered the Radio Officer. "Orbital Station 3 is maintaining a listening watch on our frequency."

There was a period of silence, broken only by the hiss and crackle of interstellar static, then the voice of the operator saying quietly, "*Freedom* to Station Three. *Freedom* to Station Three. Do you hear me? Come in, please."

Again there was silence.

"Sample the bands," said Grimes. "Listening watch only."

And then they knew that the bomb had exploded, that the results of the explosion had been as planned. There was an overheard dialogue between two beings with high, squeaky voices, similar to the voice that had been recorded in *Freedom's* signal log. There was a discussion of Estimated Time of Arrival and of arrangements for the discharge of cargo—hard to understand at first, but easier once ear and brain became attuned to the distortion of vowel sounds.

When the ports were unscreened, the outside view was as it had been prior to the launching of the bomb, but Grimes and his people knew that the worlds in orbit around those dim, far suns were not, in this Universe, under human dominion.

∽ Chapter 12 ∽

"WHAT'S THEIR RADAR LIKE?" asked Grimes.

"Judging by what's in this ship, not too good," replied Williams. "Their planet and station-based installations will have a longer range, but unless they're keepin' a special lookout they'll not pick us up at this distance."

"Good," said Grimes. "Then swing her, Commander. Put the Lorn sun dead ahead. Then calculate what deflection we shall need to make Lorn itself our planetfall."

"Reaction Drive, sir?"

"No. Mannschenn Drive."

"But we've no Mass Proximity Indicator, Skipper, and a jump of light minutes only."

"We've slipsticks, and a perfectly good computer. With any luck we shall be able to intercept that ship coming in for a landing."

"You aren't wasting any time, John," said Sonya, approval in her voice. The Commodore could see that she was alone in her sentiments. The other officers, including the Major of Marines, were staring at him as though doubtful of his sanity.

"Get on with it, Commander," snapped Grimes. "Our only hope of intercepting that ship is to make a fast approach, and one that cannot be detected. And make it Action Stations while you're about it."

"And Boarding Stations?" asked the Major. The spacegoing

soldier had recovered his poise and was regarding his superior with respect.

"Yes. Boarding Stations. Get yourself and your men into those adapted spacesuits." He added, with a touch of humor, "And don't trip over the tails."

He sat well back in his chair as the gyroscopes whined, as the ship's transparent nose with its cobweb of graticules swung slowly across the almost empty sky. And then the yellow Lorn sun was ahead and Sonya, who had taken over the computer, was saying, "Allowing a time lag of exactly one hundred and twenty seconds from . . . *now*, give her five seconds of arc left deflection."

"Preliminary thrust?" asked Williams.

"Seventy-five pounds, for exactly 0.5 second."

"Mannschenn Drive ready," reported the officer at the Remote Control.

Grimes was glad that he had ordered the time-varying device to be warmed up before the transition from one universe to the other had been made. He had foreseen the possibility of flight; he had not contemplated the possibility of initiating a fight. But, as he had told the Admiral, he was playing by ear.

He said to Sonya, "You have the con, Commander Verrill. Execute when ready."

"Ay, ay, sir. Stand by all. Commander Williams—preliminary thrust on the word 'Fire!' Mr. Cavendish, Mannschenn Drive setting 2.756. Operate for exactly 7.5 seconds immediately reaction drive has been cut. Stand by all. Ten . . . Nine . . . Eight . . . Seven . . . Six . . . Five . . ."

Like one of the ancient submarines, Grimes was thinking. *An invisible approach to the target, and not even a periscope to betray us. But did those archaic warships ever make an approach on dead reckoning? I suppose that they must have done, but only in their infancy.*

"Four . . . Three . . . Two . . . One . . . fire!"

The rockets coughed briefly, diffidently, and the normally heavy hand of acceleration delivered no more than a gentle pat. Immediately there was the sensation of both temporal and spatial disorientation as the ever-precessing gyroscopes of the Drive began to spin—a sensation that faded almost at once. And then the control room was flooded with yellow light—light that dimmed as the ports were polarized. But there was still light, a pearly radiance of reflected illumination from the eternal overcast, the familiar overcast of Lorn. That planet hung on their port beam, a great, featureless sphere, looking the same as it had always looked to the men and women at the controls of the ship.

But it was not the same.

There was that excited voice, that shrill voice spilling from the speaker: "*Whee eere yee? Wheet sheep? Wheet sheep? Wee sheell reepeert yee. Yee knee theer eet ees feerbeedeen tee eese thee Dreeve weetheen three reedeei!*"

"Almost rammed the bastards," commented Williams. "That was close, Skip."

"It was," agreed Grimes, looking at the radar repeater before his chair. "Match trajectory, Commander." He could see the other ship through the ports now. Like *Freedom*, she was in orbit about Lorn. The reflected sunlight from her metal skin was dazzling and he could not make out her name or any other details. But Sonya had put on a pair of polaroids with telescopic lenses. She reported, "Her name's *Weejee*. Seems to be just a merchantman. No armament that I can see."

"Mr. Carter!"

"Sir!" snapped the Gunnery Officer.

"See if your laser can slice off our friend's main venturi. And then the auxiliary ones."

"Ay, ay, sir."

The invisible beams stabbed out from *Freedom's* projectors. In spite of the dazzle of reflected sunlight from the other's hull the blue incandescence of melting, vaporizing metal was visible. And then Grimes was talking into the microphone that somebody had passed to him, "*Freedom* to *Weejee*. *Freedom* to *Weejee*. We are about to board you. Offer no resistance and you will not be harmed."

And then the shrill voice, hysterical now, was screaming to somebody far below on the planet's surface. "Heelp! Heelp! Eet ees thee *Deestreeyeer!* Eet ees the sleeves! Heelp!"

"Jam their signals!" ordered Grimes. How long would it be before a warship came in answer to the distress call? Perhaps there was already one in orbit, hidden by the bulk of the planet. And there would be ground to space missiles certainly—but Carter could take care of them with his laser.

Somebody came into the control room, a figure in bulky space armor, a suit that had been designed to accommodate a long, prehensile tail. For a moment Grimes thought that it was one of the rightful owners of the ship, that somehow a boarding had been effected. And then the Major's voice, distorted by the diaphragm in the snouted helmet, broke the spell. "Commodore Grimes, sir," he said formally, "my men are ready."

Grimes told him, "I don't think that our friends out there are going to open up." He added regretfully, "And we have no laser pistols."

"There are cutting and burning tools in the engineering workshop, sir. I have already issued them to my men."

"Very good, Major. You may board."

"Your instructions, sir?"

"Limit your objectives. I'd like the Log Books from her Control, and any other papers, such as manifests, that could be useful. But if there's too much resistance, don't bother. We may have to get out of here in a hurry. But I shall expect at least one prisoner."

"We shall do our best, sir."

"I know you will, Major. But as soon as I sound the Recall, come a-running."

"Very good, sir." The Marine managed a smart salute, even in the disguising armor, left the control room.

"Engaging ground to space missiles," announced the Gunnery Officer in a matter of fact voice. Looking out through the planetward ports Grimes could see tiny, distant, intensely brilliant sparks against the cloud blanket. There was nothing to worry about—yet. Carter was picking off the rockets as soon as they came within range of his weapons.

And then he saw the Marines jetting between the two ships, each man with a vapor trail that copied and then surpassed the caudal appendage of his suit. They carried boarding axes, and the men in the lead were burdened with bulky cutting tools. He watched them come to what must have been a clangorous landing on the other vessel's shell plating and then, with an ease that was the result of many drills, disperse themselves to give the tool-bearers room to work. Metal melted, flared and exploded into glowing vapor. The ragged-edged disc that had been the outer valve of the airlock was pried up and clear and sent spinning away into emptiness. There was a slight delay as the inner door was attacked—and then the armored figures were vanishing rapidly into the holed ship.

From the speaker of the transceiver that was tuned to spacesuit frequency Grimes heard the Major's voice, "Damn it all, Bronsky, that's a tool, not a weapon! Don't waste the charge!"

"He'd have got you, sir. . ."

"Never mind that. I want that airtight door down!"

And there were other sounds—clanging noises, panting, a confused scuffling. There was a scream, a human scream.

In the control room the radar officer reported. "Twelve o'clock low. Two thousand miles. Reciprocal trajectory. Two missiles launched."

"Carter!" said Grimes.

"In hand, sir," replied that officer cheerfully. "So far."

"Recall the Marines," ordered Grimes. "Secure control room for action."

The armored shutters slid over the ports. Grimes wondered how much protection the lead sheathing would give against laser, if any. But if the Major and his men were caught between the two ships their fate would be certain, unpleasantly so. And it was on the planetary side of the ship, the side from which the boarding party would return, that the exterior television scanner had been destroyed by the blast that had thrown the ship into Grimes' universe. That scanner had not been renewed. The Commodore could not tell whether or not the Major had obeyed his order; by the time that the Marines were out of the radar's blind spot they would be almost in *Freedom's* airlock. Not that the radar was of much value now, at short range; *Freedom* was enveloped in a dense cloud of metallic motes. This would shield her from the enemy's laser, although not from missiles. And the floating screen would render her own anti-missile laser ineffective. Missile against missile was all very well, but the other warship was operating from a base from which she could replenish her magazines.

"Reporting on board, sir." It was the Major's voice, coming from the intercom speaker. "With casualties—none serious—and prisoner."

Wasting no time, Grimes sized up the navigational situation. The ship would be on a safe trajectory if the reaction drive were brought into operation at once. He so ordered and then, after a short blast from the rockets, switched to Mannschenn Drive. He could sort out the ship's next destination later.

"Secure all for interstellar voyage," he ordered. Then, into the intercom microphone: "Take your prisoner to the wardroom, Major. We shall be along in a few minutes."

~ Chapter 13 ~

THE PRISONER, still with his guards, was in the wardroom when Grimes, Sonya and Mayhew got there. He was space-suited still, and manacled at wrists and ankles, and six Marines, stripped to the rags that were their uniforms aboard this ship, were standing around him, apparently at ease but with their readiness to spring at once into action betrayed by a tenseness that was felt rather than seen. But for something odd about the articulation of the legs at the knee, but for the unhuman eyes glaring redly out through the narrow transparency of the helmet, this could have been one of the Major's own men, still to be unsuited. And then Grimes noticed the tail. It was twitching inside its long, armored sheath.

"Mr. Mayhew?" asked Grimes.

"It . . . He's not human, sir," murmured the telepath. Grimes refrained from making any remarks about a blinding glimpse of the obvious. "But I can read . . . after a fashion. There is hate, and there is fear—dreadful, paralyzing fear."

The fear, thought Grimes, *that any rational being will know when his maltreated slaves turn on him, gain the upper hand.*

"Strip him, sir?" asked the Major briskly.

"Yes," agreed Grimes. "Let's see what he really looks like."

"Brown! Gilmore! Get the armor off the prisoner."

"We'll have to take the irons off him first, sir," pointed out one of the men dubiously.

"There are six of you, and only one of him. But if you want to be careful, unshackle his wrists first, then put the cuffs back on as soon as you have the upper half of his suit off."

"Very good, sir."

"I think that we should be careful," said Sonya.

"We are being careful, ma'am," snapped the Major.

Brown unclipped a key ring from his belt, found the right key and unlocked the handcuffs, cautiously, alert for any hostile action on the part of the prisoner. But the being still stood there quietly, only that twitching tail a warning of potential violence. Gilmore attended to the helmet fastenings, made a half turn and lifted the misshapen bowl of metal and plastic from the prisoner's head. All of the humans stared at the face so revealed—the gray-furred visage with the thin lips crinkled to display the sharp, yellow teeth, the pointed, bewhiskered snout, the red eyes, the huge, circular flaps that were the ears. The thing snarled shrilly, wordlessly. And there was the stink of it, vaguely familiar, nauseating.

Gilmore expertly detached air tanks and fittings, peeled the suit down to the captive's waist while Brown, whose full beard could not conceal his unease, pulled the sleeves down from the long thin arms, over the clawlike hands. The sharp click as the handcuffs were replaced coincided with his faint sigh of relief.

And when we start the interrogation, Grimes was wondering, *shall we be up against the name, rank and serial number convention?*

Gilmore called another man to help him who, after Brown had freed the prisoner's ankles, lifted one foot after the other from its magnetic contact with the deck plating. Gilmore continued stripping the captive, seemed to be getting into trouble as he tried to peel the armor from the tail. He muttered something about not having enlisted to be a valet to bleeding snakes.

Yes, it was like a snake, that tail. It was like a snake, and it whipped up suddenly, caught Gilmore about the throat and tightened, so fast that the strangling man could emit no more than a frightened grunt. And the manacled hands jerked up and then swept down violently, and had it not been for Brown's shaggy mop of hair he would have died. And a clawed foot ripped one of the other men from throat to navel.

It was all so fast, and so vicious, and the being was fighting with a ferocity that was undiminished by the wounds that he, himself was receiving, was raging through the compartment like a tornado, a flesh and blood tornado with claws and teeth. Somebody had used his knife to slash Gilmore free, but he was out of the fight, as were Brown and the Marine with the ripped torso. Globules of blood from the ragged gash mingled with the blood that spouted from the stump of the severed tail, were dispersed by the violently agitated air to form a fine, sickening mist.

Knives were out now, and Grimes shouted that he wanted the prisoner alive, not dead. Knives were out, but the taloned feet of the captive were as effective as the human weapons, and the manacled hands were a bone-crushing club.

"Be careful!" Grimes was shouting. "Careful! Don't kill him!"

But Sonya was there, and she, of all those present, had come prepared for what was now happening. She had produced from somewhere in her scanty rags a tiny pistol, no more than a toy it looked. But it was no toy, and it fired anaesthetic darts. She hovered on the outskirts of the fight, her weapon ready, waiting for the chance to use it. Once she fired—and the needle-pointed projectile sank into glistening human skin, not matted fur. Yet another of the Marines was out of action.

She had to get closer to be sure of hitting her target, the target that was at the center of a milling mass of arms and legs, human and non-human. She had to get closer, and as she approached, sliding her magnetized sandals over the deck in a deceptively rapid slouch, the being broke free of his captors, taking advantage of the sudden lapse into unconsciousness of the man whom Sonya had hit with her first shot.

She did not make a second one, the flailing arm of one of the men hit her gun hand, knocking the weapon from her grasp. And then the blood-streaked horror was on her, and the talons of one foot were hooked into the waistband of her rags and the other was upraised for a disembowelling stroke.

Without thinking, without consciously remembering all that he had been taught, Grimes threw his knife. But the lessons had been good ones, and, in this one branch of Personal Combat, the Commodore had been an apt pupil. Blood spurted from a severed carotid artery and the claws—bloody themselves, but with human blood—did not more, in their last spasmodic twitch, than inflict a shallow scratch between the woman's breasts.

Grimes ran to his wife but she pushed him away, saying, "Don't mind me. There are others more badly hurt."

And Mayhew was trying to say something to him, was babbling about his dead amplifier, Lassie, about her last and lethal dream.

It made sense, but it had made sense to Grimes before the telepath volunteered his explanation. The Commodore had recognized the nature of the prisoner, in spite of the size of the being, in spite of the cranial development. In his younger days he had boarded a pest-ridden grain ship. He had recalled the vermin that he had seen in the traps set up by the ship's crew, and the stench of them.

And he remembered the old adage—that a cornered rat will fight.

❧ Chapter 14 ❧

FREEDOM was falling down the dark dimensions, so far with no course set, so far with her destination undecided.

In Grimes' day cabin there was a meeting of the senior officers of the expedition to discuss what had already been learned, to make some sort of decision on what was to be done next. The final decision would rest with the Commodore, but he had learned, painfully, many years ago, that it is better to ask some of the questions than to know all the answers.

The Major was telling his story again: "It wasn't all that hard to get into the ship, sir. But they were waiting for us, in spacesuits, in the airlock vestibule. Some of them had pistols. As you know, we brought one back."

"Yes," said Grimes. "I've seen it. A not very effective laser weapon. I think that our workshop can turn out copies—with improvements."

"As you say, sir, not very effective. Luckily for us. And I gained the impression that they were rather scared of using them. Possibly it was the fear of doing damage to their own ship." He permitted himself a slight sneer. "Typical, I suppose, of merchant spacemen."

"It's easy to see, Major, that you've never had to write to Head Office to explain a half inch dent in the shell plating. But carry on."

"There were hordes of them, sir, literally choking the alleyways. We tried to cut and burn and bludgeon our way through them, to get to the control room, and if you hadn't recalled us we'd have done so . . ."

"If I hadn't recalled you you'd be prisoners now—or dead. And better off dead at that. But tell me, were you able to notice anything about the ship herself?"

"We were rather too busy, sir. Of course, if we'd been properly equipped, we'd have had at least two cameras. As it was . . ."

"I know. I know. You had nothing but spacesuits over your birthday suits. But surely you gained some sort of impression."

"Just a ship, sir. Alleyways, airtight doors and all the rest of it. Oh, yes. . . Fluorescent strips instead of luminescent panels. Old-fashioned."

"Sonya?"

"Sounds like a mercantile version of this wagon, John. Or like a specimen of Rim Rummers' vintage tonnage."

"Don't be catty. And you, Doctor?"

"So far," admitted the medical officer, "I've made only a superficial examination. But I'd say that our late prisoner was an Earth-type mammal. Male. Early middle age."

"And what species?"

"I don't know, Commodore. If we had thought to bring with us some laboratory white rats I could run a comparison of tissues."

"In other words, you smell a rat. Just as we all do." He was speaking softly now. "Ever since the first ship rats have been stowaways—in surface vessels, in aircraft, in spaceships. Carried to that planet in shipments of seed grain they became a major pest on Mars. But, so far, we have been lucky. There have been mutations, but never a mutation that has become a real menace to ourselves."

"Never?" asked Sonya with an arching of eyebrows.

"Never, so far as we know, in *our* Universe."

"But in this one . . ."

"Too bloody right they are," put in Williams. "Well, we know what's cookin' now, Skipper. We still have one nuclear thunderflash in our stores. I vote that we use it and blow ourselves back to where we came from."

"I wish it were as simple as all that, Commander," Grimes told him. "When we blew ourselves here, the chances were that the ship would be returned to her own Space-Time. When we attempt to reverse the process there will be, I suppose, a certain tendency for ourselves and the machinery and materials that we have installed to be sent back to our own Universe. But no more than a tendency. We shall be liable to find ourselves anywhere—or anywhen." He paused. "Not that it really worries any of us. We're all volunteers, with no close ties left behind us. But we have a job to do, and I suggest that we at least try to do it before attempting a return."

"Then what do we try to do, Skip?" demanded Williams.

"We've made a start, Commander. We know now what we're up against. Intelligent, oversized rats who've enslaved man at least on the Rim Worlds.

"Tell me, Sonya, you know more of the workings of the minds of Federation top brass, both military and political, than I do. Suppose this state of affairs had come to pass in our Universe, a hundred years ago, say, when the Rim Worlds were no more than a cluster of distant colonies always annoying the Federation by demanding independence?"

She laughed bitterly. "As you know, there are planets whose humanoid inhabitants are subjects of the Shaara Empire. And on some of those worlds the mammalian slaves of the ruling arthropods are more than merely humanoid. They are human, descendents of ships' crews and passengers cast away in the days of the Ehrenhaft Drive vessels, the so-called gaussjammers. But we'd never dream of going to war against the Shaara to liberate our own flesh and blood. It just wouldn't be . . . expedient. And I guess that in this Space-Time it just wouldn't be expedient to go to war against these mutated rats. Too, there'll be quite a large body of opinion that will say that the human Rim Worlders should be left to stew in their own juice."

"So you, our representative of the Federation's armed forces, feel that we should accomplish nothing by making for Earth to tell our story."

"Not only should we accomplish nothing, but, in all probability, our ship would be confiscated and taken apart to see what makes her tick insofar as dimension hopping is concerned. And it would take us all a couple of lifetimes to break free of the red tape with which we should be festooned."

"In other words, if we want anything done we have to do it ourselves."

"Yes."

"Then do we want anything done?" asked Grimes quietly.

He was almost frightened by the reaction provoked by his question. It seemed that not only would he have a mutiny on his hands, but also a divorce. Everybody was talking at once, loudly and indignantly. There was the Doctor's high-pitched bray: "And it was *human* flesh in the tissue culture vats!" and William's roar: "You saw the bodies of the sheilas in this ship, an' the scars on 'em!" and the Major's curt voice: "The Marine Corps will carry on even if the Navy rats!" Then Sonya, icily calm: "I thought that the old-fashioned virtues still survived on the Rim. I must have been mistaken."

"Quiet!" said Grimes. "Quiet!" he shouted. He grinned at his officers. "All right. You've made your sentiments quite clear, and I'm pleased that you have. The late owners of this ship are intelligent beings—but that does not entitle them to treat other intelligent beings as they treat their slaves. Sonya mentioned the human slaves on the worlds of the Shaara Empire, but those so-called slaves are far better off than many a free peasant on Federation worlds. They're not mistreated, and they're not livestock. But we've seen the bodies of the men, women and children who died aboard this ship. And if we can make their deaths not in vain. . ."

Sonya flashed him an apologetic smile. "But how?" she asked. "But how?"

"That's the question." He turned to Mayhew. "You've been maintaining a listening watch. Do these people have psionic radio?"

"I'm afraid they do, sir," the telepath told him unhappily. "I'm afraid they do. And . . ."

"Out with it, man."

"They use amplifiers, just as we do. But . . ."

"But what?"

"They aren't dogs' brains. They're human ones!"

☙ Chapter 15 ☙

SONYA ASKED SHARPLY, "And what else have you to report?"

"I . . . I have been listening."

"That's what you're paid for. And what have you picked up?"

"There's a general alarm out. To all ships, and to Faraway Ultimo and Thule, and to the garrisons on Tharn, Mellise and Grollor . . ."

"And to Stree?"

"No. Nothing at all to Stree."

"It makes sense," murmured the woman. "It makes sense. Tharn, with its humanoids living in the equivalent of Earth's Middle Ages. Grollor, with just the beginnings of an industrial culture. Mellise, with its intelligent amphibians and no industries, no technology at all. Our mutant friends must have found the peoples of all those worlds a push-over."

"But Stree . . . *We* don't know just what powers-psychic? psionic?—those philosophical lizards can muster, and we're on friendly terms with them. So . . ."

"So we might get help there," said Grimes. "It's worth considering. Meanwhile, Mr. Mayhew, has there been any communication with the anti-matter worlds to the Galactic West?"

"No, sir."

"And any messages to our next door neighbors—the Shakespearian Sector, the Empire of Waverly?"

"No, sir."

Grimes smiled—but it was a cold smile. "Then this is, without doubt, a matter for the Confederacy. The legalities of it all are rather fascinating . . ."

"The illegalities, Skipper," said Williams. "But I don't mind being a pirate in a good cause."

"You don't mind being a pirate. Period," said Sonya.

"Too bloody right I don't. It makes a change."

"Shall we regard ourselves as liberators?" asked Grimes, but it was more an order than a question. "Meanwhile, Commander Williams, I suggest that we set course for Stree. And you, Mr. Mayhew, maintain your listening watch. Let me know at once if there are any other vessels in our vicinity—even though they haven't Mass Proximity Indicators they can still pick up our temporal precession field, and synchronize."

"And what are your intentions when you get to Stree, sir?" asked the Major.

"As I told the Admiral, I play by ear." He unstrapped himself from his chair and, closely followed by Sonya, led the way to the control room. He secured himself in his seat and watched Williams as the Commander went through the familiar routine of setting course—Mannschenn Drive off, directional gyroscopes brought into play to swing the ship to her new heading, the target star steadied in the cartwheel sight, the brief burst of power from the reaction drive. Mannschenn Drive cut in again. The routine was familiar, and the surroundings in which it was carried out were familiar, but he still found it hard to adjust to the near nudity of himself and his officers. But Williams, with only three bands of indigo dye on each thick, hairy wrist to make his rank, was doing the job as efficiently as he would have done had those bands been gold braid on black cloth.

"On course, Skipper," he announced.

"Thank you, Commander Williams. All off duty personnel may stand down. Maintain normal deep space watches." Accompanied by his wife, he returned to his quarters.

It was, at first and in some respects, just another voyage.

In the Mannschenn Drive Room the complexity of spinning

gyroscopes precessed, tumbled, quivered on the very edge of invisibility, pulling the ship and all her people with them down the dark dimensions, through the warped continuum, down and along the empty immensities of the rim of space.

But, reported Mayhew, they were not alone. There were other ships, fortunately distant, too far away for *Freedom's* wake through Space-Time to register on their instruments.

It was more than just another voyage. There was the hate and the fear with which they were surrounded, said Mayhew. He, of course, was listening only—the other operators were sending. There were warships in orbit about Lorn, Faraway, Ultimo and Thule; there were squadrons hastening to take up positions off Tharn, Mellise, Grollor and Stree. And the orders to single vessels and to fleets were brutally simple: *Destroy on sight.*

"What else did you expect?" said Sonya, when she was told.

"I thought," said Grimes, "that they might try to capture us."

"Why should they? As far as they know we're just a bunch of escaped slaves who've already tried their hand at piracy. In any case, I should hate to be captured by those . . . things."

"Xenophobia—from *you*, of all people?"

"No . . . not xenophobia. Real aliens one can make allowances for. But these aren't real aliens. They're a familiar but dangerous pest, a feared and hated pest that's suddenly started fighting us with our own weapons. We have never had any cause to love them—human beings have gotten, at times, quite sentimental over mice, but never rats— and they've never had any cause to love us. A strong, mutual antipathy. . . ." Absently she rubbed the fading scar between her breasts with her strong fingers.

"What do you make of this squadron dispatched to Stree?"

"A precautionary measure. *They* think that we might be making for there, and that they might be able to intercept us when we emerge into normal Space-Time. But according to Mayhew, there have been no psionic messages to planetary authorities, as there have been to the military governments on Tharn, Mellise and Grollor." She said, a note of query in her voice, "We shall make it before they do?"

"I think so. I hope so. Our Mannschenn Drive unit is running flat out. It's pushed to the safety limits. And you know what will happen if the governor packs up."

"I don't know," she told him. "Nobody knows. I do know most of the spacemen's fairy stories about what *might* happen."

"Once you start playing around with Time, anything might happen," he said. "The most important thing is to be able to take advantage of what happens."

She grinned. "I think I can guess what's flitting through your apology for a mind."

"Just an idea," he said. "Just an idea. But I'd like to have a talk with those saurian philosophers before I try to do anything about it."

"If we get there before that squadron," she said.

"If we don't, we may try out the idea before we're ready to. But I think we're still leading the field."

"What's that?" she demanded suddenly.

That was not a noise. *That* was something that is even more disturbing in any powered ship traversing any medium—a sudden cessation of noise.

The buzzer that broke the tense silence was no proper substitute for the thin, high keening of the Mannschenn Drive.

It was the officer of the watch, calling from Control. "Commodore, sir, O.O.W. here. Reporting breakdown of interstellar drive."

Grimes did not need to be told. He had experienced the uncanny sensation of temporal disorientation when the precessing gyroscopes slowed, ceased to precess. He said, "Don't bother the engineers—every second spent answering the telephone means delay in effecting repairs. I'll be right up."

"Looks as though our friends might beat us to Stree after all," remarked Sonya quietly.

"That's what I'm afraid of," said Grimes.

⚒ Chapter 16 ⚒

THE BREAKDOWN of *Freedom's* Mannschenn Drive unit was a piece of bad luck—but, Grimes admitted, the luck could have been worse, much worse. The ship had made her reentry into the normal continuum many light years from any focal point and well beyond the maximum range of the radar installations of the enemy war vessels. She had Space—or, at any rate, a vast globe of emptiness—all to herself in just this situation. But, as an amateur of naval history, Grimes knew full well what an overly large part is played by sheer, blind mischance in warfare. Far too many times a hunted ship has blundered into the midst of her pursuers when all on board have considered themselves justified in relaxing their vigilance—not that vigilance is of great avail against overwhelming fire power. And fire power, whether it be the muzzle loading cannon of the days of sail or the guided missile and laser beam of today, is what makes the final decision.

But, so far, there was no need to worry about fire power. A good look-out, by all available means, was of primary importance. And so, while *Freedom* fell—but slowly, slowly, by the accepted standards of interstellar navigation—towards the distant Stree sun the long fingers of her radar pulses probed the emptiness about her and, in the cubby hole that he shared with the naked canine brain that was a poor and untrained substitute for his beloved Lassie, Mayhew listened, alert for the faintest whisper of thought that would offer some clue as to the enemy's whereabouts and intentions.

After a while, having received no reports from the engineers, Grimes went along to the Mannschenn Drive Room. He knew that the engine room staff was working hard, even desperately, and that the buzz of a telephone in such circumstances can be an almost unbearable irritation. Even so, as Captain of the ship he felt that he was entitled to know what was going on.

He stood for a while in the doorway of the compartment, watching. He could see what had happened—a seized bearing of the main rotor. That huge flywheel, in the gravitational field of an Earth type planet, would weigh at least five tons and, even with *Freedom* falling free, it still possessed considerable mass. Its spindle had to be eased clear of the damaged bearing, and great care had to be taken that it did not come into contact with and damage the smaller gyroscopes surrounding it. Finally Bronson, the Chief Engineer, pausing to wipe his sweating face, noticed the Commodore and delivered himself of a complaint.

"We should have installed one of our own units, sir."

"Why, Commander?"

"Because ours have a foolproof system of automatic lubrication, that's why. Because the bastards who built this ship don't seem to have heard of such a thing, and must rely on their sense of smell to warn them as soon as anything even starts to run hot."

"And that's possible," murmured Grimes, thinking that the mutants had not been intelligent long enough for their primitive senses to become dulled. Then he asked, "How long will you be?"

"At least two hours. At least. That's the best I can promise you."

"Very good." He paused. "And how long will it take you to modify the lubrication system, to bring it up to our standards?"

"I haven't even thought about that, Commodore. But it'd take days."

"We can't afford the time," said Grimes as much to himself as to the engineer. "Just carry on with the repairs to the main rotor, and let me know as soon as the unit is operational. I shall be in Control." As he turned to go he added, half seriously, "And it might be an idea to see that your watchkeepers possess a keen sense of smell!"

Back in the control room he felt more at home, even though this was the nerve center of a crippled ship. Officers sat at their posts and there was the reassuring glow from the screens of navigational instruments—the chart tank and the radarscopes. Space, for billions of miles on every hand, was still empty, which was just as well.

He went to stand by Sonya and Williams, told them what he had learned.

"So they beat us to Stree," commented the Executive Officer glumly.

"I'm afraid that they will, Commander."

"And then what do we do?"

"I wish I knew just what the situation is on Stree," murmured Grimes. "*They* don't seem to have taken over, as they have on the other Rim Worlds. Should we be justified in breaking through to make a landing?"

"Trying to break through, you mean," corrected Sonya.

"All right. Trying to break through. Will it be a justified risk?"

"Yes," she said firmly. "As far as I can gather from Mayhew, our rodent friends are scared of Stree—and its people. They've made contact, of course, but that's all. The general feeling seems to be one of you leave us alone and we'll leave you alone."

"I know the Streen," said Grimes. "Don't forget that it was I that made the first landing on their planet when I opened up the Eastern Circuit to trade. They're uncanny brutes—but, after all, mammals and saurians have little in common, psychologically speaking."

"Spare us the lecture, John. Furthermore, while you were nosing around in the engine room, Mayhew rang Control. He's established contact with the squadron bound for Stree."

"What! Is the man mad? Send for him at once."

"Quietly, John, quietly. Our Mr. Mayhew may be a little round the bend, like all his breed, but he's no fool. When I said that he had made contact with the enemy I didn't mean that he had been nattering with the officer commanding the squadron. Oh, he's made contact—but with the underground."

"Don't talk in riddles."

"Just a delaying action, my dear, to give you time to simmer down. I didn't want you to order that Mayhew be thrown out of the airlock without a spacesuit. The underground, as I have referred to it, is made up of the human brains that our furry friends use as psionic amplifiers."

"But it's still criminal folly. *They* will employ telepaths as psionic radio officers, just as we do. And those telepaths will read the thoughts of their amplifiers, just as Mayhew reads the thoughts of his dog's brain in aspic."

"But will they? Can they? Don't forget that our telepaths employ as amplifiers the brains of creatures considerably less intelligent than Man. Whoever heard of a dog with any sort of mental screen? *They* will be using the brains of humans who have been unlucky enough to be born with telepathic ability. And any human telepath, any trained human telepath, is able to set up a screen."

"But why should *They* use human brains? The risk of sabotage of vital communications . . ."

"What other brains are available for their use? As far as *They* are concerned, both dogs and cats are out—repeat, out!"

"Why?"

"Far too much mutual antipathy."

"Wouldn't that also apply in the case of themselves and human beings?"

"No. I doubt if they really hate us. After all, we have provided their ancestors with food, shelter and transportation for many centuries. The rats would have survived if they hadn't had the human race to bludge upon, but they wouldn't have flourished, as they have, traps and poisons notwithstanding. Oh, all right. With the exception of the occasional small boy with his albino pets, every human being has this hatred of rats. But hate isn't the only mainspring of human behavior."

"What do you mean?"

"Look at it this way. Suppose you're a telepath, born on one of the Rim Worlds in this continuum. By the time that your talent has been noted, by the time that you're . . . conscripted, you will have come to love your parents and the other members of your family. You will have made friends outside the family circle. Without being overly precocious you may even have acquired a lover."

"I think I see. Play ball, or else."

"Yes."

"Then why should the poor bastards risk the 'or else' now?"

"Because Mayhew's peddled them a line of goods. Very subtly, very carefully. Just induced dreams at first, just dreams of life as it is on the Rim Worlds in our Universe—but a somewhat glamorized version."

"I can imagine it. Mayhew's a very patriotic Rim Worlder."

"First the dreams, and then the hints. The whisper that all that they have dreamed is true, that all of it could become the way of life of their own people. The story of what actually happened to *Freedom* and to the escaped slaves. The message that we have come to help them—and the request for help for ourselves."

"But I don't understand how he could have done all this in so short a time."

"How long does a dream take? It is said that a man can dream of a lifetime's happenings in a few seconds."

Already Grimes' active mind was toying with ideas, with ruses and strategems. Deceit, he knew, has always been a legitimate technique of warfare. Not that legalities counted for overmuch in this here-and-now. Or did they? If the Federation got dragged into the mess, he and his people might well find themselves standing trial for piracy. It was unlikely—but, bearing in mind the Federation's pampering of various unpleasant nonhuman races on his time track, possible.

He grinned. The legal aspects of it all were for too complicated—and, at the moment, far too unimportant.

He said, "Send for Mr. Mayhew."

⫸ Chapter 17 ⫷

GRIMES WENT INTO CONFERENCE with Mayhew and certain others of his officers. There was Sonya, of course, and there was Williams, and there was Dangerford, the Chief Reaction Drive Engineer. Also present was one Ella Kubinsky, who held the rank of Lieutenant in the Rim Worlds Volunteer Naval Reserve. She was not a spacewoman. She was a specialist officer, and in civilian life she was an instructor at the University of Lorn, in the Department of Linguistics. Looking at her, Grimes could not help thinking that she was ideally suited for the part that she would be called upon to play. Her straggling hair was so pale as to be almost white; her chin and forehead receded sharply from her pointed nose. Her arms and legs were scrawny, her breasts meager. She had been nicknamed "The White Rat." To begin with, Grimes and Sonya questioned Mayhew closely, with Sonya playing the major part in the interrogation. They wished that they could have subjected the bodiless human telepaths aboard the enemy ships to a similar interrogation—but that, of course, was impossible. However, Mayhew said that they were sincere in their desire to help—and sincerity is almost impossible to simulate when you have thrown your mind open to another skilled, trained intelligence.

Then other, less recondite matters were discussed with Williams and Dangerford. These concerned the efficiency of various detergents and paint removers and, also, the burning off from the hull plating of certain lettering and its replacement with other letters, these characters to be fabricated in the Engineers' workshop by Dangerford and his juniors who, of course, were not involved in the repair work to the Mannschenn Drive unit. Mayhew was called upon to supply the specifications for these characters.

And then tapes were played to Ella Kubinsky. These were records of signals received from the mutants' ships. She repeated the words, imitating them in a thin, high, squeaking voice that exactly duplicated the original messages. Even Sonya expressed her satisfaction.

While this was being done, Mayhew retired to his cabin for further consultations with his fellow telepaths. There was so much that they could tell him. There was so much that they knew, as all psionic signals had to pass through their brains. When he came back to Grimes' cabin he was able to tell the Commodore what name to substitute for both *Freedom* and *Distriyir* when these sets of characters had been removed from the forward shell plating.

While Williams and his working party were engaged outside the ship, and Dangerford and his juniors were fabricating the new characters, Grimes, Sonya and Ella Kubinsky accompanied Mayhew to his quarters. It was more convenient there to rehearse and to be filled in with the necessary background details. It seemed, at times, that the disembodied presences of the human psionic amplifiers were crowded with them into the cramped compartment, bringing with them the mental stink of their hates and fears. It has been said that to know is to love—but, very often, to know is to hate. Those brains, bodiless, naked in their baths of nutrient solution, must know their unhuman masters as no intelligence clothed in flesh and blood could ever know them. And Grimes found himself pitying Mayhew's own psionic amplifier, the brain of the dog that possessed neither the knowledge nor the experience to hate the beings who had deprived it of a normal existence.

Bronson had finished the repairs to the Mannschenn before Williams and Dangerford were ready. He was glad enough to be able to snatch a brief rest before his machinery was restarted.

And then the new name was in place.

Grimes, Sonya and Williams went back to Control where, using the public address system, the Commodore told his ship's company of the plan for the landing on Stree. He sensed a feeling of disappointment. Carter, the Gunnery Officer, and the Major and his Marines had been looking forward to a fight. Well, they could be ready for one, but if all went as planned they would not be getting it.

Cirsir—*Corsair*—as she had been renamed, set course for the Stree sun. The real *Corsair* had been unable to join the squadron, being grounded for repairs on Tharn. The real *Corsair's* psionic amplifier knew, by this time, what was happening, but would not pass on the information to the unhuman psionic radio officer who was his lord and master. And the psionic amplifier aboard the other ships would let it be known that *Corsair* was hastening to join the blockade of Stree.

It was all so simple. The operation, said Sonya, was an Intelligence Officer's dream of Heaven—to know everything that the enemy was thinking, and to have full control over the enemy's communications. The pseudo *Corsair*—and Grimes found that he preferred that name to either *Freedom* or *Destroyer*—was in psionic touch with the squadron that she was hurrying to overtake. Messages were passing back and forth, messages that, from the single ship, were utterly bogus and that, from the fleet, were full of important information. Soon Grimes knew every detail of tonnage, manning and armament, and knew that he must avoid any sort of showdown. There was enough massed firepower to blow his ship into fragments in a microsecond, whereupon the laser beams, in another microsecond, would convert those fragments into puffs of incandescent vapor.

As *Corsair* closed the range the squadron ahead was detected on her instruments, the slight flickering of needles on the faces of gauges, the shallow undulation of the glowing traces in monitor tubes, showed that in the vicinity were other vessels using the interstellar drive. They were not yet visible, of course, and would not be unless temporal precession rates were synchronized. And synchronization was what Grimes did not want. As far as he knew, his *Corsair* was typical of her class (as long as her damaged side was hidden from view) but the humans (if bodiless brains could still be called human) aboard the ships of the squadron were not spacemen, knew nothing of subtle differences that can be picked up immediately by the trained eye.

Grimes wished to be able to sweep past the enemy, invisible, no more than interference on their screens, and to make his landing on Stree before the squadron fell into its orbits. That was his wish, and that was his hope, but Branson, since the breakdown, did not trust his Mannschenn Drive unit and dared not drive the machine at its full capacity. He pointed out that, even so, they were gaining slowly upon the enemy, and that was evidence that the engineers of those vessels trusted their interstellar drives even less than he, Branson, did. The Commodore was obliged to admit that his engineer was probably right in his assumption.

So it was when *Corsair*, at last, cut her Drive and reentered normal Space-Time that the blockading cruisers were already taking up their stations. Radar and radio came into play. From the transceiver in *Corsair's* control room squeaked an irritable voice: "*Heenteer* tee *Ceerseer, Heenteer* tee *Ceerseer*, teeke eep steeteen ees eerdeered."

Ella Kubinsky, who had been throughly rehearsed for just this situation, squeaked the acknowledgement.

Grimes stared out of the viewports at the golden globe that was Stree, at the silver, flitting sparks that were the other ships. He switched his regard to Williams, saw that the Executive Officer was going through the motions of maneuvering the ship into a closed orbit—and, as he had been ordered, making a deliberate botch of it.

"*Heenteer* tee *Ceerseer*. Whee ees neet yeer veeseen screen een?"

Ella Kubinsky squeaked that it was supposed to have been overhauled on Tharn, and added some unkind remarks about the poor quality of humanoid labor. Somebody—Grimes was sorry that he did not see who it was—whispered unkindly that if Ella did switch on the screen it would make no difference, anyhow. The ugly girl flushed angrily, but continued to play her part calmly enough.

Under Williams' skilled handling, the ship was falling closer and closer to the great, expanding globe of the planet. But this did not go unnoticed for long. Again there was the enraged squeaking, but in a new voice. "Thees ees thee Eedmeereel. Wheet thee heell eere yee plee-eeng et, *Ceerseer*?"

Ella told her story of an alleged overhaul of reaction drive controls and made further complaints about the quality of the dockyard labor on Tharn.

"Wheere ees yeer Cepteen? Teell heem tee speek tee mee."

Ella said that the Captain was busy, at the controls. The Admiral said that the ship would do better by herself than with such an illegitimate son of a human female handling her. Williams, hearing this, grinned and muttered, "I did *not* ride to my parents' wedding on a bicycle."

"Wheere ees thee Ceepteen?"

And there was a fresh voice: "*Heeveec* tee *Heenteer*. Wheere deed shee geet theet deemeege?"

"All right," said Grimes. "Action stations. And get her downstairs, Williams, as fast as Christ will let you!"

Gyroscopes whined viciously and rockets screamed, driving the ship down to the exosphere in a powered dive. From the vents in her sides puffed the cloud of metallic particles that would protect her from laser—until the particles themselves were destroyed by the stabbing beams. And her launching racks spewed missiles, each programmed for random action, and to seek out and destroy any target except their parent ship. Not that they stood much chance of so doing—but they would, at least, keep the enemy laser gunners busy.

Corsair hit the first, tenuous fringes of the Streen atmosphere and her internal temperature rose fast, too fast. Somehow, using rockets only, taking advantage of her aerodynamic qualities, such as they were, Williams turned her, stood her on her tail. Briefly she was a sitting duck—but Carter's beams were stabbing and slicing, swatting down the swarm of missiles that had been loosed at her.

She was falling then, stern first, falling fast but under control, balanced on her tail of incandescence, the rocket thrust that was slowing her, that would bring her to a standstill (Grimes hoped) when her vaned landing gear was only scant feet above the surface of the planet.

She was dropping through the overcast—blue-silver at first, then gradually changing hue to gold. She was dropping through the overcast, and there was no pursuit, although when she entered regions of denser atmosphere she was escorted, was surrounded by great, shadowy shapes that wheeled about them on wide wings, that glared redly at them through the control room ports.

Grimes recognized them. After all, in his own continuum he had been the first human to set foot on Stree. They were the huge flying lizards, not unlike the pterosauria of Earth's past—but in Grimes' Space-Time they had never behaved like this. They had avoided spaceships and aircraft. These showed no inclination towards doing so, and only one of the huge brutes colliding with the ship, tipping her off balance, could easily produce a situation beyond even Williams' superlative pilotage to correct.

But they kept their distance, more or less, and followed *Corsair* down, down, through the overcast and through the clear air below the cloud blanket. And beneath her was the familiar landscape—low, rolling hills, broad rivers, lush green plains that were no more than wide clearings in the omnipresent jungle.

Yes, it was familiar, and the Commodore could make out the site of his first landing—one of the smaller clearings that, by some freak of chance or nature, had the outline of a great horse.

Inevitably, as he had been on the occasion of his first landing, Grimes was reminded of a poem that he had read as a young man, that he had tried to memorize—The *Ballad of the White Horse*, by Chesterton. How did it go?

> *For the end of the world was long ago*
> *And all we stand today*
> *As children of a second birth*
> *Like some strange people left on Earth*
> *After a Judgment Day.*

Yes, the end of their world had come for the Rim colonists, in this Universe, long ago.

And could Grimes and his crew of outsiders reverse the Judgment?

❧ Chapter 18 ❧

SLOWLY, CAUTIOUSLY *Corsair* dropped to the clearing, her incandescent rocket exhaust incinerating the grasslike vegetation, raising great, roiling clouds of smoke and steam. A human-built warship would have been fitted with nozzles from which, in these circumstances, a fire-smothering foam could be ejected. But *Corsair's* builders would have considered such a device a useless refinement. Slowly she settled, then came to rest, rocking slightly on her landing gear. Up and around the control room ports billowed the dirty smoke and the white steam, gradually thinning. Except for a few desert areas, the climate of Stree was uniformly wet and nothing would burn for long.

Grimes asked Mayhew to—as he phrased it—take psionic soundings, but from his past experience of this planet he knew that it would be a waste of time. The evidence indicated that the Streen practiced telepathy among themselves but that their minds were closed to outsiders. But the saurians must have seen the ship land, and the pillar of cloud that she had created would be visible for many miles.

Slowly the smoke cleared and those in the control room were able to see, through the begrimed ports, the edge of the jungle, the tangle of lofty, fern-like growths with, between them, the interlacing entanglement of creepers. Something was coming through the jungle, its passage marked by an occasional eruption of tiny flying lizards from the crests of the tree ferns. Something was coming through the jungle, and heading towards the ship.

Grimes got up from his chair and, accompanied by Sonya, made his way down to the airlock. He smiled with wry amusement as he recalled his first landing on this world. *Then* he had been able to do things properly, had strode down the ramp in all the glory of gold braid and brass buttons, had even worn a quite useless ceremonial sword for the occasion. *Then* he had been accompanied by his staff, as formally attired as himself. *Now* he was wearing scanty, dirty rags and accompanied by a woman as nearly naked as he was. (But the Streen, who saw no need for clothing, had been more amused than impressed by his finery.)

The airlock door was open and the ramp was out. The Commodore and his wife did not descend at once to the still slightly smoking ground. One advantage of his dress uniform, thought Grimes, was that it had included half-Wellington boots. The couple watched the dark tunnel entrance in the cliff of solid greenery that marked the end of the jungle track.

A Streen emerged. He would have passed for a small dinosaur from Earth's remote past, although the trained eye of a paleontologist would have detected differences. There was one difference that was obvious even to the untrained eye—the cranial development. This being had a brain, and not a small one. The little, glittering eyes stared at the humans. A voice like the hiss of escaping steam said, "Greetings."

"Greetings," replied the Commodore.

"You come again, man Grimes." It was a statement of fact rather than a question.

"I have never been here before," said Grimes, adding, "Not in this Space-Time."

"You have been here before. The last time your body was covered with cloth and metal, trappings of no functional value. But it does not matter."

"How can you remember?"

"I cannot, but our Wise Ones remember all things. What was, what is to come, what might have been and what might be. They told me to greet you and to bring you to them."

Grimes was less than enthusiastic. On the occasion of his last visit the Wise Ones had lived not in the jungle but in a small, atypical patch of rocky desert, many miles to the north. Then he had been able to make the journey in one of *Faraway Quest's* helicopters. Now he had no flying machines at his disposal, and a spaceship is an unhandy brute to navigate in a planetary atmosphere. He did not fancy a long, long journey on foot, or even riding one of the lesser saurians that the Streen used as draught animals, along a rough track partially choken with thorny undergrowth. Once again he was acutely conscious of the inadequacy of his attire.

The native cackled. (The Streen was not devoid of a sense of humor.) He said, "The Wise Ones told me that you would not be clad for a journey. The Wise Ones await you in the village."

"Is it far?"

"It is where it was when you came before, when you landed your ship in this very place."

"No more than half an hour's walk," began Grimes, addressing Sonya, then fell suddenly silent as an intense light flickered briefly, changing and brightening the green of the jungle wall, the gaudy colors of the flowering vines. Involuntarily he looked up, but the golden overcast was unbroken. There was another flare behind the cloud blanket, blue-white, distant, and then, belatedly, the thunder of the first explosion drifted down, ominous and terrifying.

"Missiles . . ." whispered the Commodore. "And my ship's a sitting duck. . ."

"Sir," hissed the saurian, "you are not to worry. The Wise Ones have taken adequate steps for your—and our—protection."

"But you have no science, no technology!" exclaimed Grimes, realizing the stupidity of what he had said when it was too late.

"We have science, man Grimes. We have machines to pit against the machines of your enemies. But our machines, unlike yours, are of flesh and blood, not of metal—although our anti-missiles, like yours, possess only a limited degree of intelligence."

"These people," exclaimed Grimes to Sonya, "are superb biological engineers."

"I know," she said. "And I have little doubt that their air umbrella of pterodactyls will last longer than our furry friends' supply of missiles. So I suggest that we leave them to it and go to see the Wise Ones." She looked dubiously at the jungle, then turned to call to a woman inside the ship, "Peggy! Bring us out a couple of machetes!"

"You will not need them," commented the Streen, "even though your skins are too soft."

They did need them, even though their guide went ahead like a tank clearing the way for infantry. The vines and brambles were springy, reaching out with taloned tentacles as soon as the saurian had passed. Grimes and Sonya slashed until their arms were tired, but even so, their perspiration smarted painfully in the fresh scratches all over their bodies. They were far from sorry when they emerged into another clearing, a small one, almost completely roofed over with the dense foliage of the surrounding trees.

There were the usual huts, woven from still-living creepers. There was the steaming compost pile that was the hatchery. There were the domesticated lizards, large and small, engaged in their specialized tasks—digging the vegetable plots, weeding and pruning. There were the young of the Streen, looking absurdly like plucked chickens, displaying the curiosity that is common to all intelligent beings throughout the Galaxy, keeping a respectful distance from the visitors, staring at them from their black, unwinking eyes. There were the adults, equally curious, some of whom hustled the community's children out of the path of the humans, clearing a way to the door of a hut that, by Streen standards, was imposing. From the opening drifted blue eddies of smoke—aromatic, almost intoxicating. Grimes knew that the use of the so-called sacred herbs, burned in a brazier and the smoke inhaled, was confined to the Wise Ones.

There were three of the beings huddled there in the semi-darkness, grouped around the tripod from the top of which was suspended the cage in which the source of the smoke smoldered ruddily. The Commodore sneezed. The vapor, as far as he could gather, was mildly euphoric and, at the same time, hallucinogenic—but to human beings it was only an irritant to the nasal membranes. In spite of his efforts to restrain himself he sneezed again, loudly.

The Streen around the tripod cackled thinly. The Commodore, his eyes becoming accustomed to the dim lighting, could see that they were old, their scales shabby and dulled with a lichenous growth, their bones protuberant beneath their armored skins. There was something familiar about them—sensed rather than visually recognized. One of them cackled, "Our dream smoke still makes you sneeze, man Grimes."

"Yes, Wise One."

"And what do you here, man Grimes? Were you not happy in your own here-and-now? Were you not happy with the female of your kind whom you acquired since last we met, otherwhen-and-where?"

"You'd better say 'yes' to that!" muttered Sonya.

Again the thin cackling. "We are lucky, man Grimes. We do not have the problems of you mammals, with your hot blood. . . ." A pause. "But still, we love life, just as you do. And we know that out there, falling about our world, are those who would end our lives, just as they would end yours. *Now* they have not the power, but it is within their grasp."

"But would it matter to you?" asked Sonya. "I thought that you were—how shall I put it?—co-existent with yourselves in all the alternative universes. You must be. You remember John's first landing on this planet—but that was never in *this* here-and-now."

"You do not understand, woman Sonya. You cannot understand. But we will try to explain. Man Grimes—in *your* here-and-now what cargoes do your ships bring to Stree?"

"Luxuries like tea and tobacco, Wise One. And books. . . ."

"What sort of books, man Grimes?"

"History. Philosophy. Novels, even . . . poetry."

"And your poets say more in fewer words than your philosophers. There is one whom I will quote to you:

> *And he who lives more lives than one*
> *More deaths than one shall die.*

"Does that answer your question, woman Sonya?"

"I can *feel* it," she murmured. "But I can't understand it."

"It does not matter. And it does not matter if you do not understand what you are going to do—as long as you understand how to do it."

"And what is that?" asked Grimes.

"To destroy the egg before it hatches," was the reply.

❧ Chapter 19 ❧

ANYBODY meeting the seemingly primitive Streen for the first time would never dream that these saurians, for all their obvious intelligence, are engineers. Their towns and villages are, to the human way of thinking, utterly innocent of machines. But what is a living organism but a machine—an engine that derives its motive power from the combustion of hydro-carbons in an oxygen atmosphere? On Stree, a variety of semi-intelligent lizards perform the tasks that on man-colonized worlds are performed by mechanisms of metal and plastic.

Yes, the Streen *are* engineers—biological and psychological engineers—of no mean caliber.

In their dim hut, what little light there was further obscured by the acrid fumes from the brazier, the Wise Ones talked and Grimes and Sonya listened. Much of what they were told was beyond them—but there was emotional rather than intellectual acceptance. They would not altogether understand—but they could *feel*. And, after all, the symbiosis of flesh-and-blood machine and machine of metal and plastic was not too alien a concept. Such symbiosis, to a limited extent, has been known ever since the first seaman handled the first ship, learning to make that clumsy contraption of wood and fiber an extension of his own body.

Then, convinced although still not understanding, the Commodore and his wife returned to the ship. With them—slowly,

211

creakingly—walked Serressor, the most ancient of the Wise Ones, and ahead of them their original guide did his best, as before, to clear a way for them through the spiny growths.

They came to the clearing, to the charred patch of ground already speckled with the pale green sprouts of new growth. And already the air ferns had begun to take root upon protuberances from the ship's shell plating, from turrets and sponsons and antennae; already the vines were crawling up the vaned tripod of the landing gear. Williams had a working party out, men and women who were hacking ill-humoredly at the superfluous and encroaching greenery.

From the corner of his eye the Executive Officer saw the approach of the Commodore, ceased shouting directions to his crew and walked slowly to meet his superior. He said, "The game's crook, Skipper. What with lianas an' lithophytes we'll be lucky to get off the ground. An' if we do, we've had it, like as not."

"Why, Commander Williams?"

"Mayhew tells me that *They* have cottoned on to what their psionic amplifiers have been doing. So—no more psionic amplifiers. Period."

"So we can't give them false information through their own communications system," said Sonya.

"You can say that again, Mrs. Grimes."

Serressor croaked, "So you depend upon misdirection to make your escape from our world."

"That is the case, Wise One," Grimes told him.

"We have already arranged that, man Grimes."

"You have?" Williams looked at the ancient saurian, seeing him for the first time. "You have? Cor stone the bleedin' lizards, Skipper, what *is* this?"

"This, Commander Williams," said Grimes coldly, "is Serressor, Senior Wise One of the Streen. He and his people are as interested in disposing of the mutants as we are. They have told us a way in which it may be done, and Serressor will be coming with us to play his part in the operation."

"An' how will you do it?" demanded Williams, addressing the saurian.

Serressor hissed, "Destroy the egg before it is hatched."

Surprisingly, Williams did not explode into derision. He said quietly, "I'd thought o' that myself. We could do it—but it's iffy, iffy. Too bloody iffy. There're all the stories about what happens when the Drive gets out o' kilter, but nobody's ever come back to tell us if they're true."

"If we're going to use the Drive as Serressor suggests, it will have to be fitted with a special governor."

"That makes sense, Skipper. But where're we gettin' this governor from?"

"We have it—or him—right here."

"Better him than me. There're better ways o' dyin' than bein' turned inside out." He shifted his regard to the working party, who had taken the opportunity to relax their efforts. "Back to yer gardenin', yer bunch o' drongoes! I want this hull clean as a baby's bottom!"

"Shouldn't you have said 'smooth', Commander?" asked Sonya sweetly.

Before an argument could start Grimes pulled her up the ramp and into the ship. Following them slowly came the aged and decrepit saurian.

Grimes and his officers were obliged to admit that the Streen had planned well and cunningly. When *Corsair* was ready for blasting off, a veritable horde of the winged lizards assembled above her, most of them carrying in their talons fragments of metal. Obedient to the command of their masters—it seemed that the Streen were, after all, telepathic, but only insofar as their own kind were concerned—the pterosaurs grouped themselves into a formation resembling a spaceship, flapped off to the eastward. To the radar operators of the blockading squadron it would appear that *Corsair* had lifted, was navigating slowly and clumsily within the planetary atmosphere.

There were missiles, of course.

Some were intercepted by the suicidal air umbrella above the decoys, some, whose trajectory would take them into uninhabited jungle regions, were allowed to continue their fall to the ground. They had been programmed to seek and to destroy a spaceship, winged lizards, even metal-bearing lizards, they ignored.

Meanwhile, but cautiously, cautiously, with frequent and random shifts of frequency, *Corsair's* radio was probing the sky. It seemed that the mutants' squadron had swallowed the bait. Ship after ship broke from her orbit, recklessly expending her reaction mass so as to be advantageously situated when *Corsair*, the pseudo-*Corsair*, emerged from the overcast into space.

And then the way out was as clear as ever it would be. The mutants' cruisers were hull down, dropping below the round shoulder of the world. Aboard *Corsair* all hands were at their stations, and the firing chambers were warmed up in readiness.

Grimes took her upstairs himself. With a deliberately dramatic flourish he brought his hand down to the keys, as though he were smacking a ready and willing steed on the rump. It was more like being fired from a gun than a conventional blast-off. Acceleration thrust all hands deep into the padding of their chairs. The Commodore was momentarily worried by a thin, high whistling that seemed to originate inside the ship rather than outside her hull. Then, had it not been for the brutal down-drag on his facial muscles, he would have smiled. He remembered that the Streen, normally coldly unemotional, had always expressed appreciation of a trip in a space-vessel and had enjoyed, especially, violent maneuvers such as the one that he was now carrying out. If Serressor was whistling, then he was happy.

Corsair whipped through the cloud blanket as though it had been no more than a chiffon veil, and harsh sunlight beat through the control room viewports like a physical blow. From the speaker of the transceiver came a shrill gabble of order and counter-order—evidently some alert radar operator had spotted the break-out. But *Corsair* was out of laser range from the blockading squadron, was almost out of missile range. And by the time the enemy were able to close her, she would be well clear of the Van Allens, would be falling into and through the dark, twisted dimensions created about herself by her own interstellar drive.

It was time to get Serressor along to the Mannschenn Drive room. Grimes handed over to Williams, waited until he saw the Commander's capable hands resting on his own control panel, and then, slowly and painfully, levered himself out of his seat. He found it almost impossible to stand upright under the crushing pseudo-gravity—but speed had to be maintained, otherwise the ship would be englobed by her enemies. Already Carter was picking off the first missiles with his laser. The Commodore watched two burly Marines struggle to get the aged saurian to his feet. They were big men, and strong, but the task was almost beyond them.

Then, with every shuffling step calling for an almost superhuman effort, Grimes led the way to the interstellar drive compartment. There—and how long had it taken him to make that short journey?—he found Branson, Chief Interstellar Drive Engineer, with his juniors. And there was the ship's doctor, and the telepath Mayhew. Extending from the complexity of rotors, now still and silent, was a tangle of cables, each one of which terminated in a crocodile clip.

The wall speaker crackled: "Commander to M.D. room. Calling the Commodore."

"Commodore here, Commander Williams."

"Clear of Van Allens. No immediate danger from enemy fire."

"Then carry on, Commander. You know what you have to do."

"Stand by for free fall. Stand by for course correction."

The silence, as the rocket drive was cut, fell like a blow. Then, as the whining directional gyroscopes took over, the Doctor, assisted by Branson's juniors, began to clip the cable ends to various parts of Serressor's body.

The old saurian hissed gently, "You cannot hurt me, man Doctor. My scales are thick."

And then it was Mayhew's turn, and a helmet of metal mesh was fitted over his head. The telepath was pale, frightened-looking. Grimes sympathized with him, and admired him. He, as had every spaceman, heard all the stories of what happened to those trapped in the field of a malfunctioning Drive—and even though this would be (the Commodore hoped) a controlled malfunction, it would be a malfunction nonetheless. The telepath, when the situation had been explained to him, had volunteered. Grimes hoped that the decoration for which he would recommend him would not be a posthumous one.

The gentle, off-center gravitational effect of centrifugal force abruptly ceased, together with the humming of the directional gyroscope. Then the ship trembled violently and suddenly, and again. A hit? No, decided the Commodore, it was Carter firing a salvo of missiles. But the use of these weapons showed that the enemy must be getting too close for comfort.

Williams' voice from the bulkhead speaker was loud, with a certain urgency.

"On course for Lorn, Skipper!"

"Mannschenn Drive on remote control," ordered Grimes. "Serressor will give the word to switch on."

Already the Doctor and the junior engineers had left the Mannschenn Drive room, making no secret of their eagerness to be out of the compartment before things started to happen. Bronson was making some last, finicking adjustments to his machinery, his heavily bearded face worried.

"Hurry up, Commander," Grimes snapped.

The engineer grumbled, "I don't like it. This is an interstellar drive, not a Time Machine. . . ."

Again came the violent trembling, and again, and again.

Bronson finished what he was doing, then reluctantly left his domain. Grimes turned to Serressor, who now looked as though he had become enmeshed in the web of a gigantic spider. He said, "You know the risk. . ."

"I know the risk. If I am . . . everted, it will be a new experience."

And not a pleasant one, thought the Commodore, looking at Mayhew. The telepath was paler than ever, and his prominent Adam's apple wobbled as he swallowed hard. And not a pleasant one. And how could this . . . this non-human philosopher, who had never handled a metal tool in his long life, be so sure of the results of this tampering with, to him, utterly alien machinery? Sure, Serressor had read all the books (or his other-self in Grimes' own continuum had read all the books) on the theory and practice of Mannschenn Drive operation—but book knowledge, far too often, is a poor substitute for working experience.

"Good luck," said Grimes to the saurian and to Mayhew.

He left the compartment, carefully shut the door behind him.

He heard the whine, the wrong-sounding whine, as the Drive started up.

And then the dream-filled darkness closed about him.

∾ Chapter 20 ∾

IT IS SAID that a drowning man relives his life in the seconds before final dissolution.

So it was with Grimes—but he relived his life in reverse, experienced backwards the long history of triumphs and disasters, of true and false loves, of deprivations and shabby compromises, of things and people that it was good to remember, of things and people that it had been better to forget. It was the very unreality of the experience, vivid though it was, that enabled him to shrug it off, that left him, although badly shaken, in full command of his faculties when the throbbing whine of the ever-precessing gyroscopes ceased at last.

The ship had arrived.

But where?

When?

Ahead in Space and Astern in Time—that was the principle of the Mannschenn Drive. But never Full Astern—or, never *intentionally* Full Astern. Not until now. And what of the governors that had been fitted to the machine, the flesh-and-blood governors—the human telepath and the saurian philosopher, with his intuitive grasp of complexities that had baffled the finest mathematical brains of mankind?

What of the governors? Had they broken under the strain?

And what of himself, Grimes? (And what of Sonya?)

He was still Grimes, still the Commodore, with all his memories (so far as he knew) intact. He was not a beardless youth (his probing hand verified this). He was not an infant. He was not a tiny blob of protoplasm on the alleyway deck.

He opened the door.

Serressor was still there, still entangled in the shining filaments. But his scales gleamed with the luster of youth, his bright eyes were unfilmed. His voice, as he said, "Man Grimes, we were successful!" was still a croak, but no longer a senile croak. "We did it!" confirmed Mayhew, in an oddly high voice.

The telepath was oddly shrunken. The rags that had been his loin clout were in an untidy bundle about his bare feet. No, shrunken was not the word. He was smaller, younger. Much younger.

"That was the hardest part," he said. "That was the hardest part—to stop the reversal of biological time. Serressor and I were right in the field, so we were affected. But the rest of you shouldn't be changed. You still have your long, gray beard, Commodore."

But my beard wasn't gray, thought Grimes, with the beginning of panic. *Neither was it long.* He pulled a hair from it, wincing at the sudden pain, examined the evidence, (still dark brown) while Serressor cackled and Mayhew giggled.

"All right," he growled. "You've had your joke. What now?"

"We wait," Mayhew told him. "We wait, here and now, until *Sundowner* shows up. Then it's up to you, sir."

Sundowner, thought Grimes. *Jolly Swagman . . . Waltzing Matilda.* Names that belonged to the early history of the Rim Worlds. The battered star tramps of the Sundowner Line that had served the border planets in the days of their early colonization, long before secession from the Federation had been even dreamed of, long before the Rim Worlds government had, itself, become a shipowner with the Rim Runners fleet.

Sundowner. . . She had been (Grimes remembered his history) the first ship to bring a cargo of seed grain to Lorn. And that was when this alternative universe, this continuum in which Grimes and his people were invaders, had run off the historical rails. *Sundowner . . .* Serressor knew his history too. The Wise One had planned this rendezvous in Space and Time, so that Grimes could do what, in his universe, had been accomplished by plague or traps, or, even, cats or terrier dogs.

"I can hear her. . . ." murmured Mayhew distantly. "She is on time. Her people are worried. They want to get to port before their ship is taken over by the mutants."

"In this here-and-now," said Serressor, "she crashed—will crash?—in the mountains. Most of the mutants survived. But go to your control room, man Grimes. And then you will do what you have to do."

They were all very quiet in the control room, all shaken by the period of temporal disorientation through which they had passed. Grimes went first to Williams, hunched in his co-pilot's chair. He said softly, "You are ready, Commander?"

"Ready," answered the Executive Officer tonelessly.

Then the Commodore went to sit beside his wife. She was pale, subdued. She looked at him carefully, and a faint smile curved her lips. She murmured, "You aren't changed, John. I'm pleased about that. I've remembered too much, things that I thought I'd forgotten, and even though it was all backwards it was . . . shattering. I'm pleased to have you to hold on to, and I'm pleased that it *is* you, and not some puppy. . . ."

"I shouldn't have minded losing a few years in the wash," grunted Grimes.

He looked at the officers at their stations—radar, gunnery, electronic radio. He stared out of the ports at the Lorn sun, its brightness dimmed by polarization, at the great, dim-glowing Galactic lens. Here, at the very edge of the Universe, the passage of years, of centuries was not obvious to a casual glance. There were no constellations in the Rim sky that, by their slow distortions, could play the part of clocks.

"Contact," announced the radar officer softly.

The Commodore looked into his own repeater screen, saw the tiny spark that had appeared in the blackness of the tank.

The radio officer was speaking into his microphone. "*Corsair* to *Sundowner*. *Corsair* to *Sundowner*. Do you read me? Over."

The voice that answered was that of a tired man, a man who had been subjected to considerable strain. It was unsteady, seemed on the edge of hysteria. "I hear you, whoever you are. What the hell did you say your name was?"

"*Corsair*. This is *Corsair*, calling *Sundowner*. Over."

"Never heard of you. What sort of name is that, anyhow?" And there was another, fainter voice, saying, "*Corsair*? Don't like the sound of it, Captain. Could be a pirate."

"A pirate? Out here, on the Rim? Don't be so bloody silly. There just aren't the pickings to make it worth while." A pause. "If she *is* a pirate, she's welcome to *our* bloody cargo."

"*Corsair* to *Sundowner*. *Corsair* to *Sundowner*. Come in, please. Over."

"Yes, *Corsair*. I hear you. What the hell do you want?"

"Permission to board."

"Permission to board? Who the bloody hell do you think you are?"

"R.W.C.S. *Corsair*. . ."

"R.W.C.S.?" It was obvious that *Sundowner's* Captain was addressing his Mate without bothering either to switch off or to cover his microphone. "What the hell is *that*, Joe?" "Haven't got a clue," came the reply.

Grimes switched in his own microphone. He did not want to alarm *Sundowner*, did not want to send her scurrying back into the twisted continuum generated by her Mannschenn Drive. He knew that he could blow the unarmed merchantman to a puff of incandescent vapor, and that such an action would have the desired result. But he did not want to play it that way. He was acutely conscious that he was about to commit the crime of genocide—and who could say that the mutated rats were less deserving of life than the humans whom, but for Grimes' intervention, they would replace?—and did not wish, also, to have the murder of his own kind on his conscience.

"Captain," he said urgently, "this is Commodore Grimes speaking, of the naval forces of the Rim Worlds Confederacy. It is vitally important mat you allow us to board your ship. We know about the trouble you are having. We wish to help you."

"You wish to help us?"

"If we wished you ill," said Grimes patiently, "we could have opened fire on you as soon as you broke through into normal Space-Time." He paused. "You have a cargo of seed grain. There were rats in the grain. And these rats have been multiplying. Am I correct?"

"You are. But how do you know?"

"Never mind that. And these rats—there are mutants among them, aren't there? You've been coming a long time from Elsinore, haven't you? Mannschenn Drive breakdowns . . . and fluctuations in the temporal precession fields to speed up the rate of mutation."

"But, sir, how do you *know*? We have sent no messages. Our psionic radio officer was killed by the . . . the mutants."

"We know, Captain. And now—may we board?"

From the speaker came the faint voice of *Sundowner's* Mate. "Rim Ghosts are bad enough—but when they take over Quarantine it's a bit rough."

"Yes," said Grimes. "You may regard us as Rim Ghosts. But we're solid ones."

∾ Chapter 21 ∾

HIS BIG HANDS playing over his console like those of a master pianist, Williams, with short, carefully timed bursts from the auxiliary jets, jockeyed *Corsair* into a position only yards from *Sundowner*, used his braking rockets to match velocities. Grimes and his people stared out through the ports at the star tramp. She was old, old. Even now, at a time that was centuries in the past of *Corsair's* people, she was obsolete. Her hull plating was dull, pitted by years of exposure to micrometeorites. Two of the embossed letters of her name had been broken off and never replaced, although somebody had replaced the missing U and W with crudely painted characters. Grimes could guess what conditions must be like on board. She would be one of those ships in which, to give greater lift for cargo, the pile shielding had been cut to a minimum, the contents of her holds affording, in theory, protection from radiation. And her holds were full of grain, and this grain supported pests that, through rapid breeding and mutation, had become a menace rather than a mere nuisance.

"Boarders away, sir?" asked the Marine officer.

"Yes, Major. Yourself and six men should do. I and Mrs. Grimes will be coming with you."

"Side arms, sir?"

"No. That crate'll have paper-thin bulkheads and shell plating, and we can't afford any playing around with laser."

"Then knives and clubs, sir?"

"It might be advisable. Yes."

Grimes and Sonya left Control for their quarters. There, helping each other, they shrugged into their modified spacesuits. These still had the tail sheaths and helmets designed to accommodate a long-muzzled head. This had its advantages, providing stowage for a full beard. But Grimes wondered what *Sundowner's* people would think when they saw a parry of seeming aliens jetting from *Cosair* to their airlock. Anyhow, it was their own fault. They should have had their vision transmitter and receiver in order.

The boarding party assembled at the main airlock which, although it was cramped, was big enough to hold all of them. The inner door slowly closed and then, after the pumps had done their work (*Corsair* could not afford to throw away atmosphere) the outer door opened, Grimes could see, then, that an aperture had appeared in the shell plating of the other ship, only twenty feet or so distant. But it was small. It must be only an auxiliary airlock. The Captain of *Sundowner*, thought Grimes, must be a cautious man: must have determined to let the boarding party into his ship one by one instead of in a body. *And he'll be more cautious still*, thought Grimes, *when he sees these spacesuits.*

He shuffled to the door sill. He said into his helmet microphone, "There's room for only one at a time in that airlock of theirs. I'll go first."

He heard the Major acknowledge, and then he jumped, giving himself the slightest possible push-off from his own ship. He had judged well and did not have to use his suit reaction unit. Slowly, but not too slowly, he drifted across the chasm between the two vessels, extended his arms to break his fall and, with one hand, caught hold of the projecting rung above *Sundowner's* airlock door.

As he had assumed, the compartment was large enough to hold only one person—and he had to act quickly to pull his dummy tail out of the way of the closing outer valve. There were no lights in the airlock—or, if there were lights, they weren't working—but after a while he heard the hissing that told him that pressure was being built up.

Suddenly the inner door opened and glaring light blinded the

Commodore. He could just see two dark figures standing there, with what looked like pistols in their hands. Through his helmet diaphragm he heard somebody say, "What did I tell you, Captain? A bleeding kangaroo in full armor, no less. Shall I shoot the bastard?"

"Wait!" snapped Grimes. He hoped that the note of authority would not be muffled from his voice. "Wait! I'm as human as you."

"Then prove it, mister!"

Slowly the Commodore raised his gloved hands, turning them to show that they were empty. He said, "I am going to remove my helmet—unless one of you gentlemen would care to do it for me."

"Not bloody likely. Keep your distance."

"As you please." Grimes manipulated fastenings, gave the regulation half turn and lifted. At once he noticed the smell—it was like the stink that had hung around his own wardroom for days after the attempted interrogation of the prisoner.

"All right," said one of the men. "You can come in."

Grimes shuffled into the ship. The light was out of his eyes now and he could see the two men. He did not have to ask who or what they were. Uniform regulations change far more slowly than do civilian appearance. He addressed the grizzled, unshaven man with the four tarnished gold bars on his shoulder boards, "We have already spoken with each other by radio, Captain. I am Commodore Grimes. . . ."

"Of the Rim Worlds Confederacy's Navy. But what's the idea of the fancy dress, *Commodore?*"

"The fancy dress?" Then Grimes realized that the man was referring to his spacesuit, so obviously designed for a nonhuman. What would be his reaction to what Grimes was wearing underneath it—the scanty rags and the rank marks painted on to his skin? But it was of no importance. He said, "It's a long story, Captain, and I haven't time to tell it now. What I am telling you is that you must not, repeat not, attempt a landing on Lorn until I have given you clearance."

"And who the hell do you think you are, Mister so-called Commodore? We've had troubles enough this trip. What is your authority?"

"My authority?" Grimes grinned. "In my own space and time, the commission I hold, signed by the President of the Confederacy . . ."

"What did I say?" demanded the Mate. "And I'll say it again. He's some sort of bloody pirate."

"And, in the here-and-now," continued Grimes, "my missile batteries and my laser projectors."

"If you attempt to hinder me from proceeding on my lawful occasions," said the tramp Master stubbornly, "that will be piracy."

Grimes looked at him, not without sympathy. It was obvious that this man had been pushed to the very limits of human endurance—the lined face and the red-rimmed eyes told of many, too many, hours without sleep. And he had seen at least one of his officers killed. By this time he would be regarding the enemies infesting his ship as mutineers rather than mutants, and, no longer quite rational, would be determined to bring his cargo to port come Hell or high water.

And that he must not do.

Grimes lifted his helmet to put it back on. In spite of the metal with which he was surrounded he might be able to get through to Williams in *Corsair's* control room, to Williams and to Carter, to give the order that would call a laser beam to slice off *Sundowner's* main venturi. But the Mate guessed his intention, swung viciously with his right arm and knocked the helmet out of the Commodore's hand. He growled to his Captain, "We don't want the bastard callin' his little friends do we, sir?"

"It is essential that I keep in communication with my own ship," said Grimes stiffly.

"So you can do somethin' with all the fancy ironmongery you were tellin' us about!" The Mate viciously swatted the helmet which, haying rebounded from a bulkhead, was now drifting through the air.

"Gentlemen," said Grimes reasonably, looking at the two men and at the weapons they carried, automatic pistols, no more than five millimeter caliber but deadly enough. He might disarm one but the other would fire. "Gentlemen, I have come to help you. . . ."

"More of a hindrance than a bloody help," snarled the Mate. "We've enough on our plates already without having to listen to your fairy stories about some non-existent Confederacy." He turned to the Master. "What say we start up the reaction drive an' set course for Lorn? This bloke's cobbers'll not open fire so long as he's aboard."

"Yes. Do that, Mr. Holt. And then we'll put this man in irons."

So this was it, thought Grimes dully. So this was the immutability of the Past, of which he had so often read. This was the inertia of the flow of events. He had come to where and when he could best stick a finger into the pie—but the crust was too tough, too hard. He couldn't blame the tramp Captain. He, as a good shipmaster, was displaying the utmost loyalty to his charterers. And (Grimes remembered his Rim Worlds history) those consignments of seed grain had been urgently needed on Lorn.

And, more and more, every word was an effort, every action. It was as though he were immersed in some fluid, fathoms deep. He was trying to swim against the Time Stream—and it was too much for him.

Why not just drift? After all, there would be time to do something after the landing at Port Forlorn. Or would there? Hadn't somebody told him that this ship had crashed in mountainous country?

He was aroused from his despairing lethargy by a sudden clangor of alarm bells, by a frightened, distorted voice that yammered from a bulkhead speaker, "Captain! Where are you, Captain? They're attacking the control room!"

More as the result of years of training than of conscious thought he snatched his drifting helmet as he followed the Captain and his Mate when they dived into the axial shaft, as they pulled themselves hand over hand along the guidelines to the bows of the ship.

Chapter 22

"THEY'RE ATTACKING the control room!"

The words echoed through Grimes' mind. *They* must be Sonya and the Major and his men. They must have breached the ports. So far there was no diminishing of air pressure—but even such a sorry rustbucket as *Sundowner* would have her airtight doors in reasonably good working order. All the same, he deemed it prudent to pause in his negotiation of the axial shaft to put his helmet back on. Luckily the rough treatment that it had received at the hands of the Mate did not seem to have damaged it.

Ahead of him, the two *Sundowner* officers were making rapid progress. It was obvious that they were not being slowed down by emergency doors and locks. The Commodore tried to catch up with them, but he was hampered by a spacesuit.

Then, faintly through his helmet diaphragm, he heard the sounds of a struggle, a fight. There were shots—by the sharpness of the cracks fired from small calibre pistols such as the Captain and his Mate had been carrying. There were shouts and screams. And there was a dreadful, high squeaking that was familiar, too familiar. He thought that he could make out words—or the repetition of one word only:

"Kill! Kill!"

He knew, then, who *They* were, and pulled himself along the guideline with the utmost speed of which he was capable. Glancing ahead, he saw that *Sundowner's* Master and his second in command were scrambling through the open hatch at the end of the shaft, the hatch that must give access, in a ship of this type, to Control. He heard more shots, more shouts and screams. He reached the hatch himself, pulled himself through, floundered wildly for long seconds until his magnetized boot soles made contact with the deck.

They ignored him at first. Perhaps it was that they took him—in his tailed suit with its snouted helmet—for one of their own kind, although, by their standards, a giant. *They* were small, no larger than a terrier dog, but there were many of them. *They* were fighting with claws and teeth and pieces of sharpened metal that *They* were using as knives. A fine mist of blood fogged the face plate of Grimes' helmet, half blinding him. But he could see at least two human bodies, obviously dead, their throats torn out, and at least a dozen of the smaller corpses.

He did not give himself time to be shocked by the horror of the scene. (That would come later.) He tried to wipe the film of blood from his visor with a gloved hand, but only smeared it. But he could see that the fight was still going on, that in the center of the control room a knot of spacemen were still standing, still struggling. They must either have lost their pistols or exhausted their ammunition; there were no more shots.

Grimes joined the fight, his armored fists and arms flailing into the mass of furry bodies, his hands crushing them and pulling them away from the humans, throwing them from him with savage violence. At first his attack met with success—and then the mutants realized that he was another enemy. Their squeaking rose to an intolerable level, and more and more of them poured into the control room. They swarmed over the Commodore, clinging to his arms and legs, immobilizing him. *Sundowner's* officers could not help him— they, too, were fighting a losing battle for survival.

There was a scratching at Grimes' throat. One of his assailants had a knife of sorts, was trying to saw through the fabric joint It was a tough fabric, designed for wear and tear—but not such wear and tear as this. Somehow the man contrived to get his right arm clear, managed, with an effort, to bring it up to bat away the knife wielder. He succeeded—somehow. And then there was more scratching and scraping at the joint in way of his armpit.

He was blinded, helpless, submerged in a sea of furry bodies, all too conscious of the frantic gnawings of their teeth and claws and knives. His armor, hampering his every movement even in ideal conditions, could well contribute to his death rather than saving his live. He struggled still—but it was an instinctive struggle rather than one consciously directed, no more than a slow, shrugging, a series of laborious contortions to protect his vulnerable joints from sharp teeth and blades.

Then there was a respite, and he could move once more.

He saw, dimly, that the control room was more crowded than ever, that other figures, dressed as he was, had burst in, were fighting with deadly efficiency, with long, slashing blades and bone-crushing cudgels. It was a hand-to-hand battle in a fog—and the fog was a dreadful cloud of finely divided particles of freshly shed blood.

But even these reinforcements were not enough to turn the tide. Sooner or later—and probably sooner—the mutants would swamp the humans, armored and unarmored, by sheer weight of numbers.

"Abandon ship!" somebody was shouting. It was a woman's voice, Sonya's. "Abandon ship! To the boats!" And then the cry— fainter this time, heard through the helmet diaphragm rather than over his suit radio—was repeated. It is no light matter to give up one's vessel—but now, after this final fight, *Sundowner's* people were willing to admit that they were beaten.

Somehow the armored Marines managed to surround the crew— what was left of them. The Captain was still alive, although only half conscious. The Mate, apart from a few scratches, was untouched. There were two engineers and an hysterical woman with Purser's braid on her torn shirt. That was all. They were hustled by *Corsair's* men to the hatch, thrust down the axial shaft. Grimes shouted his protest as somebody pushed him after them. He realized that it was Sonya, that she was still with him. Over their heads the hatch lid slammed into its closed position.

"The Major and his men . . ." he managed to get out. "They can't stay there, in that hell!"

"They won't," she told him. "They'll manage. Our job is to get these people clear of the ship."

"And then?"

"Who's in charge of this bloody operation?" she asked tartly. "Who was it who told the Admiral that he was going to play by ear?"

Then they were out of the axial shaft and into a boat bay. They watched the Mate help the woman into the small, torpedo-like craft, then stand back to allow the two engineers to enter. He tried to assist the Captain to board—but his superior pushed him away weakly, saying, "No, Mister. I'll be the last man off *my* ship, if you please." He noticed Grimes and Sonya standing there. "And that applies to you, too, Mr. Commodore whoever you say you are. Into the boat with you—you and your mate."

"We'll follow you, Captain. It's hardly more than a step across to our own ship."

"Into the boat with you, damn you. I shall be . . . the . . . last. . ."

The man was obviously on the verge of collapse. His Mate grasped his elbow. "Sir, this is no time to insist on protocol. We have to hurry. Can't you hear *Them?*"

Through his helmet Grimes, himself, hadn't heard them until now. But the noise was there, the frenzied chittering, surely louder with every passing second. "Get into that bloody boat," he told the Mate. "We'll handle the doors."

"I . . . insist. . ." whispered the Captain. "I shall . . . be . . . the last . . . to leave . . ."

"You know what to do," Grimes told the Mate.

"And many's the time I've wanted to do it. But not in these circumstances." His fist came up to his superior's jaw. It was little more than a tap, but enough. The Master did not fall, could not fall in these conditions of zero gravity. But he swayed there, anchored to the deck by his magnetic boot soles, out on his feet. The two engineers emerged from the lifecraft, lugged the unconscious man inside.

"Hurry!" ordered Sonya.

"Make for your ship, sir?" asked the Mate. "You'll pick us up?"

"No. Sorry—but there's no time to explain. Just get the hell out and make all speed for Lorn."

"But . . ."

"You heard what the Commodore said," snapped Sonya. "Do it. If you attempt to lay your boat alongside we open fire."

"But . . ."

Grimes had removed his helmet so that his voice would not be muffled by the diaphragm. "Get into that bloody boat!" he roared. And in a softer voice, as the Mate obeyed, "Good luck."

He replaced his helmet and, as he did so, Sonya operated the controls set into the bulkhead. A door slid shut, sealing off the boat bay from the rest of the ship. The outer door opened, revealing the black emptiness of the Rim sky. Smoothly and efficiently the catapult operated, throwing the boat out and clear. Intense violet flame blossomed at her blunt stern, and then she was away, diminishing into the distance, coming around in a great arc on to the trajectory that would take her to safety.

Grimes didn't watch her for long. He said, "We'd better get back to Control, to help the Major and his men. They're trapped in there."

"They aren't trapped. They're just waiting to see that the boat's escaped."

"But how will they get out?"

"The same way that we got into this rustbucket. We sent back to the ship for a laser pistol, burned our way in. Luckily the airtight doors were all in good working order."

"You took a risk . . ."

"It was a risk we had to take. And we knew that *you* were wearing a spacesuit. But it's time we weren't here."

"After you."

"My God! Are you going to be as stuffy as that Captain?"

Grimes didn't argue, but pushed her out of the boat lock. He jumped after her, somersaulting slowly in the emptiness. He used his suit reaction unit to steady himself, and found himself facing the ship that he had just left. He saw an explosion at her bows, a billowing cloud of debris that expanded slowly—broken glass, crystallizing atmosphere, a gradually separating mass of bodies, most of which ceased to struggle after a very few seconds.

But there were the larger bodies, seven of them, spacesuited—and each of them sprouted a tail of incandescence as the Marines jetted back to their own ship. The Major used his laser pistol to break out through the control room ports—but all the mutants would not be dead. There would be survivors, sealed off in their airtight compartments by the slamming of the emergency doors.

The survivors could be disposed of by *Corsair's* main armament.

∼ Chapter 23 ∼

"WE WERE WAITING for you, Skipper," Williams told Grimes cheerfully as the Commodore re-entered his own control room.

"Very decent of you, Commander," Grimes said, remembering how the Mate of *Sundowner* had realized his long standing ambition and clobbered his Captain. "Very decent of you."

He looked out of the viewports. The grain carrier was still close, at least as close as she had been when he had boarded her. The use of missiles would be dangerous to the vessel employing them—and even later might touch off a mutually destructive explosion.

"You must still finish your task, man Grimes," Serressor reminded him.

"I know. I know." But there was no hurry. There was ample time to consider ways and means.

"All armament ready, sir."

"Thank you. To begin with, Commander Williams, we'll open the range . . ."

Then suddenly, the outline of *Sundowner* shimmered, shimmered and faded. She flickered out like a candle in a puff of wind. Grimes cursed. He should have foreseen this. The mutants had access to the Mannschenn Drive machinery—and how much, by continuous eavesdropping, had they learned? How much did they know?

"Start M.D.," he ordered. "Standard precession."

It took time—but not too long a time. Bronson was already in the Mannschenn Drive room, and Bronson had been trained to the naval way of doing things rather than the relatively leisurely procedure of the merchant service. (Himself a merchant officer, a reservist, he had always made it his boast that he could beat the navy at its own game.) There was the brief period of temporal disorientation, the uncanny feeling that time was running backwards, the giddiness, the nausea. Outside the ports the Galactic Lens assumed the appearance of a distorted Klein flask, and the Lorn sun became a pulsing spiral of multicolored light.

But there was no sign of *Sundowner*.

Grimes was speaking into the telephone. "Commander Bronson! Can you synchronize?"

"With *what?*" Then—"I'll try, sir. I'll try . . ."

Grimes could visualize the engineer watching the flickering needles of his gauges, making adjustments measured in fractions of microseconds to his controls. Subtly the keening song of the spinning, precessing gyroscopes wavered—and, as it did so, the outlines of the people and instruments in the control room lost their sharpness, while the colors of everything momentarily dulled and then became more vivid.

"There's the mucking bastard!" shouted Williams.

And there she was, close aboard them, a phantom ship adrift on a sea of impossible blackness, insubstantial, quivering on the very verge of invisibility.

"Fire at will!" ordered Grimes.

"But, sir," protested one of the officers. "If we interfere with the ship's mass while the Drive is in operation . . ."

"Fire at will!" repeated the Commodore.

"Ay, ay, sir!" acknowledged Carter happily.

But it was like shooting at a shadow. Missiles erupted from their launchers, laser beams stabbed out at the target—and nothing happened. From the bulkhead speaker of the intercom Bronson snarled, "What the hell are you playing at up there? How the hell can I hold her in synchronization?"

"Sorry, Commander," said Grimes into his microphone. "Just lock on, and hold her. Just hold her, that's all I ask."

"An' what now, Skipper?" demanded Williams. "What now?"

"We shall use the Bomb," said Grimes quietly.

"We shall use the Bomb," he said. He knew, as did all of his people, that the fusion device was their one hope of a return to their own Space and Time. But *Sundowner* must be destroyed, the Time Stream must, somehow, be diverted. Chemical explosives and destructive light beams were, in these circumstances, useless. There remained only the Sunday Punch.

The ships were close, so close that their temporal precession fields interacted. Even so, it was obvious why all the weapons so far employed had failed. Each and every discharge had meant an appreciable alteration of *Corsair's* temporal precession rate, so that each and every missile and beam had missed in Time rather than in Space. Had *Corsair* been fitted with one of the latest model synchronizers her gunnery might have been more successful—but she was not. Only Branson's skill was keeping her in visual contact with her prey.

Getting the Bomb into position was not the same as loosing off a missile. Slowly, gently, the black-painted cylinder was eased out of its bay. The merest puff from one of its compressed air jets nudged it away from *Corsair* towards the target. It fell gently through the space between the two ships, came finally to rest against *Sundowner's* scarred hull.

At an order from Grimes the thick lead shutters slid up over the control room ports. (But the thing was close, so close, too close. Even with the radar on minimum range the glowing blob that was *Sundowner* almost filled the tank.) Carter looked at Grimes, waiting for the order. His face was pale—and it was not the only pale face in Control. But Serressor—that blasted lizard!—was filling the confined space with his irritating, high, toneless whistling.

Sonya came to sit beside him.

She said quietly, "You have to do it. We have to do it."

Even her presence could not dispel the loneliness of command. "No," he told her. "*I* have to do it."

"Locking . . ." came Branson's voice from the bulkhead speaker. "Locking . . . Holding . . ."

"Fire," said Grimes.

≈ Chapter 24 ≈

TIME HAD PASSED.

How long, Grimes did not know, nor would he ever know. (Perhaps, he was often to suspect later, this was the next time around, or the time after that.)

He half opened his eyes and looked at the red haired woman who was shaking him back to wakefulness—the attractive woman with the faint scar still visible between her firm breasts. What was her name? He should know. He was married to her. Or had been married to her. It was suddenly of great importance that he should remember what she was called.

Susan . . . ?

Sarah . . .?

No . . .

Sonya . . .?

Yes, Sonya. That was it. . . .

"John, wake up! Wake up! It's all over now. The Bomb blew us back into our own continuum, back to our own Time, even! We're in touch with Port Forlorn Naval Control, and the Admiral wants to talk to you personally."

"He can wait," said Grimes, feeling the fragments of his prickly personality click back into place.

He opened his eyes properly, saw Williams sitting at his controls, saw Serressor, nearby, still youthful, and with him the gangling adolescent who was Mayhew.

For a moment he envied them. They had regained their youth—but at a dreadful risk to themselves. Even so, they had been lucky.

And so, he told himself; had been the human race—not for the first time, and not for the last.

He thought, *I hope I'm not around when our luck finally does run out.*

THE
RIM GODS

DEDICATION
For itchy-footed Susan

⮒ Part 1 ⮐
The Rim Gods

"AND WHO," demanded Commodore Grimes, "will it be this time?" He added, "Or *what?*"

"I don't know, sir, I'm sure," simpered Miss Walton.

Grimes looked at his new secretary with some distaste. There was no denying that she was far more photogenic then her predecessor, and that she possessed a far sweeter personality. But sweetness and prettiness are not everything. He bit back a sarcastic rejoinder, looked again at the signal that the girl had just handed him. It was from a ship, a vessel with the unlikely name of *Piety*. And it was not a word in some alien language that could mean *anything*—the name of the originator of the message was Terran enough. Anglo-Terran at that. William Smith. And after that prosaic appellation there was his title— but that was odd. It was not the usual Master, Captain, Officer Commanding or whatever. It was, plainly and simply, Rector.

Piety. . . . Rector. . . . That ship's name, and that title of rank, had an archaic ring to them. Grimes had always been a student of naval history, and probably knew more about the vessels that had sailed Earth's oceans in the dim and distant past than anybody on the Rim Worlds and, come to that, the vast majority of people on the home planet itself. He remembered that most of the ancient sailing ships had been given religious names. He remembered, too, that rector had once been the shipmaster's official title.

So what was this ship coming out to the Rim, giving her ETA, details of last clearance, state of health on board and all the rest of it? Some cog, some caravel, some galleass? Grimes smiled at his own fancy. Nonetheless, strange ships, very strange ships, had drifted out to the Rim.

"Miss Walton . . ." he said.

"Yes, Commodore," she replied brightly.

"This *Piety* . . . see what details Lloyd's *Register* has on her."

"Very good, sir."

The Commodore—rugged, stocky, short, iron-gray hair over a deeply tanned and seamed face, ears that in spite of suggestions made by two wives and several mistresses still protruded—paced the polished floor of his office while the little blonde punched the buttons that would actuate the Port Forlorn robot librarian. Legally, he supposed, the impending arrival of the *Piety* was the port captain's pigeon. Grimes was Astronautical Superintendent of Rim Runners, the Confederacy's shipping line. But he was also the officer commanding the Rim Worlds Naval Reserve and, as such, was concerned with matters of security and defense. He wished that Sonya, his wife, were available so that he could talk things over with her. She, before her marriage to him, had held the rank of Commander in the Intelligence branch of the Interstellar Federation's Survey Service and, when it came to mysteries and secrets of any kind, displayed the aptitudes of a highly intelligent ferret. But Sonya, after declaring that another week on Lorn would have her climbing up the wallpaper, had taken off for a long vacation—Waverley, Caribbea, Atlantia and points inward—by herself. She, when she returned, would be sorry to have missed whatever odd adventures the arrival of this queerly named ship presaged—and Grimes knew that there would be some. His premonitions were rarely, if ever, wrong.

He turned away from the banked screens and instruments that made his office look like an exceptionally well fitted spaceship's control room, walked to the wide window that took up an entire wall, which overlooked the port. It was a fine day—for Lorn. The almost perpetual overcast was thin enough to permit a hint of blue sky to show through, and the Lorn sun was a clearly defined disk rather than the usual fuzzy ball. There was almost no wind. Discharge of *Rim Leopard*, noted, seemed to be progressing satisfactorily. There was a blue flare of welding arcs about the little spacetug *Rim Mamelute*, presently undergoing her annual survey. And there, all by herself, was the ship that Grimes—to the annoyance of his wife—often referred to as his one true love, the old, battered *Faraway Quest*. She had been built how many (too many) years ago as a standard *Epsilon* Class tramp for the Interstellar Transport Commission. She had been converted into a survey ship for the Rim Worlds' government. In her, Grimes had made the first landings on the inhabited planets to the Galactic East, the worlds now referred to as the Eastern Circuit. In her he had made the first contact—but not a physical one—with the anti-matter systems to the Galactic West.

And would the arrival of the good ship *Piety* lead to her recommissioning? Grimes hoped so. He liked his job—it was interesting work, carrying both authority and responsibility—but he was often tired of being a deskborne commodore, and had always welcomed the chance to take the old *Quest* up and out into deep space again. As often in the past he had a hunch, a strong one. Something was cooking, and he would have a finger in the pie.

Miss Walton's childish treble broke into his thoughts. "Sir, I have the information on *Piety*. . . ."

"Yes?"

"She was built as *Epsilon Crucis* for the Interstellar Transport Commission fifty Terran standard years ago. She was purchased from them last year, Terran reckoning, by the Skarsten Theological Institute, whose address is listed as Nuevo Angeles on Francisco, otherwise known as Beta Puppis VI. . . ."

"I've visited Francisco," he told her. "A pleasant world, in many ways. But an odd one."

"Odd? How, sir?"

"I hope I'm not treading on any of your corns, Miss Walton, but the whole planet's no more than a breeding ground for fancy religions."

"I'm a Latter Day Reformed Methodist myself, sir," she told him severely. "And that's not fancy."

"Indeed it's not, Miss Walton." *And I'm a cynical, more or less tolerant agnostic,* he thought. He went on, "And does Lloyds condescend to tell us the category in which this renamed *Epsilon Crucis* is now listed? A missionary ship, perhaps?"

"No, sir. A survey ship."

"Oh," was all that Grimes could say.

Two days later Grimes watched, from his office window, *Piety* come in. Whatever else this Rector William Smith might or might not be he was a good ship handler. There was a nasty wind blowing across the spaceport, not quite a gale, but near enough to it; nonetheless the ship made a classic vertical descent, dropping to the exact center of the triangle formed by the berth-marker beacons. It was easy enough in theory, no more than the exact application of lateral thrust, no more than a sure and steady hand on the remote controls of the Inertial Drive. No more—and no less. Some people get the feel of ships; some never do.

This *Piety* was almost a twin to Grimes's own *Faraway Quest*. She was a newer (less old) ship, of course, but the design of the *Epsilon* Class tramps, those trusty workhorses of the Commission, had changed very little over the years. She sat there in her assigned berth, a gray, weathered spire, the bright scarlet beacons still blinking away just clear of the broad vanes of her tripedal landing gear. From her stem a telescopic mast extended itself, and from the top of the metal staff a flag broke out, whipped to quivering rigidity by the wind. The Commodore picked up his binoculars through which to study it. It was not, as he had assumed it would be, the national ensign of Francisco, the golden *crux anasta* and crescent on a scarlet ground; even with the naked eye he could see that. This was a harshly uncompromising standard: a simple white cross on a black field. *It must be,* decided Grimes, *the houseflag of the Skarsten Institute.*

The after air lock door opened and the ramp extended from it, and to it drew up the beetle-like cars of the various port officials—

port captain, customs, immigration, health. The boarding party got out of their vehicles and filed up the gangway, to where an officer was waiting to receive them. They vanished into the ship. Grimes idly wondered whether or not they would get a drink, and what the views of these Skarsten people were on alcohol. He remembered his own visit to Francisco, as a junior officer in the Federation's Survey Service, many years ago. Some of the religious sects had been rigidly abstemious, maintaining that alcohol was an invention of the devil. Others had held that wine symbolized the more beneficent aspects of the Almighty. But it was hardly a subject worthy of speculation. He would find out for himself when, after the arrival formalities were over, he paid his courtesy call on the ship's captain.

He went back to his desk, busied himself with the paperwork that made a habit of accumulating. An hour or so later he was interrupted by the buzzing of his telephone. "Grimes here!" he barked into the instrument. "Commodore Grimes," said a strange voice. It was a statement rather than a question. "This is William Smith, Commodore, Rector of *Piety*. I request an appointment."

"It will be my pleasure, er, Rector." Grimes glanced at his watch. It was almost time for his rather dreary coffee and sandwich lunch. It was not the sort of meal that one asked visitors to share. He said, "Shall we say 1400 hours, our time? In my office?"

"That will do very nicely, sir. Thank you."

"I am looking forward to meeting you," said Grimes, replacing the handset in its rest. *And shall I send Miss Walton out for some sacramental wine?* he asked himself.

William Smith was a tall man, thin, with almost all of his pale face hidden by a bushy black beard, from above which a great nose jutted like the beak of a bird of prey. His eyes under the thick, black brows were of a gray so pale as to be almost colorless, and they were cold, cold. A plain black uniform covered his spare frame, the buttons concealed by the fly front of the tunic, the four bands of black braid on the sleeves almost invisible against the cloth. There was a hint of white lace at his throat.

"I have been told, sir," he said, sitting rigidly in his chair, "that you are something of an expert on the queer conditions that prevail here, on the Rim."

"Perhaps, Rector," said Grimes, "you will tell me first the purpose of your visit here."

"Very well, sir." The man's baritone voice was as cold and as colorless as his eyes. "To begin with, we have the permission of your government, your Rim Worlds Confederacy, to conduct our pressing need of a new Revelation, a new Sinai. . . ."

"A survey, Rector? The Rim Worlds have been very well surveyed—even though I say it myself."

"Not our kind of survey. Commodore. I shall, as you would say, put you in the picture. We of the Skarsten Institute are Neo-Calvinists. We deplore the godlessness, the heresy that is ever more prevalent throughout the galaxy—yes, even upon our own planet. We feel that Mankind is in sore and pressing need of a new Revelation, a new Sinai. . . ."

"And you honestly believe that you will find your Sinai here, out on the Rim?"

"We believe that we shall find our Sinai. If not here, then elsewhere. Perhaps, even, beyond the confines of this galaxy."

"Indeed? But how can I help you, Rector?"

"You, we were told, know more about the odd distortions of the Continuum encountered here than anybody else on these planets."

"Such is fame." Grimes sighed and shrugged. "Very well, Rector, you asked for it. I'll tell you what little I know. To begin with, it is thought by many of our scientists that here, at the very edge of the expanding galaxy, the fabric of time and space is stretched thin. We have long become used to the phenomena known as Rim Ghosts, disconcerting glimpses into alternative universes."

"I believe that you, sir, have personally made the transition into their universes."

"Yes. Once when the Federation's Survey Service requested our aid in the investigation of the Rim Ghost phenomena. No doubt your people have read the Survey Service report."

"We have."

"The second time was when we, the Confederacy, took our own

steps to deal with what we decided was a very real menace—an alternative universe in which our worlds were ruled by particularly unpleasant mutants, with human beings in a state of slavery. And then there was Captain Listowel, who was master of the first experimental lightjammer. He tried to exceed the speed of light without cheating—as *we* do with our Mannschenn Drive—and experienced quite a few different time tracks."

"And tell me, sir, did you or this Captain Listowel ever feel that you were on the point of being granted the Ultimate Revelation?"

"Frankly, no, Rector. We had our bad moments—who in Space, or anywhere else, doesn't?—and anyone who has indulged in time track switching often wonders, as I do, about the reality, the permanence of both himself and the universe about him. For example, I have vague memories of ships that were equipped with only reaction drive for blast-offs and landings and short interplanetary hauls. Absurd, isn't it, but those memories are there. And my wife—I'm sorry you can't meet her, but she's off on a trip—seems to have changed. I have this half recollection of her when she first came out to the Rim, which is there in my mind alongside the real one—but what is real? She was working for the Federation's Intelligence Service then. Anyhow, in one memory she's small and blond, in one she's tall and blonde, and in one she's tall and red-headed, as she is today, Damn it—that's *three* memories!"

"Women have been known to change their hair styles and colorations, Commodore."

"Right. I wouldn't be at all surprised if she returns with her crowning glory a bright green! But that doesn't explain the coexistent memories."

"Perhaps not." Smith's voice was bitter as he went on. "But it seems such a waste of opportunities. To have been privileged to visit the many mansions of our Father's house, and to come back only with confused recollections of the color of a woman's hair!"

"And quite a few scars, Rector. Physical and psychological."

"No doubt." The man's voice was unpleasantly ironic. "But tell me, sir, what do you know of Kinsolving's Planet?"

"Not much. I suppose that we shall settle it if we're ever faced with a population explosion, which is doubtful."

"I am referring, sir, to the man who appeared there, the Stone Age savage from the remote past."

"Yes, that was a queer business. Well before my time. Nothing like that has happened there in recent years, although there is still an uneasy, brooding atmosphere about that world that makes it undesirable as a piece of real estate. The original theory is that somehow the—the loneliness of the people out here on the Rim, hanging, as it were, by their fingernails over the abyss of the Ultimate Night, became focused on that one particular planet. Now the theory is that the fabric of Time and Space is stretched extremely thin there, and that anything or anybody is liable to fall through, either way. The rock paintings are still in the caves, but there haven't been any new ones and the paint is never wet anymore."

"The Stone Age savage," said Smith, "eventually became a Franciscan citizen, and a Neo-Calvinist. He died at a very ripe old age, and among his effects was the manuscript of his life story. His great-granddaughter presented it to the Institute. It was thought, at first, that it was a work of fiction, but the surviving relatives insisted that it was not. And then I, when I made a voyage to Earth, was able to obtain access to the Survey Service records."

"And so?" asked Grimes.

"So Kinsolving's Planet is to become our new Sinai," Smith told him.

"You'd better go along, Grimes," Admiral Kravitz told him, "just to see fair play. Anyhow, it's all been arranged. You will be recalled to the active list—pay, etc., as per regulations—and ship out in this *Piety* of theirs as Rim Worlds' government observer."

"But why me, sir? If I were taking my own ship, if the old *Quest* were being recommissioned, with myself in command, it'd be different. But I don't like being a passenger."

"You'll not be a passenger, Grimes. Captain—sorry, *Rector*—Smith has indicated that he'll appreciate having you along as a sort of pilot. . . ."

"In a ship full of sky pilots—and myself a good agnostic!" He saw the bewildered expression on the Admiral's face and explained his choice of words. "In the old days, before there were any *real* sky pilots, seamen used to refer to ministers of religion as such."

"Did they, now? And what would those tarry-breeked ruffians of whom you're so fond have thought of a captain calling himself 'Rector'?"

"In the early days of sail they'd have thought nothing of it. It was the master's usual title."

"I doubt if anybody'll ever call *you* 'Bishop,'" remarked the Admiral. "Anyhow, you'll be aboard primarily to observe. And to report. In the unlikely event of anything occurring that will affect Rim Worlds' security you are to take action."

"Me—and what squad of Marines?"

"We could send a detachment of the Salvation Army with you," joked the Admiral.

"I doubt that they'd be allowed on board. As far as I can gather, these Neo-Calvinists are somewhat intolerant. Only on a world as tolerant as Francisco would they have been allowed to flourish."

"Intolerant, yes," agreed Kravitz. "But scrupulously honest. And moral."

"In short." said Grimes, "no redeeming vices."

"*Piety* lifts ship at 1800 hours tomorrow, Commodore Grimes," said the Admiral. "You will be aboard."

"Aye, aye, sir," replied Grimes resignedly.

Grimes had never enjoyed serving in a "taut ship" himself, and had never commanded one. Nonetheless, he respected those captains who were able to engender about themselves such a state of affairs. *Piety*, as was obvious from the moment that he set foot on the bottom of the ramp, was a taut ship. Everything was spotless. Every metal fitting and surface that was supposed to be polished boasted a mirror-like sheen. All the paintwork looked as though it was washed at least twice daily—which, in fact, it was. The atmosphere inside the hull bore none of the usual taints of cookery, tobacco smoke or—even though there was a mixed crew—women's perfume. But it was too chilly, and the acridity of some disinfectant made Grimes sneeze.

The junior officer who met him at the head of the ramp showed him into the elevator cage at the foot of the axial shaft. Grimes thanked him and assured the presumably young man—the full beard made it hard to determine his age—that he knew his way around this class of vessel. A captain, no matter what he calls himself or is called, is always accommodated as closely as possible to the center of control. The elevator worked smoothly, noiselessly, carrying the Commodore speedily up to the deck just below the control room. There, as in his own *Faraway Quest*, was the semi-circular suite of cabins. Over the door was a brass plate with the title RECTOR.

As Grimes approached this entrance it slid open. Smith stood there and said formally, "Welcome aboard, Commodore."

"Thank you, Rector."

"Will you come in, sir?"

There were other people in the day cabin: a tall, stout, white-headed and bearded man dressed in clothing that was very similar to Smith's uniform; a woman in a long-sleeved, high-necked, ankle-length black dress, her hair completely covered by a frilly white cap. They looked at Grimes, obviously disapproving of his gold-braided, brass-buttoned, beribboned finery. They did not get up.

"Commodore Grimes," said Smith. "Presbyter Cannan. Sister Lane."

Reluctantly the Presbyter extended his hand. Grimes took it. He was not surprised that it was cold. Sister Lane nodded slightly in his general direction.

Smith gestured stiffly toward a chair, sat down himself. Grimes lowered himself to his own seat incautiously. He should have known that it would be hard. He looked curiously at the two civilians. The Presbyter was an old edition of Rector Smith. The sister. . . ? She had him puzzled. She belonged to a type that been common enough on Francisco when he had been there—the Blossom People, they had called themselves. They preached and practiced a sort of hedonistic Zen, and claimed that their use of the wide range of drugs available to them put them in close communication with the Cosmic All. Prim she was, this Sister Lane, prim and proper in her form-concealing black, but the planes of her face were not harsh, and her unpainted lips were full, and there was a strange gentleness in her brown eyes. Properly dressed—or undressed—thought Grimes, she would be a very attractive woman. Suddenly it was important that he hear her voice.

He pulled his battered pipe out of his pocket, his tobacco pouch and lighter. He asked, addressing her, "Do you mind if I smoke?"

But it was the Presbyter who replied. "Certainly we mind, sir. As you should know, we are opposed to the use of any and all drugs."

"*All* drugs?" murmured the woman, with a sort of malicious sweetness. Her voice was almost a baritone, but it could never be mistaken for a male one.

"There are exceptions, Sister Lane," the old man told her harshly. "As you well know."

"As I well know," she concurred.

"I take it," said Grimes, "that nicotine is not among those exceptions."

"Unfortunately," she stated, "no."

"You may leave us, Sister," said Presbyter Cannan. "We have no further business to discuss with you."

"Thank you, sir." She got gracefully to her feet, made a curtsey to Cannan, walked out of the door. Her ugly clothing could not hide the fluid grace of her movements.

"Your Nursing Sister, Rector?" asked Grimes when she was gone.

"No," answered Cannan. And, *Who's running this ship?* thought Grimes irritably. But evidently the Presbyter piled on more gravs than did the ship's lawful master.

Smith must have noticed the Commodore's expression. "Sister Lane, sir," he explained, "is a member of the Presbyter's staff, not of mine."

"Thank you, Rector." Grimes rewarded him with what was intended to be a friendly smile. "I'm afraid that it will take me some time to get your ranks and ratings sorted out."

"I have no doubt," said Cannan, "that it must be confusing to one who relies upon gaudy fripperies for his authority rather than inner grace."

"Your baggage must be aboard and stowed by now, Commodore," Smith said hastily. He turned to his spiritual superior. "May I suggest, sir, that you and your people retire to your quarters? Liftoff"—he glanced at his watch—"will be in fifteen minutes."

"Very well, Rector." The old man got up, towering over the two spacemen. Smith got up. Grimes remained seated until Smith returned from seeing the Presbyter out.

He said, "I'd better be getting below myself. If you could have somebody show me to my stateroom, Rector."

"I was hoping, Commodore, that you would be coming up to Control for the lift-off."

"Thank you, Rector Smith. It will be my pleasure."

Smith led the way out of his quarters, up the short ladder that brought the two men to the control room. Grimes looked about him. The layout was a standard one: acceleration chairs before which were banks of instruments, screens, meters, chart tank, mass proximity indicator, Carlotti Beacon direction finder. All seemed to be in perfect order, and much of the equipment was new. Evidently the Skarsten Theological Institute did not believe in spoiling the ship for a ha'porth of tar.

The Rector indicated a chair, into which Grimes strapped himself, then took his own seat. The officers were already at their stations. All those bearded men, thought the Commodore, looked too much alike, and their black-on-black insignia of rank made it hard to tell who was what. But this wasn't *his* ship, and she had managed to come all the way out from Francisco without mishap.

The departure routine went smoothly enough, with the usual messages exchanged between control room and spaceport control tower. The Inertial Drive started up, and there was that brief second of weightlessness before the gentle acceleration made itself felt. The ship lifted easily, falling upward to the cloud ceiling. Briefly Grimes was able to look out through the viewports at Port Forlorn and at the dreary countryside spread out around the city like a map. And then there was nothing but gray mist outside—mist that suddenly became a pearly, luminescent white and then vanished. Overhead was a steely sun glaring out of a black sky, its light harsh even though the ports were polarized.

There was free fall for a little while, and then the gyroscopes swung the ship's head to the target star. The Inertial Drive came on again, its irregular throbbing beat a bass background for the thin, high keening of the Mannschenn Drive. Ahead, save for the iridescent spiral that was the target sun, there was only blackness. Lorn was to starboard—a vast, writhing planetary amoeba that was falling astern, that was shrinking rapidly. And out to port was the Galactic Lens, distorted by the temporal precession field of the Drive to a Klein flask blown by a drunken glass-blower.

Grimes wondered, as he had wondered before, if anybody would ever come up with another simile. But this one was so apt.

Grimes didn't like this ship.

She was beautifully kept, efficiently run, and with her cargo spaces converted to passenger accommodation she comfortably housed her crew and all the personnel from the Skarsten Institute. But she was . . . cold. She was cold, and she was too quiet. There was none of the often ribald laughter, none of the snatches of light music that lent warmth to the atmosphere of a normal vessel. There were, he noted, playmasters in all the recreation rooms; but when he examined the spools of the machine in the senior officers' mess he found that they consisted entirely of recordings of sermons and the gloomier hymns. The library was as bad. And, socially, there was complete segregation of the sexes. Deaconesses and sisters were berthed aft, and between them and the male crew and passengers were the storerooms and the "farm."

The food was not bad, but it was plain, unimaginative. And there was nothing to drink but water, and even that had a flat taste. The conversation at table was as boring as the provender. Too, Grimes was annoyed to find out that the Rector did not sit at the head of the board in the senior officers' mess; that place of honor was reserved for the Presbyter. And he talked, almost non-stop, about the Institute's internal politics, with the ship's captain interjecting an occasional quiet affirmative as required. The chief officer, surgeon and purser gobbled their meals in silence, as did Grimes, very much the outsider at the foot of the table. They were served by a young stewardess who would have been pretty in anything but that ugly, all-concealing black, who seemed to hold the domineering old man—but nobody else—in awe.

After the evening meal Grimes made his excuses and retired to his cabin. It was little more than a dogbox, and was a comedown after his suite aboard the *Quest*. He was pleased that he had brought his own reading matter with him, and pleased that he had exercised the forethought to make provision for his other little comforts. Before doing anything else, he filled and lit his pipe and then, moving slowly and easily through the blue haze of his own creation, unclipped the larger of his cases from its rack, pulled it out and opened it. He was lifting out the shirts that had acted as shock-proof packing for certain breakables when he heard a light tap at his door. He groaned. A passenger is bound by ship's regulations as much as is any crew member. But he was damned if he was going to put out his pipe. "Come in," he called.

She came in. She pulled the ugly white cap off her lustrous brown hair, tossed it on to the bunk. Then she turned back to the door, snapped on the spring lock. She tested its security, smiled, then flopped down into the one chair that the cabin possessed.

Grimes looked at her, with raised eyebrows. "Yes, Sister Lane?" he asked.

"Got a smoke, spaceman?" she growled.

"There are some cigars . . ." he began doubtfully.

"I didn't expect pot. Although if you have any . . . ?"

"I haven't." Then Grimes said virtuously, "In any case, such drugs are banned on the Rim Worlds."

"Are they? But what about the cigar you promised me?"

Grimes got a box of panatellas out of his case, opened it, offered it to her. She took one, accepted his proffered light. She inhaled luxuriously. She said, "All I need now is a drink."

"I can supply that."

"Good on you, Admiral!"

There was the bottle of absolute alcohol, and there was the case with its ranked phials of essences. "Scotch?" asked Grimes. "Rum? Brandy? Or . . . ?"

"Scotch will do."

The Commodore measured alcohol into the two glasses over the washbasin, added to each a drop of essence, topped up with cold water from the tap. She murmured, "Here's mud in your eye," and gulped from hers as soon as he handed it to her.

"Sister Lane," said Grimes doubtfully.

"You can call me Clarisse."

"Clarisse. . . . Should you be doing this?"

"Don't tell me that you're a wowser, like all those Bible-punchers."

"I'm not. But this is not my ship. . . ."

"And it's not mine, either."

"Then what are you doing here?"

"It's a long story, dearie. And if you ply me with liquor, I might just tell it to you." She sighed and stretched. "You've no idea what a relief it is to enjoy a drink and a talk and a smoke with somebody who's more or less human."

"Thank you," said Grimes stiffly.

She laughed. "Don't be offended, duckie." She put up her hands, pulled her hair back and away from her face. "Look at my ears."

Grimes looked. They were normal enough organs—save for the fact that were pointed, and were tufted with hair at the tips.

"I'm only more or less human myself," she told him. "More rather than less, perhaps. You know about the man Raul, the caveman, the Stone Age savage, who was pulled, somehow, from the remote past on Kinsolving's Planet to what was then the present. He was my great-grandfather."

"He was humanoid," said Grimes. "Not human."

"Human-schuman!" she mocked. "There is such a thing as parallel evolution, you know. And old Raul was made something of a pet by the scientists back on Earth, and when he evinced the desire to father a family the finest genetic engineers in the Galaxy were pressed into service. No, not the way that you're thinking. Commodore. You've got a low mind."

"Sorry."

"I should think so. Just for that, you can pour me another drink."

And Grimes asked himself if his liquor ration would last out until his return to Lorn.

"What are you doing here?" he asked bluntly. "In *this* ship?"

"At this very moment I'm breaking at least ninety-nine percent of the regulations laid down by the Presbyter and enforced by the Rector. But I know what you mean." Her voice deepened so that it was like Grimes's own. "What is a nasty girl like you doing in a nice place like this?"

"I wouldn't call you nasty," said Grimes.

"Thank you, sir. Then stand by for the story of my life, complete and unexpurgated. I'll start off with dear old great-granddaddy, the Noble Savage: He was an artist, you know, in his proper place and time, one of those specialists who practiced a form of sympathetic magic. He would paint or draw pictures of various animals, and the actual beasts would be drawn to the spot, there to be slaughtered by the hunters. He said that it worked, too. I can remember, when I was a little girl, that he'd put on demonstrations. He'd draw a picture of, say, the cat—and within seconds pussy would be in the room. Oh, yes—and he was a telepath, a very powerful transceiver.

"After many years on Earth, where he was latterly an instructor at the Rhine Institute, he emigrated, with his wife and children, to Francisco, where he was psionic radio officer in charge of the Port Diego Signal Station. It was there that he got religion. And with all the religions to choose from, he had to become a Neo-Calvinist! His family was converted with him—and I often wonder how much part his undeniable psychic powers played in their conversion! And the wives of his sons had to become converts, and the husbands of his daughters—yea, even unto the third and fourth generations."

She grinned. "One member of the fourth generation kicked over the traces. Me. From the Neo-Calvinists to the Blossom People was a logical step. Like most new converts I overdid things. Drinks, drugs, promiscuity—the works. The Neo-Calvinists picked me up, literally, from the gutter and nursed me back to health in their sanatorium— and, at the same time, made it quite clear that if I was predestined to go to Hell I should go there. And then, when they checked up on great-grandfather's autobiographical papers, they realized that I was predestined for something really important—especially since I, alone of his descendants, possess something of his powers."

"You mean that you can . . . ?"

There was a violent knocking on the door, and a voice shouting, "Open up! Open up, I say!"

"They know I'm here," muttered Clarisse sullenly. She got out of her chair, operated the sliding panel herself.

Rector Smith was standing outside, and with him was a tall, gaunt woman. She stared at Sister Lane in horror and snarled, "Cover your nakedness, you shameless hussy!"

Clarisse shrugged, picked up the ugly cap from where it was lying on the bunk, adjusted it over her hair, tucking all loose strands out of sight.

"Will you deal with Sister Lane, Deaconess?" asked Smith.

"That I shall, Rector."

"Miss Lane and I were merely enjoying a friendly talk," said Grimes.

"A friendly talk!" The Deaconess' voice dripped scorn. "Smoking! Wine-bibbing! You—you gilded popinjay!"

Smith had picked up the bottle of alcohol, his obvious intention being to empty it into the washbasin. "Hold it!"

Smith hesitated. Unhurriedly Grimes took the bottle from his hand, restoppered it, put it in the rack over the basin.

Then the Rector started to bluster. "Sir. I must remind you that you are a guest aboard my ship. A passenger. You are obliged to comply with ship's regulations."

"Sir," replied Grimes coldly, "I have signed no articles of agreement, and no ticket with the back covered with small print has been issued to me. I am surprised that a shipmaster should have been so neglectful of the essential legalities, and were you in the employ of the company of which I am astronautical superintendent I should find it my duty to reprimand you."

"Not only a gilded popinjay," observed the Deaconess harshly, "but a space lawyer."

"Yes, madam, a space lawyer—as any master astronaut should

be." He was warming up nicely. "But I must remind you, both of you, that I do have legal standing aboard this vessel. I am here in my capacity as official observer for the Rim Worlds Confederacy. Furthermore, I was called back to active duty in the Rim Worlds Naval Reserve, with the rank of Commodore."

"Meaningless titles," sneered the Deaconess. "A Commodore without a fleet!"

"Perhaps, madam. Perhaps. But I must remind you that we are proceeding through Rim Worlds' territorial space. And I must make it plain that any interference with my own personal liberties—*and* the infliction by yourselves of any harsh punishment on Miss Lane— will mean that *Piety* will be intercepted and seized by one of our warships." He thought, *I hope the bluff isn't called.*

Called it was.

"And just how, Mr. Commodore Grimes, do you propose to call a warship to your aid?" asked the woman.

"Easily, Deaconess, easily," said Clarisse Lane. "Have you forgotten that I am a telepath—and a good one? While this ship was on Lorn I made contact with Mr. Mayhew, Senior Psionic Radio Officer of the Rim World Navy. Even though we never met physically we became close friends. He is an old friend and shipmate of the Commodore, and asked me to keep in touch to let him know if Commodore Grimes was in any danger."

"And you will tell him, of course," said Grimes, "if *you* are subjected to any harm, or even discomfort."

"He will *know*," she said quietly.

"Yes," agreed Grimes. "He will know."

He was familiar with telepaths, was Grimes, having commenced his spacefaring career before the Carlotti direction finding and communications systems began to replace the psionic radio officers with its space- and time-twisting beamed radiations. He was familiar with telepaths, and knew how it was with them when, infrequently, one of them found a member of the opposite sex with the same talents attractive. Until this happened—and it rarely did—they would lavish all their affection on the disembodied canine brains that they used as amplifiers.

Rector Smith was the first to weaken. He muttered, "Very well, Commodore."

"And is this harlot to go unpunished?" flared the Deaconess.

"That's right, she is," Grimes told her.

She glared at him—and Grimes glared back. He regretted deeply that this was not his ship, that he had no authority aboard her.

"Rector Smith . . ." she appealed.

"I'm sorry, Deaconess," Smith told her. "But you have heard what these people have told us."

"And you will allow them to flout your authority?"

"It is better than causing the success of our mission to be jeopardized." He stiffened. "Furthermore, I order you not to lay hands upon Sister Lane, and not to order any of the other sisters to do so."

"And I suppose she's to be free to visit this—this vile seducer any time that she sees fit."

"No," said Smith at last. "No. That I will not sanction. Commodore Grimes claims that I cannot give orders to him, but my authority is still absolute insofar as all other persons aboard this vessel are concerned. Sister Lane will not be ill-treated, but she will be confined to the women's quarters until such time as her services are required."

"The Presbyter shall hear of this," said the woman.

"Indeed he shall. I shall be making my own report to him. Meanwhile, he is not, repeat not, to be disturbed." He added, "And those are *his* orders."

"Very well, then," snapped the Deaconess. And to Clarisse Lane, "Come."

"It was a good try, Commodore," said the girl, looking back wistfully at her unfinished drink, her still smoldering cigar. "It was a good try, but it could have been a better one, as far as I'm concerned. Good night."

It was a good try, thought Grimes. *Period.* He had gone as far as he could go without undermining the Master's—the Rector's—authority too much. As for the girl, he was sure that she would not, now, be maltreated, and it would do her no harm to revert to the abstemious routine of this aptly named ship.

"Good night," he said.

"May I have a word with you, sir?" asked Smith when the two women were gone.

"Surely. Stick around, Rector. This is Liberty Hall; you can spit on the mat and call the cat a bastard."

Smith looked, but did not voice, his disapproval of the figure of speech. He shut the door, snapped the lock on. Then, with a penknife taken from his pocket, he made a little adjustment to one of the securing screws of the mirror over the washbasin.

"Bugged?" asked Grimes interestedly.

"Of course—as is every compartment in the ship. But there are speakers and screens in only two cabins—my own and the Presbyter's. His Reverence, I know, took sleeping pills before retiring, but he might awaken."

"I suppose the ladies' showers are bugged, too?" asked Grimes.

A dull flush covered what little of the Rector's face was not hidden by his beard. He growled. "That, sir, is none of your business."

"And what, sir, is *your* business with me?"

"I feel, Commodore Grimes, that you should know how important that unhappy woman is to the success of our mission; then, perhaps, you will be less inclined, should the opportunity present itself again, to pander to her whims." Smith cleared his throat; then he went on. "This business upsets me, sir. You will know, as you, yourself, were once a shipmaster, how unpleasant it is to have to assert your authority."

"And talking," said Grimes, who had his telepath moments, "is thirsty work."

"If you would be so kind, sir," said Smith, after a long moment of hesitation. "I believe that brandy has always been regarded as a medicine."

Grimes sighed, and mixed fresh drinks. He motioned Smith to the single chair, sat down on the bunk. He thought of shocking the other man with one of the more obscene toasts, but merely said, "Down the hatch." The Rector said, "I needed that."

"Another, Rector Smith?"

"No, thank you, sir."

You want me to twist your arm, you sanctimonious bastard, thought Grimes, but I'm not going to do it. He put the bottle of alcohol and the little case of essences away. "And now," he said, "about Miss Lane. . . ."

"Yes, Sister Lane. As she has told you, she was one of us. But she backslid, and consorted with the fornicators and wine-bibbers who call themselves the Blossom People. But even this was in accordance with the Divine scheme of things. Whilst consorting with those— those pagans she became accustomed to the use and the abuse—but surely the use is also abuse!—of the psychedelic drugs. Already she possessed considerable psychic powers, but those vile potions enhanced them.

"You will realize, sir, that it would have been out of the question for any of our own Elect to imperil his immortal soul by tampering with such powerful, unseen and unseeable forces, but—"

"But," said Grimes, "Clarisse Lane has already demonstrated that she is damned, so you don't mind using her as your cat's-paw."

"You put it very concisely, sir," agreed Smith.

"I could say more, but I won't. I just might lose my temper. But go on."

"Sister Lane is not entirely human. She is descended from that Raul, the Stone Age savage who was brought to Earth from Kinsolving's Planet. Many factors were involved in his appearance. It could be that the very fabric of the Continuum is worn thin, here on the Rim, and that lines of force, or fault lines, intersect at that world. It could be, as the Rhine Institute claimed at the time, that the loneliness and the fear of all the dwellers on the colonized Rim Worlds are somehow focused on Kinsolving. Be that as it may, it happened. And it happened too that, in the fullness of time, this Raul was accepted into the bosom of our Church.

"Raul, as you may know, was more than a mere telepath. Much more. He was a wizard, one of those who, in his own age, drew animals to the hunters' spears by limning their likenesses on rock."

Grimes interrupted. "Doesn't the Bible say, somewhere, that thou shalt not suffer a witch to live?"

"Yes. It is so written. But we did not know of the full extent of

Raul's talents when he was admitted into our Fold. We did not know of them until after his death, when his papers came into our possession."

"But what are you playing at?" demanded Grimes. "Just what you are playing at in *our* back garden?" He had the bottle out again, and the little phial of cognac-flavored essence, and was mixing two more drinks. He held out one of them, the stronger, to Smith, who absentmindedly took it and raised it to his lips.

The Rector said, "Sir, I do not approve of your choice of words. Life is not a game. Life, death and the hereafter are not a game. We are not playing. We are working. Is it not written. 'Work, for the night is coming?' And you, sir, and I, as spacemen, know that the night is coming—the inevitable heat death of the Universe. . . ." He gulped more of his drink.

"You should visit Darsha some time," said Grimes, "and their Tower of Darkness. You should see the huge clock that is the symbol of *their* God." He added softly, "The clock is running down."

"Yes, the clock is running down, the sands of time are running out. And there is much to be done, so much to be done. . . ."

"Such as?"

"To reestablish the eternal verities. To build a new Sinai, to see the Commandments graven afresh on imperishable stone. And then, perhaps, the heathen, the idolators, will take heed and tremble. And then, surely, the rule of Jehovah will come again, before the End."

Grimes said reasonably enough, "But you people believe in predestination, don't you? Either we're damned or we aren't, and nothing we do makes any difference."

"I have learned by bitter experience," Smith told him, "that it is impossible to argue with a heretic—especially one who is foredoomed to eternal damnation. But even you must see that if the Commandments are given anew to Man then we, the Elect, shall be elevated to our rightful place in the Universe."

"Then God save us all," said Grimes.

Smith looked at him suspiciously, but went on. "It is perhaps necessary that there should be a sacrifice, and, if that be so, the Lord has already delivered her into our hands. No, sir, do not look at me like that. *We* shall not kill her, neither by knife nor fire shall we slay her. But, inevitably, she will be the plaything of supernal powers when she, on the planet of her ancestral origin, her inherited talents intensified by drugs, calls to Jehovah, the true God, the God of the Old Testament, to make Himself known again to sinful men."

There were flecks of white froth on Smith's beard around his lips, a dribble of saliva down the hair on his chin. His eyes were glaring and bloodshot. Grimes thought, *in vino veritas*. He said, with a gentleness he did not feel, actuated only by self-interest, "Don't you think that you've had enough, Rector? Isn't it time that we both turned in?"

"Eh, what? When'm ready. But you understand now that you must not interfere. *You must not interfere.*"

"I understand," said Grimes, thinking, *Too much and, not enough.* He found a tube of tablets in his suitcase, shook one into the palm of his hand. "Here," he said, offering it. "You'd better take this."

"Wha's it for?"

"It'll sweeten the breath and sober you up. It'll be too bad for you if the Presbyter sees the state you're in." *And too bad for me,* he thought.

"'M not drunk."

"Of course not. Just a little—unsteady."

"Don't really need . . . But jus' to oblige, y'un-derstan'."

Smith swallowed the tablet, his Adam's apple working convulsively. Grimes handed him a glass of cold water to wash it down. It acted almost immediately. The bearded man shuddered, then got steadily to his feet. He glared at Grimes, but it was no longer a fanatical glare. "Good night, sir," he snapped.

"Good night, Rector," Grimes replied.

When he was alone he thought of playing back the record of the evening's conversations, but thought better of it. For all he knew, Smith might be able to switch the hidden microphone and scanner back on from his own quarters—and the less he knew of the tiny device hidden in the starboard epaulet of his white mess jacket, the better.

He got out of his clothes and into his bunk, switched off the light;

but, unusually for him, his sleep was uneasy and nightmare-ridden. He supposed that it was Clarisse Lane's fault that she played a leading part in most of the dreams.

The voyage wore on, and on, and even as the ever-precessing gyroscopes of the Mannschenn Drive tumbled and receded down the dark infinities, so did the good ship *Piety* fall through the twisted Continuum. On one hand was the warped convoluted Galactic Lens and ahead, a pulsating spiral of iridescent light against the ultimate darkness, was the Kinsolving sun.

And this ship, unlike other ships of Grimes's wide experience, was no little man-made oasis of light and warmth in the vast, empty desert of the night. She was cold, cold, and her atmosphere carried always the faint acridity of disinfectant, and men and women talked in grave, low voices and did not mingle, and never was there the merest hint of laughter.

Clarisse Lane was not being maltreated—Grimes made sure of that—and was even allowed to meet the Commodore for a daily conversation, but always heavily chaperoned. She was the only telepath in the ship, which, while the interstellar drive was in operation, depended entirely upon the Carlotti equipment for deep space communication. But the Rector and the Presbyter did not doubt that she was in constant touch with Mayhew back at Port Forlorn—and Grimes did not doubt it either. She told him much during their meetings—things about which she could not possibly have known if there had not been a continual interchange of signals. Some of this intelligence was confirmed by messages addressed to Grimes and received, in the normal way, by the ship's electronic radio officer.

So they were obliged to be careful, these Neo-Calvinists. The chosen instrument for their experiment in practical theology was now also an agent for the Rim Worlds Confederacy. "But what does it matter?" Smith said to Grimes on one of the rare occasions that he spoke at length to him. "What does it matter? Perhaps it was ordained this way. Your friend Mayhew will be the witness to the truth, a witness who is not one of us. He will see through her eyes, hear with her ears, feel with every fiber of her being. The Word propagated by ourselves alone would be scoffed at. But there will be credence given it when it is propagated by an unbeliever."

"If anything happens," said Grimes.

But he couldn't argue with these people, and they couldn't argue with him. There was just no meeting of minds. He remembered a theory that he had once heard advanced by a ship's doctor. "Long ago," the man had said, "very long ago, there was a mutation. It wasn't a physically obvious one, but as a result of it Homo Sapiens was divided into two separate species: *Homo credulens*, those capable of blind faith in the unprovable, and *Homo incredulens*, those who aren't. The vast majority of people are, of course, hybrids."

Grimes had said, "And I suppose that all the pure *Homo incredulens* stock is either atheist or agnostic."

"Not so." The doctor had laughed. "Not so. Agnostic—yes. But don't forget that the atheist, like the theist, makes a definite statement for which he can produce no proof whatsoever."

An atheist would have been far less unhappy aboard this ship than a tolerant agnostic like Grimes.

But even the longest, unhappiest voyage comes to an end. A good planetfall was made—whatever they believed, *Piety's* people were excellent navigators—and, the Mannschenn Drive switched off, the Inertial Drive ticking over just enough to produce minimal gravitational field, the ship was falling in orbit about the lonely world, the blue and green mottled sphere hanging there against the blackness.

The old charts—or copies of them—were out, and Grimes was called up to the control room. "Yes," he told Smith, stabbing a finger down on the paper, "that's where the spaceport was. Probably even now the apron's not too overgrown for a safe landing. Captain Spence, when he came down in *Epsilon Eridani*, reported creepers over everything, but nothing heavy."

"It is a hundred and fifty standard years since he was here," said Smith. "At least. I would suggest one of the beaches."

"Risky," Grimes told him. "They shelve very steeply and according to our records violent storms are more frequent than otherwise." He turned to the big screen upon which a magnification of the planet was appearing. "There, just to the east of the sunrise terminator. That's the major continent—Farland, it was called—where the capital city and the spaceport were situated. You see that river, with the S bend? Step up the magnification, somebody. . . ."

Now there was only the glowing picture of the island continent, filling all the screen, and that expanded, so that there was only the sprawling, silvery S, and toward the middle of it, on either bank, a straggle of buildings was visible.

"The spaceport should be about ten miles to the west," said Grimes.

"Yes," agreed Smith, taking a long pointer to the screen. "I think that's it."

"Then make it Landing Stations, Rector," ordered Presbyter Cannan.

"Sir," demurred Smith, "you cannot put a big ship down as though she were a dinghy."

"Lord, oh Lord," almost prayed the Presbyter. "To have come so far, and then to be plagued by the dilatoriness of spacemen!"

I wish that this were my control room, thought Grimes.

But *Piety's* crew worked well and efficiently, and in a very short space of time the intercom speakers were blatting strings of orders: "Secure all for landing stations!" "All idlers to their quarters!" and the like. Gyroscopes hummed and whined and the ship tilted relative to the planet until its surface was directly beneath her, and the first of the sounding rockets, standard equipment for a survey expedition but not for landing on a world with spaceport control functioning, were fixed.

Parachutes blossomed in the upper atmosphere and the flares, each emitting a great steamer of smoke, ignited. Somebody was singing. It was the Presbyter.

> *"Let the fiery, cloudy pillar*
> *Guide me all my journey through. . . ."*

Even Grimes was touched by the spirit of the occasion. What if this crazy, this impious (for so he was beginning to think of it) experiment did work? What would happen? What would be unleashed upon the worlds of men? Who was it—the Gnostics?—who had said that the God of the Old Testament was the Devil of the New? He shivered as he sat in his acceleration chair.

She was dropping steadily, was *Piety*, following the first of her flares. But there was drift down there—perhaps a gale in the upper atmosphere, or a jet stream. The Inertial Drive generators grumbled suddenly as Smith applied lateral thrust. Down she dropped, and down, almost falling free, but under the full control of her captain. On the target screen, right in the center, highly magnified, the cluster of ruins that had been a spaceport was clearly visible, tilting like tombstones in a deserted graveyard, ghastly in the blue light of the rising sun.

Down she dropped, plunging through the wisps of cirrus, and there was a slight but appreciable rise of temperature as skin friction heated the metal of her hull. Smith slowed the rate of descent. The Presbyter started muttering irritably to himself.

There was no longer need for magnification on the screen. The great rectangle of the landing field was clearly visible, the vegetation that covered it lighter in color—eau de Nile against the surrounding indigo—than the brush outside the area. The last of the flares to have been fired was still burning there, its column of smoke rising almost vertically. The growth among which it had fallen was slowly smoldering.

Grimes looked at Smith. The man was concentrating hard. Beads of perspiration were forming on his upper cheeks, running down into his beard. But this was more important than an ordinary landing. So much hinged upon it. And, perhaps, malign (or benign) forces might be gathering their strength to overset the ship before her massive tripedal landing gear reached the safety of the planetary surface.

But she was down.

There was the gentlest of shocks, the faintest of creakings, the softest sighing of shock-absorbers. She was down, and the Inertial Drive generators muttered to themselves and then were quiet. She was down, and the soughing of the fans seemed to make the silence all the more silent.

Presbyter Cannan broke it. He turned in his chair to address Grimes. "Commodore," he asked as he pointed toward a distant peak, a black, truncated cone against the blue sky, "Commodore Grimes, what is the name of that mountain?"

"I . . . I don't know, sir."

"*I* know." The old man's voice was triumphant. "It is Sinai."

Had this been any other ship there would have been a period of relaxation. There were wild pigs and rabbits to hunt, descendants of the livestock abandoned by the original colonists. There were the famous caves, with their rock paintings, to visit. But the animals, their fear of Man long forgotten, came out of the undergrowth to stare curiously at the vessel and at the humans who busied themselves around her, opening side ports to allow the egress of the three pinnaces, already stocked with what would be required for the final stages of the expedition. And nobody was remotely interested in the caves.

Grimes managed to see Clarisse Lane. The ship was almost deserted now, so he was able to make his way down into the women's quarters without being challenged and stopped. He found her little cabin, hardly more than a cell. She was not locked in, not restrained in any way. She was sitting in her chair, a somber figure in her black dress, staring into nothingness. Her full lips moved almost imperceptibly as she vocalized her thoughts.

With a sudden start she realized that Grimes was standing before her. She whispered, "I—I was talking to Ken."

"To Mayhew?"

"Yes."

Saying goodbye, he thought. He said, "Clarisse, you don't have to go through with this."

"I am going through with it, Commodore."

"You don't have to," he insisted. "You're in touch with Mayhew. And he'll be in touch with *Rim Sword*. The Admiral told me that she'd be standing by in this sector. She's probably on her way here now. We can stall off those fanatics until she comes in."

She said, "I'm going through with it."

"But why? Why?"

"Because I want to."

"But you're not really one of them."

"I'm not."

"Sister Lane!" It was the Deaconess. "You asked for a few moments of privacy—and now I find you with this—this lecher! But come. The boat is waiting."

"I'll come with you." said Grimes.

"You will not," snapped the woman. "A place has been reserved for you in the pinnace carrying the Presbyter and the Rector. They had decided that it is meet that an infidel shall witness the handing down of the Law."

Clarisse Lane followed the Deaconess from the cabin. Grimes trailed along behind them. They went down to the main air lock, down the ramp to the overgrown apron, stumbling over the tough, straggling vines on their way to the boats. The sun was dropping fast to the western horizon. There was a hint of chill, a smell of dusk in the still air. There was the scent of growing things, and a faint hint of corruption.

Smith beckoned to Grimes from the open door of the leading pinnace. He made his way slowly toward it, walking carefully. He clambered up the retractable steps into the crowded cabin that stank of perspiration and damp, heavy clothing. He found a seat, wedged between two junior officers.

The door hissed shut. The Inertial Drive generator throbbed and snarled. Grimes could not see out of the ports, but he knew that the boat was airborne, was moving. There was no conversation in the cabin, but a metallic male voice reported from the speaker on the pilot's console, "Number Two following." After a pause a harsh female voice said, "Number Three following."

How long the flight lasted Grimes did not know; he was unable to raise his arm to look at his watch. But it seemed a long time, and it seemed a long time that they sat there after they had landed, waiting for the other boats to come down. But at last the door opened and a thin, icy wind whined through the aperture. The Presbyter was out first, then Smith, and eventually Grimes, in the middle of a huddle of officers and civilians.

The plateau was smooth, windswept, an expanse of bare rock. To one side of it were the three pinnaces, and in front of them the men were drawn up in orderly ranks, with only the Presbyter standing apart. In the middle of the circular area were the women, a ragged huddle of somber black.

Grimes's attention was caught by a blue spark far below, not far from the still gleaming, serpentine river. Had *Rim Sword* landed? No. It was only the control room windows of *Piety* reflecting the last rays of the setting sun.

There was a subdued murmuring as the women walked to stand to one side of the men. No, not all the women. Two remained in the center of the plateau. One was the Deaconess, tall and forbidding. The other was the Clarisse Lane. They had stripped her. She was wearing only a kilt cut roughly from the hide of some animal, clothing like that which had been worn by her ancestresses on this very planet. She was shivering and was hugging her full breasts to try to keep out the cold.

Stark, incongruous, an easel stood there, supporting a frame square of black canvas, and there was a battery-powered floodlight to illuminate it. At its foot were pots of pigment, and brushes. Raul, the forefather of this girl, had called animals with his paintings. What would she call? What could she call?

"Drink!" said the Deaconess, her voice rang clear over the thin whine of the bitter wind. "Drink!" She was holding out a glass of something. Clarisse took it, drained it.

Suddenly the sun was gone, and there was only the glare of the floodlight. Overhead was the almost empty black sky, and low to the east was an arc of misty luminescence that was the slowly rising Galactic Lens. The wind seemed to be coming straight from intergalactic space.

The Deaconess stalked over the rocky surface to take her stand beside the Presbyter, leaving the girl alone. Hesitantly Clarisse stooped to the pots and brushes, selected one of the latter, dipped it into paint, straightened, stood before the easel.

She stiffened into immobility, seemed to be waiting for something.

They were singing, then, the black-clad men and women drawn up in their stiff ranks before the pinnaces. They were singing. "Cwn Rhonda," it was, and even Grimes, who had always loved that old Welsh hymn tune, found it hard to refrain from joining in. They were singing, the rumbling basses, the baritones, the high tenors and the shrill sopranos.

> *Guide, me, oh Thou great Jehovah,*
> *Pilgrim through this barren land!*
> *I am weak, but Thou art mighty.*
> *Hold me with Thy powerful hand!*

They were singing, and the girl was painting. With deft, sure strokes she was depicting on the black canvas the figure of a god, white-bearded, white-robed, wrathful. She was painting, and the men and women were singing, and the air was full of unbearable tension and the wind was now howling, tugging at their clothing, buffeting them. But the easel in its circle of harsh light stood steady and the girl worked on. . . .

There was the dreadful *crack* of lightning close at hand, too close at hand, the *crack* and the dazzle, and the pungency of ozone, and the long, long streamer of blue fire licking out from above their heads and culminating on the plain far below, at the spaceport.

There was the burgeoning fireball where the ship had been.

There was the dreadful laughter, booming above the frenzy of the wind, and the metallic crash and clatter as the pinnaces, lifted and rolled over the rim of the plateau, plunged to destruction down the steep, rocky mountain slope.

And *They* were there—the robust, white-bearded deity, a lightning bolt clutched and ready in his right hand, and the naked, seductively smiling goddess, and the other naked one with her bow and her leashed hounds, and she in the white robes, carrying a book, with the owl perched on her shoulder. The lame smith was there, with his hammer, and the sea-god, with his trident, and he with the red beard and the helmet and the body armor and the sword.

Somebody screamed, and at least a score of the men and women had fallen to their knees. But the Presbyter stood his ground.

"Who are you?" he shouted. "Who are you?"

"Little man," the great voice replied, "we were, we are and we always shall be."

Grimes realized that he was laughing uncontrollably and saying, over and over to himself, "Not Sinai, but Olympus! Not Sinai, but Olympus!"

There was another supernal clap of thunder and the dark came sweeping back.

They sat around in miserable little groups on the bare mountaintop.

The Presbyter was gone, nobody knew where or how, and the Deaconess, and Smith, and perhaps a dozen of the others. It had been a long night, and a cold one, but the sun had risen at last, bringing some warmth with it.

Grimes, in shirt and trousers, stood with Clarrise Lane, who was wrapped in his jacket.

"But what happened?" he was asking. "What happened? What did you do?"

She said, "I . . . I don't know. I suppose that I do have some sort of power. And I suppose that I am, at heart, one of the Blossom People. Our religious beliefs are a sort of vague pantheism. . . . And, after all, the Father of the Gods is very similar in His attributes to the patriarchal gods of later religions. . . ." She looked at the sky. "It's lucky that I'm a telepath as well as being . . . whatever it is that I am. *Rim Sword* will be here very shortly. I hope it's soon. I have a feeling that when some of our fanatical friends recover they'll be blaming me for everything."

"*When* they recover," said Grimes. "It will take me a long time." He added, "But I don't think you'd better return to Francisco with them."

"Ken," she told him, "has already got the formalities under way that will make me a Rim Worlds citizen."

"The obvious one?"

"Yes."

"And are you going to get married in church?" he asked. "It should be interesting."

"Not if I can help it," she told him.

And so, in due course, Grimes kissed the bride and, at the reception, toasted the newlyweds in imported champagne. He did not stay long after that. He was too much the odd man out—almost all the other guests were married couples, and such few women as were unattached made little or no appeal to him. He was missing Sonya, still away on her galactic cruise. Somehow he missed her less at home, lonely though it was without her. There was still so much of her in the comfortable apartment: her books, the pictures that she had chosen, the furniture that had been specially designed to her taste.

Having left the party early, he was at his office, at the spaceport, bright and early the following morning. He received, personally, the urgent Carlottigram from *Rim Griffon*, on Tharn. He smiled as he read it. He had been deskbound for too long, and his recent voyage in the oddly named *Piety* had aggravated rather than assuaged the itching of his feet. Captain Timms, one of the Rim Runners' senior masters, was due back from annual leave within a few days and, at the moment, there was no appointment open for him. So Timms could keep the chair warm while Grimes took passage to Tharn; the scheduled departure date of *Rim Dragon* for that planet fitted in very nicely with his plans.

"Miss Walton," he said happily to the rather vapid little blonde secretary, "this is going to be a busy morning. Telephoning first, and then correspondence every which way. . . . To begin with, get me the General Manager. . . ."

⤳ Part 2 ⤳
The Bird-Brained Navigator

HER INERTIAL DRIVE throbbing softly, all hands at landing stations, all passengers save one strapped in their acceleration couches (a sudden emergency requiring the use of the auxiliary reaction drive was unlikely, but possible), the starship *Rim Dragon* dropped slowly down to Port Grimes on Tharn. The privileged passenger—although in his case it was a right rather than a privilege—was riding in the control room instead of being incarcerated in his cabin. Commodore John Grimes, Astronautical Superintendent of Rim Runners, said nothing, did nothing that could be construed as interference on his part. Legally speaking, of course, he was no more than a guest in the liner's nerve center; but at the same time he could and did exercise considerable authority over the space-going employees of Rim Runners, made the ultimate decisions in such matters as promotions and appointments. However, Captain Wenderby, *Rim Dragon's* master, was a more than competent ship-handler and at no time did Grimes feel impelled to make any suggestions, at no time did his own hands start to reach out hungrily for the controls.

So Grimes sat there, stolid and solid in his acceleration chair, not even now keeping a watchful eye on the briskly efficient Wenderby and his briskly efficient officers. They needed no advice from him, would need none. But it was easier for them than it had been for him, when he made his own first landing on Tharn—how many years ago? Too many. There had been no spaceport then, with spaceport control keeping the master fully informed of meteorological conditions during his entire descent. There had been no body of assorted officials—port captain, customs, port health and all the rest of it— standing by awaiting the ship's arrival. Grimes, in fact, had not known what or whom to expect, although his robot probes had told him that the culture of the planet was roughly analogous to that of Earth's Middle Ages. Even so, he had been lucky in that he had set *Faraway Quest* down near a city controlled by the priesthood rather than in an area under the sway of one of the robber barons.

He looked out of one of the big viewports. From this altitude he could see no signs of change—but change there must have been, change there had been. On that long ago exploration voyage in the old *Quest* he had opened up the worlds of the Eastern Circuit to commerce—and the trader does more to destroy the old ways than either the gunboat or the missionary. In this case the trader would have been the only outside influence: the Rim Worlds had always, fortunately for them, been governed by cynical, tolerant agnostics to whom gunboat diplomacy was distasteful. The Rim Worlders had always valued their own freedom too highly to wish to interfere with that of any other race.

But even commerce, thought Grimes, *is an interference. It makes people want the things that they cannot yet produce for themselves: the mass-produced entertainment, the labor-saving machines, the weapons.* Grimes sighed. *I suppose that we were right to arm the priesthood rather than the robber barons. In any case, they've been good customers.*

Captain Wenderby, still intent on his controls, spoke. "It must seem strange, coming back after all these years, sir."

"It does, Captain."

"And to see the spaceport that they named after you, for the first time."

"A man could have worse monuments."

Grimes transferred his attention from the viewport to the screen that showed, highly magnified, what was directly astern of and below the ship. Yes, there it was. Port Grimes. A great circle of gray-gleaming concrete, ringed by warehouses and administration buildings, with cranes and gantries and conveyor belts casting long shadows in the ruddy light of the westering sun. He had made the first landing on rough heathland, and for a long, heart-stopping moment had doubted that the tripedal landing gear would be able to adjust to the irregularities of the surface. And there was *Rim Griffon*, the reason for his voyage to Tharn. There was the ship whose officers refused to sail with each other and with the master. There was the mess that had to be sorted out with as few firings as possible—Rim Runners, as usual, was short of spacefaring personnel. There was the mess.

It was some little time before John Grimes could get around to doing anything about it. As he should have foreseen, he was a personality, a historical personality at that. He was the first outsider to have visited Tharn. He was responsible for the breaking of the power of the barons, for the rise to power of the priesthood and the merchants. Too, the Rim Confederacy's ambassador on Tharn had made it plain that he, and the government that he represented, would appreciate it if the Commodore played along. The delay in the departure of a very unimportant merchant vessel was far less important than the preservation of interstellar good relations.

So Grimes was wined and dined, which was no hardship, and obliged to listen to long speeches, which was. He was taken on sight-seeing tours, and was pleased to note that progress, although inevitable, had been a controlled progress, not progress for its own sake. The picturesque had been sacrificed only when essential for motives of hygiene or *real* efficiency. Electricity had supplanted the flaring natural gas jets for house-and street-lighting—but the importation and evolution of new building techniques and materials had not produced a mushroom growth of steel and concrete matchboxes or plastic domes. Architecture still retained its essentially

Tharnian character, even though the streets of the city were no longer rutted, even though the traffic on those same streets was now battery-powered cars and no longer animal-drawn vehicles. (Internal combustion engines were manufactured on the planet, but their use was prohibited within urban limits.)

And at sea change had come. At the time of Grimes's first landing the only oceangoing vessels had been the big schooners; now sail was on its way out, was being ousted by the steam turbine. Yet the ships, with their fiddle bows and their figureheads, with their raked masts and funnels, still displayed an archaic charm that was altogether lacking on Earth's seas and on the waters of most Man-colonized worlds. The Commodore, who was something of an authority on the history of marine transport, would dearly have loved to have made a voyage in one of the steamers, but he knew that time would not permit this. Once he had sorted out *Rim Griffon's* troubles he would have to return to Port Forlorn, probably in that very ship.

At last he was able to get around to the real reason for his visit to Tharn. On the morning of his fifth day on the planet he strode purposefully across the clean, well-cared-for concrete of the apron, walked decisively up the ramp to *Rim Griffon's* after air lock door. There was a junior officer waiting there to receive him; Captain Dingwall had been warned that he would be coming on board. Grimes knew the young man, as he should have; after all, he had interviewed him for a berth in the Rim Runners' service.

"Good morning, Mr. Taylor."

"Good morning, sir." The Third Officer was painfully nervous, and his prominent Adam's apple bobbled as he spoke. His ears, almost as outstanding as Grimes's own, flushed a dull red. "The Old—" The flush spread to all of Taylor's features. "Captain Dingwall is waiting for you, sir. This way, sir."

Grimes did not need a guide. This *Rim Griffon*, like most of the older units in Rim Runners' fleet, had started her career as an *Epsilon* Class tramp in the employ of the Interstellar Transport Commission. The general layout of those tried and trusted Galactic workhorses was familiar to all spacemen. However, young Mr. Taylor had been instructed by his captain to receive the Commodore and to escort him to his, Dingwall's, quarters, and Grimes had no desire to interfere with the running of the ship.

Yet.

The two men rode up in the elevator in silence, each immersed in his own thoughts. Taylor, obviously, was apprehensive. A delay of a vessel is always a serious matter, especially when her own officers are involved. And Grimes was sorting out his own impressions to date. This *Rim Griffon* was obviously not a happy ship. He could feel it— just as he could see and hear the faint yet unmistakable signs of neglect, the hints of rust and dust, the not yet anguished pleading of a machine somewhere, a fan or a pump, for lubrication. And as the elevator cage passed through the "farm" level there was a whiff of decaying vegetation; either algae vats or hydroponic tanks, or both, were overdue for cleaning out.

The elevator stopped at the captain's deck. Young Mr. Taylor led the way out of the cage, knocked diffidently at the door facing the axial shaft. It slid open. A deep voice said, "That will be all, Mr. Taylor. I'll send for you, and the other officers, when I want you. And come in, please, Commodore Grimes."

Grimes entered the day cabin. Dingwall rose to meet him—a short, stocky man, his features too large, too ruddy, his eyes too brilliantly blue under a cockatoo-crest of white hair. He extended a hand, saying, "Welcome aboard, Commodore." He did not manage to make the greeting sound convincing. "Sit down, sir. The sun's not yet over the yardarm, but I can offer you coffee."

"No thank you, Captain. Later, perhaps. Mind if I smoke?" Grimes produced his battered pipe, filled and lit it. He said through the initial acid cloud, "And now, sir, what *is* the trouble? Your ship has been held up for far too long."

"You should have asked me that five days ago, Commodore."

"Should I?" Grimes stared at Dingwall, his gray eyes bleak. "Perhaps I should. Unfortunately I was obliged to act almost in an ambassadorial capacity after I arrived here. But now I am free to attend to the real business."

"It's my officers," blurted Dingwall.

"Yes?"

"The second mate to begin with. A bird-brained navigator if ever there was one. Can you imagine anybody, with all the aids we have today, getting lost between Stree and Mellise? *He* did."

"Legally speaking," said Grimes, "the master is responsible for everything. Including the navigation of his ship,"

"I navigate myself. Now."

And I can imagine it, thought Grimes. *"Do I have to do everybody's bloody job in this bloody ship? Of course, I'm only the Captain. . . ."* He said, "You reprimanded him, of course?"

"Darn right I did." Dingwall's voice registered pleasant reminiscence. "I told him that he was incapable of navigating a plastic duck across a bathtub."

"Hmm. And your other officers?"

"There're the engineers, Commodore. The Interstellar Drive chief hates the Inertial Drive chief. Not that I've much time for either of 'em. In fact I told Willis—he's supposed to run the Inertial Drive—that he couldn't pull a soldier off his sister. That was after I almost had to use the auxiliary rockets to get clear of Grollor—"

"And the others?"

"Vacchini, Mate. He couldn't run a pie cart. And Sally Bowen, Catering Officer, can't boil water without burning it. And Pilchin, the so-called purser, can't add two and two and get the same answer twice running. And as for Sparks . . . I'd stand a better chance of getting an important message through if I just opened a control viewport and stood there and shouted."

The officer who is to blame for all this, thought Grimes, *is the doctor. He should have seen this coming on. But perhaps I'm to blame as well. Dingwall's home port is Port Forlorn, on Lorn—and his ship's been running between the worlds of the Eastern Circuit and Port Farewell, on Faraway, for the past nine standard months. And Mrs. Dingwall (Grimes had met her) is too fond of her social life to travel with him. . . .*

"Don't you like the ship, Captain?" he asked.

"The *ship's* all right," he was told.

"But the run, as far as you're concerned, could be better."

"And the officers."

"Couldn't we all, Captain Dingwall? Couldn't we all? And now, just between ourselves, who is it that refused to sail with you?"

"My bird-brained navigator. I hurt his feelings when I called him that. A very sensitive young man is our Mr. Missenden. And the Inertial Drive chief. He's a member of some fancy religion called the Neo-Calvinists. . . ."

"I've met them," said Grimes.

"What I said about his sister and the soldier really shocked him."

"And which of them refuse to sail with each other?"

"Almost everybody has it in for the second mate. He's a Latter Day Fascist and is always trying to make converts. And the two chiefs are at each other's throats. Kerholm, the Interstellar Drive specialist, is a militant atheist—"

And I was on my annual leave, thought Grimes, *when this prize bunch of square pegs was appointed to this round hole. Even so, I should have checked up. I would have checked up if I hadn't gotten involved in the fun and games on Kinsolving's Planet.*

"Captain," he said, "I appreciate your problems. But there are two sides to every story. Mr. Vacchini, for example, is a very efficient officer. As far as he is concerned, there could well be a clash of personalities. . . ."

"Perhaps," admitted Dingwall grudgingly.

"As for the others. I don't know them personally. If you could tell them all to meet in the wardroom in—say—five minutes, we can go down to try to iron things out."

"You can try," said the Captain. "I've had them all in a big way. And, to save you the bother of saying it, Commodore Grimes, they've had me likewise."

Grimes ironed things out. On his way from Lorn to Tharn he had studied the files of reports on the captain and his officers. Nonetheless, in other circumstances he would have been quite ruthless—but good spacemen do not grow on trees, especially out toward the Galactic Rim. And these were good spacemen, all of them, with the exception of Missenden, the second officer. He had been born on New Saxony, one of the worlds that had been part of the short-lived Duchy of Waldegren, and one of the worlds upon which the political perversions practiced upon Waldegren itself had lived on for years after the downfall of the Duchy. He had been an officer in the navy of New Saxony and had taken part in the action off Pelisande, the battle in which the heavy cruisers of the Survey Service had destroyed the last of the self-styled commerce raiders who were, in fact, no better than pirates.

There had been survivors, and Missenden had been one of them. (He owed his survival mainly to the circumstance that the ship of which he had been Navigator had been late in arriving at her rendezvous with the other New Saxony war vessels and had, in fact, surrendered after no more than a token resistance.) He had stood trial with other war criminals, but had escaped with a very light sentence. (Most of the witnesses who could have testified against him were dead.) As he had held a lieutenant commander's commission in the navy of New Saxony he had been able to obtain a Master Astronaut's Certificate after no more than the merest apology for an examination. Then he had drifted out to the Rim, where his New Saxony qualifications were valid; where, in fact, qualifications issued by any human authority anywhere in the galaxy were valid.

Grimes looked at Missenden. He did not like what he saw. He had not liked it when he first met the man, a few years ago, when he had engaged him as a probationary third officer—but then, as now, he had not been able to afford to turn spacemen away from his office door. The Second Officer was tall, with a jutting, arrogant beak of a nose over a wide, thin-lipped mouth, with blue eyes that looked even madder than Captain Dingwall's, his pale, freckled face topped by close-cropped red hair. He was a fanatic, that was obvious from his physical appearance, and in a ship where he, like everybody else, was unhappy his fanaticism would be enhanced. *A lean and hungry look,* thought Grimes. *He thinks too much; such men are dangerous.* He added mentally, *But only when they think about the wrong things. The late Duke Otto's* Galactic Superman, *for example, rather than Pilgren's* Principles of Interstellar Navigation.

He said, "Mr. Missenden . . ."

"Sir?" The curtly snapped word was almost an insult. The way in which it was said implied, "I'm according respect to your rank, not to *you*."

"The other officers have agreed to continue the voyage. On arrival at Port Forlorn you will all be transferred to more suitable ships, and those of you who are due will be sent on leave or time off as soon as possible. Are you agreeable?"

"No."

"And why not, Mr. Missenden?"

"I'm not prepared to make an intercontinental hop under a captain who insulted me."

"Insulted you?"

"Yes." He turned on Dingwall." Did you, or did you not, call me a bird-brained navigator?"

"I did, Mr. Missenden," snarled Captain Dingwall. "And I meant it."

"Captain," asked Grimes patiently, "are you prepared to withdraw that remark?"

"I am not, Commodore. Furthermore, as master of this ship I have the legal right to discharge any member of my crew that I see fit."

"Very well," said Grimes, "As Captain Dingwall has pointed out I can only advise and mediate. But I do possess some authority; appointments and transfers are my responsibility. Will you arrange, Captain, for Mr. Missenden to be paid, on your books, up to and including midnight, local time? Then get him off your Articles of Agreement as soon as possible, so that the second officer of *Rim Dragon* can be signed on here. And you, Mr, Missenden, will join *Rim Dragon*."

"If you say so," said Missenden, "Sir."

"I do say so. And I say, too, Mr. Missenden, that I shall see you again in my office back in Port Forlorn."

"I can hardly wait, Sir."

Captain Dingwall looked at his watch. He said, "The purser already has Mr. Missenden's payoff almost finalized. Have you made any arrangements with Captain Wenderby regarding his second officer?"

"I told him that there might be a transfer, Captain. Shall we meet at the Consul's office at 1500 hours? You probably know that he is empowered to act as shipping master insofar as our ships on Tharn are concerned."

"Yes, sir," stated Dingwall. "I know."

"You would," muttered Missenden.

The transfer of officers was nice and easy in theory—but it did not work out in practice. The purser, Grimes afterward learned, was the only person aboard *Rim Griffon* with whom the second officer was not on terms of acute enmity. Missenden persuaded him to arrange his pay-off for 1400 hours, not 1500. At the appointed time the purser of the *Griffon* was waiting in the Consul's office, and shortly afterward the purser and the second officer of *Rim Dragon* put in their appearance. The *Dragon's* second mate was paid off his old ship and signed on the Articles of his new one. But Missenden had vanished. All that *Griffon's* purser knew was that he had taken the money due him and said that he had a make a business call and that he would be back.

He did not come back.

Commodore Grimes was not in a happy mood. He had hoped to be a passenger aboard *Rim Griffon* when she lifted off from Port Grimes, but now it seemed that his departure from Tharn for the Rim Worlds would have to be indefinitely postponed. It was, of course, all Missenden's fault. Now that he had gone into smoke all sorts of unsavory facts were coming to light regarding that officer. During his ship's visits to Tharn he had made contact with various subversive elements. The Consul had not known of this—but Rim Runners' local agent, a native to the planet, had. It was the police who had told him, and he had passed the information on to Captain Dingwall. Dingwall had shrugged and growled, "What the hell else do you expect from such a drongo?" adding, "As long as I get rid of the bastard he can consort with Aldebaranian necrophiles for all I care!"

Quite suddenly, with Grimes's baggage already loaded aboard *Rim Griffon*, the mess had blown up to the proportions of an interstellar incident. Port Grimes's Customs refused outward clearance to the ship. The Rim Confederacy's Ambassador sent an urgent message to Grimes requiring him to disembark at once—after which the ship would be permitted to leave—and to report forthwith to the Embassy. With all this happening, Grimes was in no fit state to listen to Captain Wenderby's complaints that he had lost a first class second officer and now would have to sail shorthanded on completion of discharge.

The Ambassador's own car took Grimes from the spaceport to the Embassy. It was a large building, ornately turreted, with metal-bound doors that could have withstood the charge of a medium tank. These opened as the Commodore dismounted from the vehicle, and within them stood saluting Marines. *At least,* thought Grimes, *they aren't going to shoot me. Yet.* An aide in civilian clothes escorted him to the Ambassador's office.

The Honorable Clifton Weeks was a short, fat man with all of a short, fat man's personality. "Sit down, Commodore," he huffed. Then, glowering over his wide, highly polished desk at the spaceman. "Now, sir. This Missenden character. What about him? Hey?"

"He seems to have flown the coop," said Grimes.

"You amaze me, sir." Week's glower became even more pronounced. "You amaze me, sir. Not by what you said, but by the way in which you said it. Surely you, even you, have some appreciation of the seriousness of the situation?"

"Spacemen have deserted before, in foreign ports. Just as seamen used to do—still do, probably. The local police have his description. They'll pick him up, and deport him when they get him. And we'll deport him, too, when he's delivered back to the Confederacy."

"And you still don't think it's serious? Hey?"

"Frankly, no, sir."

"Commodore, you made the first landing on this planet. But what do you know about it? Nothing, sir. Nothing. You haven't lived here. I have. I know that the Confederacy will have to fight to maintain the currently favorable trade relations that we still enjoy with Tharn. Already other astronautical powers are sniffing around the worlds of the Eastern Circuit."

"During the last six months, local time," said Grimes, "three of the Empire of Waverley's ships have called here. And two from the Shakespearean Sector. And one of Trans-Galactic Clippers' cargo liners. But, as far as the rulers of Tharn are concerned, the Confederacy is still the most favored nation."

"Who *are* the rulers of Tharn?" barked the Ambassador.

"Why, the priesthood."

The Ambassador mumbled something about the political illiteracy of spacemen, then got to his feet. He waddled to the far wall of his office, on which was hung a huge map of the planet in Mercator projection, beckoned to Grimes to follow him. From a rack he took a long pointer. "The island continent of Ausiphal . . ." he said, "And here, on the eastern seaboard, Port Grimes, and University City. Where we are now."

"Yes. . . ."

The tip of the pointer described a rhumb line, almost due east. "The other island continent of the northern hemisphere, almost the twin to this one. Climatically, politically—you name it."

"Yes?"

The pointer backtracked, then stabbed viciously. "And here, well to the west of Braziperu, the island of Tangaroa. Not a continent, but still a sizable hunk of real estate."

"So?"

"So Tangaroa's the last stronghold of the robber barons, the ruffians who were struggling for power with the priests and merchants when you made your famous first landing. How many years ago was it? Hey?"

"But what's that to do with Mr. Missenden?" Grimes asked. "And me?" he added.

"Your Mr. Missenden," the Ambassador said, "served in the navy of New Saxony. The people with whom he's been mixing in University City are Tangaroan agents and sympathizers. The priesthood has allowed Tangaroa to continue to exist—in fact, there's even trade between it and Ausiphal—but has been reluctant to allow the Tangaroans access to any new knowledge, especially knowledge that could be perverted to the manufacture of weaponry. Your Mr. Missenden would be a veritable treasure house of such knowledge."

"He's not *my* Mr. Missenden!" snapped Grimes.

"But he is, sir. He is. *You* engaged him when he came out to the Rim. *You* appointed him to ships running the Eastern Circuit. *You* engineered his discharge on this world, even."

"So what am I supposed to do about him?"

"Find him, before he does any real damage. And if you, the man after whom the spaceport was named, are successful it will show the High Priest just how much we of the Confederacy have the welfare of Tharn at heart."

"But why *me*? These people have a very efficient police force. And a man with a pale, freckled face and red hair will stand out like a sore thumb among the natives."

The Honorable Mr. Weeks laughed scornfully. "Green skin dye! Dark blue hair dye! Contact lenses! And, on top of all that, a physical appearance that's common on this planet!"

"Yes," admitted Grimes. "I might recognize him, in spite of a disguise. . . ."

"Good. My car is waiting to take you to the High Priest."

The University stood on a rise to the east of the city, overlooking the broad river and, a few miles to the north, the sea. It looked more like a fortress than a seat of learning, and in Tharn's turbulent past it had, more than once, been castle rather than academy.

Grimes respected the Tharnian priesthood, and the religion that they preached and practiced made sense to him than most of the other faiths of Man. There was something of Buddhism about it, a recognition of the fact that nothing *is*, but that everything is flux, change, a continual process of becoming. There was the equation of God with Knowledge—but never that infuriating statement made by so many Terran religions, that smug, "There are things that we aren't meant to know." There was a very real wisdom—the wisdom that accepts and rejects, and that neither accepts nor rejects just because a concept is *new*. There was a reluctance to rush headlong into an industrial revolution with all its miseries; and, at the same time, no delay in the adoption of techniques that would make the life of the people longer, easier and happier.

Night had fallen when the Embassy car pulled up outside the great gates of the University. The guard turned out smartly—but in these days their function was merely ceremonial; no longer was there the need to keep either the students in or the townsfolk out. On all of Tharn—save for Tangarora—the robber barons were only an evil memory of the past.

A black-uniformed officer led Grimes through long corridors, lit by bright electric bulbs, and up stairways to the office of the High Priest. He, an elderly, black-robed man, frail, his skin darkened by age to an opaque olive, had been a young student at the time of the first landing. He claimed to have met the Commodore on that occasion, but Grimes could not remember him. But he was almost the double of the old man who had held the high office then—a clear example of the job making the man.

"Commodore Grimes," he said. "Please be seated."

"Thank you, your Wisdom."

"I am sorry to have interfered with your plans, sir. But your Mr. Weeks insisted."

"He assured me that it was important."

"And he has . . . put you in the picture?"

"Yes."

The old man produced a decanter, two graceful glasses. He poured the wine. Grimes relaxed. He remembered that the Tharnian priesthood made a point of never drinking with anybody whom they considered an enemy, with nobody who was not a friend in the true sense of the word. There was no toast, only a ceremonial raising of goblets. The liquor was good, as it always had been.

"What can I do?" asked Grimes.

The priest shrugged. "Very little. I told Mr. Weeks that our own police were quite capable of handling the situation, but he said, 'It's *his* mess. He should have his nose rubbed in it.'" The old man's teeth were very white in his dark face as he smiled.

"Tales out of school, your Wisdom." Grimes grinned. "Now I'll tell one. Mr. Weeks doesn't like spacemen. A few years ago his wife made a cruise in one of the T-G clippers—and, when the divorce came though, married the chief officer of the liner she traveled in."

The High Priest laughed. "That accounts for it. But I shall enjoy your company for the few weeks that you will have to stay on Tharn. I shall tell my people to bring your baggage from the Embassy to the University."

"That is very good of you." Grimes took another sip of the strong wine. "But I think that since I'm here I shall help in the search for Mr. Missenden. After all, he is still officially one of our nationals."

"As you please, Commodore. Tell me, if you were in charge how would you set about it?"

Grimes lapsed into silence. He looked around the office. All of the walls were covered with books, save one, and on it hung another of those big maps. He said, "He'll have to get out by sea, of course."

"Of course. We have no commercial airship service to Tangaroa, and the Tangaroans have no commerical airship service at all."

"And you have no submarines yet, and your aerial coast guard patrol will keep you informed as to the movements of all surface vessels. So he will have to make his getaway in a merchant vessel. . . . Would you know if there are any Tangaroan merchantmen in port?"

"I would know. There is one—the *Kawaroa*. She is loading textiles and agricultural machinery."

"Could she be held?"

"On what excuse, Commodore? The Tangaroans are very touchy people, and if the ship is detained their consul will at once send off a radio message to his government."

"A very touchy people, you say . . . and arrogant. And quarrelsome. Now, just suppose that there's a good, old-fashioned tavern brawl, as a result of which the master and his officers are all arrested. . . ."

"It's the sort of thing that could easily happen. It has happened, more than once."

"Just prior to sailing, shall we say? And then, with the ship immobilized, with only rather dim-witted ratings to try to hinder us, we make a thorough search—accommodations, holds, machinery spaces, storerooms, the works."

"The suggestion has its merits."

"The only snag," admitted Grimes, "is that it's very unlikely that the master and all three of his mates will rush ashore for a quick one just before sailing."

"But they always do," said the High Priest.

As they always had done, they did.

Grimes watched proceedings from the innkeeper's cubbyhole, a little compartment just above the main barroom with cunning peepholes in its floor. He would have preferred to have been among the crowd of seamen, fishermen and watersiders, but his rugged face was too well known on Tharn, and no amount of hair and skin dye could have disguised him. He watched the four burly, blue- and brass-clad men breasting the bar, drinking by themselves, tossing down pot after pot of the strong ale. He saw the fat girl whose dyed yellow hair was in vivid contrast to her green skin nuzzle up to the man who was obviously the Tangaroan captain. He wanted none of her—and Grimes sympathized with him. Even from his elevated vantage point he could see that her exposed overblown breasts were sagging, that what little there was of her dress was stained and bedraggled. But the man need not have brushed her away so brutally. She squawked like an indignant parrot as she fell sprawling to the floor with a display of fat, unlovely legs.

One of the other drinkers—a fisherman by the looks of him— came to the aid of beauty in distress. Or perhaps it was only that he was annoyed because the woman, in her fall, had jostled him, spilling his drink. Or, even more likely, he was, like the woman, one of the High Priest's agents. If such was the case, he seemed to be enjoying his work. His huge left hand grasped the captain's shoulder, turning him and holding him, and then right fist and left knee worked in unison. It was dirty, but effective.

After that, as Grimes said later, telling about it, it was on for young and old. The three mates, swinging their heavy metal drinking pots, rallied to the defense of their master. The fisherman picked up a heavy stool to use as his weapon. The woman, who had scrambled to her feet with amazing agility for one of her bulk, sailed into the fray, fell to a crouching posture, straightening abruptly, and one of the Tangaroan officers went sailing over her head as though rocket-propelled, crashing down on to a table at which three watersiders had been enjoying a quiet, peaceful drink. They, roaring their displeasure, fell upon the hapless foreigner with fists and feet.

The police officer with Grimes—his English was not too good—said, "Pity break up good fight. But must arrest very soon."

"You'd better," the Commodore told him. "Some of your people down there are pulling knives."

Yes, knives were out, gleaming wickedly in the lamplight. Knives were out, but the Tangaroans—with the exception of the victim of the lady and her stevedoring friends—had managed to retreat to a corner and there were fighting off all comers, although the captain, propped against the wall, was playing no great part in the proceedings. Like the fisherman, the two officers had picked up stools, were using them as both shields and weapons, deflecting flung pots and bottles with them, smashing them down on the heads and arms of their assailants.

The captain was recovering slowly. His hand went up to fumble inside the front of his coat. It came out, holding something that gleamed evilly—a pistol. But he fired it only once, and harmlessly. The weapon went off as his finger tightened on the trigger quite involuntarily, as the knife thrown by the yellow-haired slattern pinned his wrist to the wall.

And then the place was full of University police, tough men in black tunics who used their clubs quite indiscriminately and herded all those present out into the waiting trucks.

Quietly, Grimes and the police officer left their observation post and went down the back stairs. Outside the inn they were joined by twelve men—six police and six customs officials, used to searching ships. Their heels ringing on the damp cobblestones, they made their way through the misty night to the riverside, to the quays.

Kawaroa was ready for sea, awaiting only the pilot and, of course, her master and officers. Her derricks were stowed, her moorings had been singled up, and a feather of smoke from her tall, raked funnel showed that steam had been raised. She was not a big ship, but she looked smart, well maintained, seaworthy.

As Grimes and his party approached the vessel they saw that somebody had got there ahead of them, a dark figure who clattered hastily up the gangway. But there was no cause for hurry. The ship, with all her navigating officers either in jail or in the hospital, would not be sailing, and the harbor master had already been told not to send a pilot down to take her out.

There was no cause for hurry....

But what was that jangling of bells, loud and disturbing in the still night? The engine room telegraph? The routine testing of gear one hour before the time set for departure?

And what were those men doing, scurrying along to foc'sle head and poop?

Grimes broke into a run, and as he did so he heard somebody shouting from *Kawaroa's* bridge. The language was unfamiliar, but the voice was not. It was Missenden's. From forward there was a *thunk!* and then a splash as the end of the severed headline fell into the still water. The last of the flood caught the ship's bows and she fell away from the wharf. With the police and customs officers, who had belatedly realized what was happening, well behind him, Grimes reached the edge of the quay. It was all of five feet to the end of the still-dangling gangway and the gap was rapidly widening. Without thinking, Grimes jumped. Had he known that nobody would follow him he would never have done so. But he jumped, and his desperate fingers closed around the outboard man-ropes of the accommodation ladder and somehow, paying a heavy toll of abrasions and lacerations, he was able to squirm upward until he was kneeling on the bottom platform. Dimly he was aware of shouts from the fast receding dock. Again he heard the engine room telegraph bells, and felt the vibration as the screw began to turn. So the after lines had been cut, too, and the ship was under way. And it was—he remembered the charts that he had looked at—a straight run down river with absolutely no need for local knowledge. From above sounded a single, derisory blast from *Kawaroa's* steam whistle.

Grimes was tempted to drop from his perch, to swim back ashore. But he knew too much; he had always been a student of maritime history in all its aspects. He knew that a man going overboard from a ship making way through the water stands a very good chance of being pulled under and then cut to pieces by the screw. In any case, he had said that he would find Missenden, and he had done just that.

Slowly, painfully, he pulled himself erect, then walked up the clattering treads to deck level.

There was nobody on deck to receive him. This was not surprising; Missenden and the crew must have been too engrossed in getting away from the wharf to notice his pierhead jump. So . . . He was standing in an alleyway, open on the port side. Looking out, he saw the harbor lights sliding past, and ahead and to port there was the white-flashing fairway buoy, already dim, but from mist rather than distance. Inboard there was a varnished wooden door set in the white-painted plating of the 'midships house, obviously the entrance to the accommodation. Grimes opened it without difficulty—door handles will be invented and used by any being approximating to human structure. Inside there was a cross alleyway, brightly illuminated by electric light bulbs in well fittings. On the after bulkhead of this there was a steel door, and the mechanical hum and whine that came from behind it told Grimes that it led to the engine room. On the forward bulkhead there was another wooden door.

Grimes went through it. Another alleyway, cabins, and a companionway leading upward. At the top of this there were more cabins, and another companionway. And at the top of this . . . the captain's accommodation, obviously, even though the word on the tally over the door was no more than a meaningless squiggle to Grimes.

One more companionway—this one with a functional handrail instead of a relatively ornate balustrade. At the head of it was a curtained doorway. Grimes pushed through the heavy drape, found himself in what could only be the chart room, looked briefly at the wide chart table upon which was a plan of the harbor, together with a pair of dividers and a set of parallel rulers. The Confederacy, he remembered, had at one time exported quite large consignments of these instruments to Tharn.

On the forward bulkhead of the chart room, and to port, was the doorway leading out to the wheelhouse and bridge. Softly, Grimes stepped through it, out into the near-darkness. The only light was that showing from the compass periscope, the device that enabled the helmsman to steer by the standard magnetic compass, the binnacle of which was sited up yet one more deck, on what had been called on Earth's surface ships the "monkey island." There was the man at the wheel, intent upon his job. And there, at the fore end of the wheelhouse, were two dark figures, looking out through the wide windows. One of them, the taller one, turned suddenly, said something in Tangaroan. As before, the voice was familiar but the language was not.

The question—intonation made that plain—was repeated, and then Missenden said in English, "It's you! How the hell did you get aboard? Hold it, Commodore, hold it!" There was just enough light for Grimes to see the pistol that was pointing at his midriff.

"Turn this ship around," ordered Grimes, "and take her back into port."

"Not a chance." Missenden laughed. "Especially when I've gone to all the trouble to taking her out of port. Pity old Dingwall wasn't here to see it. Not bad, was it, for a bird-brained navigator? And keep your hands up where I can see them."

"I'm unarmed," said Grimes.

"I've only your word for it," Missenden told him. Then he said something to his companion, who replied in what, in happier circumstances, would have been a very pleasant contralto. The girl produced a mouth whistle, blew a piercing blast. In seconds two burly seamen appeared on the bridge. They grabbed Grimes and held him tightly while she ran practiced hands over his clothing. It was not the first time that she had searched a man for weapons. Then they dragged him below, unlocked a steel door and threw him into the tiny compartment beyond it. The heavily barred port made it obvious that it was the ship's brig.

They locked him in and left him there.

Grimes examined his surroundings by the light of the single dim bulb. Deck, deckhead and bulkheads were all of steel—but had they been of plyboard it would have made no difference: that blasted girl had taken from him the only possession that could possibly have been used as a weapon, his pocketknife. There was a steel-framed bunk, with a thin mattress and one sleazy blanket. There was a stained washbasin, and a single faucet which, when persuaded, emitted a trickle of rusty water. There was a bucket—plastic, not metal. Still, it could have been worse. He could sleep, perhaps, and he would not die of thirst. Fully clothed, he lay down on the bunk. He realized that he was physically tired; his desperate leap for the gangway had taken something out of him. And the ship was moving gently now, a slight, soporific roll, and the steady hum and vibration of the turbines helped further to induce slumber. There was nothing he could do, absolutely nothing, and to lose valuable sleep by useless worry would have been foolish. He slept.

It was the girl who awakened him.

She stood there, bending over him, shaking his shoulder. When he stirred she stepped sharply back. She was holding a pistol, a revolver of Terran design if not manufacture, and she looked as though she knew how to use it; and she was one of those women whose beauty is somehow accentuated by juxtaposition to lethal ironmongery. Yes, she was an attractive wench, with her greenish, translucent skin that did not look at all odd, with her fine, strong features, with her sleek, short-cut blue hair, and her slim yet rounded figure that even the rough uniform could not hide. She was an officer of some sort, although what the silver braid on the sleeves of her tunic signified Grimes could not guess. Not that he felt in the mood for guessing games; he was too conscious of his own unshaven scruffiness, of the aches and pains resulting from his athletics of the previous night and from the hardness of the mattress.

She said, in fair enough English, "Your Mr. Missenden would see you."

"He's not *my* Mr. Missenden," replied Grimes testily. Why did everybody ascribe to him the ownership of the late second officer of *Rim Dragon*?

"Come," she said, making an upward jerking motion of the pistol barrel.

"All right," grumbled Grimes. "All right."

He rolled off the narrow bunk, staggered slightly as he made his way to the washbasin. He splashed water over his face, drank some from his cupped hands. There was no towel. He made do with his handkerchief. As he was drying himself he saw that the door was open and that a seaman was standing beyond it. Any thoughts that he had entertained of jumping the girl and seizing her gun—if he could—evaporated.

"Follow that man," she ordered. "I will follow you."

Grimes followed the man, through alleyways and up companionways. They came at last to the bridge. Missenden was there, striding briskly back and forth as though he had been at sea all his life. In the wheelhouse the helmsman was intent on his own task. Grimes noted that the standard compass periscope had been withdrawn and that the man was concentrating upon the binnacle housing the ocean passage compass. So they still used that system. But why shouldn't they? It was a good one. He looked out to the sea, up to the sky. The morning was calm, but the sun was hidden by a thick, anti-cyclonic overcast. The surface of the sea was only slightly ruffled and there was a low, confused swell.

"Missenden," called the girl.

Missenden stopped his pacing, walked slowly to the wheelhouse. With his dyed hair and skin he looked like a Tharnian, a Tangaroan, and in his borrowed uniform he looked like a seaman. He also looked very pleased with himself.

"Ah, Commodore," he said, "welcome aboard. You've met Miss Ellevie, I think. Our radio officer."

"You'd better tell Miss Ellevie to send a message to the High Priest for me, Mr. Missenden."

Missenden laughed harshly. "I'll say this for you, Commodore, you do keep on trying. Why not accept the inevitable? You're in Tangaroan hands; in fact you put yourself in their—our—hands. The Council of Barons has already been informed, and they have told me that they want you alive. If possible."

"Why?" asked Grimes bluntly.

"Use your loaf, Commodore. First, it's possible that we may be able to persuade you to press for the establishment of trade relations between the Confederacy and Tangaroa. You do pile on quite a few G's in this sector of the galaxy, you know. Or should I say that you do draw a lot of water? And if you play, it could be well worth your while."

"And if I don't play?"

"Then we shall be willing to sell you back to your lords and masters. At a fair price of course. A squadron of armed atmosphere fliers? Laser weapons? Missiles with nuclear warheads?"

"That's for *your* lords and masters to decide."

Missenden flushed and the effect, with his green-dyed skin, was an odd one. He said to the girl, "That will do, Ellevie. I'll let you know when I want you again." He walked out to the wing of the bridge, beckoning Grimes to follow. When he turned to face the Commodore he was holding a pistol in his right hand.

He said, "Don't try anything. When I was in the navy of New Saxony I was expert in the use of hand guns of all descriptions. But I'd like a private talk. Ellevie knows English, so I sent her below. The man at the wheel may have a smattering, but he won't overhear from where we are now."

"Well?" asked Grimes coldly.

"We're both Earthmen."

"*I* am, Mr. Missenden."

"And I am, by ancestry. These Tharnians are an inferior breed, but if they see that *you* can be humiliated—"

"—they'll realize that *you* aren't the Galactic Superman you set yourself up to be."

Missenden ignored this, but with an effort. He said, "My position in this ship is rather . . . precarious. The crew doesn't trust me. I'm captain, yes—but only because I'm the only man on board who can navigate."

"But can you?"

"Yes, damn you! I've read the textbooks—it was all the bastards gave me to read when I was holed up down in the secret compartment. And anybody who can navigate a starship can navigate one of these hookers! Anyhow . . . anyhow, Commodore, it will be better for both of us if we maintain the pretense that you are a guest rather than a prisoner. But I must have your parole."

"My parole? What can I do?"

"I've heard stories about you."

"Have you? Very well, then, what about this? I give you my word not to attempt to seize the ship."

"Good. But not good enough. Will you also give your word not to signal, by any means, to aircraft or surface vessels?"

"Yes," agreed Grimes after a short hesitation.

"And your word not to interfere, in any way, with the ship's signaling equipment?"

"Yes."

"Then, Commodore, I feel that we may enjoy quite a pleasant cruise. I can't take you down yet; I relieved the lookout for his breakfast. You'll appreciate that we're rather shorthanded—as well as the Old Man and the three mates half the deck crew was left ashore, and two of the engineers. I can't be up here all the time, but I do have to be here a lot. And the lookouts have orders to call me at once if they sight another ship or an aircraft."

"And, as you say, you're the only navigator." *The only* human *navigator,* Grimes amended mentally.

The lookout came back to the bridge then, and Missenden took Grimes down to what was to be his cabin. It was a spare room, with its own attached toilet facilities, on the same deck as the captain's suite, which, of course, was now occupied by Missenden. It was comfortable, and the shower worked, and there was even a tube of imported depilatory cream for Grimes to use. After he had cleaned up he accompanied Missenden down to the saloon, a rather gloomy place paneled in dark, unpolished timber. Ellevie was already seated at one end of the long table, and halfway along it was an officer who had to be an engineer. Missenden took his seat at the head of the board, motioned to Grimes to sit at the right. A steward brought in cups and a pot of some steaming, aromatic brew, returning with what looked like two deep plates of fish stew.

But it wasn't bad and, in any case, it was all that there was.

After the meal Missenden returned to the bridge. Grimes

accompanied him, followed him into the chart room, where he started to potter with the things on the chart table. Grimes looked at the chart—a small-scale oceanic one. He noted that the Great Circle track was penciled on it, that neat crosses marked the plotting of dead reckoning positions at four hourly intervals. He looked from it to the ticking log clock on the forward bulkhead. He asked, "This submerged log of yours—does it run fast or slow?"

"I . . . I don't know, Commodore. But if the sky clears and I get some sights I'll soon find out."

"You think you'll be able to?"

"Yes. I've always been good with languages, and I've picked up enough Tangaroan to be able to find my way through the ephemeris and reduction tables."

"Hmm." Grimes looked at the aneroid barometer—another import. It was still high. With any luck at all the anti-cyclonic gloom would persist for the entire passage. In any case, he doubted if Missenden's first attempt to obtain a fix with sextant and chronometer would be successful.

He asked, "Do you mind if I have a look around the ship? As you know, I'm something of an authority on the history of marine transport."

"I do mind!" snapped Missenden. Then he laughed abruptly. "But what could you do? Even if you hadn't given your parole, what could you do? All the same, I'll send Ellevie with you. And I warn you, that girl is liable to be trigger happy."

"Have you known her long?"

Missenden scowled. "Too long. She's the main reason why I'm here."

Yes, thought Grimes, *the radio officer of a merchant vessel is well qualified for secret service work, and when the radio officer is also an attractive woman . . .* He felt sorry for Missenden, but only briefly. He'd had his fun; now he was paying for it.

Missenden went down with Grimes to the officers' quarters, found Ellevie in her room. She got up from her chair without any great enthusiasm, took a revolver from a drawer in her desk, thrust it into the side pocket of her tunic.

"I'll go now," said Missenden.

"All right," she answered in a flat voice. Then, to Grimes, "What you want to see?"

"I was on this world years ago," he told her.

"I know."

"And I was particularly impressed by the . . . the ocean passage compasses you had, even then, in your ships. Of course, it was all sail in those days."

"Were you?"

Grimes started pouring on the charm. "No other race in the galaxy has invented such ingenious instruments."

"No?" She was beginning to show a flicker of interest. "And did you know, Commodore Grimes, that it was not a wonderful priest who made the first one? No. It was not. It was a Baron Lennardi, one of my ancestors. He was—how do you put it? A man who hunts with birds?"

"A falconer."

"A falconer?" she repeated dubiously. "No matter. He had never been to the University, but he had clever artisans in his castle. His brother, whom he loved, was a—how do you say sea raider?"

"A pirate."

She took a key from a hook by the side of her desk. "Second Mate looks after compass," she said. "But Second Mate not here. So I do everything."

She led the way out into the alleyway, then to a locked door at the forward end of the officers' accommodation, to a room exactly on the center line of the ship, directly below the wheelhouse. She unlocked and opened the door, hooked it back. From inside came an ammonia-like odor. In the center of the deck was a cage, and in the cage was a bird—a big, ugly creature, dull gray in color, with ruffled plumage. It was obvious that its wings had been brutally amputated rather than merely clipped. Its almost globular body was imprisoned in a metallic harness, and from this cage within a cage a thin yet rigid shaft ran directly upward, through the deckhead and, Grimes knew, through a casing in the master's day cabin and, finally, to the card of the ocean passage compass. As Grimes watched, Ellevie took a bottle of water from a rack, poured some into the little trough that formed part of the harness. Then from a box she took a spoonful of some stinking brown powder, added it to the water. The bird ignored her. It seemed to be looking at something, for something, something beyond the steel bulkhead that was its only horizon, something beyond the real horizon that lay forward and outside of the metal wall. Its scaly feet scrabbled on the deck as it made a minor adjustment of course.

And it—or its forebears—had been the only compasses when Grimes had first come to this planet. Even though the Earthmen had introduced the magnetic compass and the gyro compass, this was still the most efficient for an ocean passage.

Cruelty to animals is penalized only when commerical interests are not involved.

"And your spares?" asked Grimes.

"Homeward spare—right forward," she told him. "Ausiphal compass and one spare—right aft."

"So you don't get them mixed?" he suggested. She smiled contemptuously. "No danger of that." "Can I see them?"

"Why not? May as well feed them now."

She almost pushed Grimes out of the master compass room, followed him and locked the door. She led the way to the poop, but Grimes noticed that a couple of unpleasant looking seamen tailed after him. Even though the word had been passed that he had given his parole he was not trusted.

The Ausiphal birds were in a cage in the poop house. As was the case with the Tangaroa birds, their wings had been amputated. Both of them were staring dejectedly directly astern. And both of them (even though dull and ruffled their plumage glowed with gold and scarlet) were females.

Grimes followed Ellevie into the cage, the door to which was at the forward end of the structure. He made a pretense of watching interestedly as she doled out the water and the odoriferous powder— and picked up two golden tail feathers from the filthy deck. She straightened and turned abruptly. "What you want those for?"

"Flies," he lied inspiredly, "Dry flies."

"*Flies?*"

"They're artificial lures, actually. Bait. Used for fishing."

"Nets," she stated. "Or explosives."

"Not for sport. We use a rod, and a line on the end of it, and the hook and the bait on the end of that. Fishermen are always experimenting with different baits. . . ."

The suspicion faded from her face. "Yes, I remember. Missenden gave me a book—a magazine? It was all about outdoor sports. But this fishing . . . Crazy!"

"Other people have said it, too. But I'd just like to see what sort of flies I can tie with these feathers when I get home."

"If you get home," she said nastily.

Back in his cabin, Grimes went over mentally what he had learned about the homers, which was as good a translation as any of their native name, during his visit to Tharn. They were land birds, but fared far out to sea in search of their food, which was fish. They *always* found their way back to their nests, even when blown thousands of miles away by severe storms, their powers of endurance being phenomenal. Also, whenever hurt or frightened, they headed unerringly for home—by the shortest possible route, which was a Great Circle course.

Used as master compasses, they kept the arrowhead on the card of the steering compass pointed directly toward wherever it was that they had been born—even when that was a breeding pen in one of the seaport towns. On a Mercator chart the track would be a curve, and according to a magnetic or a gyrocompass the ship would be continually changing course; but on a globe a Great Circle is the shortest distance between two points.

Only one instinct did they possess that was more powerful, more overriding than the homing instinct.

The sex instinct.

Grimes had given his word. Grimes had promised not to do certain things—and those things, he knew, were beyond his present capabilities in any case. But Grimes, as one disgruntled Rim Runners' captain had once remarked, was a stubborn old bastard. And Grimes, as the Admiral commanding the navy of the Rim Worlds Confederacy had once remarked, was a cunning old bastard. Sonya, his wife, had laughed when told of these two descriptions of her husband, and had laughed still louder when he had said plaintively that he didn't like to be called old.

Nonetheless, he was getting past the age for cloak and dagger work, mutiny on the high seas and all the rest of it. But he could still use his brains.

Kawaroa's shorthandedness was a help. If the ship had been normally manned he would have found it hard, if not impossible, to carry out his plan. But, insofar as the officers were concerned, the two engineers were on alternate watches, and off-duty hours would be spent catching up on lost sleep. That left Ellevie—but she had watches to keep, and one of these two hour stretches of duty coincided with and overlapped evening twilight. Missenden was not a watchkeeper, but he was, as he was always saying, the only navigator, and on this evening there seemed to be the possibility of breaks appearing in the overcast. There had been one or two during the day, but never where the sun happened to be. And insofar as evening stars were concerned out here on the Rim, there were very, very few. On a clear evening there would have been three, and three only, suitably placed for obtaining a fix. On this night the odds were against even one of the three appearing in a rift in the clouds before the horizon was gone.

Anyhow, there was Missenden, on the bridge, sextant in hand, the lid of the chronometer box in the chart room open, making an occasional gallop from one wing to the other when it seemed that a star might make a fleeting appearance. Grimes asked if he might help, if he could take the navigator's times for him. Missenden said no, adding that the *wrong* times would be no help at all. Grimes looked hurt, went down to the boat deck, strolled aft. The radio shack was abaft the funnel. He looked in, just to make sure that Ellevie was there. She was, and she was tapping out a message to somebody. Grimes tried to read it—then realized that even if the code was Morse the text would be in Tangaroan.

He went down to the officers' deck. All lights, with the exception of the dim police bulbs in the alleyways, were out. From one of the cabins came the sound of snoring. He found Ellevie's room without any trouble; he had been careful to memorize the squiggle over her door that meant *Radio Officer*. He walked to the desk, put his hand along the side of it. Yes, the key was there. Or *a* key. But it was the only one. He lifted it from its hook, stepped back into the alleyway, made his way forward.

Yes, it was the right key. He opened the door, shut it behind him, then groped for the light switch. The maimed, ugly bird ignored him; it was still straining at its harness, still scrabbling now and again at the deck as it made some infinitesimal adjustment of course. It ignored him—until he pulled one of the female's tail features from his pocket. It squawked loudly then, its head turning on its neck to point at the potent new attraction, its clumsy body straining to follow. But Grimes was quick. His arm, his hand holding the feather shot out, steadied over the brass strip let into the deck that marked the ship's center line. But it had been close, and he had been stupid. The man at the wheel would have noticed if the compass card had suddenly swung a full ninety degrees to starboard—and even Missenden would have noticed if the ship had followed suit. (And would he notice the discrepancies between magnetic compass and ocean passage compass? Did he ever compare compasses? Probably not. According to Captain Dingwall he was the sort of navigator who takes far too much for granted.)

Grimes, before Missenden had ordered him off the bridge, had been able to study the chart. He assumed—he had to assume—that the dead reckoning position was reasonably accurate. In that case, if the ship flew off at a tangent, as it were, from her Great Circle, if she followed a rhumb line, she would miss the north coast of Tangaroa by all of a hundred miles. And if she missed that coast, another day's steaming would bring her into the territorial waters of Braziperu. There was probably some sort of coastal patrol, and even though surface and airships would not be looking for *Kawaroa* her description would have been sent out.

The rack containing water and food containers was on the forward bulkhead of the master compass room. It was secured to the plating with screws, and between wood and metal there was a gap. Grimes pushed the quill of the feather into this crack, being careful to keep it exactly over the brass lubber's line. He remembered that the male homer had paid no attention to the not-so-artificial lure until he pulled it out of his pocket. Had his own body odor masked the smell of it? Was there a smell, or was it some more subtle emanation? He had learned once that the male birds must be kept beyond a certain distance from the females, no matter what intervened in the way of decks or bulkheads. So . . . ? His own masculine aura . . . ? The fact that he had put the feathers in the pocket that he usually kept his pipe in . . . ?

He decided to leave the merest tip of the feather showing, nonetheless. He had noted that Ellevie went through her master compass tending routine with a certain lack of enthusiasm; probably she would think that the tiny touch of gold was just another rust speck on the paintwork.

He waited in the foul-smelling compartment for what seemed like far too long a time. But he had to be sure. He decided, at last, that his scheme was working. Before the planting of the feather the maimed bird had been shifting to starboard, the merest fraction of a degree at a time, continually. Now it was motionless, just straining at its harness.

Grimes put out the light, let himself out, locked up, then returned the key to Ellevie's cabin. He went back up to the bridge, looked into the chart room. It seemed that Missenden had been able to take one star, but that his sums were refusing to come out right.

The voyage wore on. It was not a happy one, especially for Grimes. There was nothing to read, and nobody to talk to except Missenden and Ellevie—and the former was all too prone to propagandize on behalf of the Galactic Superman, while the latter treated Grimes with contempt. He was pleased to note, however, that they seemed to be getting on each other's nerves. The honeymoon, such as it had been, was almost over.

The voyage wore on. No other ships were sighted, and the heavily clouded weather persisted. Once or twice the sun showed through, and once Missenden was able to obtain a sight, to work out a position line. It was very useful as a check of distance run, being almost at right angles to the course line.

"We shall," announced Missenden proudly, "make our landfall tomorrow forenoon."

"Are you sure?" asked Grimes mildly.

"Of course I'm sure." He prodded with the points of his dividers at the chart. "Look! Within five miles of the D.R."

"Mphm," grunted Grimes.

"Cheer up, Commodore! As long as you play ball with the barons they won't boil you in oil. All you have to do is be reasonable."

"I'm always reasonable," said Grimes. "The trouble is that too many other people aren't."

The other man laughed. "We'll see what the Council of Barons has to say about that. I don't bear you any malice—well, not much— but I hope I'm allowed to watch when they bring you around to their way of thinking."

"I hope you never have the pleasure," snapped Grimes, going below to his cabin.

The trouble was that he was not sure. Tomorrow might be arrival day at Port Paraparam on Tangaroa. It might be. It might not. If he started taking too much interest in the navigation of the ship—if, for example, he took it upon himself to compare compasses—his captors would at once smell a rat. He recalled twentieth century sea stories he had read, yarns in which people, either goodies or baddies, had thrown ships off course by hiding an extra magnet in the vicinity of the steering compass binnacle. *Those old bastards had it easy,* he thought. *Magnetism is straightforward; it's not like playing around with the tail feathers of a stupid bird.*

He did not sleep well that night, and was up on bridge before breakfast, with Missenden. Through a pair of binoculars he scanned the horizon, but there was nothing there, no distant peaks in silhouette against the pale morning sky.

The two men were up on the bridge again after breakfast. Still there was nothing ahead but sea and sky. Missenden was beginning to look worried—and Grimes's spirits had started to rise. Neither of them went down for the midday meal, and it was significant that the steward did not come up to ask if they wanted anything. There was something in the atmosphere of the ship that was ugly, threatening. The watches—helmsmen and lookouts—were becoming increasingly surly.

"I shall stand on," announced Missenden that evening. "I shall stand on. The coast is well lit, and this ship has a good echometer."

"But no radar," said Grimes.

"And whose fault is that?" flared the other. "Your blasted pet priests'. *They* say that they won't introduce radar until it can be manufactured locally!"

"There are such things as balance of trade to consider," Grimes told him.

"Balance of trade!" He made it sound like an obscenity. Then: "But I can't understand what went wrong . . . the dead reckoning . . . my observed position . . ."

"The log could be running fast. And what about set? Come to that, did you allow for accumulated chronometer error?"

"Of course. In any case, we've been getting radio time signals."

"Are you sure that you used the right date in the ephemeris?"

"Commodore Grimes, as I told you before, I'm a good linguist. I can read Tangaroan almost as well as I can read English."

"What about index error on that sextant you were using?"

"We stand on," said Missenden stubbornly.

Grimes went down to his cabin. He shut the door and shot the securing bolt. He didn't like the way the crew was looking at the two Earthmen.

Morning came, and still no land.

The next morning came, and the next. The crew was becoming mutinous. To Missenden's troubles—and he was, by now, ragged from lack of sleep—were added a shortage of fresh water, the impending exhaustion of oil fuel. But he stood on stubbornly. He wore two holstered revolvers all the time, and the ship's other firearms were locked in the strong room. And what about the one that Ellevie had been waving around? wondered Grimes.

He stood on—and then, late in the afternoon, the first dark peak was faintly visible against the dark, clouded sky. Missenden rushed into the chart room, came back out. "Mount Rangararo!" he declared.

"Doesn't look like it," said Ellevie, who had come on to the bridge.

"It must be." A great weight seemed to have fallen from his shoulders. "What do you make of it, Commodore?"

"It's land," admitted Grimes.

"Of course it's land! And look! There on the starboard bow! A ship. A cruiser. Come to escort us in."

He snapped orders, and *Kawaroa's* ensign was run up to the gaff, the black mailed fist on the scarlet ground. The warship, passing on their starboard beam, was too far distant for them to see her colors. She turned, reduced speed, steered a converging course.

The dull *boom* of her cannon came a long while after the flash of orange flame from her forward turret. Ahead of *Kawaroa* the exploding shell threw up a great fountain of spray. It was Grimes who ran to the engine room telegraph and rang *Stop*. It was Ellevie who, dropping her binoculars to the deck, cried, "A Braziperuan ship!" Then she pulled her revolver from her pocket and aimed it at Missenden, yelling, "Terry traitor!" Unluckily for her she was standing just in front of Grimes, who felled her with a rabbit punch to the back of the neck. He crouched, scooped up the weapon and straightened. He said, "You'd better get ready to fight your faithful crew away from the bridge, Missenden. We should be able to hold them off until the boarding party arrives." He snapped a shot at the helmsman, who, relinquishing his now useless wheel, was advancing on them threateningly. The man turned tail and ran.

"You're behind this!" raved Missenden. "What did you do? You gave your word . . ."

"I didn't do anything that I promised not to."

"But . . . what went wrong?"

Grimes answered with insufferable smugness. "It was just a case of one bird-brained navigator trusting another."

The tidying up did not take long. Missenden's crew did not put up even a token resistance to be the boarding party sent from the warship. *Kawaroa* was taken into the nearest Braziperuan port, where her crew was interned pending decisions as to its eventual fate. Grimes and Missenden—the latter under close arrest—made the voyage back to University City by air. The Commodore did not enjoy the trip; the big blimp seemed to him to be a fantastically flimsy contraption and, as it was one of the hydrogen-filled craft, smoking was strictly forbidden.

He began to enjoy himself again when he was back in University City, although the task of having to arrange for the deportation of the sullen Missenden back to New Saxony was a distasteful one. When this had been attended to Grimes was finally able to relax and enjoy the hospitality and company of the High Priest and his acolytes, none of whom subscribed to the fallacy that scholarship goes hand and hand with asceticism. He would always remember the banquet at which he was made an Honorary Admiral of the Ausiphalian Navy.

Meanwhile, his passage had been arranged on the Lornbound *Rim Cayman*, aboard which Missenden would also be traveling on the first leg of *his* long and miserable voyage home. It came as a surprise, therefore, when he received a personal telephone call from the Honorable Clifton Weeks, the Rim Worlds' ambassador to Tharn. "I hope that you're in no hurry to be getting home, Commodore," said the fat man. Grimes could tell from the Ambassador's expression that he hoped the reverse.

"Not exactly," admitted Grimes, enjoying the poorly concealed play of expressions over the other's pudgy features.

"Hrrmph! Well, sir, it seems that our masters want you on Mellise."

"What for, sir?" asked Grimes.

"Don't ask me. I'm not a spaceman. I didn't open the bloody world up to commerce. All that I've been told is that you're to arrange for passage to that planet on the first available ship. You're the expert."

On what? wondered Grimes. He said sweetly, "I'm looking forward to the trip, Mr. Ambassador."

≈ Part 3 ≈
The Tin Fishes

COMMODORE JOHN GRIMES was proceeding homeward from Tharn the long way around—by way of Groller, Stree and Mellise, by the route that he, in the old *Faraway Quest,* had opened and charted so many years ago.

On all the worlds he was still remembered. On Tharn the spaceport was named after him. In Breardon, the planetary capital of Groller, a huge statue of him stood in Council Square. Grimes had stared up at the heroic monument with some distaste. Surely his ears didn't stand out that much, and surely his habitual expression was not quite so frog-like. He made allowances for the fact that the Grollens, although humanoid, are a batrachian people, but he still inspected himself for a long time in a full-length mirror on his return to the ship in which he was a passenger.

And then *Rim Kestrel*, in which Grimes had taken passage from Tharn, came to Mellise.

Mellise was a watery world, fully four-fifths of its surface being covered by the warm, mainly shallow seas. The nearest approach to a continent was a long, straggling chain of islands almost coincident with the equator. On one of the larger ones was the spaceport. There was no city, only a village in which the human spaceport personnel and the Rim Confederacy's ambassador and his staff lived. The Mellisans themselves were an amphibious race; like the Earthly cetacea they returned to the sea after having reached quite a high stage of evolution ashore. They could, if they had to, live and work on dry land, but they preferred the water. They dwelt in submarine villages where they were safe from the violent revolving storms that at times ravaged the surface. They tended their underwater farms, raising giant mollusks, great bivalves that yielded lustrous pearls, the main item of export. Their imports were the manufactured goods needed by an aquatic culture: nets, cordage, harpoon guns and the like. They could make these for themselves but, with the establishment of regular trade between themselves and the Confederacy, they preferred not to. Why should an essentially water-dwelling being work with fire and metals when pearl farming was so much more comfortable and pleasant?

Grimes rode down to the surface in *Rim Kestrel's* control room. Captain Paulus, the ship's master, was nervous, obviously did not like having his superior there to watch his ship-handling. But he was competent enough, although painfully cautious. Not for him the almost meteoric descent favored by other masters. His Inertial Drive delivered a thrust that nearly countered the planet's gravitational pull. The *Kestrel* drifted surfaceward like a huge balloon with barely negative buoyancy. But Paulus reacted fast enough when a jet stream took hold of the ship, canceling its effect by just the right application of lateral drive; reacted fast again when the vessel was shaken by clear air turbulence, pulling her out of the danger area with no delay. Nonetheless, Grimes was making mental notes. The efficiency of the spaceport's meteorological observatory left much to be desired; Paulus should have been warned by radio of the disturbances through which he had passed. (But he, Grimes, had made his first landing here before there was a spaceport, let alone spaceport facilities. He had brought the *Quest* down through the beginnings of a hurricane.)

The Commodore looked at the vision screen that showed, highly magnified, what lay aft and below. There were the islands, each one raggedly circular, each one ringed by a golden beach that was ringed, in its turn, by white surf. There was the cloudy green of shallow water, the clear blue of the deeper seas. Inland was the predominant purple of the vegetation.

Yes, it was a pleasant world, Mellise. Even here, out on the Rim, it could have been developed to a holiday planet, rivaling if not surpassing Caribbea. If the Mellisans had been obliged to deal with the Interstellar Federation rather than with the Rim Worlds Confederacy, this probably would have been the case. Grimes, whose first years in space had been as an officer in the Federation's Survey Service, knew all too well that the major Terran galactic power was far more concerned with the rights of other intelligent races in theory than in practice—unless there was some political advantage to be gained by posing as liberator, conservator or whatever.

He could see the white spaceport buildings now, gleaming in the light of the afternoon sun, startlingly distinct against their backdrop of purple foliage. He could see the pearly gray of the apron, and on it the black geometrical shadows cast by cranes and conveyor belts and gantries. He could even see the tiny, blinking stars that were the three beacons, the markers of the triangle in the center of which *Rim Kestrel* was to land. He wished that Paulus would get on with it. At this rate it would be after sunset by the time the ship was down.

After sunset it was, and the night had fallen with the dramatic suddenness to be expected in the low latitudes of any planet. Overhead the sky was clear and almost empty, save for the opalescent arc that was the upper limb of the Galactic Lens, low on the western horizon. Paulus had ordered all ports throughout the ship opened, and through them flowed the warm breeze, the scents of growing and flowering things that would have been cloyingly sweet had it not been for the harsh tang of salt water. There was the distant murmur of surf and, even more distant, a grumble of thunder.

"Thank you, Captain Paulus," said Grimes formally. "A very nice set-down."

And so it had been. Merchant captains, after all, are not paid to put their ships in hazard.

Port formalities were few. The Mellisans cared little about such matters as health, customs and immigration regulations. The port captain, a Rim Worlder, took care of all such details for them; and insofar as vessels owned by the Confederacy were concerned there was not even the imposition of port dues. After all, the levying of such charges would have been merely robbing Peter to pay Paul. The rare outside ships—the occasional Interstellar Transport Commission *Epsilon* Class tramp, the infrequent Empire of Waverley freighter, the once-in-a-blue-moon Shakespearian Sector trader—were, presumably, another matter. They would at least pay port dues.

Grimes sat with Captain Paulus and Stacey, the port captain, in Paulus' day cabin. Cold drinks were on the table before them. The Commodore was smoking his foul pipe, Paulus was nervously lighting one cigarette after another, and Captain Stacey had between his fleshy lips a peculiarly gnarled cigar of local manufacture. It looked as though it had been rolled from dry seaweed, and smelt like it. ("An acquired taste," Stacey had told them. "Like to try one?" They had refused.)

"Only a small shipment of pearls this time," Stacey said. "The pearl fishers—or farmers—are having their troubles."

"Disease again?" asked Paulus.

"No. Not this time. Seems to be a sort of predatory starfish. Could be a mutation. Whether it is or not, it's a vicious bastard."

"I thought, Captain Stacey," said Grimes, "that the people here were quite capable of dealing with any of the dangerous life forms in their seas."

"Not this new starfish," Stacey told him. "It's a killer." He sipped his drink. "The natives knew that you were coming here almost as soon I did, Commodore. Telepathy? Could be. But, sir, you are almost a local deity. Old Wunnaara—he's the boss in these parts—said to me only this morning, 'Grimes *Wannarbo*'—and a *Wannarbo* is roughly halfway between a high chief and the Almighty—'will us help. . . .' Really touched by his faith, I was."

"I'm not a marine biologist," said Grimes. "But couldn't you, with your local knowledge, do something, Captain Stacey?"

"I'm not a marine biologist either, Commodore. It takes all my time to run the port."

And I recommended you for this appointment, thought Grimes, looking at the fat man. *I thought that this would be an ideal job for anybody as notoriously lazy as yourself. I thought that you couldn't do any harm here, and that you'd get on well with the Mellisans. But you can't do any good either.*

"They must produce pearls," stated Paulus, "if they're to pay for their imports. They've nothing else we want."

Nothing else that we want. . . thought Grimes. *But the Rim Confederacy is not alone in the galaxy.* He said, "Surely, Captain Stacey, you've found out what sort of weapons would be most effective against these things. They could be manufactured back on Lorn or Faraway, and shipped out here. And what about protective netting for the oyster beds?"

"Useless, Commodore," Stacy told him. "The starfish just tear to shreds even the heaviest nets, made from wire rope. As for weapons— poison has always been effective in the past, but not any longer."

"We have to do something to help these people," Grimes said definitely. "And, frankly, not altogether from altrusitic motives. As you should know, both Waverly and the Shakespearian Sector are anxious to expand their spheres of influence. If they can help Mellise and we can't . . ." The unspoken words "you'll be out of a soft job" hung in the air between them.

"They seem to rely upon *you* to help them, sir," Stacey grumbled.

"And perhaps I can," Grimes told him. "Perhaps I can."

Perhaps he could—but, as he had said, he was not a marine biologist. Even so, he knew of the parallel evolution of life forms on all Earth-type planets. And in the course of his career he had tangled with unfriendly and hungry beasts on more than a century of worlds; he was still around and the hostile animals were not. Variations on familiar patterns or utterly alien, all had fallen victim to human cunning and human weaponry—and human savagery. Man, after all, was still the most dangerous animal.

He said good night to Stacey and Paulus, told them that he was going outside the ship to stretch his legs. He made his way down to the after air lock, then down the ramp to the smooth, clean concrete of the apron. He walked away from the direction of the administration buildings and the human village, found a path that must lead down to the sea. On either side of it the feathery fronds of the trees rustled in the warm breeze. Overhead, Mellise's single moon, a ruddy globe with an almost unmarked surface, rode high in the sky.

Grimes came to the beach, to the pale, gently shelving stretch of coarse sand beyond which the surf was greenly luminescent. He kicked off his sandals and, carrying them, walked slowly down to the edge of the water. He missed Sonya.

He saw that a black, humanoid shape, outlined by the phosphorescence, was waddling ashore, splashing through the shallows. From its dark head two eyes that reflected the light of the moon stared at Grimes. The teeth glinted whitely in the long muzzle as it spoke. "*Meelongee,* Grimes *Wannarbo.*" Its voice was like that of a Siamese cat.

"*Meelongee,*" replied Grimes. He remembered that this was the word of greeting.

"You have come back." The English was oddly accented but perfectly understandable. "Yes. I have come back." "You . . . help?"

"I shall try."

The native was close to Grimes now, and the Commodore could smell the not unpleasant fishy odor of him. He could see, too, that he was old; in the moonlight the white hairs about the muzzle and the white patches of fur on the chest were plainly visible.

"You me remember?" There was a short, barking laugh. "No? I was cub when first you come to Mellise, Grimes *Wannarbo.* Now I am chief. My name—Wunnaara. And you, too, are chief—not of one skyship, but of many. I am chief—but known little. You are chief—but know much."

"The *Rim Kestrel* lifts tomorrow," said Grimes.

"But you will stay, *Wannarbo?* You will stay?"

Grimes made his decision. If there was anything that he could do he would be furthering the interests of the Confederacy as well as helping the natives of Mellise. Stacey, it was obvious, would not lift one fat finger. The ambassador, like the port captain, was a no-hoper who had been sent to a planet upon which no emergencies were ever likely to arise. Grimes had not yet met him, but he knew him by repute.

"I will stay," he told the Chief.

"Then I tell my people. There is much to make ready." Wunnaara slipped back into the water, far more silently than he had emerged from it, and was gone.

The Commodore resumed his walk along the beach.

He came to a shallow bay, a crescent-like indentation in the shoreline. There was somebody out there in the water swimming—and by the flash of long, pale arms Grimes knew that it was not a native. Too, there was a pile of clothing on the sand. Grimes quickly stripped. It was a long time since he had enjoyed a swim in the sea. He divested himself of his clothing without embarrassment. Even though he was no longer a young man his body was still compact, well-muscled, had not begun to run to belly. He waded out into the warm salt water.

Suddenly he was confronted by the other swimmer. Only her head and smooth, bare shoulders were visible above the surface. Her eyes and her wide mouth were very dark against the creamy pallor of her face.

"Can't you read?" she was asking indignantly. "Didn't you see the notices? This beach is reserved for ladies only."

Her accent was not a Rim Worlds' one; it was more Pan-Terran than anything. That would account for her indignation; only on parts of the home planet did the absurd nudity taboo still persist. But this was not the home planet.

Grimes said mildly, "I'm sorry. I didn't know." He turned to leave the water.

She said, "Don't run away. We can talk, at this depth, modestly enough."

"I suppose we can."

"You're from the ship, aren't you? But of course, you must be . . . let me see, now . . . I've a good ear for accents, and you haven't quite lost the good old Terran twangs—Commodore Grimes, would it be?"

"Guilty," admitted Grimes. He was amused to note either that the tide was going out fast or that this companion had moved closer inshore. Her full breasts were fully exposed now, and there was more than a hint of the pale glimmer of the rest of her below the surface.

She said, "It's rather a pity that you're leaving tomorrow."

"I'm not leaving."

"You're not?" she asked sharply.

"No. I promised Chief Wunnaara that I'd stay to look into this plague of starfish."

"You promised Wunnaara . . ." Her voice was scornful. "But he's only a native, and has to be kept in his place. That's why I insisted on having this beach made private. I hated to think that those . . . *things* were spying on me, leering at me while I was swimming."

"And what about me, leering and spying?" Grimes asked sarcastically.

"But you're a Terran—"

"Ex-Terran, young lady. Very ex."

"—and we Terrans should stick together," she completed with a dazzling smile.

"I'm a Rim Worlder," Grimes told her severely. "And so must you be, if you're employed at the spaceport, no matter where you were born." He asked abruptly, "And what do you do, by the way?"

"I'm in the met. office," she said. "Then I shall see you tomorrow," stated Grimes.

"Good!" Her smile flashed on again.

"I shall be calling in to register a strong complaint," the Commodore went on.

He attempted to step past the girl, intending to swim out to the first line of breakers. Somehow she got in his way, and somehow both of them lost their balance and went down, floundering and splashing. Grimes got to his feet first, pulled the young woman to hers. He was suddenly conscious, as she fell against him, of the firmness and the softness of the body against his own. It was all very nice—and all a little too obvious. But he was tempted, and tempted strongly. Then, but with seeming reluctance, she broke away from him and splashed shoreward, her slim, rounded figure luminous in the moonlight.

Her voice floated back to him, "I still hope that it's a pleasant meeting tomorrow, Commodore!"

It was not as unpleasant as it could have been. The girl, Lynn Davis, was second in charge of the spaceport's meteorological office. By daylight, and clothed, she was still attractive. Her hair was a dark, dull-gleaming blonde and her eyes were so deep a blue as to be almost black. Her face was thin and intelligent, with both mouth and nose a little too pronounced for conventional prettiness. There was a resemblance to Sonya, his wife, that strongly attracted Grimes; more than a physical likeness, it was a matter of essential quality. This, at once, put Grimes on his guard. Sonya had held the rank of commander in the Federation's Survey Service, and in the Intelligence branch at that. But now Federation and Rim World Confederacy worked together, shared all information, kept no secrets from each other. Even so. . . .

Lynn Davis had all the answers ready. *Rim Kestrel* had been given no information on jet streams and clear air turbulence because there had been a breakdown of radar and other instruments. This, Grimes was made to feel, was *his* fault; the Rim Runners' Stores Department should have been more prompt in dealing with requisitions for spare parts. "And after all, Commodore," she told him sweetly, "*you* made the first landing here without any aid at all from the surface, didn't you?"

Grimes asked to see the instrument room. He thought that this request disconcerted her—but this was understandable enough. Any officer, in any service, likes to do things his own way and is apt to resent a superior's intrusion into his own little kingdom, especially when the superior is in a fault-finding mood. But she got up from behind her very tidy desk, led the Commodore out of the office and up a short flight of stairs.

At first glance the compartment looked normal enough; its counterpart could have been found at almost any human-operated spaceport throughout the galaxy. The deviations from the norm were also normal. On many worlds with a lack of recreational facilities the instrument room, with its laboratory and workshop equipment to one side of it, is an ideal place for hobbyists to work. The practice is officially frowned upon, but persists.

There was a tank there, a small aquarium, brilliantly lit. Grimes walked over to it. The only animal denizens were a dozen or so small starfish, brightly colored, spiny little beasts, unusually active. These, unlike their kind on the majority of worlds, seemed to prefer swimming to crawling as a means of locomotion, although they possessed, on the undersides of their limbs, the standard equipment of myriads of suckers.

"And who belongs to these?" asked Grimes.

"Me," she replied.

"Is marine biology your hobby?"

"I'm afraid not, Commodore. I just keep these because they're ornamental. They add something to the decor."

"Yes," he agreed. "Starfish." He walked to a bench where there was an intricacy of gleaming wire. "And what the hell's *this*?"

"A mobile," she told him. "Jeff Petersen, the met. officer, has artistic ambitions."

"And where is Mr. Peterson?"

"He's away. The crowd setting up the weather control station on Mount Llayilla asked Captain Stacey for the loan of him."

"Hmm. Well, I can't help feeling, Miss Davis, that if you and Mr. Peterson devoted more time to your work and less time to your hobbies you'd give incoming ships far better service."

She flared. "We never play around with our hobbies in our employer's time. And there's so little social life here that we must have something to occupy us when we're off duty."

"I'm not denying that, Miss Davis."

She switched on that smile again. "Why don't you call me Lynn, Commodore? Everybody else does."

He found himself smiling in reply. "Why not, Lynn?"

"Isn't that better? And, talking of social life, I'd like it very much if you came to my place some evening for dinner." She grinned rather than smiled this time. "I'm a much better cook than Mrs. Stacey."

That wouldn't be hard, thought Grimes. The Port Captain's wife, as he had learned that morning at breakfast, couldn't even fry an egg properly.

"Try to keep an evening open for me," she said.

"I'll try," he promised. He looked at his watch. "But I must go. I have an appointment with the Ambassador."

The Confederacy's Ambassador was a thin, languid and foppish man. In spite of the disparity in physical appearance he was cut from the same cloth as Captain Stacey. He was one of the barely competent, not quite bad enough to be fired but too lazy and too disinterested to be trusted with any major appointment. He drawled, "I can't order you not to stay, old man, any more than I can order you to stay. Let's face it—you pile on a few more G's (as you spacefaring types put it) than I do. But I still think that you're wasting your time. The natives'll have to pull their socks up, that's all. And tighten their belts for the time being—not that they have any belts to tighten. Ha, ha! You may have been first on this world, Commodore, but you haven't lived with these people as I have. They're a lazy, shiftless bunch. They won't stir a finger to help themselves as long as the Confederacy's handy to do it for them."

"And if the Confederacy won't," said Grimes flatly, "there's the Empire of Waverley. Or the Shakespearians. Or the Federation. Even the Shaara might find this planet interesting."

"Those communistic bumblebees? It might do the Mellisans a world of good if they did take over." He raised a slim, graceful wrist and looked at his watch. "Old Wunnaara's due about now. I don't encourage him—it takes *days* to get the fishy stink out of the Embassy—but he insisted."

"You could," pointed out Grimes, "have a room specially fitted for the reception of local dignitaries, something that duplicates, as far as possible, the conditions that they're used to."

"You don't understand, old man. It's taken me years, literally, to get this shack fitted and decorated the way that it should be. The *battles* I've had to fight with Appropriations! It's all a matter of keeping up a front, old man, showing the flag and all that. . . ."

A smartly uniformed Marine entered the elegant, too elegant *salon*.

"Chief Wunnaara, your Excellency."

"Show him in, Sergeant. Show him in. And attend to the air-conditioning, will you?"

Wunnaara was dressed for the occasion. His ungainly (on dry land) body was clad in a suit of what looked like coarse sacking, and riding high on a complicated harness-like framework was a tank, the contents of which sloshed as he walked. From this tank depended narrow tubes, connected to his clothing at various points. They dripped—both upon the cloth and upon the Ambassador's carpet. A goggled mask, water-filled, covered his eyes and the upper part of his face. The smell of fish was very evident.

"Your Excellency," he mewed. "*Meelongee*, Grimes *Wannarbo, meelongee.*"

"Greetings," replied the Ambassador, and, *"Meelongee,"* replied Grimes.

"Your Excellency, Grimes *Wannarbo* has agreed to help. He come with me now, I show him trouble."

"Do you want to go through with this, old man?" the Ambassador asked Grimes. "Really?"

"Of course. Would you know of any scuba outfits on this island? I've already asked Captain Stacey, and he says that the only ones here are privately owned."

"That is correct, Commodore. I could ask the sergeant to lend you his."

"Not necessary, Grimes *Wannarbo*," interjected the chief. "Already waiting on beach we have ship, what you call submarine."

"Good," said Grimes.

"You'd trust yourself to *that* contraption?" demanded the Ambassador in a horror-stricken voice. "It'll be one of the things that they use to take stores and equipment down to their farms."

"They work, don't they?"

"Yes, old man. But . . ."

"But I'd have thought, on a world like this, that the Ambassador would have his own, private submarine."

"I'm a diplomat, old man, not a sailor."

Grimes shrugged. He said formally. "With your permission, your Excellency, I shall accompany Chief Wunnaara."

"Permission granted, old man. Don't get your feet wet."

The submarine had been pulled up on the beach, onto a ramp that had been constructed there for that purpose, that ran from the water to a low warehouse. Apart from its wheeled undercarriage it was a conventional enough looking craft, torpedo-shaped, with a conning tower amidships and rudder and screw propeller aft, with hydroplanes forward and amidships. A wooden ladder had been placed on the ramp to give access to the conning tower. Wunnaara gestured to Grimes to board first. The Commodore clambered up the ladder with a certain lack of agility; the spacing of the rungs was adapted to the Mellisan, not the human, frame. He had the same trouble with the metal steps leading into the submarine's interior.

When he was down in what was obviously the craft's control room he looked about him curiously. It was easy enough to get a general idea of what did what to which; the Mellisans, with no written language of their own, had adopted Terran English to their requirements. There were depth gauges, steering, hydroplane and engine controls, a magnetic compass. Inside an aluminum rather than a steel hull it should, thought Grimes, function quite satisfactorily. What had him puzzled was a bundle of taut bladders, evidently taken from some sea plant. Beside them, in a rack on the bulkhead, was a sharp knife. And he did not quite approve of the flowerpot that was hanging to one side of the steering gear, in which was growing a vividly blue, fernlike plant. He recalled the conversation that he had had with Lynn Davis on the subject of hobbies.

Apart from these rather peculiar fittings the little ship was almost as she had been when built to Mellisan specifications at the Seacraft Yard on Thule: the original electric motors, a big bank of heavy-duty power cells, a capacious cargo hold (now empty) and no accommodation whatsoever. He had noticed, on his way down through the conning tower, that the compartment, with its big lookout ports, could still be used as an air lock.

Wunnaara joined him, accompanied by another native dressed as he was. The younger Mellisan went straight to the wheel, from which all the other controls were easily accessible. Wunnaara asked Grimes to return with him to the conning tower. The upper hatch, he saw, was shut now, but there was an unrestricted view all around from the big ports. And although the lower hatch remained open there was ample room, on the annular platform, to walk around it. Wunnaara yelped some order down through the opening. Slowly at first, then faster, the submarine started to move, sliding astern down the ramp on her wheels. She slipped into the water with hardly any disturbance, and when she was afloat at least half of her hull was above the surface. Electric motors hummed and she backed away from the beach, her head swinging to starboard as she did so. She came around well and easily, and when she was broadside on to the shore, starting to roll uncomfortably in the swell, the coxswain put the engines ahead and the wheel hard over to complete the swing. Then, after surprisingly little fuss and bother, she was headed seaward, pitching easily, her straight wake pearly white on the blue water under the noonday sun.

A red marker buoy indicated the location of the pearl beds. Quietly, without any fuss, the ship submerged, dropping down below the surface as her ballast tanks were filled. Grimes went back to the control room; always keenly interested in ships—the ships of the sea as well as the ships of space—he wanted to see how this submersible was handled. He was alarmed when, as he completed his cautious descent down the ladder, the coxswain snatched that nasty looking knife from the rack on the bulkhead. But the Mellisan ignored him, slashed swiftly and expertly at one of the seaweed bladders. It deflated with a loud hiss. Behind Grimes, Wunnaara hooted with laughter. When he had the Commodore's attention he pointed to the absurd potted plant hanging almost over the compass. Its fronds had turned scarlet, but were already slowly changing back to blue. Grimes chuckled as he realized what was being done. This was air regeneration at its most primitive, but still effective. These submarines, when built, had been fitted with excellent air regeneration plants but, no doubt, the Mellisans preferred their own. The oxygen released from the bladder brought with it a strong smell of wet seaweed which, to them, would be preferable to the odorless gas produced by the original apparatus.

Grimes watched the coxswain until Wunnaara called him back to the conning tower. He was impressed by the Mellisan's competence. He was doing things that in a human operated submarine would have required at least four men. Could it be, he wondered, that a real sea man must, of necessity, be also a first-class seaman? He toyed, half humorously, with the idea of recruiting a force of Mellisan mercenaries, to be hired out to those few nations—on those few worlds where there was still a multiplicity of nations—which still relied upon sea power for the maintenance of their sovereignty.

Back in the conning tower he forgot his not-quite-serious money-making schemes. The submarine—as he already knew from his inspection of the depth gauges—was not running deep, but neither was she far from the sandy bottom. Ahead, astern and on either side were the pearl beds, the orderly rows of the giant bivalves. Among them worked Mellisans—who, like similar beings on other planets, including Earth, were able to stay under water for a very long time on one lungful of air. Some of them, explained Wunnaara, were planting the irritant in the mantle of the shellfish. Others were harvesting the pearls from mollusks that had been treated months previously. These were taken to the underwater depot for cleaning and sorting and, eventually, would be loaded into the submarine for carriage to the spaceport. But, said the Chief, this would be a poor harvest. . . .

From his vantage point he conned the ship, yelping orders down to the coxswain. Finally they were drifting over a long row of opened bivalves. Considerable force had been employed in this opening, the not typical Mellisan care. They could extract the pearl without inflicting permanent injury upon the creature inside the paired shells; in many cases here the upper valve had been completely shattered. In most cases no more than a few shreds of tattered flesh remained. And in all cases what had been a pearl was now only a scattering of opalescent dust.

Now the submarine was approaching the high wire net fence that had been erected to protect the pearl farm. It looked stout enough to stop a ship of this class—but *something* had come through it. *Something* had uprooted metal posts embedded in concrete;

something had snapped wire rope like so much sewing thread. It was not something that Grimes was at all keen to meet, not even in the comparative safety of this well-designed and -built submersible.

"You see?" mewed the Chief. "You see, Grimes *Wannarbo*?"

"Yes. I see."

"Then what do, Grimes *Wannarbo*? What do?" Under stress, the old Mellisan's English tended to deteriorate.

"I . . . I don't know. I shall have to see some of the starfish. Have you any in captivity, or any dead ones?"

"No. No can catch. No can kill."

There was a steady thumping sound, transmitted through the water, amplified by the hull plating.

"Alarm!" Wunnaara cried. "Alarm! Alarm!" He shouted something in his own language to the coxswain. The submarine changed course, her motors screaming shrilly as speed was increased to full—or a little over. She skimmed over the flat sandy bottom, raising a great cloud of disturbed particles astern of her.

Ahead there was a commotion of some kind—a flurry of dark, almost human figures, an occasional explosion of silvery air bubbles, a flashing of metallic-seeming tentacles, a spreading stain in the water that looked like a frightened horse as she came full astern—and then she hung there, almost motionless, on the outskirts.

There were half a dozen of the . . . *things*, the starfish, and a dozen Mellisans. Through the now murky water could be seen the wreckage of practically an entire row of the bivalves—shattered shells, crushed pearls, torn, darkly oozing flesh. The odd thing about it all was the gentleness of the marauders. They seemed to be trying to escape—and they were succeeding—but at the same time were avoiding the infliction of serious injury upon the guardians of the beds.

And they were such flimsy things. Or they looked flimsy, as though they had been woven from fragile metallic lace. They looked flimsy, but they were not. One of them was trapped in a net of heavy wire handled by three Mellisans. Momentarily it was bunched up, and then it . . . expanded, and the wires snapped in a dozen places. One of them received a direct hit from a harpoon—and the weapon, its point blunted and broken, fell harmlessly to the bottom.

They were free and clear now, all of them, looking more like gigantic silvery snowflakes than living beings. They were free and clear, swimming toward the breached barrier, their quintuple, feathery arms flailing the water. They were free and clear, and although the Mellisans gave chase there was nothing that anybody could do about them.

"You see?" said the Chief.

"I see," said Grimes.

He saw, too, what he would have to do. He would make his own report, of course, to Rim Runners' head office, recommending that something be done on a government level to maintain the flow of commerce between Mellise and the Confederacy. And he would have to try to persuade that pitiful nong of an ambassador to recommend to *his* bosses that a team qualified to handle the problem—say marine biologists and professional fishermen from Thule—be sent at once to Mellise. But it would not be at once, of course. Nobody knew better than Grimes how slowly the tide runs through official channels.

But. . . .

What could he, Grimes do? Personally, with his own two hands, with his own brain?

There had been something oddly familiar about the appearance of those giant Astersidea, about their actions. There had been something that evoked memories of the distant past, and something much more recent. What was it? Lynn Davis' gaudy pets in the brightly lit aquarium? They swam, of course, and these giant mutants (if mutants they were) were swimmers, but there the similarity ceased.

"What do, Grimes *Wannarbo*?" Wunnaara was insistent. "What do?"

"I . . . I don't know," replied the Commodore. "But I'll do something," he promised.

But what?

That night, back in his room in the port captain's residence, he did his homework. He had managed to persuade Captain Stacey to let him have the files on all Rim Runners' personnel employed on

Mellise, and also had borrowed from the Ambassador's library all six volumes of Trantor's very comprehensive *Mellisan Marine Life*. (Trantor should have been here now, but Trantor was dead, drowned two years ago in a quite stupid and unnecessary accident in the Ultimate Sea, on Ultimo, a body of water little larger than a lake.) Grimes skimmed through Trantor's work first, paying particular attention to the excellent illustrations. Nothing, nothing at all, resembled the creatures that he had seen, although most of the smaller starfish, like the ones he had seen in Lynn Davis' tank, subsisted by making forcible entry into the homes of unfortunate bivalves.

Then he turned to the files.

About half the spaceport employees were true Rim Worlders—born out on the Rim. The other half—like Grimes himself—were not, although all of them were naturalized citizens. Judging from the educational qualifications and service records of all of them, none of them would be capable of inducing a mutation. Grimes had hoped to turn up a biological engineer, but he was disappointed. And biological engineering is not the sort of thing that anybody takes up as a hobby; in addition to the years of study and training there is the quite expensive license to practice to obtain, and the qualifications for that are moral rather than academic or practical. Mary Shelley's Frankenstein is a permanent fixture in Man's mythology.

Feeling like a Peeping Tom, another permanent fixture, he leafed through Lynn Davis' service record. She was Terran-born, of course. Her real education had been at M.I.T., where she had graduated as a Bachelor of General Physics. After that she seemed to have specialized in meteorology. There had been a spell with Weather Control, North American Continent, and another spell with Weather Prediction, satellite-based. After that she had entered the service of Trans-Galactic Clippers as Spaceport Meteorological Officer. She had seen duty on Austral, Waverly, and Caribbea, all of them planets upon which T-G maintained its own spaceports. From Waverly she had gone to Caribbea—and on Caribbea she had blotted her copybook.

So, thought Grimes, *she's a compulsive gambler. She doesn't look like one. But they never do.* It was on Caribbea that she had become a regular habitué of the New Port of Spain Casino. She had, of course, worked out a system to beat the wheel—but the system hadn't worked out for her. There had been the unhappy business of the cracking of the T-G cashier's safe, allegedly thiefproof, but (luckily) very few thieves held a degree in Physics. There had been the new banknotes, the serial numbers of which were on record, that had turned up in the safe of the casino's cashier.

After that—the Rim Worlds.

A pity, said Grimes to himself. *A pity. But it could have been worse. If she'd gone to Elsinore, in the Shakespearian Sector, where they're notorious for their gambling, she'd really be in a mess by now.*

He turned up the file on Peterson. The absentee meteorologist was another ex-Terran, and also had been employed with Trans-Galactic Clippers. Grimes noted with interest that Petersen had spent a few weeks on El Dorado, popularly known as "the planet of the filthy rich." (Grimes had been there himself as a young man, as a junior officer in the Federation's Survey Service.) It seemed that a T-G ship had called there on a millionaires' cruise, and T-G had insisted on sending its own spaceport personnel there in advance.

Women, not money, had been Petersen's trouble. Twice he had been named as correspondent in an unsavory divorce case. If the ladies had not been the wives of prominent T-G executives it wouldn't have mattered so much—but they had been.

There could be a connection, thought Grimes. *There could be. Both of them from Earth, both of them T-G. . . .* He shrugged away the idea. After all, it had been said that if you threw a brick at random aboard any Rim Runners' ship, the odds are that you will hit an ex-officer of the Interstellar Transport Federation's vessels.

So it went on—case histories, one after the other, that made depressing reading and, insofar as the quite serious crisis on Mellise was concerned, a shortage of both motive and opportunity. But money could be a motive. Suppose, tomorrow, a foreign ship dropped in, and suppose that somebody aboard her said to old Wunnaara, "*We'll* fix your starfish for you—in return for full trading rights. . . ."

And whatever else I am, thought Grimes tiredly, *I'm not a starfish fixer.*

He poured himself a stiff drink and went to bed.

She said, "I hear that you've been looking through the personnel files, John. That wasn't very gentlemanly of you."

"How did you hear?" asked Grimes. "My doing so was supposed to be as secret as the files themselves."

"There aren't any secrets on this bloody planet, in this tiny community." Her face, as she stared at him over her candlelit dining table, was hard and hostile, canceling out the effects of an excellent meal. "And did you find what you were looking for?"

"No."

"What were you looking for?"

"Somebody who's capable of doing a spot of biological engineering."

"Did you find anybody?"

"No, Lynn."

"What about the spaceport quack?"

"Frankly," said Grimes, "I wouldn't go to him with a slight head cold."

"Frankly, my dear, neither would I." She laughed, and her manner softened. "So you're still no closer to solving the Mystery of the Mutated Starfish."

"No."

"Then I'll solve it for you. There was a bad solar flare about a year ago, and our atmospheric radiation count went up no end in consequence. There's the answer. But I'm glad that you stayed on Mellise, John. You've no idea how hungry a girl gets for intelligent company."

"I'm glad that I stayed, Lynn. For personal reasons. But I really wish that I could help old Wunnaara. . . ."

She said, "I don't like His Too Precious Excellency any more than you do, John, but I often feel that he's on the right tack as far as the natives are concerned. Let them help themselves."

He said, "I discovered this world. I feel, somehow, that it's my direct responsibility."

She replied a little bitterly, "I wish that you'd start shedding some of your feelings of responsibility, *Commodore*. Don't worry so much. Start having a good time, while you can."

And I could, too, he thought. *With a quite beautiful, available woman. But. . . .*

She said, "It's a wild night. Hurricane Lynn—I named it after me. You aren't walking back to old Stacey's place in this, surely?"

He said, "It's time I was going."

"You'll be drenched," she told him.

"All right. Then go. You can let yourself out."

For a tall girl she flounced well on her way from the little dining room to her bedroom.

Grimes sighed, cursing his retentive memory, his detailed recollection of the reports from all the planets with which Rim Runners traded. But he had to be sure, and he did not wish to make any inquiries regarding this matter on Mellise. He let himself out of the little dome-shaped cottage, was at once furiously assailed by the wind. Hurricane Lynn had not yet built up to its full intensity, but it was bad enough. There were great sheets of driving rain, and with them an explosion of spray whipped from the surface of the sea.

Luckily the spaceport was downwind from the village. Grimes ran most of the way. He didn't want to, but it was easier to scud before the gale than to attempt to maintain a sedate pace. He let himself into the port captain's large house. The Staceys were abed— he had told them that he would be late—but Captain Stacey called out from his bedroom, "Is that you, Commodore?"

"Who else, Captain? I shall be going out again shortly."

"What the hell for?" testily.

"I have to send a message. An important one."

"Telephone it through to the Carlotti Communications Office from here."

"I want to make sure it goes."

Grimes faintly overheard something about distrustful old bastards as he went to his own room, but ignored it.

There was a very cunning secret compartment built into his suitcase. The Commodore opened it, took from it a slim book. Then, with scratch pad and stylus, he worked rapidly and efficiently, finishing up with eleven gibberish groups. He put the book back in its hiding place, pocketed the pad. Then he had to face the stormy night again.

The duty operator in the Carlotti Office was awake, but only just. Had it not been for the growing uproar of the hurricane, penetrating even the insulated walls, he would not have been. He reluctantly put down his luridly covered book and, recognizing Grimes, said, "Sir?"

"I want this to go at once. To my office at Port Forlorn. Urgent." He managed a grin. "That's the worst of space travel. It's so hard to keep track of dates. But my secretary will be able to lay on flowers for the occasion."

The operator grinned back. Judging by the way that he was making a play for that snooty Lynn Davis the Commodore must be a gay old dog, he figured. He said, a little enviously, "Your message will be winging its way over the light-years in a jiffy, sir." He handed the Commodore a signals pad.

Grimes put down the address, transcribed the groups from his own pad, filled in his name and the other details in the space provided. He said, "Let me know how much it is. It's private."

The young man winked. "Rim Runners'll never know, sir."

"Still, I prefer to pay," said Grimes.

He watched the miniature Carlotti Beacon—it was like a Mobius Strip distorted to a long oval—turn on its mounting in the big star tank until it was pointing directly at the spark that represented the Lorn sun. He hoped that the big beacon on the roof of the building was turning, too. But it had to be. If it stopped, jammed, the little indicator would seize up in sympathy. In any case, it was shielded from the weather by its own dome.

The operator's key rattled rapidly in staccato Morse, still the best method of transmitting messages over vast distances. From the wall speaker blurted the dots and dashes of acknowledgment. Then the message itself was sent, and acknowledged.

"Thank you," said Grimes. "If there's a reply phone it through to me, please. I shall be at Captain Stacey's house."

"Very good, sir."

Grimes was relaxing under a hot shower when he heard the

telephone buzz. Wrapping a towel around himself, he hurried out of the bathroom, colliding with Captain Stacey.

"It's probably for me," he said.

"It would be," growled Stacey.

It was. It was in reply to Grimes's signal which, when decoded, had read, *Urgently require information on solar flares Mellise sun last year local.* It said, after Grimes had used his little book, *No repeat no solar flares Mellise sun past ten years.*

Somebody's lying, thought Grimes, *and I don't think it's my secretary.*

Hurricane Lynn, while it lasted, put a stop to any further investigations by Grimes. Apart from anything else, the sea people were keeping to their underwater houses, each of which was well stocked with air bladders and the carbon dioxide absorbing plants. He managed, however, to get back on friendly terms with Lynn Davis—or she with him; he was never quite sure which was the case. He found her increasingly attractive; she possessed a maturity that was lacking in all the other young women in the tiny human community. He liked her, but he suspected her—but of what? It was rather more than a hunch: there had been, for example, that deliberate lie about the solar flares. Grimes, who was an omnivorous reader, was well aware that fictional detectives frequently solved their cases by sleeping with the suspects. He wasn't quite ready to go that far; he had always considered such a *modus operandi* distinctly ungentlemanly.

Then Hurricane Lynn blew itself out and normally fine weather returned to the equatorial belt. Flying was once again possible, and Petersen came back to the spaceport from Mount Llayilla. Grimes didn't like him. He was a tall, athletic young man, deeply tanned, with sun-bleached hair and startlingly pale blue eyes. His features were too regular, and his mouth too sensual. The filed stories of his past amatory indiscretions made sense. And he was jealously possessive insofar as Lynn Davis was concerned. *She's nice, Commodore,* was the unspoken message that Grimes received, loud and clear. *She's mine. Keep your dirty paws off her.*

Grimes didn't like it, and neither did the girl. But the Commodore, now that the storm was over, was busy again. At least once daily he argued with the Ambassador, trying to persuade that gentleman to request the services of a team of marine biologists and professional fishermen. He composed and sent his own report to Rim Runners' head office. And, whenever conditions were suitable, he was out to the pearl beds with Wunnaara, at first in the little submarine and then in a skin diving outfit that the spaceport's repair staff had improvised for him. It was a bastard sort of rig, to quote the chief mechanic, but it worked. There was a spacesuit helmet with compressed air tanks, suitably modified. There was a pair of flippers cut from a sheet of thick, tough plastic. There was a spear gun and a supply of especially made harpoons, each of which had an explosive warhead, fused for impact. As long as these were not used at close range the person firing them should be reasonably safe.

Lynn Davis came into the maintenance workshop while Grimes was examining one of the projectiles.

"What's that, John?" she asked.

"Just a new kind of spear," he replied shortly.

"New—an' nasty," volunteered the chief mechanic, ignoring Grimes's glare. "Pack too much of a wallop for my taste. If you're too close to the target when one o' these goes off, you've had it."

"Explosive?" she asked.

"That's right."

She turned back to Grimes. "Are these safe, John?"

"Safe enough, as long as they're used carefully."

"But against starfish! Like using an elephant gun against a gnat!"

"There are starfish and starfish," he told her. "As everybody on this planet should know by this time."

"You think this will kill them?"

"It's worth giving it a go."

"Yes," she admitted. "I suppose so. . . ." Then, more briskly, "And when are you giving your secret weapon a trial?"

"There are a few modifications to be made," Grimes told her.

"They'll all be ready for you tomorrow morning," said the mechanic. "As promised."

She turned on her dazzling smile. "Then you'd better dine with me tonight, John. If you insist on playing with these dangerous toys there mightn't be another time." She laughed, but that odd, underlying note of seriousness persisted. She went on. "And Jeff will be out of our hair, I promise you that. There's a party on in the Carlotti Operations' Mess, and he *never* misses those."

"I've a pile of paper work, Lynn," Grimes told her.

"That can wait."

He made his decision. "All right, then. What time?"

"Whatever time suits you; 1800 hours, shall we say? For a few drinks first . . . ?" "Good. I'll be there."

He dressed carefully for the dinner party, paying even more attention to the contents of his pockets than to the clothes themselves. He had one of his hunches, and he knew he'd need the things that he was taking from the secret compartment of his suitcase. There was the Minetti automatic, with a spare clip, neither of which made more than a slight bulge in the inside breast pocket of his jacket. There was the pack of cigarillos. (Two of the slim, brown cylinders possessed very special properties, and were marked in such a way that only Grimes would be able to identify them.) *Marriage to an Intelligence officer,* he thought, *has its points. Something is bound to rub off.* There was the button on his suit that was a camera, and the other button that was a miniaturized recorder.

On the way from his room to the front door he passed through the lounge where Captain and Mrs. Stacey were watching a rather witless variety program on the screen of their playmaster. The Captain looked up and around, his fat, heavy face serious. He said, "I know that it's none of my business, Commodore, and that you're technically my superior, but we—Lucy and myself—think that you should be warned. Miss Davis is a dangerous woman. . . ."

"Indeed, Captain?"

"Yes, indeed. She leads men on, and then that Jeff Petersen is apt to turn nasty."

"Oh?"

An ugly flush suffused Stacey's face. "Frankly, sir, I don't give a damn if you are beaten up for playing around with a girl young enough to be your granddaughter. But because you're Astronautical Superintendent of Rim Runners there'd be a scandal, a very nasty scandal. And I don't want one in *my* spaceport."

"Very concisely put, Captain. But I can look after myself."

"I hope that you can, Commodore. Good night to you."

"Good night, Captain Stacey."

Grimes let himself out. The pieces of the jigsaw puzzle were beginning to fall into place; his suspicions were about to be confirmed. He smiled grimly as he walked along the narrow street toward the row of neat little bungalows where Lynn Davis lived. Night was falling fast, and already lights were coming on in the houses. From open windows drifted the sound of music. The scene was being set for a romantic—romantic?—assignation.

Lynn Davis met him at her door. She was dressed in something loose and, Grimes noted as she stood with the lamp behind her, almost transparent. She took his hand, led him into her living room, gently pushed him down into a deep chair. Close by it was a tray of drinks, and a dish upon which exotic delicacies were displayed. Real Terran olives—and a score of those would make a nasty hole in the weekly pay of an assistant met. officer. Sea dragon caviar from Atlantia . . . pickled rock frogs from Dunartil . . .

The playmaster was on, its volume turned well down. A woman was singing. It was an old song, dating back to the twentieth century, its lyrics modernized, its melody still sweet with lost archaic lilt.

> *Spaceman, the stars are calling,*
> *Spaceman, you have to roam . . .*
> *Spaceman, through light-years falling,*
> *Turn back at last to home. . . .*

"Sherry, John?" asked Lynn Davis. She was sitting on the arm of his chair. He could see the gleam of her smooth flesh through her sheer robe. "Amontillado?"

He said. "You're doing me proud."

"It's not often I entertain such an important guest as you."

He sipped the wine from the fragile glass she had filled for him. She had measured her own drink from the same decanter. He did not think that there was anything wrong with it—any connoisseur would have told him, indignantly that there was *nothing* wrong with it—but at the first hint of muzziness he would smoke a cigarillo. . . .

She was leaning closer to him, almost against him. Her robe was falling open in front. She was wearing nothing underneath it. She said, "Aren't you hot? Why not take your jacket off?"

"Later, perhaps." He managed a quite creditable leer, "after all, we've all night."

"Why waste time?" Her mouth was slightly parted in frank invitation. *What the hell?* thought Grimes, and accepted. Her body was pliant in his arms, her lips on his warm and moist. But his mind, his cold, calculating mind, was still in full command of the situation. He heard the door open softly, heard feet sliding over the thick carpet. He pushed the girl away from him, from the corner of his eye saw her fall to the floor, a delectable sprawl of exposed, gleaming body and limbs.

"So," snarled Jeff Petersen. "So this is what you get up to, Mr. Commodore Dirty Old Man Grimes! What did you promise her, you swine? Promotion and a transfer to a better station?"

Petersen, Grimes noted, was not a slave to this instincts any more than he, Grimes, had been. Superficially his voice was that of the wronged, jealous lover, but there was an artificial quality in his rage.

Grimes said equally, "I can explain. . . ."

"Yes." Petersen was advancing slowly. "You can explain after I've torn off your right arm and beaten your brains out with it."

Suddenly the tiny pistol was in Grimes's right hand. It cracked once, and once only, a sound disproportionate to its dimensions. Petersen halted, staggered, staring stupidly. He swayed on his feet for long seconds and then crashed to the floor, overturning the low table, spilling wine over the sprawling body of the girl. She exploded up from the carpet like a tigress, all teeth and claws. Grimes was hampered by the chair in which he was confined but fought her off somehow. He did not want to use the gun again.

"You bastard!" She was sobbing. "You ruthless bastard! You killed him. And we were careful not to kill—not even the natives!"

"I didn't kill him," Grimes managed to say at last, after he had imprisoned her hands behind her back, after he had clasped her legs between his own. "I didn't kill him. This pistol is loaded with anesthetic needles. He'll be out for twelve hours—no more, no less."

"He's not . . . dead?"

"Do dead men snore?" asked Grimes practically.

"I . . . I suppose not." Her manner changed abruptly. "Well, he asked for it, John, and this time he got it. Poor Jeff." There was little sympathy in her voice. "So . . ."

"So what?"

"So we might as well be hung for sheep as lambs. We might as well have the game as well as the name."

He said admiringly, "You're a cold-blooded bitch, aren't you?"

"Just realistic." She bent her head forward, but it was not to bite. After the kiss Grimes released her. She pulled slowly away from him, walked undulatingly to the door of the bedroom, shedding the torn remnants of her robe as she went.

Grimes sighed, then got up and followed.

She said, "That was good. . . ."

"It was."

"Stay there, darling, and I'll make us some coffee. We don't want to waste time sleeping."

A sleep, thought Grimes, *is just what I would like. The sleep of the just—the just after.*

He sprawled at ease on the wide couch, watched her appreciatively as she left him, as she walked gracefully to the door. In the subdued light she was all rosy bronze. In any sort of light she was, as he knew, beautiful. He heard a slight clattering from the kitchenette, imposed upon the still stertorous snores of the hapless Jeff. After a while she came back with a tray on which were a pot and two cups. She poured. "Sugar, darling? Cream?" The steam from the coffee was deliciously fragrant. He reached out for his cup, accidentally? put his fingers on the handle of hers. She gently pushed his hand away. "Mine hasn't sugar," she told him.

"You're sweet enough as you are," he said, asking himself, *How corny can you get?*

So he took three sips of the coffee that was intended for him, and at once felt the onset of heavy drowsiness, even though there was no warning flavor. He mumbled, "Like a smoke. . . . Would you mind, Lynn? In my pocket . . . on chair . . ."

She reached out to his clothing, produced the packet of cigarillos and his lighter. She, he already knew, did not smoke herself, which was just as well. She handed him the packet. In his condition, in the dim lighting, he could hardly make out the distinguishing mark. He hoped that he had the right one. Here and now, the special effects of the other one would be more spectacular than useful.

She lit the cigarillo for him, smiling condescendingly down at him. He inhaled the smoke, retained it for long seconds before blowing it out. He took one more sip of coffee, then let a dribble of the hot fluid fall on to his naked chest. He was careful not to wince. He mumbled indistinctly, then fell back against the pillows. His right hand, with the little smoldering cylinder between his fingers, fell limply onto his belly. He could smell the acridity of burning body hair, felt the sharp beginnings of pain. With a great effort of will he remained in his relaxed posture.

He heard her mutter, "I should let the old bastard burn, but. . ." Her cool, slim fingers removed the miniature cigar from his hand. He felt very grateful to her.

He heard her dressing, heard her walk rapidly from the bedroom. He heard, eventually, the front door open and shut. He gave her time to get clear of the house.

When he got down from the bed he expected to feel sick and dizzy, with drug and antidote still at war within his system. But he did not, although he was conscious of the minor burns. He dressed rapidly, checked his possessions. He was pleased to find that the Minetti was still in his pocket; probably whatever it was in the coffee was supposed to put him under for a longer period than the anesthetic needle-bullet that he had used on Jeff Petersen.

The street outside the house was deserted. Everybody was indoors, and everybody seemed to be having a party. He grinned. He had had one too. He walked briskly away from the spaceport, in the direction of the beach where he had first met Lynn Davis. The signs that had been affixed to the trunks of trees were a help. By what moonlight there was he could read, PRIVATE. LADIES ONLY. And how would she have managed, he wondered, if the other human ladies on Mellise had shared her views on outdoor nudity?

The beach was deserted. Backing the narrow strip of sand were the trees, and between their boles was undergrowth, affording effective cover. Grimes settled down to wait. He slipped the magazine from his automatic, exchanged it for the other one; the needle-bullets in this one were no more lethal than the first had been, but they differed from them in one or two respects. He took the remaining marked cigarillo from its packet, put it carefully into his breast pocket. This one had a friction fuse.

At last she came, walking barefooted over the sand, her shoes in her left hand, a heavy case in the other. She dropped the shoes, put the case down carefully. She opened it, then pulled out a silvery telescopic antenna to its full extent. She squatted down, making even this normally ungainly posture graceful, appeared to be adjusting controls of some sort. There was a high, barely audible whine.

Something was coming in from the sea. It was not a native. It came scuttling ashore like a huge crab—like a huge, five-legged crab. Then there was another, and another, and another, until two dozen of the beasts stood there waiting. For orders—or programming?

Grimes walked slowly and deliberately out from the shadows, his Minetti in his right hand. He said quietly, "I'm sorry, Lynn, but the game's up."

She whirled grotesquely like a Russian dancer.

"You!" she snarled, making it seem like a curse.

"Yes. Me. If you come quietly and make a full confession I'll see to it that things go easy for you."

"Like hell I will!"

She turned swiftly back to the transmitter, kicking up a flurry of sand. The whining note abruptly changed to an irregular beat. And then the starfish were coming for him, slowly at first, but faster and faster. He swatted out instinctively at the leading one, felt the skin of his hand tear on metal spines. In his other hand was the gun. He fired—almost a full burst. The minute projectiles tore though the transmitter. Some of them, a few of them, were bound to sever connections, to shatter transistors. They did. There was a sputtering shower of blue sparks. The metal monsters froze into immobility.

But Lynn did not. She had her own gun out, a heavier weapon than Grimes's own. He felt the wind of her first bullet. And then, with one of the few remaining rounds in his magazine, he shot her.

He stood there, looking down at her. She was paralyzed, but her eyes could still move, and her lips, and her tongue. She was paralyzed—and when the drug took hold properly she would feel the compulsion to talk.

She asked bitterly, "How long will this last?"

"Days, unless I let you have the antidote."

She demanded, "How did you *know?*"

"I didn't *know*. I guessed, and I added two and two to make a quite convincing and logical four. Suppose I tell you—then you can fill in the details."

"That'll be the sunny Friday!"

"Will it?" Grimes squatted down beside her. "You had things easy here, didn't you? You and Jeff Petersen. Such a prize bunch of nongs and no-hopers, from the Ambassador and the port captain on down. I shouldn't have said that; I forgot that this is being recorded.

"Well, one thing that started to make me suspicious of you, especially, was that lie you told me about the solar flares. I checked up; there are very complete records of all phenomena in this sector of space in my office at Port Forlorn. Then there was the shortage of spares for your equipment—I remembered that the requisitions for electronic bits and pieces have been abnormally heavy ever since you and Mr. Petersen were appointed here. There was that ornamental tank of little starfish—and that so-called mobile almost alongside it. Petersen's hobby. The construction that, I realized later, looked very much like the tin starfish I saw raiding the pearl beds. There was the behavior of these same tin starfish: the way in which they attacked the bivalves with absolute viciousness but seemed very careful not to hurt the Mellisans.

"That tied in with the few weeks that Petersen spent on El Dorado.

"They have watchbirds there, Lynn, and similar semi-robots that function either on the ground or in the water. Animal brains in metal bodies. Absolute faithfulness and obedience to their human masters. As a skilled technician, Petersen would have been able to mingle, to a certain extent, with the gifted amateurs who play around with that sort on El Dorado. He must have picked up some of their techniques, and passed them on to you. You two modified them, probably improved upon them. A starfish hasn't any brain to speak of, so probably you have the entire animal incorporated into your destructive servants. Probably, too, there's an electronic brain built in somewhere, that gets its orders by radio and that can be programmed.

"You were going to recall the local . . . flock, pack, school? What does it matter? . . . tonight, weren't you? For reprogramming. Some preset course of action that would enable them to deal with the threat of spears with explosive warheads. It wouldn't do to have tin tentacles littering the ocean floor, would it? When the Mellisans brought in the evidence even the Ambassador would have to do something about it.

"And, tonight being the night, I had to be got out of the way. Plan A failed, so you switched to Plan B. Correct?"

"Correct," she muttered.

"And for whom were you working?" he asked sharply and suddenly.

"T-G." The answer had slipped out before she could stop it.

"Trans-Galactic Clippers. . . . Why does T-G want Mellise?"

"A tourist resort." She was speaking rapidly now, in obvious catharsis. "We were to destroy the economy, the trade with the Confederacy. And then T-G would step in, and pay handsomely for rights and leases."

"And you and Mr. Petersen would be suitably rewarded. . . ." He paused. "Tell me, Lynn. . . did you enjoy tonight? Between the disposal of Jeff and the disposal of myself, I mean."

"Yes," she told him.

"I'm glad you said that. It makes what I'm going to do a lot easier. I was going to do it in any case; I always like to pay my bills." As he spoke, he pulled the cigarillo from his breast pocket, scratched the friction fuse with his thumbnail. The thing ignited at once, fizzed, ejected a bright blue pyrotechnic star. "I'm letting you go free," Grimes went on, "both of you. You will have to resign, of course, from the Rim Runners' service, but as T-G is your real employer that shouldn't mean any hardship. The records I have made"—he tapped the two buttons of his jacket—"stay with me. To be used, if required. Meanwhile my friends"—he turned to wave to Wunnaara and a dozen other natives who were wading up from the sea—"will dispose of the evidence. The story will be that they, without any outside aid, have succeeded in coping with the starfish plague. You will furnish them, of course, with transmitters like the one you used tonight so that your pets in other parts of the sea can be rounded up."

"Haven't much option, have I?" she asked.

"No."

"There's just one thing I'd like to say. That question you asked me, about my enjoying myself . . . I'm damned sorry this truth drug of yours made me give the right answer."

"I'm not," said Grimes.

It was nice while it lasted, thought the Commodore, *but I'm really not cut out for these James Bond capers, any more than I would be for the odd antics of any of the other peculiar heroes of twentieth century fiction.* He filled and lit his pipe—he preferred it to the little cigars, even to those without the built-in devices—and looked out over the blue sea. The sun was warm on his naked body. He wished that Sonya were with him. But it wouldn't be long now.

～ Part 4 ～
The Last Dreamer

JOHN GRIMES was really homeward bound at last.

On both Tharn and Mellise he had been obliged to leave the ships in which he had taken passage when requested by the rulers of those planets to assist them in the solution of rather complicated problems. He had not minded at all; he had welcomed the prospect of action after too long a time as a desk-borne commodore. But now he was beginning to become a little impatient. Sonya, his wife, would be back soon from her galactic cruise and then the major city of Lorn would be—as far as Grimes was concerned—forlorn in name only. He was pleased that *Rim Jaguar* would be making a direct run from Mellise to Port Forlorn with no time-expanding calls *en route*. All being well, he would have a few days in which to put things in order prior to Sonya's homecoming.

It promised to be an uneventful voyage—and in deep space uneventful voyages are the rule rather than the exception. *Rim Jaguar* was one of the more modern units of Rim Runners' fleet, built for them to modified *Epsilon* Class design. She was well found, well manned and reasonably happy. Grimes was the only passenger, and as Rim Runners' Astronautical Superintendent he was given the run of the vessel. He did not abuse the privilege. He would never have dreamed of interfering, and he made suggestions only when asked to do so. Nonetheless he enjoyed the long hours that he spent in the control room, yarning with the officer of the watch, looking out through the wide viewports at the great, distant Galactic Lens, unperturbed by its weird, apparent distortion, the result of the warped space-time through which the ship was falling. He was Earth-born but, like so many spacemen who had made their various ways to this frontier of the dark, he belonged on the Rim, had come to accept that almost empty sky—the sparsely scattered, unreachable island universes, the galaxy itself no more than a dim-glowing ellipsoid—as being altogether right and proper and, somehow, far more natural than worlds in toward the center.

He was sitting in *Rim Jaguar's* control room now, at ease in his acceleration chair, his seamed, pitted face and his still youthful gray eyes almost obscured by the cloud of acrid smoke from his vile, battered pipe. He was listening tolerantly to the third officer's long list of grievances; shortly after departure from Mellise he had made it quite plain that he wouldn't bite and also that anything told to him by the ship's people would not be taken down and used as evidence against them.

"And annual leave, sir," the young man was saying. "I realize that it isn't always possible to release an officer on the exact date due, but when there's a delay of two, or even three months . . ."

"We just haven't enough personnel, Mr. Sanderson," Grimes told him, "to ensure a prompt relief. Also, when it comes to appointments I try to avoid putting square pegs into round holes. *You* know what *that* can lead to."

"The *Rim Griffon* business, sir?"

"Yes. Everybody hating everybody, and the ship suffering in consequence. A very sorry affair."

"I see your point, sir, but—" An alarm pinged sharply. "Excuse me."

It was the Mass Proximity Indicator that had sounded off, the only piece of navigational equipment, apart from the Carlotti Direction Finder, that was functional while the Interstellar Drive was in operation. Grimes swiveled his chair so that he could look at the globular tank that was the screen of the device. Yes, there was something there all right, something that had no business to be there, something that, in the screen, was only a little to one side of the glowing filament that was the extrapolation of the ship's trajectory.

Sanderson was speaking briskly into the telephone. "Control Room here, sir. Unidentified object 000 01.5, range 3,000, closing. Bearing opening."

Grimes heard Captain Drakenberg's reply. "I'll be right up, Mr. Sanderson."

Drakenberg, an untidy bear of a man, looked into the screen and grunted. He turned to Grimes. "And what do you make of it, sir?"

"It's *something*. . . ."

"I could have told you that, Commodore."

Grimes felt his prominent ears redden. Drakenberg was a highly competent shipmaster, popular rather than otherwise with his officers, but at times lacking in the social graces.

The third officer said, "According to Traffic Control there are no ships in this sector. . . ."

"Would it be a Rim Ghost?" asked the Captain. "You're something of an expert on them, Commodore. Would one show up on the M.P.I.?"

"Conditions would have to be exactly right," said Grimes. "We would have had to slip into its continuum, or it into ours. The same applies, of course, to any attempt to establish radio communication."

"We'll try that, sir," said Drakenberg bluntly. Then, to Sanderson, "Line up the Carlotti."

The watch officer switched on the control room Carlotti communicator, a miniature version of the main set in the ship's radio office, which was a miniature version of the huge, planet-based beacons. The elliptical Mobius Strip that was the antenna began to rotate about its long axis, fading into apparent insubstantiality as it did so. Sanderson threw the switch that hooked it up with the Mass Proximity Indicator. At once the antenna began to swing on its universal mounting, turning unsteadily, hesitantly in a wide arc. After its major oscillations had ceased it hunted for a few seconds, finally locked on.

"Pass me the microphone," Drakenberg ordered. Then he said,

speaking slowly and very distinctly, *"Rim Jaguar* calling unidentified vessel. *Rim Jaguar* calling unidentified vessel. Come in, please. Come in, please."

There was a silence, broken by Grimes. "Perhaps she hasn't got M.P.I.," he suggested. "Perhaps she hasn't seen us."

"It's a compulsory fitting, isn't it?" growled the master.

"For the Federation's ships. And for ours. But the Empire of Waverley hasn't made it compulsory yet. Or the Shakespearian Sector." He got out of his chair, moved to the screen. "Besides, I don't think that this target *is* a ship. Not with a blip that size, and at this range. . . ."

"What the hell else can it be?" demanded Drakenberg.

"I don't know," admitted Grimes. "I don't know. . . ."

It hung there against the unrelieved blackness of Rim Space, a planet where no planet should have been, illuminated by a sun that wasn't there at all. There was an atmosphere, with cloud masses. There were seas and continents. There were polar icecaps. And it was real, solid, with enough mass to hold the ship—her Inertial Drive and her Mannschenn Drive shut down—in a stable orbit about it. An Earth-type world it was, according to *Rim Jaguar's* instruments—an inhabited world, with the scintillant lights of cities clearly visible scattered over its night hemisphere.

All attempts at communication had failed. The inhabitants did not seem to have radio, either for entertainment or for the transmission of messages. Grimes, still in the control room, looked with some distaste at the useless Carlotti transceiver. Until the invention of this device, whereby ships could talk with each other, and with shore stations regardless of range and with no time lag, psionic radio officers had always been carried. In circumstances such as these a trained telepath would have been invaluable, would have been able to achieve contact with a least a few minds on the planet below. Psionic radio officers were still carried by fighting ships and by survey vessels, but *Rim Jaguar* was neither. She was a merchantman, and the employment of personnel required for duty only upon very special occasions would have been uneconomical.

She did not carry sounding rockets, even. Grimes, as Astronautical Superintendent of Rim Runners, had been responsible for that piece of economy, had succeeded in having the regulations amended. He had argued that ships trading only in a well charted sector of space had no need for such expensive toys. It had not been anticipated that an unknown planet—matter or anti-matter?—would appear suddenly upon the track between Mellise and Lorn.

But the construction of a small liquid fuel rocket is little more than a matter of plumbing, and the *Jaguar's* engineers were able to oblige. Her second officer—as well as being the ship's navigator he specialized in gunnery in the Confederacy's Naval Reserve—produced a crude but effective homing device for the thing. It was hardly necessary. The range was short and the target a big one.

The rocket was fired on such a trajectory that it would hit the night side while the ship was directly over the hemisphere. Radar tracked it down to the outer reaches of the atmosphere, where it disintegrated. But it was a normal, meteoric destruction by impact and friction, not the flare of released energy that would have told of the meeting of matter and anti-matter. That was that. The initial reports of the sighting, together with all the relevant coordinates, had already been sent to Lorn; all that remained now was to report the results of the sounding rocket experiment. Grimes was scribbling the message down on a signal pad, and Drakenberg was busy with the preliminaries of putting the ship back on to trajectory, when the radio officer came into the control room. He was carrying three envelopes, one of which he handed to the Captain, giving the two to the Commodore. Grimes knew what their contents would be, and sighed audibly. Over the years he had become too much of an expert on the dimensional oddities encountered out on the rim of the galaxy. And he was the man on the spot—just when he was in a hurry to be getting home.

The first message was from Rim Runners' Board of Management and read, *Act as instructed by Admiral Commanding Confederate Navy.* The second one was from Admiral Kravinsky. *Carry out full investigation of strange planet.* Drakenberg, scowling, handed Grimes the flimsy that had been inside his own envelope. Its content was clear enough, *Place self and vessel under orders of Commodore Grimes, Rim Worlds Naval Reserve.*

"Keep the ship in orbit, Captain," ordered Grimes resignedly.

A dust mote in the emptiness, *Rim Jaguar's* number two lifeboat fell toward the mysterious planet. In it were two men only—Grimes and Sanderson, the freighter's third officer. There had been no shortage of volunteers, from the Master on down, but Grimes, although a high ranking officer of the Naval Reserve, was still an employee of a commercial shipping line. To make a landing on an unknown world with horse, foot and artillery is all very well when you have the large crew of a warship to draw upon; should the initial expedition come to grief there is sufficient personnel left aboard the vessel to handle her and, if necessary, to man her weaponry. But insofar as manning is concerned, a merchant ship is run on a shoestring. There are no expendable ratings, and the loss of even one officer from any department means, at least, considerable inconvenience.

Grimes's decision to take only Sanderson with him had not been a popular one, but the young man had been the obvious choice. He was unmarried—was an orphan. He did not have a steady girlfriend, even. Furthermore, he had just completed a period of Naval Reserve training and rather fancied himself a small arms expert.

Rim Jaguar, however did not carry much of an armory. Grimes had with him his own Minetti and one of the ship's laser handguns. Sanderson had one of the other lasers—there were only three on board—and a vicious ten millimeter projectile pistol. There were spare power packs and a good supply of ammunition for all weapons.

The third officer, who was handling the boat, was talkative on the way down. Grimes did not mind—as long as the young man kept his trap shut and concentrated on his piloting as soon as the little craft hit the atmosphere.

"This is a rum go," he was saying. "How do you explain it, sir? All that obvious sunlight, and no sun at all in the sky . . ."

"I've seen worse," Grimes told him. Like, he thought, the series of alternative universes he had explored—although not thoroughly—

in that voyage of the *Faraway Quest* that somebody had referred to as a Wild Ghost Chase. And that other universe, into which he had quite literally blown his ship, the one in which those evil non-human mutants had ruled the Rim. On both of those occasions Sonya had been with him. She should have been with him now—not this lanky, blond, blue-eyed puppy. But that wasn't Sanderson's fault, and in any case Grimes did not think that he would find the young man lacking in any respect.

"I suppose," the third officer rattled on, "that it's all something to do with different dimensions. Here we're at the very edge of the expanding galaxy, and the barriers between continua must be stretched thin, very thin. That planet's popped through into our continuum, but only half through, if you see what I mean. Its primary has stayed put on the other side of the boundary...."

"A fairish hypothesis," admitted Grimes. "It will have to do until we can think of a better one."

And, he told himself, *there must be a better one.* As far as he knew the difference between the universes were cultural rather than cosmological. There just couldn't be a planet here—or a sun with a family of planets.

"And I wonder what the people are like, sir. Would they be humanoid, do you think, or even human? They must be civilized. They have cities."

Grimes muttered something about plastic jungles.

"Not plastic, sir. They haven't radio, so the chances are that they don't run to chemical engineering. Concrete jungles ... would that be better?"

Grimes allowed himself to suppose that it might be.

"You couldn't have timed it better, sir. That large town you decided on will be just clear of the terminator when we get down."

In the Federation's Survey Service, thought Grimes, we were drilled so that such timing became second nature. How had that instructor put it? "Make your first landing just west of the terminator, and unless some bastard chases you off you've the whole day to play silly buggers in."

"Better fasten seat belts, sir."

Grimes pulled the webbing taut across his body, snapped shut the buckle. In a boat fitted with Inertial Drive the ride down to the planetary surface should be a smooth one, provided that there was no atmosphere turbulence. But here there was no spaceport control to give information on meteorological conditions. He spoke into the microphone of the transceiver. "Commodore to *Rim Jaguar*. We are now entering exosphere. So far all in going as planned." He heard Drakenberg acknowledge.

The air below the boat was clear, abnormally so. The lights of the cities were like star clusters. For a brief second Grimes entertained the crazy idea that they *were* star clusters, that he and Sanderson had broken through into some other time and space, were somehow adrift in regions toward the heart of a galaxy. He looked upward for reassurance. But he did not, through the transparency of the overhead viewport, see the familiar, almost empty Rim sky. The firmament was ablaze with unfamiliar constellations. It was frightening. Had Sanderson, somehow, turned the boat over just as Grimes had shifted his regard? He had not, as a glance at the instrument panel made obvious. He had not—and below were still the city lights, and from zenith to horizon there were the stars, and low to the west was a great golden moon. Astern, the first rosy flush of dawn was in the sky.

His voice unemotional, deliberately flat, Grimes reported his observations to the ship.

Swiftly the boat fell through the atmosphere, so fast that interior temperature rose appreciably. But Sanderson was a first class pilot and at no time did he allow the speed of descent to approach dangerous limits. Swiftly the boat fell, her Inertial Drive purring gently, resisting but not overcoming the gravitational field that had her in its grip. Through the morning twilight she dropped, and above her only the brighter stars were visible in the pale sky, and below her the land masses were gray-green rather than black, and the city lights had lost their sharp scintillance and were going out, street by street.

It was toward what looked like a park that Sanderson, on Grimes's instructions, was steering, an irregular rectangle of comparative darkness outlined by such lights as were still burning. There were trees there, the men could see as the boat lost altitude; there were trees, and there were dull-gleaming ribbons and amoeboid shapes that looked like water, and featureless patches that must be clear level ground. Bordering the park were the towers of the city— tall, fantastically turreted and, when struck by the first bright rays of the rising sun, shining like jewels in the reflected radiance.

The boat grounded gently on a soft, resilient surface. Grimes looked at Sanderson and Sanderson looked at Grimes, and then they both stared out of the viewports. They had landed in the middle of the park, on what looked like a lawn of emerald green grass, not far from the banks of a stream. There were trees in the foreground, low, static explosions of dark foliage among which gleamed, scarlet and crimson and gold, what were either fruit or flowers. In the background were the distant towers, upthrusting like the suddenly frozen spray of some great fountain, an opalescent tracery against the clear blue sky.

"Open up, sir?" asked the young officer at last.

"Yes," said Grimes. An itemized list of all the precautions that should be taken before setting foot on a strange planet briefly flashed before his mind's eye, but he ignored it. And to wear a spacesuit in this huge, gorgeous garden would be heresy. But not all of his training could be dismissed so easily. Reluctantly he picked up the microphone, made his report to the ship. He concluded with the words, "We're going out, now, to make contact with the natives. You have your instructions, Captain."

"Yes, Commodore Grimes." Grimes wondered why Drakenberg should sound so anxious. "If I don't hear from you again twenty-four standard hours from now, at the latest, I'm to make a report directly to the Admiralty and await their orders." He hesitated, then brought out the final words with some difficulty. "And on no account am I to attempt another landing."

"That is correct, Captain Drakenberg. Over."

"Good luck, Commodore Grimes. Over and out."

Sanderson already had both air lock doors open and the cool breeze had eddied gently through the little cabin, flushing out the acridity of hot oil and machinery, bringing with it the scent of flowers, of dew-wet grass. There were birds singing outside and then, faint yet clear, the sound of a great clock somewhere in the city striking the hour. Automatically Grimes looked at his watch, made to reset it and then smiled at his foolishness. He did not know yet what sort of time it was that these people kept.

He was first out of the boat, jumping down onto the velvety turf, joined almost at once by Sanderson. "This is beautiful!" exclaimed the young man. "I hope that the natives come up to what we've seen so far." He added, "The girls especially."

Grimes should have reproved him, but he didn't. He was too busy wondering what it was that made everything, so far, so familiar. He had never seen this world before, or any planet like it, and yet. . . How did he know, for example, that this city's name was Ayonoree? How could he know?

"Which way do we go, sir?" Sanderson was asking.

Which way? The memory, if it was memory, wasn't quite good enough. "We'll follow the stream," he decided.

It was a short walk to the near bank of the little river, along which ran a path of flagstones. The water was crystal clear, gently flowing. On it floated great lily pads, and on one of these sat a huge frog, all gold and emerald, staring at them with bright, protuberant eyes. It croaked loudly.

"It's saying something!" cried Sanderson.

"Rubbish!" snapped Grimes, who was trying to break the odd spell that had been cast over them. But were those words that they could hear?

Follow stream stay in the dream.
Follow stream stay in the dream.

"You!" shouted Sanderson. "What do you mean?"

In reply the batrachian croaked derisively, splashed into the water and struck out slowly for the further shore.

So we follow the stream, thought Grimes. He set off along the path, the young man tailing behind. Suddenly he stopped. There was a tree, gracefully trailing its tendril-like branches almost to the water, to one side of the flagstones, another tree a few yards inshore from it. Between the trunks was a huge, glittering web. There was a spider, too, disgustingly hairy, as large as a man's clenched fist, scuttling toward the center of its fragile-seeming net. And there was an insect of some kind, a confused fluttering of gauzy wings, snared by the viscous strands.

Grimes made to detour around the landward tree. After all, spiders were entitled to a meal, just as he was. Insofar as the uglier sides of Nature were concerned he tried to maintain his neutrality. He did not especially like spiders—but, in all probability, that oversized insect in the web was something even more unpleasant.

Behind him he heard Sanderson cry out, heard the hiss of his laser pistol and felt the heat of the beam that narrowly missed his right ear. The fleshy body of the spider exploded and hung there, tattered and steaming. There was a sickening stench of burned flesh.

Grimes turned angrily on the young man. "What the hell do you think you're doing? For all we know, spiders are sacred on this world!"

"More likely *these* are!"

Sanderson had pushed past Grimes and, with gentle hands, was freeing the trapped creature. "Look!" he was saying. "Look!"

The Commodore looked. This was not, as he assumed, an insect. It was humanoid, a winged woman, but tiny, tiny. Her lustrous golden hair hung to her waist, and beneath her filmy green robe was the hint of perfectly formed breasts. Her mouth was scarlet and her eyes blue, and her features were perfectly formed. She sat there in the third officer's cupped hands, looking up at him. Her voice, when she spoke, was like the tinkling of a little silver bell.

"Follow stream, and follow river,

"When danger threatens do not quiver;

"Follow stream to Ogre's Keep,

"Wake the Princess from her sleep!"

"What princess?" demanded Grimes.

She turned to glare to him.

"Prince's servitors like you,

"Should only speak when spoken to."

Sanderson was shocked. "This is the Commodore," he said severely to the winged being.

"Commodore, Schmommodore!" she replied sweetly—and then, with hardly a quiver of those impractical looking pinions, was gone.

"So you're promoted," said Grimes dryly. "And I'm demoted."

"All the same, sir, it was absolute sauce on her part." Then he went on a little smugly. "The odd part is that I *am* a prince. My father was King of Tavistock, until they threw him out."

"And your great-grandfather," said Grimes, "who founded the dynasty, was a semi-piratical tramp skipper. I know the history."

"Do we follow the stream, sir?"

"Yes. It's as good a way to explore this world as any."

They followed the stream. Through the great park it led them, past enormous beds of fantastic, glowing flowers, through a grove of gaunt, contorted trees. The transition from parkland to city street was abrupt; suddenly there were cobbles underfoot instead of the worn flagstones, and on every hand towered multi-colored buildings, convoluted structures that made nonsense of all the laws of architecture and engineering.

People were abroad now, men and women, a great number of children. They were human enough in outward appearance at least, but there was an oddness about them, an oversimplification of all features, a peculiar blend of stylization and caricature. There was no vehicular traffic, but there were riders—some upon horses, some upon camels, some upon the lizard-like roadrunners indigenous to Tarizeel, some upon beasts that were utterly strange even to the widely traveled Grimes.

The two explorers marched on, ignored by the brightly dressed natives, ignoring them. They should, Grimes knew, have tried to make contact, which would not have been hard. From the scraps of conversation they overheard it was obvious that Anglo-Terran was the language of this planet. They should have demanded to be taken to the king, president or whatever authority it was that ruled this world. But it was not important. What was important was to find the Ogre's Keep, to awaken the sleeping princess. It was as though some outside power had taken control of them. The feeling should have been nightmarish, but it was not. Grimes was oddly grateful that somebody—or something—else was making the decisions that he should have been making.

The stream joined a river, and the path continued along the bank of the larger body of water, taking the two men clear of the city. They walked on steadily, feeling no fatigue, maintaining a brisk pace. They were away from the crowds of the city, met only an occasional pedestrian, and now and again a peasant man or woman pushing a barrow high-laden with produce in to market. One of these latter, a wizened, black-clad crone dragging a little cart fitted with pumpkins, accosted them. Raising high a skinny claw she declaimed in a cracked voice,

"Dare the dragon! Storm the Keep!

"Save us all from endless sleep!"

"The dragon, madam?" inquired Grimes politely.

But she was given no time to answer him. From the cloudless sky crackled a bolt of lightning, dazzling, terrifying, striking the path between her and the two men. She wailed, "I didn't say anything! I didn't say anything!" and was gone, scuttling toward the city, the cart bouncing along behind her, a trail of bruised and burst pumpkins in her wake.

"Somebody Up There doesn't like her," remarked Sanderson. Then, brightly, "Do you feel in the mood for dragon-slaying, sir?"

"Why not?" countered Grimes. After all, it would be no more outrageous than any of their other encounters to date. *Outrageous?* He repeated the word mentally. Where had he got it from? Nothing, so far, justified its use: the frog, the fairy in the spider's web, all the talk of ogres' keeps and sleeping princesses and dragons, it had all been perfectly natural. In any well-regulated world sleeping princesses were there to be awakened, and ogres' keeps to be stormed, and the dragons to be slain. Of course, the way he and the young prince were dressed was all wrong—more like peasants than like knights errant. But that could not be helped. Disguise was allowable.

"Shall we press on, Your Highness?" he suggested.

"Yes, Sir John. No doubt the dragon awaits us eagerly."

Sanderson pulled the projectile pistol from its holster, spun it carelessly with his right forefinger through the trigger guard. "Methinks that our magic weapons will prove more efficacious than swords."

"Mehopes that you're right, Your Highness."

"Then come, Sir John. Time's a-wasting."

They walked on—and then, just ahead of them, Grimes saw a pontoon landing dock on the river. There was a ship alongside it, an archaic side-wheel paddle steamer, smoke issuing from its tall funnel. At the shoreward side of the stage was a notice board and on it, in big black letters on a white ground, the sign:

RIVER TRIPS TO OGRE'S KEEP.
HALF A FLORIN. VERY CHEAP.

"Your Highness," said Grimes, "let's take the boat and rest awhile, then face the dragon with a smile."

"Have you the wherewithal, Sir John, to pay the fare agreed upon?"

"I have a pass, Prince Sanderson. And so have you—your trusty gun."

Something at the back of the Commodore's mind winced at the doggerel and cried voicelessly, *You're a spaceman, not a character out of a children's book!* Grimes almost ignored it, tried to ignore it, but the nagging doubt that had been engendered persisted.

They marched on to the pontoon, their sturdily shod feet ringing on the planking, their weapons drawn and ready. Side by side, but with Sanderson slightly in the lead, they tramped up the gangway. At the head of it stood a man in uniform—and, incongruously, his trappings were those of a purser in the Waverley Royal Mail Line. He held out his hand." Good knights, if you would board this ship, pay passage money for your trip."

"Varlet, stand back! The ride is free for this, the bold Sir John, and me!"

"And here, as you can plainly see," added Grimes, making a meaningful gesture with his Minetti, "is our loud-voiced authority."

"Sir, it speaks loud enough for me," admitted the purser, standing to one side. As they passed him Grimes heard him mutter. "The Royal Mail could not be worse. *They* never made me speak in verse."

Grimes, who was always at home aboard ships of any kind, led the way down to the saloon, a large compartment, darkly paneled, with black leather upholstery on chairs and settees. At one end of it there was a bar, but it was shut. Along both sides were big windows, barely clear of the surface of the water. There were no other passengers.

Overhead there was the thudding of feet on planking. Then there was a jangling of bells, followed at once by the noise of machinery below decks. From above came the long mournful note of a steam whistle, and then came the steady *chunk, chunk, chunk* of the paddles. The ship was underway, heading down river. On either side the banks were sliding past, a shifting panorama of forest and village, with only rarely what looked like a cultivated field, but very often a huge, frowning, battlemented castle.

The rhythm of paddles and engines was a soothing one and Grimes, at least, found that it made him drowsy. He lolled back in his deep chair, halfway between consciousness and sleep. When he was in this state his real memories, his very real doubts and worries came suddenly to the surface of his mind. He heard his companion murmur, "Speed, bonny boat, like a bird through the sky. Carry us where the dragon must die."

"Come off it, Sanderson," ordered the Commodore sharply.

"Sir John, please take yourself in hand. Such insolence I will not stand!"

"Come off it!" ordered Grimes again—and then the spell, which had been so briefly broken, took charge again. "Your Highness, I spoke out of turn. But courtesy I'll try to learn."

"My good Sir John, you better had. Bad manners always make me mad. But look through yonder port, my friend. Methinks we neareth journey's end."

Journey's end or not, there was a landing stage there toward which the paddle steamer was standing in. Inshore from it the land was thickly wooded and rose steeply. On the crest of the hill glowered the castle, a grim pile of gray stone, square-built, ugly, with a turret at each corner. There was a tall staff from which floated a flag. Even from a distance the two men could make out the emblem: a white skull-and-crossbones in a black ground. And then, as the ship neared the shore, the view was shut out and, finally, only the slime-covered side of the pontoon could be seen through the window.

The paddle steamer came alongside with a gentle crunch and, briefly, the engines were reversed to take the way off her. From forward and aft there was a brief rattle of steam winches as she was moored, and then there were no more mechanical noises.

The purser appeared in the saloon entrance. "Good knights, you now must leave this wagon. So fare you forth to face the dragon."

"And you will wait till we are done?" asked Grimes.

"We can't, Sir Knight, not on this run.

"Come rain, come shine, come wind, come snow,

"Back and forth our ferries go.

"Like clockwork yet, sir, you should try 'em,

"And even set your wristwatch by 'em."

"Enough, Sir John," said Sanderson, "this wordy wight will keep us gabbing here all night. In truth, he tells a pretty tale—this lackey from the Royal Mail!"

The spell was broken again. "You noticed too!" exclaimed Grimes.

"Yes. I noticed. That cap badge with a crown over the silver rocket." Sanderson laughed. "It was when I tried to find a rhyme for *tale* that things sort of clicked into place."

Grimes turned on the purser. "What the hell's going on here?" he demanded.

"Alas, Sir Knight, I cannot say. *I cannot say*?" The young man's pudgy face stiffened with resolution. "*No!* Come what may . . ."

Whatever it was that came, it was sudden. He was standing there, struggling to speak, and then he was . . . gone, vanished in a gentle thunderclap as the air rushed in to fill the vacuum where he had stood. Then another man stamped into the saloon, in captain's uniform with the same familiar trappings.

"Begone, good knights," he shouted, "to meet your fate! Get off my ship, I'm running late."

"Sir," began Grimes—and then that influence gripped his mind again. He said, "Thank you for passage, sir. Goodbye. We fare forth now, to do or die!"

"Well said, Sir John," declaimed Sanderson. "Well said, my friend. We go—to shape the story's end."

"I hope, good knights, you gallant two," growled the captain, "that story's end does not shape you." He led the way from the saloon up to the gangway.

They stood on the pontoon, watching the little steamer round the first bend on her voyage up river, then walked to the bridge that spanned the gap between landing stage and bank. Overhead the sky was darkening and the air was chill. The westering sun had vanished behind a bank of low clouds. Grimes, his shirt and slacks suddenly inadequate, shivered. *What am I doing here?* he asked himself. And then, quite suddenly, *Who am I?* It was a silly question, and he at once knew how foolish it was. The answer shaped itself in his mind. *I am the one they call Sir John, true comrade to Prince Sanderson.*

"We forward march," announced the Prince, "my cobber bold, to meet the perils long foretold. Up yonder hill, let us then, to beard the dragon in his den."

"The dragon wastes no time on fuss," remarked Grimes. "He's coming down, and bearding us."

Yes, the beast was coming down, either from the castle or from somewhere else atop the hill. It was airborne—and even in his bemused state Grimes realized that it should never have gotten off the ground. Its head and body were too large, its wings too small, too skimpy. But it was a terrifying sight, a monstrous, batwinged crocodile, its mouth, crowded with jagged teeth, agape, the long, sharp claws of its forefeet extended. It dived down on them, roaring, ignoring the laser beams that the two men directed at it, even though its metallic scales glowed cherry red where they scored hits. It dived down on them—and there was more than mere sound issuing from that horrid maw. The great gout of smoky flame was real enough, and Grimes and Sanderson escaped it only by diving into the undergrowth on either side of the steep path.

The beast pulled out of its dive and flapped away slowly, regaining altitude. The men watched it until it was only a darker speck in the dark sky, then realized that the speck was rapidly increasing in size. It was coming for them again.

Something was wrong, very wrong. In the fairy stories the dragons never kill the heroes . . . but this dragon looked like being the exception to prove the rule. Grimes holstered his laser pistol, pulled out his Minetti. He doubted that the little weapon would be of any avail against the armored monstrosity, but it might be worth trying. From the corner of his eyes he saw that Sanderson had out and ready his heavy projectile pistol. "Courage, Sir John," called the young man. "Aim for his head. We've no cold steel; we'll try hot lead!"

"Cold steel, forsooth!" swore Grimes. "Hot lead, indeed! A silver bullet's what we need!"

"Stand firm, Sir John, and don't talk rot! Don't whine for what we haven't got!"

Grimes loosed off a clip at the diving dragon on full automatic. Sanderson, the magazine of whose pistol held only ten rounds, fired in a more leisurely manner. Both men tried to put their shots into the open mouth, the most obviously vulnerable target. Whether or not they succeeded they never knew. Again they had to tumble hastily off the path just as the jet of flame roared out at them. This time it narrowly missed Grimes's face. It was like being shaved with a blowtorch.

He got groggily to his feet, fumbled another clip of cartridges out of the pouch at his belt, reloaded the little automatic. He saw that Sanderson was pushing a fresh magazine into the butt of his heavy pistol. The young man smiled grimly and said, "Sir John, the ammo's running low. When all is spent, what shall we do?"

"The beast will get us if we run. Would that we'd friends to call upon!"

"Many did give us good advice. If they gave us more it would be nice."

"What of the fairy Lynnimame?"

"And how, Sir John, do you know her name?"

The dragon was coming in again, barely visible in the fast gathering dusk. The men held their fire until the last possible moment—and it was almost the last moment for both of them. Barely did they scramble clear of the roaring, stinking flame, and as they rolled in the brush both of them were frantically beating out their smoldering clothing. The winged monster, as before, seemed to be uninjured.

Suddenly Sanderson cried out, swung to turn his just reloaded pistol on a new menace. It was Grimes who stopped him, who knocked his arm down before he could fire. In the glowing ovoid of light was a tiny human figure, female, with gauzy wings. She hung there over the rough, stony path. She was smiling sweetly, and her voice, when she spoke, was a silvery tintinnabulation. "Prince, your companion called my name. I am the fairy Lynnimame. I am she who, this very morn, from the jaws of the spider foul was torn. I pay my debts; you rescued me. I'll rescue you, if that's your fee."

"Too right it is, you lovesome sprite."

"Then take this, Prince. And now, good night."

She put something into Sanderson's hand and vanished. Before she flickered into invisibility Grimes, by the pale luminosity of her, saw what it was. It was a cartridge case, ordinary enough in appearance except that the tip of the bullet looked too bright to be lead. "A silver bullet!" marveled Sanderson. "A silver bullet. We are saved. He'll play Goliath to my David!"

"Unless you load, you pious prig, he'll play the chef to your long pig!"

Hastily Sanderson pulled the magazine from the butt of his pistol, ejected the first cartridge, replaced it with the silver bullet. He shoved the clip back home with a loud *click*. He was just in time; the dragon was upon them again, dropping almost vertically. The first lurid flames were gushing from its gaping mouth when the third officer fired. The result was spectacular. The thing exploded in mid-air, and the force of the blast sent Grimes tumbling head over heels into the bushes, with only a confused impression of a great, scarlet flower burgeoning against the night.

He recovered consciousness slowly. As before, when he had

dozed briefly aboard the river steamer, he was aware of his identity, knew what he was supposed to be doing. And then Sanderson's words severed the link with reality, recast the spell.

"Arise, Sir John! No time for sleep! We march against the Ogre's Keep!"

They marched against the Ogre's Keep—but it was more an undignified scramble up the steep path than a march. Luckily the moon was up now, somewhere above the overcast, and its diffused light was helpful, showed them the dark mass of briars that barred their way before they blundered into the thorny growth. Luckily they had not lost their weapons, and with their laser pistols they slashed, and slashed again, and slashed until their wrists ached with fatigue and their thumbs were numb from the continual pressure on the firing studs. For a long while they made no headway at all; it seemed that the severed, spiny tendrils were growing back faster than they were being destroyed. When the power packs in the pistols were exhausted they were actually forced back a few feet while they were reloading. It was Grimes who thought of renewing the attack with a wide setting instead of the needle beams that they had been using at first. The prickly bushes went up with a great *whoosh* of smoky flame, and the two men scrambled rather than ran through the gap thus cleared, and even then the barbed thorns were clutching at skin and clothing.

Then, with the fire behind them, they climbed on, bruised, torn and weary. They climbed, because it was the only thing to do. At last they were high enough up the hillside to see the castle again, black and forbidding against the gray sky. The few squares of yellow light that were windows accentuated rather than relieved the darkness.

They gained the rock-strewn plateau in the center of which towered the Keep. They stumbled across the uneven surface, making their way between the huge boulders, avoiding somehow the fissures that made the ground a crazy pattern of cracks. From some of these sounded ominous hissings and croakings and gruntings, from some there was a baleful gleaming of red eyes, but nothing actively molested them. And there was a rising wind now, damp and cold, that made a mockery of their rent, inadequate clothing, that whined and muttered in their ears like unquiet ghosts.

But they kept on at a staggering, faltering pace and came at last to the great iron-studded doorway. Barely within Sanderson's reach—and he was a tall man—was a huge knocker, forged in the semblance of a snarling lion's head. The young officer had to stretch to reach it; and as he put his hand to it, it moved of its own accord, emitting a thunderous clangor like an artillery barrage. *Boom, boom! Boom, boom! Boom!*

Almost as loud were the heavy footsteps that sounded thunderously behind the door. Almost as loud was the deep voice that asked, "Who on this night, so bleak and frore, disturbs the Giant Blunderbore?"

The double doors crashed outward. Standing there, silhouetted against the light, was a human figure. It was all of ten feet tall, and broad in proportion. It looked down at them, its eyes gleaming yellow in the black face, and bellowed, "Enter, Princeling! Enter, Knight! *Ye* shall be my guests tonight." Then, as the two men drew back, it went on, "Come in, come in! This is Liberty Hall—you can spit on the mat and call the cat a bastard!"

The lapse from rhymed couplets and the use of an expression that had never failed to annoy him snapped Grimes back to reality. He was Commodore John Grimes, of the Rim Worlds Naval Reserve, not Sir John, and he was supposed to be investigating this crazy planet. But the castle was real enough, as was the giant who loomed there in the open doorway, as were the bruises on his body that still ached, the scratches and burns that still smarted.

"What's the matter?" he asked nastily. "Can't you find a rhyme for 'bastard'? And who are you, anyhow?"

"And who are you? All I know is that you are outsiders, and I'm supposed to stop you. Not that I want to. This damn foolishness has gone on too long. Much too long."

From the sky thundered a great voice, "Blunderbore, your duty's plain! These prying strangers must be slain!"

The giant stared upward, growled, "—you. I've had you, chum, in a big way."

The answer was a sizzling bolt of lightning, a crackling streak of dazzling energy that should have incinerated Blunderbore where he stood. But he caught it with a huge hand, laughed and hurled it back like a flaming javelin, shouting, "Try that on for size, damn you!"

"What's going on?" Sanderson whimpered. "What's going on here?"

"It's a long story," Blunderbore told him.

"It's a story, all right," agreed Grimes. "The city of Ayonoree . . . the Frog Prince . . . the Fairy Lynnimame . . . and you, Blunderbore." Yes, it was all coming back to him, and it was all making a fantastic kind of sense.

"Can you be killed?" Blunderbore was asking.

"I suppose so," said Grimes, conscious of the smart of his wounds. "Yes, I fear so. We're the outsiders. We don't belong in the series, do we? And you and the others go on from installment to installment. . . ."

"Only because we're trapped. But come in. You have to wake the Princess. It's the only way out, for all of us."

The huge man stood to one side as Grimes and Sanderson hurried into the castle. They were barely in time, were almost knocked from their feet by the wind from the crashing volley of great rocks that fell from the black sky. Splinters stung the backs of their legs painfully. Grunting, Blunderbore pushed past them, seized the two sides of the door in his big hands, pulled them shut just as another shower of boulders crashed against the stout, iron-bound timbers. "Hurry!" he shouted. "He's turning nasty!"

The giant led the way across the flagstoned floor, to the far end of the enormous, gloomy hall. He staggered as he ran—and with cause. The very earth was growling beneath their feet, and each successive tremor was more violent than the last. From above came a crash of toppling masonry.

The air was thickening. Tendrils of yellow fog clutched at the running, stumbling men, and the writhing mist had substance. Half-seen, evil faces leered at them, distorted visages that were all teeth and dull-gleaming eyes. Vaporous claws reached out for them, solidifying as they did so. Behind Grimes Sanderson screamed, and the Commodore stopped and turned, slashing with his laser at the gelatinous obscenity that had the young officer in its grip. It piped shrilly as it disintegrated, stinking sulfurously.

"Hurry!" Blunderbore was still shouting. "Hurry!"

The stone floor was crackling underfoot, heaving and buckling, and from the high, vaulted ceiling ominous groans resounded. The castle could not withstand this punishment for long. The flaring torches were going out and there was a strong smell of escaping gas. Then, as a chance spark reignited the explosive mixture, there was a fiery blast that almost finished the destructive work initiated by the earthquake.

Almost finished.

But Blunderbore and the two spacemen were still on their feet, somehow, and there were still walls around them, although crumbling and tottering, and over their heads the last stone arch still held, despite the torrential rain of rubble that was clattering upon and around it. Ahead of them was the great fireplace, into which the giant jumped without stooping. Then he bent slowly and fumbled among the dead ashes, and straightened even more slowly, the muscles of his naked back and arms bulging and glistening. He grunted as he came erect, holding before him an enormous slab of stone. He cast it from him—and the noise of its fall and its shattering was lost amid the general uproar.

Under the slab was a spiral stairway, a helix of rusty iron running down, and down, down to murky depths where an eerie blue glimmer flickered. The prospect was not an inviting one; how long would the walls of the shaft withstand the incessant tremors? Even so, the fire was yet to come, whereas the frying pan was becoming hotter and hotter. Great sheets of flame from the ruptured gas mains were shrieking across the ruined hall, and through them crashed increasingly heavy falls of debris. And the writhing phantasms were back, multiplying in spite of the geysers of burning, exploding gas, coalescing, solidifying, piping and tittering. They were insubstantial no longer; their claws and their teeth were sharp.

"Down with you!" bellowed Blunderbore. "Down with you! It's the only way!"

"You lead!" gasped Grimes, using his laser like a sword, slashing at the half-materialized things that were closing in upon them.

"No . . . I'll hold . . . them off. . . ." The giant had wrenched the great iron spit from its sockets on either side of the fireplace, was flailing away with it, grunting with every stroke. Tattered rags of ectoplasm clung to its ends, eddied through the smoke- and dust-filled air.

Grimes paused briefly at the head of the spiral staircase, then barked to Sanderson, "Come on!" He clattered down the shaking treads, his left hand on the outer guard rail, his pistol clenched in his right fist. The central column seemed to be trying to tie itself into a knot, but it held, although the steps were canting at odd angles. The walls of the shaft were starting to bulge inward.

Grimes ran—down, down, round, round—keeping his footing in spite of the earthquake shocks, in spite of his increasing dizziness. He ran, and after him ran the third officer. Up there above Blunderbore was still fighting; his joyous bellowing came rolling down on them like thunder, loud even above the clangorous destruction of the Ogre's Keep.

Down, down. . . .

Grimes staggered on, forcing his legs to move, to go on moving, taking great gasps of the damp, fetid air. Something barred his way, something long and serpent-like, with absurdly small forelegs, with curved poison-fangs and a flickering black tongue. The Commodore tried to stop, tried to bring his pistol up to a firing position, but could not. His impetus carried him on. Then he was *through* the monster; its body offered no more resistance than wet tissue paper.

Down, down. . . .

It was more of a fall than a run.

It was a fall.

Grimes thudded gently into something thick and soft, lay sprawled on the soft bed of moss, breathing in great, painful gulps. Slowly he became aware of his surroundings: the cave, lit by a soft, rosy radiance with no apparent source, the opalescent colonnades of stalactite and stalagmite, the tinkling, glittering waterfalls. He focused his attention upon his immediate vicinity. The Prince was still with him, was himself slowly stirring into wakefulness. Sir John knew where he was. This was the Witch's Cave, the home of the wicked Melinee.

She was standing over them, a tall woman, white of skin, black of hair, vividly red of mouth, clad in a robe of misty gray. In either hand she held a crystal goblet, bedewed with condensation. She murmured, "Rest you awhile, good knights and true, and pray accept this cooling brew."

Sanderson reached greedily for the vessel she held out to him—and Grimes, firing from his supine position, exploded it into a spray of splinters and acrid steam.

"It's not the mess," protested Sanderson, "but it's the waste! I never even got a taste!"

"Prince, had we quaffed the witch's wine," Grimes told him, "it would have turned us into swine."

Melinee laughed, a low, throaty gurgle. "You know too much, too much by far. But you'll be more fun the way you are." She looked at Sanderson as she said this. The invitation in her black eyes, her parted scarlet lips, was unmistakable.

The young officer reacted. He got gracefully to his feet, took a step toward the witch. He said gallantly. "Who needs wine when you're around, beautiful?"

"Careful!" warned Grimes.

"Have we been careful so far, sir? We've been collecting all the kicks—it's time that we got our paws on some of the ha'pence." Then, to the woman, "Isn't there somewhere around here a little more private?"

She smiled. "My bower, behind the waterfall . . ."

"Sanderson! I order you to keep away from this female!"

"*I* give the orders around here, old man," said Melinee sweetly. "This is *my* cave, and whatever your rank may be it means nothing as long as you're on my property." She turned again to Sanderson. The filmy robe was already slipping down from one smooth shoulder and it was obvious that she was wearing nothing underneath it. "Come," she murmured.

The admonitory voice boomed from the roof of the cavern. "Melinee, you forget yourself!"

"I don't!" she shouted. "I'm remembering myself. I'm a real person, not a character in some stupid children's fairy story! If *you* can't write adult fiction, buster, *I'm* taking charge of the plot. I'm supposed to be stopping these men from going any further, aren't I? Then shut up and let me do it my way!"

"Melinee!"

"That's not my name, and you know it." She turned again to Sanderson. "Don't be shy, spaceman. I'll show you just how wicked a wicked witch can be!"

"Mr. Sanderson!" Grimes's voice crackled with authority. "Leave that woman alone!"

The young man stood there, obviously thinking mutinous thoughts but not daring to express them. The woman stood there, looking at him, a contemptuous little smile curving her full lips. And then she turned, began to walk slowly and gracefully toward the waterfall. Her robe was almost transparent.

"Melinee!" The voice from the roof expressed entreaty as well as anger. And why, Grimes asked himself suddenly, *should I be on his side?* He said aloud, but quietly, "All right, Mr. Sanderson. Go with her."

Sanderson shook his head bewilderedly. "First you tell me not to, and now you say that I can. . . . After all, we *are* on duty."

"Go with her," repeated Grimes. It was more of an order than a suggestion. "But, sir . . ."

"Damn it all, when I was your age I didn't have to be told twice."

The Wicked Witch called over her shoulder, "Do as the nice man says, darling."

The third officer made a sort of growling noise deep in his throat, glared defiantly at the Commodore, then started after the woman. She had reached the shimmering curtain of the waterfall, was passing through it. As she turned to look back through the rippling transparency Sanderson quickened his pace. Grimes chuckled, pulled from his pocket the battered pipe that somehow had survived unbroken, filled it, then ostentatiously used his laser pistol as a lighter. It was a dangerous trick, but an impressive one.

From beyond the cascade came the sound of a crooning female

voice. "Mirror, mirror on the wall, who is the fairest one of all?" Then there was a crash of splintering glass and a scream. "No! No! You can't do that to me! I'll fix you! I'll fix you, you . . . you fairy story-teller!"

Melinee burst back into the main cavern. She was shaking with murderous fury. "Look!" she yelled. "Look what that bastard did to me!"

Grimes looked. Sanderson looked. "But—" the latter started to say. Grimes interjected hastily, "It's shocking!" He was lying—as the mirror must have done.

"Come on!" she snarled. "This joke's gone on quite long enough!"

She led the way into her bower, through the curtain of falling water. As Grimes passed through it he heard behind him the clatter of falling stalactites, felt the brief wave of scalding heat as the waterfall flashed into steam. But it was too late to harm him, and the others were well clear.

On the far wall of the bower was the mirror—or what had been the mirror. Now it was only an elaborately molded golden frame set into the rock face. Melinee scrambled through it, ignoring the sharp edges that ripped her robe from hip to ankle. Sanderson followed her, then Grimes. The tunnel beyond it was unpleasantly organic in appearance, a convoluted tube, with smooth and pinkly glistening walls, winding, pulsing underfoot, writhing.

Melinee ran on, sure-footed. Somewhere she had lost her sandals, had probably used one of them to smash the lying, libelous looking-glass. The men, in their shoes, slipped and slithered, but they kept up with her. Down they went, and down, losing all sense of direction, losing their footing, putting hands out to steady themselves against smooth, warm walls that shrank away from the touch. Down they went, and down, gasping in the hot air, suddenly conscious that the red-glowing walls were steadily contracting. Soon there would be no going any further ahead, and no turning back.

They were crouching, and then they were slithering on their bellies. Grimes, who had passed Sanderson while it was still possible, while there was still freedom of movement, suddenly found his way blocked, realized that the crown of his head was pressing against the soles of Melinee's bare feet. Faintly her voice came back to him. "We're there . . . at the air lock. But . . . I don't know how to open it. . . ."

"I . . . I have to crawl past you . . ." gasped Grimes. Then, urgently, "Make yourself small, woman! Breathe out!"

"I'll . . . try."

Like an earthworm in its tunnel—but with far less agility, far less speed—the Commodore edged forward. Somehow he managed to get both arms ahead of his body, clutched filmy fabric and the firm flesh beneath. He heard her give a little scream, but he ignored it. Cloth tore, and then he had a firm grip on her waist, just above her hips. His face was over her heels, and then pressing down on her ankles. Somehow he was still able to draw an occasional breath. His nose was sliding—but slowly, slowly—up the valley between her calves. He hunched his back, and the resilient wall above him gave a little.

He grunted as he wriggled forward. Somehow he negotiated her buttocks; then his fingers were on her shoulders. He pulled himself ahead, more rapidly now. He spat out a mouthful of hair, then slid his hands along her upreaching bare arms. And then there was metal, blessedly hard and solid to the touch—and touch was the only sense that he and to guide him.

Was this an air lock door? He did not know; he had only her word for it. And if it were, indeed, an air lock door, was it of the standard pattern? It had to be; otherwise the situation was utterly hopeless. Cramped as he was, Grimes could never get his laser pistol out of its holster—and even if he could its employment in this confined space might well prove fatal to himself and the others.

His fingers groped, scrabbled, feeling nothing at first but smooth, seamless metal. He had almost given up hope when he found what he was looking for: the neat little hole, large enough to admit a space-gloved digit. He had to squirm and contort himself to get his hand to the right angle. Under him Melinee whimpered a little, but did not complain.

The tip of his index finger crept over the faired rim of the hole, pushed into it, at first encountering nothing at all and then, after what seemed an eternity, smooth plastic. Grimes pushed, felt the surface give. He maintained the pressure, relaxed it, pushed again, and again, making "O" in Morse Code—"O" for "Open."

He heard the faint whir of machinery, a noise that suddenly became louder. The inward opening door almost took his finger with it. And then he was in the air lock, closely followed by Sanderson.

Melinee had vanished.

Slowly Grimes and Sanderson walked through the silent, the too silent alleyways of the ship, fighting the lassitude that threatened to close down upon them, forcing their way through air that seemed to possess the viscosity of cold treacle. But they were not alone. In their ears—or in their minds?—sounded the croaking voice of the Frog Prince, the tinkling soprano of the Fairy Lynnimame, the husky whisper of Melinee. "You must not give in. You have come so far; you must not give in. Waken the Princess. Waken the Princess." And there was Blunderbore's urgent muttering, and the faint voices of the *River Queen's* captain and purser. "Wake the Princess. Wake the Princess."

They stumbled on, weakening, through the gelid air, the internal atmosphere that didn't even smell right, that didn't smell at all, that lacked the familiar taints of hot oil and machinery, of tobacco smoke and women's perfume, the clean, garden scents of the hydroponics deck. They staggered on, through alleyways and up companionways, fighting every inch of the way, sustained somehow by the fairytale characters whom they had encountered.

And Grimes knew what was wrong, knew the nature of the stasis that must, soon, make them part of itself, unless they reached the Mannschenn Drive room in time. He had read of, but had never until now experienced, the almost impossible balance of forces, the canceling out of opposing temporal precession fields that would freeze a ship and all her people in an eternal *Now,* forever adrift down and between the dimensions. That had been one of the theories advanced to account for the vanishing, without trace, of that Waverley Royal Mail liner ten standard years ago—the ship aboard which the writer Clay Wilton had been a passenger.

Grimes could remember, vividly, the blurb on the dust jacket of the book that he had bought as a present for the small daughter of a friend. "The last of the dreamers," the author had been called. He had skimmed through it, had laughed at the excellent illustrations and then, to his amazement, had been gripped by the story. It was about a world that never was and was never could be, a planet where sorcery was everyday practice, where talking animals and good fairies and wicked witches interfered in the affairs of men and women.

"You are beginning to understand," whispered Lynnimame.

There was the door ahead of them, with MANNSCHENN DRIVE in shining metal letters above it. The door was closed, stubborn; it would not yield. Human muscles were powerless against the stasis; human muscles with strength flowing into them from outside, somehow, were still powerless. The handle snapped off cleanly in Grimes's hand.

"Let me, sir," Sanderson was saying. "Let me try."

The Commodore stepped slowly to one side, his motions those of a deep-sea diver. He saw that the young man had his laser weapon out of its holster, was struggling to raise it against the dreadful inertia.

He pressed the firing stud.

Slowly, fantastically, the beam of intense light extruded itself from the muzzle, creeping toward that immovable door. After an eternity it made contact, and after another eternity the paint began to bubble. Aeons passed, and there was a crater. More aeons dragged by—and the crater was a hole. Still Sanderson, his face rigid with strain, held the weapon steady. Grimes could imagine that luminous, purple worm crawling across the space from the door to the switchboard. Then Sanderson gasped, "I can't keep it up!" and the muzzle of the pistol wavered, sagged until it was pointing at the deck.

We tried, thought Grimes. Then he wondered, *Will Wilton add us to his permanent cast of characters?*

Suddenly there was sound again—the dying, deepening whine of a stopped Mannschenn Drive unit, of spinning, precessing gyroscopes slowing to final immobility. Like a bullet fired from a gun deflected after the pulling of the trigger, the laser beam had reached its target. There was sound again: fans, and pumps, the irregular throbbing of the Inertial Drive, and all the bubble and clamor of a suddenly awakened ship. From bulkhead speakers boomed a voice, that of the captain of the river steamer. "Whoever you are, come up to the main saloon, please. And whoever you are—thank you."

Grimes sprawled comfortably in an easy chair, a cold drink ready to hand. He had decided to stay aboard this ship, the *Princess of Troon*, having persuaded her captain to set trajectory for Lorn. After all, he was already ten years late—a few more weeks would make very little difference. During the voyage the Commodore would be able to question the *Princess'* personnel still further, to work on his report. He was keeping young Sanderson with him. Drakenberg had not been at all pleased when deprived of the service of a watch officer, but the Commodore piled on far more G's than he did.

Already Grimes was beginning to wonder if his report would be believed, in spite of all the corroborative evidence from the personnel of both ships, *Rim Jaguar* and *Princess of Troon*. He recalled vividly the scene in the passenger liner's main saloon when he and Sanderson had made their way into that compartment. The stasis must have been closed down while everybody was at dinner; dishes on the tables were still steaming.

They had all been there: the frog-like Grollan, the old lady who had been the peasant woman encountered on the towpath, the pretty fragile blonde whose name should have been Lynnimame, but was not; all of them looking like the characters in the illustrations to the Clay Wilton books. And there was the big—but not all that big—Negro, who was a physicist, not an ogre, and the captain, and the purser. There was the beautiful woman who could have been the model for the Melinee in the pictures and who was, in fact, Mrs. Wilton. There were other officers, other passengers, and among them was Clay Wilton himself. He had the beginnings of a black eye, and a trickle of blood still dribbled from the corner of his mouth. Ship's staff had formed a protective cordon about him, but made it quite obvious that this was only because they had been ordered to do so.

After the first excitement there had been the conference, during which all concerned tried to work out what had happened, and why.

Blundell, the big physicist—it had been hard not to think of him as Blunderbore—had said, "I've my own ideas, Commodore Grimes. But you, sir, are the recognized authority on Rim phenomena. . . ."

Grimes was flattered, and tried not to show it. He made a major production of filling and lighting his pipe. After he had it going he said, "I can *try* to explain. The way I see it is this. The ship went into stasis, and somehow drifted out from the Waverley sector toward the Rim. And out here, at the very edge of the expanding galaxy, there's always an . . . oddness. Time and space are not inclined to follow the laws that obtain elsewhere. Too, thought seems to have more power—physical power, I mean—than in the regions more toward the center. It's all part and parcel of the vagueness—that's not quite the right word—of . . . of everything. We get along with it. We're used to it.

"Look at it this way. You were all frozen in your ever-lasting *Now,* but you could still think, and you could still dream. And who was the most expert dreamer among you? It had to be Clay Wilton; after all, his publishers refer to him as 'the last of the dreamers.' Mr. Wilton dreamed out the story that he was working on at the time when your Mannschenn Drive went on the blink. Then he dreamed of the next story in the series, and the next, and the next. . . . Somehow a world shaped itself about his dreams. Out here, on the Rim, there must be the raw material for the creation of new galaxies. Somehow that world shaped itself, a solid world, with atmosphere, and vegetation, and people. It was real enough to register on all *Rim Jaguar's* instruments, even though it vanished when this ship came out of stasis. It was real enough, but, with a few exceptions, the people weren't real. They were little more than mobile scenery. The exceptions, of course, were those characters drawn from real life. And they led a sort of double existence. One body here, aboard the ship, and another body on the surface of that impossible planet, dancing like a puppet as Mr. Wilton manipulated the strings. Toward the end, the puppets were getting restive. . . ."

"You can say that again, Commodore," grinned Blundell.

"Yes, the puppets were getting restive, and realized that they, too, could become puppet-masters, could use Mr. Sanderson and myself to break the stasis. And, at the same time, Mr. Wilton was trying to work us into his current plot." Grimes turned to the writer. "And tell me, sir, did you intend to kill us?"

"Nobody dies in my stories," muttered the man. "Not even the baddies."

"But there has to be a first time for everything. That dragon of yours was far too enthusiastic. And so was your destruction of Blunderbore's castle."

"I'd gotten kind of attached to the place, too," grumbled the physicist.

"I meant no harm." Wilton's voice was sullen.

"Don't you believe him!" flared Mrs. Wilton—Melinee, the Wicked Witch. "He has a nasty, cruel streak in him, and only writes the sweetness and light fairy-tale rubbish because it makes good money. But that trick of his with my mirror will be grounds for divorce. Any judge, anywhere, will admit that it was mental cruelty."

"But what did you do to *me*?" demanded the weedy little man, taking a pitiful offensive. "You destroyed my world."

But did we? Grimes was wondering. Did *we*?

Sanderson and the fragile little blonde had come into the small smoking room, had not noticed him sitting there; they were sharing a settee only a few feet from him.

"The really fantastic thing about it all, Lynnimame—I like to call you that; after all, it was your name when I first met you. You don't mind, do you?" Sanderson was saying.

"Of course not, Henry. If you like it, *I* like it."

"Good. But as I was saying, the really fantastic thing about it all, the way that I fitted into old Wilton's story, is that I *am* a prince. . . ."

"But I think," said Grimes coldly as he got up from his chair, "that the Wicked Witch will be able to vouch that you're not a fairy prince."

And would they all live happily ever after? he wondered as he made his way to his cabin. At least he was finally on his way home.

⟾ Grimes at Glenrowan ⟾

Captain Chandler reports that he wrote his first story after meeting John W. Campbell, the late, great editor of Astounding/Analog SF, during WWII. During the war years, the author became a regular contributor to the SF magazines, but almost dropped out of the field when he was promoted to Chief Officer in the British-Australian steamship service. His second wife, Susan, encouraged him to take up writing again; the Rim Worlds and the Rim Runners series is a result.

COMMODORE JOHN GRIMES of the Rim Worlds Naval Reserve, currently Master of the survey ship *Faraway Quest*, was relaxing in his day cabin aboard that elderly but trustworthy vessel. That morning, local time, he had brought the old ship down to a landing at Port Fortinbras, on Elsinore, the one habitable planet in orbit about the Hamlet sun. It was Grimes's first visit to Elsinore for very many years. This call was to be no more—and no less—than a showing of the flag of the Confederacy. The *Quest* had been carrying out a survey of a newly discovered planetary system rather closer to the Shakespearian Sector than to the Rim Worlds and Grimes's lords and masters back on Lorn had instructed him, on completion of this task, to pay a friendly call on their opposite numbers on Elsinore.

However, he would be seeing nobody of any real importance until this evening, when he would attend a reception being held in his honour at the President's palace. So he had time to relax, at ease in his shipboard shorts and shirt, puffing contentedly at his vile pipe, watching the local trivi programmes on his playmaster. That way he would catch up on the planetary news, learn something of Elsinorian attitudes and prejudices. He was, after all, visiting this world in an ambassadorial capacity.

He looked with wry amusement into the screen. There he was or, to be more exact, there was *Faraway Quest*—coming down. *Not bad,* he admitted smugly, *not bad at all.* There had been a nasty, gusty wind at ground level about which Aerospace Control had failed to warn him—but he had coped. He watched the plump, dull-silver spindle that was his ship sagging to leeward, leaning into the veering breeze, then settling almost exactly into the center of the triangle of bright flashing marker beacons, midway between the Shakespearian Line's *Oberon* and the Commission's *Epsilon Orionis*. He recalled having made a rather feeble joke about O'Brian and O'Ryan. (His officers had laughed dutifully.) He watched the beetle-like ground cars carrying the port officials scurry out across the grey apron as the *Quest*'s ramp was extruded from her after airlock. He chuckled softly at the sight of Timmins, his Chief Officer, resplendent in his best uniform, standing at the head of the gangway to receive the boarding party. Although only a reservist—like Grimes himself—that young man put on the airs and graces of a First Lieutenant of a Constellation Class battlewagon, a flagship at that. But he was a good spaceman and that was all that really mattered.

After a short interval, filled with the chatter of the commentator, he was privileged to watch himself being interviewed by the newsman who had accompanied the officials on board. Did he really look as crusty as that? he wondered. And wasn't there something in what Sonya, his wife, was always saying—and what other ladies had said long before he first met her—about his ears? Stun's'l ears, jughandle ears. Only a very minor operation would be required to make them less outstanding, but . . . He permitted himself another chuckle. He liked him the way that he was and if the ladies didn't they had yet to show it.

The intercom telephone buzzed. Grimes turned to look at Timmins's face in the little screen. He made a downward gesture of his hand towards the playmaster, and his own voice and that of the interviewer at once faded into inaudibility. "Yes, Mr. Timmins?" he asked.

"Sir, there is a lady here to see you."

A *lady?* wondered Grimes. Elsinore was one of the few worlds upon which he had failed to enjoy a temporary romance. He had been there only once before, when he was a junior officer in the Federation's Survey Service. He recalled (it still rankled) that he had had his shore leave stopped for some minor misdemeanor.

"A lady?" he repeated. Then, "What does she want?"

"She says that she is from Station Yorick, sir. She would like to interview you."

"But I've already been interviewed," said Grimes.

"Not by Station Yorick," a female voice told him. "Elsinore's purveyors of entertainment and philosophy."

Timmins's face in the little screen had been replaced by that of a girl—a woman, rather. Glossy black hair, short cut, over a thin, creamily pale face with strong bone structure and delicately cleft chin . . . a wide, scarlet mouth . . . almost indigo blue eyes set off by black lashes.

"Mphm," grunted Grimes approvingly. "Mphm . . ."

"Commodore Grimes?" she asked in a musical contralto. "*The* Commodore Grimes?"

"There's only one of me as far as I know," he told her. "And you?"

She smiled whitely. "Kitty, of Kitty's Korner. With a 'K'. And I'd like a *real* interview for *my* audience, not the sort of boring question-and-answer session that you've just been watching."

"Mphm," grunted Grimes again. What harm could it do?, he asked himself. This would be quite a good way of passing what otherwise would be a dull afternoon. And Elsinore was in the Shakespearian Sector, wasn't it? Might not he, Grimes, play Othello to this newshen's Desdemona, wooing her with his tall tales of peril and adventure all over the Galaxy? And in his private grog locker were still six bottles of Antarean Crystal Gold laid aside for emergencies such as this, a potent liquor coarsely referred to by spacemen as a leg-opener, certainly a better loosener of inhibitions than the generality of alcoholic beverages. He would have to partake of it with her, of course, but a couple or three soberups would put him right for the cocktail party.

"Ask Mr. Timmins to show you up," he said.

He looked at her over the rim of his glass. He liked what he saw. The small screen of the intercom, showing only her face, had not done her full justice. She sat facing him in an easy chair, making a fine display of slender, well-formed thigh under the high-riding apology for a skirt. (Hemlines were down again, almost to ankle length, in the Rim Worlds and Grimes had not approved of the change in fashion.) The upper part of her green dress was not quite transparent but it was obvious that she neither wore nor needed a bust support.

She looked at him over the rim of her glass. She smiled. He said, "Here's to Yorick, the Jester . . ."

She said, "And the philosopher: We have our serious side." They sipped. The wine was cold, mellow fire.

He said, "Don't we all?"

"You especially," she told him. "You must be more of a philosopher than most men, Commodore. Your interdimensional experiences—"

"So you've heard of them . . . Kitty."

"Yes. Even here. Didn't somebody once say, 'If there's a crack in the Continuum, Grimes is sure to fall into it—and come up with the Shaara Crown Jewels clutched in his hot little hands.'?"

He laughed. "I've never laid my paws on the Shaara Crown Jewels yet—although I've had my troubles with the Shaara. There was the time that I was in business as an interstellar courier and got tangled with a Rogue Queen—"

But she was not interested in the Shaara. She pressed on, "It seems that it's only out on the Rim proper, on worlds like Kinsolving, that you find these . . . cracks in the Continuum. . . ."

Grimes refilled the glasses saying, "Thirsty work, talking. . . ."

"But we've talked hardly at all," she said. "And I *want* you to talk. I want *you* to talk. If all I wanted was stories of high adventure and low adventure in *this* universe I'd only have to interview any of our own space captains. What I want, what Station Yorick wants, what our public wants is a story such as only *you* can tell. One of your adventures on Kinsolving. . ."

He laughed. "It's not only on Kinsolving's Planet that you can fall through a crack in the Continuum." He was conscious of the desire to impress her. "In fact, the first time that it happened was on Earth. . . ."

She was suitably incredulous.

"On Earth?" she demanded.

"Too right," he said.

I'm a Rim Worlder now [he told her] but I wasn't born out on the Rim. As far as the accident of birth is concerned I'm Terran. I started my spacefaring career in the Interstellar Federation's Survey Service. My long leaves I always spent on Earth, where my parents lived.

Anyhow, just to visualize me as I was then: a Survey Service JG Lieutenant with money in his pocket, time on his hands and, if you must know, between girlfriends. I'd been expecting that—What was her name? Oh, yes. Vanessa. I'd been expecting that she'd be still waiting for me when I got back from my tour of duty. She wasn't. She'd married—of all people!—a sewage conversion engineer.

Anyhow, I spent the obligatory couple of weeks with my parents in The Alice. (The Alice? Oh, that's what Australians call Alice Springs, a city in the very middle of the island continent.) My father was an author. He specialised in historical romances. He was always saying that the baddies of history are much more interesting than the goodies—and that the good baddies and the bad goodies are the most fascinating of all. You've a fine example of that in this planetary system of yours. The names, I mean. The Hamlet sun and all that. Hamlet was rather a devious bastard, wasn't he? And although he wasn't an out and out baddie he could hardly be classed as a goodie.

Well, the Old Man was working on yet another historical novel, this one to be set in Australia. All about the life and hard times of Ned Kelly. You've probably never heard of him—very few people outside Australia have—but he was a notorious bushranger. Bushrangers were sort of highway robbers. Just as the English have Dick Turpin and the Americans have Jesse James, so we have the Kelly Gang. (Australia had rather a late start as a nation so has always made the most of its relatively short history.)

According to my respected father this Ned Kelly was more, much more, than a mere bushranger. He was a freedom fighter, striking valiant blows on behalf of the oppressed masses, a sort of Robin Hood. And, like that probably-mythical Robin Hood, he was something of a military genius. Until the end he outwitted the troopers—as the police were called in his day—with ease. He was a superb horseman. He was an innovator. His suit of homemade armor, breast and back-plates and an odd cylindrical helmet—was famous. It was proof against rifle and pistol fire. He was very big and strong and could carry the weight of it.

It was at a place called Glenrowan that he finally came unstuck. In his day it was only a village, a hamlet. (No pun intended.) It was on the railway line from Melbourne to points north. Anyhow, Ned had committed some crime or other at a place called Wangaratta and a party of police was on the way there from Melbourne by special train, not knowing that the Kelly gang had ridden back to Glenrowan. Like all guerrilla leaders throughout history Kelly had an excellent intelligence service. He knew that the train was on the way and would be passing through Glenrowan. He persuaded a gang of Irish workmen—platelayers, they were called—to tear up the railway tracks just north of the village. The idea was that the train would be derailed and the policemen massacred. While the bushrangers were waiting they enjoyed quite a party in the Glenrowan Hotel; Kelly and his gang were more popular than otherwise among the locals. But the schoolmaster—who was *not* a Kelly supporter—managed to creep away from the festivities and, with a lantern and his wife's red scarf, flagged the train down.

The hotel was besieged. It was set on fire. The only man who was not killed at once was Kelly himself. He came out of the smoke and the flames, wearing his armor, a revolver (a primitive multi-shot projectile pistol) in each hand, blazing away at his enemies. One of the troopers had the intelligence to fire at his legs, which were not protected by the armor, and brought him down.

He was later hanged.

Well, as I've indicated, my Old Man was up to the eyebrows in his research into the Ned Kelly legend, and some of his enthusiasm rubbed off on to me. I thought that I'd like to have a look at this Glenrowan place. Father was quite amused. He told me that Glenrowan *now* was nothing at all like Glenrowan *then*, that instead of a tiny huddle of shacks by the railway line I should find a not-so-small city sitting snugly in the middle of all-the-year-round-producing orchards under the usual featureless plastic domes. There was, he conceded, a sort of reconstruction of the famous hotel standing beside a railway line—all right for tourists, he sneered, but definitely not for historians.

I suppose that he was a historian—he certainly always took his researches seriously enough—but I wasn't. I was just a spaceman with time on my hands. And—which probably decided me—there was a quite fantastic shortage of unattached popsies in The Alice and my luck might be better elsewhere.

So I took one of the tourist airships from Alice Springs to Melbourne and then a really antique railway train—steam-driven yet, although the coal in the tender was only for show; it was a minireactor that boiled the water—from Melbourne to Glenrowan. This primitive means of locomotion, of course, was for the benefit of tourists.

When I dismounted from that horribly uncomfortable coach at Glenrowan Station I ran straight into an old shipmate. Oddly enough—although, as it turned out later, it wasn't so odd—his name was Kelly. He'd been one of the junior interstellar drive engineer officers in the old *Aries*. I'd never liked him much—or him me—but when you're surrounded by planetlubbers you greet a fellow spaceman as though he were a long-lost brother.

"Grimes!" he shouted. "Gutsy Grimes in person!"

[No, Kitty, I didn't get that nickname because I'm exceptionally brave. It was just that some people thought I had an abnormally hearty appetite and would eat *anything*.]

"An' what are *you* doin' here?" he demanded. His Irish accent, as Irish accents usually do, sounded phoney as all hell.

I told him that I was on leave and asked him if he was too. He told me that he'd resigned his commission some time ago and that so had his cousin, Spooky Byrne. Byrne hadn't been with us in *Aries* but I had met him. He was a PCO—Psionic Communications Officer. A Commissioned Teacup Reader, as we used to call them. A trained and qualified telepath. You don't find many of 'em these days in the various merchant services—the Carlotti Communications System is a far more reliable way of handling instantaneous communications over the light-years. But most navies still employ them—a telepath is good for much more than the mere transmission and reception of signals.

So, Kelly and Spooky Byrne, both in Glenrowan. And me, also in Glenrowan. There are some locations in some cities where, it is said, if you loaf around long enough you're sure to meet everybody you know. An exaggeration, of course, but there *are* focal points. But I wouldn't put the Glenrowan Hotel—that artificially tumbledown wooden shack with its bark roof—synthetic bark, of course—in that category. It looked very small and sordid among the tall, shining buildings of the modern city. Small and sordid? Yes, but—somehow—even though it was an obvious, trashy tourist trap it possessed a certain character. Something of the atmosphere of the original building seemed to have clung to the site.

Kelly said, using one of my own favourite expressions, "Come on in, Grimes. The sun's over the yardarm."

I must have looked a bit dubious. My onetime shipmate had been quite notorious for never paying for a drink when he could get somebody else to do it. He read my expression. He laughed. "Don't worry, Gutsy. I'm a rich man now—which is more than I was when I was having to make do on my beggarly stipend in the Survey Service—may God rot their cotton socks! Come on in!"

Well, we went into the pub. The inside came up to—or down to—my worst expectations. There was a long bar of rough wood with thirsty tourists lined up along it. There was a sagging calico ceiling. There was a wide variety of antique ironmongery hanging on the walls—kitchen implements, firearms, rusty cutlasses. There were simulated flames flickering in the glass chimneys of battered but well-polished brass oil lamps. The wenches behind the bar were dressed in sort of Victorian costumes—long, black skirts, high-collared, frilly white blouses—although I don't think that in good Queen Victoria's day those blouses would have been as near as dammit transparent and worn over no underwear.

We had rum—not the light, dry spirit that most people are used to these days but sweet, treacly, almost-knife-and-fork stuff. Kelly paid, peeling off credits from a roll that could almost have been used as a bolster. We had more rum. Kelly tried to pay again but I wouldn't let him—although I hoped this party wouldn't last all day. Those prices, in that clipjoint, were making a nasty dent in my holiday money. Then Spooky Byrne drifted in, as colorless and weedy as ever, looking like a streak of ectoplasm frayed at the edges.

He stared at me as though he were seeing a ghost. "Grimes, of all people!" he whispered intensely. "Here, of all places!"

[I sensed, somehow, that his surprise was not genuine.]

"An' why not?" demanded his burly, deceptively jovial cousin. "Spacemen are only tourists in uniform. An' as Grimes is in civvies that makes him even more a tourist."

"The . . . coincidence," hissed Spooky. Whatever his act was he was persisting with it.

"Coincidences are always happenin'," said Kelly, playing up to him.

"Yes, Eddie, but—"

"But what?" I demanded, since it seemed expected of me.

"Mr. Grimes," Spooky told me, "would it surprise you if I told you that one of your ancestors was *here*? Was here *then*?"

"Too right it would," I said. "Going back to the old style Twentieth Century, and the Nineteenth, and further back still, most of my male forebears were seamen." The rum was making me boastfully talkative. "I have a pirate in my family tree. And an Admiral of the Royal Navy, on my mother's side. Her family name is Hornblower. So, Spooky, what the hell would either a Grimes or a Hornblower have been doing here, miles inland, in this nest of highway robbers?" Both Kelly and Byrne gave me dirty looks. "All right, then. Not highway robbers. Bushrangers, if it makes you feel any happier."

"And not bushrangers either!" growled Kelly. "Freedom fighters!"

"Hah!" I snorted.

"Freedom fighters!" stated Kelly belligerently. "All right, so they did rob a bank or two. An' so what? In, that period rebel organizations often robbed the capitalists to get funds to buy arms and all the rest of it. It was no more than S.O.P."

"Mphm," I grunted.

"In any case," said Kelly, "your ancestor was so here. We *know*. Come home with us an' we'll convince you."

So I let those two bastards talk me into accompanying them to their apartment, which was a penthouse atop the Glenrowan Tower. This wasn't by any means the tallest building in the city although it had been, I learned, when it was built. I remarked somewhat enviously that this was a palatial pad for a spaceman and Kelly told me that he wasn't a spaceman but a businessman and that he'd succeeded, by either clever or lucky investments, in converting a winning ticket in the New Irish Sweep into a substantial fortune. Byrne told him that he should give some credit where credit was due. Kelly told Byrne that graduates of the Rhine Institute are bound, by oath, not to use their psionic gifts for personal enrichment. Byrne shut up.

The living quarters of the penthouse were furnished in period fashion—the Victorian period. Gilt and red plush—dark, carved, varnished wood heavily framed, sepia-tinted photographs—no, not holograms, but those old *flat* photographs—of heavily bearded worthies hanging on the crimson-and-gold papered walls. One of them I recognized from the research material my father had been using. It was Ned Kelly.

"Fascinating," I said.

"This atmosphere is necessary to our researches," said Byrne. Then, "But come through to the laboratory."

I don't know what I was expecting to see in the other room into which they led me. Certainly not what first caught my attention. That caught my attention? That *demanded* my attention. It was, at first glance, a Mannschenn Drive unit—not a full sized one such as would be found in even a small ship but certainly a bigger one than the mini-Mannschenns you find in lifeboats.

[You've never seen a Mannschenn Drive unit? I must show you ours before you go ashore. And you don't understand how they work? Neither do I, frankly. But it boils down, essentially, to gyroscopes precessing in time, setting up a temporal precession field, so that our ships aren't really breaking the light barrier but going astern in time while they're going ahead in space.]

"A Mannschenn Drive unit," I said unnecessarily.

"I built it," said Kelly, not without pride.

"What for?" I asked. "Time Travel?" I sneered.

"Yes," he said.

I laughed. "But it's known to be impossible. A negative field would require the energy of the entire galaxy—"

"Not physical Time Travel," said Spooky Byrne smugly. "Psionic Time Travel, back along the world line stemming from an ancestor. Eddie's ancestor was at Glenrowan. So was mine. So was yours."

"Ned Kelly wasn't married," I said triumphantly.

"And so you have to be married to father a child?" asked Byrnes sardonically. "Come off it, Grimes! You should know better than that."

[I did, as a matter of fact. This was after that odd business I'd gotten involved in on El Dorado.]

"All right," I said. "Your ancestors might have been present at the Siege of Glenrowan. Mine was not. At or about that time he was, according to my father—and he's the family historian—second mate of a tramp windjammer. He got himself paid off in Melbourne and, not so long afterwards, was master of a little brig running between Australia and New Zealand. He did leave an autobiography, you know."

"Autobiographies are often self-censored," said Byrne. "That long-ago Captain Grimes, that smugly respectable shipmaster, a pillar, no doubt, of Church and State, had episodes in his past that he would prefer to forget. He did not pay off from his ship in Melbourne in the normal way. He—what was the expression?—jumped ship. He'd had words with his captain, who was a notorious bully. He'd exchanged blows. So he deserted and thought that he'd be safer miles inland. The only work that he could find was with the Irish laborers on the railway."

"How do you know all this?" I asked. "*If* it's true—"

"He told me," said Byrne. "Or he told my ancestor—but I was inside his mind at the time. . . ."

"Let's send him back," said Kelly. "That'll convince him."

"Not . . . yet," whispered Byrne. "Let's show him first what will happen if the special train is, after all, derailed. Let's convince him that it's to his interests to play along with us. The . . . alternative, since Grimes showed up here, is much . . . firmer. But we shall need—did need?—that British seaman Grimes, just as George Washington needed his British seaman John Paul Jones. . . ."

"Are you trying to tell me, " I asked, "that the squalid squabble at Glenrowan was a crucial point in history?"

"Yes," said Kelly.

I realised that I'd been maneuvered to one of the three chairs facing the Mannschenn Drive unit, that I'd been eased quite gently on to the seat. The chair was made of tubular metal, with a high back, at the top of which was a helmet of metal mesh. This Kelly rapidly adjusted over my head. The only explanation that I can find for my submitting so tamely to all this is that Spooky Byrne must have possessed hypnotic powers.

Anyhow, I sat in that chair, which was comfortable enough. I watched Kelly fussing around with the Mannschenn Drive controls while Byrne did things to his own console—which looked more like an aquarium in which luminous, insubstantial, formless fish were swimming than anything else. The drive rotors started to turn, to spin, to precess. I wanted to close my eyes; after all, it is dinned into us from boyhood up never to look directly at the Mannshchenn Drive in operation. I wanted to close my eyes, but couldn't. I watched those blasted, shimmering wheels spinning, tumbling, fading, always on the verge of invisibility but ever pulsatingly a-glimmer. . . .

I listened to the familiar thin, high whine of the machine. . . .

That sound persisted; otherwise the experience was like watching one of those ancient silent films in an entertainments museum. There was no other noise, although that of the Drive unit could almost have come from an archaic projector. There were no smells, no sensations. There were just pictures, mostly out of focus and with the colors not quite right. But I saw Kelly—the here-and-now Kelly, not his villainous ancestor—recognizable in spite of the full beard that he was wearing, in some sort of sumptuous regalia, a golden crown in which emeralds gleamed set on his head. And there was Byrne, more soberly but still richly attired, reminding me somehow of the legendary wizard Merlin who was the power behind King Arthur's throne. And there were glimpses of a flag, a glowing green banner with a golden harp in the upper canton, the stars of the Southern Cross, also in gold, on the fly. And I saw myself. It was me, all right. I was wearing a green uniform with gold braid up to the elbows. The badge on my cap, with its bullion-encrusted peak, was a golden crown over a winged, golden harp. . . .

The lights went out, came on again. I was sitting in the chair looking at the motionless machine, at Kelly and Byrne, who were looking at me.

Kelly said, "There are crucial points in history. The 'ifs' of history. *If* Napoleon had accepted Fulton's offer of steamships . . . just imagine a squadron of steam frigates at Trafalgar! *If* Pickett's charge at Gettysburg had been successful . . . *If* Admiral Torrance had met the Waverley Navy head on off New Dunedine instead of despatching his forces in a fruitless chase of Commodore McWhirter and his raiding squadron.

"And. . . .

"*If* Thomas Curnow had not succeeded in flagging down the special train before it reached Glenrowan.

"You've seen what could have been, what can be. The extrapolation. Myself king. Spooky my chief minister. You—an admiral."

I laughed. In spite of what I'd just seen it still seemed absurd. "All right," I said. "You might be king. But why should I be an admiral?"

He said, "It could be a sort of hereditary rank granted, in the first instance, to that ancestor of yours for services rendered. When you're fighting a war at the end of long lines of supply somebody on your staff who knows about ships is useful—"

"I've looked," said Spooky Byrne. "I've seen how things were after the massacre of the police outside Glenrowan. I've seen the rising of the poor, the oppressed, spreading from Victoria to New South Wales, under the flag of the Golden Harp and Southern Cross. I've seen the gunboats on the Murray, the armored paddlewheelers with their steam-powered Gatling cannon, an' the armoured trains ranging up an' down the countryside. An' it was yourself, Grimes— or your ancestor—who put to good use the supplies that were comin' in from our Fenian brothers in America an' even from the German emperor. I've watched the Battle of Port Phillip Bay—the English warships an' troop transports, with the *Pope's Eye* battery wreakin' havoc among 'em until a lucky shot found its magazine. An' then your flimsy gasbags came a-sailin' over, droppin' their bombs, an' not a gun could be brought to bear on 'em. . . ."

"Airships?" I demanded. "You certainly have been seeing things, Spooky!"

"Yes, airships. There was a man called Bland in Sydney, somethin' of a rebel himself, who designed an airship years before Ned was ever heard of. An' you—or your ancestor—could have found those plans. You, in your ancestor's mind, sort of nudgin'—just as Eddie an' meself'll be doing our own nudgin'. . . ."

I wasn't quite sober so, in spite of my protestations, what Spooky was saying, combined with what I had seen, seemed to make sense. So when Kelly said that we should now, all three of us, return to the past, to the year 1880, old reckoning, I did not object. I realized dimly that they had been expecting me, waiting for me. That they were needing me. I must have been an obnoxious puppy in those days— but aren't we all when still wet behind the ears? I actually thought of bargaining. A dukedom on top of the admiral's commission . . . the Duke of Alice . . . ? It sounded good.

Kelly and Byrne were seated now, one on either side of me. There were controls set in the armrests of their chairs. Latticework skeps, like the one that I was wearing, were over their heads. The rotors started to spin, to spin and precess, glimmering, fading, tumbling, dragging our *essences* down the dark dimensions while our bodies remained solidly seated in the here and now.

I listened to the familiar thin, high whine of the machine. . . .

To the babble of rough voices, male and female. . . . To the piano-accordion being not too inexpertly played. . . . An Irish song it was—*The Wearin' Of The Green*. . . . I smelled tobacco smoke, the fumes of beer and of strong liquor. . . . I opened my eyes and looked around me. It was real—far more real than the unconvincing reconstruction in the here-and-now Glenrowan had been. The slatternly women were a far cry from those barmaids tarted up in allegedly period costume. And here there were no tourists, gaily dressed and hung around with all manner of expensive recording equipment. Here were burly, bearded, rough-clad men and it was weapons, antique revolvers, that they carried, not the very latest trivoders.

But the group of men of whom I was one were not armed. They were laborers, not bushrangers—but they looked up to the arrogant giant who was holding forth just as much as did his fellow . . . criminals? Yes, they were that. They had held up coaches, robbed banks, murdered. Yet to these Irish laborers he was a hero, a deliverer. He stood for the Little Man against the Establishment. He stood for a warmly human religion against one whose priests were never recruited from the ranks of the ordinary people, the peasants, the workers.

Mind you, I was seeing him through the eyes of that ancestral Grimes who was (temporarily) a criminal himself, who was (temporarily) a rebel, who was on the run (he thought) from the forces of Law and Order. I had full access to his memories. I was, more or less, him. More or less, I say. Nonetheless, I, Grimes the spaceman, was a guest in the mind of Grimes the seaman. I could remember that quarrel on the poop of the *Lady Lucan* and how Captain Jenkins, whose language was always foul, had excelled himself, calling me what was, in those days, an impossibly vile epithet.

I lost my temper, Jenkins lost a few teeth, and I lost my job, hastily leaving the ship in Melbourne before Jenkins could have me arrested on a charge of mutiny on the high seas.

And now, mainly because of the circumstances in which I found myself, I was on the point of becoming one of those middle class technicians who, through the ages, have thrown in their lot with charismatic rebel leaders, without whom those same alleged deliverers of the oppressed masses would have gotten no place at all. I—now—regard with abhorrence the idea of derailing a special train on the way to apprehend a rather vicious criminal. That ancestral Grimes, in his later years, must have felt the same sentiments—so much so that he never admitted to anybody that he was among those present at the Siege of Glenrowan.

But Ned Kelly. . . . He was in good form, although there was something odd about him. He seemed to be . . . possessed. So was the man—Joe Byrne—standing beside him. And so, of course, was John Grimes, lately second mate of the good ship *Lady Lucan*. Kelly— which Kelly?—must have realized that he was drawing some odd looks from his adherents. He broke the tension by putting on his famous helmet—the sheet-iron cylinder with only a slit for the eyes— and singing while he was wearing it. This drew both laughter and applause. Did you ever see those singing robots that were quite a craze a few years back? The effect was rather similar. Great art it was not but it was good for a laugh.

Nobody saw the schoolmaster, Thomas Curnow, sneaking out but me. That was rather odd as he, fancying himself a cut above the others making merry in the hotel, had been keeping himself to himself, saying little, drinking sparingly. This should have made him conspicuous but, somehow, it had the reverse effect. He was the outsider, being studiously ignored. I tried to attract Kelly's attention, Byrne's attention, but I might as well just not have been there. After all I—or my host— was an outsider too. I was the solitary Englishman among the Australians and the Irish. The gang with whom I'd been working on the railway had never liked me. The word had gotten around that I was an officer. The fact that I was (temporarily, as it happened) an ex-officer made no difference. I was automatically suspect.

But I still wanted to be an admiral. I still wanted to command those squadrons of gunboats on the Murray River, the air fleet that would turn the tide at Port Phillip Bay. (How much of my inward voice was the rum speaking, how much was me? How much did the John Grimes whose brain I was taking over ever know about it, remember about it?)

I followed Curnow, out into the cold, clear night. The railway track was silvery in the light of the lopsided moon, near its meridian. On either side, dark and ominous, was the bush. Some nocturnal bird or animal called out, a raucous cry, and something else answered it. And faint—but growing louder—there was a sort of chuffing rattle coming up from the south'ard. The pilot engine, I thought, and then the special train.

Ahead of me Curnow's lantern, a yellow star where no star should have been, was bobbing along between the tracks. I remembered the story. He had the lantern, and his wife's red scarf. He would wave them. The train would stop. Superintendent Hare, Inspector O'Connor, the white troopers, and the black trackers would pile out. And then the shooting, and the siege, and the fire, and that great, armoured figure, like some humanoid robot before its time, stumbling out through the smoke and the flame for the final showdown with his enemies.

And it was up to me to change the course of history.

Have you ever tried walking along a railway line, especially when you're in something of a hurry? The sleepers or the ties or whatever they're called are spaced at just the wrong distance for a normal human stride. Curnow was doing better than I was. Well, he was more used to it. Neither as a seaman nor as a spaceman had I ever had occasion to take a walk such as this.

And then—he fell. He'd tripped, I suppose. He'd fallen with such force as to knock himself out. When I came up to him I found that he'd tried to save that precious lantern from damage. It was on its side but the chimney was unbroken, although one side of the glass was blackened by the smoke from the burning oil.

And the train was coming. I could see it now—the glaring yellow headlight of the leading locomotive, the orange glow from the fireboxes, a shower of sparks mingling with the smoke from the funnels. I had to get Curnow off the line. I tried to lift him but one foot was somehow jammed under the sleeper over which he had tripped. But his lantern, as I have already said, was still burning. I hastily turned it the right side up; only one side of the chimney was smoked into opacity. And that flimsy, translucent red scarf was still there.

I lifted the lantern, held it so that the colored fabric acted as a filter. I waved it—not fast, for fear that the light would be blown out, but slowly, deliberately. The train, the metal monster, kept on coming. I knew that I'd soon have to look after myself but was determined to stand there until the last possible second.

The whistle of the leading locomotive, the pilot engine, sounded—a long, mournful note. There was a screaming of brakes, a great, hissing roar of escaping steam, shouting. . . .

I realised that Curnow had recovered, had scrambled to his feet, was standing beside me. I thrust the lantern and the scarf into his hand, ran into the bushes at the side of the track. He could do all the explaining. I—or that ancestral Grimes—had no desire to meet the police. For all I—or he—knew they would regard the capture of a mutineer and deserter as well as a gang of bushrangers as an unexpected bonus.

I stayed in my hiding place—cold, bewildered, more than a little scared. After a while I heard the shooting, the shouting and the screaming. I saw the flames. I was too far away to see Ned Kelly's last desperate stand; all that I observed was distant, shadowy figures in silhouette against the burning hotel.

Suddenly, without warning, I was back in my chair in that other Kelly's laboratory. The machine, the modified Mannschenn Drive unit, had stopped. I looked at Byrne. I knew, without examining him, that he, too, had . . . stopped. Kelly was alive but not yet fully conscious. His mouth was working. I could just hear what he was muttering; "It had to come to this." And those, I recalled, had been the last words of Ned Kelly, the bushranger, just before they hanged him.

I reasoned, insofar as I was capable of reasoning, that Kelly and Byrne had entered too deeply into the minds of their criminal ancestors. Joe Byrne had died in the siege and his descendant had died with him. Kelly had been badly wounded, although he recovered sufficiently to stand trial. I'd been lucky enough to escape almost unscathed.

I'm not at all proud of what I did then. I just got up and left them—the dead man, his semi-conscious cousin. I got out of there, fast. When I left the Glenrowan Tower I took a cab to the airport and there bought a ticket on the first flight out of the city. It was going to Perth, a place that I'd never much wanted to visit, but at least it was putting distance between me and the scene of that hapless experiment, that presumptuous attempt at tinkering with Time.

I've often wondered what would have happened if I'd left Curnow to his fate, if I hadn't stopped the train. The course of history might well have been changed—but would it have been for the better? I don't think so. An Irish Australia, a New Erin, a Harp in the South . . . New Erin allied with the Boers against hated England during the wars in South Africa . . . New Erin quite possibly allied with Germany against England during the First World War . . . The Irish, in many ways, are a great people—but they carry a grudge to absurd lengths. They have far too long a memory for their own wrongs.

And I think that I like me better as I am now than as an Hereditary Admiral of the New Erin Navy in an alternate universe that, fortunately, didn't happen.

She said, "Thank you, Commodore, for a very interesting story." She switched off her trivoder, folded flat its projections, closed the carrying case about it. She got to her feet.

She said, "I have to be going."

He looked at the bulkhead clock, he said, "There's no hurry, Kitty. We've time for another drink or two." He sensed a coldness in the atmosphere and tried to warm things up with an attempt at humour. "Sit down again. Make yourself comfortable. This ship is Liberty Hall, you know. You can spit on that mat and call the cat a bastard."

She said, "The only tom cats I've seen aboard this wagon haven't been of the four-legged variety. And, talking of legs, do you think that I haven't noticed the way that you've been eyeing mine?"

His prominent ears reddened angrily but he persisted. "Will you be at the cocktail party tonight?"

"No, Commodore Grimes. Station Yorick isn't interested in boring social functions."

"But I'll be seeing more of you, I hope. . . ."

"You will not, in either sense of the words." She turned to go. "You said, Commodore, that the Irish have a long memory for their own wrongs. Perhaps you are right. Be that as it may—you might be interested to learn that my family name is Kelly."

When she was gone Grimes reflected wryly that now there was yet another alternate universe, differing from his here-and-now only in a strictly personal sense, which he would never enter.

❧ Grimes at the ❧
Great Race

"I DIDN'T THINK that I'd be seeing you again," said Grimes.

"Or I you," Kitty Kelly told him. "But Station Yorick's customers liked that first interview. The grizzled old spacedog, pipe in mouth, glass in hand, spinning a yarn. . . . So when my bosses learned that you're stuck here until your engineers manage to fit a new rubber band to your inertial drive they said, in these very words, 'Get your arse down to the spaceport, Kitty, and try to wheedle another tall tale out of the old bastard!'"

"Mphm," grunted Grimes, acutely conscious that his prominent ears had reddened angrily.

Kitty smiled sweetly. She was an attractive girl, black Irish, wide-mouthed, creamy-skinned, with vivid blue eyes. Grimes would have thought her much more attractive had she not been making it obvious that she still nursed the resentment engendered by his first story, a tale of odd happenings at long-ago and far-away Glenrowan where, thanks to Grimes, an ancestral Kelly had met his downfall.

Grimes looked at her, at her translucent, emerald green blouse that concealed little, at the long, shapely legs under the skirt that concealed even less. He thought, *There's one of the Irish, right here, that I'd like to lay on.*

With deliberate awkwardness he asked, "If I'm supposed to avoid giving offense to anybody—and you Elsinoreans must carry the blood of about every race and nation on Old Earth—what can I talk about?"

She made a great show of cogitation, frowning, staring down at the tips of her glossy green shoes. Then she smiled. "Racing, of course! On this world we're great followers of the horses." She frowned again. "But no. Somehow I just can't see you as a sporting man, Commodore."

"As a matter of fact," said Grimes stiffly, "I did once take part in a race. And for high stakes."

"I just can't imagine *you* on a horse."

"Who said anything about horses?"

"What were you riding, then?"

"Do you want the story or don't you? If I'm going to tell it, I'll tell it my way."

She sighed, muttered, "All right, all right." She opened her case, brought out the trivi recorder, set it up on the deck of the day cabin. She aimed one lens at the chair in which Grimes was sitting, the other at the one that she would occupy. She squinted into the viewfinder. "Pipe in mouth," she ordered. "Glass in hand . . . Where is the glass, Commodore? And aren't you going to offer *me* a drink?"

He gestured towards the liquor cabinet. "You fix it. I'll have a pink gin, on the rocks."

"Then I'll have the same. It'll be better than the sickly muck you poured down me last time I was aboard your ship!"

Grimes's ears flushed again. The "sickly muck" had failed to have the desired effect.

My first command in the Survey Service [he began] was of a Serpent Class Courier, *Adder.* The captains of these little ships were lieutenants, their officers lieutenants and ensigns. There were no petty officers or ratings to worry about, no stewards or stewardesses to look after us. We made our own beds, cooked our own meals. We used to take turns playing with the rather primitive autochef. We didn't starve; in fact we lived quite well.

There was some passenger accommodation; the couriers were—and probably still are—sometimes used to get VIPs from Point A to Point B in a hurry. And they carried Service mail and dispatches hither and yon. If there was any odd job to do we did it.

This particular job was a very odd one. You've heard of Darban? No? Well, it's an Earth-type planet in the Tauran Sector. Quite a pleasant world although the atmosphere's a bit too dense for some tastes. But if it wcre what we call Earth-normal I mightn't be sitting here talking to you now. Darban's within the Terran sphere of influence with a Carlotti Beacon Station, a Survey Service Base, and all the rest of it. At the time of which I'm talking, though, it wasn't in anybody's sphere of influence, although Terran star tramps and Hallichek and Shaara ships had been calling there for quite some time. There was quite a demand for the so-called living opals—although how any woman could bear to have a slimy, squirming necklace of luminous worms strung about her neck beats me!

She interrupted him. "These Hallicheki and Shaara . . . non-human races, aren't they?"

"Non-human and non-humanoid. The Hallicheki are avian, with a matriarchal society. The Shaara are winged arthropods, not unlike the Terran bees, although very much larger and with a somewhat different internal structure."

"There'll be pictures of them in our library. We'll show them to our viewers. But go on, please."

The merchant captains [he continued] had been an unusually law-abiding crowd. They'd bartered for the living opals but had been careful not to give in exchange any artifacts that would unduly accelerate local industrial evolution. No advanced technology—if the Darbanese wanted spaceships they'd have to work out for themselves how to build them—and, above all, no sophisticated weaponry. Mind you, some of those skippers would have been quite capable of flogging a few hand lasers or the like to thc natives but the Grand Governor of Barkara—the nation that, by its relatively early development of airships and firearms, had established *de facto* if not *de jure* sovereignty over the entire planet—made sure that nothing was imported that could be a threat to his rule. A situation rather analogous, perhaps, to that on Earth centuries ago when the Japanese Shoguns and their samurai took a dim view of the muskets and cannon that, in the wrong hands, would have meant their downfall.

Then the old Grand Governor died. His successor intimated that he would be willing to allow Darban to be drawn into the Federation of Worlds and to reap the benefits accruing therefrom. But whose Federation? Our Interstellar Federation? The Hallichek Hegemony? The Shaara Galactic Hive?

Our Intelligence people, just for once, started to earn their keep. According to them the Shaara had dispatched a major warship to Darban, the captain of which had been given full authority to dicker with the Grand Governor. The Hallicheki had done likewise. And— not for the first time!—our lords and masters had been caught with their pants down. It was at the time of the Waverley Confrontation; and Lindisfarne Base, as a result, was right out of major warships. Even more fantastically the only spaceship available was my little *Adder*—and she was in the throes of a refit. Oh, there were ships at Scapa and Mikasa Bases but both of these were one helluva long way from Darban.

I was called before the Admiral and told that I must get off Lindisfarne as soon as possible, if not before, to make all possible speed for Darban, there to establish and maintain a Terran presence until such time as a senior officer could take over from me. I was to report on the actions of the Shaara and the Hallicheki. I was to avoid direct confrontation with either. And I was not, repeat not, to take any action at any time without direct authorization from Base. I was told that a civilian linguistic expert would be travelling in *Adder*—a Miss Mary Marsden—and that she would be assisting me as required.

What rankled was the way in which the Admiral implied that he was being obliged to send a boy on a man's errand. And I wasn't at all happy about having Mary Marsden along. She was an attractive enough girl—what little one could see of her!—but she was a super wowser. She was a member of one of the more puritanical religious sects flourishing on Francisco—and Francisco, as you know, is a hotbed of freak religions. Mary took hers seriously. She had insisted on retaining her civilian status because she did not approve of the short-skirted uniforms in which the Survey Service clad its female personnel. She always wore long-skirted, long-sleeved, high-necked dresses and a bonnet over her auburn hair. She didn't smoke—not even tobacco—or drink anything stronger than milk.

And yet, as far as we could see, she was a very pretty girl. Eyes that were more green than any other color. A pale—but not unhealthily so—skin. A straight nose that, a millimeter longer, would have been too big. A wide, full mouth that didn't need any artificial coloring. A firm, rather square chin. Good teeth—which she needed when it was the turn of Beadle, my first lieutenant, to do the cooking. Beadle had a passion for pies and his crusts always turned out like concrete. . . .

Well, we lifted off from Lindisfarne Base. We set trajectory for Darban. And before we were halfway there we suffered a complete communications black-out. Insofar as the Carlotti deep space radio was concerned I couldn't really blame Slovotny, my Sparks. The Base technicians, in their haste to get us off the premises, had botched the overhaul of the transceiver and, to make matters worse, hadn't replaced the spares they had used. When two circuit trays blew, that was that.

Spooky Deane, my psionic communications officer, I could and did blame for the shortcomings of *his* department. As you probably know, it's just not possible for even the most highly trained and talented telepath to transmit his thoughts across light years without an amplifier. The amplifier most commonly used is the brain of that highly telepathic animal, the Terran dog, removed from the skull of its hapless owner and kept alive in a tank of nutrient solution with all the necessary life-support systems. PCOs are lonely people; they're inclined to regard themselves as the only true humans in shiploads of sub-men. They make pets of their horrid amplifiers, to which they can talk telepathically. And—as lonely men do—they drink.

What happened aboard *Adder* was an all-too-frequent occurrence. The PCO would be going on a solitary bender and would get to the stage of wanting to share his bottle with his pet. When neat gin—or whatever—is poured into nutrient solution the results are invariably fatal to whatever it is that's being nourished.

So—no psionic amplifier. No Carlotti deep space radio. No contact with Base.

"And aren't you going to share your *bottle with* your *pet, Commodore?"*

"I didn't think that you were a pet of mine, Miss Kelly, or I of yours. But it's time we had a pause for refreshment."

We stood on for Darban [he continued]. Frankly, I was pleased rather than otherwise at being entirely on my own, knowing that now I would have to use my own initiative, that I would not have the Lord Commissioners of the Admiralty peering over my shoulder all the time, expecting me to ask their permission before I so much as blew my nose. Beadle, my first lieutenant, did try to persuade me to return to Lindisfarne—he was a very capable officer but far too inclined to regard Survey Service Regulations as Holy Writ. (I did find later that, given the right inducement, he was capable of bending those same regulations.) Nonetheless, he was, in many ways, rather a pain in the arse.

But Beadle was in the minority. The other young gentlemen were behind me, all in favour of carrying on. Mary Marsden, flaunting her civilian status, remained neutral.

We passed the time swotting up on Darban, watching and listening to the tapes that had been put on board prior to our departure from Lindisfarne.

We gained the impression of a very pleasant, almost Earth-type planet with flora and fauna not too outrageously different from what the likes of us are used to. Parallel evolution and all that. A humanoid—but not human—dominant race, furry bipeds that would have passed for cat-faced apes in a bad light. Civilized, with a level of technology roughly that of Earth during the late nineteenth century, old reckoning. Steam engines. Railways. Electricity, and the electric telegraph. Airships. Firearms. One nation—that with command of the air and a monopoly of telegraphic communications—*de facto* if not entirely *de jure* ruler of the entire planet.

The spaceport, such as it was, consisted of clearings in a big forest some kilometers south of Barkara, the capital city of Bandooran. Bandooran, of course, was the most highly developed nation, the one that imposed its will on all of Darban. Landing elsewhere was . . . discouraged. The Dog Star Line at one time tried to steal a march on the competition by instructing one of their captains to land near a city called Droobar, there to set up the Dog Star Line's own trading station. The news must have been telegraphed to Barkara almost immediately. A couple of dirigibles drifted over, laying H.E. and incendiary eggs on the city. The surviving city fathers begged the Dog Star line captain to take himself and his ship elsewhere. Also, according to our tapes, the Dog Star Line was heavily fined shortly thereafter by the High Council of the Interstellar Federation.

But the spaceport . . . just clearings, as I have said, in the forest. Local airships were used to pick up incoming cargo and to deliver the tanks of "living opals" to the spaceships. No Aerospace Control, of course, although there would be once a base and a Carlotti Beacon Station had been established. Incoming traffic just came in, unannounced. Unannounced officially, that is. As you know, the inertial drive is far from being the quietest machine ever devised by Man; everybody in Barkara and for kilometers around would know when a spaceship was dropping down.

And we dropped in, one fine, sunny morning. After one preliminary orbit we'd been able to identify Barkara without any difficulty. The forest was there, just where our charts said it should be. There were those odd, circular holes in the mass of greenery—the clearings. In two of them there was the glint of metal. As we lost altitude we were able to identify the Shaara vessel—it's odd (or is it?) how their ships always look like giant beehives—and a typical, Hallicheki oversized silver egg sitting in a sort of latticework egg cup.

We came in early; none of the Shaara or Hallicheki were yet out and about although the noise of our drive must have alerted them. I set *Adder* down as far as possible from the other two ships. From my control room I could just see the blunt bows of them above the treetops.

We went down to the wardroom for breakfast, leaving Slovotny to enjoy his meal in solitary state in the control room; he would let us know if anybody approached while we were eating. He buzzed down just as I'd reached the toast and marmalade stage. I went right up. But the local authorities hadn't yet condescended to take notice of us; the airship that came nosing over was a Shaara blimp, not a Darbanese rigid job. And then there was a flight of three Hallicheki, disdaining mechanical aids and using their own wings. One of the horrid things evacuated her bowels when she was almost overhead, making careful allowance for what little wind there was. It made a filthy splash all down one of my viewports.

At last the Darbanese came. Their ship was of the Zeppelin type, the fabric of the envelope stretched taut over a framework of wood or metal. It hovered over the clearing, its engines turning over just sufficiently to offset the effect of the breeze. That airship captain, I thought, knew his job. A cage detached itself from the gondola, was lowered rapidly to the ground. A figure jumped out of it just before it touched and the airship went up like a rocket after the loss of weight. I wondered what would happen if that cage fouled anything before it was rehoisted, but I needn't have worried. As I've said, the airship captain was an expert.

We went down to the after airlock. We passed through it, making the transition from our own atmosphere into something that, at first, felt like warm soup. But it was quite breathable. Mary Marsden, as the linguist of the party, accompanied me down the ramp. I wondered how she could bear to go around muffled up to the eyebrows on such a beautiful morning as this; I was finding even shorts and shirt uniform too heavy for a warm day.

The native looked at us. We looked at him. He was dressed in a dull green smock that came down to mid-thigh and that left his arms bare. A fine collection of glittering brass badges was pinned to the breast and shoulders of his garment. He saluted, raising his three-fingered hands to shoulder level, palms out. His wide mouth opened in what I hoped was a smile, displaying pointed, yellow teeth that were in sharp contrast to the black fur covering his face.

He asked, in quite passable Standard English, "You the captain are?"

I said that I was.

He said, "Greetings I bring from the High Governor." Then, making a statement rather than asking a question, "You do not come in trade."

So we—or a Federation warship of some kind—had been expected. And *Adder*, little as she was, did not look like a merchantman—too many guns for too small a tonnage.

He went on, "So you are envoy. Same as—" He waved a hand in the general direction of where the other ships were berthed. "—the Shaara, the Hallicheki. Then you will please to attend the meeting that this morning has been arranged." He pulled a big, fat watch on a chain from one of his pockets. "In—in forty-five of your minutes from now."

While the exchange was taking place Mary was glowering a little. She was the linguistic expert and it was beginning to look as though her services would not be required. She listened quietly while arrangements were being made. We would proceed to the city in my boat, with the Governor's messenger acting as pilot—pilot in the marine sense of the word, that is, just giving me the benefit of his local knowledge.

We all went back on board *Adder*. The messenger assured me that there was no need for me to have internal pressure adjusted to his requirements; he had often been aboard outworld spaceships and, too, he was an airshipman.

I decided that there was no time for me to change into dress uniform so I compromised by pinning my miniatures—two good attendance medals and the Distinguished Conduct Star that I'd got after the Battle of Dartura—to the left breast of my shirt, buckling on my sword belt with the wedding cake cutter in its gold-braided sheath. While I was tarting myself up, Mary entertained the messenger to coffee and biscuits in the wardroom (his English, she admitted to me later, was better than her Darbanese) and Beadle, with Dalgleish, the engineer, got the boat out of its bay and down to the ground by the ramp.

Mary was coming with me to the city and so was Spooky Deane—a trained telepath is often more useful than a linguist. We got into the boat. It was obvious that our new friend was used to this means of transportation, must often have ridden in the auxiliary craft of visiting merchant vessels. He sat beside me to give directions. Mary and Spooky were in the back.

As we flew towards the city—red brick, grey-roofed houses on the outskirts, tall, cylindrical towers, also of red brick, in the center— we saw the Shaara and the Hallicheki ahead of us, flying in from their ships. A Queen-Captain, I thought, using my binoculars, with a princess and an escort of drones. A Hallichek Nest Leader accompanied by two old hens as scrawny and ugly as herself. The Shaara weren't using their blimp and the Hallicheki consider it beneath their dignity to employ mechanical means of flight inside an atmosphere. Which made *us* the wingless wonders.

I reduced speed a little to allow the opposition to make their landings on the flat roof of one of the tallest towers first. After all, they were both very senior to me, holding ranks equivalent to at least that of a four-ring captain in the Survey Service, and I was a mere lieutenant, my command notwithstanding. I came in slowly over the streets of the city. There were people abroad—pedestrians mainly, although there were vehicles drawn by scaly, huge-footed draught animals and the occasional steam car—and they raised their black-furred faces to stare at us. One or two of them waved.

When we got to the roof of the tower the Shaara and the Hallicheki had gone down but there were a half-dozen blue-smocked guards to receive us. They saluted as we disembarked. One of them led the way to a sort of penthouse which, as a matter of fact, merely provided cover for the stairhead. The stairs themselves were . . . wrong. They'd been designed, of course, to suit the length and jointure of the average Darbanese leg, which wasn't anything like ours. Luckily the Council Chamber was only two flights down.

It was a big room, oblong save for the curvature of the two end walls, in which were high windows. There was a huge, long table, at one end of which was a sort of ornate throne in which sat the High

Governor. He was of far slighter stature than the majority of his compatriots but made up for it by the richness of his attire. His smock was of a crimson, velvetlike material and festooned with gold chains of office.

He remained seated but inclined his head in our direction. He said—I learned afterwards that these were the only words of English that he knew; he must have picked them up from some visiting space captain—"Come in. This is Liberty Hall; you can spit on the mat and call the cat a bastard!"

"I was wondering," said Kitty Kelly coldly, "just when you were going to get around to saying that."

"He said it, not me. But I have to use that greeting once in every story. It's one of my conditions of employment."

And where was I [he went on] before I was interrupted? Oh, yes. The Council Chamber, with the High Governor all dressed up like a Christmas tree. Various ministers and other notables, not as richly attired as their boss. All male, I found out later, with the exception of the Governor's lady, who was sitting on her husband's right. There were secondary sexual characteristics, of course, but so slight as to be unrecognizable by an outworlder. To me she—and I didn't know that she was "she"—was just another Darbanese.

But the fair sex was well represented. There was the Queen-Captain, her iridescent wings folded on her back, the velvety brown fur of her thorax almost concealed by the sparkling jewels that were her badges of high rank. There was the Shaara princess, less decorated but more elegant than her mistress. There was the Nest Leader; she was nowhere nearly as splendid as the Queen-Captain. She wasn't splendid at all. Her plumage was dun and dusty, the talons of the "hands" at the elbow joints of her wings unpolished. She wore no glittering insignia, only a wide band of cheap-looking yellow plastic about her scrawny neck. Yet she had her dignity, and her cruel beak was that of a bird of prey rather than that of the barnyard fowl she otherwise resembled. She was attended by two hen officers, equally drab.

And, of course, there was Mary, almost as drab as the Hallicheki. The Governor launched into his spiel, speaking through an interpreter. I was pleased to discover that Standard English was to be the language used. It made sense, of course. English is the common language of Space just as it used to be the common language of the sea, back on Earth. And as the majority of the merchant vessels landing on Darban had been of Terran registry, the local merchants and officials had learned English.

The Governor, through his mouthpiece, said that he welcomed us all. He said that he was pleased that Imperial Earth had sent her representative, albeit belatedly, to this meeting of cultures. Blah, blah, blah. He agreed with the representatives of the Great Space-faring Powers that it was desirable for some sort of permanent base to be established on Darban. But . . . but whichever of us was given the privilege of taking up residence on his fair planet would have to prove capability to conform, to mix. . . . (By this time the interpreter was having trouble in getting the idea across but he managed somehow.) The Darbanese, the Governor told us, were a sporting people and in Barkara there was one sport preferred to all others. This was racing. It would be in keeping with Darbanese tradition if the Treaty were made with whichever of us proved the most expert in a competition of this nature. . . .

"*Racing?*" I whispered. In a foot race we'd probably be able to beat the Shaara and the Hallicheki, but I didn't think that it was foot racing that was implied. Horse racing or its local equivalent? That didn't seem right either.

"Balloon racing," muttered Spooky Deane, who had been flapping his psionic ears.

I just didn't see how balloon racing could be a spectator sport— but the tapes on Darban with which we had been supplied were far from comprehensive. As we soon found out.

"*Balloon racing?*" *asked Kitty Kelly.* "*From the spectators' viewpoint it must have been like watching grass grow.*"

"*This balloon racing certainly wasn't,*" *Grimes told her.*

The Darbanese racing balloons [he went on] were ingenious aircraft: dirigible, gravity-powered. Something very like them was, as a matter of fact, invented by a man called Adams back on Earth in the nineteenth century. Although it performed successfully, the Adams airship never got off the ground, commercially speaking. But it did work. The idea was that the thing would progress by soaring and swooping, soaring and swooping. The envelope containing the gas cells was a planing surface and the altitude of the contraption was controlled by the shifting of weights in the car—ballast, the bodies of the crew. Initially, positive buoyancy was obtained by the dumping of ballast and the thing would plane upwards. Then, when gas was valved, there would be negative buoyancy and a glide downwards. Sooner or later, of course, you'd be out of gas to valve or ballast to dump. That would be the end of the penny section.

I remembered about the Adams airship while the interpreter did his best to explain balloon racing to us. I thought that it was a beautiful case of parallel mechanical evolution on two worlds many light years apart.

The Queen-Captain got the drift of it quite soon—after all, the Shaara *know* airships. Her agreement, even though it was made through her artificial voice box, sounded more enthusiastic than otherwise. The Nest Leader took her time making up her mind but finally squawked yes. I would have been outvoted if I hadn't wanted to take part in the contest.

There was a party then, complete with drinks and sweet and savoury things to nibble. The Shaara made pigs of themselves on a sticky liqueur and candy. Spooky Deane got stuck into something rather like gin. I found a sort of beer that wasn't too bad—although it was served unchilled—with little, spicy sausages as blotting paper. Mary, although she seemed to enjoy the sweetmeats, would drink only water. Obviously our hosts thought that she was odd, almost as odd as the Hallicheki who, although drinking water, would eat nothing.

They're *nasty* people, those avians. They have no redeeming vices—and when it comes to *real* vices their main one is cruelty. *Their* idea of a banquet is a shrieking squabble over a table loaded with little mammals, alive but not kicking—they're hamstrung before the feast so that they can't fight or run away—which they tear to pieces with those beaks of theirs.

After quite a while the party broke up. The Nest Leader and her officers were the first to leave, anxious no doubt to fly back to their ship for a tasty dish of live worms. The Queen-Captain and her party were the next to go. They were in rather a bad way. They were still on the rooftop when Mary and I, supporting him between us, managed to get Spooky Deane up the stairs and to the boat.

None of the locals offered to help us; it is considered bad manners on Darban to draw the attention of a guest to his insobriety. We said our goodbyes to those officials, including the interpreter, who had come to see us off. We clambered into our boat and lifted. On our way back to *Adder* we saw the Shaara blimp coming to pick up the Queen-Captain. I wasn't surprised. If she'd tried to take off from the roof in the state that she was in she'd have made a nasty splash on the cobblestones under the tower.

And I wasn't at all sorry to get back to the ship to have a good snore. Spooky was fast asleep by the time that I landed by the after airlock and Mary was looking at both of us with great distaste.

"I'm not a wowser," said Kitty Kelly.

"Help yourself, then. And freshen my glass while you're about it."

Bright and early the next morning [he went on, after a refreshing sip] two racing balloons and an instructor were delivered by a small rigid airship. Our trainer was a young native called Robiliyi. He spoke very good English; as a matter of fact he was a student at the University of Barkara and studying for a degree in Outworld Languages. He was also a famous amateur balloon jockey and had won several prizes. Under his supervision we assembled one of the balloons, inflating it from the cylinders of hydrogen that had been brought from the city. Imagine a huge air mattress with a flimsy, wickerwork car slung under it. That's what the thing looked like. The only control surface was a huge rudder at the after end of the car. There were two tillers—one forward and one aft.

Dalgleish inspected the aircraft, which was moored by lines secured to metal pegs driven into the ground. He said, "I'm not happy about all this valving of gas. You know how the Shaara control buoyancy in their blimps?"

I said that I did.

He said that it should be possible to modify one of the balloons—

the one that we should use for the race itself—so as to obviate the necessity of valving gas for the downward glide. I prodded the envelope with a cautious finger and said that I didn't think that the fabric of the gas cells would stand the strain of being compressed in a net. He said that he didn't think so either. *So that was that,* I thought. *Too bad.* Then he went on to tell me that in the ship's stores was a bolt of plastic cloth that, a long time ago, had been part of an urgent shipment of supplies to the Survey Service base on Zephyria, a world notorious for its violent windstorms. (Whoever named that planet had a warped sense of humour!) The material was intended for making emergency repairs to the domes housing the base facilities. They were always being punctured by wind-borne boulders and the like. When *Adder* got to Zephyria it was found that somebody had experienced a long overdue rush of brains to the head and put everything underground. There had been the usual lack of liaison between departments and nobody had been told not to load the plastic.

Anyhow, Dalgleish thought that he'd be able to make gas cells from the stuff. He added that the Shaara would almost certainly be modifying their own racer, using the extremely tough silk from which the gas cells of their blimps were made.

I asked Robiliyi's opinion. He told me that it would be quite in order to use machinery as long as it was hand-powered.

Dalgleish went into a huddle with him. They decided that only the three central, sausage-like gas cells need be compressed to produce negative buoyancy; also that it would be advisable to replace the wickerwork frame enclosing the "mattress" with one of light but rigid metal. Too, it would be necessary to put a sheet of the plastic over the assembly of gas cells so as to maintain a planing surface in all conditions.

Then it was time for my first lesson. Leaving Dalgleish and the others to putter around with the still unassembled balloon I followed Robiliyi into the flimsy car of the one that was ready for use. The wickerwork creaked under my weight. I sat down, very carefully, amidships, and tried to keep out of the way. Robiliyi started scooping sand out of one of the ballast bags, dropping it overside. The bottom of the car lifted off the mossy ground but the balloon was still held down by the mooring lines, two forward and two aft. Robiliyi scampered, catlike, from one end of the car to the other, pulling the metal pegs clear of the soil with expert jerks. We lifted, rising vertically. I looked down at the faces of my shipmates. *Better him than us,* their expressions seemed to be saying.

Then we were at treetop height, then above the trees, still lifting. Robiliyi scrambled to the rear of the craft, calling me to follow. He grabbed the after tiller. The platform tilted and above us the raft of gas cells did likewise, presenting an inclined plane to the air. We were sliding through the atmosphere at a steep angle. I wasn't sure whether or not I was enjoying the experience. I'd always liked ballooning, back on Earth, but the gondolas of the hot air balloons in which I'd flown were far safer than this flimsy basket. There was nothing resembling an altimeter in the car; there were no instruments at all. I hoped that somewhere in the nested gas cells there was a relief valve that would function if we got too high. And how high was too high, anyhow? I noticed that the underskin of the balloon, which had been wrinkled when we lifted off, was now taut.

Robiliyi shouted shrilly, "Front end! Front end!" We scuttled forward. He pulled on a dangling lanyard; there was an audible hiss of escaping gas from above. He put the front-end tiller over and as we swooped downward we turned. The treetops, which had seemed far too distant, were now dangerously close. And there was the clearing from which we had lifted with *Adder* standing there, bright silver in the sunlight. But we weren't landing yet. We shifted weight aft, jettisoned ballast, soared. I was beginning to get the hang of it, starting to enjoy myself. Robiliyi let me take the tiller so that I could get the feel of the airship. She handled surprisingly well.

We did not return to earth until we had dumped all our ballast. I asked Robiliyi what we could do if, for some reason, we wanted to get upstairs again in a hurry after valving gas. He grinned, stripped off his tunic, made as though to throw it overboard. He grinned again, showing all his sharp, yellow teeth. "And if *that* is not enough," he said, "there is always your crew person. . . ."

We landed shortly after this. Robiliyi reinflated the depleted cells from one of the bottles while Beadle and Spooky collected ballast sand from the banks of a nearby brook.

Then it was Mary's turn to start her training.

"Mary? Was she your crew, your co-pilot, for the race?"

"Yes."

"But you've impressed me as being a male chauvinist pig."

"Have I? Well, frankly, I'd sooner have had one of my officers. But Mary volunteered, and she was far better qualified than any of them. Apart from myself she was the only one in Adder *with lighter-than-air experience. It seems that the sect of which she was a member went in for ballooning quite a lot. It tied in somehow with their religion. Nearer my God to Thee, and all that."*

Well [he went on], we trained, both in the balloon that Dalgleish had modified and in the one that was still as it had been when delivered to us. The modifications? Oh, quite simple. A coffee-mill hand winch, an arrangement of webbing that compressed the three central, longitudinal gas cells. The modified balloon we exercised secretly, flying it only over a circuit that was similar in many ways to the official, triangular race track. The unmodified balloon we flew over the actual course. The Shaara and the Hallicheki did likewise, in craft that did not appear to have had anything done to them. I strongly suspected that they were doing the same as we were, keeping their dark horses out of sight until the Big Day. The Shaara, I was certain, had done to theirs what we had done to ours—after all, it was a Shaara idea that we had borrowed. But the Hallicheki? We just couldn't guess.

And we trained, and we trained. At first it was Robiliyi with Mary or Robiliyi with myself. Then it was Mary and I. I'll say this for her— she made good balloon crew. And I kidded myself that she was becoming far less untouchable. In that narrow car we just couldn't help coming into physical contact quite frequently.

Then the time was upon us and we were as ready as ever we would be. On the eve of the Great Day the three contending balloons were taken to the airport. The Shaara towed theirs in behind one of their blimps; it was entirely concealed in a sort of gauzy cocoon. The

Hallicheki towed theirs in, four hefty crew hens doing the work. There was no attempt at concealment. We towed ours in astern of our flier. It was completely swathed in a sheet of light plastic.

The racers were maneuvered into a big hangar to be inspected by the judges. I heard later, from Robiliyi, that the Nest Leader had insinuated that the Shaara and ourselves had installed miniature inertial drive units disguised as hand winches. (It was the sort of thing that *they* would have done if they'd thought that they could get away with it.)

We all returned to our ships. I don't know how the Shaara and the Hallicheki spent the night but we dined and turned in early. I took a stiff nightcap to help me to sleep. Mary had her usual warm milk.

The next morning we returned in the flier to the airport. It was already a warm day. I was wearing a shirt-and-shorts uniform but intended to discard cap, long socks, and shoes before clambering into the wickerwork car of the balloon. Mary was suitably—according to her odd lights—dressed but what she had on was very little more revealing than her usual high-necked, longsleeved, long-skirted dress; it did little more than establish the fact that she was, after all, a biped. It was a hooded, long-sleeved cover-all suit with its legs terminating in soft shoes. It was so padded that it was quite impossible to do more than guess at the shape of the body under it.

Young Robiliyi was waiting for us at the airport, standing guard over our green and gold racer. Close by was the Shaara entry, its envelope displaying orange polka dots on a blue ground. The Shaara crew stood by their balloon—the pilot, a bejeweled drone, and his crew, a husky worker. Then there were the Hallicheki—officers both, to judge from the yellow plastic bands about their scrawny necks. The envelope of their racer was a dull brown.

On a stand, some distance from the starting line, sat the Governor with his entourage. With him were the Queen-Captain and the Nest Leader with their senior officers. The judges were already aboard the small, rigid airship which, at its mooring mast, was ready to cast off as soon as the race started. It would fly over the course with us, its people alert for any infraction of the rules.

Two of the airport ground crew wheeled out a carriage on which was mounted a highly polished little brass cannon. The starting gun. I kicked off my shoes, peeled off my socks, left them, with my cap, in Robiliyi's charge. I climbed into the flimsy car, took my place at the after tiller. Mary followed me, stationed herself at the winch amidships. She released the brake. The gas cells rustled as they expanded; we were held down now only by the taut mooring lines fore and aft. I looked over at the others. The Shaara, too, were ready. The Hallicheki had just finished the initial dumping of sand ballast.

One of the gunners jerked a long lanyard. There was a bang and a great flash of orange flame, a cloud of dirty white smoke. I yanked the two after mooring lines, pulling free the iron pegs. Forward Mary did the same, a fraction of a second later. It wasn't a good start. The forward moorings should have been released first to get our leading edge starting to lift. Mary scrambled aft, redistributing weight, but the Shaara and the Hallicheki, planing upwards with slowly increasing speed, were already ahead.

Almost directly beneath us was Airport Road and in the middle distance was the railway to Brinn with the Brinn Highway running parallel to it. I can remember how the track was gleaming like silver in the morning sunlight. To the north, distant but already below the expanding horizon, was the Cardan Knoll, a remarkable dome-shaped hill with lesser domes grouped about it. We would have to pass to the west and north of this before steering a south-easterly course for the Porgidor Tower.

Shaara and Hallicheki were racing neck and neck, still climbing. I was still falling behind. I brought the dangling mooring lines inboard to reduce drag. It may have made a little difference, but not much. Ahead of us the Shaara balloon reached its ceiling, compressed gas and began the first downward glide. A second or so later the Hallicheki reduced buoyancy to follow suit. I looked up. The underskin of my gas cells was still slightly wrinkled; there was still climbing to do.

The last wrinkles vanished. I told Mary to compress. The pawls clicked loudly as she turned the winch handle. Then we scuttled to the front end of the car. I took hold of the forward tiller. We swooped down, gathering speed rapidly. The farm buildings and the grazing animals in the fields were less and less toylike as we lost altitude. I steered straight for an ungainly beast that looked like an armour-plated cow. It lifted its head to stare at us in stupid amazement.

I didn't want to hit the thing. I sort of half ran, half crawled aft as Mary released the winch brake. We lifted sweetly—no doubt to the great relief of the bewildered herbivore. I looked ahead. The opposition were well into their second upward beat, the Hallicheki soaring more steeply than the Shaara. But taking advantage of thermals is an art that every bird learns as soon as it is able to fly; there must be, I thought, a considerable updraught of warm air from the railroad and the black-surfaced Brinn Highway. But the higher the Hallicheki went the more gas they would have to valve, and if they were not careful they would lose all their reserve buoyancy before the circuit was completed.

The Shaara reached their ceiling and started their downward glide. The Hallicheki were still lifting, gaining altitude but losing ground. I couldn't understand why they were not gliding down their lift. And I was still lifting. Then I saw that, ahead, the Hallicheki had at last valved gas and were dropping. I pulled to starboard to avoid them. It meant putting on some distance but I daren't risk a mid-air collision. The Hallicheki had wings of their own and could bail out in safety. Mary and I hadn't and couldn't.

But there was no danger of our becoming entangled with the Hallicheki. They had put on considerable speed during their dive and were swooping down on the Shaara balloon like a hawk on its prey. They were directly above it—and then, although they were still well clear of the ground, were rising again. A failure of nerve? It didn't fit in with what I knew of their psychology. But ballast must have been dumped and it would mean an additional soar and swoop for them before rounding the Cardan Knoll.

And I was gaining on them.

But where were the Shaara?

Mary seemed to have read my thought. She said, "They're in trouble."

I looked down to where she was pointing. Yes, they were in

trouble all right. They had lost considerable altitude and the car of their balloon was entangled with the topmost branches of a tall tree. The drone and the worker were tugging ineffectually with all their limbs, buzzing about it. But they would never get it clear. They'd lost all their lift. The sausage-like gas cells were limp, more than half deflated.

But that was their worry. We flew on. Ahead, the Knoll was getting closer. I pulled over to port to pass to the west'ard of the brush-covered domes. The Hallicheki were already rounding the Knoll, lost briefly to sight as they passed to north of it. Then I was coming round to starboard in a tight, rising turn. I didn't realize until it was almost too late that the slight northerly breeze was setting me down onto the hill; I had to put the tiller hard over to try to claw to wind'ard. The deck of our car just brushed the branches of a tree and there was a clattering, screeching explosion of small, flying reptiles from the foliage. Luckily they were more scared of us than we were of them.

Ahead, now, was the railway to Garardan and the Garardan Road. Beyond road and railway was the Blord River and, far to the southeast, I could see the crumbling stonework of the Porgidor Tower. Over road and railway, I reasoned, there would be thermals but over the river, which ran ice-cold from the high hills, there would be a downdraught. . . Yes, there were thermals all right. The Hallicheki were taking full advantage of them, going up like a balloon. Literally. What were they playing at? Why weren't they gliding down the lift? And they were keeping well to starboard, to the south'ard of the track, putting on distance as they would have to come to port to pass to north and east of the tower.

I looked astern. The judges' airship was following, watching. If the Hallicheki tried to cut off a corner they'd be disqualified.

I kept the Porgidor Tower fine on my starboard bow; whatever the Hallicheki were playing at, I would run the minimum distance. And then, as I was lifting on the thermals over the railway, I saw that there was some method in the opposition's madness. There were more thermals over the power station on the west bank of the river and I had missed out on them.

Swoop and soar, swoop and soar. Compress, decompress. Our muscles were aching with the stooped scrambles forward and aft in the cramped confines of the car. It must have been even worse for Mary than for me because of the absurdly bulky and heavy clothing that she was wearing. But we were holding our own, more than holding our own. That thermal-hunting had cost the Hallicheki their lead.

Then there was the Porgidor Tower close on our starboard hand, with quite a crowd of spectators waving from the battered battlements. And we were on the last leg of the course, over boulder-strewn bushland, with the twin ribbons of the Saarkaar Road and Railway ahead and beyond them the river again, and beyond that the mooring masts and hangars of the airport.

Swoop and soar, swoop and soar. . . .

I swooped into the thermals rising from the road and the railway so that I could manage a steep, fast glide with no loss of altitude. I began to feel smugly self-congratulatory.

But where were the Hallicheki?

Not ahead any longer. All that they had gained by their use of thermals was altitude. They were neither ahead nor to either side, and certainly not below, where the only artifact visible was a little sidewheel paddle steamer chugging fussily up river.

Then there was the anticipated downdraught that I countered with decompression.

Suddenly there was a sharp pattering noise from directly above and I saw a shower of glittering particles driving down on each side of the car. Rain? Hail? But neither fall from a clear sky.

Mary was quicker on the uptake than I was. "The Hallicheki," she shouted. "They dumped their ballast on us!"

Not only had they dumped ballast on us, they'd holed the gas cells. Some of the viciously pointed steel darts had gone through every surface, dropping to the deck of the car. If we'd been in the way of them they'd have gone through us too. Razor-sharp, tungsten tipped (as I discovered later). So this was what had happened to the Shaara racer. . . .

"Ballast!" I yelled. "Dump ballast!"

But we didn't have any to dump. I thought briefly of the mooring lines with their metal pegs but the ropes were spliced to the pins and to the structure of the car. And I didn't have a knife. (All right, all right, I should have had one but I'd forgotten it.) Then I remembered my first flight with Robiliyi and what he had told me when I'd asked him what to do when there was no ballast left to dump. I stripped off my shirt, dropped it over the side. It didn't seem to make much difference. I sacrificed my shorts. I looked up. All the cells were punctured and three of them looked as though they were empty. But the planing surface above them must still be reasonably intact. I hoped. If only I could gain enough altitude I could glide home. Forgetting the company that I was in I took off my briefs, sent the scrap of fabric after the other garments.

I heard Mary make a noise half way between a scream and a gasp.

I looked at her. She looked at me. Her face was one huge blush.
I felt my own ears burning in sympathy.
I said, "We're still dropping. We have to get upstairs. Fast."
She asked, "You mean . . . ?"
I said, "Yes."
She asked, her voice little more than a whisper, "Must I?"
I said that she must.

But you could have knocked me over with a feather when her hand went to the throat of her coveralls, when her finger ran down the sealseam. She stepped out of the garment, kicked it overside. Her underwear was thick and revealed little; nonetheless I could see that that fantastic blush of hers suffused the skin of her neck and shoulders, even the narrow strip of belly that was visible. *That will do*, I was going to say, but she gave me no time to say it. Her expression had me baffled. Her halter came off and was jettisoned, then her remaining garment.

I'll be frank. She wouldn't have attracted a second glance on a nudist beach; her figure was good but not outstanding. But this was not a nudist beach. A naked woman in an incongruous situation is so much more naked than she would be in the right surroundings. She looked at me steadily, defiantly. Her blush had faded. Her skin was smoothly creamy rather than white. I felt myself becoming interested.

She asked, "Do you like it?" I thought at first that she meant the strip show that she had put on for me. She went on, "*I* do! I've often thought about it but I had no idea what it would really be like! The feel of the sun and the air on my skin . . . "

I wanted to go on looking at her. I wanted to do more than that— but there's a time and a place for everything and this was neither. It could have been quite a good place in other circumstances but not with a race to be flown to a finish.

I tore my eyes away from her naked body—I heard a ripping noise, but it was only one of the rents in the envelope enlarging itself—and looked around and up and down to see what was happening. Mary's supreme sacrifice was bringing results. We were lifting—sluggishly, but lifting. And so, just ahead of us, were the Hallicheki. The gas cells of their balloon were flabby and wrinkled; they must have squandered buoyancy recklessly in their attacks on the Shaara and ourselves. And then I *saw* one of the great, ugly brutes clambering out of the car. They were abandoning ship, I thought. They were dropping out of the race. Then I realized what they were doing. The one who had gone outboard was gripping the forward rail of the car with her feet, was beating her wings powerfully, towing the balloon. Legal or illegal? I didn't know. That would be for the judges to decide, just as they would have to make a decision on the use of potentially lethal ballast. But as no machinery was being used, the Hallicheki might be declared the winners of the race.

What else did we have to dump? We would have to gain altitude, and fast, for the last swoop in. The hand winch? It was of no further use to us. It was held down to the deck of the car only by wing nuts, and they loosened fairly easily. We unscrewed them, threw them out. We were rising a little faster. Then there were the shackles securing the downhaul to the compression webbing. Overboard they went. The winch itself I decided to keep as a last reserve of disposable ballast.

High enough?

I thought so.

I valved gas—for the first and only time during our flight—and Mary and I shifted our weight forward. We swooped, overtaking the crawling, under tow, Hallicheki balloon. We were making headway all right but losing too much altitude. The winch would have to go.

It was insinuated that my jettisoning it when we were directly above the Hallicheki was an act of spite. I said in my report that it was accidental, that the Hallicheki just happened to be in the wrong place at the wrong time. Or the right time. I'll not deny that we cheered when we saw the hunk of machinery hit that great, flabby mattress almost dead center. It tore through it, rupturing at least four of the gas cells. The envelope crumpled, fell in about itself. The two hen officers struggled to keep the crippled racer in the air, ripping the balloon fabric to shreds with their clawed feet as their wings flapped frenziedly. Meanwhile *we* were going up like a rocket.

The Hallicheki gave up the attempt to keep their craft airborne. They let it flutter earthwards, trailing streamers of ragged cloth. They started to come after us, climbing powerfully. I could sense somehow that they were in a vile temper. I imagined those sharp claws and beaks ripping into the fabric of our balloon and didn't feel at all happy. *We* didn't have wings of our own. We didn't even have parachutes.

It was time for the final swoop—if only those blasted birds let us make it. There was no need to valve any more gas; the rents in the fabric of the gas cells had enlarged themselves. We shifted our weight forward. Astern and overhead I heard the throbbing of engines; it was the judges' airship escorting us to the finish line. The Hallicheki wouldn't dare to try anything now. I hoped. My hope was realized. They squawked loudly and viciously, sheared off.

Overhead, as I've said, there was the throbbing of airship engines—and, fainter, the irregular beat of an inertial drive unit. *Adder*'s atmosphere flier, I thought at first, standing by in case of accidents. But it didn't sound quite right, somehow. Too deep a note. But I'd too much on my plate to be able to devote any thought to matters of no immediate importance.

We swept into the airport, steering for the red flag on the apron that marked the finish. We were more of a hang glider now than a balloon but I *knew* somehow that we'd make it. The underside of the car brushed the branches of a tree—to have made a detour would have been out of the question—and a large section of decking was torn away. That gave us just the little extra buoyancy that we needed. We cleared the spiky hedge that marked the airport boundary. We actually hit the flagpole before we hit the ground, knocking it over. Before the tattered, deflated envelope collapsed over us completely we heard the cries of applause, the thunder of flat hands on thighs.

It was quite a job getting out from under that smothering fabric. During the struggle we came into contact, very close contact. At least once I almost . . . Well, I didn't. I'm not boasting about it, my alleged self-control, I mean. There comes a time in life when you feel more remorse for the uncommitted sins—if sins they are—than for the committed ones.

At last we crawled out of the wreckage. The first thing we noticed was that the applause had ceased. My first thought was that the natives were shocked by our nudity and then, as I looked around, saw that they were all staring upwards. The clangor of the strange inertial drive was sounding louder and louder.

We looked up too. There was a pinnace—a big pinnace, such as are carried by major warships—coming down. It displayed Survey Service markings. I could read the name, in large letters, ARIES II. *Aries'* number-two pinnace . . . *Aries*—a Constellation Class cruiser— I knew quite well. I'd once served in her as a junior watch-keeper. She must still be in orbit, I thought. This would be the preliminary landing party.

The pinnace grounded not far from where Mary and I were standing. Or where *I* was standing; Mary was on her hands and knees desperately trying to tear off a strip of fabric from the ruined envelope to cover herself. The outer airlock door opened. A group of officers in full dress blues disembarked. Captain Daintree was in the lead. I knew him. He was a strict disciplinarian, a martinet. He was one of the reasons why I had not been sorry to leave *Aries*.

He glared at us. He recognized me in spite of my non-regulation attire. He stood there, stiff as a ramrod, his right hand on the pommel of his dress sword. I still think that he'd have loved to use that weapon on me. His face registered shock, disbelief, horror, you name it.

He spoke at last, his voice low but carrying easily over the distance between us.

"Mr. Grimes, correct me if I am wrong, but your instructions, I believe, were merely to maintain a Terran presence on this planet until such time as an officer of higher rank could take over." I admitted that this was so.

"You were not, I am certain, authorised to start a nudist club. Or is this, perhaps, some sort of love-in?"

"But, sir," I blurted, "I won the race!" Even he could not take that triumph from me. "I won the race!"

"And did you win the prize, Commodore?" asked Kitty Kelly.

"Oh, yes. A very nice trophy. A model, in solid gold, of a racing balloon, suitably inscribed. I have it still, at home in Port Forlorn."

"Not that prize. It's the body beautiful I mean. The inhibition-and-clothing-shedding Miss Marsden."

"Yes," said Grimes. "She shed her inhibitions all right. But I muffed it. I should have struck while the iron was hot, before she had time to decide that it was really Beadle—of all people!—whom she fancied. He reaped what I'd sown—all the way back to Lindisfarne Base!

"When you get to my age you'll realise that there's no justice in the Universe."

"Isn't there?" she asked, rather too sweetly.

⪜ Grimes Among the ⪜ Gourmets

COMMODORE GRIMES, although he hated to admit it even to himself, was coming to look forward to the visits paid by Kitty Kelly to his ship. *Faraway Quest* was immobilized at Port Fortinbras, on Elsinore, and would remain so until such time as her engineers were able to effect repairs to the old vessel's inertial drive. Originally an Epsilon Class star tramp, built for the Interstellar Transport Commission, she had been obsolescent when she entered the service of the Rim Worlds Confederacy. Her main propulsive machinery was hopelessly out of date and engineroom spares were not easily procurable. New eccentrics—but conforming to a long outmoded design—were being fabricated in Rim Runners' workshops in Port Forlorn, on Lorn. Nobody was busting a gut on the job. Meanwhile the venerable *Quest*, her future employment a matter of no great urgency, stayed put.

Shortly after the Rim Worlds survey ship's arrival at Port Fortinbras, Grimes had been interviewed by Kitty Kelly of Station Yorick. He had been inveigled into spinning her a yarn about one of his adventures during his younger days in the Federation Survey Service, which she had recorded. It had been broadcast on her Kitty's Korner tri-vi programme and Station Yorick's viewers had lapped it up. She had been told to wheedle more tall stories out of the crusty old spacedog. Grimes had not been at all displeased to learn that most of his crew now watched, and enjoyed, Kitty's Korner.

This day she had told him that she would, if it suited his convenience, be calling aboard at a later time than usual. He suggested that she take dinner with him before the recording session. She was pleased to accept the invitation.

Grimes's paymaster—who was also the ship's catering officer—was Miss Keiko Otoguro. Learning that the commodore would be dining with his guest in his day cabin she asked him if she could serve one of the traditional meals of her ancestral people. She told him that she had been for a ramble along the seashore and had collected various seaweeds that would be suitable for the menu that she had in mind. Grimes assented happily. He had always loved exotic foods. And, he thought and hoped, a sumptuous repast laid on especially for the beautiful, blue-eyed, black-haired Kitty Kelly might soften her attitude towards him. (He had already tried the "candy is dandy but liquor is quicker" approach but it hadn't worked.)

So Kitty Kelly was sitting in an easy chair in the commodore's day cabin, displaying her excellent legs. Grimes, seated facing her, was admiring the scenery. Both were sipping large pink gins.

She said, "I enjoy a meal aboard a ship now and again, even though autochefs tend to make everything taste the same."

"Not necessarily," he told her. "A lot depends upon how much imagination is employed in the programming and upon what spices are available. But the dinner that we shall be enjoying is not from the autochef. My paymaster prepared it with her own fair hands . . ."

There was a light tap at the door. Miss Otoguro entered the cabin, carrying a lacquered tray with bottles, glasses and tiny porcelain cups. She was followed by two stewardesses with larger trays upon which the food had been set out. There was just enough room on the big coffee table for the meal and the drinks.

She uncapped a bottle of cold beer, poured into two glasses. Then, from a gracefully shaped porcelain bottle, she filled two of the little cups.

She said formally, "Dinner is served, Commodore-san."

He replied with equal formality, "Thank you, Paymaster-san," then added, "there's no need for you to play Mama-san, Keiko. We can help ourselves."

She smiled but there was a hint of disappointment in her voice as she said, "As you please, Commodore."

When she and the girls had left Grimes said, "She has very old-fashioned ideas about the proper place of women in the universe. But she's not a Rimworlder by birth. She was brought up on Mikasa . . ."

Kitty was looking at the meal laid out on her tray.

"But this is beautiful. . ." she whispered. "Like flowers . . . It looks too good, almost, to eat. . ."

"Keiko's specialty," he told her. "Only for very honored guests."

He raised his saki cup in a silent toast. She raised hers, sipped. She made a grimace.

"But this is *warm* . . ."

"That's the way it should be served."

"Oh. I think I'll stick to beer. And didn't your Miss Keiko forget knives and forks?"

Grimes picked up his ivory chopsticks, used them to mix mustard with the soy sauce in a little bowl. He then picked up what looked like a pink and white and green blossom with the implements, dipped it in the sauce, brought it to his mouth. He chewed and swallowed appreciatively.

She watched him, tried to follow suit. She did not manage too badly. Then her lips twisted in revulsion. She swallowed with an effort.

"*Raw* fish!" she exclaimed.

"Of course. With boiled rice, and seaweed . . ."

"I'm sorry," she said, "but I can't eat this. It looks pretty but it tastes like what it really is."

"But it's *sushi*. . ."

"I don't give a damn what it's called."

It was just as well that materials for making snacks were to hand in Grimes's refrigerator. With any luck at all Miss Otoguro would never know that the feast which she had so lovingly prepared had been devoured by only one person. (And even if she ever did find out all that would really matter to her was that the commodore had enjoyed it.)

The stewardesses had cleared away the debris of the meal and Kitty Kelly set up her recorder, one lens trained on Grimes, the other upon herself.

"Carry on drinking saki," she ordered. "That bottle and the tiny cup will look interesting . . . Now—and I promise you that this isn't for broadcasting unless you agree—isn't it true that your nickname when you were in the Federation Survey Service was Gutsy Grimes?"

His prominent ears flushed. "Yes, it is true. I admit that I've always liked my tucker. But I'm a gourmet rather than a gourmand. The meal that we've just enjoyed is proof of that."

"That *you've* just enjoyed, you mean."

"All right. I enjoyed it."

"Do you always enjoy exotic foods?"

"Almost always."

"Can you recall any occasion in your long career upon which exotic foods played a big part, Commodore?"

Grimes grinned. He put down his saki cup, picked up his pipe, slowly filled and lit it. He said, through the acrid, wreathing cloud, "As a matter of fact I can . . ."

"It was (he said) when I was captain of the Survey Service's census ship *Seeker*. I'd been given a sort of roving commission, checking up on human colonies in the Argo sector. Also I'd been told to show the flag on one or two inhabited planets with whose people, even though they weren't human, strictly speaking, the Federation wanted to keep on friendly terms. Spheres of influence and all that. Even though the Interstellar Federation was—and still is—the Big Boy, other, smaller spacefaring powers wanted to be Big Boys too. The Duchy of Waldegren, for example. The Empire of Waverley . . ."

"And now," she interrupted him, "the Rim Worlds Confederacy."

"We," he said stiffly, "have no Imperial ambitions."

"Spoken like a true Rimworlder, even though you were once a Terrie."

All right, all right, so I was a Terrie then (he went on). I held the rank of lieutenant commander in the Federation Survey Service. I was captain of FSS *Seeker*, one of the census ships. I was counting noses and, at the same time, showing the flag. I'd been ordered to do this latter on Werrississa, the home planet of a non-human civilization.

Not that the Werrississians are all that non-human. There are, in fact, some far-fetched theories to the effect that Werrississa was colonised from Earth by some pre-Atlantean culture. The resemblances between them and us do seem to be too close to be accounted for by parallel evolution—but, given enough time, evolution can come up with *anything*. And, although sexual intercourse is possible between humans and Werrississians, such unions are always sterile.

What do they look like, you ask? To begin with, they're tall, the adults, male and female, running to two meters and up. They're slender, although their women are subtly rounded in the right places. They're wide-mouthed but thin-lipped. Their noses tend to be aquiline. Their eyes are huge, like those of some nocturnal mammals on Earth and other worlds. Hair coloring? From black through brown through gold to silver, but that silver is no indicator of age. Long, slender hands and feet, four-digited.

Clothing? Except for occasions when working gear is required, translucent, ankle-length robes, usually white, are worn by both sexes. Sandals tend—or tended when I was there—to be ornate. Both sexes wear jewelry—rings, ear-clips, bracelets, anklets.

They regard outsiders—rightly so, in many cases—as uncultured barbarians. They set great value on face. They attach great importance to etiquette. Their highest art form is cookery.

"For you," she said, "a paradise."

"It would not have been for you," he told her, "after the way in which you turned up your nose at that excellent dinner." "Do they like their food raw too?" she asked.

Seeker being a survey ship proper rather than a warship (he went on) she carried quite an assortment of scientists. Men dressed as spacemen, as the saying goes. Women dressed as spacewomen. Commissioned ranks, of course. One of them was Dr.—or Commander—Maggie Lazenby. She outranked me, although I was still the captain. She was my tame ethologist. She was supposed to be able to tell me what made alien people tick.

Shortly after we set down at the spaceport just outside Wistererri City she gave me a good talking to. She was good at that. "These are people," she said, "who were civilized while we were still living in caves."

"So how come," I asked, "that they'd only gotten as far as the airship when we made our first landings on this world in our interstellar vessels?"

"Civilization and advanced technology," she told me, "do not necessarily go together. But these," she continued, "are a very civilized people. Perhaps too civilized. There's a certain rigidity, and too great a tendency to regard all outworlders as uncultured barbarians. In matters of dress, for example. We tend to be casual—even in uniform unless it's some sort of state occasion. Short-sleeved shirts, shorts— and for women very short skirts. Luckily you received the local dignitaries in full dress, with all your officers, including myself, attired likewise. But I couldn't help noticing the horror with which the City Governor and his entourage regarded the stewardesses who brought in the refreshments . . ."

"They were correctly and respectably dressed," I said.

"By *our* standards. And on my home world nudity wouldn't have caused so much as a raised eyebrow." (Maggie came from Arcadia, where naturism is the accepted way of life.) "But I'm not running around naked here. And you and your crew are not going to run around half naked when you go ashore. Arms and knees, female as well as male, must, repeat must, be covered."

"But it's summer. It's *hot*."

"A good sweat will get some of your fat off," she said.

So . . . When in Rome, and all that. But I didn't like it. My crew didn't like it, even after I'd explained the reason for my order. But it wasn't too bad for the women. Maggie went into a huddle with the paymaster—oddly enough she was, like Miss Otoguro, in this ship, of Japanese origin—and between the pair of them they cooked up a shoregoing rig based on the traditional kimono, made up from extremely lightweight material. Miss Hayashi looked very attractive in hers. Maggie looked odd at first—to my eyes, anyhow—but I had to admit that it suited her; the green, silky cloth matched her eyes and was an agreeable contrast to her red hair . . .

"You seem to have had quite a crush on this Maggie," commented Miss Kelly.
"Mphm. Yes."

So there was shore leave. The male personnel suffered; even the nights were uncomfortably warm and nowhere was there air-conditioning. The ladies, in their filmy but all-concealing dresses, flourished. For daytime excursions Yoshie Hayashi issued parasols and also, for all occasions, paper fans. Oh, we could have used the parasols, and the fans too, but neither, somehow, seemed masculine. And we sweated. By the Odd Gods of the Galaxy, how we sweated! Official banquets are bad enough at any time but they're absolute purgatory when you're wrestling with unfamiliar eating irons and literally stewing inside a dress uniform.

"The eating irons?"

You've seen me using chopsticks—but the Werrississians use a sort of *single* chopstick. They come in three varieties. There's what is, in effect, just a sharp-pointed skewer, quite good for spearing chunks of meat or whatever. Then there's a long handled affair with a sort of small, shallow spoon on the end of it. You can eat a bowl of soup with the thing, but it's a long process and, if you hold it properly, unless you have a very steady hand most of the fluid food finishes up in your lap. And the last one's a real beauty. At the end of it is an auger with a left-handed thread. And it's used only for a very special dish.

You didn't like Keiko's *sushi*. It's just as well that she didn't prepare *sashimi* for us. It's also raw fish, but even more so, if you know what I mean. You don't? Well, the fish is only stunned, not killed, before being prepared. While you're picking the bite-sized pieces off the skeleton it comes back to life and twitches its fins and *looks* at you . . . I came quite to like it while I was stationed on Mikasa Base for a while; the junior officers' mess, where I took most of my meals, specialized in a traditionally Japanese cuisine. So, having eaten and enjoyed *sashimi*, I was quite able to cope with *leeleeoosa*. It's a sort of thick worm. Alive and wriggling. The skin's rather tough and rubbery but it tends to dissolve when you chew it, this process being initiated by the sauce, mildly acid in flavour, into which you dip it.

So you have these . . . worms swimming around in a bowl of tepid water. You select your next victim. You jab, then twist left-handed. You dip in the sauce, bring it to your mouth and chew. The flavor? Not bad. Rather like rare steak, with a touch of garlic.

Fortunately I'd been able to get in some practice before the first official dinner at which *leeleeoosa* was served. Maggie had done her homework before we came to Werrississa. She, like me, enjoyed exotic foods. The ship's artificers, acting on her instructions, had run up a few sets of working tools. Of course, we weren't able to test our skills on real live and wriggling *leeleeoosa* until after we'd set down and Miss Hayashi had been able to do some shopping. But we'd sort of trained on *sukiyaki*, the strips of meat bobbing around in boiling water made a fair substitute for the real thing. It was the lefthanded thread on the skewer that took the most getting used to.

Then HIMS *William Wallace*, one of the *big* ships of the Navy of the Empire of Waverley, dropped in. Her classification was more or less—more rather than less—of our Constellation Class battle cruisers. Her commanding officer was Captain Sir Hamish McDiarmid, Knight of the Order of the Golden Thistle &c, &c *and &c*. Like me, he was showing the flag. *His* flag. He had a far bigger ship to wear it on. But she was a warship, not a survey ship. She was long on specialists in the martial arts but short on scientists. Ethologists especially. Nonetheless, I was to discover later, he had done some research into local lore before inflicting his presence on the Werrississians.

But national pride influenced him. The kilt, in a variety of tartans, is worn throughout the Empire on all occasions, by both men and women, with uniform and with civilian clothing. Longish, heavy kilts are for winter, short, lightweight kilts are for summer. Traditionally nothing is worn under these garments—all well and good when they're long and heavy but liable to offend the prudish when they're short and light.

Not that the Werrississians were prudish. It was just that, as far as they were concerned, there were things that are done and things that just definitely aren't done. They were prepared to tolerate outworlders and their odd ways but they didn't have to like them when such odd ways were offensive. I was grateful to Maggie for her good advice. Here was (comparatively) little, lightly armed *Seeker* whose people were happily conforming, and there was the huge *William Wallace* whose men strode arrogantly along the avenues of the city flaunting their bare knees—and more on a breezy day. They realized that the natives liked us while thinking that *they* were something that the cat had dragged in in an off moment. They resented this. They openly jeered at our women in their long gowns, carrying their parasols, calling them Madam Butterfly. I heard that they were referring to me as Lieutenant Pinkerton . . .

"Who were they, when they were up and dressed?" asked Kitty.

"Two characters in an opera who were dressed more or less as we were dressed," said Grimes. *"Very unsuitably—as far as Pinkerton was concerned—for the climate."*

But, as I said, Sir Hamish had done some research before his landing on Werrississa. I learned later that he had earned quite a reputation as a gourmet. He had even been known to sneer at the Waverley national dish, the haggis. He had, as I had done, insisted that all his people familiarize themselves with local dishes and eating implements. They even carried their own working tools with them, tucked into their sporrans, when they went ashore. It was reported to me by some of my officers, who had dined in the same restaurants, that the *William Wallace* personnel were quite skilful with these, even with the *skirroo*, the implement used when eating *leeleeoosa*. Yet it wasn't enough. They might eat like civilized people but they dressed like barbarians. We both ate and dressed properly.

And yet we were all members of the same race, whereas the Werrississians, for all their similarities, weren't. There had to be some fraternization between the two crews. I invited Sir Hamish to take lunch with me aboard *Seeker*—and, unlike some people whom I will not name, he thoroughly enjoyed his *sushi*. He told me that he was planning a dinner aboard *William Wallace* for local dignitaries and would be pleased if I would attend together with three of my senior officers. I was happy to accept the invitation. Then—we'd had quite a few drinks and were getting quite matey—I asked him if he'd be serving haggis, piped in the traditional way. He wasn't offended. He laughed and said, "Not likely, Grimes. I ken well that you people are putting on a big act o' being civilized while we're just hairy-kneed barbarians. But I'll demonstrate that, when it comes to civilized living, we're as good as anybody. It'll be a Werrississian menu, prepared by my chefs . . ."

"Dress?" I asked.

"Formal, o' course. Ye'll be wearin' your dinner uniforms. We'll be wearin' ours. An' we'll be cooler than you'll be—from the waist down, anyhow. My private dining room will have to conform to local ideas of comfort, temperaturewise . . ."

I was rather sorry then that I couldn't back out, but it was too late. Later, when I passed the word around, nobody was keen to accompany me. At last Maggie said that she'd come to hold my hand. The other two victims were MacMorris, my chief engineer, and Marlene Deveson, one of the scientists. A geologist, as a matter of fact. Not that it matters.

Then the Big Day came round. Or the Big Night. We met in the air-conditioned comfort of my day cabin for a drink before walking the short distance to Sir Hamish's ship. We were all tarted up in our best mess dress, tropical. It would still be too hot for comfort with the white bum-freezer over the starched white shirt, the long, black trousers. The two ladies were slightly better off, with high-collared, epauletted, long-sleeved shirts only on top of their ankle-length black skirts. At least they were not required to wear jackets. Maggie looked good, as she always did, no matter what she was or wasn't wearing. Marlene looked a mess. She was a short girl, fat rather than plump.

Her round face was already sweaty. Her hair, greasily black, was a tangle. Two of her shirt buttons had come undone.

We allowed ourselves one small whisky each. Sir Hamish would be serving Scotch and it wouldn't do to mix drinks. Then Maggie made a check of Marlene's appearance, frowned, took her into my bathroom to make repairs and adjustments. When they came out shirt buttons had been done up and hair combed and brushed into a semblance of order.

We took the elevator down to the airlock, walked slowly down the ramp. *William Wallace* was a great, dark, turreted tower in ominous silhouette against the city lights. (Sir Hamish did not believe on wasting money on floodlighting, even when he was showing the Thistle Flag.) It was a hot night. I'd started perspiring already. I had little doubt that the others were doing likewise. We made our way slowly across the apron. The heat of the day was beating up from the concrete.

We climbed the ramp to *William Wallace*'s after airlock. The Imperial Marine on duty—white, sleeveless shirt over a kilt with black and red tartan, sturdy legs in calf-length boots—saluted smartly. I replied. Inside the chamber we were received by a junior officer, clad as was the Marine but with black and gold tartan and gold-braided shoulder boards on his shirt. More saluting. We were ushered into the elevator, carried swiftly up to Sir Hamish's suite.

He received us personally. He looked very distinguished. From the waist up he was dressed as I was—although he had more gold braid on his epaulettes than I did, more brightly ribboned miniature medals on the left breast of his mess jacket. And he was wearing a kilt, of course, summer weight and length, in the Imperial Navy's black and gold tartan. His long socks were black, with gold at the turnover. There were gold buckles on his highly polished black shoes.

And he, I was pleased to see, was feeling the heat too. His craggy face under the closely cropped white hair was flushed and shining with perspiration. But he was jovial enough.

He exclaimed, "Come in, come in! This is Liberty Hall. Ye can spit on the mat an' call the haggis a bastard!"

"Are ye givin' us haggis, then, sir?" asked MacMorris eagerly.

"No. 'twas just an expression of your captain's that I modified to suit *my* ship. *We* don't carry tabbies in the Waverley Navy."

Both Maggie and Marlene gave him dirty looks.

"Tabbies?" asked Kitty Kelly.

"In the old days of passenger carrying surface ships on Earth they used to call stewardesses that. Today all female spacegoing personnel, regardless of rank or department, are called tabbies. But not to their faces."

"I should hope not."

We were the first guests to arrive. We were taken into Sir Hamish's sitting room—he had quarters that would have made a Survey Service admiral green with envy—introduced to his senior officers, plied with excellent Scotch. Then the young officer who had received us on board ushered in the native guests. There were six of them, three male and three female. They looked pale wraiths. They accepted drinks from the mini-kilted mess steward although they regarded his hairy knees with distaste. Rather pointedly they made polite conversation only with those of us from *Seeker*, we were properly dressed even though our hosts were not. Their command of standard English was quite good.

A skirling of bagpipes came over the intercom. I assumed that it was the mess call. I was right. Sir Hamish led the way into his dining room. The long table, with its surface of gleaming tiles, each with a different tartan design, was already set. Sir Hamish's artificers had done him proud, were doing us all proud. At each place were the native eating utensils in polished bronze—*slup, splik* and *skirroo*. There were the bronze wine flasks, the cups made from the same alloy. There were place cards, with names both in English and the flowing Werrississian script.

Sir Hamish took the head of the table, of course, with a local lady on his right and her "social function husband" on his left. (The Werrississians have a multiplicity of wives and husbands—mates for all occasions.) I sat below the native woman and Maggie below the man. Then another native couple, then Marlene and MacMorris, then

the last Werrississian pair. Below them was the covey of Imperial
Navy commanders—(E), (N), (C), (S) and (G)—all looking rather
peeved at having to sit below the salt.

Sir Hamish's mess waiters were well trained, efficient. They were
drilled in local customs. First they poured each of us a goblet of the
sweet, sticky wine—it was, as it should have been, at room
temperature but I'd have preferred it chilled—and there was a round
of toasts. We toasted the Emperor James XIV of Waverley, whose
gold-framed, purple-draped portrait was on the bulkhead behind Sir
Hamish's chair. The gentlemen toasted the ladies. The ladies toasted
the gentlemen. We all toasted our host. By this time it was necessary
to bring in a fresh supply of the bronze flasks. Unluckily it was still the
same sickly but potent tipple. I looked rather anxiously at MacMorris.
He didn't have a very good head for drinks and was liable after only
one too many to insist on dancing a Highland fling. But I needn't
have worried about him. He was a Scot more than he was a Terran
and it was obvious that he, aboard a warship owned by the only
essentially Scottish spacefaring power, was determined to be on his
very best behavior. It was an effort but he was capable of making it.
The toasting over, he was taking merely token sips from his cup.

I looked at Marlene. I knew little about her drinking capacity and
behavior. What I saw worried me. She was downing goblet after
goblet of the wine as fast as the steward could refill them. Her hair was
becoming unfixed. The black, floppy bow at the neck of her shirt was
now lopsided. One button on the front of the garment was undone.

The first course came in.

I've forgotten its native name but it was, essentially, bite-sized
cubes of meat, fish, vegetables and other things coated in a savoury
batter and deep fried. For these we used the *spliks,* the long, sharp
skewers. The Werrississian guests made complimentary noises and,
as was their custom, ate rapidly, their implements clicking on the
china plates with their thistle pattern. Sir Hamish and his officers ate
almost as fast and so did we *Seeker* people—with the exception of
Marlene. It seemed to me that about half of her meal was going on to
the table and the other half on to her lap, and from there to the deck.
I was very sorry that Maggie wasn't sitting beside me instead of

opposite. Had I been next to her I could have whispered to her, begged her to do something, anything, about her fellow scientific officer before she disgraced us.

The table was cleared but the *spliks* were left for use on the next course. This consisted of cubes of a melon-like fruit rolled in a sort of aromatic sugar. To my great relief Marlene seemed to have regained control of herself and succeeded in putting at least seventy-five percent of the sweet morsels into her broad mouth, although by this time her lipstick was smeared badly.

Plates and *spliks* were removed by the attentive stewards. Goblets—where necessary—were refilled. I looked imploringly at Sir Hamish; surely he must realize that Marlene had had enough to drink, more than enough. He looked at me. There was a sardonic expression on his craggy face that I didn't like at all. I looked at Maggie. She knew what was passing through my mind. I could read her expression. It said, *What can I do about it?*

Plashish was next—a sort of clear soup, with shreds of something like cheese floating in it, served in shallow bowls. We all plied our *slups*, the long-handled spoons, holding them as we had been taught, by the very end of the shaft. *All?* No, there was one exception. Marlene, of course. She *did* try, I admit, but gave it up as a bad job. Then she lifted the bowl to her mouth, with two hands, and *lapped* from it . . .

The *William Wallace* people were trying to look even more shocked than their native guests but I knew that the bastards were glorying in the discomfiture of the Sassenachs. Us. And Sir Hamish— may the Odd Gods of the Galaxy rot his cotton socks!—was looking insufferably smug. He had shown the Werrississians that even though the representatives of Waverley insisted on wearing their own native dress they could comport themselves at table far more decently than the minions of Terra. And the Werrississians? They were gravely embarrassed. Their complexions had faded from the usual pale cream to an ashy grey. They were obviously avoiding looking at Marlene.

The *plashish* course was over. The *leeleeoosa* was (were?) brought in—the deep bowls of lukewarm water in which the meaty worms were swimming, the smaller bowls of sauce. I daren't look at Marlene to see how she was managing. I was having my own troubles, anyhow. So was Maggie. So was MacMorris. We'd practised enough with *skirmos*—both aboard *Seeker* and in restaurants ashore—but somehow our acquired skill seemed to have deserted us. We'd stab, and make contact with our prey, and twist—yet every time our intended victims would wriggle free. But Sir Hamish and his people were eating as expertly as the Werrississian guests . . .

It was Maggie first who twigged what was wrong. She stared at me across the table. She raised her left hand with forefinger extended, made a circular motion. I finally realised what she was driving at. The *skirroos* at our places, those long, bronze augers, had right-handed threads. I impaled one of the tasty worms without trouble then, dipped it in the sauce, brought it up to my mouth, chewed. I felt that I'd earned it. MacMorris, as befitting an engineer, had made the discovery himself. He was eating fast and happily.

I looked down and across the table at Marlene. She was having her troubles. I tried to catch her attention but she was concentrating too hard on her bowl of *leeleeoosa*. She had her *skirroo* in both hands. She brought it down like a harpoon. She must have driven the point through the tough, rubbery skin of a worm by sheer force. She lifted it out of the bowl. She didn't bother to dip it in the sauce but brought the wriggling thing straight up to her open mouth. If it had made the distance it wouldn't have mattered, but . . . It slipped off the end of the *skirroo*. It fell on to Marlene's ample bosom. It found the gap in her shirt front where the gilt button had come undone. It squirmed into the opening.

Marlene screamed. She jumped to her feet, oversetting her *leeleeoosa* bowl. There were worms everywhere. Maggie guessed her intentions but did not reach her in time to stop her from ripping off her shirt. She was wearing nothing under it. Her breasts were her best feature, but they were *big*. It seemed as though somebody had launched a couple of Shaara blimps into Sir Hamish's dining room.

The Waverley officers stared appreciatively. The Werrississians, male and female, covered their eyes with both hands. Sir Hamish got to his feet, glared at me—but I knew that this was a histrionic display put on for the benefit of his native guests.

"Commander Grimes," he said, "you and your officers have abused my hospitality and gravely embarrassed my other guests. You will please leave my ship. I shall be vastly obliged if you never set foot aboard her again."

"Sir Hamish," I said to him, "none of this would have happened if our places had been set with the correctly left-hand-threaded *skirroos*."

He said, "I thought that I was doing you a favor. All my people have found it far easier to use right-handed *skirroos* of our own manufacture."

And so we slunk off *William Wallace* in disgrace, what little dignity remaining to us dissipated by the tussle that we had with Marlene to stop her from stripping completely; she was convinced that one of the spilled worms had wriggled from the floor up her leg.

Back aboard *Seeker* we almost literally threw the fat, drunken girl into her cabin. MacMorris—whose mind was reeling under the shock of having been thrown off a Scottish ship—went to his quarters to sulk and to console himself with whisky.

Maggie came up to my flat to console me. We held a post mortem on the disastrous evening. We'd thought that we, playing along with the local prudery regarding dress while the Waverley crew flaunted their short kilts, had made ourselves the most favored aliens. But Sir Hamish had turned the tables on us. Of course, Marlene's strip act had been an unexpected bonus to him.

So that was that. I had to carry the can back, of course—after all, I was the captain. My popularity rating with the Lords Commissioners of the Admiralty sank to what I thought must be an all time low.

"If you had the sense to stick to civilized food," said Kitty Kelly, *"that sort of thing would never happen . . . But I don't know much about the Galaxy outside the Shakespearian Sector. This Werri-whatever-it-is . . . I suppose that it's now well and truly inside the Waverley sphere of influence."*

Grimes laughed. "As a matter of fact it isn't. I heard that after we'd left Sir Hamish and his senior officers were invited to a very genteel garden party thrown by no less a dignitary than the Grand Coordinator. It was a windy day. They should have had sense enough to wear their winter weight kilts . . .

"It was the Shaara, of all people, who got a foothold (talonhold?) on Werrississa. After all, you don't expect a really alien alien to have the same nudity taboos, the same table manners, as you do. We humans are so like the Werrississians that every difference was exaggerated."

"Just as differences between members of the same species are," she said. "Some like raw fish and seaweed. Some don't."

⮞ Grimes and the ⮜
Odd Gods

FARAWAY QUEST, the Rim Worlds Confederacy survey ship, was still berthed at Port Fortinbras, on Elsinore. She was still awaiting replacements for the rotors of her outmoded inertial drive unit. More than once, in strongly worded Carlottigrams, Commodore Grimes had requested, demanded almost, that he be allowed to put the repairs in the hands of one of the several local shipyards. Each time he received a terse reply from the Rim Worlds Admiralty's Bureau of Engineering which, translated from Officialese to English, boiled down to *Father knows best.* He unburdened his soul to the Rim Worlds ambassador on Elsinore.

"Can't *you* do something, Your Excellency?" he asked. "There's my ship been sitting here for weeks now. My crew's becoming more and more demoralized. . . ."

"As well I know, Commodore," the ambassador agreed. "You've some hearty drinkers aboard your vessel, and when they drink they brawl. Perhaps you could stop the shore leave of the worst offenders. . . ."

"And have them drinking and brawling aboard the *Quest*? Or, if I really put my foot down, slouching around in a state of sullen sobriety? There's only one thing to do. Get them off this bloody planet and back where they belong, back to their wives and families or, in the case of the tabbies, to their boyfriends."

"Some of your female personnel are even greater nuisances than the men," said the ambassador.

"You're telling *me*. But as an ambassador, Your Excellency, you pile on far more Gs than a mere commodore, a commodore on the reserve list at that. Can't *you* do something?"

"I've tried, Grimes. I've tried. But it's all a matter of economics. The Confederacy just does not have the funds in any bank in the Shakespearean Sector to pay for a major repair and replacement job. Those rotors will have to be manufactured on Lorn, and then carried out here in whatever ship of the Rim Runners fleet is due to make a scheduled call to Elsinore. . . ."

"And meanwhile," the commodore said, "there are mounting port dues. And the wages that everybody aboard *Faraway Quest* is getting for doing nothing. And the three square meals a day, plus snacks, that all hands expect as their right. And. . . ."

"I'm a diplomat, Grimes, not an economist."

"And I'm just a spaceman. Oh, well. Theirs not to reason why, and all that. And now I'll be getting back to my ship, Your Excellency."

"What's the hurry, Commodore? I was hoping that you would stay for a few drinks and, possibly, dinner."

"I have an appointment," said Grimes.

The ambassador laughed. "Another interview for Kitty's Korner? I always watch that program myself. And I've heard that Station Yorick's ratings have improved enormously since Miss Kelly persuaded you to treat her viewers and listeners to your never-ending series of tall tales."

"Not so tall," growled Grimes.

"Perhaps not. You have had an interesting life, haven't you?"

An hour or so later, in his sitting room aboard the old ship, Grimes and Kitty Kelly were enjoying the simple yet satisfying meal that had been brought to them by one of the stewardesses. There were sandwiches constructed from crisply crusty new bread, straight from *Faraway Quest*'s own bakery, and thick slices of juicy Waldegren ham, the flavor of which derived from the smoldering sugar pine sawdust over which the meat had been smoked. (Almost alone among the ship's personnel, Grimes liked this delicacy; that was a good supply of it in the ship's cool stores. He was pleased that Kitty, hitherto inclined to be an unadventurous eater, enjoyed it, too.) There was a variety of cheeses—Ultimo Blue, Aquarian Sea Cream, and Caribbean Pineapple and Pepper—altogether with assorted pickles and the especially hot radishes that Grimes had insisted be cultivated in the ship's hydroponic farm. There was Australian beer—some while ago Grimes had done a private deal with the master of a Federation star tramp not long out from Earth—served in condensation-bedewed pewter pots.

Nibbling a last radish with her strong while teeth, Kitty slumped back in her chair. Grimes regarded her appreciatively. As she always did, she was wearing green, this time a long, filmy, flowing dress with long, loose sleeves. Above it, the food and the drink had brought a slight flush to the normal creamy pallor of her face, a healthy pallor, set off by the wide scarlet slash of her lips. Below her black glossy hair, this evening braided into a sort of coronet, her startlingly blue eyes looked back at Grimes.

She murmured, "Thank you for the meal, Commodore. It was very good."

He asked, "And will you sing for your supper?"

She said, "You're the one who's going to do the singing." She looked at the bulkhead clock. "It's almost time that we got the show on the road again. And what are you going to talk about tonight? Your adventures as a pirate?"

"Not a pirate," he corrected her stiffly. "A privateer."

"Who knows the difference? And who cares? Or what about when you were governor general of that anarchist planet?"

"Too long a story, Kitty," he said. "And too complicated. By All the Odd Gods of the Galaxy, there never were, before or since, such complications!"

She said thoughtfully, "That . . . that oath you often use . . . By All the Odd Gods of the Galaxy . . . Did you ever get tangled with any of these Odd Gods?"

He told her, "I'm an agnostic. But . . . there have been experiences."

She got up from her chair, went to the case containing her audiovisual recorder, opened it, pulled out the extensions with their lenses and microphones.

She said, peering into the monitor screen. "Yes, that's it. Pipe in one hand, tankard in the other . . . And now, *talk*."

"What about?"

"The Odd Gods, of course. Or, at the very least, One Odd God."

He said, "Oh, all right. But I must get my pipe going first."

As you know (he started at last), I left the Federation Survey Service under something of a cloud after the *Discovery* mutiny. For a while I was yachtmaster to the Baroness Michelle d'Estang, an El Doradan aristocrat, and on the termination of this employment she gave me the yacht's pinnace, which was practically a deep-space ship in miniature, as a parting gift. I called her—the pinnace, not the baroness—*Little Sister* and set up shop as Far Traveler Courier Services. I'd carry anything or anybody anywhere, as long as I got paid. There would be small parcels of special cargo. There would be people waiting to get to planets well off the normal interstellar trade routes.

It was a living.

I didn't make a fortune, but there was usually enough in the bank to pay port's dues and such and to keep me in life's little luxuries. It was lonely for quite a lot of the time but, now and again, there were passengers who were pleasant enough company . . . Yes, female ones sometimes, if you must know. But it was the female ones who usually got me into all kinds of trouble. Mphm.

Well, I'd carried a small parcel of urgently needed medical supplies to a world called Warrenhome—no, the inhabitants weren't descended from rabbits but the name of the captain who made the first landing was Warren—where they were having some sort of plague. A mutated virus. After I'd made delivery and received the balance of the payment due to me, I lost no time in placing the usual advertisements in the usual media. I decided that I'd wait around for a week and then, if nothing came up, get off the planet. There was talk that that virus, a nasty one, might mutate again.

Luckily (I thought at the time) I didn't have long to wait for my next job. I returned to *Little Sister*, after a yarn with the Port Captain, just before any usual lunchtime. I saw that a tall woman was approaching the airlock door from the opposite direction to myself. She was dressed in severe, ankle-length black with touches of white at throat and wrists. On her head was an odd sort of hat, black, with a wide, stiff brim. The skin of her strong-featured face was white; even the lips of her wide mouth were pale. Her eyes were a hard, steely blue.

She stated rather than asked, "Captain Grimes."

Her voice was deep for a woman, resonant.

I said, "I have that honor, Miz . . . ?"

She said, "You may call me Madame Bishop."

I asked, "And what can I do for you, Miz Bishop?"

She said coldly, "Bishop is my title, Captain Grimes, not my surname. I understand that you are seeking employment for yourself and your ship. I shall employ you."

I let us both into the ship, seated her at the table in the cabin while I went through into the little galley. I asked her what she would like to drink. She told me coldly that she would appreciate a glass of water. I brought her one, and a pink gin for myself. She looked at this disapprovingly. I pulled out my pipe and filled it. She as good as ordered me to put it away. It wasn't so much the words that she used but the way in which she said them. But I had been learning, ever since I set up in business for myself, that the customer is always right. I put my pipe back in my pocket.

She asked, "How soon can you lift ship, Captain Grimes?"

I said, "As soon as I've paid on my bills and cleared outwards."

"Today?"

"Yes."

She asked, "Are you capable of making the voyage to Stagatha?"

I'd never heard of that world, but *Little Sister* was capable of going just about anywhere in the galaxy. I told her yes.

"What will be the single fare for one passenger?"

I couldn't answer this at once. I didn't know where Stagatha was or how far it was from Warrenhome. I asked her to wait while I switched on the playmaster. She told me that she did not approve of frivolous entertainment. I told her that the playmaster screen served as the read-out for *Little Sister*'s computer and library bank. I don't think she believed me until the requested data began to appear.

In a short while I had all the information required. The voyage would take six weeks. Then there were all the various expenses accruing over this period—depreciation, insurance, consumption of stores, the salary that I—as owner—was paying to myself as master. And so on, and so on. After all, I had to show a profit. I told her how much I should be asking.

She said, "We are not a rich church, Captain Grimes, but we are not a poor one. And has it not been written that the laborer is worthy of his hire?" She allowed herself the merest hint of a smile. "Too, you are the only laborer available at this moment of time."

"Is this voyage a matter of some urgency?" I asked.

"The Lord's work is always urgent," she told me.

And so it was that I contracted to carry Bishop Agatha Lewis, of the Church Of The Only Salvation, from Warrenhome to Stagatha.

He paused, looking down into his now-empty tankard. Kitty refilled it for him, refilled her own.

She said, "So far we haven't had any Odd Gods. These Only Salvation people seem to have been just another nut cult, probably with their own translation of the Christian Bible slanted to make it fit their own beliefs."

He said, "Even without special translations you can interpret the Bible in a very wide variety of ways, find in it Divine Authority for just about every aberration of which the human race is capable. But the Church Of The Only Salvation did have its own Bible. Bishop Lewis gave me a copy. I tried to read it but the writing was appallingly bad. As far as I'm concerned there is only one Bible. The King James version."

After she was gone, to get herself organized, I made myself a sandwich lunch and tried to get more information about Stagatha from the library bank. It was an Earth-type planet with about the same proportion of land to water. The inhabitants were humanoid. I've often wondered why there are so many humanoid, as near as dammit human, races throughout the galaxy. Was there some Expansion, from Somewhere, before the dawn of history? But on every world there is the evolutionary evidence that cannot be denied that Man descended from lower life forms. Or is there some Divine Plan?

But I'm just a spaceman, not a philosopher.

There were photographs of typical Stagathans. These could have been taken on practically any beach on Earth or any Man-colonized planet. The males were, to all outward appearances, well-endowed (but not abnormally so) men. The females tended to be busty, but firm-breasted. The only thing odd was that these photographs had been taken in the streets of a Stagathan town, not at a seaside resort. I finally got around to looking at the vehicles and buildings in the background. Electric cars (I thought). Dwellings, offices, shops—but nothing over one story and everything with a flat roof.

And that was all. There was no trade with other worlds, no exports, no imports. There had been very little contact with outsiders since the first landing by Commodore Shakespeare, that same Commodore Shakespeare after whom your Shakespearean Sector was named. Every so often some minor vessel of the Survey Service would drop in, just showing the flag and for rest and recreation. But why, I wondered, should the Church Of The Only Salvation be interested in the planet?

But I had things to do. Bills to pay, outward clearance to be obtained and all the rest of it. Not much was required in the way of stores; my tissue culture vats were in good order and I could program the autochef to turn out quite fair imitations of Scotch whiskey and London gin. Flour I needed, and fresh eggs, and a few cases of the not-too-bad local table wines. Regarding these, I based my order on what I regarded as normal consumption by two people for the duration of the voyage. I could have cut that order by half. . . .

I made my pre-liftoff checks. Everything was in order, as it almost always was. She was a reliable little brute, was *Little Sister*. When I was walking around the outside of her, just admiring her, a small motorcade approached from the spaceport gates. There were four archaic-looking ground cars, black-painted, steam-driven, each emitting a thick cloud of dirty smoke from its funnel. From the first one Bishop Agatha Lewis disembarked, followed by half a dozen men and women, dressed in plain black and with broad-brimmed black hats like the one she was wearing. The men were all heavily bearded. Similar parties got out from the other three cars.

I walked up to the she-bishop and threw her a smart salute. She did not quite ignore me, but her curt nod was of the don't-bother-me-now variety. She made no attempt to introduce me to the assembled elders and deaconesses and deacons or whatever they were. Oh, well, I was only the captain. *And* the owner. I was only a space-going cabbie. I went back inside the ship to sulk.

Before long an elderly woman, followed by four men, carrying between them two heavy trunks, came in. She asked me, quite politely, "Where do we put these?" I showed them. The men went back outside.

She sat down at the table, noticed the tea things that I had not cleared away yet after my afternoon break.

She asked, in a whisper, "Do you think that I might have a cup, Captain?"

I made a fresh pot and, with a clean cup, brought it in to her. I could hear some sort of hymn being sung outside, one of those *dreary* ones all about the blood of the lamb and so forth.

She murmured, as she sipped appreciatively, "We shall all miss the dear bishop. But we, the synod, decided that she would be the right and proper person to send to Stagatha." She helped herself to a chocolate biscuit, crunched into it greedily. "Surely the similarity of the names is no coincidence. There was a St. Agatha, you know. Not that we approve of the Popish church and their beliefs." She poured herself more tea, added cream and was generous with the sugar. "Yes. We shall all of us miss the dear bishop—although, perhaps, her interpretation of the Word has been a mite too strict."

I said, "I still haven't been told why Bishop Lewis is going to Stagatha."

She said, "I thought that you knew. It is because those unhappy people, on that world, are living in a state of darkness, are brands to be plucked from the burning. We heard about it from a spaceman, a young fellow called Terry Gowan, one of the engineers aboard the *Cartographer*, a Survey Service ship. Would you know him?"

I said that I didn't. (It is truly amazing how so many planetlubbers have the erroneous idea that everybody in Space, naval or mercantile, knows everybody else.)

"A very nice young man. A *religious* young man. His ship set down here a few weeks after a visit to Stagatha. One of our people went on board her with books and pamphlets. The only one of the crew who was interested was Terry. He came to our prayer meetings. He talked about Stagatha. He brought us audio-visual records that he had taken. We were shocked. Those people, as human as you and me, going about completely . . . unclothed. And their *heathen* religion! Do you know, they worship their sun. . . ."

I didn't see much wrong with that. After all, sun-worship is logical. And as long as you don't go to the horrid extreme of tearing the still-beating hearts out of the breasts of sacrificial virgins, it has much to recommend it. The sun, after all—your sun, Earth's sun, Stagatha's sun, anybody's sun—is the source of all life. And there are Man-colonized planets, such as Arcadia, where naturism is a way of life, although the Arcadians don't quite make a religion of it.

"None of the other churches," the old lady went on, "has sent a missionary to Stagatha. But *somebody* has to. . . ."

"And Bishop Lewis was your obvious choice," I said.

"Why, yes," she almost laughed.

I was beginning to like the old dear. She had told me, as plainly as she could, that dear Agatha was being kicked upstairs. Literally.

Suddenly she stiffened and with a swift motion pushed her half-full teacup across the table so that it was in front of me. She was just in time. Bishop Lewis came into the cabin and stood there, staring down at us suspiciously.

She asked, "Why are you still here, Sister Lucille?"

The old lady got to her feet and bowed deferentially and said, "I was just keeping Captain Grimes company while he had his tea, Your Reverence. And I was telling him about our work."

"Indeed?" Her voice was very cold. "Since when were you one of our missioners, Sister Lucille?"

That business with the teacup had been a fair indication of which way the wind was blowing, but I made sure.

I asked, "Would you care for tea, Madame Bishop? I asked Sister Lucille to join me, but she refused."

"As she should have done, Captain Grimes, and as I shall do. Nowhere in Holy Writ are such unclean beverages as tea or coffee mentioned. Members of our Church are forbidden to partake of them."

And that was that.

He paused for refreshment, sipping from his newly filled tankard. Kitty asked, "And what about wine? That's mentioned quite a few times."

"Yes," said Grimes. "Noah planted a vineyard and then made his own wine after he ran the Ark aground on Mount Ararat. Then he got drunk on his own tipple and the Almighty did not approve."

"But, in the New Testament, there's the story of the wedding feast and the water-into-wine miracle."

"According to Bishop Agatha, and according to her Church's own translation of the Bible, that wine was no more than unfermented fruit juice."

I'll not bore you (he went on) with a long account of the voyage out to Stagatha. It was not one of the happiest voyages in my life. On previous occasions, when carrying a female passenger, I found that familiarity breeds attempt. Mutual attempt. But there just wasn't any familiarity. At nights—we maintained a routine based on the twenty-hour day of Warrenhome—the portable screen was always in place, dividing the cabin into two sleeping compartments. Once we were out and clear and on the way, I put on my usual shirt-and-shorts uniform and Her Reverence ordered me—ordered *me*, aboard my own ship—to cover myself decently. Smoking was forbidden, except in the control cab with the communicating door *sealed*. Meals were a misery. I regard myself as quite a fair cook and can make an autochef do things that its makers would never have so much as dreamed of, but . . . Boiled meat and vegetables for lunch, the same for dinner. Breakfast—boiled eggs. No ham or bacon, of course. The wine that I had stocked up with went almost untouched; I just don't like drinking it during a meal while my companion sticks to water. And *she* soon went through the ship's stock of orange juice—she liked that—leaving me with none to put with my gin.

She had brought her own supply of tapes for the playmaster, mainly sermons of the fire-and-brimstone variety and uninspiring hymns sung by remarkably untuneful choirs. Some of those sermons were delivered by herself. I had to admit she had something. She was a born rabble rouser. Had she been peddling some line of goods with greater appeal than the dreary doctrines of her freak religion, she might have finished up as dictator of a planet rather than as the not-very-popular boss cocky of an obscure sect. Might have finished up? But I'm getting ahead of myself.

I dutifully read the Bible, in that horridly pedestrian translation, which she had given me. I did not think that I should ever become a convert. Unluckily, I was rather low on reading matter of my own choice—books, that is—and my stock of microfilmed novels I could not enjoy because of her continuous monopoly of the playmaster.

Anyhow, at last the time came when I stopped the Mannschenn Drive unit and *Little Sister* sagged back into the normal Continuum. There were the usual phenomena, the warped perspective and all that, and (for me) a brief session of déjà vu. I saw Agatha Lewis as a sort of goddess in flowing black robes, brandishing a whip. It frightened me. And then things snapped back to normal.

I had made a good planetfall. We were only two days' run from Stagatha and made our approach to the world, under inertial drive, from north of the plane of ecliptic. There was no need for me to get in radio touch with Aero-space Control. There wasn't any Aero-space Control. As far as I could gather from the information in my library banks, Entry Procedure for just about every known planet in the galaxy, one just came in, keeping a sharp lookout for airships, selected a landing place, and landed. It all seemed rather slipshod, but if the Stagathans liked it, who was I to complain?

The planet looked good from Space. Blue seas, green and brown land masses, relatively small polar ice-caps. There was very little cloud except for a dark and dirty-looking patch of dense vapor that practically obscured from view most of a large island almost on the equator. I studied it through the control cab binoculars and could see flickers of ruddy light within it. It could only be Stagatha's only active volcano. According to Survey Service accounts, it was unnamed and regarded with a sort of superstitious horror. Nobody ever went near it. Looking down at it I thought that I could understand why. Even from a great distance I got the impression of utter ugliness.

Whenever possible, when making a landing on a strange planet with no spaceport facilities, I adhere to Survey Service standard practice, timing my descent from close orbit to coincide with sunrise. That way every irregularity of the ground is shown up by the long shadows. Agatha Lewis had told me to set the ship down as close as possible to one of the cities. Not that there were any *real* cities, just largish country towns, most of them on the banks of rivers, set among fields and forests.

So I dropped down through the early-morning sky, feeling the usual sense of pleasurable anticipation. I enjoy shiphandling and, too, this to me would be a new and almost certainly interesting world. But I wasn't as happy as I should have been. *She* insisted on coming into the control cab with me, which meant that I was not able to smoke my pipe.

My own intention had been not to pass low over the town. Inertial drive units are *noisy*—to anybody outside the ship, that is— and it would be, I thought, stupid to annoy the citizenry by waking them before sparrowfart. But Agatha Lewis insisted that I make what I considered to be the ill-mannered approach. As it turned out, I needn't have worried about disturbing the sleep of the natives. But I did interrupt their dawn service. They were in the central plaza, all of them—men, women, and children—wearing their symbolic black cloaks that they threw aside as the first rays of the rising sun struck through between and over the low buildings. They stared up at us. We stared down. The bishop hissed in disgust at the sight of all that suddenly revealed nakedness.

She . . . she snarled, "Now you know why I have come to this world. To save these poor sinners from their utter degradation."

I said, "They didn't look all that degraded to me. They were clean, healthy. Quite attractive, some of them. . . ."

"But their heathen worship, Captain Grimes! The baring of their bodies. . . ."

I said, "If God had meant us to go around without clothes we'd have been born naked."

"Ha, ha," interjected Kitty Kelly.

"You're as hard as she was," Grimes told her. "She didn't think that it was very funny either. But it shut her up. I was able to land Little Sister in peace and quiet."

"And then you got your gear off and went to romp with the happy nudists, I suppose."

"Ha, ha. Not with her around."

So I landed in the middle of this grassy field. Well, it looked like grass, and some odd-looking quadrupeds were grazing on it until we scared them off with the racket of the inertial drive. I made the routine tests of the atmosphere, not that it was really necessary as the Survey Service had already certified it fit for human consumption. I opened up both airlock doors. Bishop Agatha was first out of the ship. She stood there, in her stifling black clothing, glaring disapprovingly at the sun. I joined her. The fresh air tasted good, was fragrant with the scent of the grass that we had crushed with our set-down, with that of the gaudy purple flowers decorating clumps of low, green-blue foliaged bushes.

I thought that whether or not *she* approved, I was going to wear shirt-and-shorts rig while on this planet. I didn't know for how long I should have to stay; the agreement was that I should wait until the mission was well established and, at intervals, send reports to Warrenhome by means of my Carlotti radio. I couldn't get through directly, of course. The messages would have to be beamed to Baniskil, the nearest planetary Carlotti station, and relayed from there. After I was gone, Agatha would have to wait for the next Survey

Service ship to make a call—which might be a matter of months, or even years—before she could make further contact with those who had been her flock.

Anyhow, we stood there in the sunlight, the warm breeze, myself enjoying the environment, she obviously not. We did not talk. We watched the small crowd walking out from the town. As they grew closer, I could see how like they were to humans—our kind of humans—and how unlike. Their faces had eyes and nose and mouth, but their ears were long, pointed, and mobile. The hair on their heads was uniformly short and a sort of dark olive green in color. There was a complete absence of body hair. Their skins were golden brown. There was a something . . . odd about their lower limbs. (Their ancestors, I discovered later, had been animals not dissimilar to the Terran kangaroo.) But they all possessed what we would regard as human sexual characteristics. Apart from necklaces and bracelets and anklets of gold and glittering jewels, they were all of them naked.

Their leader, a tall man with a strong, pleasant, rather horselike face, walked up to me, stiffened to what was almost attention and threw me quite a smart salute with his six-fingered hand. Obviously he was not unused to dealing with visiting spacemen and, even though he himself went naked, knew the meaning of uniforms and badges of rank.

He said, in almost accentless Standard English, "Welcome to Stagatha, Captain."

I returned his salute and said, "I am pleased to be here, sir."

This did not suit the lady bishop. She was the VIP, not myself. She said a few words in a language strange to me. I was not entirely surprised. I knew that each night during the voyage she had retired to her bed with a slutor—a sleep tutor. She must, somehow, have obtained the necessary language capsules from that visiting Survey Service ship, *Cartographer.* I should have made some attempt myself to learn the language—but linguistically I'm a lazy bastard and always have been. Wherever I've gone I've always found somebody who could speak English.

The Stagathan turned to Agatha Lewis and bowed. Despite his lack of clothing it was a very dignified gesture. She returned this salutation with the slightest of nods. She went on talking in a harsh, angry voice. He grinned, looked down at himself and gave a very human shrug. She went on talking.

He turned to me and said, "For you I am very sorry, Captain. Now we go."

They went.

After I had gazed my fill upon a fine selection of retreating naked female buttocks, I turned to the bishop and asked, "What was all that about, Your Reverence?"

She looked at me very coldly and said, "I was telling these heathen, in their own language, to cover their nakedness."

I said, greatly daring, "They are dressed more suitably for this climate than we."

She said something about lecherous spacemen and then returned to the ship. I followed her. I busied myself with various minor chores while she opened one of the large trunks that had been put aboard before we left Warrenhome. She seemed to be unpacking. It was clothing, I noticed, that she was pulling out and spreading over the deck. She must be looking, I thought, for something cool to wear during the heat of the day. The next time I looked at her she was stowing a quantity of drab raiment into a large backpack.

When she was finished she said, "We will now go to the city, Captain Grimes."

"We haven't had lunch yet," I told her.

"Doing the Lord's work, according to His bidding, will be nourishment enough," she told me. "Please pick up the bag that I have packed and follow me."

"Why?" I demanded.

"It is essential," she said, "that we arrive in the central square prior to the noon service."

"Why?"

"It is not for you to question the Lord's bidding."

I said that I was a spaceship pilot, not a porter. She said that as long as I was on the payroll of her Church I was obliged to do as she required. I wasn't sure of the legality of it all but . . . After all, I had to live with the woman. Anything-for-a-quiet-life Grimes, that's me. I did, however, insist that I dress more suitably for the expedition than in what I was wearing at the time—long trousers, shirt, necktie, and uniform jacket. I went into the shower cubicle with a change of clothing and emerged in short-sleeved, open-necked shirt, kilt, and sandals. She glared at me.

"Are you going native, Captain?"

"No, Your Reverence. I have changed into suitable shore-going civilian rig."

"You are not to accompany *me* dressed like that."

"Then hump your own bluey," I told her.

She didn't know what I meant, of course, so I had to translate from Australian into Standard English.

"Then carry your own bag," I said.

She didn't like it but realized that if we wasted any more time in argument we should be late for the noon service. She swept out of the ship with me, her beast of burden, plodding behind. It was too hot a day to be encumbered with a heavy backpack but, at least, I was less uncomfortable than I should have been in formal uniform.

In other circumstances I should have enjoyed the walk—that springy almost-grass underfoot, the tuneful stridulations of what I assumed to be the local version of insects, occasional colorful flights of what I assumed to be birds but later discovered to be small, gaudy flying mammals.

But I was unable to loiter. Her Reverence set the pace, and a spanking one it was. That woman, I thought, must have ice water in her veins, to be able to stride along like that while wearing all that heavy, body-muffling clothing. We came to the boundary of the field, to a dirt road, to the beginnings of the houses. There were people abroad, coming out of the low buildings, setting off in the same direction as the one that we were taking. There were men and women and children. They looked at us curiously—as well they might!—but not in an unmannerly fashion. They were dressed—undressed—for the climate. Her Reverence was suitably attired for a midwinter stroll over a polar icecap.

We came to the central square. It was paved with marble slabs but, breaking the expanse of gleaming stone, were beds of flowering bushes and fountains in the spray of which the sun was making rainbows. In the middle of the square was a tall obelisk, surrounded by concentric rings of gleaming metal—brass? gold?—set in the marble. Hard by this was a tripod made of some black metal from which was suspended a huge brass gong. A tall, heavily muscled man—I'll call him a man, at any nude resort on Earth or any Terran colony world the only glances that he would have attracted would have been admiration—naked apart from his ornaments of gold and jewels, was standing by the tripod, holding, as though it were a ceremonial spear, a long-handled striker with leather-padded head. A woman—and she was truly beautiful—was sitting cross-legged, all her attention on the slow, almost imperceptible shortening of the shadow cast by the obelisk.

She turned to the man by the gong, uttered one short word. His muscles flexed as he raised the striker, brought the head of it, with a powerful sweeping motion, into contact with the surface, radiant with reflected sunlight, of the great brass disc.

A single booming note rolled out and the people, from streets and alleys, came flooding into the plaza. They were marching rather than merely walking, dancing rather than marching, and the clashing of their glittering cymbals was not without an odd, compelling rhythm. They were unclothed (of course), all of them—the men, the women, and the children—although bright metal and jewels glowed on glowing, naked flesh. They formed up into groups, all of them facing inwards, towards the central obelisk. The . . . the timekeeper was standing now, arms upraised above her head. She was singing, in a high, sweet voice. It was not the sort of noise that normally I should have classed as music, the tonality was not one that I was accustomed to, the rhythms too subtle, but here, in these circumstances, it was . . . right. The man at the gong was accompanying her, stroking the metal surface with the head of his striker, producing a deep murmuring sound. And all the people were singing.

I didn't need to understand the words to know that it was a hymn of praise.

"What are you *standing* there for?" demanded the she-bishop.

"What else should I do?" I countered.

She snarled wordlessly, literally tore the backpack from my

shoulders. She opened it, spilled the drab heap of secondhand clothing onto the marble paving. Close by us were children, about twenty in this group, who, until now, had been ignoring us. Her Reverence snatched up a rust black dress, forced it down over the body of a struggling, bewildered little girl. "Can't you help?" she snarled at me. By the time that she got her second victim clothed, the first one was naked again and running to the timekeeper, the priestess, bawling with fright and bewilderment.

Things started to happen then.

I was unarmed, of course, with not so much as a stungun on low power. Contrary to so many space stories the toting of firearms by spacemen, merchant spacemen especially, on other people's planets is not encouraged. It didn't take long for two hefty wenches to immobilize me, one on each side of me, both of them holding me tightly. I could do nothing but watch as four men seized Agatha, threw her down to the paving and, despite her frenzied struggles, stripped her. A knife gleamed and I yelled wordlessly—but it was being used as a tool, not a weapon, to slice through cloth and not through skin. Her long body, revealed as the last of underwear was slashed away, was disgustingly pallid. It needn't have been. She could have made use of the UV lamps every time that she had a shower during the passage out, as I had done. She was pallid and she was flabby, physically (at least) far inferior to those who were punishing her for her act of . . . sacrilege. Yes. Sacrilege. They held her there, in the blazing noonday sunlight, while the rags of her clothing were gathered up, and those other rags, those donations of used clothing with which she had tried to clothe the happily naked.

There was that pile of drab, tattered cloth and there was that big lens, a great burning glass, that was brought to bear upon the rubbish, concentrating upon it the purifying rays of the sun. There was the acrid smoke, and then the first red glimmer of smolder, and then flames, almost invisible in the strong sunlight.

And all the time Agatha was writhing and screaming, calling out not in Standard English but in the Stagathan language that she had learned. What she was saying I did not know, but it sounded like (and probably was) curses.

The bonfire died down.

A man whom I recognized as the leader of the party that had come out to the ship strode up to me. His face was grave.

"Captain," he said, "take this woman from here. She has insulted our God."

I said lamely, "She means well."

He said, "The path of the Mountain We Do Not Name is paved with good intentions."

My two captors released me.

The four men holding Agatha Lewis's wrists and ankles let go of her. She stumbled to her feet and stood there in that classic pose, one arm shielding her breasts, the other hand over her pudenda. With a younger, more shapely woman the attitude would have been prettily appealing; with her it was merely ludicrous. Her face was scarlet with humiliation. But it wasn't only her face. And it wasn't only humiliation. It was sunburn.

Kitty said, "When you mentioned the gleam of a knife I thought that you were going to tell us that Bishop Agatha suffered the same sort of martyrdom as Saint Agatha. Her breasts were cut off."

Grimes said, "I know. I did some checking up. There was so much odd parallelism about the whole business. But my Agatha suffered no worse than severely frizzled nipples. Very painful, I believe. I lent her my shirt for the walk back to the ship but, by that time, it was too late."

So we got ourselves back to the ship (he continued) with Her Reverence in a state of shock. It had all been such a blow to her pride, her prudery, her own kind of piety. The pyschological effects were more severe than the physical ones, painful as those most obviously were. And she had to let me apply the soothing lotions to her body. Oh, she *hated* me.

Once she was muffled up in a robe, wincing as every slightest motion brought the fabric into contact with her inflamed breasts, I said, "It is obvious, Your Reverence, that you are not welcome here. I suggest that we get off the planet."

She said, "We shall do no such thing."

She wanted her bunk set up then and the privacy screen put in position. I busied myself with various small tasks about the ship, trying not to make too much noise. But I needn't have bothered. I could hear her; the partition was not soundproof. First of all she was sobbing, and then she was praying. It was all very embarrassing, far more so than her nudity had been.

Late in the afternoon she came out. As well as a long, black robe, she was wearing her wide-brimmed hat and almost opaque dark glasses. She walked slowly to the airlock and then out onto the grassy ground. I followed her. She stood there, staring at the westering sun. Her expression frightened me. Rarely have I seen such naked hate on anybody's face.

"Your Reverence," I said, "I am still of the opinion that we should leave this world."

"Are you, an Earthman, frightened of a bunch of naked savages?" she sneered.

"Naked, perhaps," I said, "but not savages." I pointed almost directly upwards to where one of the big solar-powered airships, on its regular cargo and passenger run, was sailing overhead. "Savages could never have made a thing like that."

"Savagery and technology," she said, "can coexist. As *you* should know."

"But these people are not savages," I insisted.

"You dare to say that, Captain Grimes, after you witnessed what they did to *me*, the messenger of God."

"Of *your* God. And, anyhow, you asked for it."

Even from behind her dark glasses her eyes were like twin lasers aimed at me.

"Enough," she said coldly. "I would remind you, Captain Grimes, that you are still my servant and, through me, of the Almighty. Please prepare to lift ship."

"Then you are taking my advice?"

"Of course not. We shall proceed forthwith to the Mountain That Is Not Named."

Oh, well, if she wanted to do some sight-seeing, I did not object. Tourism would get us into far less trouble (I thought) than attempting to interfere with perfectly innocent and rather beautiful religious rituals. Quite happily I went back into the ship, straight to the control cab, and started to do my sums or, to be more exact, told the pilot-computer to do my sums for me. *Little Sister*, although a deep-space ship in miniature, was also a pinnace quite capable of flights, short or long, within a planetary atmosphere. *She* joined me as I was studying the readouts, looking at the chart and the extrapolation of the Great Circle course.

"Well," she asked.

"If we lift now we can be at Nameless Mountain by sunrise tomorrow, without busting a gut."

"There is no need to be vulgar, Captain. But sunrise will be a good time. It will coincide with *their* dawn service."

I didn't bother to try to explain to her the concept of longitudinal time differences and, in any case, possibly some town or city was on the same meridian as the volcano—but then, of course, there would be other factors, such as latitude and the sun's declination, to be considered. So I just agreed with her. And then, with the ship buttoned up, I got upstairs.

It was an uneventful flight. I had the controls on full automatic so there was no need for me to stay in the cab. Too, according to the information at my disposal, there was very little (if any) traffic in Stagatha's night skies. The sun ruled their lives.

We were both of us back in the control cab as we approached the volcano. She was looking disapprovingly at the mug of coffee from which I was sipping. I hoped sardonically that she had enjoyed the glass of water with which she had started her day. Outside the ship it was getting light, although not as light as it should have been at this hour. We were flying through dense smoke and steam, with visibility less than a couple of meters in any direction. Not that I had any worries. The three-dimensional radar screen was showing a clear picture of what was below, what was ahead. It was not a pretty picture but one not devoid of a certain horrid beauty. Towering, contorted rock pinnacles, evilly bubbling lava pools, spouting mud geysers. . . . The ship, still on automatic, swerved to steer around one of these that was hurling great rocks into the air. . . .

I said, "We're here."

She said, "We have yet to reach the main crater rim."

"The main crater rim?" I repeated.

"You're not afraid, Captain, are you? Didn't you tell me that this ship of yours can take anything that anybody cares to throw at her?"

"But . . . An active volcano . . . One that seems to be on the verge of blowing its top in a major eruption. . . ."

"Are you a vulcanologist, Captain?"

So we stood on, feeling our way through the murk. There was more than volcanic activity among the special effects. Lightning writhed around us, a torrent—flowing upwards or downwards?—of ghastly violet radiance that would have been blinding had it not been for the automatic polarization of the viewports. And ahead was sullen, ruddy glare . . . No, not *glare*. It was more like a negation of light than normal luminosity. It was the Ultimate Darkness made visible.

Little Sister maintained a steady course despite the buffeting that she must be getting. And then she was in clear air, the eye of the storm as it were. We could see things visually instead of having to rely upon the radar screens. We were over the vast crater, the lake of dull, liquid fire, the semi-solid, dark glowing crust through cracks in which glared white incandescence. In the center of this lake was a sort of island, a black, truncated cone.

"Set us down there," *she* said.

"Not bloody likely," I said.

"Set us down there."

She was standing now and her hand was on my shoulder, gripping it painfully. And . . . And . . . How can I describe it? It was as though some power were flowing from her to me, through me. I fought it. I tried to fight it. And then I tried to rationalize. After all, the metal of which *Little Sister* was built, an isotope of gold, was virtually guaranteed to be proof against *anything*. If anything should happen to her I could go to her builders on Electra and demand my money back. (Not that my money had paid for her in the first place.) Joke.

I had the ship back on manual control. I made a slow approach to the central island, hovered above it. I had been expecting trouble, difficulty in holding the ship where I wanted her, but it was easy. Too easy. Suspiciously easy.

I let her fall, slowly, slowly, the inertial drive just ticking over. I felt the faint jar, a very faint jar, as she landed on the flat top, the perfectly smooth top of the truncated cone.

She said, "Open the airlock doors."

I tried to protest but the words wouldn't come.

She said, "Open the airlock doors."

I thought, *And so we fill the ship with stinking, sulfurous gases. But the internal atmosphere can soon be purified.*

On the console before me I saw the glowing words as I actuated the switch. INNER DOOR OPEN. OUTER DOOR OPEN.

She was gone from behind me, back into the main cabin. I got up from my chair, followed her. She was going outside, I realized. She should have asked me for a spacesuit; it would have given her some protection against the heat, against an almost certainly poisonous atmosphere. Some of this was already getting inside the ship, an acridity that made my eyes water, made me sneeze. But it didn't seem to be worrying her.

She passed through both doors.

I stood in the little chamber, watching her. She was standing on the heat-smoothed rock, near, too near to the edge of the little plateau. Was the silly bitch going to commit spectacular and painful suicide? But I was reluctant to leave the security—the illusory security?—of my ship to attempt to drag her to safety. No, it wasn't cowardice. Not altogether. I just *knew* that she knew what she was doing.

(If I'd known more I should have been justified in going out to give her a push!)

She stood there, very straight and tall, in black silhouette against the dull glow from the lake of fire. Her form wavered, became indistinct as a dark column of smoke eddied about her. Still she stood there while the smoke thinned, vanished. It was as though it had been absorbed by her body.

But that was impossible, wasn't it?

She walked back to the airlock. The skin of her face seemed to be much darker than it had been—but that was not surprising. It seemed to me—but that must have been imagination—that her feet did not touch the surface over which she was walking.

She said as she approached me, "Take me back to the city."

I obeyed. No matter what her order had been, no matter how absurd or dangerous, I should have obeyed. When first I had met her I had been conscious of her charisma but had learned to live with it, to distrust it and to despise it. Now neither distrust nor contempt would have been possible.

We got upstairs.

No sooner were we on course than the volcano blew up. The blast of it hit us like a blow from something solid. I wasn't able to watch as I was too busy trying to keep the ship under some sort of control as she plunged through the fiery turbulence, through the smoke and the steam and the fiery pulverized dust, through the down-stabbing and up-thrusting lightning bolts.

And, through it all, *she* was laughing.

It was the first time that I had heard her laugh.

It was an experience that I could well have done without.

"I need some more beer," he said, "to wash the taste of that volcanic dust out of my throat. After all the years I still remember it." She refilled his mug, and then her own. "Did the dust get inside your ship?" she asked. "It got everywhere," he told her. "All over the entire bloody planet."

We set down in that same field where we had made our first landing. According to the chronometer it wanted only an hour to local, apparent noon, but the sky was overcast. The air was chilly. *She* ordered me to open one of her trunks. In it was a further supply of the cast-off clothing that she had brought from Warrenhome. And there were books. Bibles, I assumed, or the perversion of Holy Writ adopted by *Her* church. I opened one but was unable, of course, to read the odd, flowing Stagathan characters.

I filled a backpack with the clothing. While I was so doing she took something else from the trunk. It was a whip; haft and tapering lash were all of three meters long. It was an evil-looking thing.

We left the ship. She took the lead. I trudged behind. As she passed one of the flowering bushes, its blossoms drab in the dismal gray light, she slashed out with the whip, cracking it expertly, severing stems and twigs, sending tattered petals fluttering to the ground.

We walked into the city.

We came to the central square, with the obelisk (but it was casting no shadow), the great gong (but it was now no more than an ugly disk of dull, pitted metal), the celebrants and the worshippers.

But there was nothing for them to worship. The sky was one uniform gray with not so much as a diffuse indication of the position of the sun. The people were all, as they had been at that other service, naked but now their nudity was . . . ugly. A thin drizzle was starting to fall, but it was mud rather than ordinary rain, streaking the shivering skins of the miserable people.

The priest standing by the gong, the man with the striker, was the first to see us. He pointed at us, shouting angrily. He advanced towards us, still shouting, menacing us with his hammer. Behind him others were now shouting, and screaming. They were blaming us for the dense cloud that had hidden their god from sight.

She stood her ground.

Suddenly her lash snaked out, whipped itself around the striker and tore it from the priest's hands, sent it clattering to the mud-slimed marble paving. It cracked out again, the tip of it slashing across the man's face, across his eyes. He screamed, and that merciless whip played over his body, drawing blood with every stroke.

And *She* was declaiming in a strong, resonant voice, with one foot planted firmly upon the squirming body of the hapless, blinded priest, who had fallen to the ground, laying about her with the whip.

Even then, at the cost of a few injuries, they could have overpowered her, have taken her from behind. But the heart was gone from them. Their god had forsaken them. And *She* . . . *She* was speaking with the voice of a god. Or was a god speaking through her? She was possessed. The black charisma of her was overpowering. I opened the backpack and began to distribute the cast-off clothing.

Hands—the hands of men, women, and children—snatched the drab rags from me eagerly. And there was something odd about it. It seemed as though that backpack were a bottomless bag. It could never have held sufficient clothing to cover the nakedness of a crowd of several thousand people. Sometime later, of course, I worked things out. Converts must have gone back into their homes for the ceremonial black robes that they doffed at the dawn service and resumed at sunset. But, even so . . . How could those robes have assumed the appearance of, say, ill-cut, baggy trousers? Imagination, it must have been. Even though I could not understand what she was saying, I was under the spell of Her voice.

And it frightened me.

I felt my agnosticism wavering.

And I *like* being an agnostic.

Oh, well, at a time of crisis there is always one thing better than presence of mind—and that is absence of body.

I left her preaching to the multitude and walked back to the ship. I did worse than that. When I was back on board I collected everything of hers, every last thing, and lugged it out through the airlock on to a plastic sheet that I spread on the wet grass, covered it with another sheet.

And then I lifted off.

After all, I had done what I had contracted to do. I had carried her from Warrenhome to Stagatha (and the money for her fare had been deposited in my bank). I had stayed around until she had become established as a missionary. (Well, she had, hadn't she?)

I broke through that filthy overcast into bright sunlight. I began to feel less unhappy. I looked down at Stagatha. The entire planet, from pole to pole, was shrouded with smoke, or steam, or dust or—although this was unlikely—just ordinary cloud.

I wondered when their god would next show himself to the Stagathans and set course for Pengram, the nearest Man-colonized planet, where I hoped to be able to find further employment for *Little Sister* and myself.

"*I don't think much of your Odd Gods,*" said Kitty Kelly. "*After*

*all, sun-worship is common enough. And so are evangelists of either
sex who preach peculiar perversions of Christianity and are
charismatic enough to make converts. But I would have expected you
to behave more responsibly. To go flying off, the way you did, leaving
that poor woman to her fate. . . ."*

*"Poor woman? I was there, Kitty. You weren't. Too, I haven't
finished yet."*

I'd almost forgotten about Stagatha (he went on) when, some
standard years later, I ran into Commander Blivens, captain of the
survey ship *Cartographer*. I'd known Blivens slightly when I was in
the Survey Service myself. Anyhow, I was at Port Royal, on Caribbea,
owner-master of *Sister Sue*, which vessel had started her life as one of
the Interstellar Transport Commission's Epsilon Class star tramps,
Epsilon Scorpii. (She finally finished up as the Rim Worlds
Confederacy's survey ship *Faraway Quest*. Yes, this very ship that
we're aboard now.) But to get back to Blivens . . . I was in the Trade
Winds Bar with my chief officer, Billy Williams, quietly absorbing
planter's punches when I heard somebody call my name. I couldn't
place him at first but finally did so.

Then, for a while, it was the usual sort of conversation for those
circumstances. What happened to old so-and-so? Did you hear that
thingummy actually made rear admiral? And so on.

I got around to asking Blivens what he was doing on Carribea.

"Just a spell of rest and recreation for my boys and girls," he told
me. "And for myself. At one time I used to regard a rather odd but
very human world called Stagatha as my R & R planet. The people as
near human as makes no difference. Sun worshippers they were,
happy sun worshippers. Unpolluted atmosphere, solar power used
for everything. And not, like this overpriced dump, commercialized.

"But it's ruined now."

"How so?" I asked him.

"They've changed their religion. Some high-powered female
missionary decided to save their souls. I suppose that some money-
hungry tramp skipper carried her from her own planet,
Warrenhome, to Stagatha. Somebody should find out who the

bastard was and shoot him. And then, really to put the tin hat on things, there was a catastrophic volcanic eruption which threw the gods alone know how many tons of dust into the upper atmosphere and completely buggered the climate. So there was a switch from solar power to the not-very-efficient burning of fossil fuels—and still more airborne muck to obscure the sunlight.

"The missionary—the Lady Bishop, she called herself—called aboard to see me. She scared me, I don't mind admitting it. You'll never guess what her staff of office was. A dirty great whip. She demanded that I release one of my engineer officers to her service. The odd part was that she knew his name—Terry Gowan—and all about him. And Mr. Gowan seemed to know of her. It made sense, I suppose. He was one of those morose, Bible-bashing bastards himself. And, apart from the Bible in some odd version, his only reading was books on the engineering techniques in use during the Victorian era on Earth. He used to make models, working models, of steam engines and things like that.

"I gave him his discharge—which, as a Survey Service captain, I was entitled to do. You know the regulation. *Should a properly constituted planetary authority request the services of a specialist officer, petty officer or rating for any period, and provided that such officer, petty officer or rating signifies his or her willingness to enter the service of such planetary authority, and provided that the safe management of the ship not be affected by the discharge of one of her personnel with no replacement immediately available, then the commanding officer shall release such officer, petty officer or rating, paying him or her all monies due and with the understanding that seniority shall continue to accrue until the return of the officer, petty officer or rating to the Survey Service.*

"Anyhow, I don't think that anybody aboard *Cartographer* shed a tear for Gloomy Gowan, as he was known, when he was paid off. And he, I suppose, has been happy erecting dark, satanic mills all over the landscape for Her Holiness."

"And so everybody was happy," I said sarcastically.

"A bloody good planet ruined," grumbled Blivens.

A few more years went by.

Again I ran into Blivens—Captain Blivens now—quite by chance. He was now commanding officer of the Survey Service base on New Colorado and I had been chartered by the Service—they often threw odd jobs my way—to bring in a shipment of fancy foodstuffs and tipples for the various messes.

I dined with Blivens in his quite palatial quarters.

He said, towards the end of the meal, "You remember when I last met you, Grimes . . . I was captain of *Cartographer* then and we were talking about Stagatha. . . ."

"I remember," I said.

"Well, I went there again. For the last time. Just one of those checking-up-showing-the-flag voyages that I had to make. But there wasn't any Stagatha. Not anymore. The sun had gone nova. And as there hadn't been a Carlotti station on the planet no word had gotten out. . . ."

The news shocked me.

All those people, incinerated.

And I couldn't help feeling that I was somehow responsible.

But it was just a coincidence.

Wasn't it?

"Of course it was," said Kitty Kelly brightly.

"Was it?" whispered Grimes. And then: "For I am a jealous God. . . ."

≈ Grimes and the ≈ Jailbirds

"HAVE YOU EVER, in the course of your long and distinguished career, been in jail, Commodore?" asked Kitty Kelly after she had adjusted the lenses and microphones of her recording equipment to her satisfaction.

"As a matter of fact I have," said Grimes. He made a major production of filling and lighting his pipe. "It was quite a few years ago, but I still remember the occasion vividly. It's not among my more pleasant memories. . . ."

"I should imagine not," she concurred sympathetically. "What were you in for? Piracy? Smuggling? Gunrunning?"

"I wasn't in in the sense that you assume," he told her. "After all, there are more people in a jail than the convicts. The governor, the warders, the innocent bystanders. . . ."

"Such as yourself?"

"Such as myself."

≈≈≈≈

468

It was (he said) when I was owner-master of *Little Sister*. She was the flagship and the only ship of Far Traveler Couriers, the business title under which I operated. She was a deep-space pinnace, and I ran her single-handed, carrying small parcels of special cargo hither and yon, the occasional passenger. Oh, it was a living of sorts, quite a good living at times, although, at other times, my bank balance would be at a perilously low ebb.

Well, I'd carried a consignment of express mail from Davinia to Helmskirk—none of the major lines had anything making a direct run between the two planets—and I was now berthed at Port Helms waiting for something to turn up. The worst of it all was that Helmskirk is not the sort of world upon which to spend an enforced vacation—or, come to that, any sort of vacation. There is a distinct shortage of bright lights. The first settlers had all been members of a wowserish religious sect misnamed the Children of Light—it was founded on Earth in the late twentieth century, Old Reckoning. Over the years their descendants had become more and more wowserish.

The manufacture, vending, and consumption of alcoholic beverages were strictly prohibited. So was smoking—and by "smoking" I mean smoking anything. There were laws regulating the standards of dress—and not only in the streets of the cities and towns. Can you imagine a public bathing beach where people of both sexes—even children—are compelled to wear neck-to-ankle, skirted swimming costumes?

There were theaters, showing both live and recorded entertainment, but the plays presented were all of the improving variety, with virtue triumphant and vice defeated at the end of the last act. I admit that some of the clumsily contrived situations were quite funny, although not intentionally so. I found this out when I laughed as a stern father turned his frail, blonde daughter, who had been discovered smoking a smuggled cigarette, out into a raging snowstorm. Immediately after my outbreak of unseemly mirth, I was turned out myself, by two burly ushers. Oh, well, it wasn't snowing, and it was almost the end of the play, anyhow.

It wouldn't have been so bad if the local customs authorities had not done their best to make sure that visiting spacemen conformed to Helmskirkian standards whilst on the surface of their planet. They inspected my library of playmaster cassettes and seized anything that could be classed as pornographic—much of it the sort of entertainment that your maiden aunt, on most worlds, could watch without a blush. These tapes, they told me, would be kept under bond in the customs warehouse and returned to me just prior to my final lift-off from the Helmskirk System. They impounded the contents of my grog locker and even all my pipe tobacco. Fortunately, I can, when pushed to it, make an autochef do things never intended by its manufacturer, and so it didn't take me long to replenish my stock of gin. And lettuce leaves from my hydroponics minifarm, dried and suitably treated, made a not-too-bad tobacco substitute.

Nonetheless, I'd have gotten the hell off Helmskirk as soon as the bags of express mail had been discharged if I'd had any definite place to go. But when you're tramping around, as I was, you put your affairs into the hands of an agent and wait hopefully for news of an advantageous charter.

So Messrs. Muggeridge, Whitelaw, and Nile were supposed to be keeping their ears to the ground on my behalf, and I was getting more and more bored, and every day doing my sums—or having the ship's computer do them for me—and trying to work out how long it would be before the profit made on my last voyage was completely eaten up by port charges and the like. For the lack of better entertainment I haunted the Port Helms municipal library—at least it was free—and embarked on a study course on the history of this dreary colony. Someday I shall write a book—The Galactic Guide to Places to Stay Away From. . . .

The fiction in the library was not of the variety that is written to inflame the passions. It was all what, during the Victorian era on Earth, would have been called "improving." The factual works were of far greater interest. From them I learned that the incidence of crime—real crime, not such petty offenses as trying to grow your own tobacco or brew your own beer—on Helmskirk was surprisingly high. Cork a bottle of some fermenting mixture—and any human society is such a mixture—too tightly and the pressures will build up.

There was an alarmingly high incidence of violent crime—armed robbery, assault, rape, murder.

I began to appreciate the necessity for Helmskirk's penal satellite, a smallish natural moon in a just under twenty-four-hour orbit about its primary. Not only was it a place of correction and/or punishment for the really bad bastards, but it also housed a large population of people who'd been caught playing cards for money, reading banned books, and similar heinous offenses. If I'd been so unfortunate as to have been born on Helmskirk, I thought, almost certainly I should have been acquainted with the maze of caverns and tunnels, artificial and natural, that honeycombed the ball of rock.

As the days wore on I'd settled into a regular routine. The morning I'd devote to minor maintenance jobs. Then I'd have lunch. Before leaving the ship after this meal, I'd make a telephone call to my agents to see if they'd anything for me. Then I'd stroll ashore to the library. It was a dreary walk through streets of drably functional buildings, but it was exercise. I'd try to keep myself amused until late afternoon, and then drop briefly into the agents' office on the way back to *Little Sister*.

Then the routine was disrupted.

As I entered the premises, old Mr. Muggeridge looked up accusingly from his desk, saying, "We've been trying to get hold of you, Captain."

I said, "I wasn't far away. I was in the municipal library."

"Hmph. I never took you for a studious type. Well, anyway, I've a time charter for you. A matter of six local weeks, minimum."

"Where to?" I asked hopefully.

"It will not be taking you outside the Helmskirk System," he told me rather spitefully. "The prison tender, the *Jerry Falwell*, has broken down. I am not acquainted with all the technical details, but I understand that the trouble is with its inertial drive unit. The authorities have offered you employment until such time as the tender is back in operation."

I went through the charter party carefully, looking for any clauses that might be turned to my disadvantage. But Muggeridge, Whitelaw, and Nile had been looking after my interests. After all, why shouldn't they? The more I got, the more their rake-off would be.

So I signed in the places indicated and learned that I was to load various items of stores for the prison the following morning, lifting off as soon as these were on board and stowed to my satisfaction. Oh, well, it was a job and would keep me solvent until something better turned up.

It was a job, but it wasn't one that I much cared for. I classed it as being on a regular run from nowhere to nowhere. The atmosphere of Helmskirk I had found oppressive; that of the penal satellite was even more so. The voyage out took a little over two days, during which time I should have been able to enjoy my favorite playmaster cassettes if the customs officers had seen fit to release them. But rules were rules, and I was not leaving the Helmskirk System. And the moon, which was called Sheol, was very much part of it.

On my first visit I did not endear myself to the prison governor. I'd jockeyed *Little Sister* into a large air lock set into the satellite's surface and then left my control room for the main cabin. I opened the air lock doors and then sat down to await whatever boarders there would be—somebody with the inevitable papers to sign, a working party to discharge my cargo, and so on and so forth. I was not expecting the ruler of this tiny world to pay a call in person.

He strode into the ship, a tall man in dark gray civilian clothes, long-nosed, sour-featured, followed by an entourage of black-uniformed warders. "Come in, come in!" I called. "This is Liberty Hall. You can spit on the mat and call the cat a bastard!"

He said, "I do not see any cat. Where is the animal? The importation of any livestock into Sheol is strictly contrary to regulations."

I said, "It was only a figure of speech."

"And a remarkably foul-mouthed one." He sat down uninvited. "I am the governor of this colony, Mr. Grimes. During each of your visits here you will observe the regulations, a copy of which will be provided you. You will be allowed, should time permit, to make the occasional conducted tour of Sheol so that you may become aware of the superiority of our penal system to that on other worlds. There will, however, be no fraternization between yourself and any of our inmates. There will be no attempt by you to smuggle in any small luxuries. One of the officers of the *Jerry Falwell* made such an attempt some months back. He is now among our . . . guests, serving a long sentence."

"What did he try to smuggle in?" I asked.

"It is none of your business, Mr. Grimes. But I will tell you. It was cigarettes that he had illegally obtained from a visiting star tramp. And I will tell you what he hoped to receive in exchange. Mood opals. And the penalty for smuggling out mood opals is even greater than that for smuggling in cigarettes."

"What are mood opals?" asked Kitty.

"Don't you know? They were, for a while, very popular and very expensive precious stones on Earth and other planets, especially the Shaara worlds. The Shaara loved them. They weren't opals, although they looked rather like them. But they were much fierier, and the colors shifted, according, it was said, to the mood of the wearer, although probably it was due to no more than changes in temperature and atmospheric humidity. They were found only on—or in, rather—Sheol. They were actually coprolites, fossilized excrement, all that remained of some weird, rock-eating creatures that inhabited Sheol and became extinct ages before the colonization of Helmskirk. The mood opals became one of Helmskirk's major moneymaking exports. They were never worn by anybody on Helmskirk itself, such frivolity as personal jewelry being illegal."

"How come," asked Kitty, "that we've never seen mood opals here? Most Terran fads drift out to this part of the Galaxy eventually."

"There aren't any mood opals anymore," Grimes told her. "It seems that the polishing process, which removed the outer crust, exposed the jewels to the atmosphere and to radiation of all kinds. After a few years of such exposure, the once-precious stones would crumble into worthless dust."

Well (he went on), that was my first visit to Sheol. Naturally it sparked my interest in the mood opal trade. I suggested to my agents that they try to organize for me the shipment of the next parcel of precious stones to wherever it was they were going. But the Interstellar Transport Commission had that trade tied up. Every six months one of their Epsilon-class freighters would make a very slight deviation during her voyage from Waverly to Earth, and it was on Earth—in Australia, in fact—where the opal polishers plied their trade. I pointed out that it was only a short hop, relatively speaking, from Helmskirk to Baroom, the nearest Shaara colony world, Surely, I said, the Shaara could polish their own mood opals. But it was no-go. They always had been polished in some place called Coober Peedy, and they always would be polished in Coober Peedy, and that was that.

Meanwhile, I made friends among the warders on Sheol. Some of them were almost human. Their close association with the quote, criminal, unquote classes had rubbed off much of the arrogant sanctimoniousness so prevalent on the primary. There was one—Don Smith was his name—whom I even trusted with one of my guilty secrets. He would share morning coffee, generously spiked with the rum that I had persuaded the autochef to produce, with me. When there was any delay between the discharge of the cargo I had brought and the loading of the mood opals that I should be taking back, he would take me on conducted tours of the prison.

There were the hydroponic farms, where most of the workers were women, some of them, despite their hideous zebra-striped coveralls, quite attractive. Some of them, and not only the attractive ones, would waggle their hips suggestively and coo, "Hello; spaceman! I'll do it for a cigarette!" And Don would grin and say, "They would, you know. I can arrange it for you." But I refused the offer. I didn't trust him all that much. Besides, my stock of cigarettes—which I kept aboard only for hospitality and not for my own use—had been impounded by the blasted customs.

There were the workshops, where convict labor, all men, assembled machines at whose purpose I could do no more than guess; I haven't a mechanical mind. There was the printery and there was the bookbindery. I was invited to help myself from the stacks of new books, but I did not take advantage of the offer. Collections of sermons of the hellfire-and-damnation kind are not my idea of light reading to while away a voyage. There was the tailor's shop, where both warders' uniforms and convicts' uniforms were made. There were the kitchens and there were the messrooms. (The prison officers' food was plain but wholesome; that for the convicts, just plain, definitely so.) There were the tunnels in which the mood-opal miners worked. It was in one of these that I was accosted by a man with a dirt-streaked face and sweat- and dust-stained coveralls.

"Hey, Skipper!" he called. "How about my hitching a ride in your space buggy away from here? I can make it worth your while!"

I stared at him. I didn't like the cut of his jib. Under the dirt that partially obscured his features was a hard viciousness. He had the kind of very light and bright blue eyes that are often referred to as "mad." He looked as though he'd be quite willing to use the small pickax he was holding on a human being rather than on a rock.

I decided to ignore him.

"Stuck-up bastard, aren't you, Skipper. Like all your breed. You deep-spacers think yourselves too high and mighty to talk to orbital boys!"

"That will do, Wallace!" said Don sharply.

"Who's talking? You're not in charge of this work party."

"But I am." Another warder had come up. He was holding one of the modified stun guns that were the main weaponry of the guards; on the right setting (or the wrong setting, if you were on the receiving end) they could deliver a most painful shock. "Get back to work, Wallace. You're nowhere near your quota for the shift—and you know what that means!"

Apparently Wallace did and he moved away. Don and I moved on.

"A nasty piece of work," I said.

"He is that," agreed Don, "even though he is a spaceman like yourself."

"Not too like me, I hope."

"All right. Not too like you. He got as high as mate of the *Jerry Falwell*, and then he was caught smuggling cigarettes and booze in and mood opals out. If only the bloody fool had done his dealing with the right people and not with the convicts! I suppose that it's poetic justice that he's serving his time here as an opal miner."

I supposed that it was.

And then we wandered back to *Little Sister*, where, after half an hour or so, I loaded two small bags of mood opals—in their rough state they looked like mummified dog-droppings—and embarked a couple of prison officers who were returning to the primary for a spell of leave. Although they were (a) female and (b) not unattractive, they were not very good company for the voyage.

My next trip back from Sheol to Helmskirk I had company again. Unexpected company. For some reason I decided to check the stowage in the cargo compartment; there was a nagging feeling that everything was not as it should be. This time there were no mood opals, but there were half a dozen bales of clothing, civilian work coveralls, that had been manufactured in the prison's tailor's shop. At first glance nothing seemed amiss. And then I saw a pool of moisture slowly spreading on the deck from the underside of one of the bales. Aboard a ship, any kind of ship, leaking pipes can be dangerous. But there were no pipes running through and under the deck of the compartment; such as there were were all in plain view on the bulkheads, and all of them were intact.

Almost I dipped my finger into the seepage to bring it back to my mouth to taste it. Almost. I was glad that I hadn't done so. I smelled the faint but unmistakable acridity of human urine.

I went back to the main cabin, to my arms locker, and got out a stun gun and stuck it into my belt. And then, very cautiously, I unsnapped the fasteners of the metal straps holding the bale together. The outer layers of folded clothing fell to the deck. I stepped back and drew my stun gun and told whoever it was inside the bale, in as stern a voice as I could muster, to come out. More layers of clothing fell away, revealing a sort of cage of heavy wire in which crouched a young woman. She straightened up and stepped out of the cage, looking at me with an odd mixture of shame and defiance.

She said, "I shouldn't have had that last drink of water, but I thought that I should half die of thirst if I didn't. . . ." She looked down at the sodden legs of her civilian coveralls and managed an embarrassed grin. "And now I suppose, Captain, that you'll be putting back to Sheol and handing me over."

I said, "I can hand you over just as well at Port Helms."

She shrugged. "As you please. In that case, could I ask a favor? The use of your shower facilities and the loan of a robe to wear while my clothes are drying . . . I have to wash them, you know."

I thought, You're a cool customer. And I thought, I rather like you.

Despite her ugly and now sadly bedraggled attire, she was an attractive wench: blonde, blue-eyed, and with a wide mouth under a nose that was just retrousse enough, just enough, no more. She had found some way to tint her lips an enticing scarlet. (The women convicts, I had already learned, used all sorts of dyes for this purpose, although cosmetics were banned.) And I remembered, too, all the fuss there'd been about taking showers and such, all the simpering prudery, when I had carried those two women prison officers.

So I let her use my shower and hang her clothes in my drying room, and lent her my best Corlabian spider silk bathrobe, and asked her what she would like for dinner. She said that she would like a drink first and that she would leave the ordering of the meal to me.

It was good to be having dinner with a pretty girl, especially one who was enjoying her food as much as she was. The autochef did us proud, from soup—mulligatawny, as I remember—to pecan pie. The wines could have been better; an autochef properly programmed can make quite a good job of beer or almost any of the potable spirits, but as far as, say, claret is concerned, is capable of producing only a mildly alcoholic red ink. Not that it really mattered on this occasion. Everything that I gave my guest to eat and drink was immeasurably superior to the prison food—and, come to that, streets ahead of anything that could have been obtained in any restaurant on Helmskirk.

After the meal we relaxed. I filled and lit my pipe. She watched me enviously. I let her have one of my spare pipes. She filled it with my shredded, dried, and treated lettuce leaf tobacco substitute. She lit it, took one puff, and decided that it was better than nothing, but only just.

"Thank you, Captain," she said. "This has been a real treat. The drinks, the meal, your company. . . ." She smiled. "And I think that you've been enjoying my company, too. . . ."

"I have," I admitted.

"And won't you feel just a little bit remorseful when you turn me in after we arrive at Port Helms? But I suppose that you've already been in touch with the authorities by radio, while I was having my shower, to tell them that you found me stowed away. . . ."

I said, "I'll get around to it later."

Her manner brightened. "Suppose you never do it, Captain? I could . . . work my passage. . . ." The dressing gown was falling open as she talked and gesticulated, and what I could see looked very tempting—and I had been celibate for quite a while. "Before we set down at Port Helms, you can put me back in the bale. The consignees of the clothing are members of a sort of . . . underground. They have helped escaped convicts before."

"So your crime was political?"

"You could call it that. There are those of us, not a large number but growing, who are fighting for a liberalization of the laws—a relaxation of censorship, more freedom of thought and opinion. . . . You're an off-worlder. You must have noticed how repressive the regime on Helmskirk is."

I said that the repression had not escaped my notice.

"But," she went on, "I do not expect you to help me for no reward. There is only one way that I can reward you. . . ."

"No," I said.

"No?" she echoed in a hurt, a very hurt, voice.

"No," I repeated.

Oh, I'm no plaster saint, never have been one. But I have my standards. If I were going to help this girl, I'd do it out of the kindness of my heart and not for reward. I realize now that I was doing her no kindness. In fact, she was to tell me just that on a later occasion. A roll in the hay was just what she was needing just then. But I had my moments of high-minded priggishness, and this was one of them. (Now, of course, I'm at an age when I feel remorse for all the sins that I did not commit when I had the chance.)

She said, "People have often told me that I'm attractive. I would have thought. . . . But I can read you. You're a businessman as well as a spaceman. You own this little ship. You have to make a profit. You're afraid that if it's discovered that you helped me, you'll lose your profitable charter. Perhaps you're afraid that you'll become one of the inmates of Sheol yourself, like Wallace. . . ."

"I never said that I wasn't going to help you," I told her. "But there are conditions. One condition. That if you are picked up again, you say nothing about my part in your escape."

When she kissed me, with warm thoroughness, I weakened—but not enough, not enough. And before the sleep period I rigged the privacy screen in the main cabin, and she stayed on her side of it and I stayed on mine. The next "day"—and I maintained Port Helms standard time while in space—she dressed in her all-concealing coveralls, which were now dry, instead of in my too-revealing bathrobe. We had one or two practice sessions of repacking her in the bale. And before long it was time for me to repack her for good—as far as I was concerned.

And I made my descent to the apron at Port Helms.

There was, of course, something of a flap about the escape of a prisoner from Sheol. The authorities, of course, knew that if she had escaped, she must have done so in *Little Sister*—but I was in the clear. The ship was under guard all the time that she was berthed in the air lock. Too, there was a certain element of doubt. In the past convicts had hidden for quite a while in unexplored tunnels, and some had even died there. Convicts had been murdered by fellow inmates and their bodies fed into waste disposal machinery.

And then Evangeline—that was her name—was picked up, in Calvinville. She had been caught leaving pamphlets in various public places. She was tried and found guilty and given another heavy sentence, tacked on to the unexpired portion of her previous one. She kept her word insofar as I was concerned, saying nothing of my complicity. She even managed to protect the clothing wholesalers to whom her bale had been consigned. Her story was that this bale could be opened from the inside, and that after her escape from it, at night, she had tidied up after herself before leaving the warehouse.

Inevitably, I got the job of returning her to incarceration. (The repairs to the prison tender *Jerry Falwell* were dragging on, and on, and on.) She was accompanied by two sourpussed female prison officers returning to Sheol from planet leave. These tried to persuade me—persuade? Those arrogant bitches tried to order me—that during the short voyage there should be two menus, one for the master, me, and the warders, and the other, approximating prison fare, for the convict. I refused to play, of course. The poor girl would eat well while she still had the chance. But there were no drinks before, with, or after meals, and I even laid off smoking for the trip.

And so I disembarked my passengers and discharged my cargo at Sheol. I'd not been able to exchange so much as a couple of words with Evangeline during the trip, but the look she gave me before she was escorted from the ship said, Thanks for everything.

So it went on, trip after trip.

Then it happened. I was having an unusually long stopover on Sheol, and my friend, Don Smith, suggested that I might wish to see, as he put it, the animals feed. I wasn't all that keen—I've never been one to enjoy the spectacle of other people's misery—but there was nothing much else to do, and so I accompanied him through the maze of tunnels to one of the mess halls used by the male prisoners. Have you ever seen any of those antique films about prison life made on Earth in the latter half of the twentieth century? It was like that. The rows of long tables, covered with some shiny gray plastic, and the benches. The counter behind which stood the prisoners on mess duty, with aprons tied on over their zebra-striped coveralls, ladling out a most unsavory-looking—and -smelling—stew into the bowls held out by the shuffling queue of convicts. The guards stationed around the walls, all of them armed with stun guns and all of them looking bored rather than alert. . . . The only novel touch was that it was all being acted out in the slow motion imposed by conditions of low gravity.

Finally, all the convicts were seated at the long tables, their sluggishly steaming plastic bowls—those that were still steaming, that is; by this time, the meals of those first in the queue must have been almost cold—before them, waiting for the prison padre, standing at his lectern, to intone grace. It was on the lines of: For what we about to receive this day may the Lord make us truly thankful.

As soon as he was finished, there was a commotion near the head of one of the tables. A man jumped to his feet. It was, I saw, Wallace, the ex-spaceman.

"Thankful for this shit, you smarmy bastard?" he shouted. "This isn't fit for pigs, and you know it!"

The guards suddenly became alert. They converged upon Wallace with their stun guns out and ready. They made the mistake of assuming that Wallace was the only troublemaker. The guards were tripped, some of them, and others blinded by the bowls of stew flung into their faces. Their pistols were snatched from their hands.

"Get out of here, John," said Don Smith urgently. He pulled me back from the entrance to the mess hall. "Get out of here! There's nothing you can do. Get back to your ship. Use your radio to tell Helmskirk what's happening. . . ."

"But surely your people," I said, "will have things under control. . . ."

"I . . . I hope so. But this has been brewing for quite some time."

By this time we were well away from the mess hall, but the noise coming from it gave us some idea of what was happening—and what was happening wasn't at all pleasant for the guards. And there were similar noises coming from other parts of the prison complex. And there was a clangor of alarm bells and a shrieking of sirens and an amplified voice, repeating over and over, "All prison officers report at once to the citadel! All prison officers report at once to the citadel!"

Don Smith said, "You'd better come with me."

I said, "I have to get back to my ship."

He said, "You'll never find the way to the air lock."

I said, "I've got a good sense of direction."

So he went one way and I went another. My sense of direction might have served me better if I had not been obliged to make detours to avoid what sounded like small-scale battles ahead of me in that maze of tunnels. And the lights kept going out and coming on again, and when they were on kept flickering in an epilepsy-inducing rhythm. I'm not an epileptic, but I felt as though I were about to become one. During one period of darkness I tripped over something soft, and when the lights came on found that it was a body, that of one of the female prison officers. Her uniform had been stripped from the lower part of her body, and it was obvious what had been done to her before her throat had been cut. And there was nothing that I could do for her.

At last, at long, long last, more by good luck than otherwise, I stumbled into the big air lock chamber in which *Little Sister* was berthed. There were people standing by her. The guards, I thought at first, still at their posts. Then the lights temporarily flared into normal brightness, and I saw that the uniform coveralls were zebra-striped. But I kept on walking. After all, I was just an innocent bystander, wasn't I?

Wallace—it had to be he—snarled, "You took your time getting here."

"What are you doing here?" I demanded.

"What the hell do you think? But we wouldn't be here now if we could get your air lock door open."

"And suppose you could, what then?"

"That, Skipper, is a remarkably stupid question."

I looked at Wallace and his two companions. I looked at the sacks at their feet. I could guess what was in them. The lights were bright again, and I saw that the other two convicts were women—and that one of them was Evangeline. She looked at me, her face expressionless.

"What are you waiting for, Skipper?" almost shouted Wallace.

I'm playing for time, I thought, although I hadn't a clue as to what I could do with any time I gained.

Wallace shot me with his stun gun. It wasn't on the Stun setting but one that which gave the victim a very painful shock, one that lasted for as long as the person using the gun wished. It seemed to be a very long time in this case, although it could have been no more than seconds. When it was over, I was trembling in every limb and soaked in cold perspiration.

"Want another dose, Skipper?" Wallace demanded.

"You'd better open up, Captain," said Evangeline in an

emotionless voice. She was holding a gun, too, pointed in my direction. So was the other woman.

So what could I do? Three, armed, against one, unarmed.

There was more than one way of getting into *Little Sister*. The one that I favored, if the ship was in an atmosphere, was by voice. It always amused guests. And it worked only for me, although I suppose that a really good actor, using the right words, could have gained ingress.

"Open Sesame," I said.

The door slid open.

And while Wallace and the woman whom I didn't know had their attention distracted by this minor miracle, Evangeline shot them both with her stun gun.

"Hurry," she said to me, throwing the sacks of mood opals into the air lock chamber. "Lend a hand, can't you?"

No, I didn't lend a hand, but I accompanied her into the ship. I used the manual air lock controls to seal the lock. I went forward to the control cab, my intention being to try to raise somebody, anybody, on my radio telephone to tell them what had been happening—and to try to find out what was still happening.

She said, from just behind me, "Get us out of here, Captain."

I asked, "Do you expect me to ram my way out of the air lock chamber?"

She said, "Wallace's men have taken over the air lock control room. If they hear my voice and see my face in their telescreen, they'll open up."

"But there's also a screen," I said, "that gives a picture of the air lock chamber. They must have seen what happened outside the ship, when you buzzed Wallace and the girl."

"Very luckily," she said, "that screen got smashed during the fight when we took over the control center."

She'd seen me operate the NST transceiver when I was making my approach to Port Helms the voyage that she'd stowed away. She got it switched on—the controls were simple—without having to ask for instruction except for the last important one.

"What channel do I call on?"

A. Bertram Chandler

"Hold it," I said. I had acquired quite a dislike for Wallace but had nothing against his girlfriend. "The air's going to be exhausted from the chamber before the outer doors open."

"Oh, I hadn't thought of that. . . ."

I activated the screens that showed me what was going on outside the ship. (From the control cab our only view was forward.) I saw that Wallace was just getting groggily to his feet, assisted by the girl, who must have made a faster recovery that he had. I spoke into the microphone that allowed me to talk to anybody outside the hull.

"Wallace," I said, "get out of the chamber, fast! It's going to open up—and you know what that means!"

He did know. He raised his right hand and shook his fist. I saw his mouth forming words, and I could guess what sort of words they were. Then he turned from *Little Sister* and made for the door leading into the interior of Sheol at a shambling run, with the girl trailing after. No women and children first as far as he was concerned.

"Channel six," I told Evangeline. "Evangeline here," I heard her say. "We're all aboard, and the stones. Open up."

"We're relying on you to spend the money you get for the stones where it will do the most good! I hope Wallace can find his way to the nearest Shaara world, where there'll be a market and no questions asked!"

"We'll persuade Grimes to do the navigating."

"Are you taking him with you?" I was annoyed by the lack of interest and regretted, briefly, having allowed Wallace to escape from certain asphyxiation. "Stand by. Opening up. Bon voyage."

But opening up took time. The air had to be exhausted from the chamber first. How long would it take Wallace to reach the control center? From my own controls I had a direct view overhead. At last I saw the two valves of the air lock door coming apart, could see the black sky and the occasional star in the widening gap. I had *Little Sister*'s inertial drive running in neutral and then applied gentle thrust. We lifted, until we were hovering just below the slowly opening doors.

Was there enough room?

Yes, barely.

I poured on the thrust and we scraped through, almost literally. And just in time. In the belly-view screen I saw that the doors were closing again, fast. Wallace had reached the control center just too late.

And I kept going.

"Back to Helmskirk," said Kitty Kelly, "to hand that poor girl back to the authorities. They must really have put the boot in this time."

"I said," Grimes told her, "that I kept on going. Not to Port Helms. To a Shaara world called Varoom, where we could flog those stones with no awkward questions asked. I considered that I owed far more loyalty to Evangeline than to the Helmskirk wowsers."

"But what about those prison guards under siege in their citadel? Didn't you owe them some loyalty?"

"One or two of them, perhaps," he admitted. "But what could I have done? And, as a shipmaster, my main loyalty was to my ship."

"But you could have carried reinforcements, police, from Port Helms to Sheol."

"In *Little Sister*? She was only a pinnace, you know. Aboard her, four was a crowd. Too, there was one of the Commission's Epsilon-class tramps in port. She could be requisitioned as a troopship."

"But that time charter, Commodore . . . weren't you tied by that?"

"Oddly enough, no. The original six weeks had expired and it was being renewed week by week. At the time of the mutiny it was due for renewal."

"And the girl. Evangeline. Did you dump her on that Shaara planet?"

"Of course not," said Grimes virtuously. "I was rather too fond of her by that time. After we sold the jewels, I carried her to Freedonia, a colony founded by a bunch of idealists who'd take in anybody as long as he or she could claim to be a political refugee. I'd have liked to keep her with me, but there were too many legal complications. She had no papers of any kind, and the authorities on most planets demand documentation from visitors, crew as well as passengers.

I got into enough trouble myself for having left Helmskirk without my Outward Clearance."

"And during your wanderings, before you got to Freedonia, did you lose your priggish high-mindedness?"

He laughed reminiscently. "Yes. I did let her work her passage, as she put it. And I accepted, as a farewell gift, quite a substantial share of the mood opal money."

She said, not admiringly, "You bastard. I'd just hate to owe you a favor."

"You've got it wrong," Grimes told her. "I took what she offered because I owed her one."

THE
COMMODORE
AT SEA

DEDICATION
For my favorite wife.

❧ Hall of Fame ❧

SONYA GRIMES was unpacking. Grimes watched her contentedly. She was back at last from her galactic cruise, and the apartment was no longer just a place in which to live after a fashion, in which to eat lonely meals, in which to sleep in a lonely bed. It was, once more, home.

She asked lightly, "And have you been *good* while I've been away?"

"Yes," he replied without hesitation, bending the truth only slightly. There had been that girl on Mellise, of course, but it had all been in the line of duty. A reminiscent grin softened his craggy features. "So good, in fact, that I was given the honorary rank of Admiral on Tharn . . ."

She laughed. "Then I'd better give you something too, my dear. Something I know you'll like . . ." She fell gracefully to her knees beside a suitcase that she had not yet opened, unsnapped and lifted up the lid, plunged a slender hand into a froth of gossamer undergarments. "Ah, here it is. I didn't want it to get broken . . ."

It was a leather case and, although it obviously had been well cared for, it was worn and cracked, was ancient rather than merely old. The Commodore took it carefully from his wife, looked at it with some puzzlement. Its shape was clue enough to what it contained, but Grimes had never guessed that such homely and familiar masculine accessories could ever possess any value other than a strictly utilitarian one.

"Open it!" she urged.

Grimes opened the case, stared in some bewilderment at the meerschaum pipe that was revealed, archaic and fragile in its nest of faded plush.

"There was a little shop in Baker Street," she said, speaking rapidly. "An antique shop. They had this. I knew you'd like it . . ."

"Baker Street . . ." he repeated. "In London? On Earth?"

"Of course, John. And you *know* who lived there . . ."

Yes, thought Grimes. *I know who lived there. And he smoked a pipe, and he wore something called a deerstalker hat. The only trouble is that he never lived at all in real life. Oh Sonya, Sonya, they must have seen you coming. And how much did you pay for . . . this?*

"Think of it," she went on. "Sherlock Holmes's own pipe . . ."

"Fantastic."

"You don't like it?" Neither of them was a true telepath, but each was quick to sense the mood of the other. "You don't like it?"

"I do," he lied. But was it a lie? The thought behind the gift was more important, much more important than the gift itself. "I do," he said, and this time there was no smallest hint of insincerity in his voice. He put the precious pipe down carefully on the coffee table. "But you've brought yourself back, and you're worth more to me than Sherlock Holmes's pipe, or Julius Caesar's bloodstained toga, or King Solomon's mines. Come here, woman!"

"That's an odd-looking weapon you've got, Grimes," remarked Admiral Kravinsky.

The Commodore laughed. "Yes, and there's quite a story attached to it, sir. Sonya bought it for me in London—and you'd think that a woman who holds a commission in the Intelligence Branch of the Survey Service would have more intelligence than to be taken in by phony antiques! This, sir, is alleged to be the actual pipe smoked by the great Sherlock Holmes himself."

"Really?"

"Yes, really. But I'll say this for Sonya, she's got a sense of humor. After I'd explained to her in words of one syllable that Sherlock

Holmes was no more than a fictional character she saw the joke, even though it was on her . . ."

"And on you."

"I suppose so. When I think of all the first class London briars that could have been purchased for the same money . . ."

"I'm surprised that you're smoking *that*. After all, a secondhand pipe . . ."

"Sonya's thorough. She took the thing to the nearest forensic laboratory to have it examined. They assured her that it was untouched by human hand—or lip. It's a perfectly good meerschaum, recently manufactured and artificially aged. So she said that she liked to see her husband smoking the most expensive pipe in the Rim Worlds. It's not a bad smoke either . . ."

"Don't drop it," warned the Admiral. "Whatever you do, don't drop it." Then the tolerant smile vanished from his broad, ruddy features. "But I didn't send for you to discuss your filthy smoking habits." He selected a gnarled, black cigar from the box on his desk, lit it. "I've a job for you, Grimes. I've already spoken to Rim Runners' management and arranged for your release for service with the Reserve."

Normally Grimes would have been pleased, but with Sonya *just* back . . .

"The Federation has a finger in this particular pie as well, Grimes. And as their Commander Sonya Verrill is back in Port Forlorn she may as well go along with you."

Grimes's face cleared.

"And this *will* please you, Commodore. I haven't any warships to spare, and so your beloved *Faraway Quest* will be recommissioned, with you in full command. The selection of personnel will be up to you."

"And what is the job, sir?" asked Grimes.

"A detailed, leisurely investigation of Kinsolving's Planet. We all of us tend to shy away from that ruddy world—but, after all, it is in our back garden. And after those outsiders from Francisco landed there to carry out their odd experiments . . ."

"I was there too," said Grimes.

"Well I bloody well know it. And I had to organize the rescue party. Anyhow, you're our expert on Rim World oddities. Things seem to happen around you rather than to you. If anybody falls through a crack in the continuum the odds are at least a hundred to one that Commodore Grimes, Rim Worlds Naval Reserve, will be lurking somewhere in the background . . ."

"I've been in the foreground too, sir."

"I know, Grimes, I know. But you always survive, and the people with you usually survive. I had no hesitation in recommending you for this . . . survey. Yes, I suppose you could call it that, although what you'll be surveying God knows."

"Which god?" asked Grimes, remembering vividly what had happened to the expedition from Francisco.

"Fill me in," ordered Sonya. "Put me in the picture."

"I wrote to you," said Grimes. "I told you all about it."

"I never received the letter."

"It must still be chasing you. Well, you know of Kinsolving's Planet, of course . . ."

"Not as much as I should, my dear. So just make believe that I've just come out to the Rim, and that I was never in the Intelligence Branch of the Survey Service. Start from there."

"You have access to all the official reports, including mine."

"I prefer to hear the story in less formal language. I never did care for officialese."

"Very well, then. Now, Kinsolving's Planet. It's one of the Rim Worlds, and it was colonized at the same time as the others, but the colonization didn't stick. There's something . . . odd about the atmosphere of the place. No, not chemically, or physically. Psychologically. There are all sorts of fancy theories to account for it; one of the more recent is that Kinsolving lies at the intersection of stress lines; that there the very fabric of space and time is stretched almost to bursting; that the boundaries between *then* and *now*, between *here* and *there*, are so thin as to be almost nonexistent. Oh, I know that the same sort of thing has been said often enough about the Rim Worlds in general—but nowhere is the effect so pronounced as on Kinsolving. People just didn't like living on a world where they could never feel sure of *anything*, where there was always the dread at the back of their minds that the Change Winds would reach gale force at any tick of the clock. So, when their suicide rate had risen to an unprecedented level and their nut hatches were crammed to capacity, they got the hell out.

"That was that. And then, a century and a half ago, Galactic Standard, one of the Commission's tramps, *Epsilon Eridani*, made an emergency landing at the spaceport. She had to recalibrate the controls of her Mannschenn Drive and, as you know, that's best done on a planetary surface. It could be that the temporal precession fields set up while this was being done triggered some sort of continuum-warping chain reaction . . . Anyhow, a few of the officers were allowed shore leave, and they decided to explore the famous caves, which were not far distant. In these caves are remarkably well-preserved rock paintings, made by the Stone Age aborigines who once lived on Kinsolving. (What happened to *them*, nobody knows. They just vanished, millennia before the first humans landed.) They returned to their ship in quite a dither, reporting that the paint of some of the pictures of various animals was *wet*.

"The Federation's Survey Service finally got to hear about this and sent a small team of investigators, one of them a very well-qualified young lady from the Rhine Institute. They found the rock paintings without any trouble—and found that a new one had been added, one depicting men in the standard spaceman's rig of that period. While they were standing around marveling they were pounced upon by a horde of cavemen and made prisoner.

"But the Rhine Institute's star graduate was equal to the occasion. Telepathy, teleportation, psychokinesis—you name it, she had it. The party escaped with a prisoner of their own, the artist in person. His name was Raul. . .

"And, back on Earth, Raul became a pet of the Rhine Institute himself. He was a very specialized kind of painter. When he drew an animal, that animal was drawn, in the other sense of the word, to within range of the weapons of the hunters. He was also a telepath, and after the Institute had just about sucked him dry he went to

Francisco to become chief psionic radio officer of the Deep Space Communications Station on that world. By this time he'd married the wench who'd captured him and, although he wasn't human, strictly speaking, the genetic engineers were able to make certain modifications to his body so that the union was a fruitful one.

"You've been to Francisco, of course. You know how religion is almost a primary industry on that planet. Raul got religion—and became, of all things, a neo-Calvinist, as did all his family. His great-granddaughter fell from grace with a loud thud and became one of the so-called Blossom People. . ."

"So there's a woman mixed up in it!" commented Sonya.

"Look around, my dear, and you'll find a woman mixed up in almost everything. But where was I? Yes, Clarisse. She rather overdid things—drink, sex, drugs—and was picked up out of the gutter and brought back into the fold. But the neo-Calvinists weren't being charitable. They knew that she had inherited her ancestor's talents, and they knew that certain of the psychedelic drugs amplified these same talents, and so . . ."

"And so?" she echoed.

"And so some perverted genius cooked up a scheme that even now makes me shudder. The idea was that she should be taken to Kinsolving and there, on a suitable mountain top, invoke by her graphic art and magic the God of the Old Testament, in the pious hope that He would provide for the neo-Calvinists a new edition of the Ten Commandments. That bunch of unspeakable wowsers had to get the permission of the Confederacy, of course, before they could land on Kinsolving—and so my lords and masters decided that Commodore Grimes, Rim Worlds Naval Reserve, should go along as an observer . . ."

"You never tell me anything."

"I wrote to you about it. And it's all in the reports that you, as the senior representative of the Survey Service's Intelligence Branch on the Rim Worlds, should have read by now. Besides, I've hardly had a chance to get a word in edgewise since you came home."

"Never mind that. What happened?"

"They set up shop on top of the mountain that they'd decided was the new Sinai. Clarisse, after the proper preparations, painted a picture of a suitably irate-looking, white-bearded deity . . . The trouble was, of course, that so many of those patriarchal gods looked alike. And the Blossom People's religion is a pantheistic one. Cutting a long and sad story short—what we got wasn't Sinai, but Olympus . . ."

There was a long silence. And then, "If I didn't know you, and if I didn't know from personal experience what odd things do happen out on the Rim, I'd say that you'd missed your vocation, that you should be a writer of fairy stories . . . But you assure me that all this is in the reports?"

"It is. And Clarisse is still on Lorn. She married Mayhew. I was thinking that we might have them round tomorrow evening. And they'll be coming with us in the *Quest*, in any case."

"But what's our expedition supposed to be in aid of?" she demanded. "You're leading it, and I shall be your second-in-command; and two more unlikely people to be involved in any sort of religious research, I can't think of."

The Commodore smiled a little crookedly. "I'll tell you what Kravinsky said to me. 'It boils down to this, Grimes. Both the Confederacy and our big brothers of the Federation think that something should be done about Kinsolving. Nobody is quite sure what. So I'm sending you, with your usual crew of offbeats and misfits, and if you bumble around in your inimitable manner *something* is bound to happen . . .'"

Sonya grinned back at him. "The man could be right," she said.

Finally—the recommissioning of a long laid up vessel takes time, *Faraway Quest*, Commodore John Grimes commanding, lifted slowly from Port Forlorn. She was well-manned; Grimes had selected his crew, both spacefaring personnel and civilian scientists and technicians, with care. The officers of all departments were, like the Commodore himself, naval reservists, specialists in navigation and gunnery and engineering: in ship's biochemistry. And there was the Major of Marines—also, as were his men, a specialist. Grimes hoped that the spaceborne soldiers' services would not be needed, but it was good to have them along, just in case. There was Mayhew, one of the few psionic radio officers still on active service, youthful in appearance but old in years; and Clarisse, really beautiful since her marriage and her breakaway from the neo-Calvinists and their severe rules regarding dress and decorum, her hair styling revealing the pointed ears inherited from her nonhuman ancestor. There were the two fat, jolly men from the Dowser's Guild who, even in this day and age, were shunned by the majority of the scientists. There were men and women whose specialty was the measururement of radiation, others whose field was chemistry, organic and inorganic. There were archeologists, and paleontologists, and . . .

"One more specialist, Grimes," Admiral Kravinsky had growled, "and that old bitch of yours won't be able to lift a millimeter . . ."

But a converted freighter, with all space properly utilized, has quite amazing capacity insofar as the carrying of passengers is concerned.

So she lifted, her inertial drive running sweetly and uncomplainingly, with Grimes himself at the controls, all the old skill flowing back into his fingers, the ship an extension of his fit, stocky body, obedient to his will, as were his officers grouped around him in the control room, each in his own chair with his own bank of instruments before him.

She lifted, accelerating smoothly, soaring up to the low cloud ceiling, and through it, breaking out into the steely sunlight of high altitudes, driving up to the purple sky that soon deepened to black, into the darkness where glimmered the few, faint stars of the Rim, where, rising above the gleaming arc that was the sunlit limb of the planet, glowed the misty ellipsoid that was the Galactic Lens.

Sonya, who had traveled vast distances as a passenger, said quietly, "It's good to see this from a control room again."

"It's always good . . ." said Grimes.

Faraway Quest was clear of the atmosphere now, still lifting, and below them the planet presented the appearance of a huge, mottled ball, an enormous flawed pearl lustrous against the black immensities. She was clear of the Van Allen, and Grimes snapped an order. The Senior Communications Officer spoke quietly into his intercom microphone. "Attention all! Attention all! There will be a short countdown, from ten to zero. The inertial drive will be shut off, after which there will be a period of free fall, with brief lateral accelerations as trajectory is adjusted." He turned to the Commodore. "Ready, sir?"

Grimes studied the chart tank. "Now!" he said.

"Ten . . ." began the officer. "Nine . . ."

Grimes looked to Sonya, raised his heavy eyebrows and shrugged. She shrugged back, and made even this gesture graceful. She knew, as he knew, that all this formality was necessary only because there were so many civilians aboard.

". . . Zero!"

The irregular, throbbing beat of the inertial drive suddenly ceased and there was brief weightlessness and a short silence. Then there was the hum of the maneuvering gyroscopes, rising to a whine, and centrifugal force gently pressed those in Control to the sides of their chairs. Slowly, slowly, the target star, the Kinsolving sun, drifted across the black sky until the glittering spark was centered in the cartwheel sight, wavered, then held steady. The inertial drive came on again, its broken rumble a bass background to the thin, high keening of the ever-precessing rotors of the Mannschenn Drive. Ahead, save for the tiny, iridescent spiral that was the target sun, there was only emptiness. Lorn was to starboard; a vast, writhing planetary amoeba that was dropping back to the quarter, that was dwindling rapidly. And out to port was the Galactic Lens, distorted by the temporal precession field of the Drive to the similitude of a Klein flask blown by a drunken glassblower.

Grimes rather wished, as he had often wished before, that somebody would come up with another way of describing it. He doubted if anybody ever would.

This was a far more pleasant voyage than the one that he had made to Kinsolving in the unhappy *Piety*. To begin with, he had Sonya with him. Second, he was in command, and the ship was being run his way. *Faraway Quest* was no luxury liner, but she was warm, comfortable. Her internal atmosphere carried the scents of women's perfume, of tobacco smoke, of good cooking—not that omnipresent acridity of disinfectant. The snatches of music that drifted through her alleyways from the playmasters in the public rooms were anything and everything from grand opera to the latest pop, never the morbid hymns and psalms in which the neo-Calvinists had specialized. He spoke of this to Clarisse. She grinned and said, "You're not with it, Dad. You're just not with it. By *our* standards this wagon is bitter endsville, just a spaceborne morgue."

He grinned back. "If the best that the Blossom People can do is to resurrect the hip talk of the middle twentieth century, I doubt if you're with it either."

"Every religion," she told him seriously, "uses archaic language in its scriptures and in its rituals." Then she laughed. "I'm not complaining, John. Believe me, I'm not complaining. When I look back to the *Piety*, and Rector Smith and Presbyter Cannan, and that she-dragon of a deaconess, I realize how lucky I am. Of course, I could have been luckier . . ."

"How so?"

"That tall, beautiful redhead of yours could have been left behind."

"To say nothing of that highly capable telepath you're married to."

Her face softened. "I was joking, John. Before I met Ken—before I met him physically, that is—something might have been possible between us. But I'm well content now, and I feel that I owe it all to you. Ken was against our coming on this expedition, but I insisted. I'll do anything I can to aid your . . . researches."

"Even to a repeat performance?"

"Even to a repeat performance."

"I hope it doesn't come to that."

"Frankly, John, so do I."

The voyage was over. *Faraway Quest*, her Mannschenn Drive shut down, her inertial drive ticking over just sufficiently to induce a minimal gravitational field, was falling in orbit about the lonely world, the blue and green mottled sphere hanging there against the blackness. The old charts were out, and the new ones too, made by

Grimes himself with the assistance of the officers of *Rim Sword*.
"Here," said the Commodore, stabbing a blunt forefinger down onto
the paper, "is where the spaceport *was*. There's only a crater there
now. Whoever or whatever destroyed *Piety* made a thorough job of
it. And here's the city—Enderston it was called—on the east bank of
the Weary River . . ."

"'Where even the weariest river winds somewhere safe to
sea . . .'" quoted Sonya. "They must have been a cheerful bunch, those
first colonists."

"I've already told you that the very atmosphere of the planet
engenders morbidity. And there, on the shore of Darkling Tarn, is
what was the Sports Stadium, where *Rim Sword* landed. In the
absence of any spaceport facilities it's as good a place as any." He
turned from the chart to the big screen upon which a magnification
of the planet was presented. "You can see it all there—just to the east
of the sunrise terminator. That river, with all the S bends, is the
Weary, and that lake which looks like an octopus run over by a
streamroller is Darkling Tarn. The city's too overgrown for it to show
up at this range."

"You're the boss," said Sonya.

"Yes. So I suppose I'd better do something about something." He
turned to his executive officer. "Make it landing stations,
Commander Williams."

"Landing stations it is, sir."

The officers went to their acceleration chairs, strapped themselves
in. In seconds the intercom speakers were blatting, "Secure all for
landing stations! Secure all for landing stations! All idlers to their
quarters!" And then the maneuvering gyroscopes hummed and
whined as the ship was tilted relative to the planet until the surface
was directly beneath her. The sounding rockets were discharged as
she began her descent, each of them releasing a parachute flare in the
upper atmosphere, each of them emitting a long, long streamer of
white smoke.

Faraway Quest dropped steadily—not too fast and not too slow.
Grimes made allowance for drift and, as the first of the flares was
swept west by a jet stream, he applied lateral thrust. Down she

dropped, and down, almost falling free, but always under the full control of her master. The picture of the surface on the target screen expanded. The city could be seen now, a huddle of ruins on the river bank, and beside the lake there was the oval of the Stadium, *Eau de Nil* in the midst of the indigo of the older growth. The last of the flares to have been fired was still burning down there, the column of smoke rising almost vertically. The brush among which it had fallen was slowly smoldering.

Grimes shivered. The feeling of *déjà vu* was chillingly uncanny. But he had seen this before. He had been here before—and, save for the different choice of landing site, circumstances had been almost exactly duplicated, even to that luckily unenthusiastic bush fire. And again there was the sensation that supernal forces—malign or beneficent?—were mustering to resist the landing of the ship.

But she was down at last.

There was the gentlest of shocks, the faintest of creakings, the softest sighing of the shock absorbers as the great mass of the vessel settled in her tripodal landing gear. She was down. "Finished with engines!" said Grimes softly. Telegraph bells jangled, and the inertial drive generators muttered to themselves and then were still. She was down, and the soughing of the fans intensified the silence.

Grimes turned in his swivel chair, looked toward the distant mountain peak, the black, truncated cone sharp against the blue sky. "Sinai," Presbyter Cannan had named it. "Olympus," Grimes had called it on his new charts. It was there that the neo-Calvinists had attempted to invoke Jehovah, and there that the old gods of the Greek pantheon had made their disastrous appearance. Grimes hoped that he would never have to set foot upon that mountain top again.

He was not first off the ship; after all, this was no newly discovered planet, this was not a historic first landing of Man. The honor fell to the Major of Marines, who marched smartly down the ramp at the head of his clattering column of space soldiers. He barked orders and the detachment broke up into its component parts, fanning out from the landing site, trampling through the bushes. From somewhere came a sharp rattle of machine-pistol fire. The

Commodore was not concerned. He said, "There'll be fresh pork or rabbit on the table in the Marines' mess tonight. Or pigburger or rabbitburger if the man who fired was too enthusiastic."

"Pigs? Rabbits?" inquired Sonya.

"Descendants of the livestock brought here by the original colonists. They—the pigs, probably—seem to have wiped out most of the indigenous fauna. And, come to that, the hens and the sheep and the cattle." He lit his pipe. "They were, I suppose, the two species best fitted to survive. The pigs with their intelligence, the rabbits with their ability to go underground and to breed . . . like rabbits."

She said, "I could do with some fresh air after weeks of the tinned variety. What's good enough for pigs and rabbits and Marines is good enough for me."

"Just as well that the gallant Major didn't hear you say that. Commander Williams!"

"Sir!" replied the burly Executive Officer.

"Shore leave is in order, as long as a full working watch—and that includes the manning of weaponry—is left aboard the ship at all times. And every party of boffins is to be accompanied by at least one officer or one Marine other rank, armed. Nobody is to go down the ramp without checking out or without wearing his personal transceiver. Apart from that, we'll make this a day of general relaxation. After all, there are no physical dangers on this world. As for the other kind—I doubt if the Federation's Grand Fleet could cope with them."

"Good-oh, Skipper," replied Williams.

Grimes glared at him, then laughed. "I wondered how long it would be before the veneer of your last drill in the Reserve wore off. Anyhow, those are the orders—and just try to remember now and again that this is an auxiliary cruiser of the Rim Worlds Navy, not your beloved *Rim Mamelute*." He closed on a formal note. "The ship is yours, sir, until my return."

"The ship is mine, sir, until your return."

Then Grimes and Sonya went down to their quarters, replaced their light uniform sandals with knee-high boots, strapped on their wrist transceivers, buckled on the belts from which depended their holstered hand weapons. The Commodore was sure that these would never be required but, as leader of the expedition, he could not break the orders that he had issued. It was, he already knew, warm outside; the slate grey shorts and shirts that he and his wife were wearing would be adequate.

They made their way down to the after airlock, checked out with the officer on gangway duty, walked slowly down the ramp. The fresh air was good, and the last traces of smoke from the now dead fire added a pleasant tang to it. The light of the sun, past its meridian and now dropping slowly to the west, was warm on the exposed portions of their bodies. (*I made much better time down than Rector Smith did in his* Piety, thought Grimes smugly. It had been late afternoon when that ship had landed.) And yet there was a chill in the air— psychological rather than physical. There was a chill in the air, and with the scent of green growing things there was a hint of corruption.

Sonya shivered. "There's something . . . wrong," she stated.

"That's why we're here," Grimes told her.

They were met by the Major. He was returning to the ship, seven of his men behind him. Four of them carried the bodies of two large boars, slung on branches; the others were loaded down with rabbits. The young officer saluted cheerfully. "Enemy beaten off, sir, with heavy casualties."

"So I see, Major. But this is more than a hunting party, you know."

"I know, sir. I've set alarms all around the field so that we shall be alerted if anything large and dangerous approaches."

"Good."

Grimes and Sonya walked on, picking their way with care over the tangle of tough vines, making their slow way toward what had once been the Stadium's grandstand, now a terraced, artificial hillock overgrown with flowering creepers. They saw the two dowsers, stumbling about happily with their gleaming divining rods in their hands, trailed by a bored-looking junior officer. They passed a party of the more orthodox scientists setting up a piece of apparatus that looked like a miniature radio telescope. They met Mayhew and Clarisse.

"Do *you* feel it?" demanded the Psionic Radio Officer. "Do *you* feel it, sir? None of these others seem to."

"Yes, I feel it. And so does Sonya."

"Like something that has been waiting for us for a long time. Like something getting ready to pounce. But it's not sure that it has the strength anymore . . ."

"Yes . . . I thought myself that the ominous atmosphere wasn't quite so pronounced as when I was here last. What do you think, Clarisse? You were here too."

"I'm not as scared as I was then, John. But there are reasons for that."

"It's pronounced enough for me," said Sonya.

"It's here still," admitted Grimes. "But it could be fading. It could be that this planet has been at the very focus of . . . forces, and now the focus is shifting." He laughed. "We shan't be at all popular if, after our masters have sent us here at enormous expense, nothing happens."

"Frankly," said Clarisse, "I hope nothing does."

Nothing did.

Day followed day, and the parties of scientists spread out from around the landing site, on foot and in *Faraway Quest*'s pinnaces. The archeologists grubbed happily in kitchen middens that they discovered on the banks of the lake and the river, penetrated the caves and photographed the famous paintings in a wide range of illuminations. Nothing new was found in the middens, no evidence that would throw any light at all on the disappearance of the aboriginal race. The rock paintings were just rock paintings, the pigments dry and ancient. The dowsers dowsed, and discovered deposits of metals that would be valuable if the planet were ever recolonized, and found oil, and mapped the meanderings of underground streams in desert areas. The other specialists plotted and measured and calculated—and found nothing that could not have been found on any Earth type planet.

"At least," said Grimes, "we've proven that this world is suitable for resettlement." He, with Sonya and Clarisse and Mayhew, was sitting over after dinner coffee in his comfortable day cabin. "All hands are really enjoying a marvelous outdoor holiday."

"Except us," said Sonya in a somber voice.

"There's a reason for that, my dear. You're sensitive to my moods, as I am to yours. And I had such a scare thrown into me when I was here last that I could never feel at ease on this planet. And Clarisse was more frightened than I was—and with good reason!—and all the time she was in telepathic touch with Mayhew."

"I still say that there's something wrong," insisted Mayhew. "I still say that we should be absolutely sure before we put in a report recommending another attempt at colonization."

Grimes looked at Clarisse. "Would you be willing to repeat that experiment?" he asked.

She replied without hesitation. "Yes. I was going to suggest it. I've talked it over with Ken. And I feel that if I try to call those old gods, rather than the deity of the neo-Calvinists, the results might be better. It could be that it is in their interests that this world be peopled again—this time with potential worshippers."

"Like your Blossom People," said Mayhew, unmaliciously.

"Yes. Like the Blossom People. After all, the slogan *Make love, Not War*, would appeal to Aphrodite if not to Ares . . ."

Grimes laughed, but without real humor. "All right, Clarisse. We'll arrange it for tomorrow night. And we'll have all hands out of the ship and well scattered just in case Zeus is too handy with his thunderbolts again. Williams has been getting too fat and lazy; it'll do him good to have a job of organization thrown suddenly onto his lap . . ."

Williams enjoyed himself; things had been altogether too quiet for his taste. And then, with the ship quiet and deserted, Grimes, with Sonya and Clarisse and Mayhew, and with a full dozen of assorted scientists, boarded one of the pinnaces, in which the necessary materials had already been stowed.

It was just before sunset when they landed on the smooth, windswept plateau that was the summit of the mountain. A thin, icy wind swept into the little cabin as the door opened. One by one,

Grimes in the lead, the members of the party clambered down on to the bare, barren rock, the last ones to emerge handing down the equipment before making their own exits. There was an easel, as before, a floodlight, pots of paint, brushes. There were cameras, still and cinematographic, one of which would transmit a television picture to receivers on the plain below the mountain. There were sound recorders.

Silently, slowly, Mayhew and his wife walked to the center of the plateau, accompanied by Grimes and Sonya, carrying what she would be using. Grimes set up the easel, with its stretched black canvas, and the powerful floodlight. Sonya placed the painting materials at its foot. Mayhew, his thin face pale and anxious, lifted the heavy cloak from Clarisse's shoulders. She stood there as she had stood before, naked save for the brief, rough kilt of animal hide, her arms crossed over her full breasts for warmth rather than from modesty. She looked, thought Grimes (again) as her remote ancestresses on this very world must have looked, was about to practice the magic that they had practiced. Mayhew had produced from a pocket a little bottle and a tiny glass—the psychedelic drug. He filled the glass, held it out to her. "Drink this, my dear," he ordered gently.

She took it from him, drained it, threw it down. It shattered with a crystalline crash, surprisingly loud in spite of the wind. "Your bare feet . . ." muttered Mayhew. He squatted down, carefully picking up the glittering fragments. She did not appear to see what he was doing, stood like a statue when he, on his feet again, laid his free hand on her bare shoulder in an attempted gesture of reassurance and . . . farewell?

He whispered to Grimes, his voice taut with strain and worry, "I can't get through to her. Somebody, something's got hold of her . . ."

The three of them walked back to where the scientists were standing by the pinnace, their recording apparatus set up and ready. And suddenly the sun was gone, and there was only the glare of the floodlight, in which Clarisse was standing. Overhead was the almost empty black sky with its sparse scatter of dim stars, and low to the east was the arc of misty luminescence that was the slowly rising Galactic Lens. The wind could have been blowing straight from intergalactic space.

Conditions were almost the same as they had been on the previous occasion. Almost. It was the human element that was different. This time those on the mountain top were skeptics and earnest inquirers, not true believers. But the feeling of almost unendurable tension was the same.

Hesitantly, Clarisse stooped to the clutter of materials at her feet. She selected a brush. She dipped it into one of the pots, then straightened. With swift, sure strokes she began to paint.

But it was wrong, Grimes realized. It was all wrong. It was white paint that she had used before; this time she was applying a bright, fluorescent pigment to the canvas. A figure was taking shape—that of a tall, slender man in red tights, with a pointed beard, a mocking smile . . . A man? But men do not have neat little goatlike horns growing from their heads; neither do they have long, lissome tails ending in a barbed point. . .

A god?

Pan, perhaps.

No, not Pan. Pan never looked like that.

There was a dreadful crack of lightning close at hand, too close at hand, but the flash was not blue-white but a dull, unnatural crimson. There was a choking, sulphurous stench. And then *he* was standing there, laughing; amid the roiling clouds of black smoke, laughing.

Grimes heard one of the scientists almost scream, "What the devil. . . ?"

And the devil advanced, still laughing, his very white and very sharp teeth flashing. His surprisingly elegant right hand stretched out to rest on the Commodore's wrist. "You are under arrest," he said. "And I must warn you that anything you say will be taken down and may be used as evidence."

"By what authority?" Grimes heard Sonya cry. "By what . . .?"

And then there was darkness deeper than that between the universes, and absolute silence.

How long did the journey last? An eternity, or a fraction of a microsecond? It could have been either.

There was light again; not bright, but dim and misty. There was light, and there was solidity underfoot—and there was still the pressure of that restraining hand on his wrist. Grimes looked down— he was reluctant to look up—and saw what looked like a marble pavement. At last he allowed his eyes slowly to elevate. There were the slim, pointed red shoes, inches from his own. There were the slender yet muscular legs in their skintight scarlet hose. There were the elaborately puffed trunks. There was the scarlet, gold-trimmed doublet . . . Suddenly Grimes felt less frightened. This was the Mephistopheles of fancy dress balls, and of opera, rather than a real and living embodiment of unutterable evil. But when he came to the face his assurance began to ebb. There was a reckless handsomeness, but there was power, too much power, power that would be used recklessly and selfishly.

Behind Grimes a very English voice was saying, "We must congratulate our friend on his speedy arrest, Watson."

A deeper voice replied, "Yes, yes, my dear Holmes. But are we sure that we have the right man? After all, to judge by his uniform, he's an officer, and presumably a gentleman . . ."

Mephistopheles laughed sneeringly. "Well I know the villainies of which so-called gentlemen are capable. But I have carried out my part of the bargain and now I shall return to my own place; it's too infernally cold here for comfort."

There was a flash of dull crimson light, the stench of burning sulphur, and he was gone.

"Turn around, fellow, and let us look at you," ordered the first English voice.

Slowly Grimes turned, and what he saw was no surprise to him. There was the tall man with aquiline features, wearing peculiar garments that he knew were a Norfolk jacket, an Inverness cape and a deerstalker cap. There was the short, stout man with the walrus moustache, formally clad, even to black frock coat and gleaming top hat.

Grimes looked at them, and they looked at him.

Then, "Hand it over, sir," ordered the tall man. "Hand it over, and I shall prefer no charges."

"Hand what over?" asked Grimes, bewildered.

"My pipe, of course."

Silently the Commodore drew the leather case from his pocket, placed it in the outstretched hand.

"A remarkable piece of deduction, my dear Holmes," huffed the stout man. "It baffles me how you did it."

"Elementary, my dear Watson. It should be obvious, even to you, that a crime, any crime, cannot take place in the three dimensions of space only. The additional factor, the fourth dimension, time, must always be taken into account. I reasoned that the thief must be somebody living so far in our future that our fictional origin will be forgotten. Then I enlisted the aid of the London branch of the Baker Street Irregulars—those fellows are always absurdly flattered when I condescend to share their dreams! Through them I maintained a round the clock watch on the antique shop that stands where our lodgings used to be. At last it was reported to me that my pipe had been purchased by a red-haired young lady of striking appearance. I learned, too—once again through the invaluable Irregulars—that she was the wife of one Commodore Grimes, of the Rim Worlds Naval Reserve, and would shortly be returning to her husband, who was resident in a city called Port Forlorn, on a planet called Lorn, one of the Rim Worlds. These Rim Worlds are outside our ambit, but I was able to persuade that learned colleague of yours who dabbles in magic to persuade his ... er ... colleague, Mephistopheles, to place his services at my disposal. Between us we were able to lay a very subtle psychological trap on yet another planet, one with the unlikely name of Kinsolving ..." Holmes opened the case, took out the pipe, looked at it, sniffed it. His face darkened. "Sir, have you been *smoking* this?"

"Yes," admitted Grimes.

Watson intervened. "It will be a simple matter, Holmes, to sterilize it. Just a jet of steam from a boiling kettle, back in our lodgings ..."

"Very well, Watson. Let us proceed with the purification rites forthwith."

The two men walked rapidly away, their forms becoming indistinct in the mist. Grimes heard Watson say, "And when I chronicle this case, I shall call it 'The Adventure of the Missing Meerschaum . . .'"

And what about 'The Case of the Kidnapped Commodore'? wondered Grimes. But before he could start in pursuit of the great detective and his friend another figure had appeared, blocking his way.

He, too, was English, most respectably dressed in the style of the early twentieth century, in black jacket and trousers with a gray waistcoat, a stiff white collar and a black necktie. He was inclined to stoutness, but the ladies of the servants' hall must often have referred to him—but never in his dignified hearing—as "a fine figure of a man."

He raised his bowler hat, and Grimes had sufficient presence of mind to bring the edge of his right hand to the peak of his cap to return the salute. He said, his voice deferential but far from servile, "Welcome aboard, sir." He contrived to enclose the words between quotation marks.

"Er . . . Thank you."

"Perhaps, sir, you will accompany me. I am the only member of my profession in this place, and so it has become my duty—and my pleasure, sir—to welcome new arrivals and to arrange for their accommodation."

"That's very good of you, er . . ."

"Jeeves, sir. At your service. This way, Commodore—I take it that the braid on your epaulettes still has the same significance as in my time—if you please."

"Where are you taking me?"

"I took the liberty, sir, of arranging for your accommodation at the Senior Service Club. There are other naval gentlemen in residence. There is Admiral—Lord Hornblower, that is. You must have heard of him. And there is Commander Bond—a very likable young gentleman, but not quite my idea of what a naval officer should be. And . . ." a flicker of distaste crossed Jeeves's plump face . . . "a certain Lieutenant Commander Queeg, who somehow appointed himself club secretary. He even tried to have Captain Ahab evicted from the premises. How did he put it?" Jeeves's voice acquired a nasal twang. "'How can I run a taut ship with that damned whaling skipper stomping around the decks on his peg leg? He'll be putting that pet whale of his in the swimming bath next. I kid you not.' But the Admiral—he's president; although old Captain Noah is the senior member he's really not much interested in anything—asked my advice. So Commander Bond was ordered to act as a one-man press gang—a form of activity for which he seemed well qualified—and, after Captain Ahab had been pressed into the King's service he was promptly commissioned by Lord Hornblower. As an officer of the Royal Navy he was really more entitled to Club membership—it's a very British institution—than Commander Queeg . . ."

"Very ingenious," commented Grimes.

"I am always happy to oblige, sir." Jeeves raised his hat to a tall woman who had appeared out of the mist, a striking brunette, barefooted, wearing a long white nightgown. "Good morning, Your Ladyship."

She ignored him but concentrated on Grimes. She glared at him from slightly mad, dark eyes, and all the time her hands were making peculiar wringing motions. "Ye havena brought any decent soap wi' ye?" she demanded.

"Soap, madam?"

"Aye, soap, ye lackwitted Sassenach!"

"I'm afraid not. If I'd known that I was coming here . . ."

The woman brushed past him, muttering, "Will *nothing* wash these white hands?"

"I have tried to help her, sir," said Jeeves, "But I can only do so much. After all, I am not a qualified psychiatrist. But many of the guests in this establishment are more odd than otherwise." He gestured toward a break in the mist, through which Grimes glimpsed lush greenery, vivid flowers, a veritable jungle. And surely that was the coughing roar of a lion, followed by the shrill chattering of disturbed tropical birds . . . "Lord Greystoke lives there, sir, with his wife, the Lady Jane. They have a house in a big tree, and they consort with *apes* . . . And the people next door, in the next estate—like an English woodland, it is—live in a gamekeeper's cottage. A Mr. Mellors and a Lady Constance Chatterley. You would think that with their mutual love of nature the two couples would be on *very* friendly terms. But no. Lady Chatterley said to me once when I mentioned it—it was when I had invited her and Mr. Mellors to my quarters for a real English afternoon tea, and we were discussing the Greystokes—'The only nature I'm interested in, Jeeves, is *human* nature.'" Again he raised his hat. "Good morning, Colonel."

"Who was that?" asked Grimes, staring after the figure in the fringed buckskin shirt, with a revolver slung at each hip.

"Colonel William Cody, sir. I feel sorry for the gentleman. You see, he isn't really one of us. As well as living an actual life on the printed page he was also a flesh and blood person. As I understand it, a New York publishing house of his time commissioned a writer to produce a series of stories about the Wild West, and this writer, instead of creating a character, used one who was already in existence in the flesh and blood world, calling him Buffalo Bill. And this, you will understand, makes him, insofar as *we* are concerned, illegitimate. But he is not the only one. There are the Greek ladies and gentlemen—Helen, and Cassandra, and Odysseus, and Achilles, and Oedipus . . . And others. And, of course, there is the Prince, although His Highness claims that he was cribbed from an earlier work of fiction and not from what the flesh and blood people call real life."

"So I'm not real?" demanded Grimes.

"But you are, sir, otherwise you could never have come here. You are, like the rest of us, a creation, a product of the imagination of some gifted writer." He stopped suddenly, and Grimes stopped with him. "But, sir, are you an *enduring* product?" He walked around the Commodore like a tailor inspecting the fit and cut of a new uniform. "This is indeed unfortunate, sir. Already I detect a hint of insubstantiality . . ." He paused, turned to face a newcomer, bowed. "Good morning, Your Highness."

The tall, thin, pale man in form-fitting black, with the white lace at throat and cuffs, did not reply to the salutation. Instead he said in a sonorous voice, "To be or not to be, that is the question . . ."

"Too right," agreed Grimes.

The Prince of Denmark looked down at the age-mottled skull that he held in his right hand. "Alas, poor Yorick, I knew him well . . ."

He stared at the Commodore. "But you I do not know." He turned on his heel, strode away.

"Good night, sweet Prince," said Grimes bitterly.

"Do not mind His Highness," said Jeeves. "He has a sardonic sense of humor."

"Maybe he has. But you must have had other . . . characters here who were not, as you put it, enduring products. What happened to them?"

"They . . . faded, sir. There was a young man dressed up in old woman's clothing who called himself 'Charley's Aunt.' He lasted quite a few years, Earth Time, but he's vanished now. And there have been many gentlemen like yourself, spacemen. None of them lasted long."

"But what happens to them? To *us?*"

"I cannot say, sir. When the last book in which you appeared has crumbled into dust, when your last reader has gone to wherever the flesh and blood people go, what then?"

"There must be *some* way," muttered Grimes. Then, aloud "All right. I'm scared. I admit it. But my own case is different. All you others came here, I suppose, after the death of your authors. You're immortality—perhaps—for the men who created you. But I was brought here before my time. I was the victim of a plot cooked up— and what more unlikely fellow conspirators could there ever be!—by Sherlock Holmes and Dr. Faustus. And Mephistopheles."

Jeeves laughed quietly. "I knew that Mr. Holmes had lost his pipe. I offered to assist him in its recovery; but he, of course, was too proud to accept my humble services. He always likes to do things his own way. And you, sir, I take it, are the innocent victim."

"You can say that again. I was shanghaied away from my own universe to this . . . limbo . . ."

"We prefer, sir, to call it the Hall of Fame."

"And I'm not the only victim. Back there I've a wife, and a ship . . . I must get back to them."

"I appreciate your anxiety, sir, and I admit that there could be need for haste. Time is measured differently here than elsewhere, sir, and already you are becoming quite diaphanous . . ."

Grimes held out his hand, looked at it. He could see the marble flooring through skin and flesh and blood and bone.

"Hurry, sir," urged Jeeves.

They hurried. Nonetheless, Grimes retained a confused memory of their nightmarish gallop. Men and women stopped to stare at them; and some of them Grimes recognized; and some were hauntingly familiar; and a very few struck no chords in his memory whatsoever. There were occasional rifts in the eddying mists to afford fleeting glimpses of buildings, and, like the clothing of the people, the architecture was of all historical periods. Turreted Camelot, its towers aflutter with gay pennons, they sped by; and beyond its walls was a barren and dusty plain whereon a solitary knight, a scarecrow figure astride a skeletal horse, tilted at windmills. Then there was Sherwood Forest, where the outlaws in Lincoln green paused in their archery practice to cheer on the two runners.

And for a while there was the shambling monstrosity that lurched along beside them, keeping pace, like a large, unlovely dog trying to make friends. Grimes glanced at this giant, who seemed to have been put together from not quite matching parts pilfered from the graveyard, then looked hastily away, sickened by the sight of him and by the charnel stench that emanated from the crudely humanoid form. Then there was the other monster, the handsome man in nineteenth century dress finery who hovered above them on black bat's wings. Jeeves, who did not suffer from lack of wind, muttered something uncomplimentary about Eastern European aristocracy.

At last there loomed before them the house that was their destination. All high gables it was, and oak beams, with narrow, diamond-paned windows. Set high on the stout, iron-bound door was the black, iron knocker—metal cast in the form of an inverted crucifix. Jeeves reached for it, rapped smartly.

Slowly the door creaked open. An old, graybearded man peered out at them suspiciously. He was dressed in a rusty black robe upon which cabalistic symbols gleamed with a dull luster and a tall, conical, black hat. His blue eyes were so faded as to be almost white.

He demanded querulously, "Who disturbs my rest?"

"It is I, Jeeves, Herr Doktor . . ."

"And this other? This . . . phantasm?"

"The innocent victim, Dr. Faustus, of the peculiar machinations set in motion by yourself and Mr. Holmes."

"What is done cannot be undone." He glared at Grimes, through Grimes. "And do *you* cry, 'Oh, Lord, put back Thy Universe, and give me back my yesterday'?"

"I have done so," whispered Grimes. "As who has not?"

"*I* cannot help you." The door was starting to close.

But Jeeves had inserted a stout, highly polished shoe into the narrowing opening. "Do not forget that *I* have helped you, Dr. Faustus. Have I not sent patients to you?" He added nastily, "Although Achilles still limps, and Oedipus still chases after older women . . ."

"My name is Faustus, not Freud," grumbled the old man.

"Furthermore," continued Jeeves, "both you and your partner rely upon me for the supply of the luxuries that were unavailable in your own day and age."

The door opened abruptly. "Come in!" snarled the old doctor.

Inside it was dark, the only light coming from a brazier over which a cauldron bubbled. The room was a large one, but it was so cluttered with a fantastic miscellany of objects that it was hard to move without fouling something. Grimes ducked hastily to avoid striking his head on a stuffed crocodile that hung from the low ceiling, then almost tripped over a beautiful—but woefully inaccurate—celestial globe that stood on the stone floor. He would have tripped had his body been solid, but his shadowy leg passed through the obstacle with no more than the faintest hint of resistance.

Grumbling, the old man shuffled to a bench littered with the apparatus of alchemy. "Chalk . . ." he muttered, "for the pentagram . . . Where did I put it? And the sulphur candles . . ."

"There's no time for that, Doctor. Can't you see? This gentleman needs help urgently."

"But *He* will not like it if I do not observe protocol."

"*He* won't like it if he has to go thirsty from now on."

"Very well, very well. But I warn you—*He* will be bad tempered."

Dr. Faustus tottered to a low table upon which stood a large, stuffed owl. He lifted the bird, which was hollow, revealing a jarringly anachronistic telephone. He handed the owl to Jeeves, who regarded it with some distaste, then took the handset from its rest, punched a number.

"Yes," he croaked into the instrument. "At once." There was a pause. "Yes, I know that you always insist that the proper procedure be followed, but Mr. Jeeves says that this is urgent." There was another pause. "You'd better come, unless you want to do without your brandy and cigars . . ."

This time there was no thunder, no crimson lightning, no clouds of black, sulphurous smoke. But Mephistopheles was standing there, his arms folded over his muscular chest, scowling down at Grimes. "Yes?" he demanded shortly. "Yes, my man?"

The Commodore, his voice a barely audible whisper, said, "Take me back to where I belong."

The Commodore stepped silently forward, peered over the writer's shoulder. He read, *He was standing in a ship's cabin. The carpeted deck swayed and lurched under his feet . . .* Then the carpeted deck lurched really heavily. Grimes put out a hand, to the back of the other man's chair, to steady himself.

The writer started violently, exclaimed, "What the hell!" He twisted in his seat, stared at Grimes. His pipe fell from his mouth, clattered to the deck. "No . . ." he said slowly. "No. It can't be. Go away."

"I wish that I could," Grimes told him.

"Then why the hell don't you?"

"You, sir, should know the answer to that question," said Grimes, reasonably enough. He looked curiously at the other man, his . . . creator? His . . . parent? But there was no physical resemblance to himself. He, Grimes, was short and stocky, and his ears were his most prominent facial feature. The writer was tall, with normal enough ears, but too much nose.

"You, sir, should know the answer to that question," repeated Grimes.

"I'm sorry, Commodore, but I don't. Not yet, anyhow." Then, in a tone of forced cheerfulness, "But this is only a silly dream. It must be."

"It's not, Captain." The man's gold-braided epaulettes and the uniform cap, with the scrambled egg on its peak, hanging on a hook just inside the curtained door made this a safe enough guess. "It's not, Captain. Pinch yourself."

"Damn it! That hurt."

"Good. Do you mind if I sit down?" Carefully, Grimes eased himself on to the settee that ran along one bulkhead of the day cabin. He feared at first that he was going to sink through the cushion, but it had substance (or he had substance) and supported him, although only just. He shut his eyes for a moment, trying to dispel the faintness that was creeping over him. It was the result of shock, he realized, of shock and of disappointment. He had expected to find himself aboard his own ship, the old, familiar, tried and trusted *Faraway Quest*, to be welcomed back by his wife. But where was he now? *When* was he? On Earth, the mother world of humankind? Aboard some sort of surface vessel?

The writer answered the unspoken questions. He said, "I'll put you in the picture, Commodore. You're aboard the good ship *Kantara*, which same plies between Melbourne and the port of Macquarie, on the wild west coast of Tasmania. We load pyritic ore in Macquarie for Melbourne, and make the return trip (as we are doing now) in ballast. I doubt very much if you have anything like this trade in your day and age, sir. Macquarie's one of those places that you can't get into when you're outside, and that you can't get out of when you're inside. To begin with, the tides are absolutely unpredictable, and it's safe to work the entrance—it's called Hell's Gates, by the way—only at slack water. If you tried to come in against a seven knot ebb you'd be in trouble! And the Inner Bar and the Outer Bar are always silting up, and with strong north westerlies— which we've been having—Outer Bar breaks badly. I've been riding out a howling westerly gale, keeping well to seaward, as I just don't like being caught on a lee shore in a small, underpowered and underballasted ship. But the wind's backed to the south'ard and is moderating, and the glass is rising, and all the weather reports and forecasts look good. So I'm standing in from my last observed position—P.M. star sights—until I'm just inside the extreme range of Cape Sorell light, and then I'll just stand off and on until daylight, keeping within easy reach of the port. Come the dawn, I'll have a natter with the harbor master on the radio telephone, and as soon as he's able to convince me that conditions are favorable I'll rush in."

"Why bother with the extreme range of the light?" asked Grimes, becoming interested in spite of all his troubles. "You have radar, don't you?"

"I do. I have radar and echo sounder. But my radar gets old and tired after only a few hours' operation, and my echo sounder's on the blink. I've nothing against electronic gadgetry *as long as it can be relied upon.* At the moment, mine can't be." The writer laughed. "But this is crazy. To sit here discussing navigation with a navigator from the distant future! I hope that none of my officers comes in to find me carrying on a conversation with myself!"

"I'm real, Captain. And I'm here. And I think that you should do something about getting me back to where I belong."

"What can I do, Commodore? People have said, more than once, that my stories just *happen.* And that's true, you know. Furthermore, I've always given *you* a free hand. Time and time again I've had to make plot changes because you've insisted on going your own way."

"So you can't help me . . ."

"I wish that I could. Believe me, I wish that I could. Do you think that I want to be haunted by you for the rest of my life?"

"There could be a way . . ." whispered Grimes. *Yes,* he thought, *there could be a way.* Life in that Hall of Fame would not be at all bad as long as he—*and Sonya*—were assured of the same degree of permanence as the others: Oedipus Rex, Hamlet, Sherlock Holmes, James Bond . . . He said, "I shan't mind a bit going back to that peculiar Elysium you cooked up as long as my status there is better than that of an ephemeral gate crasher. And, of course, I'd like Sonya with me."

"And just how can I arrange that for you, Commodore?"

"Easily, Captain. All you have to do is write a best seller, a series of best sellers."

The other man grinned. "It's a pity you can't meet my wife." He gestured toward a peculiarly two-dimensional photograph in a frame over the desk. The auburn-haired woman who looked out at them reminded Grimes of Sonya. "That's what she's always telling me."

There was a sharp buzz from the telephone on the desk. The writer picked up the handset. "Master here."

"Third Officer here, sir," Grimes heard faintly. "I've just picked up Cape Sorell light, at extreme range, right ahead . . ."

"Good, Mr. Tallent. Turn her on to the reciprocal course. Yes, keep her on half speed. I'll be right up."

Grimes followed the shipmaster out of the day cabin, up the narrow companionway to the chartroom, out of the glass-enclosed wheelhouse, then out through a sliding door to the wing of the bridge. The night was clear, and the stars (would he ever see them again as more than lights in the sky?) were bright. Astern was the winking, group-flashing light, an intermittent spark on the far horizon. And then the light itself was gone, only a flash recurring at regular intervals marking its position as the lantern dipped below the planet's curvature.

The captain grunted his satisfaction, then turned to stare forward. There was still quite a sea running, the wave crests faintly phosphorescent in the darkness; there was still a stiff breeze, broad on the port bow, but there was no weight to it. The ship was lifting easily to the swell, the motion not at all uncomfortable. The captain grunted again, went back to the chartroom. Grimes looked over his shoulder as he bent over the chart, noted the range circle with Cape Sorell as its center, the dot on it in the middle of its own tiny, penciled circle with the time—2235—along it, and another, cryptic notation, 33.5. On the chart, to one side, was a message pad. *Final Gale Warning*, it was headed. "Wind and sea moderating in all areas," read Grimes. "All pressures rising."

The shipmaster was busy now with parallel rulers, pencil and dividers. From the observed position he laid off a course—270° True. With the dividers he stepped off a distance, marked it with a cross and wrote alongside it "0200?" Grimes realized that the officer of the watch had come into the chartroom. He could see the young man, but the young man, it seemed, could not see him.

"Mr. Tallent," said the shipmaster, "we'll stand out to this position, then bring her around to 090 True. All being well, we shall be within comfortable VHF range at daylight, and with any luck at all the Bar will have stopped breaking and we shall have slack water. I'll not write up my night orders yet; I'll see the second officer at midnight before I turn in . . ."

"We should get in tomorrow all right, sir," said the officer.

"Don't be so bloody sure. You can never tell with this bloody place!"

"Good night, sir."

"Good night, Mr. Tallent."

Back in the day cabin, Grimes said, "You can see, Captain, that I have no real existence *here* and *now*. You *must* try to make me real *somewhere*."

"Or somewhen."

"Or somewhen."

"More easily said than done, Commodore. Especially in the existing circumstances. At the moment of writing *I* am master of this little rustbucket. Master under God, as Lloyd's puts it. This ship is my responsibility—and *you* should be able to appreciate that. This evening I was writing just as relaxation, one hand on the keyboard, the other ready to pick up the telephone . . ."

Grimes said, "You take yourself too bloody seriously. This is only a small ship with a small crew on an unimportant trade."

"Nonetheless," the shipmaster told him, "this is *my* ship. And the crew is *my* crew. The trade? That's the Company's worry; but, as Master, it's up to me to see that the ship shows a profit."

"And I'm your responsibility too," Grimes pointed out.

"Are you? As I've already said, Commodore, you've proven yourself able to go your own sweet way in any story that I've written. But if I *am* responsible, just bear in mind that I could kill you off as easily as I could swat a fly. More easily. How do you want it? Act of

God, the King's enemies, or pirates? Nuclear blast—or a knife between the ribs?"

"You're joking, surely."

"Am I? Has it never occurred to you, Commodore, that a writer gets rather tired of his own pet characters? Sir Arthur Conan Doyle killed off Sherlock Holmes, but had to drag him back to life to please his public. Ian Fleming was becoming more than somewhat browned off with James Bond when he, himself, kicked the bucket. . ."

Grimes looked toward the photograph over the desk. "But you like Sonya," he said.

"I do. She's too good for you."

"Be that as it may. She's part of my world, my time . . ."

"So?"

"Well, I thought . . ."

The telephone buzzed. The shipmaster picked up the handset. "Yes?"

"The wind's freshening, sir, and it's veered to west."

"Put her back on full speed, Mr. Tallent." The captain got up from his chair, went to the aneroid barometer mounted on the bulkhead. He tapped it. The needle jerked in a counterclockwise direction. "Just what I need," he said. "A bloody secondary."

"What does that mean, Captain?"

"It means, Commodore, that those *Final Gale Warnings* aren't worth the paper that Sparks typed them on. Very often, too often, in these waters the secondary depression is more vicious than the so-called primary."

"What can you do?"

"Stand out. Make offing. Get the hell off this bloody lee shore."

Again the telephone buzzed. "Master here."

"Sir, we've lifted Cape Sorell again . . ."

"Tell the engineers to give her all they've got. I'll be right up."

The ship was lurching, was rolling heavily as she fell away from the wind. She was pounding as her fore part lifted and then slammed back down into the trough. Her screw was racing each time that her stern came clear of the water, and as the propeller lost purchase, so did the rudder. "Sir," complained the helmsman, "the wheel's hard over, but she's not coming back . . ."

"Keep it hard over until she answers," ordered the Master. He was looking into the radar screen. It was not a very good picture. There was spoking, and there was too much clutter. But there, right astern, was the faint outline of the rocky coast, a ragged luminosity. And there were the range circles—and slowly, slowly, the coastline was drifting from the 24 mile to the 20 mile ring. Even Grimes, peering over the other man's shoulder, could appreciate what was happening.

"Mr. Tallent!"

"Sir?"

"Call the Chief Officer. Tell him to flood the afterhold."

"*Flood* the afterhold, sir?"

"You heard me. We have to get the arse down somehow, to give the screw and the rudder some sort of grip on the water."

"Very good, sir."

"She's logging three knots," whispered the Master. "But she's making one knot—*astern*. And that coast is nothing but rocks . . ."

"And flooding the hold will help?" asked Grimes.

"It'd better. It's all I can do."

They went back out to the wing of the bridge, struggling to retain their balance as the wind hit them. Cape Sorell light was brightly visible again, right astern, and even to the naked eye it had lifted well clear of the sea horizon. A shadowy figure joined them there—the Chief Officer, decided Grimes.

"I've got two fire hoses running into the hold, sir. What depth of water do you want?"

"I want 100 tons. Go below and work it out roughly."

"What if the ceiling lifts?"

"Let it lift. Put in your hundred tons."

"Very good, sir."

Another officer came onto the bridge—big, burly, bearded. This must be, realized Grimes, the midnight change of watch. "Keep her as she's going, sir?" he asked.

"Yes. Keep her as she's going, Mr. Mackenzie. She'll be steering better once we get some weight in aft, and racing less. But you might tell the engineers to put on the second steering motor . . ."

"Will do, sir."

The shipmaster made his way back into the wheelhouse, staggering a little as the vessel lurched in the heavy swell. He went to the radar unit, looked down into the screen with Grimes peering over his shoulder. Right astern, the ragged outline of Cape Sorell was touching the twenty mile ring. Slowly the range decreased—slowly, but inexorably.

The Chief Officer was back. "About two foot six should do it, sir." "Make it that . . ."

Then, gradually, the range was opening again. The range was opening, and the frequent heavy vibrations caused by the racing screw were becoming less. The wind was still shrieking in from the westward, whipping the crests off the seas, splattering them against the wheelhouse windows in shrapnel bursts of spray, but the ship was steering again, keeping her nose into it, clawing away from the rocks that had claimed, over the years, too many victims.

Grimes followed the Master down to the afterdeck, stood with him as he looked down a trunkway into the flooded hold. Swirling in the filthy water were the timbers of the hold ceiling, crashing against the bulkheads fore and aft, splintering themselves against frames and brackets and the hold ladders, self-destroying battering rams driven by the force of the ship's pitching and rolling. There would be damage, even Grimes could see that. There would be damage—and, inevitably, the writing of reports with carbon copies every which way.

Grimes knew this, and he should have had more sense than to attempt to bring up the subject again of his own, private worries.

He said, "This hold flooding seems to have worked . . ."

"Yes."

"Then perhaps, Captain, you could spare the time to discuss the question of returning me to my own place and period . . ."

". . . off!" snarled the shipmaster. "I've more important things on my plate than your troubles. . . . Off!"

The screaming wind took hold of Grimes, whirling him away into the darkness. But, before he was gone, he heard the Chief Officer ask his captain, "Who was that, sir? I thought I saw somebody standing there with you, a stranger in an odd-looking uniform . . ."

"Just a figment of the imagination, Mr. Briggs. Just a figment of the imagination."

He was standing in his own day cabin, aboard *Faraway Quest*. He was staring at Sonya, and she, her face white under the auburn hair, was staring at him.

"John! You're back!"

"Yes."

"I've been holding the ship, here on Kinsolving, but our lords and masters have been putting the pressure on us to return . . ."

"It wouldn't have mattered," Grimes told her.

"Why not?"

"Because wherever *you* are, that's where I belong."

He was sitting in his day cabin, trying to relax over a stiff drink. He had brought his ship into port, scurrying in during a lull between two depressions, pumping out after ballast to compensate for the weight of water in the flooded hold, clearing the Bar without touching. He was overtired and knew that sleep was out of the question. But there was nothing for him to do; his Chief Officer was capably overseeing the pumping out of the flooded compartment and would, as soon as possible, put the necessary repairs in hand.

He thought, *I might as well finish that bloody story.* He inserted paper into his typewriter, refueled and lit his pipe, began to write. As the final words shaped themselves on the white sheet he looked up at the photograph of the red-haired woman over his desk. *Because wherever you are, that's where I belong . . .*

"And I hope you're satisfied, you cantankerous old bastard," he muttered.

"And it all actually happened . . ." murmured Admiral Kravinsky, indicating the thick report that lay on his desk.

"I . . . I suppose so . . ." said Grimes uncertainly.

"You should know, man. You were there."

"But *where* was *there?*"

"Don't go all metaphysical on me, Grimes." The Admiral selected a gnarled cheroot from the box before him, lit it. In self-defense the Commodore filled and ignited a battered briar pipe. He regretted, he realized, having lost that meerschaum during his last adventure.

Kravinsky regarded the swirling clouds of acrid blue smoke thoughtfully. He said at last, "It was rummy, all the same. Very rummy."

"You're telling *me*," concurred Grimes.

"I think that we shall be leaving Kinsolving severely alone for quite a while. I don't like this business about our just being a figment of the imagination or an imagination of the figment or whatever . . ."

"*You* don't like it. . ." muttered Grimes.

"All right, all right, my heart fair bleeds for you. Satisfied? And now, Admiral, I have a job for you that should be right up your alley."

"Admiral? Have I been promoted, sir?"

"That'd be the sunny Friday! But, Grimes, I seem to remember that you're an honorary admiral in the Tharn Navy, and that same Navy consists of seagoing surface vessels. The rank, meaningless though it is, should be useful to you when we send you to Aquarius."

"The rank's not meaningless, sir," protested Grimes.

"So much the better, then. On your way, Admiral. Weigh anchor, splice the main brace, heave the lead or whatever it is you seafaring types do when you get under way."

"It should be interesting," said Grimes.

"With you around to complicate matters, it's bound to be."

❧ The Sister Ships ❧

CAPTAIN JOHN GRIMES stood impassively in the port wing of his bridge as his ship, the round-the-world tramp *Sonya Winneck*, slid gently in toward her berth. But although his stocky body was immobile his brain was active. He was gauging speed, distances, the effect of the tide. His engines were stopped, but the vessel still seemed to be carrying too much way. He was stemming the ebb, but, according to the Port Directions there was sometimes—not always— an eddy, a counter current along this line of wharfage. In any case, it would be a tight fit. Ahead of him was *Iron Baron*, one of the steel trade ships: a huge, beamy brute with gigantic deck cranes almost capable of lifting her by her own bootstraps. In the berth astern was the Lone Star Line's *Orionic*, with even more beam to her than the *Baron*.

"Port!" ordered Grimes. "Hard over!"

"Hard aport, sir!" replied the quartermaster.

Sonya Winneck was accosting the wharf at a fairly steep angle now, her stem aimed at a bollard just abaft *Iron Baron*'s stern. Grimes lifted his mouth whistle to his lips, blew one short, sharp blast. From the fo'c'sle head came the rattle of chain cable as the starboard anchor was let go, then one stroke of the bell to signal that the first shackle was in the pipe.

Grimes looked aft. *Sonya Winneck*'s quarter was now clear of *Orionic*'s bows. "Midships! Slow astern!"

He heard the replies of the man at the wheel and the Third Officer. He felt the vibration as the reversed screw bit into the water. But would slow astern be enough? He was about to order half astern, then realized that this was what he was getting, if not more. The transverse thrust of the screw threw *Sonya Winneck*'s stern to port even as her headway was killed. Already a heaving line was ashore forward, and snaking after it the first of the mooring lines. Aft, the Second Mate was ready to get his first line ashore.

"Stop her," ordered Grimes. "That will do the wheel, thank you."

On fo'c'sle head and poop the self-tensioning winches were whining. Grimes, looking down from the bridge wing to the marker flag on the wharf, saw that he was exactly in position. He made the traditional "arms crossed above the head" gesture—*Make her fast as she is*—to the Chief Officer forward, the Second Officer aft. Then he walked slowly into the wheelhouse. The Third Officer was still standing by the engine control pedestal.

"Finished with engines, Mr. Denham," said Grimes coldly.

"Finished with engines, sir." The young man put the lever to that position. There was a jangling of bells drifting up from below.

"Mr. Denham . . ."

"Sir?" The officer's voice was an almost inaudible squeak. He looked frightened, and, thought Grimes, well he might be.

"Mr. Denham, I am well aware that in your opinion I'm an outsider who should never have been appointed to command of this vessel. I am well aware, too, that in your opinion, at least, your local knowledge far surpasses mine. Even so, I shall be obliged if you will carry out my orders, although you will still have the right, the obligation, in fact, to query them—but not when I'm in the middle of berthing the bloody ship!" Grimes simmered down. "For your information, Mr. Denham, even I realized that slow astern would not be sufficient. I was about to order more stern power, then saw that you had taken matters into your own possibly capable but definitely unqualified hands."

"But, sir . . ."

Grimes's prominent ears had reddened. "There are no 'buts.'"

"But, sir, I *tried* to put her to slow astern. The lever jerked out of my hand to full."

"Thank you, Mr. Denham," said Grimes at last. He knew that the young man was not lying. "You'd better see the Engineer, or the Electrician, and get those controls fixed. The next time they might do the wrong thing, instead of the right one."

He went through the chartroom and then down to his quarters. Sonya, who had watched the berthing from the lower bridge, was there waiting for him. She got up from her chair as he entered the day cabin and stood there, tall and slim and graceful. Her right hand snapped up to the widow's peak of her shining auburn hair.

She said, "I salute you, Cap'n. A masterly piece of ship handling."

"Mphm," grunted Grimes.

"But, John, it was like something out of one of your own books." She went to the case on the bulkhead in which were both privately owned volumes and those considered by the Winneck Line to be fit and proper reading for its masters. From the Company's shelf she lifted *The Inter-Island Steamer Express.* by John Grimes. She read aloud, ". . . These captains, maintaining their timetables and berthing and unberthing their big, seagoing passenger ferries in the most appalling weather conditions, were, without doubt, among the world's finest ship handlers . . ."

"The weather conditions this morning aren't appalling," said Grimes. "In any case, that was on Earth. This is Aquarius."

Aquarius, as its name implies, is a watery world.

It lies in toward the center from the Rim Worlds, fifty or so light-years to the galactic east of the Shakespearean Sector. It is Earth-type insofar as gravitation, atmosphere and climate are concerned, but geographically is dissimilar to the "home planet." There are no great land masses; there are only chains of islands: some large, some small, some no more than fly specks on even a medium scale chart. In this respect it is like Mellise, one of the planets of the Eastern Circuit. Unlike Mellise, it possesses no indigenous intelligent life. Men colonized it during the Second Expansion—and, as was the case with most Second Expansion colonizations, it was discovery and settlement by chance rather than by design. Time and time again it happened, that disastrous, often tragic sequence of events. The magnetic storm, the gaussjammer thrown light millennia off course, her pile dead and the hungry emergency diesels gulping precious hydrocarbons to feed power to the Ehrenhaft generators, the long plunge into and through the Unknown; the desperate search for a world, any world, that would sustain human life . . .

Lode Messenger stumbled upon Aquarius and made a safe landing in the vicinity of the North Magnetic Pole. Like all the later ships of her period she carried a stock of fertilized ova, human and animal, a wide variety of plant seeds and an extensive technical library. (Even when the gaussjammers were on regular runs, as *Lode Messenger* had been, there was always the possibility that their people would finish up as founders of a new colony.) When the planet was rediscovered by Commodore Shakespeare, during his voyage of exploration out toward the Rim, the settlement was already well established. With the Third Expansion it accepted its quota of immigrants, but insisted that all newcomers work for a probationary period in the merchant or fishing fleets before, if they so wished, taking up employment ashore. Somebody once said that if you wanted to emigrate to Aquarius you had to hold at least an "Able-bodied seaman's" papers. This is not quite true, but it is not far from the truth. It has also been said that Aquarians have an inborn dislike and distrust of spaceships but love seagoing ships. This is true.

Grimes, although not an immigrant, was a seaman of sorts. He was on the planet by invitation, having been asked by its rulers—the Havenmaster and the Master Wardens—to write a history of the colony. For that he was well qualified, being acknowledged as the leading maritime historian, specializing in Terran marine history, in the Rim Worlds. His books: *The Inter-Island Steamer Express*, *The Flag Of The Southern Cross*, *The Western Ocean Greyhounds*, *Times of Transition*—had sold especially well on Aquarius, although in the worlds of the Rim Confederacy they were to be found mainly only in libraries, and in very few libraries at that.

And Commodore Grimes, Rim Worlds Naval Reserve, Master Astronaut, was more than just a writer about the sea. He held the rank of admiral—honorary, but salt water admiral nonetheless—in the Ausiphalian Navy, on Tharn. Captain Thornton, the Havenmaster, had said, "Legally speaking, that commission of yours entitles you to a Certificate of Competency as a Master Mariner. Then you can sail in command of one of our ships, to get the real feel of life at sea."

"I'm not altogether happy about it, Tom," Grimes had objected, not too strongly.

"I'm the boss here," Thornton assured him. "And, in any case, I'm not turning you loose until you've been through crash courses in navigation, seamanship, meteorology, cargo stowage and stability."

"I'm tempted . . ." Grimes had admitted.

"Tempted?" scoffed Sonya. "He's just dying to strut his bridge like the ancient mariners he's always writing about. His only regret will be that you Aquarians didn't re-create the days of sail while you were about it."

"Now and again I regret it myself," admitted the Havenmaster. "Fore and aft rig, a diesel auxiliary, electrical deck machinery—there'd be something quite fast enough for some of our trades and economical to boot. But I'm well known as an enemy of progress—progress for its own sake, that is."

"A man after my own heart," said Grimes.

"You're just a pair of reactionaries," Sonya had told them.

I suppose I am a reactionary, Grimes had thought. But he enjoyed this world. It was efficiently run, but it was always recognized that there are things more important than efficiency. There was automation up to a certain point, but up to that certain point only. (But the Havenmaster had admitted that he was fighting a rearguard action to try to keep control of the ships in the hands of the seamen officers . . .) There was a love of and a respect for the sea. It was understandable. From the first beginnings of the colony these people had grown up on a watery world, and the books in their technical library most in demand had been those on shipbuilding, seamanship and navigation. Aquarius was poor in radioactives but rich in mineral oil, so the physicists had never been able, as they have on so many worlds, to take charge. The steam engine and the diesel engine were still the prime movers, even in the air, where the big passenger-carrying airships did the work that on other planets is performed by jet planes and rockets.

The surface ships were, by modern standards, archaic. Very few of them ran to bow thrusters—and those only ferries, cargo and passenger, to whom the strict adherence to a timetable was of paramount importance, whose masters could not afford to make a leisurely job of backing into a roll-on-roll-off berth and therefore required the additional maneuvering aid. There was some containerization, but it was not carried to extremes, it being recognized that the personnel of the cargo carriers were entitled to leisure time in port. Self-tensioning winches and, for cargo handling, cranes rather than derricks cut down the number of hands required on deck, and engine rooms were almost fully automated, with bridge control for arrival and departure maneuvers.

There were electronic navigational aids aplenty—radar, echometer, loran, shoran, an inertial system, position fixing by artificial satellite—but these the Havenmaster frowned upon, as did most of the senior shipmasters. He quoted from Grimes's own book, *Times Of Transition*, "The electronic wizards of the day, who were not seamen, failed to realize that a competent navigator, armed only with sextant, chronometer and ephemeris, together with a reasonably accurate log, can always fix the position of his ship with reasonable accuracy provided that there is an occasional break in the clouds for an identifiable celestial body to shine through. Such a navigator is never at the mercy of a single fuse . . ."

"And that, John, is what I'm trying to avoid," said Thornton. "Unless we're careful our ships will be officered by mere button pushers, incapable of running a series of P/Ls. Unluckily, not all the Master Wardens think as I do. Too many of them are engineers, and businessmen—and in my experience such people have far less sales resistance than we simple sailors."

"And what pups have they been sold?" asked Grimes.

"One that's a real bitch from my viewpoint, and probably from yours. You've heard of Elektra?"

"Yes," broke in Sonya. "Carinthian Sector. Third Expansion colonization." She grinned a little unkindly. "It's a planet where the minimum qualification for immigration is a doctorate in one of the sciences, preferably physics. But they have to let in occasional chemists, biologists and the like to keep the dump habitable."

"And they have quite a few, now, with degrees in salesmanship," went on the Havenmaster. "One of them was here a few years back."

"And he sold you this female pup," said Grimes.

"He did that. The Purcell Navigator. It's named, I suppose, after its inventor. It's a sealed box, with the gods know what sort of mess of memory fields and the like inside it. It's hooked up to all the ship's electronic navigational gear: gyro compass, radar, echometer, loran, shoran . . . Just name a pie and it's got a finger in it. Or a tentacle. It knows just where the ship is at any given second. If you ask it nicely it might condescend to tell you."

"You don't like it," said Grimes.

"I don't like it. To begin with, some of the shipowners—and this is a private enterprise planet, remember—feel that now the bridge can be automated to the same extent as the engine room, with just one man, the Master, in charge, snoring his head off on the chartroom settee and being awakened by an alarm bell just in time to rub the sleep out of his eyes and take his ship into port. But that's not the worst of it. Now the Institute of Marine Engineers is saying, 'If navigation is only a matter of pushing buttons, we're at least as well qualified as deck officers.'"

"I've heard that often enough," said Grimes. "Even in space."

"Does anybody know how these Purcell Navigators work?" asked Sonya.

"No. One of the terms of sale is that they must be installed by technicians from the world of manufacture, Elektra. Another is that they must not, repeat not, be tampered with in any way. As a matter of fact the Chief Electrician of the Carrington Yard did try to find out what made one tick. He was lucky to lose only a hand."

"It seems," said Grimes, "that I came here just in time."

"What do you mean, John?"

"Well, I shall be able to enjoy the last of the old days, the good old days, on Aquarius, and I shall have the material for a few more chapters to my *Times Of Transition*."

"He likes being morbid," said Sonya. "Almost as much as he likes being reactionary."

"Mphm," grunted Grimes. "Old-fashioned sounds better."

He got up from his chair, walked soundlessly over the carpeted floor to the bookshelves that formed a space divider in the huge, circular room that was called the Havenmaster's Lookout. He stared at the rows of books, most of them old (but in recent printings), only a few of them new. And they were *real* books, all of them, not spools of microfilm. There were the standard works on the old arts of the seaman, hopelessly out of date on most worlds, but not (yet) on this one. Brown, Nicholl, Norie, Riesenberg . . . Lecky . . . Thomas . . . And the chronicles of the ancient explorers and navigators: Hakluyt, Dampier, Cook, Flinders, Bligh . . . Then there were the novels: Conrad (of course), McFee, Monsarrat, Herman Wouk, Forester . . . Grimes's hand went out to Melville's *Moby Dick*, and he remembered that odd Hall of Fame to which he had been whisked from the mountaintop on Kinsolving, and felt regret that he had not been able to meet Lieutenant Commander Queeg, Admiral Hornblower and Captain Ahab. (Were there any white whales in the Aquarian seas?)

He turned, saw that his wife and Captain Thornton had risen from their own seats, were standing staring out through the huge window that formed the entire outer wall of the Lookout that, in its turn, was the top level of the two thousand foot high Havenmaster's Control Tower. Above it was only the mast from which sprouted antennae, radar scanners, anemometers and the like, that was topped by the powerful, group-flashing Steep Island light.

Grimes walked slowly to join Sonya and his host, gazed out through the clear glass into the darkness. At regular intervals the beam of the light, a sword of misty radiance, swept overhead. Far to the south, a loom of luminescence on the distant sea horizon, was Port Stellar, and to east and west, fainter still, were other hazy luminosities, island cities, island states. Almost directly below was a great passenger liner, from this height no more than a gaudy, glittering insect crawling over the black carpet of the sea.

In spite of the insulation, the soundproofing, the thin, high whine of the wind was evident.

Sonya shivered. "The winds of change are blowing," she whispered.

"A seaman should be able to cope with the wind," said the Havenmaster. Then, to Grimes, "I wonder how you'll cope, John? I've arranged for you to take over *Sonya Winneck* at Port Stellar tomorrow."

"I'll get by," said Grimes.

"He always does," said Sonya. "Somehow."

Grimes fell in love with *Sonya Winneck* from the very start. She was, of course, his first sea command; nonetheless, she made an immediate appeal to the eye, even to the eye of one who, for all his admiral's commission, had very little practical knowledge of oceangoing ships. The lady was a tramp, but the tramp was also a lady.

Five hundred feet long overall, she was, with a seventy-foot beam. Bridge and funnel—the latter scarlet, with a black top and two narrow black bands—were amidships. Her upperworks and deck cranes were white, her hull green with a yellow ribbon. The boot-topping was red.

There is more to a ship than outward appearance, however. And Grimes, himself a shipmaster of long standing, knew this as well as the most seasoned master mariner on the oceans of Aquarius. But she had, he discovered, a fair turn of speed, her diesel-electric drive pushing her through the water at a good twenty knots. She was single screw, with a right-handed propeller. Her wheelhouse and chartroom reminded him almost of the spaceships that he was accustomed to command, but the electronic gadgetry was not unfamiliar to him after the sessions he had put in on the various simulators in the Havenmaster's Control Tower. The only thing that he did not like was the Purcell Navigator squatting like a sinister octopus in its own cage abaft the chartroom. Oh, well, he would make sure that his young gentlemen had no truck with the electronic monster. He hoped.

"I don't like it either," said the tall, skinny, morose Captain

Harrell, whom Grimes was relieving. "But it works. Even I have to admit that. It works."

Then Harrell led Grimes down to the big, comfortable day cabin where the two wives—Mrs. Harrell very dumpy and mousy alongside the slender Sonya—were waiting. The Harrells' baggage, packed and ready to be carried ashore, was against one bulkhead. On a table stood bottles and glasses, a bowl of cracked ice. The officers came in then, neat in their slate grey shirt-and-shorts uniforms, their black, gold-braided shoulderboards, to say good-bye to their old captain, to greet their new one. There was Wilcox, Chief Officer, a burly, blond young (but not too young) giant. There was Andersen, the Second, another giant, but red-haired. There was Viccini, the Third, slight and dark. And Jones, the Engineer, a fat, bald man who could have been any age, came up to be introduced, and with him he brought Mary Hales, the Electrician, a fragile, silver-headed little girl who looked incapable of changing a fuse. Finally there came Sally Fielding, Stewardess-Purser, plump and motherly.

Glasses were charged. "Well, Captain," began Harrell. "Or should I say Commodore, or Admiral?"

"Captain," Grimes told him.

"Well, Captain, your name's on the Register and the Articles. You've signed the Receipt for Items Handed Over. You've a good ship, and a good team of officers. Happy sailing!"

"Happy sailing," everybody repeated.

"Thank you, Captain," replied Grimes. "And I'm sure that we all wish you an enjoyable leave."

"And how are you spending it, Mrs, Harrell?" asked Sonya.

"We've a yacht," the other woman told her. "Most of the time we shall be cruising around the Coral Sea."

"A busman's holiday," commented Grimes.

"Not at all," Harrell told him, grinning for the first time. "There'll just be the two of us, so there'll be no crew problems. And no electronic gadgetry to get in my hair either."

"Happy sailing," said Grimes, raising his glass.

"Happy sailing," they all said again.

❧❧❧❧❧

And it was happy sailing at first.

It did not take Grimes long to find his feet, his sea legs. "After all," he said to Sonya, "a ship is a ship is a ship . . ." He had been afraid at first that his officers and crew would resent him, an outsider appointed to command with no probationary period in the junior grades—but there hung about him the spurious glamour of that honorary admiral's commission, and his reputation as a maritime historian earned him respect. *Sonya Winneck*'s people knew that he was on Aquarius to do a job, a useful job, and that his sailing as master of her was part of it.

Sonya enjoyed herself too. She made friends with the other women aboard: with Mary Hales, with Sally Fielding, with the darkly opulent Vanessa Wilcox, who had joined just before departure from Port Stellar, with Tessa and Teena, the Assistant Stewardesses, with the massive Jemima Brown who was queen of the beautifully mechanized galley. This shipboard life—*surface* shipboard life—was all so new to her, in spite of its inevitable resemblances to life aboard a spaceship. There was so much to see, so much to inquire into . . .

The weather was fine, mainly, with warm days and nights with just sufficient chill to provide a pleasant contrast. Grimes played with the sextant he had purchased in Port Stellar, became skilled in its use, taking altitude after altitude of the sun, of the planet's two moons, of such stars, planets and artificial satellites as were visible at morning and evening twilight. His officers watched with a certain amusement as he plotted position after position on the working chart, congratulated him when these coincided with those for the same times shown on the chart that was displayed on the screen of the Purcell Navigator. And they, he was pleased to note, tended to ignore that contraption, consulting it only when there was a wide variance between positions taken by two observers.

A shipmaster, however, is more than a navigator. Pilotage was not compulsory for the majority of the ports visited by *Sonya Winneck*, although in each one of them pilots were available. Grimes had taken a pilot sailing from Port Stellar, but after the six-day run between that harbor and Tallisport decided to try to berth the ship himself. After all, he had spent hours in the simulator and, since joining his ship, had read Ardley's *Harbor Pilotage* from cover to cover.

This book, a standard Terran twentieth-century work on the handling and mooring of ships, had been given him by the Havenmaster, who had said, "You should find this useful, John. Ardley was one of *the* authorities of his time. One thing I like about him—he says that anchors are there to be used. For maneuvering, I mean . . ." He laughed, then added, "But don't go making too much of a habit of it. It annoys chief officers!"

And so, having made a careful study of the large-scale chart, the plan and the "sailing directions," Grimes stood in to Tallisport shortly after sunrise. The wheel was manned, the engines on standby. According to the Tide Tables it was just two hours after first high water, which meant that *Sonya Winneck* would be stemming the ebb on her way in. (But, Wilcox had told him, complications were bound to crop up in this river harbor. All wharfage was on the western bank of the river, on the starboard hand entering—and to berth starboard side to is to risk damage in a vessel with a right-handed single screw, especially when the master is an inexperienced ship handler. Sometimes, however, an eddy, a countercurrent, set strongly along the line of wharfage, giving the effect of flood tide. If this eddy were running—and only visual observation when approaching the berth would confirm this or not—Grimes would be able to bring the ship's head to starboard, letting go the starboard anchor to stub her around, and then ease her alongside, port side to, with the anchor still on the bottom.)

Grimes stood into Tallisport. With his naked eye he could now see the Main Leads, two white towers, nicely in line. He told the Harbor Quartermaster to steer for them, to keep them right ahead. Yes, and there was the breakwater to port, with its red beacon . . . The red beacon was abeam now, and *Sonya Winneck* was sweeping into the harbor in fine style.

"Hadn't you better reduce speed, sir?" suggested the Third Officer.

"Mphm. Thank you, Mr. Viccini. Better make it slow—no, dead slow." "Dead slow, sir."

The rhythmic thudding of the diesel generators was unchanged, but there was a subtle diminution of vibration as the propeller revolutions decreased. The Main Leads were still ahead, but coming abeam to starboard were the two white obelisks that were the Leads into the Swinging Basin. "Port ten degrees," ordered Grimes. Would it be enough? Then he saw the ship's head swinging easily, heard the clicking of the gyro repeater. "Midships. Steady!"

He went out to the starboard wing of the bridge, looked aft. The Swinging Basin Leads were coming into line astern nicely. "Steady as you go!" he called.

Now *Sonya Winneck* was creeping up the last navigable reach of the river. To starboard was the line of wharfage, and behind it the clumps of greenery, spangled with blossoms like jewels, the white-walled houses, all clean and bright in the morning sun. But Grimes had no eye for scenery; he was too new to the game. Through his binoculars he studied the quay at which he was to berth, the furthest up river. Beyond it was a mess of dredging equipment, all part and parcel of the port expansion plan. Which side to would it be? He had still to make up his mind.

"Sir," said the Third Officer.

"Yes?"

"It doesn't look as though the eddy, the countercurrent, is running, sir."

"What makes you think that, Mr. Viccini?"

The young man pointed to the small craft—a yacht, two fishing vessels—past which they were sliding. Their upstream moorings were bar taut, their downstream lines hanging in bights. "Mphm," grunted Grimes. So it was ebb all over the river. He made up his mind. "Tell the Chief and Second Officers it will be starboard side to. Tell Mr. Wilcox to have his port anchor ready."

He came to starboard, lined the ship's head up on the up river end of the wharf. With his mouth whistle he blew one short, sharp blast. The chain cable of the port anchor rattled out through the pipe, the grip of the flukes in the mud acted as a brake. *Sonya Winneck* was still making way, but with the ebb against her and the drag of the anchor she was almost stopped.

This, thought Grimes, *is easy,* as he nosed in toward his berth.

But there was an eddy after all, and as soon as the ship was well inside it she was swept upstream toward the dredges, buoys and pipelines. "Hard a-starboard!" Grimes ordered. The anchor was still holding, luckily, and it acted as a fulcrum, checking the upstream motion of the stem while the stern was free to swing. The vessel was broadside on to the line of the river now, still approaching the wharf, but head on.

"Swing her, sir," suggested Viccini. "Get a headline ashore and tell the linesmen to run it to the down-river end of the berth . . ."

Yes, thought Grimes, *it'll work. It'd better . . .*

A heaving line snaked ashore from the fo'c'sle head, was caught by one of the waiting linesmen. He and another man ran with it to the post indicated by the Chief Officer. Then the self-tensioning winch, whining, took the weight. Belatedly Grimes thought that he had better stop the engines, had better go astern before the ship's stem crashed through the wharf stringer. But the order had been anticipated. *A good lad, Viccini . . .* he thought. *But he'd better not make a habit of this sort of thing.*

Now *Sonya Winneck*'s bows were being pulled downriver against the countercurrent, her stern still only a few feet from the stringer, the stern swinging in easily. "Stop her," Grimes ordered. She was alongside now, with the very gentlest of impacts, and the leading hand of the mooring gang was shouting up that she was in position.

Grimes filled and lit his pipe. "Make fast fore and aft," he said. "That'll do the wheel. Finished with engines." And then, "Mr. Viccini, I appreciate your help. Don't get me wrong, I like an officer to show initiative. But I think you should try to remember there's only one Master on the bridge."

"But, sir . . ."

"That's all right, Mr. Viccini. You did the right things, and I appreciate it. I'll try to do the right things myself in future."

Probably the Third Officer would have made a full explanation to Grimes during the day, but as soon as the gangway was out the Winneck Line's local agent came aboard with the mail, and among it was a letter saying that Viccini was to be paid off to commence his annual leave and would be relieved that morning by a Mr. Denham.

Sonya Winneck continued her steady, round-the-planet progress, rarely straying north or south of the tropics. The met. screen in the chartroom rarely showed indications of disturbed weather conditions, and when it did these were invariably hundreds of miles from the ship's track. It was, Mr. Wilcox said to Grimes, the sort of weather you sign on for. The days and the nights passed pleasantly. At sea, there was sunbathing, swimming in the ship's pool that, when inflated, occupied all the foredeck between the forward and after cranes of the main hatch, deck golf and, in the evenings, a variety of games or a wide selection of programs on the playmasters installed throughout the accommodation. In port, the day's business over, there was so much to see, so much to do. There was *real* swimming from sun-washed, golden beaches, and surfing; and now and again Grimes was able to hire a small sailing yacht for the day and found this sport much more enjoyable than on the lakes of Lorn, where there was wind enough but it was always bitter. There were the waterfront taverns—and both Grimes and Sonya loved seafood. The Terran lobster, prawn, oyster and herring had all done well in the Aquarian seas, and there were the local delicacies: the sand crawlers, which were something like Earth's trilobites must have been, the butterfly fish and the sea steaks.

It was, for both of them, a holiday, but for Sonya it was a holiday that palled in time. It was all right for Grimes; he had his navigation to play with, his pilotage and, when he got around to it, research to carry out on the projected history and a chapter or so of it to write. His wife, however, was becoming bored.

It was a longish run between Lynnhaven and Port Johnson, all of seven days. During it Sonya found stacks of magazines in one of the lockers in the ship's office, back numbers of the *Merchant Shipping Journal*, dating back for years. She brought a pile of them up to the master's day cabin. She said, "These could be useful to you, John." Grimes picked one up, leafed through it. "Mphm. All rather *dry* stuff. At the moment I'm trying to get the essential *feel* of this planet."

"But they're full of information."

"So's a dictionary."

She said, "Suppose I go through them, making notes of anything that might be useful to you . . ."

"That," he told her, "is very sweet of you, Sonya."

She made a grimace at him, then settled down with the supply of factual reading matter. Everything was there: specifications of new tonnage, sales, breakings up, wrecks, strandings, collisions, courts of inquiry. These latter were of interest to her. She could see how, time and time again, the unfortunate Master was given only seconds to decide what to do, while learned judges, counsel and marine assessors had weeks to decide what should have been done. And then, as she read on, nagging hints of some sort of pattern began to form in her mind, her trained mind. After all, she had been an intelligence officer, and a good one, in the Federation's Survey Service.

It seemed to her that the Winneck Line ships were getting into more than their fair share of trouble, with Lone Star Line running a close second. She knew little about the Lone Star Line, although she had seen their ships often enough in various ports and, with Grimes, had been a guest aboard a few of them for drinks and meals. They were well-run, well-maintained vessels. She could speak with more authority regarding the Winneck Line; *Sonya Winneck* was typical of their newer tonnage. There wasn't the same spit and polish as in the Lone Star, but there was a very real efficiency.

She read again the details of one of the collision cases. *Olga Winneck* had been bound up the Great Muddy River to Steelport, *Suzanne Winneck* had been outbound. The ships had passed each other—or had attempted to pass each other—in Collier's Reach, the navigable channel in that locality being both deep and wide. Suddenly *Olga Winneck* had taken a sheer to port and, in spite of the efforts of both Masters to avert collision, had struck *Suzanne Winneck* on her port quarter, holing her so badly that she was obliged to return to dock for repairs.

There was the transcription of evidence:

Mr. Younghusband (counsel for Havenmaster's Office): Can you tell me, Mr. Margolies, what orders were given by Captain Hazzard?

Mr. Margolies (Third Officer of *Olga Winneck*): Yes, sir. The Master ordered, "Hard a-starboard! Stop engines! Full astern!"

Mr. Younghusband: And were these orders carried out?

Mr. Margolies: Of course. I at once put the controls to full astern.

Mr. Younghusband: And what about the wheel? Quartermasters have been known to put the helm the wrong way, especially in an emergency.

Mr. Margolies: The quartermaster put the wheel hard to starboard.

Mr. Younghusband: And did you look at the rudder indicator? It has been suggested that steering gear failure was a cause of the collision.

Mr. Margolies: Yes, I looked. The pointer was hard over to starboard.

And so it went on. It was established finally that both Masters had done all the right things, although Captain Hazzard should have realized that a delay was inevitable when switching directly from full ahead to full astern. It was thought that a tidal eddy had been responsible for the collision. The court recommended that ships passing in Collier's Reach keep each well to their own sides of the channel, also that speed be reduced.

That was one case. There were others, and Sonya made notes, drew up tables. There had been collisions in narrow channels and in the open sea. Some had been in clear weather, some in conditions of reduced visibility. The causes were various: tidal eddies, steering gear failure, radar breakdown and, inevitably, errors of judgment. And the Winneck Line and the Lone Star Line were having more than their fair share of marine casualties . . . It was odd, she thought. Odd. There was something rotten in the state of Aquarius.

She asked Grimes if she could browse through the ship's files of correspondence. He said, "Of course. They aren't top secret." She found the one labeled *Damage Reports*. It wasn't especially bulky. But its contents were interesting.

"Sir, (she read)

I regret to have to report that whilst berthing this morning at

No.3 Inner East, Port Kantor, the stem of the vessel came into heavy contact with the starboard side of the Lone Star Line's *Canopic*. Damage to *Sonya Winneck* was superficial only—please see enclosed sketch—but that to the other ship was considerable and, I am informed by *Canopic*'s master, will necessitate dry-docking.

I entered the harbor at 0545 hrs., standing in on the Main Leads. When clear of the breakwaters I reduced to dead slow and altered course to port, steering for the shore end of No.3 Jetty. Visibility was good, wind was ENE at about 10 knots, tidal influence, it being just after low water slack, was negligible.

When my bridge was just abeam of *Canopic*'s stern, however, *Sonya Winneck* took a sudden sheer to port. I at once ordered a hard a-starboard, stopped the engines and ordered full astern. Also I signaled to the Chief Officer to let go the starboard anchor, but unfortunately it jammed in the pipe, and was released too late to have any effect. In spite of the application of full starboard rudder and full stern power, contact occurred at 0555 hrs.

It is possible that I underestimated the force of the wind while standing in to my berth, but, even so, find it hard to account for the sudden sheer to port . . ."

But *Sonya Winneck* was sometimes at the receiving end.

"Sir,

I have to report that this afternoon, at 1327 hrs., the vessel was struck by the Company's *Elizabeth Winneck*, which same was proceeding down river, bound for sea. Unfortunately, it being Saturday afternoon, with no work in progress, no officers were on deck at the time of the contact, and the Company's gangway watchman was at his place of duty, at the head of the gangway, on the inshore side of the vessel.

Damage, fortunately, was not extensive and all above the waterline. My Chief Officer's report is enclosed herewith. No doubt you will be hearing from Captain Pardoe of *Elizabeth Winneck* . . ."

There were several more letters, some going into great detail, others composed on the good old principle of "least said, soonest mended." With two exceptions the other ships concerned were units of either the Winneck or the Lone Star fleets. One of the exceptions was the contact with *Iron Duchess*. On that occasion Captain Harrell, Grimes's predecessor, had been trying to berth his ship during a howling gale. The other occasion was a collision with a ferry steamer in Carrington Harbor, with fortunately no loss of life.

So, Sonya wondered, just what was the connection between the Winneck Line and the Lone Star Line? She borrowed from the Chief Officer's office the bulky *Aquarian Registry* in which was listed comprehensive details of all the commercial shipping of the planet. Against the name of each ship were the lines of information: tonnage, gross, net and deadweight; propulsion; speed; length overall, length between posts, breadth . . . And builders.

She looked up her namesake first. She had been built by the Carrington State Dockyard. She looked up *Canopic*. Her builders were Varley's Dockyard, in Steelport. She looked up *Elizabeth Winneck*—another Varley's job. So it went on. The majority of the collisions had occurred between ships constructed at those two yards.

And what about the contact that her husband, Grimes, had so narrowly averted, that time coming into Newhaven? What was the name of the ship that he had almost (but not quite) hit? *Orionic* . . . She looked it up. Carrington State Dockyard. She murmured, "All us Carrington girls must stick together . . ."

"What was that?" demanded Grimes, looking up from his book.

"Just a thought," she told him. "Just a passing thought."

"Mphm."

"Do ships *really* have personalities?" she asked.

He grinned. "Spacemen and seamen like to kid themselves that they do. Look at it this way. You're bringing a ship in—a spaceship or a surface ship—and you've failed to allow for *all* the factors affecting her handling. Your landing or berthing isn't up to your usual standard. But you kid yourself, and your officers that it wasn't *your* fault. You say, 'She was a proper little bitch, wasn't she? Wouldn't do a thing right . . .' But *you* were the one who wasn't doing a thing right."

She said, "I've handled ships too."

"I know, my dear. I've seen you do it. Your landing technique is a little too flashy for my taste."

"Never mind that now. I'm talking about surface ships. Is there any reason to believe, John, that two ships built to the same design, but in different yards, would have conflicting personalities?"

Grimes was starting to get annoyed with his wife. "Damn it all," he expostulated, "spacemen's superstitions are bad enough! But I'm surprised that you, of all people, should pay any heed to seamen's superstitions."

"But are they superstitions? Couldn't a machine absorb, somehow, something of the personalities of the people who built it, the people who handle it?"

"Hogwash," said Grimes.

"If that's the way you feel about it . . ." She slumped in her deep chair, struck a cigarillo on her thumbnail, put it to her mouth, looked at her husband through the wreathing smoke. "All right. Before you get back to your precious research, what do the initials P N mean?"

"In what context?"

Sonya nudged with a slim, sandaled foot the bulky *Aquarian Registry*, which lay open on the deck in front of her. "It's printed against the names of some of the ships, the newer ships—but only those built by the Carrington State Dockyard or Varley's."

"P . . . N . . ." muttered Grimes. "P . . . N . . . ? We can ask the Mate, I suppose . . ."

"But you don't like to," she scoffed. "You're the Captain, you know everything."

"Almost everything," he qualified smugly. The ship lurched suddenly, and Grimes knew the reason. When last he had been on the bridge he had been slightly perturbed by the chart presented in the met. screen, televised from one of the weather satellites. Ahead of *Sonya Winneck* was a deepening depression, almost stationary. He had considered altering course to try to avoid it—but, after all, he had a big, powerful ship under his feet, well found, stoutly constructed. And, he had thought, he would not like to be remembered on this world as a fair weather sailor. Even so, he saw in his mind's eye that chart—the crowded isobars, the wind arrows with their clockwise circulation. Now the heavy swell running outward from the center, like ripples from a pebble dropped into a pond, was beginning to make itself felt. He looked at the aneroid barometer on the bulkhead. The needle had fallen ten millibars since he had last set the pointer, two hours ago.

He said, "I fear we're in for a dirty night."

She said, "It's what you're paid for."

He grunted, got up from his chair, went up to the bridge by the inside companionway to the chartroom. He looked at the instruments over the chart table. According to the Chernikeeff Log, speed through the water had already dropped by half a knot. The barograph showed a fairly steep fall in pressure. The met. screen, set for the area through which the ship was passing, showed a chart almost identical with the one that he had last seen.

He went out to the bridge. The sky was mainly overcast now, with the larger of the two Aquarian moons, almost full, showing fitfully through ragged breaks in the cloud. There was high altitude wind, although it had yet to be felt at sea level. But the swell seemed to be increasing.

Young Mr. Denham, the Third Officer, came across from the wing of the bridge. He said, rather too cheerfully, "Looks like a blow, sir."

"We can't expect fine weather all the time," Grimes told him. He stood with his legs well apart, braced against the motion of the ship. He wondered if he would be seasick, then consoled himself with the thought that both the actual Lord Nelson and the fictional Lord Hornblower had been afflicted by this malady.

Mr. Denham—since Grimes had torn that strip off him regarding the unauthorized engine movements he had tended to overcompensate—went on chirpily, "At this time of the year, sir, the revolving storms in these waters are unpredictable. In theory the center should be traveling east, away from us, but in practice it's liable to do anything."

"Oh?"

"Yes, sir. I remember one when I was in the old *Sally—Sara Winneck*, that is. Captain Tregenza tried to outmaneuver it; we had a pile of deck cargo that trip, teak logs from Port Mandalay. But it was almost as though it had a brain of its own. Finally it sat right on top of us and matched speed and course, no matter which way we steered. We lost all the cargo off the foredeck, and the wheelhouse windows were smashed in . . ."

Cheerful little swine . . . thought Grimes. He stared ahead into the intermittently moonlit night, at the long swell that was coming in at an angle to the ship's course. *Sonya Winneck*'s bows lifted then dipped, plunging into and through the moving dune of water. They lifted again, and a white cascade poured aft from the break of the fo'c'sle, spangled with jewels of luminescence. Grimes said, "Anyhow, we have no deck cargo this trip."

"No, sir."

He remained on the bridge a while longer. There was nothing that he could do, and he knew it. The ship was far from unseaworthy, capable of riding out a hurricane. There was ample sea room; the Low Grenadines were many miles to the north of her track. And yet he felt uneasy, could not shake off a nagging premonition. Something, he somehow knew, was cooking. But what, when and where?

At last he grunted, "You know where to find me if you want me. Good night, Mr. Denham."

"Good night, sir."

Back in his quarters his uneasiness persisted. He told Sonya that he would sleep on the settee in his day cabin, so as to be more readily available in the event of any emergency. She did not argue with him; she, too, felt a growing tension in the air. It could have been that she was sensitive to his moods but, she told him, she didn't think so. She quoted, *"By the pricking of my thumbs something wicked this way comes."*

He laughed. "A tropical revolving storm is not wicked, my dear. Like any other manifestation of the forces of nature it is neither good nor evil."

She repeated, "Something wicked this way comes."

They said good night then, and she retired to the bedroom and he disposed himself comfortably on the settee. He was rather surprised that sleep was not long in coming.

But he did not enjoy his slumber for more than a couple of hours. A particularly violent lurch awakened him, almost pitched him off his couch. He switched on a light, looked at the aneroid barometer. The needle was down another twenty millibars. And, in spite of the well-insulated plating of the accommodation, he could hear the wind, both hear and feel the crash of the heavy water on deck. He thrust his feet into his sandals and, clad only in his shorts (Master's privilege) went up to the bridge. He found the Second Officer—it was now the middle watch—in the wheelhouse, looking ahead through the big clear view screen. Grimes joined him. When his eyes became accustomed to the semi-darkness he could see that the wind was broad on the starboard bow; he could see, too, that with each gust it was veering, working gradually around from southeast to south. *Southern Hemisphere*, he thought. *Clockwise circulation, and the low barometer on my left hand* . . . Now that he had something to work on he might as well avoid the center with its confused, heavy seas. "Bring her round to starboard easily," he told the Second Officer. "Bring wind and sea ahead."

"Wind and sea ahead, sir." The officer went to the controls of the autopilot. Grimes watched the bows swinging slowly, then said, "That should do, Mr. Andersen."

"Course one three five now, sir."

Grimes went back into the chartroom, looked down at the chart, busied himself briefly with parallel rulers and dividers. He grunted his satisfaction. This new course took him even further clear of the Low Grenadines, that chain of rocky islets that were little more than reefs. There was nothing to worry about.

He was aware that Sonya was standing behind him; there was a hint of her perfume, the awareness of her proximity. He said without turning around, "Passengers not allowed on the bridge."

She asked, "Where are we?"

He indicated with the points of the dividers the penciled cross of the position, the new course line extending from it. "I'm more or less, not quite heaving to. But she's easier on this heading, and it pulls her away from the eye of the storm."

She said, "There's a lot to be said for spaceships. They don't pitch and roll. When you're in your virtuous couch you're not slung out of it."

"We take what comes," he told her.

"We haven't much option, have we?"

Then they went below again, and she made coffee, and they talked for awhile, and eventually Grimes settled down to another installment of his broken night's sleep.

The next time he awakened it was by the insistent buzzing of the bridge telephone, which was in his bedroom. He rolled off the settee, stumbled through the curtained doorway. Sonya, looking rather hostile, lifted the instrument off its rest, handed it to him.

"Master here," said Grimes into the mouthpiece.

"Second Officer, sir. There's a Mayday . . ."

"I'll be right up."

The Second Mate was in the chartroom, plotting positions on the chart. He straightened as Grimes came in, turned to speak to him. "It's *Iron Warrior*, sir. One of their big bulk carriers. She's broken down, lying in the trough, and her cargo's shifted. Zinc concentrates."

"Not good. Where is she?"

The young man stood away from the chart so that Grimes could see, indicated the other ship's position with the point of a pencil. "Here, sir. Just twenty miles south of the Low Grenadines. And she reports a southerly gale, the same as we're getting."

"Not good," said Grimes again. "Not good at all. She'll be making leeway, drifting . . ." Swiftly he measured the distance between *Sonya Winneck*'s last recorded position—electronic navigation had its good points!—and that given by the disabled ship. One hundred and fifty nautical miles . . . And *Sonya Winneck* would have to turn, putting the wind right aft. With her high superstructure this should mean a marked increase of speed . . . Suppose she made twenty knots over the ground . . . Twenty into one hundred and fifty . . . Seven and a half hours . . . He looked at the chartroom clock. Oh three thirty . . .

"Put your standby man on the wheel, Mr. Andersen," he ordered. "I'm bringing her round manually."

He went out into the wheelhouse. Both moons were down, but the sky had cleared. Overhead the scattered stars were bright; and bright, too, were the living stars thrown aloft and back in the sheets of spray each time that the ship's prow crashed down to meet the racing seas. Grimes stood there, waiting, hoping for a lull, however brief. He glanced behind him, saw that the wheel was manned and that Andersen was standing beside the helmsman.

He looked ahead again. It seemed to him that the pitching of the ship was a little less pronounced, that sea and swell were a little less steep. "Port," he ordered. "Easily, easily . . ." He heard the clicking of the gyro-repeater as the ship's head started to come round. And then he saw it, broad on the starboard bow, a towering cliff of water, white capped, a freak sea. "Hard a-port!" Grimes shouted. "Hard over!"

She responded beautifully, and the clicking of the repeater was almost one continuous note. She responded beautifully, but not quite fast enough. The crest of the dreadful sea was overhanging the bridge now, poised to fall and smash. Still she turned, and then she heeled far over to port, flinging Grimes and the Second Officer and the helmsman into an untidy huddle on that side of the wheelhouse. She shuddered as the tons of angry water crashed down to her poop, surged forward along her decks, even onto the bridge itself. There was a banging and clattering of loose gear, cries and screams from below. But miraculously she steadied, righted herself, surging forward with only a not very violent pitching motion.

Somehow Grimes got to his feet, disentangling himself from the other two men. He staggered to the untended wheel, grasped the spokes. He looked at the repeater card. Three two oh . . . Carefully he applied starboard rudder, brought the lubber's line to the course that had been laid off on the chart, three three five. He saw that Andersen and the seaman had recovered their footing, were standing by awaiting further orders.

"Put her back on automatic," he told the Second Officer. "On this course." He relinquished the wheel as soon as this had been done. "Then take your watch with you and make rounds through the accommodation. Let me know if anybody's been hurt."

"Who the hell's rocking the bloody boat?" It was Wilcox, the Chief Officer. Then, as he saw Grimes by the binnacle, "Sorry, sir."

"It's an emergency, Mr. Wilcox. A Mayday call. *Iron Warrior*, broken down and drifting on to the Low Grenadines. We're going to her assistance."

"What time do you estimate that we shall reach her, Captain?"

"About eleven hundred hours."

"I'd better start getting things ready," replied the Mate.

Grimes went back into the chartroom, to the transceiver that had been switched on as soon as the auto-alarm had been actuated by the Mayday call. "*Sonya Winneck* to Ocean Control, Area Five," he said.

"Ocean Control to *Sonya Winneck*. I receive you. Pass your message."

"I am now proceeding to the assistance of *Iron Warrior*. Estimated time of visual contact ten thirty hours, Zone Plus Seven."

"Thank you, *Sonya Winneck*. *Pleiaidic* cannot be in the vicinity until thirteen hundred hours at the earliest. Please use Channel Six when working *Iron Warrior*. Call me on Sixteen to keep me informed. Over."

He switched to Channel Six. "*Sonya Winneck* to *Iron Warrior*..."

"*Iron Warrior* here, *Sonya Winneck*." The other Captain's voice, was, perhaps, a little too calm.

"How are things with you, *Iron Warrior*?"

"Bloody awful, to be frank. A twenty degree list, and my boats and rafts smashed on the weather side. Estimated rate of drift, two knots."

"I should be with you in seven hours," said Grimes. "I shall try to take you in tow."

"We'll have everything ready, Captain,"

"Good. We shall be seeing you shortly. Over and standing by."

Wilcox had come into the chartroom. He said, "Everybody's been informed, sir. The Chief reckons that he can squeeze out another half knot."

"Anybody hurt when she went over?"

"Only minor lacerations and contusions, sir."

"Such as this," announced Sonya, who had joined the others in the chartroom, putting a cautious hand up to the beginnings of a black eye. "But it's in a good cause."

Iron Warrior was not a pretty sight.

She lay wallowing in a welter of white water, like a dying sea beast. The seas broke over her rust-colored hull in great explosions of spray, but now and again, during brief lulls, the extent of the damage that she had sustained could be made out. She was a typical bulk carrier, with all the accommodation aft, with only a stumpy mast right forward and her mainmast growing out of her funnel, and no cargo gear but for one crane on the poop for ship's stores and the like. That crane, Grimes could see through his binoculars, was a twisted tangle of wreckage. That would explain why the *Warrior*'s Captain had not used oil to minimize the effect of breaking waves; probably the entrance to the storerooms was blocked. And there must be some other reason why it had not been possible to pump diesel fuel overside—even though a mineral oil is not as effective as vegetable or animal oil it is better than nothing. The side of the bridge seemed to be stove in, and under the boat davits dangled a mess of fiberglass splinters.

Beyond her—and not far beyond her, a mere three miles—was the black, jagged spine of Devlin's Islet, dead to leeward. It seemed more alive, somehow, than the stricken ship, looked like a great, malevolent sea monster creeping nearer and ever nearer through the boiling surf toward its dying prey.

Grimes was using oil, a thin trickle of it from his scuppers, wads of waste soaked in it thrown overside to leeward. Luckily there had been plenty of it in *Sonya Winneck*'s storerooms—fish oil for the preservation of exposed wire ropes, a heavy vegetable oil for the treatment of wooden decks and brightwork. It was beginning to have effect; the thin, glistening surface film was a skin over the water between the two ships, an integument that contained the sea, forcing some semblance of form upon it. The swell was still there—heavy, too heavy—but the waves were no longer breaking, their violence suppressed.

Aft, Andersen and his men were standing by the rocket gun. The heavy insurance wire was already flaked out ready for running, its inboard end taken not only around both pairs of bitts—these, in a ship with self-tensioning winches, were rarely used for mooring, but there was always the possibility of a tow—but also around the poop house. The sisal messenger was coiled down handy to the line-throwing apparatus.

On the bridge, Grimes conned his ship. She was creeping along parallel to *Iron Warrior* now, at reduced speed. She was making too much leeway for Grimes's taste; unless he was careful there would be two wrecks instead of only one. Too, with the swell broad on the beam *Sonya Winneck* was rolling heavily, so much so that accurate shooting would be impossible. But the necessary maneuvers had been worked out in advance. At the right moment Grimes would come hard to port, presenting his stern to the *Iron Warrior*. Andersen would loose off his rocket, aiming for a point just abaft the break of the other ship's fo'c'sle head, where men were already standing by. They would grab the light, nylon rocket line, use it to pull aboard the heavier messenger, use that to drag the end of the towing wire aboard, shackling it to the port anchor cable. After that, it would be plain sailing (Grimes hoped). He would come ahead slowly, slowly, taking the weight gently, trying to avoid the imposition of overmuch strain on either vessel. Slowly but surely he would pull the wounded *Warrior* away from the hostile fortifications. (*Come off it, Grimes,* he told himself sternly. *Don't be so bloody literary.*)

"Hard a-port!" he ordered.

"Hard a-port, sir!" The clicking of the repeater was audible above the shrieking of the wind.

"Ease her . . . Midships . . . Steady! Steady as you go!"

Sonya Winneck hung there, her stern a bare two cables from the side of *Iron Warrior*. Grimes thought, *I cut that ratlier too close. But at this range it'll be impossible for Andersen to miss.* To the Third Officer, at the radar, he called, "Are we opening the range?"

"Slowly, sir."

It was time that Andersen got his rocket away. The ship was not pitching too badly; firing at just the right moment should not be difficult. As long as the missile passed over the target it would be a successful shot. Grimes went out to the wing of the bridge to watch. The air scoop dodger deflected the wind, throwing it up and over, so it was not too uncomfortable away from the wheelhouse.

Andersen fired—and at precisely the wrong moment the ship's head fell off heavily to starboard. The rocket streaked through the air, arcing high, a brief orange flare against the gray, ragged clouds, a streamer of white smoke, and behind it the fluorescent yellow filament of the nylon line. Inevitably it missed, finally splashing to the sea well forward of and beyond *Iron Warrior*'s bows.

Grimes didn't see it drop. He stormed into the wheel-house, bawled at the helmsman, "What the hell do you think you're playing at?"

"It's the wheel, sir," The man's voice was frightened. "It turned in my hands. I can't budge it!"

The ship was coming round still, turning all the time to starboard. The gale force wind and her own engines were driving her down on to the helpless *Warrior*. "Stop her!" ordered Grimes. "Full astern!"

Denham was still at the radar, so Wilcox jumped to the engine controls. He slammed the lever hard over to the after position. Still the ship was making headway—but, at last slowing. She stopped at last, her stern scant feet from *Iron Warrior*'s exposed side. Grimes could see the white faces of her people as they stared at him, as they watched, in horrified disbelief, this rescuer turned assassin.

Sonya Winneck was backing away now, her stern coming up into the wind. She was backing away, but reluctantly, Wilcox shouted, "Denham, come and give me a hand! I can't keep this bloody handle down!"

Grimes dragged his attention away from the ship he had so nearly rammed to what was happening on his own bridge. Both the Chief and Third Officer—and Wilcox was a big, strong man—were having to exert all their strength to keep the metal lever in its astern position. It was jerking, forcing itself up against their hands.

Sonya—who until now had been keeping well out of the way—grabbed him by the arm. "Tell the Chief to put the engine controls on manual!" she screamed. "I know what's happening!"

"What's happening?"

"No time now to tell you. Just put her on manual, and get Lecky up here!"

Grimes went to the telephone, rang down to the engine-room. "Manual control, your end, Mr. Jones," he ordered. "Keep her on full astern until I order otherwise. And send Miss Hales up to the bridge. At once."

Thankfully, Wilcox and Denham released their painful grip on the bridge control lever. On the console the revolution indicator still showed maximum stern power. Ahead, the distance between the two ships was fast diminishing. From the VHF transceiver came a frightened voice, "What's happening, *Sonya Winneck?* What's happening?"

"Tell him," said Grimes to Denham, "that we're having trouble with our bridge controls. We'll get a line aboard as soon as we can."

Wilcox, watching the indicator, yelled, "She's stopped! The bitch is coming ahead again!"

Sonya said urgently, "There's only one thing to do, John. Shut off the Purcell Navigator. *Iron Warrior* has P N against her name in the Registry—and she was built by Varley's." She turned to Mary Hales, who had just come onto the bridge. "Mary, switch off that bloody tin brain, or pull fuses, or something—*but kill it!*"

The pretty little blonde was no longer so pretty. On one side of her head the hair was charred and frizzled, and her smooth face was marred by an angry burn. "We've been trying to," she gasped. "The Chief and I. It won't let us."

"She's coming astern again," announced Wilcox. "She's . . . No, she's stopped . . ."

"Watch her, Mr. Wilcox," ordered Grimes. He ran with his wife and the Electrician to the house abaft the chartroom in which the Purcell Navigator lived. It squatted there sullenly on its four stumpy legs, the dials set around its spherical body glaring at them like eyes. From its underside ran armored cables, some thick and some thin— that one leading aft and down must be the main power supply, the ones leading into the wheelhouse and chartroom would be connected to various controls and navigational equipment. On the after bulkhead of the house was a switchboard and fuse box. Mary Hales went straight to this, put out her hand to the main switch. There was a sudden, intense violet flare, a sharp crackling, the tang of overheated metal. The girl staggered back, her blistered hands covering her eyes. "That's what happened to the engine room switchboard!" she wailed. "It's welded itself in the *On* position!" Then, using language more seamanlike than ladylike, she threw herself at the fuse box. She was too late—but perhaps this was as well. Had she got the lid open she would have been blinded.

Still cursing softly, she grabbed a spanner from her belt. Her intention was obvious; she would unscrew the retaining nut holding the main supply lead firmly in its socket. But an invisible force yanked the tool out of her hand, threw it out of the open door.

Grimes watched, helpless. Then he heard Sonya snarling, "Do something. *Do* something, damn you!" She thrust something into his right hand. He looked down at it. It was the big fire ax from its rack in the chartroom. He got both hands about the haft, tried to swing up the head of the weapon, staggered as the magnetic fields which now were the machine's main defense tugged at it. But he lifted the ax somehow, brought it crashing down—and missed his own right foot by a millimeter. Again he raised the ax, straining with all his strength, and again struck at the thick cable. The ship lurched heavily, deflecting his aim, and, fantastically, the magnetic deflection brought the head back to its target. The armored cable writhed away from the blow, but not in time, not enough. The keen edge bit home, in a coruscation of violet sparks. And Mary Hales, with a smaller ax that she had found somewhere, was chopping away, sobbing and cursing; and Sonya was jabbing with a heavy screwdriver at the thing's "eyes"—and so, at last, it died.

And so it died, damaged beyond its built-in powers of self-regeneration. (Mary Hales made sure of that.) And so Grimes was able to get a line aboard *Iron Warrior*, and the *Warrior*'s people got the towing wire shackled onto their anchor cable, and slowly, slowly but surely, the crippled ship was dragged to safety, away from the avidly waiting fangs and talons of Devlin's Islet; the rocky teeth and claws that, when the tow finally commenced, had been less than half a mile distant.

The Purcell Navigator was dead, and its last flares of energy had destroyed or damaged much more than itself. The gyro-compass and the autopilot were inoperative (but the ship had a magnetic compass and hand steering). Loran and radar were burned out, inertial navigator and echometer were beyond repair, even the Chernikeeff

Log was useless. But Grimes was not worried. He had sextant, chronometer, ephemeris and tables—and the great navigators of Earth's past had circled their globe with much less in the way of equipment. In the extremely unlikely event of his not knowing where he was he could always ask *Iron Warrior* for a fix—but he did not think that he would have to do so.

He did, however, urge the *Warrior*'s Master to put his own Purcell Navigator out of commission, explaining why in some detail. Then he went to the house abaft the chartroom where, under the direction of Mary Hales, Wilcox and his men were loosening the holding down bolts, disconnecting the cables that had not already been cut. (There might still be a flicker of life in the thing, some capability of self-repair.) He watched happily as the Mate and three brawny ratings lifted the spherical casing from the deck, staggered with it out the door.

"What shall we do with it, sir?" asked the Mate.

"Give it a buoyancy test," ordered Grimes. He followed the men to the side rail of the bridge, watched as they tipped it over. It sank without a trace.

Grimes was relieved of his command in Longhaven, after the successful completion of the tow, and flown back to Steep Island, accompanied by Sonya. Neither he nor his wife felt very strong when they boarded the airship—the crews of both *Sonya Winneck* and *Iron Warrior* had united in laying on a farewell party more enthusiastic than restrained. ("You *must* be glad to see the back of us," Sonya had remarked at one stage of the proceedings.) Even so, old and tired as he was feeling, Grimes had insisted on seeing the airship's captain so as to be assured that the craft was not fitted with a Purcell Navigator. Then, he and his wife went to their cabin and collapsed into their bunks.

Steep Island, although not officially an airport, had a mooring mast, so a direct flight was possible. When the time came for Grimes and Sonya to disembark they were feeling better and, in fact, had been able to put the finishing touches to their report.

Captain Thornton, the Havenmaster, welcomed them warmly but was obviously anxious to hear what they had to tell him. In minutes only they were all seated in the Havenmaster's Lookout and Thornton was listening intently as they talked.

When they were finished, he smiled grimly, "This is good enough," he said. "It's good enough even for the Council of Master Wardens. I shall issue orders that those infernal machines are to be rendered inoperative in every ship fitted with them, and that no more are to be put aboard any Aquarian vessel. Then we make arrangements to ship them all back to where they came from."

Grimes was surprised, and said so. He was used to having his recommendations adopted eventually, but in most cases there was a lot of argument first.

Thornton laughed. "What you've said is what I've been saying, John, for months. But nobody listens to me. I'm just a reactionary old shellback. But you, sir, as well as being a well-known maritime historian, have also one foot—at least—in what to us is still the future. You're a master astronaut, you hold the rank of commodore in the Space Navy of your Confederacy. They'll listen to you, when they won't listen to me."

"It's Sonya they should listen to," Grimes said. "She's a spacewoman *and* an intelligence officer. She tied the loose ends together."

"But it was all so obvious," she said smugly. "Two yards, and two yards only, on this planet licensed to fit the Purcell Navigator: Varley's and the Carrington State Dockyard. Two ... sororities? Yes, two sororities of ships, the Varley Sisterhood and the Carrington Sisterhood, each hating the other. Limited intelligence, but, somehow, a strong, built-in spite, and also a strong sense of self-preservation. That much, I think, was intended by those electronic geniuses on Elektra—and possibly more, but I'll come to that later.

"Anyhow, if a Carrington sister saw a chance of taking a swipe at a Varley sister without much risk of damage to herself she'd take it. And *vice versa*. Hence all the collisions, and all the minor berthing accidents. Now and again, of course, the sense of self-preservation worked to everybody's benefit . . ." She smiled at her husband rather too sweetly. "I know of at least one bungled berthing where everything, almost miraculously, came right in the end . . ."

"But what's behind it all?" asked the Havenmaster. "You're the Intelligence Officer. Is it, do you think, intentional on somebody's part?"

"I don't know, Tom. I'd have to snoop around on Elecktra to find out, and I doubt if the Elektrans would let me. But try this idea on for size . . . What if the Elektrans want to make Aquarius absolutely dependent upon them?"

"It could be . . ." mused Thornton. "It could be . . ." He went up, walked to the bookshelves, took out a book, opened it. It was Grimes's own *Times Of Transition*. The Havenmaster leafed through it to find the right place. He read aloud, " 'And so was engendered a most unseamanlike breed of navigator, competent enough technicians whose working tools were screwdrivers and voltmeters rather than sextants and chronometers. Of them it could never be said *Every hair a ropeyarn, every fingernail a marlinespike, every drop of blood pure Stockholm tar.* They were servants to rather than masters of their machines, and ever they were at the mercy of a single fuse . . .'" He shut the book with a slam. He said, "It can't happen here."

"Famous last words," scoffed Sonya, but her voice was serious.

"It mustn't happen here," said Grimes.

The Man Who Sailed The Sky

It was fortunate, Sonya always said, that the Federation Survey Service's *Star Pioneer* dropped down to Port Stellar, on Aquarius, when she did. Had not transport back to the Rim Worlds, although it was by a roundabout route, become available it is quite possible that her husband would have become a naturalized Aquarian citizen. Seafaring is no more (and no less) a religion than spacefaring; be that as it may, John Grimes, Master Astronaut, Commodore of the Rim Confederacy's Naval Reserve, Honorary Admiral of the Ausiphalian Navy and, lately, Master Mariner, was exhibiting all the zeal of the new convert. For some months he had sailed in command of an Aquarian merchantman and, although his real job was to find out the cause of the rapidly increasing number of marine casualties, he had made it plain that insofar as his own ship was concerned he was no mere figurehead. Although (or because) only at sea a dog watch, he was taking great pride in his navigation, his seamanship, his pilotage and his ship handling.

"Damn it all," he grumbled to Sonya, "if our lords and masters wanted us back they'd send a ship for us. I know that *Rim Eland* isn't due here for another six weeks, on her normal commercial voyage—but what's wrong with giving the Navy a spot of deep space training? The Admiralty could send a corvette . . ."

"You aren't all that important, John."

"I suppose not. I'm only the Officer Commanding the Naval Reserve, and the Astronautical Superintendent of Rim Runners . . . Oh, well—if *they* don't want me, there're some people who do."

"What do you mean?" she asked sharply.

"Tom told me that my Master Mariner's Certificate of Competency and my Pilotage Exemption Certificates are valid for all time. He told me, too, that the Winneck Line will give me another appointment as soon as I ask for it. There's just one condition . . ."

"Which is?"

"That we take out naturalization papers."

"No," she told him. "No, repeat, capitalize, underscore, no."

"Why not, my dear?"

"Because this world is the bitter end. I always thought that the Rim Worlds were bad enough, but I put up with them for your sake and, in any case, they've been improving enormously over the past few years. But Aquarius . . . It's way back in the twentieth century!"

"That's its charm."

"For you, perhaps. Don't get me wrong. I enjoyed our voyage in *Sonya Winneck*—but it was no more than a holiday cruise . . ."

"An odd sort of holiday."

"You enjoyed it too. But after not too long a time you'd find the life of a seafaring commercial shipmaster even more boring than that of a spacefaring one. Do you want to be stuck on the surface of one planet for the rest of your life?"

"But there's more variety of experience at sea than there is in space . . ."

Before she could reply there was a tap on the door. "Enter!" called Grimes.

Captain Thornton, the Havenmaster of Aquarius, came into the suite. He looked inquiringly at his guests. "Am I interrupting something?" he asked.

"You are, Tom," Sonya told him. "But you're welcome to join the argument, even though it will be the two of you against me. John's talking of settling down on Aquarius to continue his seafaring career."

"He could do worse," said Thornton.

Sonya glared at the two men, at the tall, lean, silver-haired ruler of Aquarius, at her stocky, ragged husband whose prominent ears, already flushing, were a thermometer of his rising temper. Grimes, looking at her, had the temerity to smile slightly, appreciatively. Like the majority of auburn-haired women she was at her most attractive when about to blow her top.

"What are you grinning at, you big ape?" she demanded. "You."

Before she could explode Thornton hastily intervened. He said, "I came in with some news that should interest you, both of you. I've just got the buzz that the Federation's *Star Pioneer* is putting in to Port Stellar. I know that you used to be in the Survey Service, John, and that Sonya still holds a Reserve commission, and it could be that you'll be meeting some old shipmates . . ."

"Doubtful," said Grimes. "The Survey Service has a very large fleet, and it's many years since I resigned . . ."

"Since you were asked to resign," remarked Sonya.

"You were still in your cradle, so you know nothing about the circumstances. But there might be some people aboard that Sonya would know."

"We shall soon find out. I have to throw a party for the Captain and officers—and you, of course, will be among the guests."

Grimes knew none of *Star Pioneer*'s officers, but Sonya was acquainted with Commander James Farrell, the survey ship's captain. How well acquainted? Grimes felt a twinge of jealousy as he watched them chatting animatedly, then strolled over to the buffet for another generous helping of the excellent chowder. There he was engaged in conversation by two of the *Pioneer*'s junior lieutenants. "You know, sir," said one of them, "your name's quite a legend in the Service . . ."

"Indeed?" Grimes felt flattered.

The other young man laughed—and Grimes did not feel quite so smug. "Yes, sir. Any piece of insubordination-justifiable insubordination, of course—is referred to as 'doing a Grimes . . .'"

"Indeed?" The Commodore's voice was cold.

The first young man hastened to make amends. "But I've heard very senior officers, admirals and commodores, say that you should never have been allowed to resign . . ."

Grimes was not mollified. "*Allowed* to resign? It was a matter of choice, *my* choice. Furthermore . . ." And then he became aware that Sonya, with Commander Farrell in tow, was making her way toward him through the crowd. She was smiling happily. Grimes groaned inwardly. He knew that smile.

"John," she said, "I've good news."

"Tell me."

"Jimmy, here, says that I'm entitled to a free passage in his ship."

"Oh."

"I haven't finished. The Survey Service Regulations have been modified since *your* time. The spouses of commissioned officers, even those on the Reserve List, are also entitled to a free passage if suitable accommodation is available. *Star Pioneer* has ample passenger accommodation, and she will be making a courtesy call at Port Forlorn after her tour of the Carlotti Beacon Stations in this sector of space . . ."

"We shall be delighted to have you aboard, sir," said Farrell.

"Thank you," replied Grimes. He had already decided that he did not much care for the young Commander who, with his close-cropped sandy hair, his pug nose and his disingenuous blue eyes, was altogether too much the idealized Space Scout of the recruiting posters. "Thank you. I'll think about it."

"We'll think about it," said Sonya.

"There's no mad rush, sir," Farrell told him, with a flash of white, even teeth. "But it should be an interesting trip. Glebe, Parramatta, Wyong and Esquel . . ."

Yes, admitted Grimes to himself, *it could be interesting.* Like Aquarius, Glebe, Parramatta and Wyong were rediscovered Lost Colonies, settled originally by the lodejammers of the New Australia Squadron. Esquel was peopled by a more or less humanoid race that, like the Grollons, had achieved the beginnings of a technological civilization. Grimes had read about these worlds, but had never visited them. And then, through the open windows of the hall, drifted the harsh, salty smell of the sea, the thunderous murmur of the breakers against the cliff far below.

I can think about it, he thought. *But that's as far as it need go.*

"We'll think about it," Sonya had said—and now she was saying more. "Please yourself, John, but I'm going. You can follow me when *Rim Eland* comes in. If you want to."

"You'll not consider staying here on Aquarius?"

"I've already made myself quite clear on that point. And since you're hankering after a seafaring life so badly it'll be better if you make the break *now*, rather than hang about waiting for the Rim Runners' ship. Another few weeks here and it'll be even harder for you to tear yourself away."

Grimes looked at his wife. "Not with you already on the way home."

She smiled. "That's what I thought. That's why I took Jimmy's offer. He is rather sweet, isn't he?"

"All the more reason why I should accompany you aboard his blasted ship."

She laughed. "The old, old tactics always work, don't they?"

"Jealousy, you mean?" It was his turn to laugh. "Me, jealous of that puppy!"

"Jealous," she insisted, "but not of *him*. Jealous of the Survey Service. You had your love affair with the Service many years ago, and you've gotten over it. You've other mistresses now—Rim Runners and the Rim Worlds Naval Reserve. But I was still in the middle of mine when I came under the fatal spell of your charm. And I've only to say the word and the Service'd have me back; a Reserve Officer can always transfer back to the Active List . . ." She silenced Grimes with an upraised hand. "Let me finish. If I'd taken passage by myself in *Rim Eland* there'd have been no chance at all of my flying the coop. There's so much of *you* in all the Rim Runners' ships. And the Master and his officers would never have let me forget that I was Mrs. Commodore Grimes. Aboard *Star Pioneer*, with you not there, I'd soon revert to being Commander Sonya Verrill. . ."

Slowly, Grimes filled and lit his pipe. Through the wreathing smoke he studied Sonya's face, grave and intent under the gleaming corona of auburn hair. He knew that she was right. If he persisted in the pursuit of this new love for oceangoing steamships, she could return to her old love for the far-ranging vessels of the Interstellar Federation's military and exploratory arm. They might meet again sometime in the distant future, they might not. And always there would be the knowledge that they were sailing under different flags.

"All right," he said abruptly. "Better tell your boyfriend to get the V.I.P. suite ready."

"I've already told him," she said. She grinned. "Although as a mere Reserve Commander, traveling by myself, I shouldn't have rated it."

The last farewells had been said, not without real regrets on either side, and slowly, the irregular throbbing of her inertial drive drowning the brassy strains of the traditional *Anchors Aweigh*, *Star Pioneer* lifted from the Port Stellar apron. Guests in her control room were Grimes and Sonya. Usually on such occasions the Commodore would be watching the ship handling technique of his host, but today he was not. He was looking down to the watery world fast falling away below. Through borrowed binoculars he was staring down at the slender shape that had just cleared the breakwaters of the Port Stellar seaport, that was proceeding seawards on yet another voyage; and he knew that on her bridge *Sonja Winneck*'s officers would be staring upward at the receding, diminishing ship of space. He sighed, not loudly, but Sonya looked at him with sympathy. That was yet another chapter of his life over, he thought. Never again would he be called upon to exercise the age-old skills of the seaman. But there were worse things than being a spaceman.

He pulled his attention away from the viewport, took an interest in what was going on in the control room. It was all much as he remembered it from his own Survey Service days—dials and gauges and display units, telltale lights, the remote controls for inertial, auxiliary rocket and Mannschenn Drives, the keyboard of the Gunnery Officer's "battle organ." And, apart from the armament accessories, it was very little different from the control room of any modern merchantman.

The people manning it weren't quite the same as merchant officers; and, come to that, weren't quite the same as the officers of the

Rim Worlds Navy. There was that little bit of extra smartness in the uniforms, even to the wearing of caps inside the ship. There were the splashes of fruit salad on the left breast of almost every uniform shirt. There was the crispness of the Captain's orders, the almost exaggerated crispness of his officers' responses, with never a departure from standard Naval terminology. This was a taut ship, not unpleasantly taut, but taut nonetheless. (One of Grimes's shortcomings in the Survey Service had been his inability, when in command, to maintain the requisite degree of tension.) Even so, it was pleasant to experience it once again—especially as a passenger, an outsider. Grimes looked at Sonya. She was enjoying it too. Was she enjoying it too much?

Still accelerating, although not uncomfortably, the ship drove through the thin, high wisps of cirrus. Overhead the sky was indigo, below Aquarius was already visibly a sphere, an enormous mottled ball of white and gold and green and blue—mainly blue. Over to the west'ard was what looked like the beginnings of a tropical revolving storm. And who would be caught in it? Grimes wondered. Anybody he knew? In deep space there were no storms to worry about, not now, although in the days of the lodejammers magnetic storms had been an ever-present danger.

"Secure all!" snapped Commander Farrell.

"Hear this! Hear this!" the Executive Officer said sharply into his microphone. "All hands. Secure for free fall. Report."

Another officer began to announce, "Sick Bay—secure, secure. Enlisted men—secure. Hydroponics—secure . . ." It was a long list. Grimes studied the sweep second hand of his wristwatch. By this time a Rim Runners' tramp would be well on her way. Quite possibly, he admitted, with some shocking mess in the galley or on the farm deck. ". . . Mannschenn Drive Room—secure. Inertial drive room—secure. Auxiliary rocket room—secure. All secure, sir."

"All stations secure, sir," the Executive Officer repeated to the Captain.

"Free fall—execute!"

The throb of the inertial drive faltered and died in mid-beat.

"Centrifugal effect—stand by!"

"Centrifugal effect—stand by!"

"Hunting—execute!"

"Hunting—execute!"

The mighty gyroscopes hummed, then whined. Turning about them, the ship swung to find the target star, the distant sun of Glebe, lined it up in the exact center of the Captain's cartwheel sights and then fell away the few degrees necessary to allow for galactic drift.

"Belay gyroscopes!"

"Belay gyroscopes!"

"One gravity acceleration—stand by!"

"One gravity acceleration—stand by!"

"One gravity acceleration—execute!"

"One gravity acceleration—execute!"

The inertial drive came to life again.

"Time distortion—stand by!"

"Time distortion—stand by!"

"Mannschenn Drive—stand by!"

"Mannschenn Drive—stand by!"

"Mannschenn Drive—3 lyps—*On!*"

"Mannschenn Drive—3 lyps—*On!*"

There was the familiar thin, high keening of the ever-precessing gyroscopes, the fleeting second (or century) of temporal disorientation, the brief spasm of nausea; and then, ahead, the sparse stars were no longer steely points of light but iridescent, pulsating spirals, and astern the fast diminishing globe of Aquarius could have been a mass of multi-hued, writhing gases. *Star Pioneer* was falling down the dark dimensions, through the warped continuum toward her destination.

And about time, thought Grimes, looking at his watch again. *And about bloody time.*

Glebe, Parramatta, Wyong . . . Pleasant enough planets, with something of the Rim Worlds about them, but with a flavor of their own. Lost Colonies they had been, settled by chance, discovered by the ships of the New Australia Squadron after those hapless lodejammers had been thrown light-years off course by a magnetic storm, named after those same ships. For generations they had developed in their own way, isolated from the rest of the man-colonized galaxy. Their development, Commander Farrell complained, had been more of a retrogression than anything else. Commodore Grimes put forward his opinion, which was that these worlds were what the Rim Worlds should have been, and would have been if too many highly efficient types from the Federation had not been allowed to immigrate.

Sonya took sides in the ensuing argument—the wrong side at that. "The trouble with you, John," she told him, "is that you're just naturally against all progress. That's why you so enjoyed playing at being a twentieth century sailor on Aquarius. That's why you don't squirm, as *we* do, every time that you hear one of these blown away Aussies drawl, 'She'll be right . . .'"

"But it's true, ninety-nine percent of the time." He turned to Farrell. "I know that you and your smart young technicians were appalled at the untidiness of the Carlotti Stations on all three of these planets, at the slovenly bookkeeping and all the rest of it. But the beacons work and work well, even though the beacon keepers are wearing ragged khaki shorts instead of spotless white overalls. And what about the repairs to the one on Glebe? They knew that it'd be months before the spares for which they'd requisitioned trickled down through the Federation's official channels, and so they made do with the materials at hand . . ."

"The strip patched with beaten out oil drums . . ." muttered Farrell. "Insulators contrived from beer bottles . . ."

"But that beacon works, Commander, with no loss of accuracy."

"But it shouldn't," Farrell complained.

Sonya laughed. "This archaic setup appeals to John, Jimmy. I always used to think that the Rim Worlds were his spiritual home—but I was wrong. He's much happier on these New Australian planets, which have all the shortcomings of the Rim but nary a one of the few, the very few good points."

"What good points are you talking about?" demanded Grimes. "Overreliance on machinery is one of them, I suppose. That's what I liked about Aquarius, and what I like about these worlds—the tacit determination that the machine shall be geared to man, not the other way round . . ."

"But," said Sonya. "The contrast. Every time that we step ashore it hits us in the eye. Jimmy's ship, with everything spick and span, every officer and every rating going about his duties at the very peak of efficiency—and this city (if you can call it that) with everybody shambling around at least half-asleep, where things get done after a fashion, if they get done at all. It must be obvious even to an old-fashioned . . . seaman like yourself."

"Aboard a ship," admitted Grimes, "any sort of ship, one has to have some efficiency. But not too much."

The three of them were sitting at a table on the wide veranda of the Digger's Arms, one of the principal hotels in the city of Paddington, the capital (such as it was) of Wyong. There were glasses before them, and a bottle, its outer surface clouded with condensation. Outside the high sun blazed down on the dusty street, but it was pleasant enough where they were, the rustling of the breeze in the leaves of the vines trailing around the veranda posts giving an illusion of coolness, the elaborate iron lace of pillars and railing contributing its own archaic charm.

A man came in from outside, removing his broad-brimmed hat as soon as he was in the shade. His heavy boots were noisy on the polished wooden floor. Farrell and Sonya looked with some disapproval at his sun-faded khaki shirt, the khaki shorts that could have been cleaner and better pressed.

"Mrs. Grimes," he said. "How yer goin'?"

"Fine, thank you, Captain," she replied coldly.

"How's tricks, Commodore?"

"Could be worse," admitted Grimes.

"An' how's the world treatin' you, Commander?"

"I can't complain," answered Farrell, making it sound like a polite lie.

The newcomer—it was Captain Dalby, the Port Master—pulled up a chair to the table and sat down with an audible *thump*. A shirt-sleeved waiter appeared. "Beer, Garry," ordered Dalby. "A schooner of old. An' bring another coupla bottles for me friends." Then, while the drinks were coming, he said, "Your Number One said I might find you here, Commander."

"If it's anything important you want me for," Farrell told him, "you could have telephoned."

"Yair. Suppose I could. But yer ship'll not be ready ter lift off fer another coupla days, an' I thought the walk'd do me good . . ." He raised the large glass that the waiter had brought to his lips. "Here's lookin' at yer."

Farrell was already on his feet. "If it's anything serious, Captain Dalby, I'd better get back at once."

"Hold yer horses, Commander. There's nothin' you can do till you get there."

"Get *where?*"

"Esquel, o' course."

"What's wrong on Esquel?"

"Don't rightly know." He drank some more beer, taking his time over it. "But a signal just came in from the skipper of the *Epileptic Virgin* that the Esquel beacon's on the blink."

"*Epsilon Virginis,*" corrected Farrell automatically. Then—"But this could be serious . . ."

"Nothin' ter work up a lather over, Commander. It's an unwatched beacon, so there's no need to worry about the safety of human personnel. An' it's not an important one. Any nog who can't find his way through this sector o' space without it ain't fit ter navigate a plastic duck across a bathtub!"

"Even so . . ." began Farrell.

"Sit down and finish your beer," said Grimes.

"Yer a man after me own heart, Commodore," Dalby told him.

"Did the Master of *Epsilon Virginis* have any ideas as to what might have happened?" asked Sonya.

"If he had, Mrs. Grimes, he didn't say so. Mechanical breakdown, earthquake, lightnin'—you name it." He grinned happily at Farrell. "But it suits me down ter the ground that you're here, Commander. If you weren't, I'd have ter take me own maintenance crew to Esquel an' fix the bloody thing meself. I don't like the place, nor its people . . ." He noticed that Sonya was beginning to look at him in a rather hostile manner. "Mind yer, I've nothin' against wogs, as long as they keep ter their own world an' I keep ter mine."

"So you've been on Esquel?" asked Sonya in a friendly enough voice.

"Too right. More'n once. When the beacon was first installed, an' three times fer maintenance. It's too bleedin' hot, for a start. It just ain't a white man's planet. An' the people . . . Little, gibberin' purple monkeys—chatter, chatter, chatter, jabber, jabber, jabber. Fair gets on yer nerves. I s'pose their boss cockies ain't all that bad when yer get ter know 'em—but they know what side their bread's buttered on an' try ter keep in our good books. If they hate our guts they don't show it. But the others—the lower classes I s'pose you'd call 'em—do hate our guts, an' they do show it."

"It often is the way, Captain," said Sonya. "Very often two absolutely dissimilar races are on far friendlier terms than two similar ones. I've never been to Esquel, but I've seen photographs of the natives and they're very like Terran apes or monkeys; and the apes and monkeys are our not so distant cousins. You and your men probably thought of the Esquelians as caricatures in very bad taste of human beings, and they thought of you in the same way."

"Yair. Could be. But I'm glad it's not me that has ter fix the beacon."

"Somebody has to," said Farrell virtuously.

Star *Pioneer* was on her way once more, driving along the trajectory between Wyong and Esquel, her inertial drive maintaining a normal one standard gravity acceleration, her Mannschenn Drive set for cruising temporal precession rate. Farrell had discussed matters with Grimes and Sonya and with his own senior officers. All agreed that there was no need for urgency; the Esquel beacon was not an essential navigational aid in this sector of space; had it been so it would have been manned.

There was, of course, no communication with the world toward which the ship was bound. The Carlotti beacons are, of course, used for faster-than-light radio communication between distant ships and planets, but the one on Esquel was a direction finding device only. A team of skilled technicians could have made short work of a conversion job, rendering the beacon capable of the transmission and reception of FTL radio signals—but there were no human technicians on Esquel. Yet. Imperialism has long been a dirty word; but the idea persists even though it is never vocalized. The Carlotti beacon on Esquel was the thin end of the wedge, the foot inside the door. Sooner or later the Esquelian rulers would come to rely upon that income derived from the rental of the beacon site, the imports (mainly luxuries) that they could buy with it; and then, not blatantly but most definitely, yet another planet would be absorbed into the Federation's economic empire.

There was conventional radio on Esquel, but *Star Pioneer* would not be able to pick up any messages while her time and space warping interstellar drive was in operation, and not until she was within spitting distance of the planet. There were almost certainly at least a few Esquelian telepaths—but the Survey Service ship was without a psionic radio officer. One should have been carried; one had been carried, in fact, but she had engineered her discharge on Glebe, where she had become wildly enamored of a wealthy grazier. Farrell had let her go; now he was rather wishing that he had not done so.

The *Pioneer* fell down the dark dimensions between the stars, and life aboard her was normal enough. There was no hurry. Unmanned beacons had broken down before, would do so again. Meanwhile there was the pleasant routine of a ship of war in deep space, the regular meals, the card-playing, the chess and what few games of a more physically demanding nature were possible in the rather cramped conditions. Sonya was enjoying it, Grimes was not. He had been too long away from the spit and polish of the Survey Service. And Farrell—unwisely for one in his position—was starting to take sides. Sonya, he not very subtly insinuated, was his breed of cat. Grimes might have been once, but he was no longer. Not only had he resigned from the finest body of astronauts in the galaxy, known or unknown, but he had slammed the door behind him. And as for this craze of his for—of all things!—seamanship . . . Grimes was pained, but not surprised, when Sonya told him, one night, that aboard this ship he was known as the Ancient Mariner.

Ahead, the Esquel sun burgeoned; and then came the day, the hour and the minute when the Mannschenn Drive was shut down and the ship reemerged into the normal continuum. She was still some weeks from Esquel itself, hut she was in no hurry—until the first messages started coming in.

Grimes sat with Sonya and Farrell in the control room. He listened to the squeaky voice issuing from the transceiver. "Calling Earth ship . . . Calling any Earth ship . . . Help . . . Help . . . Help . . ."

It went on and on without break, although it was obvious that a succession of operators was working a more or less regular system of reliefs at the microphone. Farrel acknowledged. It would be minutes before the radio waves carrying his voice reached the Esquelian receiver, more minutes for a reply to come back. He said, as they were waiting for this, that he hoped that whoever was making the distress call had more than one transceiver in operation.

Abruptly the gibbering plea for unspecified aid ceased. A new voice came on the speaker. "I talk for Cabarar, High King of Esquel. There has been . . . revolution. We are . . . besieged on Drarg Island. Cannot hold out . . . much longer. Help. You must . . . help."

There was a long silence, broken by Farrell. "Number One," he ordered, "maximum thrust."

"Maximum thrust, sir." Then, into the intercom, "All hands to acceleration couches! Maximum thrust!"

The backs of the control room chairs fell to the horizontal, the leg rests lifted. The irregular beat of the inertial drive quickened, maddening in its noisy nonrhythm. Acceleration stamped frail human bodies deep into the resilient padding of the couches.

I'm getting too old for this sort of thing, thought Grimes. But he retained his keen interest in all that was going on about him. He heard Farrell say, every word an effort, "Pilot . . . Give me . . . data . . . on . . . Drarg . . ."

"Data . . . on . . . Drarg . . . sir . . ." replied the Navigator.

From the corner of his eye Grimes could see the young officer stretched supine on his couch, saw the fingers of his right hand crawling among the buttons in the arm rest like crippled white worms. A screen came into being overhead, a Mercator map of

Esquel, with the greens and yellows and browns of sprawling continents, the oceanic blue. The map expanded; it was as though a television camera was falling rapidly to a position roughly in the middle of one of the seas. There was a speck there in the blueness. It expanded, but not to any extent. It was obvious that Drarg was only a very small island.

The map was succeeded by pictorial representations of the beacon station. There were high, rugged cliffs, with the sea foaming angrily through the jagged rocks at the water-line. There was a short, spidery jetty. And, over all, was the slowly rotating antenna of the Carlotti beacon, an ellipsoid Mobius strip that seemed ever on the point of vanishment as it turned about its long axis, stark yet insubstantial against the stormy sky.

Farrell, speaking a little more easily now, said, "There's room on that plateau to land a boat—but to put the ship down is out of the question . . ."

Nobody suggested a landing at the spaceport. It must be in rebel hands; and those same rebels, in all probability, possessed at least a share of Earth-manufactured weapons and would be willing to use them against the Earthmen whose lackeys their rulers had been. *Star Pioneer* was armed, of course—but too active participation in other people's wars is frowned upon.

"You could land on the water," said Grimes. "To leeward of the island."

"I'm not a master mariner, Commodore," Farrell told him rather nastily. "But this is *my* ship, and I'm not hazarding her. We'll orbit about Esquel and send down a boat."

I hope that one boat will be enough, thought Grimes, not without sympathy. *The mess isn't of your making, Jimmy boy, but you'll have to answer the "please explains." And as human beings we have some responsibility for the nongs and drongoes we've been propping up with Terran bayonets—or Terran credits, which have been used to purchase Terran bayonets or their present day equivalent.*

"Whatever his shortcomings," commented Sonya, "High King Cabrarar used his brains. He knew that if the beacon ceased functioning there'd be an investigation . . ."

"And better us to make it," said Farrell, "than Dalby and his bunch of no hopers."

"Why?" asked Grimes coldly.

"We're disciplined, armed . . ."

"And if you'll take my advice, Commander, you'll not be in a hurry to use your arms. The top brass is apt to take a dim view of active intervention in outsiders' private squabbles."

"But Cabrarar . . ."

". . . *was* the Federation's blue-eyed boy. His kingdom now is limited to one tiny island. I've no doubt that your lords and masters are already considering dickering with whatever new scum comes to the top."

"Sir . . ." One of the officers was trying to break into the conversation.

"Yes, Mr. Penrose?"

"A signal, sir, from Officer Commanding Lindisfarne Base . . ."

The young man crawled slowly and painfully to where his captain was stretched out on the acceleration couch, with a visible effort stretched out the hand holding the flimsy. Farrell took it, managed to maneuver it to where his eyes could focus on it.

After a long pause he read aloud, "Evacuate King Cabrarar and entourage. Otherwise do nothing, repeat nothing, to antagonize new regime on Esquel."

"As I've been saying," commented Grimes. "But at least they're exhibiting some faint flickers of conscience."

Shortly thereafter Farrell ordered a half hour's reduction of acceleration to one G, a break necessary to allow personnel to do whatever they had to do essential to their comfort. Grimes and Sonya—she with some reluctance—left the control room and retired to their own quarters.

Star Pioneer was in orbit about Esquel. Free fall, after the bone-crushing emergency acceleration, was a luxury—but it was not one that Commander Farrell and those making up the landing party were allowed to enjoy for long. Farrell had decided to send down only one boat—the pinnace. There was insufficient level ground on the island for more than one craft to make a safe landing. He had learned from King Cabrarar that the rebels had control of the air, and that their aircraft were equipped with air-to-air missiles. An air-spacecraft hovering, awaiting its turn to land, would be a tempting target—and effective self-defense on its part could easily be the beginnings of a nasty incident.

The deposed monarch and his party comprised three hundred beings, in terms of mass equivalent to two hundred Earthmen. In addition to its crew the pinnace could lift fifty men; so four rescue trips would be necessary. While the evacuation was in process a small party from the ship would remain on the island, deciding what in the way of stores, equipment and documents would be destroyed, what lifted off. Sonya had volunteered to be one of the party, pointing out that she was the only representative of the Intelligence Branch of the Survey Service in the ship, Reserve commission notwithstanding. Too, Esquelian was one of the many languages at her command; some years ago it had been intended that she visit Esquel, at the time of the installation of the Carlotti beacon, but these orders had been canceled when she was sent elsewhere on a more urgent mission. So, even though she had never set foot on the planet, she could make herself understood and—much more important—understand what was being said in her hearing.

Grimes insisted on accompanying his wife. He was an outsider, with no standing—but, as he pointed out to Farrell, this could prove advantageous. He would have more freedom of action than *Star Pioneer*'s people, not being subject to the orders of the distant Flag Officer at Lindisfarne Base. Farrell was inclined to agree with him on this point, then said, "But it still doesn't let *me* off the hook, Commodore. Suppose you shoot somebody who, in the opinion of my lords and masters, shouldn't have been shot . . . And suppose I say, 'But, sir, it was Commodore Grimes, of the Rim Worlds Naval Reserve, who did the shooting . . .' What do *they* say?"

"Why the bloody hell did you let him?" replied Grimes, laughing. "But I promise to restrain my trigger finger, James."

"He's made up his mind to come," Sonya said. "But not to worry. After all his playing at being a merchant sea captain he'll not know one end of a gun from the other . . ."

So, with the landing party aboard, the pinnace broke out of its bay and detached itself from the mother ship. The young lieutenant at the controls was a superb boat handler, driving the craft down to the first tenuous wisps of atmosphere, then decelerating before friction could overheat the skin. Drarg Island was in the sunlit hemisphere, the sky over which was unusually clear—so clear that there was no likelihood of mistaking the smoke from at least two burning cities for natural cloud. Navigation presented no problems. All that the officer had to do was to home on a continuous signal from the transmitter on the island. Grimes would have liked to have played with the bubble sextant and the ephemerides—produced by *Star Pioneer*'s navigator just in case they would be needed—that were part of the boat's equipment, but when he suggested so doing Sonya gave him such a scornful look that he desisted.

There was the island: a slowly expanding speck in the white-flecked sea. And there, a long way to the westward, were two airships, ungainly dirigible balloons. They must have seen the pinnace on her way down, but they made no attempt to intercept; a blimp is not an ideal aircraft in which to practice the *kamikaze* technique. But, remarked Farrell, they would be reporting this Terran intervention to their base. The radio operator found their working frequency and Sonya was able to translate the high-pitched squeakings and gibberings.

"As near as I can render it," she reported, "they're saying, 'The bastard king's bastard friends have come . . .' In the original it's much more picturesque." The operator turned up the gain to get the reply. "'Keep the bastards under observation,'" said Sonya. Then, "'Use Code 17A . . .'"

"They can use any code they please," commented Farrell. "With what weaponry there is on this world, the island's impregnable. It'll be more impregnable still after we've landed a few of our toys."

"Never underrate primitive peoples," Grimes told him. He dredged up a maritime historical snippet from his capacious memory. "In one of the wars on Earth—the Sino-Japanese War in the first half of the twentieth century—a modern Japanese destroyer was sent to the bottom by the fire of a concealed battery of primitive muzzle-loading cannon, loaded with old nails, broken bottles and horseshoes for luck . . ."

"Fascinating, Commodore, fascinating," said Farrell. "If you see any muzzle-loaders pointed our way, let me know, will you?"

Sonya laughed unkindly.

Grimes, who had brought two pipes with him, took out and filled and lit the one most badly in need of a clean.

They dropped down almost vertically on to the island, the lieutenant in charge of the pinnace making due allowance for drift. As they got lower they could see that the elliptical Mobius strip that was the antenna of the Carlotti beacon was still, was not rotating about its long axis. Draped around it were rags of fabric streaming to leeward in the stiff breeze. It looked, at first, as though somebody had improvised a wind sock for the benefit of the landing party—and then it was obvious that the fluttering tatters were the remains of a gasbag. A little to one side of the machinery house was a crumpled tangle of wickerwork and more fabric, the wreckage of the gondola of the crashed airship. Some, at least, of the refugees on the island must have come by air.

Landing would have been easy if the Esquelians had bothered to clear away the wreckage. The lieutenant suggested setting the pinnace down on top of it, but Farrell stopped him. Perhaps he was remembering Grimes's story about that thin-skinned Japanese destroyer. He said, "There's metal there, Mr. Smith—the engine, and weapons, perhaps, and other odds and ends. We don't want to go punching holes in ourselves . . ."

So the pinnace hovered for a while, vibrating to the noisy, irregular throb of her inertial drive, while the spidery, purple-furred humanoids on the ground capered and gesticulated. Finally, after Sonya had screamed orders at them through the ship's loudhailer, a party of them dragged the wreckage to the edge of the cliff, succeeded in pushing it over. It plunged untidily down to the rocks far below. There was a brilliant orange flash, a billowing of dirty white-brown smoke, a shock wave that rocked the pinnace dangerously. There must have been ammunition of some kind in that heap of debris.

Farrell said nothing. But if looks could have killed, the King, standing aloof from his loyal subjects, distinguishable by the elaborate basketwork of gold and jewels on his little, round head, would have died. Somebody muttered, "Slovenly bastards . . ." Grimes wondered if the rebels were any more efficient than the ruling class they had deposed, decided that they almost certainly must be. It was such a familiar historical pattern.

The pinnace grounded. The noise of the inertial drive faded to an irritable mumble, then ceased. Farrell unbuckled his seat belt, then put on his cap, then got up. Sonya—who was also wearing a uniform for the occasion—did likewise. Somehow, the pair of them conveyed the impression that Grimes had not been invited to the party, but he followed them to the airlock, trying to look like a duly accredited observer from the Rim Worlds Confederacy. The airlock doors, inner and outer, opened. The Commodore sniffed appreciatively the breeze that gusted in, the harsh tang of salt water that is the same on all oceanic worlds. His second sniff was not such a deep one; the air of the island was tainted with the effluvium of too many people cooped up in far too small a space.

The ramp extended. Farrell walked slowly down it, followed by Sonya, followed by Grimes, followed by two ratings with machine pistols at the ready. The King stood a few yards away, watching them, surrounded by his own officers, monkeylike beings on the purple fur of whose bodies gleamed the golden ornaments that were badges of rank.

Stiffly (reluctantly?) Farrell saluted.

Limply the King half raised a six-fingered hand in acknowledgment. The rings on his long fingers sparkled in the afternoon sunlight. He turned to one of the staff, gibbering.

The being faced Farrell, baring yellow teeth as he spoke. "His Majesty say, why you no come earlier?"

"We came as soon as we were able," said Farrell.

There was more gibbering, unintelligible to all save Sonya. Then—"His Majesty say, where *big* ship? When you start bomb cities, kill rebels?"

Farrell turned to face his own people. He said, "Take over, please,

Commander Verrill. You know the language. You might be able to explain things more diplomatically than me. You know the orders."

"I know the orders, Commander Farrell," said Sonya. She stepped forward to face the King, speaking fluently and rapidly. Even when delivered by her voice, thought Grimes, this Esquelian language was still ugly, but she took the curse off it.

The King replied to her directly. He was literally hopping from one splayed foot to the other with rage. Spittle sprayed from between his jagged, yellow teeth. The elaborate crown on his head was grotesquely awry. He raised a long, thin arm as though to strike the woman.

Grimes pulled from his pocket the deadly little Minetti automatic that was his favorite firearm. Viciously, Farrell knocked his hand down, whispering, "Hold it, Commodore! Don't forget that we represent the Federation . . ."

"*You* might," snarled Grimes.

But the King had seen the show of weapons; Grimes learned later that the two spacemen had also made threatening gestures with their machine pistols. He let his arm fall to his side. His clawed fingers slowly straightened. At last he spoke again—and the unpleasant gibbering was less high-pitched, less hysterical.

Sonya translated. "His Majesty is . . . disappointed. He feels that he has been . . . betrayed."

"Tell his Majesty," said Farrell, "that my own rulers forbid me to take part in this civil war. But His Majesty and those loyal to him will be transported to a suitable world, where they will want for nothing."

Grimes tried to read the expression on the King's face. Resignation? Misery? It could have been either, or both. Then his attention was attracted by the glint of metal evident in the crowd behind the deposed monarch. He saw that most of the Esquelians were armed, some with vicious-looking swords, others with projectile weapons, archaic in design, but probably effective enough. He doubted if any of the natives would be able to fly the pinnace—but a human pilot might do what he was told with a knife at his throat.

Farrell spoke again. "Tell His Majesty, Commander Verrill, that if he has any ideas about seizing my pinnace he'd better forget 'em. Tell him that those odd-looking antennae poking out from their turrets are laser cannon, and that at the first sign of trouble this plateau will be one big, beautiful barbecue. Tell him to look at that bird, there . . ." he pointed . . . "over to the eastward." He raised his wrist to his mouth, snapped an order into the microphone.

After Sonya finished her translation, everybody looked at the bird—if bird it was. It was a flying creature of some kind, big, with a wide wing span. It was a carrion eater, perhaps, hovering to leeward of the island in the hope of a meal. It died suddenly in a flare of flame, a gout of greasy smoke. A sparse sprinkling of smoldering fragments drifted down to the surface of the sea.

There was an outburst of squealing and gibbering. The Esquelians, with quite advanced armaments of their own at the time of Man's first landing on their world, had never, until now, been treated to a demonstration of the more sophisticated Terran weaponry. But they were people who knew that it is not the *bang* of a firearm that kills.

"His Majesty," said Sonya, "demands that he and his people be taken off this island, as soon as possible, if not before." She grinned. "That last is a rather rough translation, but it conveys the essential meaning."

"I am happy to obey," replied Farrell. "But he and his people will have to leave all weapons behind."

There was more argument, and another demonstration of the pinnace's firepower, and then the evacuation was gotten under way.

It had been intended, when the beacon was established on Drarg Island, that the island itself should serve as a base for some future survey party. The rock was honeycombed with chambers and tunnels, providing accommodation, should it be required, for several hundred humans. At the lowest level of all was the power station, fully automated, generating electricity for lights and fans as well as for the Carlotti beacon. The refugees had been able to live there in reasonable comfort—and in considerable squalor. Grimes decided that, as soon as things quietened down, he would get Sonya to inquire as to whether or not the flush toilet had been invented on Esquel. In spite of the excellent ventilation system, the stench was appalling.

But it was necessary for Sonya, at least, to go down into those noisome passages. In spite of the King's protests, Farrell had ordered that no property be lifted from the island; his orders were to save life, and life only. There were tons, literally, of gold and precious stones. There were tons of documents. These latter were, of course, of interest, and Sonya was the only member of *Star Pioneer*'s party able to read them. And so, accompanied by Grimes and two junior officers, she went into the room in which the papers had been stacked, skimmed through them, committing those that she thought might be important to microfilm. Now and again, for the benefit of her helpers, she translated. "This," she told them, "seems to be the wages sheet, for the palace staff . . . No less than fourteen cooks, and then fifty odd scullions and such . . . And a food taster . . . And a wine taster . . . And, last of all, and the most highly paid of the lot, a torturer. He got twice what the executioner did . . ." She passed the sheet to the Ensign who was acting as photographer, picked up the next one. "H'm. Interesting. This is the pay list for the Royal Guard. The Kardonar—roughly equivalent to Colonel—got less than the Third Cook . . ."

"This could be just yet another Colonels' Revolt," commented Grimes. He looked at his watch, which had been adjusted to local time. "Midnight. Time we had a break. This stink is getting me down."

"You can say that again, sir," agreed one of the Ensigns.

"All right," said Sonya at last. "I think we've skimmed the cream down here."

"Cream?" asked Grimes sardonically.

They made their way up the winding ramps, through the tunnels with their walls of fused rock, came at last to the surface. The plateau was brightly illumined by the floodlights that Farrell's men had set up. The pinnace was away on a shuttle trip, and only a handful of natives remained, huddling together for warmth in the lee of the beacon machinery house. The King, Grimes noted sardonically, was not among them; obviously he was not one of those captains who are last to leave the sinking ship. He was quite content to let Farrell be his stand in.

The Commander walked slowly to Grimes and Sonya. "How's it going, Commander Verrill?" he asked.

"Well enough," she replied. "We've enough evidence to show that this was a thoroughly corrupt regime."

"Physically, as well as in all the other ways," added Grimes. "This fresh air tastes good! How are you off for deodorants aboard *Star Pioneer*, Commander Farrell?"

"Not as well as I'd like to be, Commodore. But I'll put the bulk of the passengers in deep freeze, so it shouldn't be too bad." He looked up at the sky. "It'll be a while before the pinnace is back. Perhaps, sir, you might like a look at some of the surface craft that these people came out to the island in. There's a half dozen of them at the jetty; rather odd-looking contraptions . . ."

"I'd like to," said Grimes.

Farrell led the way to the edge of the plateau, to a stairway, railed at the seaward edge, running down the cliff face to a sheltered inlet in which was a short pier. Moored untidily alongside this were six sizable boats, and there was enough light from the floods at the cliff top for Grimes to make out details before he and the others commenced their descent.

"Yes, I'd like a closer look," he said. "Steam, I'd say, with those funnels. Paddle steamers. Stern-wheelers. Efficient in smooth water, but not in a seaway . . ."

He led the way down the stairs, his feet clattering on the iron treads. He said, "I'd like a trip in one of those, just to see how they handle . . ."

"Out of the question, Commodore," laughed Farrell.

"I know," said Grimes; as Sonya sneered, "You and your bloody seamanship!"

They stepped from the stairway on to the concrete apron, walked across it to the foot of the jetty. Grimes stopped suddenly, said, "Look!"

"At what?" demanded Sonya.

"At that craft with the red funnel . . . That's smoke, and a wisp of steam . . . She's got steam up . . ."

Farrell's laser pistol was out of its holster, and so was Sonya's.

Grimes pulled his own Minetti out of his pocket. Cautiously they advanced along the pier, trying to make as little noise as possible. But the natives who erupted from the tunnel at the base of the cliff were completely noiseless on their broad, bare feet and, without having a chance to use their weapons, to utter more than a strangled shout, the three Terrans went down under a wave of evil-smelling, furry bodies.

Grimes recovered slowly. Something hard had hit him behind the right ear, and he was suffering from a splitting headache. He was, he realized, propped in a sitting posture, his back against a wall of some kind. No, not a wall—a bulkhead. The deck under his buttocks had a gentle rolling motion, and—his head was throbbing in synchronization—there was the steady *chunk, chunk, chunk* of a paddle wheel. Grimes tried to lift his hands to his aching head, discovered that his wrists were bound. So were his ankles.

He heard a familiar voice. "You and your bloody boats!"

He opened his eyes. He turned his head, saw that Sonya was propped up beside him. Her face, in the light of the flickering oil lamp, was pale and drawn. She muttered sardonically, "Welcome aboard, Commodore." Beyond her was Farrell, trussed as were the other two. Nonetheless, he was able to say severely, "This is no time for humor, Commander Verrill."

"But it is, James," she told him sweetly.

"What. . . what happened?" asked Grimes.

"We were jumped, that's what. It seems that a bunch of the loyalists—quote and unquote—suffered a change of mind. They'd sooner take their chances with the rebels than on some strange and terrifying planet . . ."

"Better the devil you know . . ." said Grimes.

"Precisely."

"But where do *we* come in?" asked the Commodore.

"They had to stop us from stopping them from making their getaway," explained Farrell, as though to a mentally retarded child.

"There's more to it than that, James," Sonya told him. "There's a radio telephone of some kind in the compartment forward of this.

Battery powered, I suppose. Not that it matters. Our friends have been arranging a rendezvous with a rebel patrol craft. They've made it plain that they're willing to buy their freedom, their lives. And the price is . . ."

"Us," completed Grimes. "What's the current market value of a full Commander in the Survey Service these days, Farrell? I've no doubt that the rebels will wish to show a profit on the deal."

"And how many laser cannon, complete with instruction manuals, is the Confederacy willing to pay for you, Commodore?" asked Commander Farrell.

"Shut up!" snapped Sonya.

The cabin was silent again, save for the creaking of timbers, the faint thudding of the engines, the *chunk, chunk, chunk* of the paddle. And then, audible in spite of the intervening bulkhead, there was the high-pitched gibbering, in bursts, that, in spite of the strange language, carried the sense of *"over," "roger"* and all the rest of the standard radio telephone procedure.

Sonya whispered, "As far as I can gather, hearing only one end of the conversation, the patrol craft has sighted this tub that we're in. We've been told to heave to, to await the boarding party . . ." As she spoke, the engines and the paddle wheel slowed, stopped.

There was comparative silence again. Grimes strained his ears for the noise of an approaching stern-wheeler, but in vain. There was, he realized, a new mechanical sound, but it came from overhead. Then it, too, ceased. He was about to speak when there was a loud *thud* from the deck outside, another, and another . . . There was an outbreak of excited gibbering. Shockingly, there were screams, almost human, and three startlingly loud reports.

Abruptly the cabin door slammed open. Two Esquelians came in. There was dark, glistening blood on the fur of one of them, but it did not seem to be his own. They grabbed Grimes by the upper arms, dragged him roughly out on deck, jarring his lower spine painfully on the low sill of the door. They left him there, went back in for Sonya, and then Farrell.

Grimes lay where they had dropped him, looking upward. There were lights there, dim, but bright against the black sky, the sparse, faint stars. As his eyes grew accustomed to the darkness he could make out the great, baggy shape of the dirigible balloon, the comparative rigidity of the gondola slung under it. While he was trying to distinguish more details a rope was slipped about his body and he was hoisted aloft, like a sack of potatoes, by a creakingly complaining hand winch.

"And what now, Commodore? What now?" asked Farrell. By his tone of voice he implied, *You've been in far more irregular situations than me . . .*

Grimes chuckled. "To begin with, we thank all the odd gods of the galaxy that real life so very often copies fiction . . ."

Sonya snarled, "What the hell are you nattering about?"

Grimes chuckled again. "How often, in thrillers, have the baddies tied up the goodies and then carelessly left them with something sharp or abrasive to rub their bonds against. . . ?"

"You aren't kidding?" she asked. Then—"And since when have you been a goodie?"

"You'd be surprised . . ." Grimes swore then, briefly and vividly. The sharp edge in the wickerwork of which the airship's car was constructed had nicked his wrist quite painfully. He grunted, "But in fiction it's usually much easier . . ."

He worked on, sawing away with his bound hands, even though his wrists were slippery with blood. He was afraid that one of the airship's crew would come into the cabin to look at the prisoners, but the four Esquelians in the control room at the forward end of the gondola seemed fully occupied with navigation and, presumably, the two who were aft were devoting all their time to the engine of the thing.

Hell! That rope was tough—tougher than the edge against which he was rubbing it, tougher than his skin. Not being able to see what he was doing made it worse. He began to wonder if the first result that he would achieve would be the slitting of an artery. He had never heard of that happening to a fictional hero; but there has to be a first time for everything. Sonya whispered, very real concern in her voice, "John! You're only hurting yourself! Stop it, before you do yourself some real damage!"

"It's dogged as does it!" he replied.

"John! It's not as though they're going to kill us. We're more value to them alive than dead!"

"Could be," he admitted. "But I've heard too many stories about samples from the bodies of kidnap victims being sent to their potential ransomers to speed up negotiations. Our furry friends strike me as being just the kind of businessmen who'd stoop to such a practice!"

"After the way in which they slaughtered the crew of the steamboat," put in Farrell, "I'm inclined to agree with the Commodore."

"The vote is two against one," said Grimes. And then the rope parted.

He brought his hands slowly round in front of him. There was a lamp in the cabin, a dim, incandescent bulb, and by its feeble light he could see that his wrists were in a mess. But the blood was dripping slowly, not spurting. He was in no immediate danger of bleeding to death. And he could work his fingers, although it seemed a long time before repeated flexings and wrigglings rendered them capable of use.

He started on the rope about his ankles then. He muttered something about Chinese bowlines, Portuguese pig knots and unseamanlike bastards in general. He complained, "I can't find an end to work on." Then, with an attempt at humor, "Somebody must have cut it off!"

"Talking of cutting . . ." Sonya's voice had a sharp edge to it. "Talking of cutting, if you can get your paws on to the heel of one of my shoes . . ."

Yes, of course, thought Grimes. Sonya was in uniform, and the uniform of a Survey Service officer contained quite a few concealed weapons. Sophisticated captors would soon have found these, but the Esquelians, to whom clothing was strange, had yet to learn the strange uses to which it could be put. Without overmuch contortion Grimes was able to get his hand around the heel of his wife's left shoe. He twisted, pulled—and was armed with a short but useful knife. To slash through his remaining bonds was a matter of seconds.

The Esquelian came through into the cabin from forward just as

Grimes was getting shakily to his feet. He was wearing a belt, and from this belt depended a holster. He was quick neither on the draw nor the uptake, but the Commodore was half crippled by impeded circulation to his ankles and feet. The native got his pistol—a clumsy revolver—out before Grimes was on him. He fired two shots, each of them too close for comfort, one of them almost parting the Commodore's close-cropped hair.

Grimes's intention—he told himself afterward—had been to disable only, to disarm. It was unfortunate, perhaps, that the airship at that moment dived steeply. The Earthman plunged forward in a staggering run, the knife held before him, stabbing deep into the furry chest. The Esquelian screamed shrilly as a disgustingly warm fluid gushed from his body over Grimes's hands, tumbled to the deck. As he fell, Grimes snatched the pistol. He was more at home with firearms than with bladed weapons.

Surprisingly it fitted his hand as though made for him—but there is parallel evolution of artifacts as well as of life forms. Holding it, almost stumbling over the body of the dead native, Grimes continued his forward progress, coming into the control cabin. It was light in there, wide windows admitting the morning twilight. Gibbering, the three Esquelians deserted their controls. One of them had a pistol, the other two snatched knives from a handy rack. Grimes fired, coldly and deliberately. The one with the revolver was his first target, then the nearer of the knife wielders, then his mate. At this range, even with an unfamiliar weapon with a stiff action, a man who in his younger days had been a small arms specialist could hardly miss. Grimes did not, even though he had to shoot one of the airmen twice, even though the last convulsive stab of a broad-bladed knife missed his foot by a millimeter.

He did not know whether or not the gun that he had been using was empty; he did not bother to check. Stooping, he quickly snatched up the one dropped by the dead pilot. It had never been fired. He turned, ran back into the cabin. He was just in time. One of the engineers was just about to bring a heavy spanner crashing down on Sonya's head but was thrown back by the heavy slug that smashed his own skull.

Saying nothing, Grimes carried on aft. The other engineer was dead already, killed by the first wild shot of the encounter. Grimes thought at first that the loud dripping noise was being made by his blood. But it was not. It came from the fuel tank, which had been pierced by a stray bullet. Before Grimes could do anything about it, the steam turbine ground to a halt.

The sun was up. It was a fine morning, calm insofar as those in the disabled airship were concerned, although the whitecaps on the sea were evidence of a strong breeze. To port was the coastline: rugged cliffs, orange beaches, blue-green vegetation inland, a sizable city far to the south'ard. It was receding quite rapidly as the aircraft, broadside on to the offshore wind, scudded to leeward.

The bodies of the airmen had been dragged into the cabin in which the Terrans had been imprisoned. Farrell and Sonya had wanted to throw them overside, but Grimes had talked them out of it. From his historical researches he knew something—not much, but something—about the handling of lighter-than-air flying machines. Until he had familiarized himself with the controls of this brute, he had no intention of dumping ballast.

He had succeeded in fixing the ship's position. In the control room there was a binnacle, and there were sight vanes on the compass. There were charts, and presumably the one that had been in use at the time of the escape was the one that covered this section of coast. The compass was strange; it was divided into 400 degrees, not 360. The latitude and longitude divisions on the chart were strange, too, but it wasn't hard to work out that the Esquelians worked on 100 minutes to a degree, 100 degrees to a right angle. There was a certain lack of logic involved—human beings, with their five-fingered hands, have a passion for reckoning things in twelves. The Esquelians, six-fingered, seemed to prefer reckoning by tens. Even so, compass, sight vanes and charts were a fine example of the parallel evolution of artifacts.

There was the compass rose, showing the variation (Grimes assumed) between True North and Magnetic North. There was that city to the south. There were two prominent mountain peaks, the mountains being shown by what were obviously contour lines. Grimes laid off his cross bearings, using a roller, ruler and a crayon. The cocked hat was a very small one. After fifteen minutes he did it again. The line between the two fixes coincided with the estimated wind direction. And where would that take them?

Transferring the position to a small scale chart presented no problems. Neither did extending the course line. The only trouble was that it missed the fly speck that represented Drarg Island by at least twenty miles, regarding one minute on the latitude scale as being a mile. Sonya, recruited in her linguistic capacity, confirmed that the (to Grimes) meaningless squiggles alongside the dot on the chart did translate to "Drarg."

The trouble was that the unlucky shot that had immobilized the airship's engines had also immobilized her generator. There were batteries—but they were flat. (During a revolution quite important matters tend to be neglected.) The radio telephone was, in consequence, quite useless. Had there been power it would have been possible to raise the party on the island, to get them to send the pinnace to pick them up when the aircraft was ditched, or, even, to tow them in.

"At least we're drifting away from the land," said Farrell, looking on the bright side. "I don't think that we should be too popular if we came down ashore." He added, rather petulantly, "Apart from anything else, my orders were that there was to be no intervention . . ." He implied that all the killing had been quite unnecessary.

"Self-defense," Grimes told him. "Not intervention. But if you ever make it back to Lindisfame Base, James, you can tell the Admiral that it was the wicked Rim Worlders who played hell with a big stick."

"We're all in this, Commodore," said Farrell stiffly. "And this expedition is under *my* command, after all."

"This is no time for inessentials," snapped Sonya. She straightened up from the chart, which she had been studying. "As I see it, they'll sight us from the island, and assume that we're just one of the rebel patrol craft. They might try to intercept us, trying to find out what's happened to us. On the other hand . . ."

"On the other hand," contributed Farrell, "my bright Exec does everything by the book. He'll insist on getting direct orders from Lindisfarne before he does *anything*."

"How does this thing work?" asked Sonya. "Can you *do* anything, John? The way that you were talking earlier you conveyed the impression that you knew something about airships."

Grimes prowled through the control compartment like a big cat in a small cupboard. He complained, "If I had power, I could get someplace. This wheel here, abaft the binnacle, is obviously for steering. This other wheel, with what looks like a crude altimeter above it, will be for the altitude coxswain. The first actuates a vertical steering surface, the rudder. The second actuates the horizontal control surfaces, for aerodynamic lift. . ."

"I thought that in an airship you dumped ballast or valved gas if you wanted to go up or down, "said Sonya.

"You can do that, too." Grimes indicated toggled cords that ran down into the control room from above. "These, I *think*, open valves if you pull them. So we can come down." He added grimly, "And we've plenty of ballast to throw out if we want to get upstairs in a hurry."

"Then what's all the bellyaching about?" asked Farrell. "We can control our altitude by either of two ways, and we can steer. If the rudder's not working we can soon fix it."

Grimes looked at him coldly. "Commander Farrell," he said at last, "there is one helluva difference between a free balloon and a dirigible balloon. This brute, with no propulsive power, is a free balloon." He paused while he sought for and found an analogy. "She's like a surface ship, broken down, drifting wherever wind and current take her. The surface ship is part of the current if she has neither sails nor engines. A balloon is part of the wind. We can wiggle our rudder as much as we like and it will have no effect whatsoever . . ." Once again he tried to find a seamanlike analogy—and found something more important. He whispered, "Riverhead . . ."

"Riverhead?" echoed Farrell. "What's that, Commodore?"

"Shut up, James," murmured Sonya. "Let the man think."

Grimes was thinking, and remembering. During his spell of command of *Sonya Winneck*, on Aquarius, he had been faced with an occasional knotty problem. One such had been the delivery of a consignment of earth-moving machinery to Riverhead, a new port miles inland—equipment which was to be used for the excavation of a swinging basin off the wharfage. The channel was deep enough— but at its upper end it was not as wide as *Sonya Winneck* was long. However, everything had been arranged nicely. Grimes was to come alongside, discharge his cargo and then, with the aid of a tug, proceed stern first down river until he had room to swing in Carradine's Reach. Unfortunately the tug had suffered a major breakdown so that *Sonya Winneck*, if she waited for the repairs to be completed, would be at least ten days, idle, alongside at the new wharf.

Grimes had decided not to wait and had successfully dredged down river on the ebb.

He said slowly, "Yes, I think we could dredge . . ."

"Dredge?" asked Farrell.

Grimes decided that he would explain. People obey orders much more cheerfully when they know that what they are being told to do makes sense. He said, "Yes, I've done it before, but in a surface ship. I had to proceed five miles down a narrow channel, stern first . . ."

"But you had engines?"

"Yes, I had engines, but I didn't use them. I couldn't use them. Very few surface ships, only specialized vessels, will steer when going astern. The rudder, you see, must be in the screw race. Y'ou must have that motion of water past and around the rudder from forward to aft . . .

"The dredging technique is simple enough. You put an anchor on the bottom, not enough chain out so that it holds, but just enough so that it acts as a drag, keeping your head up into the current. You're still drifting *with* the current, of course, but not as fast. So the water is sliding past your rudder in the right direction, from forward, so you can steer after a fashion."

"It works?"

"Yes," said Sonya. "It works all right But with all the ear bashing I got before and after I was inclined to think that John was the only man who'd ever made it work."

"You can do it here?" asked Farrell.

"I think so. It's worth trying."

The hand winch was aft, in the engine compartment. To dismount it would have taken too much time, so Grimes had the rope fall run off it, brought forward and coiled down in the control room. To its end he made fast four large canvas buckets; what they had been used for he did not know, nor ever did know, but they formed an ideal drogue. Farrell, using the spanner that had been the dead engineer's weapon, smashed outward the forward window. It was glass, and not heavy enough to offer much resistance. Grimes told him to make sure that there were no jagged pieces left on the sill to cut the dragline. Then, carefully, he lowered his cluster of buckets down toward the water. The line was not long enough to reach.

Carefully Grimes belayed it to the base of the binnacle, which fitting seemed to be securely mounted. He went back forward, looked out and down. He called back, over his shoulder, "We have to valve gas . . ."

"Which control?" asked Sonya.

"Oh, the middle one, I suppose . . ."

That made sense, he thought. One of the others might have an effect on the airship's trim, or give it a heavy list to port or starboard. *And so,* he told himself, *might this one.*

He was aware of a hissing noise coming from overhead. The airship was dropping rapidly, too rapidly. "That will do!" he ordered sharply.

"The bloody thing's stuck!" he heard Sonya call. Then, "I've got it clear!"

The airship was still falling, and the drogue made its first contact with the waves—close now, too close below-skipping over them. The line tightened with a jerk and the flimsy structure of the gondola creaked in protest. The ship came round head to wind, and an icy gale swept through the broken window. The ship bounced upward and there was a brief period of relative calm, sagged, and once again was subjected to the atmospheric turbulence.

"Ballast!" gasped Grimes, clinging desperately to the sill. It seemed a long time before anything happened, and then the ship soared, lifting the drogue well clear of the water.

"Got rid . . . of one . . . of our late friends . . ." gasped Farrell.

"Justifiable, in the circumstances," conceded Grimes grudgingly. "But before we go any further we have to rig a windscreen . . . I saw some canvas, or what looks like canvas, aft . . ."

"How will you keep a lookout?" asked Farrell.

"The lookout will be kept astern, from the engine compartment. That's the way that we shall be going. Now give me a hand to get this hole plugged."

They got the canvas over the empty window frame, lashed it and, with a hammer and nails from the engine room tool kit, tacked it into place. Grimes hoped that it would hold. He discovered that he could see the surface of the sea quite well from the side windows, so had no worries on that score. Before doing anything else he retrieved the crumpled chart from the corner into which it had blown, spread it out on the desk, made an estimation of the drift since the last observed position, laid off a course for Drarg Island. Once he had the ship under control he would steer a reciprocal of this course, send Sonya right aft to keep a lookout astern, with Farrell stationed amidships to relay information and orders. First of all, however, there was more juggling to be done with gas and ballast.

Grimes descended cautiously, calling instructions to Sonya as he watched the white-crested waves coming up to meet him. The drogue touched surface—and still the ship fell, jerkily, until the buckets bit and held, sinking as they filled. There was a vile draft in the control room as the wind whistled through chinks in the makeshift windshield.

"All right," ordered Grimes. "Man the lookout!"

The others scrambled aft, while the Commodore took the wheel. He knew that he would have to keep the lubber's line steady on a figure that looked like a misshapen, convoluted 7, saw that the ship's head was all of twenty degrees to starboard off this heading. He applied port rudder, was surprised as well as pleased when she came round easily. He risked a sidewise glance at the altimeter. The needle was steady enough—but it could not possibly drop much lower. The instrument had not been designed for wave hopping.

He yelled, hoping that Farrell would be able to hear him, "If you think we're getting too low, dump some more ballast!"

"Will do!" came the reply.

He concentrated on his steering. It was not as easy as he thought it would be. Now and again he had taken the wheel of *Sonya Winneck*, just to get the feel of her—but *her* wheel could be put over with one finger, all the real work being done by the powerful steering motors aft. Here it was a case of Armstrong Patent.

But he kept the lubber's line on the course, his arms aching, his legs trembling, his clothing soaked with perspiration in spite of the freezing draft. He wished that he knew what speed the airship was making. He wanted a drink, badly, and thought longingly of ice-cold water. He wanted a smoke, and was tempted. He thought that the airship was helium filled, was almost certain that she was helium filled, but dared take no risks. But the stem of his cold, empty pipe between his teeth was some small comfort.

Faintly he heard Sonya call out something.

Farrell echoed her. "Land, ho!"

"Where away?" yelled Grimes over his shoulder, his pipe clattering unheeded to the deck.

"Astern! To port! About fifteen degrees!"

Carefully, Grimes brought the ship round to the new course. She held it, almost without attention on his part. There must, he thought, have been a shift of wind.

"As she goes!" came the hail. "Steady as she goes!"

"Steady," grunted Grimes. "Steady . . ."

How much longer? He concentrated on his steering, on the swaying compass card, on the outlandish numerals that seemed to writhe as he watched them, *How much longer?*

He heard Sonya scream, "We're coming in fast! Too low! The cliffs!"

"Ballast!" yelled Grimes.

Farrell had not waited for the order, already had the trap in the cabin deck open, was pushing out another of the dead Esquelians, then another. The deck lifted under Grimes's feet, lifted and tilted, throwing him forward onto his now useless wheel. A violent jerk flung him aft, breaking his grip on the spokes.

After what seemed a very long time he tried to get to his feet. Suddenly Sonya was with him, helping him up, supporting him in his uphill scramble toward the stern of the ship, over decking that canted and swayed uneasily. They stumbled over the dead bodies, skirting the open hatch. Grimes was surprised to see bare rock only a foot or so below the aperture. They came to the engine room, jumped down through the door to the ground. It was only a short drop.

"We were lucky," said Grimes, assessing the situation. The airship had barely cleared the cliff edge, had been brought up short by its dragline a few feet short of the Carlotti beacon.

"Bloody lucky!" Farrell said. "Some Execs would have opened fire first and waited for orders afterward . . ."

His Executive Officer flushed. "Well, sir, I thought it might be you." He added, tactlessly, "After all, we've heard so many stories about Commodore Grimes . . ."

Farrell was generous. He said, "Excellent airmanship, Commodore."

"Seamanship," corrected Grimes huffily.

Sonya laughed—but it was with him, not at him.

The voyage between Esquel and Tallis, where the King and his entourage were disembarked, was not a pleasant one. Insofar as the Terrans were concerned, the Esquelians stank. Insofar as the Esquelians were concerned, the Terrans stank—and that verb could be used both literally and metaphorically. Commander Farrell thought, oddly enough, that the King should be humbly grateful. The King, not so oddly, was of the opinion that he had been let down, badly, by his allies. Grimes, on one occasion when he allowed himself to be drawn into an argument, made himself unpopular with both sides by saying that the universe would be a far happier place if people did not permit political expediency to influence their choice of friends.

But at last, and none too soon, *Star Pioneer* dropped gently down to her berth between the marker beacons at Tallisport, and the ramp was extended, and, gibbering dejectedly, the Esquelians filed down it to be received by the Terran High Commissioner.

Farrell, watching from a control room viewport, turned to Grimes and Sonya. He said thankfully, "My first order will be 'Clean ship.' And there'll be no shore leave for anybody until it's done."

"And don't economize on the disinfectant, Jimmy," Sonya told him.

∾ The Rub ∾

SLOWLY GRIMES awakened from his nightmare.

It had been so real, too real, and the worst part of it was always the deep sense of loss. There was that shocking contrast between the dreary life that he was living (in the dream) and the rich and full life that he somehow knew that he should be living. There was his wife—that drab, unimaginative woman with her irritating mannerisms—and that memory of somebody else, somebody whom he had never met, never would meet, somebody elegant and slim, somebody with whom he had far more in common than just the physical side of marriage, somebody who knew books and music and the visual arts and yet evinced a deep appreciation of the peculiar psychology of the spaceman.

Slowly Grimes awakened.

Slowly he realized that he was not in his bedroom in the Base Commander's quarters on Zetland. He listened to the small, comforting noises: the irregular throbbing of the inertial drive, the sobbing of pumps, the soughing of the ventilation system, the thin, high whine of the Mannschenn Drive unit. And there was the soft, steady breathing of the woman in the bed with him. (That other one snored.)

But—such was the impression that his dream had made upon him—he had to be sure. (All cats are gray in the dark.) Without too much fumbling he found the stud of the light switch on his side of the bed. His reading lamp came on. Its light was soft, subdued—but it was enough to wake Sonya.

She looked up at him irritably, her lean face framed by the auburn hair that somehow retained its neatness, its sleekness, even after sleep. She demanded sharply, "What is it, John?"

He said, "I'm sorry. Sorry I woke you, that is. But I had to be sure."

Her face and voice immediately softened. "That dream of yours again?"

"Yes. The worst part of it is knowing that *you* are somewhere, somewhen, but that I shall never meet you."

"But you did." She laughed with him, not at him. "And that's your bad luck."

"My good luck," he corrected. "*Our* good luck."

"I suppose that we could have done worse . . ." he admitted.

Grimes was awakened again by the soft chiming of the alarm. From his side of the bed he could reach the service hatch in the bulkhead. He opened it, revealing the tray with its silver coffee service.

"The usual?" he asked Sonya, who was making a lazy attempt to sit up in bed.

"Yes, John. You should know by this time."

Grimes poured a cup for his wife—black, unsweetened—then one for himself. He liked sugar, rather too much of it, and cream.

"I shall be rather sorry when this voyage is over," said Sonya. "Jimmy is doing us well. We shouldn't be pampered like this in an *Alpha* Class liner."

"After all, I am a Commodore," said Grimes smugly.

"Not in the Survey Service, you aren't," Sonya told him.

In that dream, that recurring nightmare, Grimes was still an officer in the Federation's Survey Service. But he had never gotten past Commander, and never would. He was passing his days, and would end his days, as commanding officer of an unimportant base on a world that somebody had once described as a planetwide lower middle class suburb.

"Perhaps not," Grimes admitted, "but I pile on enough Gees to be accorded V.I.P. treatment aboard a Survey Service ship."

"*You* do? I was under the impression that it was because of me that Jimmy let us have the V.I.P. suite."

"Not you. You're only a mere Commander, and on the Reserve list at that."

"Don't be so bloody rank conscious!"

She took a swipe at him with her pillow. Grimes cursed as hot coffee splashed onto his bare chest. Then, "I don't know what your precious Jimmy will think when he sees the mess on the sheets."

"He'll not see it—and his laundrobot won't worry about it. Pour yourself some more coffee, and I'll use the bathroom while you're drinking it." Then, as she slid out of the bed, "And go easy on the sugar. You're getting a paunch . . ."

Grimes remembered the fat and slovenly Commander of Zetland Base.

Commander James Farrell, the Captain of *Star Pioneer*, prided himself on running a taut ship. Attendance at every meal was mandatory for his officers. As he and Sonya took their seats at the captain's table, Grimes wondered how Farrell would cope with the reluctance of middle watch keepers aboard merchant vessels to appear at breakfast.

All of *Star Pioneer*'s officers were here, in their places, except for those actually on duty. Smartly uniformed messgirls circulated among the tables, taking orders, bringing dishes. Farrell sat, of course, at the head of his own table, with Sonya to his right and Grimes to his left. At the foot of the table was Lieutenant Commander Malleson, the Senior Engineering Officer. There was little to distinguish him from his captain but the badges of rank. There was little to distinguish any of the officers one from the other. They were all tall young men, all with close-cropped hair, all with standardized good looks, each and every one of them a refugee from a Survey Service recruiting poster. *In my young days*, thought Grimes, *there was room for individuality . . .* He smiled to himself. *And where did it get me? Oh you bloody tee, that's where.*

"What's the joke, John?" asked Sonya. "Share it, please."

Grimes's prominent ears reddened. "Just a thought, dear." He was saved by a messgirl, who presented the menu to him. "Nathia juice, please. Ham and eggs—sunny-side up—to follow, with just a hint of French fries. And coffee."

"You keep a good table, Jimmy," Sonya said to Farrell. Then, looking at her husband, "Rather too good, perhaps."

"I'm afraid, Sonya," Farrell told her, "that our meals from now on will be rather lacking in variety. It seems that our Esquelian passengers brought some local virus aboard with 'em. The biologists in the first survey expeditions found nothing at all on Esquel in any way dangerous to human life, so perhaps we didn't take the precautions we should have done when we embarked the King and his followers. Even so, while they were on board their excretory matter was excluded from the ship's closed ecology. But after they were disembarked on Tallis the plumbing wasn't properly disinfected . . ."

Not a very suitable topic of conversation for the breakfast table, thought Grimes, sipping his fruit juice. "So?" asked Sonya interestedly.

"So there's been a plague running its course in the 'farm.' It's just been the tissue culture vats that have been affected, luckily. We could make do indefinitely on yeasts and algae—but who wants to?" He grinned at Grimes, who was lifting a forkload of yolk-coated ham to his mouth. "Who wants to?"

"Not me, Captain," admitted Grimes.

"Or me, Commodore. The beef's dead, and the pork, and the chicken. The quack says that the lamb's not fit for human consumption. So far the mutton seems to be unaffected, but we can't even be sure of that."

"You'll be able to stock up when we get to Port Forlorn," said Grimes.

"That's a long way off." Farrell looked steadily at Grimes as he buttered a piece of toast. "I've a job for you, Commodore."

"A job for *me*, Commander Farrell?"

"Yes, you, Commodore Grimes. By virtue of your rank you

represent the Rim Worlds Confederacy aboard this vessel. Kinsolving's Planet, although no longer colonized, is one of the Rim Worlds. I want to put down there."

"Why?" asked Grimes.

"Correct me if I'm wrong, Commodore, but I understand that the original settlers introduced Earth-type flora and fauna, some of which have not only survived, but flourished. It's not the flora that I'm interested in, of course—but I've heard that there are the descendants of the original rabbits, pigs, cattle and hens running wild there."

"No cattle," Grimes told him. "And no hens. Probably the pigs did for 'em before they could become established."

"Rabbit's a good substitute for chicken," said Farrell.

"Jimmy," reproved Sonya, "I do believe that you like your tummy."

"I do, Sonya, I do," said the young man.

"And so do I," said Lieutenant Commander Malleson, who until now had been eating in dedicated silence.

"But I don't like Kinsolving," grumbled Grimes. "And, in any case, we shall have to get permission to land."

"You will get it, John," said Sonya firmly.

Later that ship's morning, Farrell discussed the proposed landing on Kinsolving with Grimes and Sonya.

"Frankly," he told them, "I'm glad of an excuse to visit the planet. Not so long ago the Survey Service released a report on the three expeditions, starting off with that odd wet paint affair . . ."

"That was over a hundred and fifty years ago," said Grimes.

"Yes. I know. And I know, too, that you've been twice to Kinsolving—the first time as an observer with the neo-Calvinists, the second time in command of your own show . . ."

"And both times," admitted Grimes, "I was scared. Badly."

"You don't frighten easily, Commodore, as well I know. But what actually did happen? The official reports that have been released to the likes of us don't give much away. It was hinted—no more, just hinted—that the neo-Calvinists tried to call up the God of the Old

Testament, and raised the entire Greek pantheon instead. And you, sir, attempted to repeat the experiment, and got tangled with a Mephistopheles straight out of Gounod's *Faust*."

"Cutting extraneous cackle," said Grimes, "that's just what did happen."

"What I'm getting at, Commodore, is this. Were your experiences objective or subjective?"

"That first time, Commander, the neo-Calvinists' ship, *Piety*, was destroyed, as well as her pinnaces. Their leaders—the Presbyter, the Rector, the Deaconess and thirteen others, men and women— completely vanished. That was objective enough for anybody. The second time—I vanished."

"I can vouch for that," stated Sonya.

"But you came back. Obviously."

"More by luck than judgment." Grimes laughed, without humor. "When you do a deal with the Devil it's as well to read the small print."

"But at no time was there any actual physical harm to anybody."

"There could have been. And we don't know what happened to the neo-Calvinist boss cockies . . ."

"Probably being converted to hedonism on Mount Olympus," said Sonya.

"But we don't know."

Farrell grinned. "And aren't those very words a challenge to any officer in the Survey Service? You used to be one of us yourself, sir, and Sonya is still on our Reserve list. Kinsolving is almost directly on the track from Tallis to Lorn. I have a perfectly valid excuse to make a landing. And even in these decadent days . . ." He grinned again at the Commodore . . . "my Lords Commissioners do not discourage initiative and zeal on the part of their captains."

Reluctantly, Grimes grinned back. It was becoming evident that Farrell possessed depths of character not apparent on first acquaintance. True, he worked by the book—and had Grimes done so he would have risen to the rank of Admiral in the Survey Service— but he was also capable of reading between the lines. A deviation from his original cruise pattern—the evacuation of the King and his supporters from Esquel—had brought him to within easy reach of Kinsolving; he was making the most of the new circumstances. Fleetingly Grimes wondered if the destruction of the ship's fresh meat supply had been intentional rather than accidental, but dismissed the thought. Not even he, Grimes, had ever done a thing like that.

"Later," said Farrell, "if it's all right with you, sir, we'll go over the official reports, and you can fill in the gaps. But what is it that makes Kinsolving the way it is?"

"Your guess is as good as anybody's, Commander. It's just that the atmosphere is . . . odd. Psychologically odd, not chemically or physically. A terrifying queerness. A sense of impending doom . . . Kinsolving was settled at the same time as the other Rim Worlds. Physically speaking, it's a far more desirable piece of real estate than any of them. But the colonists lost heart. Their suicide rate rose to an abnormal level. Their mental institutions were soon overcrowded. And so on. So they pulled out.

"The reason for it all? There have been many theories. One of the latest is that the Kinsolving system lies at some intersection of . . . of stress lines. Stress lines in *what*? Don't ask me. But the very fabric of the continuum is thin, ragged, and the dividing lines between *then* and *now*, *here* and *there*, *what is* and *what might be* are virtually nonexistent . . ."

"Quite a place," commented Farrell. "But you're willing to visit it a third time, sir?"

"Yes," agreed Grimes after a long pause. "But I'm not prepared to make a third attempt at awakening ancient deities from their well-earned rest. In any case, we lack the . . . I suppose you could call her the medium. She's on Lorn, and even if she were here I doubt if she'd play."

"Good. I'll adjust trajectory for Kinsolving, and then we'll send Carlottigrams to our respective lords and masters requesting permission to land. I don't think that they'll turn it down."

"Unfortunately," said Grimes, but the faint smile that lightened his craggy features belied the word.

Slowly, cautiously Farrell eased *Star Pioneer* down to the sunlit hemisphere of Kinsolving, to a position a little to the west of the morning terminator. Grimes had advised a landing at the site used by the Confederacy's *Rim Sword* and, later, by his own *Faraway Quest*. The destruction of the neo-Calvinists' *Piety* had made the spaceport unusable. This landing place was hard by the deserted city of Enderston, on the shore of the Darkling Tarn. It had been the Sports Stadium.

Conditions were ideal for the landing. The sounding rockets, fired when the ship was descending through the first tenuous fringes of the atmosphere, had revealed a remarkable absence of turbulence. The parachute flares discharged by them at varying altitudes were falling straight down, each trailing its long, unwavering streamer of white smoke.

Grimes and Sonya were in the control room. "There's Enderston," the Commodore said, "on the east bank of the Weary River. We can't see much from this altitude; everything's overgrown. That's the Darkling Tarn . . ." With a ruler that he had picked up he pointed to the amoebalike glimmer of water among the dull green that now was showing up clearly on the big approach screen. "You can't miss it. That fairly well-defined oval of paler green is the Stadium . . ."

The inertial drive throbbed more loudly as Farrell made minor adjustments and then, when the Stadium was in the exact center of the screen, settled down again to its almost inaudible muttering.

At Farrell's curt order they all went to their acceleration chairs, strapped themselves in. Grimes, with the others, watched the expanding picture on the screen. It was all so familiar, too familiar, even to the minor brush fire started by the last of the parachute flares. And, as on the previous two occasions, there was the feeling that supernatural forces were mustering to resist the landing of the ship, to destroy her and all aboard her.

He looked at Farrell. The young Captain's face was pale, strained—and this, after all, was a setting down in almost ideal conditions. There were not, it is true, any ground approach aids. But neither was there wind, or cloud, or clear air turbulence. And Survey Service officers were trained to bring their ships down on worlds with no spaceport facilities.

So Farrell was feeling it too. The knowledge made Grimes less unhappy. *Now you begin to know what it's like, Jimmy boy,* he thought smugly.

But she was down at last.

There was almost no shock at all, and only an almost inaudible complaint from the ship's structure, and a faint sighing of shock absorbers as the great mass of the vessel settled in the cradle of her tripodal landing gear. She was down. "Secure main engines," ordered Farrell at last. Telegraph bells jangled sharply, and the inertial drive generators muttered to themselves and then were still. She was down, and the silence was intensified by the soft soughing of the ventilation fans.

Grimes swiveled in his chair, gazed out through the viewport toward the distant mountain peak, the black, truncated cone hard and sharp against the pale blue sky. "Sinai," Presbyter Cannon had named it. "Olympus," Grimes had labeled it on his new charts of the planetary surface. But that name was no longer apt. On its summit the neo-Calvinists had attempted to invoke Jehovah—and Zeus had answered their call. On its summit Grimes had tried to invoke the gods of the Greek pantheon—and had been snatched into an oddly peopled Limbo by Mephistopheles himself.

This time on Kinsolving the Commodore was going to be cautious. Wild horses—assuming that there were any on this planet, and assuming that they should be possessed by such a strange ambition—would not be able to drag him up to the top of the mountain.

Nonetheless, Grimes did revisit the mountaintop, taken there by the tamed horsepower of *Star Pioneer*'s pinnace rather than by wild horses. Nothing happened. Nothing could happen unless Clarisse, descendant of the long dead artist-magicians, was there to make it happen. There was nothing to see, except the view. All that remained of the two disastrous experiments was a weathered spattering of pigments where the witch girl's easel had stood.

Everybody visited the famous caves, of course, and stared at and photographed the rock paintings, the startlingly lifelike depiction of beasts and their hunters. And the paint was dry, and the paintings were old, old, even though some faint hint of their original magic still lingered.

Even so, this was an uneasy world. Men and women never walked alone, were always conscious of something lurking in the greenery, in the ruins. Farrell, reluctant as he was to break the Survey Service's uniform regulations, issued strict orders that everybody ashore on any business whatsoever was to wear a bright scarlet jacket over his other clothing. This was after two hunting parties had opened fire upon each other; luckily nobody was killed, but four men and three women would be in the sick bay for days with bullet wounds.

Grimes said to Farrell, "Don't you think it's time that we were lifting ship, Captain?"

"Not for a while, Commodore. We have to be sure that the new tissue cultures will be successful."

"That's just an excuse."

"All right, it's just an excuse."

"You're waiting for something to happen."

"Yes. Damn it all, Commodore, this sensation of brooding menace is getting me down; it's getting all of us down. But I want to have something definite to report to my Lords Commissioners . . ."

"Don't pay too high a price for that fourth ring on your sleeve, James."

"It's more than promotion that's at stake, sir, although I shall welcome it. It's just that I hate being up against an enemy that I can't see, can't touch. It's just that I want to accomplish something. It's just that I don't want to go slinking off like a dog with his tail between his legs."

"The original colony did just that."

"But they . . ." Farrell stopped abruptly.

"I'll finish it for you, James. But they were only civilians. They weren't wearing the Survey Service badge on their caps, Survey Service braid on their sleeves or shoulders. They weren't disciplined. And how long do you think your ship's discipline is going to stand up to the strain, gold braid and brass buttons notwithstanding?"

"For long enough."

Sonya broke in. "This is Jimmy's show, John. He makes the decisions. And I agree with him that we should stay on Kinsolving until we have something to show for our visit."

"Thank you, Sonya," said Farrell. Then, "You must excuse me. I have things to attend to."

When the young man had left their cabin, Sonya turned to her husband. "You're getting too old and cautious, John. Or are you sulking because *you're* not running things?"

"I don't like this world, my dear. I've reasons not to."

"You're letting it get you down. You look as though you haven't slept for a week."

"I haven't. Not to speak of."

"Why didn't you let me know?"

"It's so damned silly. It's that bloody nightmare of mine—you know the one. Every time I shut my eyes it recurs."

"You should have told me."

"I should have done." He got slowly to his feet. "Probably some good, healthy exercise will make me sleep better. A long walk . . ."

"I'll come with you."

She fetched from the wardrobe the scarlet jackets that they had been given. Grimes took from a drawer his deadly little Minetti, put it in one pocket, a spare clip of cartridges in the other. Heavier handguns and miniaturized transceivers they would collect from the duty officer at the airlock.

Within a few minutes they were walking down the ramp to the path that had been hacked and burned and trodden through the encroaching greenery, the trail that led to the ruined city.

It was early afternoon. The sun was still high in the pale sky, but the breeze, what there was of it, was chilly. And the shadows, surely, were darker here than on any other world that Grimes had ever visited, and seemed to possess a life of their own. But that was only imagination.

They walked steadily but carefully, watching where they put their feet, avoiding the vines and brambles that seemed deliberately to try to trip them. On either side of the rough track the vegetation was locked in silent, bitter warfare: indigenous trees and shrubs, importations from Earth and other worlds, and parasites upon parasites. In spite of the overly luxuriant growth the overweening impression was of death rather than of life, and the most readily identifiable scent on the chill air was that of decay.

They came to the outskirts of the city, picking their way over the tilted slabs of concrete, thrust up and aside by root and trunk, that had once been a road. Once the buildings between which it ran had been drably utilitarian; now the madly proliferating and destructive ivy clothed them in somber, Gothic splendor. An abandoned ground car, the glass of its headlights by some freak of circumstances unobscured, glared at them like a crouching, green-furred beast.

Grimes tried to imagine what this place had been like before its evacuation. Probably it had been very similar to any sizable town on Lorn or Faraway, Ultimo or Thule—architecturally. But there had been one difference, and a very important one. There had been the uncanny atmosphere, that omnipresent premonition of . . . Of . . . ? That fear of the cold and the dark, of the Ultimate Night. Other cities on other worlds had their haunted houses; here every house had been haunted.

He said, "The sooner young Farrell lifts ship off this deserted graveyard, the better."

"At least it's not raining," Sonya told him, with an attempt at cheerfulness.

"Thank the odd gods of the galaxy for one small mercy," grumbled Grimes.

"Talking of odd gods . . ." she said.

"What about them?"

"Sally Veerhausen, the Biochemist, told me that there's a very odd church on a side street that runs off the main drag."

"Oh?"

"Yes. It's to the right, and it's little more than an alley, and you turn into it just before you get to a tall tower with a latticework radio mast still standing on top of it. . ."

"That it there, to the right?"

"Must be. Shall we investigate?"

"What is there to investigate?" he asked.

"Nothing, probably. But I seem to recall a period when you exhibited a passion for what you referred to as freak religions. This could be one to add to your collection."

"I doubt it," he told her.

But after a few minutes' careful walking they were turning off the main street, making their way along an alley between walls overgrown with the ubiquitous ivy that had been brought to the world by some long dead, homesick colonist.

The church was there.

It was only a small building, a masonry cube with its angles somehow and subtly wrong. And it was different from its neighbors. Perhaps the stone, natural or synthetic, from which it had been constructed possessed some quality, physical or chemical, lacking in the building materials in more general use. Its dull grey facade was unmarked by creeper, lichen or moss. Its door, grey like the walls, but of metal, was uncorroded. Over the plain rectangle of the entrance were the embossed letters in some matte black substance— TEMPLE OF THE PRINCIPLE.

Grimes snorted almost inaudibly. Then, "What Principle?" he demanded. "There have been so many."

"Perhaps," said Sonya seriously, "the greatest and most mysterious one of all."

"The Golden Way? The greatest, I admit . . ."

"No. Sally got her paws onto such records as still exist—the vaults in the city hall kept their contents quite intact—and found out that there was a cult here that worshipped, or tried to worship, the Uncertainty Principle . . ."

"Mphm. Could have been quite a suitable religion for this world. Inexplicable forces playing hell with anything and everything, so, if you can't lick 'em, join 'em."

"Or get the hell out."

"Or get the hell out. But—who knows?—this freak religion might just have worked. Shall we go inside?"

"Why not?"

The door opened easily, too easily. It was almost as though they had been expected. But this, Grimes told himself, was absurd thinking. The officers from the ship who had found this place must have oiled the hinges. And had they done something about the lighting system too? It should have been dark inside the huge, windowless room, but it was not. The gray, subtly shifting twilight was worse than darkness would have been. It accentuated the wrongness of the angles where wall met wall, ceiling and floor. It seemed to concentrate, in a formless blob of pallid luminescence, over the coffin-shaped altar that stood almost in the middle of the oddly lopsided hall. *Almost* in the middle . . . Its positioning was in keeping with the rest of the warped geometries of this place.

"I don't like it," said Grimes. "I don't like it at all."

"Neither do I," whispered Sonya.

Yet neither of them made any attempt to retreat to the comparative light and warmth and sanity of the alley outside.

"What rites did they practice?" whispered the Commodore. "What prayers did they chant? And to *what?*"

"I'd rather not find out."

But still they did not withdraw, still, hand in hand, they advanced slowly toward the black altar, the coffin-shaped . . . coffin-shaped? No. Its planes and angles shifted. It was more of a cube. It was more than a cube. It was. . .

Grimes, knew, suddenly, what it was. It was a tesseract. And he knew, too, that he should never have come again to this world. Twice he had visited Kinsolving before, and on the second occasion had become more deeply involved than on the first. Whatever the forces were that ruled this planet, he was becoming more and more attuned to them.

And this was the third time.

"John!" he heard Sonya's distant voice. *"John!"*

He tightened the grasp of his right hand, but the warmth of hers was no longer within it.

"John . . ."

It was no more than a fading whisper. "John . . ."

"Grmph . . ." He didn't want to wake up. Full awareness would mean maximum appreciation of his nagging headache. His eyes were gummed shut, and he had the impression that small and noisome animals had fought and done other things inside his mouth.

"*John!*"

Blast the woman, he thought.

"*JOHN!*" She was shaking him now.

He flailed out blindly, felt one fist connect with something soft, heard a startled gasp of pain. "Never touch an officer," he enunciated thickly. " 'Gainst regulations."

"You . . . You *hit* me. You brute."

"Own fault."

"Wake up, damn you!"

He got his eyes open somehow, stared blearily at the plump, faded woman in the shabby robe who was staring down at him with distaste.

Who are you? he demanded silently. *Who are you?* The memory of someone slim, sleek and elegant persisted in his befuddled brain. Then—*Where am I? Who am I?*

"You've got a job to do," the woman told him in a voice that was an unpleasant whine. "You'd better get your stinking carcass out of that bed and start doing it. I like to go on eating, even if you don't."

A starvation diet would do you the world of good, he thought. He said, "Coffee."

"Coffee *what?* Where's your manners?"

"Coffee, please."

She left him then, and he rolled out of the rumpled bed. He looked down with distaste at his sagging drinker's paunch, then got to his feet and walked unsteadily to the bathroom. He was surprised at the weakness he felt, the near nausea, the protests of a body allowed to degenerate into a state of general unfitness. It all seemed wrong. Surely he had always taken pride in maintaining himself in good condition.

He stood under the shower, and gradually the mists cleared from his brain. In a little while John Grimes, Officer Commanding the Zetland Base, passed over Commander, would be ready to begin his dreary day.

Nobody quite knew why the Federation maintained a base on Zetland. Once, a long time ago, the planet had been strategically important when it seemed possible that the Federation and the expanding Shaara Empire might clash, but the Treaty of Danzenorg, respected by both cultures, had neatly parceled up the entire galaxy into spheres of influence. True, there were other spacefaring races who belonged neither to the Federation nor the Empire, but their planets were many, many light years distant from Zetland and their trade routes passed nowhere near this world.

There was a base on Zetland. There always had been one; there always would be one. The taxpayer had bottomless pockets. There were spaceport facilities, of a sort. There were repair facilities, also of a sort. There was a Carlotti beacon, which was an absolutely inessential part of the navigational network in this sector of space, and relay station. The whole setup, such as it was, could have been run efficiently by a lieutenant junior grade, with a handful of petty officers and ratings. But a base commander must have scrambled egg on the peak of his cap. The Commander of a base like Zetland is almost invariably on the way up or the way down.

Commander John Grimes was not on the way up.

Nonetheless, he did have that scrambled egg on the peak of his cap. There was also a smear of egg yolk at the corner of his mouth, and a spatter of it on the lapel of his jacket. His enlisted woman driver, waiting for him in the ground car outside the Base Commander's bungalow, looked at him with some distaste—apart from anything else, she had been there for all of twenty minutes—clambered reluctantly out of the vehicle (her legs, noted Grimes, were too thick and more than a little hairy) and threw him a salute that almost, but not quite, qualified as "dumb insolence." Grimes returned it contemptuously. She opened the rear door of the car for him. He got in, thanking her as an afterthought, sagged into the seat. She got back behind the controls, clumsily stirred and prodded the machine into reluctant motion.

It was only a short drive to the military spaceport. The Commander thought, as he had thought many times before, that he should walk to his office rather than ride; the exercise would do him good. But somehow he never felt up to it. He stared unseeingly through the dirty windows. The view was as it always was: flat fields with an occasional low farmhouse, uninteresting machines trudging through the dirt on their caterpillar treads sowing or reaping or fertilizing the proteinuts which were Zetland's only export—and that only to worlds too poverty-stricken to send anything worthwhile in exchange. Ahead was the base—administration buildings, barracks, control tower and the lopsided ellipsoid that was the Carlotti beacon, slowly rotating.

The car rolled over the concrete apron, jerked to a halt outside the control tower. The girl driver got out clumsily, opened the Commander's door. Grimes got out, muttered, " 'K you."

She replied sweetly, "It was a pleasure, sir."

Saucy bitch, thought Grimes sourly.

He did not take the elevator to his office on the top level of the tower. Thoughts about his lack of physical fitness had been nagging him all morning. He used the stairs, taking them two at a time at first. He soon had to abandon this practice. By the time that he reached the door with BASE COMMANDER on it in tarnished gilt lettering he was perspiring and out of breath and his heart was hammering uncomfortably.

Ensign Mavis Davis, his secretary, got up from her desk as he entered the office. She was a tall woman, and very plain, and old for her junior rank. She was also highly efficent, and was one of the few persons on this world whom Grimes liked.

"Good morning, Commander," she greeted him, a little too brightly.

"What's good about it?" He scaled his cap in the general direction of its peg, missed as usual. "Oh, well, it's the only one we've got."

She said, holding out a message flimsy, "This came in a few minutes ago . . ."

"Have we declared war on somebody?"

She frowned at him. She was too essentially good a person to regard war as a joking matter. "No. It's from *Draconis*. She's making an unscheduled call here . . ."

A Constellation Class cruiser, thought Grimes. *Just what I need . . .* He asked, "When is she due?"

"Eleven hundred hours this morning."

"What?" Grimes managed a grin. "The fleet's in port, or almost in port, and not a whore in the house washed . . ."

"That's not funny, Commander," she said reprovingly.

"Indeed it's not, Mavis," he agreed. Indeed it wasn't. He thought of the huge cruiser, with all her spit and polish, and thought of his own, slovenly, planet-based command, with its cracked, peeling paint, with dusty surfaces everywhere, with equipment only just working after a fashion, with personnel looking as though they had slept in their uniforms—as many of them, all too probably, had. He groaned, went to the robot librarian's console, switched on. "Fleet List," he said. "*Draconis.* Name of commanding officer."

"Yes, sir." The mechanical voice was tinny, absolutely unhuman. "Captain Francis Delamere, O.G.C., D.C.O., F.M.H. . . ." Grimes switched off.

Franky Delamere, he thought. *A lieutenant when I was a two and a half ringer. A real Space Scout, and without the brains to come in out of the rain, but a stickler for regulations. And now he's a four ring captain . . .*

"John . . ." There was sympathy in the Ensign's voice.

"Yes, Mavis?"

She was abruptly businesslike. "We haven't much time, but I issued orders in your name to get the place cleaned up a bit. And the Ground Control approach crew are at their stations, and the beacons should be in position by now . . ."

Grimes went to the wide window. "Yes," he said, looking down at the triangle of intensely bright red lights that had been set out on the gray concrete of the apron, "they are. Thank you."

"Do you wish to monitor G.C.A.?"

"Please."

She touched a switch, and almost immediately there was the sound of a crisply efficient voice. "*Draconis* to Zetland Base. E.T.A., surface contact, still 1100 hours. Is all ready?"

"All ready, *Draconis*," came the reply in accents that were crisp enough.

"Just one small thing, John," said Mavis. She stood very close to him, and with a dampened tissue removed the flecks of egg yolk from the corner of his mouth, from his uniform. "Now, let 'em all come," she declared.

"Let 'em all come," he echoed.

He remembered a historical romance he had read recently. It was about a famous English regiment whose proud epitaph was, *They died with their boots clean.*

Living with your boots clean can be harder.

Draconis was heard long before she was seen, the irregular throb of her inertial drive beating down from beyond the overcast. And then, suddenly, she was below the cloud ceiling, a great, gleaming spindle, the flaring vanes of her landing gear at her stern. Grimes wondered if Francis Delamere were doing his own pilotage; very often the captains of these big ships let their navigating officers handle the controls during an approach. He thought smugly that this was probably the case now; when Delamere had served under Grimes he had been no great shakes as a ship handler.

Whoever was bringing the cruiser down, he was making a good job of it. Just a touch of lateral thrust to compensate for the wind, a steady increase of vertical thrust as altitude diminished, so that what at first had seemed an almost uncontrolled free fall was, at the moment of ground contact, a downward drift as gentle as that of a soap bubble.

She was tall, a shining metallic tower, the control room at her sharp stem well above the level of Grimes's office. Abruptly her inertial drive was silent. "Eleven oh oh oh seven . . ." announced Mavis Davis.

"Mphm," grunted Grimes.

He retrieved his cap from the floor, let the Ensign, who had found a clothes brush somewhere, brush its crown and peak. He put it on. He said to the girl, "Look after the shop. I have to go visiting." He left his office, took the elevator down to ground level.

He was joined by the Base Supply Officer, the Base Medical Officer and the Base Engineering Officer. All three of them, he noted, looked reasonably respectable. Grimes in the lead, they marched out to the ramp that was just being extended from *Draconis*'s after airlock.

It was good to be boarding a ship again, thought Grimes, *even one commanded by a man who had once been his junior and who was now his senior.* As he climbed the ramp he threw his shoulders back and sucked in his belly. He returned the salute of the junior officer at the airlock smartly and then, followed by his own officers, strode into the elevator cage. The woman operator needed no instructions; in a very few seconds the party from the base was being ushered into the Captain's day room.

"Ah," said Delamere, "Commander Grimes, isn't it?" He had changed little over the years; his close-cropped hair was touched with gray, but he was as boyishly slim and handsome as ever. The four gold rings gleamed bravely on each sleeve, and the left breast of his uniform was gaudy with ribbons. "Welcome aboard, Commander."

"Thank you, Captain." Grimes had no intention of addressing the other as "sir."

"You're putting on weight, John," said the Specialist Commander who was one of the group of officers behind Delamere.

"Maggie!"

"Commander Lazenby," said the Captain stiffly, "this touching reunion can be deferred until such time as the Base Commander and I have discussed business."

"Aye, aye, sir," snapped Margaret Lazenby, just a little too crisply.

Delamere glared at her, John Grimes looked at her wistfully. *She* hadn't put on weight. She had hardly changed since they had been shipmates in the census ship *Seeker.* Her red hair gleamed under her cap, her figure was as slim and trim as ever. But . . .

But she was not the slender, auburn-haired woman who haunted his dreams.

"Commander Grimes," said Delamere. Then, more loudly, "Commander Grimes!"

"Yes, Captain?"

"Perhaps we can get the introductions over with, and then you and I can get down to business."

"Certainly, Captain. This is Lieutenant Commander Dufay, the Base Medical Officer. Lieutenant Danby, Supplies. Lieutenant Roscoe, Engineering."

Delamere introduced his own people, and then the specialist officers went below, leaving the Captain to conduct business with Grimes.

"A drink, Commander?"

"Please, Captain. Gin, if I may."

"You may. Sit down, Grimes." Delamere poured the drinks, took a chair facing the other. "Down the hatch."

"Down the hatch."

The Captain grinned. "Well, Grimes, I don't seem to have caught you with your pants down. Frankly, I was rather hoping I would . . ."

"What do you mean?"

"I haven't forgotten that bad report you put in on me . . ."

"It was truthful," said Grimes. "You were a lousy ship handler." Then, "By the way, who brought *Draconis* in?"

"None of your business," snapped Delamere, an angry flush on his face. After a second or so he continued. "For your information, Grimes, an economy wave is sweeping the Service. There is a cutting out of deadwood in progress. Certain ships, *Draconis* among them, have been selected by our lords and masters to make the rounds of bases such as this one, and to report upon them. My last call was at Wuggis III. The Base Commander who was in charge is now on the retired list. His G.C.A. was in such a state that I was obliged to use the commercial spaceport."

"How nice for you," commented Grimes.

The Captain ignored this. "I'm giving you fair warning, Commander. You'd better be prepared. For the purposes of this exercise a state of war is deemed to exist. *Draconis* has limped into your base with 75% casualties, including all technical officers. These same technical officers are, even now, arranging a simulation of extensive damage. The Mannschenn Drive, for example, will require a new governor and will have to have its controls recalibrated. Only one inertial drive unit is functional, and that is held together with spit and string. My laser cannon are burned out. My yeast, algae and tissue culture vats contain only slimy, dead messes utterly unfit for human—or even unhuman—consumption." He laughed. "All the parts that have been removed from machinery and weapons are, of course, securely locked in my storerooms, where your people won't be able to get their greasy paws on them. *You*, Grimes, starting from scratch, using your people, your workshops, starting from scratch, will have to bring *Draconis* back to a state of full fighting efficiency, as soon as possible if not before."

"Then I'd better get cracking," said Grimes. He got to his feet, glanced briefly and regretfully at his almost untouched glass. It was good liquor, far better than any that could be obtained locally—but, even now, he was rather fussy about whom he drank with.

"You'd better," agreed Delamere. "Oh, you haven't finished your drink, Commander."

"Your ship's in such a sorry simulated state," Grimes told him, "that we'll make believe that you need it yourself."

He forgot to salute on the way out.

"I knew something like this would happen," complained Marian tearfully. "What shall we do, John? What can we do? A commander's pension is not much."

"Too right it isn't." He looked thoughtfully at the half inch of oily gin remaining in his glass, brought it to his mouth and swallowed it, gagging slightly. He reached for the bottle, poured himself another generous shot.

"You drink too much," flared his wife.

"I do," he agreed, looking at her. She was almost passable when alcohol had dimmed the sharp edges of his perception. He murmured:

> *"Malt does more than Milton can*
> *To justify God's ways to Man . . ."*

"What?"

"Housman," he explained. "A poet. Twentieth century or thereabouts."

"Poetry!" she sneered contemptuously. "But what are you doing about Captain Delamere? He was such a *nice* young man when he was one of your officers, when we were all happy at Lindisfarne Base . . ."

"Yes, Franky was always good at sucking up to captains' and commodores' and admirals' wives."

"But you must have *done* something to him, John. Couldn't you apologize?"

"Like hell," growled Grimes. "Like adjectival, qualified hell."

"Don't swear at me!"

"I wasn't swearing."

"You were thinking it."

"All right, I was thinking it." He finished his drink, got up, put on his cap. "I'd better get down to the ship to see what sort of mess my butterfly-brained apes are making of her."

"What difference will your being there make?"

"I'm still Commander of this bloody base!" he roared.

He looked back at her briefly as he reached the door, felt a spasm of pity. She was such a mess. She had let herself go. (As he had let himself go.) Only faint traces remained of the attractive Ensign Marian Hall, Supply Branch, whom he, on the rebound, had married. Physically there was no longer any attraction. Mentally there was— nothing. She read only trash, was incapable of intelligent conversation, and could never join Grimes in his favorite pastime of kicking ideas around to see if they yelped. He wondered how things would have worked out if he and Maggie Lazenby had made a go of things. But to have Maggie here, on this world, at this juncture, was too much.

He walked to the military spaceport. The night was mild, not unpleasant in spite of the wisps of drizzle that drifted over the flat landscape. Now and again Zetland's twin moons appeared briefly in breaks in the clouds, but their light was faint and pallid in comparison to the glare of the working floods around *Draconis*.

He tramped slowly up the ramp to the airlock, returned the salute of the O.O.D., one of Delamere's men. The elevator was unmanned—but, after all, the ship had suffered heavy simulated casualties, so ratings could not be spared for nonessential duties. He went first to the "Farm." The vats had been cleaned out, but the stink still lingered. The cruiser's Biochemist had carried out his "sabotage under orders" a little too enthusiastically. He exchanged a few words with Lieutenant Commander Dufay, in charge of operations here, then went down a couple of decks to the inertial drive room. He looked at the confusion without understanding it. Roscoe and his artificers had bits and pieces scattered everywhere. It was like a mechanical jigsaw puzzle.

"She'll be right, Commander," said the Engineer Lieutenant. He didn't seem to be convinced by his own words. Grimes certainly wasn't.

"She'd better be right," he said.

Somebody else was using the elevator, so he decided to take the companionway up to Control—he *did* know more than a little about navigational equipment—rather than wait. His journey took him through Officers' Country. He was not altogether surprised when he was accosted by Commander Lazenby.

"Hi, John."

"Hi, Maggie."

"Are you busy?"

He shrugged. "I should be."

"But we haven't seen each other for years. Come into my dogbox for a drink and a yarn. It's all right—the Boy Wonder's being wined and dined by the Governor in Zeehan City."

"He might have told me."

"Why should he? In any case, he's on the Simulated Casualty List. He's probably awarded himself a posthumous Grand Galactic Cross."

"With golden comets."

"And a platinum spiral nebula." She laughed. "Come in, John. Take the weight off your feet." The door to her day cabin opened for her. "This is Liberty Hall. You can spit on the mat and call the cat a bastard."

"You haven't changed, Maggie," he said ruefully, looking at her. "I wish . . ."

She finished it for him. "You wish that you'd married me instead of that little commissioned grocer's clerk. But you were always rather scared of me, John, weren't you? You were afraid that you, a spacehound pure and simple, wouldn't be able to cope with me, a qualified ethologist. But as an ethologist I could have seen to it that things worked out for us."

She sat down on her settee, crossing her slim, sleek legs. Her thin, intelligent face under the red hair was serious. He looked at her wistfully. He murmured—and it was as much a question as a statement—"It's too late now."

"Yes. It's too late. You've changed too much. You did the wrong thing, John. You should have resigned after that court martial. You could have gone out to the Rim Worlds to make a fresh start."

"I wanted to, Maggie. But Marian—she's incurably Terran. She made it quite plain that she'd not go out to live among the horrid, rough colonials. As far as she's concerned, everywhere there's a Survey Service Base there's a little bit of Old Earth, with society neatly stratified. Mrs. Commander is just a cut above Mrs. Lieutenant Commander, and so on down." He fumbled for his pipe, filled and lit it. "She had the idea, too, that My Lords Commissioners would one day forgive me and that she'd finish up as Mrs. Admiral Grimes . . ."

"My heart fair bleeds for you both," she said drily. "But mix us drinks, John. You'll find the wherewithal in that locker."

"For you?"

"The same as always. BVG, with just a touch of lime."

There was a hologram over the grog locker, a little, brightly glowing window onto another, happier world. It was a beach scene: golden sand, creamy surf, blue sea and sky, and the golden brown bodies of the naked men and women.

Grimes asked, "Do you still spend your long leaves on Arcadia, Maggie?"

"Too right I do. It's the only possible planet for an ethologist who takes the 'Back To Nature' slogan seriously."

"You look happy enough in this hologram . . ." Grimes inspected the three-dimensional picture more closely. *"Who is that with you?"*

"Peter Cowley. He's a Senior Biochemist with Trans-Galactic Clippers."

"No. Not *him*. The woman."

She got up to come to stand beside him. "Oh, her. That's Sonya Verrill. Yet another of the Commanders with whom the Survey Service is infested. She's Intelligence. Do you know her?"

Grimes stared at the depiction of the nude woman. She was like Maggie Lazenby in many ways, her figure, her coloring, her facial features, could almost have been her sister. He looked more closely. There should be a mole on her left hip. There was.

"Do you know her?" asked Maggie again.

"Yes . . . No . . ."

"Make your mind up."

I don't know her, thought Grimes. *I have never met her. But I have dreamed about her. I thought it was Maggie in my dreams, a somehow different Maggie, but she hasn't a mole anywhere on her body . . .*

He said, "No, I don't know her. But she *is* like you, isn't she?"

"I can't see any resemblance. You know, she was almost going to call here; she's sculling around this neck of the woods in one of those little, fully automated armed yachts. Some hush-hush Intelligence deal. But when she heard that this was one of the Boy Wonder's ports of call she decided to play by herself somewhere."

"Has *he* met her?" asked Grimes, feeling absurdly jealous.

"Yes. They do not, repeat not, like each other."

"Then there must be some good in her," said Grimes, with a quite irrational surge of relief.

"Never mind her. What about me? I'm thirsty."

"All right, all right," said Grimes, mixing the drinks.

When he got home Marian was waiting up for him. "You've been drinking," she accused him.

"And so, to coin a phrase, what?"

"I don't mind that so much. But you've been with that . . . bitch, that Maggie Lazenby."

"I had a couple of drinks with her, that was all."

"Don't lie to me!"

"I'm not lying."

No, he wasn't lying. Maggie, in her woman's way, had offered him more than a drink, but he had turned it down. Even now he was not sure why he had done so. Or he was sure, but would not admit it to himself. It was all so crazy, so utterly crazy. He had been loyal to a woman whom he had never met, whose hologram he had seen for the first time, in Maggie's day cabin.

"After all I've done for you, and you going sniffing around that carroty alley cat. You're no good, you're just no good. You never were, and you never will be . . ."

Grimes brushed past her, into the living room, the Service severity of which had been marred by his wife's tasteless attempts at interior decoration.

"Say something, damn you! Say something, you waster. Haven't you even the guts to defend yourself?"

The telephone buzzed urgently. Grimes went to it, flipped down the switch. The screen came alive and the plain, almost ugly face of Mavis Davis looked out at him. "Commander, there's an emergency . . ."

"Yes?" *And what was it? Had his fumbling repair squads wreaked some irreparable damage upon the cruiser? He'd better start packing his bags.*

"A Mayday."

"Who?" he demanded. "Where?"

"The armed yacht *Grebe*. In solar orbit between Zetland and Freiad." She rattled off coordinates. "Meteor swarm. Extensive hull and machinery damage. Loss of atmosphere. Orbit decaying."

"Mavis, send a car for me. At once."

"Wilco, Commander."

"And what can *you* do?" his wife sneered. "Captain Delamere's got a cruiser and hundreds of really efficient men and women. What have *you* got?"

"Out of my way!" he snarled.

"John! You can't go. I forbid you!" She clung to his sleeve but, brutally, he shook her off. She followed him for a little way as he strode out of the house, along the dark road, then gave up. "John!" she called. "John!"

The lights of the car were ahead, approaching rapidly. It passed him, turned, braked. Mavis Davis was driving. He got in beside her.

She said, as she restarted the vehicle. *"Husky?"*

Of course, it had to be the base's space tug *Husky*. Delamere's cruiser was out of commission and the tug at the civilian spaceport was, Grimes knew, undergoing annual survey. *Husky* was the only ship on Zetland capable of getting upstairs in a hurry.

And she was Grimes's toy, his pet. She was more than a toy, much more. In her he could feel the satisfaction of real command, or symbiosis with his ship. She was the only piece of equipment on the base in absolutely first class condition—and Grimes and Mavis, working with their own hands, had kept her so. She was referred to as "the Old Man's private yacht."

"I told Petty Officer Willis to warm her up," said Mavis.

"Good girl."

"Can . . . Can I come with you?"

"I'd like you to." She was a clerical officer, trained as such, but she should have been an engineer. She possessed the inborn skills, the talents and a keen mathematical mind. Often she had accompanied Grimes on his short jaunts outside the atmosphere. "You know the little bitch better than anybody else on the base."

"Thank you, John."

The car screamed on to the apron, circled the great, useless, floodlit hulk of *Draconis*. *Husky* was in her own berth, tucked away behind the workshops, a dull metal ovoid standing in her tripodal landing gear like a gray egg in an egg-cup. A circle of yellow light marked her airlock door.

As the car stopped Grimes heard a noise in the sky. It was a jet, coming in fast. The shriek of its exhaust varied in pitch as its turret drive was used first to brake and then to ease the aircraft to a vertical touchdown. The aircraft slammed to the concrete just a few feet from the car.

A man jumped out of the cabin, confronted Grimes. It was Delamere, still in his mess dress, starched white linen, black bow tie, tinkling miniatures and all.

"Is she ready?" he demanded.

"Yes, Captain. I'll have her up and away as soon as the airlock's sealed."

"You aren't taking her up, Grimes. I am." Delamere grinned whitely. "Life's been a little too dull lately."

"Like hell you're taking her up, Delamere. This is *my* base, and *my* tug."

"And *I* am your superior officer, Grimes. You'd better not forget it."

"You're not likely to let me, are you? But this is a rescue operation—and *I* know how to handle a ship."

"Out of my way, you insolent bastard!"

Grimes swung clumsily, but with all his weight behind the blow, and the weight of all the years of misery and frustration. Delamere wasn't as fit as he looked. Grimes's fist sank deep into his midriff, under the black silk cummerbund. The air was expelled from the Captain's lungs in an explosive *oof!* He sat down hard and abruptly. He gasped something about striking a superior officer, about mutiny.

"Willis," Grimes called to the Petty Officer, who had appeared in the airlock, "drag the Captain clear of the blast area. I'm going to use the auxiliary rockets. And keep clear yourself."

"But, sir . . ."

"You don't want to be up with me on a charge of mutiny. Get out of here, and take the Captain with you. That goes for you too, Mavis."

"Like hell it does!"

Grimes paused briefly. He could manage the tug single-handed, but with rescue operations involved it would be asking for trouble. He grabbed Mavis by her bony shoulder. "Scream!" he whispered. "I'm dragging you aboard by force!"

She screamed, shrieked, "Let go of me!" From where Delamere was sprawled the struggle would look convincing enough. And then they were in the airlock, and as the door shut Grimes saw that Willis already had Delamere well clear. The Commander hurried up to the little control room while Mavis went to the engines. He plumped down into the pilot's chair and, as he strapped himself in, cast an experienced eye over the telltale lights. REACTION DRIVE—READY.

INERTIAL DRIVE—READY. MANNSCHENN DRIVE—STAND BY.

His fingers found the firing studs in the arm of his chair. He said into the microphone hanging before him, "Secure all. Secure all for blast off."

Mavis's voice came in reply. "All secure, Captain."

"Then—*blast!*" almost shouted Grimes.

He pressed the button, and *Husky* screamed upstairs like a bat out of hell.

There was only one person aboard the crippled *Grebe*, a woman. Her voice was faint, almost incoherent. She was in her suit, she said. She had a broken arm, and possible internal injuries. She thought that she would be able to ship a new air bottle when the one in use was exhausted . . .

"Can you actuate your Carlotti transceiver?" demanded Grimes urgently.

"I . . . I think so . . ."

"Try. I'm going to switch to Mannschenn Drive. I'll home on your Carlotti."

"Mannschenn Drive?" asked Mavis, who had come up to Control.

"Yes. I want to be there in minutes, not days, and the Mannschenn Drive's the only way. I know it's risky, but . . ."

It *was* risky, to operate the Drive in a planetary system with its tangle of gravitational and magnetic fields, but it had to be done. Grimes jockeyed the free-falling *Husky* around on her gyroscope, lining her up on the faint signals from the survivor's suit radio. He started the Drive. There was the usual second or so of disorientation in space and time, and then, astern of them, Zetland assumed the appearance of a writhing, convoluted ball of luminous gas, and ahead and to starboard the sun became an iridescent spiral. Grimes paid no attention. He heard the faint voice from his own Carlotti speaker— "Carlotti *on*."

"Can you fix it so that it sends a continuous note? Turn up the gain . . ."

"Wilco."

A faint, continuous squeal came from the speaker.

Good. Grimes watched the quivering antenna of his Carlotti direction finder and communicator, the ellipsoid Mobius strip that was rotating slowly about its long axis. He restarted the inertial drive and then, with lateral thrust, using the antenna as a compass needle, headed the tug directly for the distant wreck. He pushed the inertial drive control to full ahead. The irregular throbbing shook the little ship. "Mavis," he said, "see if you can coax a few more revs out of the bone shaker . . ."

"I'll try," she told him, and was gone.

A fresh voice came from the speaker. It was Delamere. "Grimes. Captain Delamere calling ex-Commander Grimes. Do you read me?"

"Loud and clear, Delamere. Get off the air. I'm busy."

"Grimes, I order you to return at once. Ensign Davis, I authorize you to use force if necessary to overcome the mutineer and to assume command of *Husky*."

Grimes watched the antenna. It showed a continual drift of the target in a three o'clock direction. The wreck was in orbit, of course. He would have to allow for that. He did so, applying just the right amount of lateral thrust.

"Grimes! Ensign Davis! Do you hear me?"

Damn the man. So far the antenna was keeping lined up on the signal from the disabled *Grebe*, but with the base transmitting at full power it was liable to topple at any second.

"Grimes! Ensign Davis!"

"Grimes here. I can't give any orders, but I can appeal to those of you in the Carlotti room. This is a rescue operation. I'm homing on *Grebe*'s Carlotti beacon. There's a woman out there, in the wreck, and she can't last much longer. Please get off the air, and stay off."

He was never to know what happened, but he thought he heard the sound of a scuffle. He thought he heard a voice—Maggie's voice— whisper, "Pull the fuse!"

He transferred his attention to the spherical tank of the mass proximity indicator. Yes, there it was, a tiny, glowing spark, barely visible. It was drifting fast in toward the center of the globe. Too fast?

Not really. For a collision to occur, two vessels must occupy the same space at the same time, and as long as *Husky*'s Mannschenn Drive was operating she was in a time of her own. But—talking of time— he didn't want to waste any. "Mavis," he said into the intercom mike, "when I put her on full astern I *want* full astern. No half measures."

"You'll get it," she assured him.

The spark was brighter now, crossing one concentric ring after another. Grimes adjusted the scale of the indicator, pushing the target back to the outernost circle. Still it drove in. Grimes adjusted the scale again, and again, and once more. Target spark merged with the bead of luminosity that represented *Husky*. For a microsecond there was an uncanny sensation of merging—not of ships, but of two personalities. "Mannschenn Drive—off!" snapped Grimes, executing his order. "Inertial drive—full astern!"

The ship shuddered, striving to tear herself apart. Colors sagged down the spectrum as the ever-precessing gyroscopes of the Mannschenn Drive were braked to a halt—but outside the viewports the stars, vibrating madly, still looked as they had done while the drive was in operation.

"Stop all!" muttered Grimes, jerking the lever to its central position.

And there, scant feet away, rotating slowly about some cockeyed axis, was the torn, buckled hull of the space yacht *Grebe*.

Mavis Davis came up to Control while Grimes was putting on his suit. She was bleeding slightly from an abrasion on her forehead. Like many another plain woman she was beautiful in conditions of emotional and physical stress. Before she lowered the helmet onto his shoulder she kissed him. It was a brief contact, but surprisingly warm. Grimes wished that it could have been longer.

She said, "Good-bye. It's been nice knowing you, John."

"What the hell's this, Mavis?"

She grinned lopsidedly. "I have my fey moments—especially when somebody is playing silly buggers with the Mannschenn Drive . . ." Then she was securing the helmet and further speech was impossible.

Grimes collected what tools he would require on his way down to the airlock. When the outer door opened he found that he could almost step across to *Grebe*. He pushed himself away from his own little ship, made contact with the hull of the other with the magnetic soles of his boots and palms of his gloves. He clambered over her like a clumsy, four-legged spider. He soon discovered that it would be impossible to open *Grebe*'s airlock door. But it didn't matter. A few feet away from it was a hole large enough for him to crawl through.

He said into his helmet microphone, "I'm here."

The faint voice that replied, at long last, held an oddly familiar astringent quality. "And about time."

"I came as quickly as I could. Where are you?"

"In the control room."

Grimes made his way forward, using cutting torch and crowbar when he had to. When he found her she was in the pilot's chair, held there by the seat belt. Moving feebly, she contrived to swivel to look at him. *Husky*'s floods were on, glaring through the viewports, but her face, inside the helmet, was in shadow.

She said, "I hate to have to admit it, but you're right, John."

"What do you mean?"

"What you always say when you deliver yourself of one of your diatribes against automation. 'Never put yourself at the mercy of a single fuse.' My meteor shield might as well have not been there, and by the time the alarm sounded it was too late to do anything . . ."

He was beside her now, holding her, cursing the heavy suits that were between them.

"Sonya, I've got to get you out of here. Aboard *Husky*." He fumbled with the strap that held her.

"Too . . . late." She coughed, and the sound of it, telling of fluid-filled lungs, was terrifying. "Too . . . late. I hung on as long . . . as I could. Start . . . Mannschenn Drive. Should be some . . . power . . . in batteries . . ."

"Sonya! I'm getting you out of here!"

"No. No! Start. . . Drive . . ."

But he persisted in trying to unstrap her. Summoning her last reserves of strength she pushed him away. He lost contact with the deck, drifted away from her. He clutched at something—a lever?—that moved in his hand.

He did not hear the Drive starting; there was no air in the ship to carry the sound. But he felt the vibration as its rotors stirred into life, was aware that the harsh light of *Husky*'s floods had deepened from white to a sullen red. Around him, around Sonya, the universe lost its substance. But he was solid still, as she was, and her hand was firm in his.

And . . .

She was saying, "We found each other again. We found each other again . . ."

Grimes looked at her, looked at her a long time, dreadfully afraid that she would vanish. He held her hand tightly. Then, but cautiously, he stared around him at the temple. It seemed to have lost its alien magic. It was just a large, featureless room with the dimensions of a cube. On the floor, annoyingly off center, was a block of black stone in the shape of a coffin.

He said, "That dream . . . If it was a dream . . ."

She said, "There is a fourth rate Survey Service Base on Zetland . . ."

He said, "The last I heard of Delamere he'd been kicked upstairs to become a deskbound commodore . . ."

She said, "Damn your silly dream. Forget about it."

"I'll try," he promised. And then, unbidden, familiar words formed themselves in his mind. He said them aloud:

> "*To sleep, perchance to dream . . .*
> *Ay, there's the rub . . .*"

Something about the emphasis he used made her ask, "What's the rub, John?"

"What *is* the dream? *That* or *this?*"

"What does it matter?" she asked practically. "We just make the best of what we've got." Then, as they walked out of the drab temple, "Damn! My ribs are still hurting!"